KNIGHT OF THE FLAME

Children of the Old War, book 1

H John Spriggs

ISBN: 1497430496

ISBN-13: 978-1497430495

For my father, who always encouraged me to write.

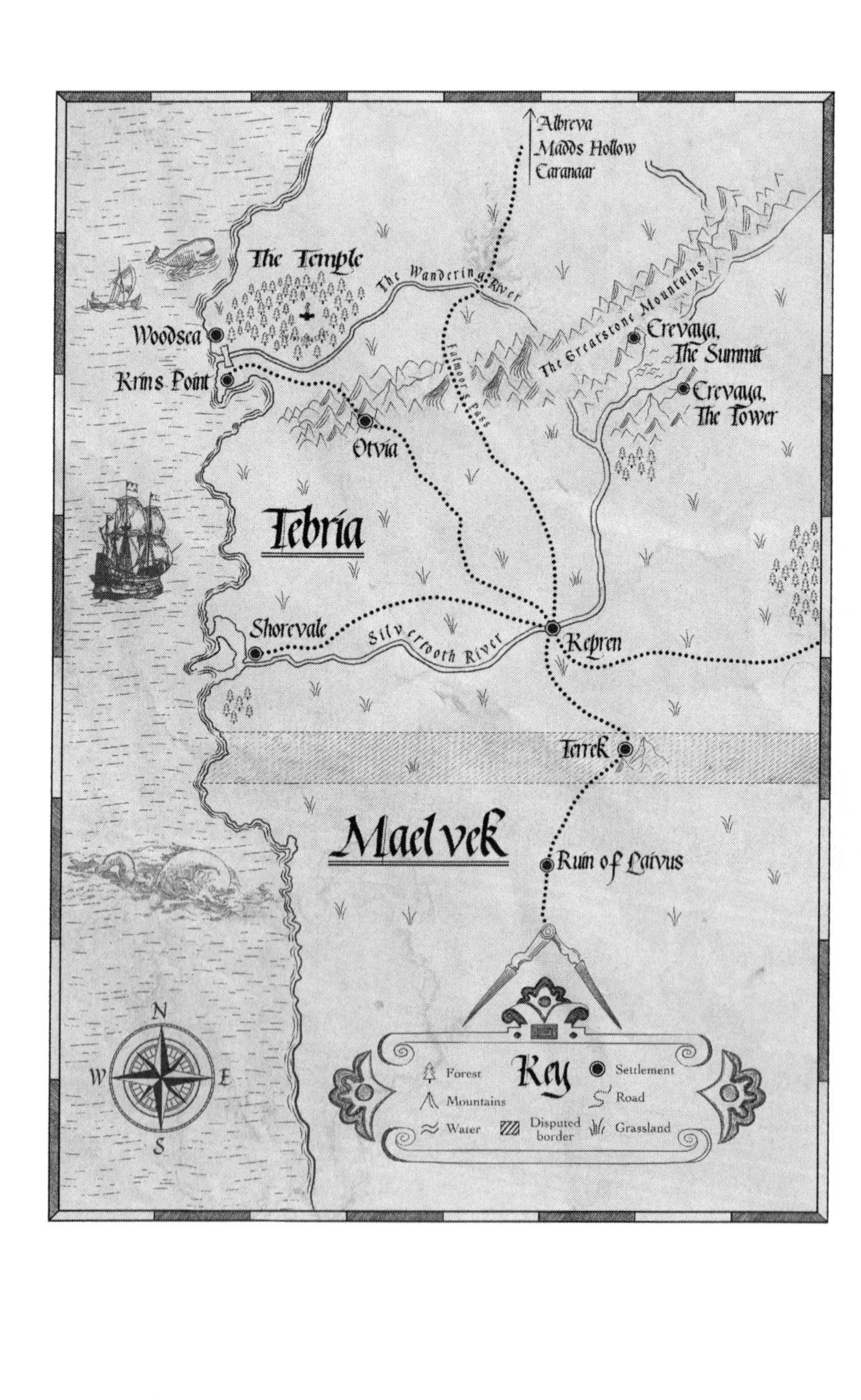

Albreva
Madds Hollow
Caranaar
The Temple
The Wandering River
Woodsea
Krin's Point
Fatmoor's Pass
The Greatstone Mountains
Crevaya,
The Summit
Crevaya,
The Tower
Otvia
Tebria
Shorevale
Silvertooth River
Repren
Terrek
Maelvek
Ruin of Laivus
N
W
E
S
Key
Forest
Mountains
Water
Disputed border
Settlement
Road
Grassland

Prologue

The shed door, thin and flimsy, squeaked on rusting hinges as it opened, and Caymus looked in with a mixture of apprehension and excitement. The first thing he always checked was the ceiling, and he sighed, relieved, at what he discovered. The shed was full of supplies, sure, but at least the ceiling was high. He ducked under the door's frame, then smiled victoriously as he stood up straight. The world always seemed a bit too small for Caymus, and so each time he walked into a building and didn't have to stoop, he counted it as a small triumph.

The shed, being the place where tools and materials for the Number Four Dry Dock were stored, was filled with the various implements a person might need if they were going to build or refit a ship. Caymus didn't imagine people came in here all that often though, considering how messy the place was. Some things were organized on to shelves, and some were hanging on nailboards on the walls. Other items were just piled or stacked so high that they blocked what little light came through the windows. He had a job to do though, and so he began peering into the dimly lit spaces, searching for the item he'd been sent here to retrieve.

The first corner he examined was home to a number of carpenter's tools, including planes, hand drills, mallets, saws, and an assortment of chisels. Caymus thought that was odd. Any ship's carpenter worth his salt would have his own tools, so why have a supply here?

The next corner was piled high with lengths and spools of rope that reached all the way to the ceiling, completely blocking out a window. Stacks of sailcloth filled this area too, and Caymus was disappointed to see mold growing on some of the material. Wasn't anybody taking care of this stuff?

Beside the cloth was the place where the caulking materials were kept. Dozens of different caulking irons—foot-long lengths of metal that either narrowed down to points or flared out into dulled blades—filled a handful of shelves against the wall, as did a few of the big, arm-sized mallets that caulkers employed. There were a couple of measuring rods and pry bars too, but the bulk of the area was dominated by several dozen spools, big and small, of cotton rope and oakum.

Caymus sighed, glad he'd found the thing he'd come in here for so easily. This was the first day of his apprenticeship, and he was anxious about making a complete mess of it.

As he approached the spools in the corner, however, his attention was caught by the sound of the shed door opening again, after which he heard a voice speaking.

"...selling your tools for drinking money," the voice said, "then you won't be working here very long. You can't just keep taking irons from—"

When the voice stopped abruptly, Caymus turned around to discover two boys—young men about his own age—looking at him with surprise and astonishment as the door squeaked its way closed again.

Actually, only one of them looked astonished. The first boy, who was both taller and darker than his companion, merely seemed startled to have found anybody in here. The second boy, whose hair was sandy, whose chest was thick, and whose face seemed about as expressive as a pile of vegetables, was the one standing there with his mouth open.

Caymus, who hadn't had a chance to meet anybody at the dock yet, wasn't quite sure what to do. Both boys seemed about a year or two his senior, being somewhere between eighteen and twenty years old. From the black-stained aprons they both wore, he guessed they worked as pitchers. They'd been so surprised to find him here though, and he started to worry whether he was in the right place, or if he'd done something else wrong.

He supposed there was nothing to do but introduce himself, and so he stepped forward and began extending his hand. "Hi," he said, "I'm Cay—"

But surprise had evaporated, leaving in its place a kind of resentful anger. "We know who you are!" the first boy said, stepping forward and sneering. "You're the hull master's kid, aren't you? From Woodsea, right?"

As though punctuating his words, the second boy spat on the ground. Both then closed the distance between themselves and Caymus.

Caymus, startled by the sudden vitriol, frowned. "Yeah," he said. "I'm Caymus. I—"

"I don't want to know your name, Woodsea!" said the first boy, incredulously. "You're not going to be here long enough for me to need to know your name!" He was standing so close to Caymus now that he was practically stepping on his toes. Had they been the same height, they'd have been staring each other in the face. As it was, the boys were both craning their necks to look up at Caymus, disgust permeating their expressions.

Caymus quietly sighed to himself. He could see where this was going; he might not be well-travelled or worldly, but he knew a bully when he saw one. The next few minutes were going to be a struggle, and he was going to have to be very, very careful.

He knew what he was supposed to do though, how he was meant to handle this: keeping his eyes on the two boys, he turned his concentration inward and did his best to shut their words out of his mind. Instead, he quickly conjured an image of the hearth in his mother's kitchen and tried to imagine himself sitting in front of it, watching the cooking fire burn.

"I'm only going to tell you once, Woodsea," said the first boy, "we've had about enough of your kind coming 'round here and just taking what they want from good, solid Pointers." His eyes flicked toward his companion. "Ain't we, Fent?"

The second boy nodded and balled up his fists.

Caymus tried to keep from frowning, tried to see the fire, to see the colors dance, to hear the crackle of the wood in his ears. He knew, however, what these boys were building toward, and that it was coming soon.

"And," said the first boy, "I'll tell you something else!"

That was it, the moment Caymus had been waiting for. The first boy, his eyes filled to the brim with hate, sneered, lowered his eyes, and drew back his arm.

Caymus winced and held his breath. As his watched the punch coming, the muscles of his chest and stomach tensed. When the blow landed, he managed not to cry out or gasp, even though the impact of the clenched fist knocked breath from his lungs, rattled his spine, and briefly displaced skin and organs.

Caymus wasn't scared. He didn't fear for his safety. He was very aware that the two boys were both more than a foot shorter than he, that if he fought back, he could probably overpower them. The attack, though, while predictable, had been so sudden and unprovoked that his mind prickled with shock and confusion. Why were they doing this? Why did they hate him so much? He was used to a certain amount of trepidation from strangers—the only people larger than Caymus were the giants in the mountains—but hatred? Hatred was new.

After the first boy's arm retreated, Caymus, being fairly certain these two wouldn't be satisfied with just one punch, took a breath and steeled himself, trying to keep the flickering fire in his mind's eye.

"Go home, Woodsea," hissed the first boy up into Caymus's face, "we don't want you here."

Then, in the next instant, the second boy, who seemed accustomed to following the lead of the first, wound back and took his turn at punching Caymus squarely in the stomach. "Nobody wants you here!" he snarled, soaking the words in venom. He delivered two more blows to Caymus's middle. "Go home before something happens to you."

Caymus saw it all happening to him in exquisite detail, almost as though time had slowed down to afford him a better view. He noticed the way the second boy's fair hair flew about and then fell into his face every time his head moved. He noticed the way he glanced at the first boy before every little action he took, as though checking for permission. He saw the way his eyes glowed with satisfaction each time he swung his arm. He clearly enjoyed hitting people, and he was glad to have an excuse to do it.

The first boy then reached up, grabbed Caymus by the tunic, and pulled. Clearly, he'd meant to yank Caymus down to his level, but Caymus was so much larger that he wasn't able to shift his great mass by more than a couple of inches. The boy seemed satisfied that he'd vanquished his quarry though, so he carried on, regardless.

"I don't care what you have to do, Woodsea," he said, "just make sure you leave Krin's today, and that you never *ever* come back." He pulled Caymus's tunic a little harder, moving him just another fraction of an inch. "I mean it," he continued, "if I see you here tomorrow, something very bad is going to happen to you." He sneered. "And the hull master too, come to think of it. The fire-masters come down here sometimes, you know, and they've taught me a trick or two."

Just like that, the tranquil kitchen hearth was gone from Caymus' mind, and rage began flooding his senses. Before the anger overwhelmed him completely though, he experienced a brief flash of irritation: why couldn't this stupid bully have just kept punching him and threatening him? Why did he have to go and threaten his father? His family!

He recognized familiar sensations as they exploded within his body. The muscles of his chest and arms tightened, pulling thick ropes of tension through his face, his neck, all the way through to his spine and the back of his throat. He felt heat on his cheeks and prickles along his forearms. He felt his hands curl into fists, felt them tighten so much that he thought his fingers might break. He watched the edges of his vision blacken, and suddenly all he could see were the faces of his tormentors, stark and sharp.

He was going to teach them! He was going to teach them not to pick on people they'd just met! He was going to teach them not to threaten the people he loved! He was going to show them what happened when they attacked somebody who was a whole lot bigger than they were!

Some small part of him cried out that this was bad, knew that he was losing control, knew what could happen when he lost his temper. That part of him was drowned out, though, by the rage pumping through his heart, by the hot fury that flowed through every capillary; it was terrified of what might be coming next—of what *must* come next!

The first boy's eyes went very wide, and he suddenly let go of Caymus's tunic and took a half-step backward; Caymus didn't know if it was the look on his face, the tension all over his body, or something else entirely, but the fool had clearly seen something that had scared him just enough to make him make him flinch toward the door.

The second boy was different. He'd been watching his friend, rather than Caymus, and so he was simply surprised by his friend's reaction. When he looked back at Caymus, his expression was so suddenly and utterly confused that he looked like a dog that had just been handed a set of keys.

The effect of the two expressions—concern paired with confusion—was so unexpectedly funny that Caymus very suddenly wanted to laugh aloud. The moment served as a much-needed distraction—a needle to puncture his anger—and a clear space opened up in the fog that had clouded his vision. The reasonable part of his mind found purchase again, and he began the process of calming himself down.

He reminded himself that these boys didn't know him, that he'd never done or said anything to provoke them. This, he concluded, meant they must have confused him with someone else, or perhaps that they'd been told something about him that wasn't true. He also reminded himself that this was his very first day in the shipyards, and that he was making his first impression on a lot of people; whoever these two were, they clearly worked at the dock too, and if Caymus were to knock the stuffing out of his workmates on the first hour of his first day, that impression wouldn't exactly be favorable.

Finally, he reminded himself what had happened the last time—the only time—he'd truly lost his temper, that he could never afford himself that luxury again. Smaller people tended to get hurt when bigger people lost control.

I know it sometimes feels good to get angry, his father liked to say, *but unless the world is actually ending, it's not a very useful thing to do.*

With quickness and clarity, Caymus tamped down the worst of what remained of his anger. The red veil dropped from his eyes, and he began to feel like himself again. As he did so, he remembered the claim that the first boy had made about learning from the fire masters. That, too, made him want to laugh. Caymus had encountered the priests of the fire realm on two separate occasions in his life; both times, he'd found them to be caustic, frightening people. The idea that one of them had taken time out of his day to teach a kid one of his "tricks" was patently absurd.

Now that Caymus could see his tormentors clearly again, he noticed that they were both standing a bit farther away from him than before. They looked confused and apprehensive. Perhaps they'd sensed the danger that had just passed through this space?

Caymus, noting his chance to escape, shrugged at the pair and presented a stony . "Sorry," he said, "I would go home, but the day just started."

With that, he grabbed the large spool of oakum that he'd come in here for, then he stepped around the pair and strode out of the shack's door. The boys didn't offer any resistance: whether they were afraid, or whether they were just confused about what he'd said, Caymus wasn't sure. The slightly unpinned expressions they wore made him suspect it was a bit more the former than the latter.

The bright, morning sky assaulted Caymus's eyes when he stepped out into the dockyard, as did the many sensations of a working dry dock. The sounds of hammers and chisels, not to mention those of voices shouting instructions at one another, mingled with the calls of sea birds and the steady, morning hum of the city of Krin's Point. The wonderful scent of new wood mixed with the reek of boiling pitch, creating a sensation in Caymus's nose that was, at the same time, both unpleasant and comfortably familiar. Behind that glorious miasma, however, was the intoxicating smell of salt: the smell of the sea.

Before him, as though waiting for him, stood the *Pride of the Expanse.* The massive barque had been raised from the water a few days previously, and the scaffolders had placed it in a strong, wooden cage that kept it a foot off the ground, allowing caulkers like him easy access to the bottom-most parts of the hull. Caymus smiled, eager to get to work.

The deck crew, he knew, being entirely composed of workers from here in Krin's Point, had started their work the previous day; Caymus couldn't see them, but he could hear their hammers working on the other side of the ship. The hull crew, on the other hand, had been waiting on their leader—Caymus's father, hull master Aster Bolwerc—to arrive in town. Caymus and his father had travelled from their home in Woodsea yesterday, having arrived at the northernmost gates of Krin's Point late the previous evening; that meant that this was the morning that work on the hull could finally begin.

Barely ten minutes ago, the hull master and his crew had gathered together to make their plans: that was when Caymus had been sent off to grab some oakum.

Caymus glanced around. Not a single member of the hull crew remained in sight. They must have all boarded the ship already. Caymus, feeling nervous and excited, took a long, steadying breath, and then made his way toward the ship, looking for his father.

As he crossed the hundred or so yards between himself and the *Pride*, he reached up with his free hand and felt his abdomen. It was sore, certainly, but not so sore that he wouldn't be able to work today. He sighed. The next day, he knew, was when the bruising would really get started. That was when it would start to really hurt. Oh well. Nothing to do but grit his teeth and do his best. He wondered why those two had hated him so much, though. In all his sixteen years, he'd never encountered anyone quite so immediately angry like that before.

Caymus aimed for the stern of the *Pride*, having heard that there was a ladder back there that would allow him up onto the deck. As he got within a dozen yards, the smell of boiling pitch became quite strong, which was surprising. If they were already boiling that much of the sticky, black substance, then the deck crew must already have made a great deal of progress.

Once Caymus stepped around the rudder, he was met by the sight of members, both of the deck and hull crews, of the Dry Dock Number Four Company—about ten of the twenty or so people working on the ship that day.

Down on the ground, the hull crew were just getting started. The two master carpenters, one Woodsean and one Pointer, were checking on the health of the wood that comprised the hull's exterior while their apprentices got on with the job of scraping barnacles and other marine life away. Others were either talking in groups of two or three or were gathering tools together. Up above him, he could hear the members of the deck crew going about the business of working the planks which could repaired and replacing those which couldn't.

There were members of other crews milling about, he knew, but they were just keeping an eye on things for now. The work of refitting a vessel's sails, steering, and pumps always came after the body of that vessel was reported to be sound by the carpenters of the hull and deck crews.

"Caymus, right?" called a woman's voice.

Caymus, who'd been looking up at the deck, turned his attention down and saw a woman of about twenty years walking toward him. She had short, blonde hair and a face full of large freckles. When she smiled, as she was doing now, she revealed that one of her eye teeth was missing. She wiped sweat from her brow as she approached.

He nodded. "That's me," he said, trying to smile just enough to seem polite, but not over-friendly.

She half-sighed, half-chucked. "Yeah, I figured," she said. "He said you'd be hard to miss." She stood before him and gazed up at him with an expression that lay somewhere between amusement and incredulity. "By the waves, you really are tall, aren't you?"

Before Caymus could answer, she looked down and pointed at the spool in his hand. "That my oakum?" she said.

Caymus was suddenly confused. "I…" he said, looking down at it. "My d— the hull master told me to fetch it from the shed, but he didn't really say what to do with it after."

When she craned her neck to look up at him again, she was grinning. "Well," she said, "we're just gathering supplies down here at the moment, so give it here and I'll add it to the pile."

Caymus did as he was told and held the spool out to the woman, who needed two hands to take it from him. Once she was clutching the thing securely to her chest, she nodded toward Caymus's left side. "Your dad," she indicated, "is checking the bilge. Said you should meet him there."

Caymus followed her gaze and discovered the rope-and-board ladder he'd been looking for just behind his left shoulder. He followed the rungs upward with his eyes until they met the deck, where he could just see one side of a young man on his hands and knees using a small decanter to pour pitch between deck boards. "They're pitching the deck already?" he said, half to the woman, half to himself.

"Sure are," she said. "We're getting a late start, for sure, but that's what happens when a third of your crew is out-of-towners."

Caymus looked down at her again, uncertain as to whether her tone had carried resentment in it or not. She was flashing a gap-toothed, but thoroughly genuine, smile though. "Hey," she said, "doesn't bother me, waiting a bit." She then leaned in closer and whispered, "everybody knows the best shipbuilders in the world come from Woodsea." She then glanced around, conspiratorially. "Don't tell anyone else I said that, though, okay?"

Caymus smiled, glad after his encounter in the shed to have met someone friendly. "I won't," he said, and he tapped the side of his nose with his finger.

The woman stepped back and laughed. "Oh, you're Aster's kid, alright," she said. "Go on, I expect he's waiting on you." Then, she turned away and walked toward the other workers, shaking her head as she went.

Caymus sighed, suddenly feeling an immense, unexpected sense of relief. Then, he turned, took hold of the ladder, and put his weight on one of the boards. The thing creaked under his great mass, but it otherwise held him without incident, and so he ascended.

Once he reached the deck, he looked around, getting his bearings. The deck crew was getting on with their work, as expected. The smell of the pitch, in fact, made him think to turn and look over the side, seeking the spot where they must be boiling the stuff. He found it near the bow of the ship: a large pot suspended over red coals on an iron stand. There was a dark-looking figure—the man was wearing a hood over his head—standing by the pot, stirring the awful stuff with a long rod or stick. The pitch was a bit closer to the ship than Caymus would have liked, but he knew that the deck crew, as his own, was led by a master of their craft, and that gave him confidence in their methods.

He'd been about to turn his attention back to the deck when he saw the two boys who'd just beaten him up come walking around the bow. Caymus, suddenly curious, watched them as they strode up to the pitch-pot and began talking—arguing, in fact—with the hooded figure. Caymus was genuinely surprised by the interaction. The boys kept pointing to the pot and talking loudly to the man; the man looked up at them occasionally, but just kept stirring. Caymus was too far away to hear anything he might have said in return.

Caymus sighed, then he turned away and started looking for the steps down to the lower decks. At least he knew it wasn't just him: those two didn't appear to get along with anybody! He tried, with some success, to stop thinking about them as he found some steps and went belowdecks.

The lower deck assaulted his senses as he moved through it. The area, though wide, had a ceiling of only moderate height, and so he had to duck down quite a lot in order to make his way. The deck crew was still caulking down here too, and the sounds of huge mallets striking chisels rattled his eardrums. He was also surprised by how dry things smelled down here. Usually, a ship's hull took days, even weeks, to air out properly, but his nose didn't detect any dampness at all. He supposed that meant the *Pride of the Expanse* had been in dry dock for quite a while. That must have been expensive. Whoever owned the ship must have had a lot of money to spare.

At least there was a fair amount of light, let in through the half dozen portholes on either side of the deck. Caymus was grateful: he'd been in a handful of large ships very like this one, and most had been so dark down below that he couldn't see his own hands, much less loose boards or giant holes in the deck.

The portholes also let in the odor of the pitch outside, and he found himself considering the two boys again, wondering how they could have hated him so much, so quickly.

He did his best to shake himself out of his consternation as he made his way down the two further sets of steps that led to the bowels of the ship—the bilge—where a familiar voice greeted him.

"Careful of the loose timber there," the voice said. "The deckers seem to think the bilge is a good place to keep their discards."

Caymus saw the pile of castoffs and stepped over them. "Well, there's no deck in the bilge, so why wouldn't they?" he said, pleased with his small epiphany. "Thanks Dad. How does it look down here?"

Caymus's father, a quiet figure of unremarkable height and build, was standing in the center of the space—likely at precisely the halfway point between the bow and the stern if Caymus knew the man at all—with his usual calm demeanor. One of his hands held the well-worn, leather roll that contained his hand-tools. The other was holding one of his caulking irons—a foot-long, wood-handled length of metal with a flanged, flattened tip—up to his bearded chin. "Oh," he said, "I think we'll have plenty to do for the rest of the week."

He pointed the iron around the space. "They went too long without a refit," he continued. "The oakum wasn't packed in hard enough in some places and the water started getting through. See the discolored areas all along the starboard side?"

Caymus looked and saw, though to his eyes there was nothing too remarkable about it. "I thought all bilges leaked?" he said. "That's why they put the pumps in, isn't it?"

Caymus's father turned to him, offered a warm, serene smile, and topped it with a wink. "*My* bilges don't leak," he said. "Stick around long enough, and yours won't either." The man then uncrossed his arms and walked up to Caymus. "So," he continued, "you meet everyone out there yet?"

Caymus's hand reflexively reached to his stomach again. "A few people," he said, and some of his cheerfulness evaporated. He frowned. "Dad, why do people here hate people from Woodsea so much?"

His father's expression turned to one of concern. "Something happen?"

"No," said Caymus, a bit too quickly. "Well, yes." He put his hand down. "I mean, just a couple of people from the deck crew didn't seem to like where I came from." He shrugged. "It's nothing I can't handle, but…why?"

Caymus's father nodded then gave him a half-shrug, as though indicating *that's the way it is*. "Well," he said, "I'm sure I don't need to tell you that our little town is home to some gifted artisans, yes?"

Caymus nodded.

"The big *ports*, though," the hull master continued, "are here, in Krin's Point, and so we have to come down here to find work, and every job one of us does is a job a Pointer doesn't get to do." He frowned, though only slightly. "I reckon I know exactly which young man might be giving you trouble."

Caymus, suddenly panicked, raised a halting hand. "Dad," he said, "please don't—"

But his father held up a hand of his own, as well as a reassuring smile. "Don't worry, son," he said. "I'm not planning on doing anything to or about him. I was an apprentice once, you know?"

Caymus put his hand down, relieved, and his father did the same.

"But," said his father, "if you're talking about a dark-haired boy, about your age, who works the pitching detail, then you're talking about Marton. Marton, you see, lost his father a couple of years ago when a brace of scaffolding collapsed under a galleon."

"Oh," said Caymus, frowning. "That's awful."

"It was," said his father. "The man was an experienced craftsman, and not half-bad at building a ship. Right up until the accident, he was set to become the leader of the hull crew for Dock Number Four." He gave his son a sad smile. "Now he's dead; now I'm the hull master."

"Oh," repeated Caymus, and then, "Oh!" Well, that certainly explained it. No wonder the boy had attacked him! "So," he concluded, "people from here, they don't all hate us, then?"

His father smiled. "No," he said. "I mean, there's always going to be some resentment when outsiders start taking up the work here, but most people know the docks are better off with us Woodseans around. Marton's a special case." He narrowed his eyes. "Nothing…happened, did it?"

Caymus, who knew exactly what his father meant, shook his head. "No," he said. "Came close, but I managed to stay on top of it."

"Good," sighed his father, "good. The trick with thinking about the kitchen is helping, then?"

"Well…" said Caymus, "it does help, yeah." He shrugged. "In the end though, they did something that just kind of snapped me out of it. I guess that means the real trick was to keep paying attention and not just lose myself in it all."

His father nodded, scratched his beard with the iron, and gave his son an appraising look. "That temper of yours," he sighed. "Your mother and I both thought you'd end up having entirely earthish qualities." He chuckled. "We were so sure of it; we were actually a little worried the average person would find you boring!" He shook his head. "I don't know where you get all this fire from, but I'm glad you're learning to control it."

Caymus, who didn't really like talking about this, nodded and looked away, thinking about the best way to change the subject.

He also realized he suddenly felt very nervous. No, not nervous… apprehensive? His spine was tingling as though there was a dagger suspended over him on a fraying bit of twine. The sensation was unnerving; where had it come from? Maybe it had something to do with the altercation, earlier?

"I'm glad you're here, son," said his father, interrupting the thought. "I'd always thought it would be fun to work a hull together. Now, here we are."

Caymus did his best to ignore the sensation tingling along the back of his neck; maybe it was something to do with the punches he'd just received? Instead, he looked back at his father and saw the warm, heartfelt expression on his face. He smiled, realizing that, beyond the apprehensiveness, beyond the jitters he'd been feeling about his first day of work, what he really felt today was pride, not to mention a sense of immense gratitude. "I'm glad I could be here too," he said.

He took a deep breath, doing his best to calm his nerves, and looked around the bilge. "Speaking of which, what do you want me to do, now that I'm here?"

The hull master nodded. "Well," he began, "I need to spend some more time down here." He indicated the hull again. "Most of this will be salvageable, but I won't know how much until I dig into it a little bit." He nodded downward, toward his feet. "Plus, we're going to have to get at the keel at some point and see how that's holding up from this end."

He then pointed his caulking iron at Caymus. "You," he said, "are going to learn how to recaulk a hull today. There's a woman I want you to go find out there. Hard to miss. Blonde hair. Missing front tooth."

"Oh," smiled Caymus. "I met her, actually. She was the one that told me where to find you. She's…" He froze, suddenly embarrassed to realize he hadn't thought to ask the woman's name.

His father grinned a friendly grin. "Her name is Yvonne," he said, "and she's an excellent caulker. Let her show you how it's done, and you'll be an expert within the week, a master in a month."

Caymus nodded with satisfaction, relieved to hear this particular bit of news. He'd spent the entire trip to Krin's worried about this part. He was happy enough to work with his father, sure, but his father was the hull master, and the hull master was responsible for everyone in his crew, not just his own son. That meant Caymus would almost certainly be spending the bulk of his time working with people he didn't know. The altercation in the shed had made him worry that this was going to be a really bad day. Working with this Yvonne person, though? That sounded like it might actually be fun.

He wished he knew where the nervous sensation was coming from though, as it was getting worse. By now, he felt like icy fingers were running up and down his spine and tickling the back of his neck.

"Alright, dad," he said, trying to shake the feeling, "I'll go find her again, then. Need me to do anything else?"

He father smiled warmly. "Nah," he said, "I'll be up in a few minutes, once I've had a good look around." He gave his son a wink. "Be steadfast, kiddo," he said. "Oh, and try to have some fun, while you're at it."

Caymus grinned. "Yeah?"

His father chuckled. "Might as well," he shrugged. "Gotta be here, anyway."

Caymus couldn't argue the point. He nodded, then he made his way up the nearby steps to the next deck. As he climbed, he found himself imagining his life beyond today. If all went well with the *Pride*, then he'd be signed on as an official apprentice at the Krin's Point Docks and would start working on lots of ships down here, every week. Between work shifts at Krin's, his father would spend his days teaching him all he knew about shipbuilding and woodwork, and so he should become an official dockhand within a year. From there, it was a long, though predictable, road to becoming a master of a craft. Maybe he'd be a hull master, like his father, or maybe he'd be a carpenter. Perhaps he'd learn the art of designing these great vessels and become a shipwright. That, he knew, would make both of his parents very happy.

A world of possibilities stretched out before him, and he was already on his way to meeting it. Just wait until he told Gerud and Willet, back home, about it all!

Once he was back to the first of the lower decks, he met the rows of portholes again, and, of course, the smell of the pitch. It was so very strong today—stronger than he'd ever thought it would be. The smell triggered the nervous sensation at the back of his neck again, which was a surprise. Why would a smell he'd come across dozens of times in his life make him so—

That was when he realized that it wasn't just pitch he was smelling, that there was another scent mixed in with it, too.

It was smoke.

"Fire!" came a call from outside. "The ship's on fire! Get away! Get away!"

Caymus, every nerve suddenly standing to attention, ran up the remaining steps to get to the top deck. Once he got there, he took in what was happening. All along the starboard side of the craft, smoke was pouring up into the sky. He could hear the sounds of crackling flames, but he couldn't see them. What had the fools with the pitch done? He knew the fire had been too close!

All around him, people were running. Some of them were pushing toward the rope ladder, taking their chances with the smoke. Others were clambering over the port side, presumably hoping to climb down the scaffolding. Two or three were looking over the edge, as though deciding whether to simply jump.

Caymus, unsure which route to take, tried to think. He could hear the fire getting louder, more intense, and knew he didn't have much time to act. The flames must have started down by the pitch—how in the world had the ship caught so quickly?—which meant the hull itself was what was on fire…

Caymus's eyes went wide.

"Dad!" he shouted, and he ran back to the steps leading belowdecks. The fire must have started just outside the bilge!

As he clambered his way down the steps, he met other people climbing up.

"Other way, fool!" they shouted. "The ship's on fire!" Most of them tried to push him the other way, but Caymus was bigger, and he was going down, and so he eventually shoved past every obstacle. Each of the encounters cost him time though, and as the precious moments passed by, smoke began to fill his nostrils and heat began to play upon his skin.

"Go up, idiot!" shouted a figure as Caymus pushed down another set of steps. He kept hoping one of the voices he was hearing would belong to his father, but he hadn't seen him yet, and he knew he was running out of time.

Once he was two decks down, he stopped meeting fleeing people. Instead, he met the fire. Rather, more than anything, he met smoke. The stuff pushed against him like it had a will, stinging his eyes so badly he had to fight to keep them open. Almost immediately, he started coughing, and he held his tunic up to his mouth in an attempt to keep the horrid stuff out of his lungs. He couldn't see the flames yet, but he could hear them, feel their heat.

He had to find his father, had to make sure he was okay. He'd been the only person in the bilge; for all Caymus knew, nobody else on the ship had even known he was down there. Nobody else would be looking for him, and so it had to be Caymus. And so, coughing so hard he felt like retching, his eyes burning as though acid had been poured into them, he leaped down the final set of steps

At last, he reached the bilge, and Caymus felt, for the first time, an impulse to abandon all hope. The smoke was so thick down here that he might as well have been wearing a sack over his head. He couldn't see his father, couldn't even see his own hand covering his mouth.

He could see the fire though, glowing a deep, blood red through the black haze. It was burning ferociously, somewhere near the bow, menacing, threatening. There was so much heat, too. Caymus felt like he'd just put his face and hands mere inches over a cook-fire. How long could a person survive down here?

"Dad!" he shouted, still holding onto the steps. "Dad, are you down here!"

He didn't know what to do. He couldn't see, and the fire and the shouting outside were so loud that even if his father had been crying for help, he knew he'd never have heard him. "Dad, where are you?" he whined, and tears which had nothing to do with the smoke welled in his eyes.

Caymus decided to try feeling around the spot where his father had been standing, earlier. He didn't really expect him to still be there, but what else could he do? He was completely blind, and the smoke was making him woozy, but he couldn't leave without at least trying to find his father. He had to *try*!

When he took his first step forward, he immediately stumbled as his foot hit something dense, yet soft. Suddenly hopeful, he reached down and felt cloth, an arm, a shoulder…the back of a head! He'd found him! He'd been so close this whole time! Caymus then remembered the pile of timber; his father must have been casting for the steps in the darkness and fallen over it!

Caymus wanted to feel his father's chest, to put his face near his lips and check for breath, but he knew there was no time. He could hear the flames raging with even greater ferocity now, and it was so hot! If he didn't hurry, it would mean the end for both of them.

Moving as fast as he dared, he turned his father over, put arms under his legs and torso, and picked him up. The man was surprisingly easy to lift, easy to carry, as though the smoke had somehow lightened his flesh. Caymus was very suddenly glad that he was so much taller than either of his parents, though a momentary spell of dizziness made him abandon the thought almost immediately.

Once he was securely holding his father, Caymus pushed himself back up the steps to the next deck. The smoke here was thicker than it had been before, but at least Caymus could just about see his father's face now. He could also see that the flames had found their way to this deck, and that they were burning away the front of the ship.

No time to waste, he made his way to the next set of steps, and began ascending…

Crack! The entire set of steps collapsed under his weight and something heavy fell down from above. Caymus was suddenly on his back, beating some kind of burning detritus away from both himself and his father!

Once he was satisfied that neither of them was actually on fire, Caymus realized he was suddenly able to see more clearly. Of course! The smoke would be rising to the ceiling It wouldn't be as thick at the floor!

The things he could now see, however, didn't give him much hope. A large section of the starboard side of the bow was on fire. In fact, despite a total lack of portholes on this deck, Caymus could actually see daylight from this position. It seemed that the flames had been so intense that they'd already burned away a huge section of the hull. He wasn't sure just how much of what he was looking at was burning hull and how much was just flames, but there was definitely a sizable hole at the front of the ship. Caymus winced, realizing that the entire structure of the ship could collapse at any moment!

What had fallen on him? He glanced to his other side and realized that the burning thing he'd just pushed away from him had once been steps from the upper decks of the ship. That meant the upper decks were on fire too. How? How in the world had that the fire jumped from the ground all the way up there so fast?

He supposed that didn't matter, though. What mattered was that he was now trapped. He couldn't go up, as the steps were gone; he couldn't go back down, else the smoke would choke him; he couldn't stay where he was for more than a few more minutes. There was nowhere to go, and he was so tired—so very tired—that he felt like it might be best if he just gave up and let the flames take him.

Then, his eyes caught movement nearby, and he saw his father through the smoke. His father, who'd cared for him his whole life, who'd taught him how to fish, how to sail, how to start a campfire, who'd told him how to talk to girls and had showed him how to use a razor…was breathing! His eyelids were fluttering too, as though he was fighting for consciousness: he was alive!

In that singular moment, Caymus decided he didn't care what happened to himself anymore; he couldn't let his father burn though, not if there was even the smallest chance of saving him!

He had to move, had to get up.

But his muscles felt so weak, his eyes stung, and his lungs were on fire. He was so tired. All he had to do was lie here for a few more moments, and it would all be over…

"No!" Caymus screamed out loud, inviting fresh spasms of coughing. "Get up!" he rasped at himself. "Get! Up!"

With that, he struggled against the tiredness in his bones, raged against his desire to simply give up and die. His muscles screamed as he fought his way to his knees, and as he picked his father up again, he wondered if they might actually tear from the effort. He planted one foot on the ground, nearly lost his balance, then planted the other foot.

Then, somehow, he was standing, albeit hunched and half-dead, and looking for the flames at the bow.

He knew his father only had one chance, and so he took it. Screaming with agony, with fury, he took one step forward then another, pushing himself toward the inferno at the bow of the ship, toward the only way out he could see.

He couldn't see what was in that fire. He knew he was sure to be stopped by some still-solid beam in there, was sure to singe all the skin from his flesh, but it didn't matter. If only he could get his father out…

He stumbled, ran, stumbled again, felt heat so searing that he was sure it had killed him…

And then was falling through empty air. He hit two…somethings…as he fell, and then he felt the ground rise up and strike him hard in the shoulder and the back of the head, felt himself lose his grip on his father's body.

As he lay there, numb to the desires of the world, he thought about how quiet everything suddenly seemed. He could hear shouting voices, could feel hands on his flesh, could feel the world moving underneath him. Was he being dragged? It didn't matter. What mattered was the thing he'd set out to do. His neck hurt, but he still managed to turn his head and look.

The search was a short one. His father was right beside him, being carried off to who-knew-where. Caymus watched intently for a few moments until he saw the tell-tale rise and fall of the man's chest.

Satisfied, and so very, very tired, Caymus closed his eyes. A fatigue more profound than any he'd ever known lay upon him, and, seeing no further reason that he should fight, he surrendered to it, and knew peace.

Chapter 1

Feel the flame.

The words echoed in Caymus's mind, again and again. Eyes closed, back straight, legs crossed upon the cold stone of the chamber, he did his best to still his mind, and once again practiced the Ritual of Embers.

Feel the flame.

First, he slowed his breathing. The fires in his body would rage like a blacksmith's furnace with too much air; he needed those fires to dampen, to quiet, that he might be able to see past them.

Next, he began to relax his muscles. He started at his center, then worked his way out towards his extremities, tensing each fiber, that he might become aware of it, then letting it calm. As the muscles relaxed, so too did the organs which supplied them with blood—the hot, liquid fire of life—and so his heartbeat slowed and the fires in his body quieted, calmed, stilled.

Feel the flame.

The flames were quiet. Caymus took a quick moment to be pleased with his success. Embers was about making the body calm, about making the fires within diminish to the point that a person's mind could see past their distraction. He'd been practicing this ritual every day since joining the Second Circle, but he'd never achieved this result so quickly before.

"Boy…" came Be'Var's warning voice.

The instant of pleasure had caused his heart to beat faster. Caymus chided himself for the moment of distraction, then went through the process again. Very quickly, he reached the state of quiet he sought.

A soft glow, not a raging fire: that was what Embers was about.

"Good. Now have a look around."

Feel the flame.

Now that the fires within his own being had been reduced to embers,

Caymus became aware of those flames without. He could feel them out there, everywhere: little pools of fire, burning at various intensities all around him. Though he was satisfied with the sensations, he knew not to become too interested in them yet. Instead, he reached out beyond the confines of his body and tried, as he has been taught, to see widely, to make a survey of his environment without using his eyes, to sense the fire within the chamber with his mind, rather than his skin.

Feel the flame.

The first thing he felt was fire's absence in the floor beneath him. He felt the chill of the stone against his legs, felt it sap what fire remained in his flesh. He felt the very air of the room slowly leeching heat from his body as though it were an animal feeding on him. He could envision the warmth of his body seeping out him in this way, could feel how it would lead to his demise if not for the warm core of his center radiating like the sun, making up for the losses.

Feel the flame.

He next became aware of the other students—all six of them—who were standing around the perimeter of the small chamber. Two of them were clearly practicing Embers themselves, as they radiated less heat than the rest; those must have been Gren and Phelyn. In stark contrast to them was Wrentyl, who had been working outside at seventh bell and had run to be in time for the lesson. Caymus could feel the heat radiating from him as though he was a torch; even the drops of sweat dripping from his nose and chin were warm.

The remaining students appeared disinterested in Caymus's lesson. Caymus could feel the way they were scuffing their feet against the floor, the way they were rocking, unconsciously, from foot to foot.

He wondered where Sannet, the eighth member of Master Be'Var's advanced class, was. He was a little disappointed that his friend wasn't in attendance.

Feel the flame.

Master Be'Var was leaning against the wall too, apart from his disciples and in front of Caymus. Caymus could barely sense the master's presence though, not like he could his fellow students. The old man seemed to control how much heat he radiated, as though he had learned not to waste energy keeping himself any warmer than necessary. His breathing was slow and easy, too. Caymus marveled at the man's discipline. Would he ever be able to do that?

Feel the flame.

The flame itself was small and timid. Had his eyes been open, Caymus wouldn't have been able to see by its flickering light. Having just gained purchase on the dry wood in the center of the room, it did not yet crackle or spurt. Instead, it held steady as it reached toward the ceiling and attempted to grow outward, to consume more of the fuel it fed upon. It did not dare burn too fiercely. Not yet. Not until it was larger, until it could draw enough air so as not to smother itself.

Feel the flame.

Caymus reached out to the flame with his mind, felt its heat, felt its tiny, flickering boundaries. There was great and terrible power contained within that flame, though there was warmth and comfort, too. Fire was a destroyer, but it was also safety on a dark night.

"Nearly…" said Be'Var, his gruff voice barely more than a whisper. "Now find out where it leads."

Caymus struggled, relaxed, struggled again, relaxed again. He knew he what he was trying to do, though he didn't yet know how. He'd grasped the flame itself, but now he needed to reach *beyond* it, *through* it. He needed to place his conscious mind inside the fire somehow, that he might feel every dimension.

Feel the flame.

In the span of a single moment, his thoughts drifted in a way he did not yet understand, and he became linked with the flame. He consumed it, was consumed by it. He felt the little fire feeding upon the wood, and the fire's hunger was his own hunger. He felt the consumption of the air in the room, and his own breaths became the fire's breaths. He breathed in, and the flame grew slightly larger; he breathed out, and it diminished. He'd done it. He felt like celebrating, but he knew he wasn't yet finished. He still needed to do what the master had said, and find out where the flame led. Taking one more deep, heavy breath, he steadied his thoughts and reached past the fire.

Feel the flame.

He felt it, and he experienced such a sense of perfect, ecstatic joy that he nearly wept.

Though every body, every surface, every single "thing" in the small chamber interacted, to some degree, with the element of fire, either soaking it inward or radiating it out, the little flame was different. It had no surface, no mass. Indeed, it could barely be thought to exist in the same way everything else did. Rather, the flame existed due to the presence of a conduit, a path torn through the fabric of reality from another place, another realm, and the conduit allowed a portion of that realm through.

The Conflagration. The Realm of Fire.

It was a realm where no living thing roamed, a place where flames burned eternally, where there existed nothing but searing fire in any direction one could think to travel, where vast and terrible flame-lords screamed their angry battle cries and dreamed of furious victory. There were those in the world who believed it to be an idea, a story that parents told their children around campfires. Most believed that there had to be some truth to those stories though, else how could the fire masters accomplish their terrible feats. Yet such foreign, intangible ideas could exert no influence upon the lives if most people, and so they were largely ignored.

For Caymus, who'd been studying for nearly two years just to reach this very moment, the Conflagration was as real as the realm around him. The two realms existed side-by-side, completely separate, but occasionally linked by conduits such as the one burning on the log before him.

But he could feel that he connection to the Conflagration was tenuous. It was so vast! It was so terrible! There was so much power! Caymus could feel his hold on the conduit, and yet he could also feel that hold slipping away! He was trying to concentrate, to hold the connection, but the more he held on, the more the power of the Conflagration threatened to overwhelm him!

"You have it, don't you, boy?" Be'Var's voice was harsh and menacing, yet it also conveyed the same genuine concern for his student that it always did. In his mind's eye, Caymus could picture the master furrowing both his brow and half his bald scalp as he directed his piercing, gray eyes to stare directly into his student's soul.

"I…I think so," Caymus replied. His face was tight with concentration and effort. As he spoke, he felt beads of sweat forming at his forehead, running down the lengths of his eyebrows, and dripping down his cheeks.

He felt Be'Var move from the wall. "Not nearly good enough," he said, his tone scolding. "You can't *think*; you need to *know*. You need to be completely certain of your connection. The Conflagration is many things, but it is *not* forgiving. It doesn't feel remorse, and it doesn't feel pity. So if you try to draw on it without a *very* firm grip, it will burn you to cinders."

Again, Caymus felt and probed around the flame, searching for a better hold, attempting to form a stronger connection with this conduit, to find his way through to the roaring inferno beyond. He wasn't even entirely sure how he'd made the connection in the first place, though, and so he wasn't sure how to fix what was breaking. He struggled with it as though a child on his first fishing trip, unsure what to do with lines, lures, or slippery, wriggling worms. His face tightened further, his expression became a painful frown, and the muscles of his neck, chest, and arms bunched as tendons tensed against one another.

"Relax, Caymus. Stop trying to force it." Be'Var's voice was calmer now: less scolding; more instructive. It sounded loud in Caymus's ears, as though the man were standing mere inches away from him. "Stop fighting and return to Embers. If you keep struggling, you're just going to push it farther away."

Caymus took a deep breath and did his best to obey the master's instructions. Relax. He needed to relax, to get back to a place where his mind and body were still. Once again, he sought the peace and calm of Embers, and the practiced ritual came to him easily. Slowly, the muscles in his face relaxed and his breathing slowed and became gentle. Slowly, he felt the connection he'd been seeking, and his efforts began to take shape.

Caymus's mind was clear, his thoughts washed clean by the Ritual of Embers. He found his consciousness merging completely with the young flame, felt the warm of it, the radiance of it. And through it, he once again felt the tantalizing sensation of the Conflagration. He'd only caught the slightest glimpse before; now he felt the sheer radiance of the realm of fire bathing his thoughts. The sensation caught him unprepared, and he felt his eyes well up with tears at the sheer beauty of it.

He felt the flame flit this way and that as small, barely perceptible currents of air wafted across it. Caymus allowed himself to feel the room again, and he realized that the students were making way for Master Be'Var to move. After just a moment, the old priest was sitting across from him, just the other side of the hearth.

"Good," Be'Var said. "Now, boy, I want you to make the flame hotter."

Caymus felt his brow furrow. "How?"

"On the other side of that conduit," grunted Be'Var, "is the Conflagration. The fire is a part of it, a tendril of the fire realm intruding into our world. If your connection is strong enough, you can pull on that tendril and draw more power out. Understand?"

Caymus's frown deepened. "What do I pull on?" he asked. "The flame or the conduit?"

"Neither," replied Be'Var. "Both. It's not about what you're pulling on; it's about your connection. If you've made a good connection, it should feel as intuitive as lifting your own arm."

Caymus nodded, though he didn't yet understand. "Okay."

"Be careful, though," warned the master. "Have a *firm* grip before you try it. What I said before about being incinerated hasn't changed."

Caymus did his best to stifle his frustration with the old man's commands. He reached for Embers again, letting his mind cool, letting his thoughts relax. Once he felt a sense of calmness washing over him, he places his conscious self, once again, into the flame. What was he supposed to be pulling—

—oh.

Caymus could see what the old man meant. Rather, he could feel it. The Conflagration flowed into his world through this budding fire, and now that he was so intimately connected with it, he could sense the possibility of pulling more power through. The potential sat there before him, almost daring him to try.

Be'Var was right: he couldn't really say what he needed to pull against

—one might as well ask what to pull on in order to take a breath—but he knew instinctively what to do. He could feel the Conflagration on the other side of the conduit, could feel the raw, immediate power contained within it; all he needed to do was draw it through.

With some effort, he centered his mind, placed his consciousness into the hottest part of the flame, and pulled.

Nothing happened. He'd expected a glorious torrent of energy to suddenly flow his way, but no such torrent came. The little fire continued to burn steadily. It was slightly larger now, but it grew naturally, as it would have done without his presence. To Caymus, the quiet of the chamber was suddenly overwhelming.

He took a breath, tried to understand what he'd felt during his attempt. He knew he'd lost his grip, somehow, that he'd failed to really get a good hold on the stream of energy coming through the conduit. His consciousness was infusing the flame, was part of it now, but the stream of fire itself, the connection to the Conflagration, had slipped away when he'd reached for it. He didn't feel like he'd done anything wrong, though. Maybe it had just been bad luck?

Taking a deep breath, he tried again. He calmed his conscious self as much as possible, though in the back of his mind, a voice screamed in terrified anxiety, reminding him that what he was doing was dangerous, that more than one disciple at this Temple had scarred himself for life, or even died, attempting to do this very thing for the first time.

He was slightly relieved, in fact, when he failed for a second time. He felt as though he was trying to retrieve some small item from a dark nest of venomous snakes; he hadn't accomplished anything, but at least he hadn't angered the vipers either.

With some consternation, Caymus backed off and assessed his situation. The rest of the process had felt fairly natural to him, but now that he was trying to actually pull more energy through, he was stumbling, not even coming close to succeeding. What was he doing wrong? His body was relaxed and his mind was clear. Infusing the conduit with his own consciousness had felt been simple enough, and he could easily detect the filaments of energy within, so why did those filaments seem to melt through his hands like tree sap whenever he tried to grasp them?

Then, he realized there might be another way.

There were four distinct parts to the puzzle he was looking at here. The Conflagration itself was the source of all fire in the world. The flame in the center of the room was a projection of the Conflagration's power. There was the conduit connecting them, of course, but there was also the thread of energy running through from the Conflagration, through the conduit, and into the flame. The filament, he now understood, was the thing he'd been trying to pull on, but he couldn't seem to grasp it. It was almost as though the conduit was a pipe and the filament was the water running through it. He could no more grasp the filament than he could a stream of water.

However, while he couldn't seem to get a grip on the Conflagration's energies, he *did* have a very firm hold on the conduit itself. He should be able to bend and stretch *that* as easily as he flexed a muscle! If he simply narrowed the conduit around the filament, the same amount of energy would have to flow faster, like water crashing through a rapid, and the faster flowing energy should make the flame hotter.

It should work. He wasn't certain of the mechanics of it all, but it *felt* right.

But, wait. Was this actually what Be'Var wanted him to do? It couldn't be. Could it? The master was talking about pulling more energy through, and Caymus was considering moving and shaping the conduit through which the energy flowed. The master wanted the flame to be hotter; did it really matter how he did it? Perhaps that was the point? Perhaps this exercise was designed around getting him to figure this out! With that thought in mind, he engulfed the conduit completely within his own consciousness, then he began to squeeze.

The results came quickly. In fact, they came much more quickly than he'd been expecting. The flame's outline constricted slightly and deepened from a lazy, comfortable orange to an angry yellow, and the wood fuel gave a loud pop as the flame quickly burned through the layer of bark it had been chewing on. The students gasped, impressed by the display. Caymus could feel the heat of their bodies crowding in around the hearth, but then he felt the same heat move backward again as Be'Var waved them away.

"Boy?" came the master's voice. "What are you doing?"

"Making it hotter," said Caymus, his tone a bit more nonchalant than he'd intended. The flame was growing faster now, and its increased appetite meant it was drawing more and more energy from the Conflagration as each moment passed. "I think," he continued, beginning to sweat with effort, "I think I can do better."

Again, he squeezed the conduit, and again the fire grew hotter, angrier. The flame's hue turned to a much brighter yellow as it sizzled through the wood in the hearth, which popped and sputtered under the onslaught. In the small room, the temperature was beginning to rise noticeably.

"All right," said Be'Var, "that's enough." As he spoke, the master couldn't quite keep the apprehension out of his voice. This was clearly more than the master had been expecting to see today.

"Wait, Master," Caymus's voice was trilling with excitement now, "just a little bit more." He squeezed hard this time, and the results were immediate. The yellow flame melted away, leaving a roaring white beast in the center of the room. Gone was the sizzling sound of burning wood, and in its place was a furious buzz, like that of a swarm of hornets preparing to attack. The stone floor of the room increased dramatically in temperature, and Caymus even noticed his breathing getting difficult as the very air around him turned hot. The other students, now pressed against the circular wall—some gasping for air—were beginning to panic.

There was nothing timid in Be'Var's voice now. "I said that's *enough*!"

Whether he would actually have been able to relax his grip on the conduit and lower the flame's intensity again, Caymus would never know. By then, the searing white fire had burned through the remainder of its fuel. It quickly sputtered and died, leaving only a smoking hearth and a darkened room. Caymus's body stung slightly as the conduit of energy was ripped away from him so suddenly. He opened his eyes. He was surprised to find himself sitting not only in total silence, but also in a stark darkness.

For several long seconds, the darkness engulfed the little classroom, and Caymus only had the sounds of his fellow students slowly catching their breath to listen to. Eventually, he heard Master Be'Var lift himself up from the floor and step over to the classroom's single, wooden door. He opened it into the hallway beyond, and flickering torchlight spilled into the room.

Caymus, his eyes stinging at the new light, looked at his instructor with a sheepish grin. "I'm sorry, Master," he said. "It was just so amazing, and I—"

But Be'Var wasn't interested in explanations. "Don't you ever do that again, boy!" he shouted. Despite his years, his voice was loud and strong, and his entire body seemed to vibrate with anger. He pointed a calloused finger at Caymus. "I do not care how good at this you might think you are. Disciples are here to learn, not to do as they please and get themselves incinerated by their own idiotic curiosities, so when I say stop, you stop! Do you understand me, boy?"

Caymus, suddenly realizing just how grievous an error he'd just committed, cast his eyes downward and spoke very softly. "I'm sorry, Master," he said. "It won't happen again."

"It had better not!" said Be'Var, still yelling. "Mistakes, lapses in judgement, moments of foolhardiness: they have consequences. Do you understand that if that hearth had been furnished with even one more branch of everwood, you could very easily have suffocated everyone in this room?"

At that, Caymus glanced around and noted the concern on some of the faces of his fellow students. There was fear in a few of those eyes, too, though whether that was fear of what he'd just done or fear of Be'Var, he wasn't sure. It was clearly his fault, though; he'd have to apologize to them when he got the chance.

Be'Var seemed ready to yell again, but he instead closed his eyes, placed a hand over his face and rubbed the bridge of his nose. He then took a deep breath and waved the other hand around the room. "This is over," he said more calmly, addressing the other students. "I'll meet you all in the sanctuary in an hour."

With that, the other young men quietly and gratefully filed out the door. Caymus, however, sensed that he wasn't dismissed yet, and so he sat still. He suddenly became acutely aware of his own size, of how conspicuous he must seem. The room, one of fifteen classrooms of its type in the Temple, was cylindrical in shape and barely a dozen feet in diameter. It might have been considered cramped if not for its high ceilings, ending in the six blackened ventilation holes, that were designed to carry the smoke from the room. Caymus had never thought of the space as being particularly small before; it sure felt small to him in that moment, though.

After the last student had filed out, Be'Var allowed the door to swing closed, then master and disciple were left alone together in darkness. The old man then lit a torch on the opposite side of the room and shuffled toward his student.

"Caymus," the master sighed, sitting down again on the opposite side of the hearth and looking down at the ash and char.

Caymus raised his head, slightly concerned that Be'Var was addressing him by his name, rather than the usual, "boy". The master was shaking his head and silently moving his lips, as though searching for the right words. Then, the old man lifted his eyes and looked his pupil over. Caymus was again reminded of his unusually large size. He'd grown even larger during his years at the Temple: he was just a hair under seven feet tall now, and at eighteen years old he'd gained broad shoulders to go along with his great height. He nervously ran a hand over his scalp as he waited for the master's judgement: that was a habit he'd picked up since he'd cut his sandy brown hair short, a requirement for boys upon first joining the Temple.

Be'Var sighed again, then looked Caymus in the eyes. "Caymus, you are a problem. Do you know that?"

Caymus surprised by the admission, didn't know what to say, and so he just shook his head.

Be'Var nodded. "Well, you are. You see, you have this enormous affinity for fire, this…intuition for the Conflagration. Where your fellow disciples have to study and fret over lessons, you just pick things up as though the masters were just teaching you how to breathe in and out. There are plenty of other disciples here who aren't terribly fond of you for that, but that's because they know what you and I both know: you're going to be a fine master one day, a priest of the Conflagration who will do amazing things. The fact that you're due to take your Trial of Courage more than a year before your twentieth is proof enough of that." He narrowed his eyes. "I'm actually not even sure if that's been done before."

The old man paused, seemingly nodding to himself. Caymus wondered if he should be saying something.

"That," continued Be'Var, "however, isn't the problem." He looked Caymus in the eye again. "The problem is that talent breeds confidence, and confidence can very easily turn into *over*-confidence." He raised a meaningful eyebrow at his pupil. "Normally, I wouldn't think you capable of such a thing, yet here you are," he lifted a hand and indicated the spent hearth, "breaking rules, acting recklessly, and adding to the general confusion."

The master looked back down at the burnt-out hearth, a frustrated sadness in his eyes. "You're in the advanced class, the one with the most gifted and most studious disciples in this building, and if the rest of them see you acting with reckless abandon, they might think it's a good idea too, and that kind of thing leads to chaos." He frowned. "Fire is chaotic enough without help from you. Got it?"

Caymus nodded, feeling no small amount of shame.

"It's the kind of behavior that prods the masters into voting for a disciple's removal from this place."

Caymus's eyes went wide with alarm.

"*More to the point,*" said Be'Var, his voice raising in anger, "it's the kind of thing that gets a disciple fried to a crisp because he started something he couldn't control! Tell me you understand that, boy." The man's visage calmed somewhat. "Tell me you understand how dangerous what you just did was."

Caymus took a deep breath and nodded, truthfully. In the coolness of reason and the wisdom of hindsight, he could understand why what he'd done had been foolish. "I understand, master," he said. "I got caught up in the moment, and that's something I know I shouldn't do."

Be'Var seemed satisfied with that. As he nodded, he glanced back down at the hearth, then back up at Caymus, a quizzical expression on his face. "Just what did you do, anyway?" he asked. "I wasn't watching closely enough to see the details, but I know you didn't do what I told you."

Caymus thought for a while before responding. "I did try it your way, Master. I tried to hold on to those…to the filaments of fire inside the conduit and pull more of them through, but…but I just couldn't get a grip. Then, I noticed that I could do the same thing—make the fire hotter —by changing the shape of the conduit instead."

"The shape?" said Be'Var, raising an eyebrow.

"Yes. The fire got hotter after I did that, and that burned through the wood faster, which got more energy flowing through…" he trailed off, then shrugged, timidly. "I thought maybe, that was the point?" He considered his next words very carefully. "I know I should have stopped the moment you told me to, master. I really am sorry."

Be'Var seemed to consider this. He shuffled backwards on his legs until his back was against the circular wall. He leaned back against the stone, and his eyes were distant, thoughtful, as though he was remembering something. "No," he said. "It certainly wasn't the point. However, if what you say is true, we may have just learned something very interesting about you."

It was Caymus's turn to frown. "Something interesting?"

Be'Var looked back and, surprisingly, instead of the usual scowl, his face was offering up a small grin.

Caymus didn't know just how old Be'Var was—in his seventies, at the very least, if the creased, leathery skin of his face was any indication—but he was always surprised at how young and alive the man's eyes seemed to be. None of the other masters had eyes like that, not even Eavuk, who was the youngest of them by far.

"No," Be'Var said, shaking his head. Then he stood up, dusting off his hands. "No, I need to look a couple of things up before I start spouting off half-baked theories. But trust me: if I'm right, it's very interesting indeed."

He then looked down at the smoking remains of Caymus's handiwork and sighed. "I meant what I said, Caymus. Mistakes like the one you just committed are exactly the reason the hearths aren't built any larger. Flame needs air to live, but so do people. You really could have killed somebody today—several somebodies, in fact." He pointedly raised an eyebrow. "Including me." He glanced briefly at the door to the chamber. "The students will talk, of course, so the other masters will find out about the incident soon enough. I doubt there will be a vote to cast out or anything, but the idea will cross a few minds, I'm sure."

Caymus opened his mouth to apologize again, but Be'Var halted him with a wave of his hand. "Just promise me I won't have to raise my voice with you again, boy," he said, "all right?"

Caymus stood also, nodding towards his mentor. "I promise, Master."

"Good," said Be'Var, nodding as he looked around the room. "Well, I suppose misbehavior requires penance. Porindus could use a break from rebuilding the hearths tonight, so I think I'll have you do it instead. Think you can handle that?"

Caymus winced. "All six of them?"

Be'Var emitted an evil chuckle. "Ten," he corrected. "Don't forget the hearths in the masters' rooms."

Caymus sighed, resigned to his fate. "Yes, Master Be'Var," he said, and as Be'Var left for the sanctuary, the young disciple went in search of a broom, a pan, and several bundles of everwood, beginning a project he knew would keep him busy right through the evening meal.

~~~

About an hour before ninth bell, which would signal the curfew hour for disciples of the Temple of the Conflagration, Caymus stumbled into the dormitory he shared with his two roommates, Rill and Sannet. The two boys were there already. Sannet was sitting up in his cot in the corner, reading as usual. Rill was lying on the top bunk of the bed he and Caymus were meant to share.

Caymus spared a passing glance for the bottom of the two beds. He'd had passed on it when the trio were first getting settled in three years ago, opting instead for a mat on the floor. Mattresses never seemed to be quite big enough for him; plus, he liked being able to see the night sky out of their third-story window. The bed, therefore held Rill's and Caymus's storage trunks, rather than pillows and blankets.

Rill sat up the moment Caymus entered. "Hey big guy, we missed you at supper. What happened?"

Caymus pulled his mat from its resting place against the wall, threw it onto the floor, and promptly fell on it. "Penance," he said, exhaling dramatically. "Be'Var had me rebuild all the hearths in the east wing tonight." He rubbed his eyes with the heels of his hands and tried to ignore sudden hunger pangs. "I…I kind of made a mistake."

"Really?" said Rill, his face breaking into a grin. "And here I thought we were a bit old for the whole, 'send you to bed without supper,' routine."

Caymus dropped his hands to his sides and turned his head to look at his friend. "Heard of it, have you?"

Rill's grin grew broader, and he reached behind himself and pulled out a small pouch, which he then lightly tossed in Caymus's direction. "You know, I might have come across it once or twice," he said.

Caymus caught the pouch. It smelled like food.

"And," Rill continued, "have you ever noticed how all of the classrooms with hearths in them are in the east wing, but the masters store all the dried everwood in the west wing?"

"I noticed today," sighed Caymus as he opened the pouch. It was jerked mutton, no doubt filched from the kitchen on his behalf. He chuckled, then rose to a sitting position and held the pouch up. "Rill, my friend, you are a lifesaver." A few pieces of dry meat weren't exactly a
~~~

filling meal, but they would at least quiet his stomach until morning. Greedily, he ate.

Rill shifted, making the old bed creak, then sat up, dangling his feet off the side. He was grinning like an idiot, and his vivid blue eyes, perched above his crooked nose, twinkled with delight. "Any time, Caymus. Just try to remember my lifesaving skills next time you notice me conspicuously absent at the evening meal."

Caymus chuckled. "I'll do that."

"You're just encouraging him, you know," remarked Sannet, his face hidden behind a particularly heavy-looking tome.

"To do what?" said Rill.

Sannet laid the book flat on his lap and turned his spectacled eyes toward Rill, an ironic smile on his face. He held up three fingers and started counting them off, one-by-one. "To break the rules," he said, "to act recklessly," he continued.

"To add to the general confusion!" they all said in unison, each boy doing his best to imitate Master Be'Var.

After the chuckles had died down, Sannet's smile faded and his expression took a more serious turn. "Seriously though, Caymus, I heard you put on quite a display today." Sannet's meaning was clear. "Mistake, you say?"

Caymus let his shoulders slump as he answered. "Yes," he said. "Yes, I think that's the kindest term for it."

Sannet sat up straight, looking both concerned and more than a little stern. "Way I heard things, it was very nearly a disaster. You should have seen how wide Wrentyl's eyes were when he was telling me about it at dinner tonight. He said he could hardly breathe at one point."

Rill turned to Caymus. "Whoa, what's this? That doesn't sound like you."

"No, Wrentyl's right," said Caymus. He didn't really want to get into it, but Rill's staring, probing eyes told him he wasn't really going to get a choice in the matter. He sighed. "Be'Var decided it was time to test my ability to pull today. It went well, to a point. Then I kind of took it too far."

Rill's mouth hung open. "Pulling? Really? They let you try pulling?"

"Really," said Caymus.

Sannet chimed in. "It's really not that surprising, is it Rill? I mean, Caymus is set to take his Trial of Courage tomorrow. It's not as though it's unusual for the masters to start training disciples in more advanced topics a few days before they enter the Third Circle." He gave Caymus an appraising look. "I just hope he hasn't spoiled anything for the rest of us. I still think I might make Third by the end of the year."

He then removed his spectacles and began cleaning them on his ink-stained tunic. "Well, I'm genuinely sorry I missed it. I was in a tutorial with Parson for most of the afternoon, else I'd have been there to see this 'mistake' of yours."

Sannet's eyes brightened just a little. "So," he said as he squinted at Caymus, "don't keep us in suspense. How was it?"

Caymus smiled, realizing he was glad for the question. "It was amazing, Sannet. Really connecting with the Conflagration lake that: it's like nothing you've ever felt before. It's..." he raised his hands, searching for the words, then he put them down again. "I don't really think I can explain it," he admitted, looking between the two of them. "You're going to have to find out for yourselves, I suppose."

Rill sighed. "Yeah, when—*if*—I ever get past the Second Circle." He flopped back down on the bunk, defeated.

"You worry about that too much, Rill," said Caymus. "Determination and lots of practice; Master Eavuk keeps saying anyone can become a master with enough work."

Sannet chuckled. "You're hardly one to give advice, Caymus," he said. "I mean, no offense, but what would you know about determination *or* practice when it all just comes so easy to you? After tonight you'll be stepping into the Conduit for your third trial—what is it, a year-and-a-half sooner than anyone else in the history of this building?"

"Fifteen months," Caymus replied, opting for a mock-defensive tone. "And, hey, I can't help it if the masters think I'm the greatest thing to walk these halls in a thousand years." Grinning, he looked at his friends in turn. "I'm just…gifted, that's all. I'm the Gifted Disci—"

He was cut short when a well-aimed pillow from Sannet's direction hit him in the face. Rill laughed out loud. "What was that?" He chuckled. "Sorry, the gifted dis?"

"Yes," mused Sannet. "Gifted Dis. That's what I heard, too."

"Apologies Gifted Dis," said Rill, "but, we mere mortals are too dumb to understand your ever-so-holy words. What were you saying?"

Caymus grinned as he threw Sannet's pillow back to him. "Oh, I forget," he said. "Nothing important."

Caymus folded his hands behind his head and lay back, satisfied to be among his friends after the stresses of the evening. As he stared at the grey, stone ceiling of the dormitory, he took a moment to ponder what Sannet had said, his friend's words echoing what Be'Var had told him just a few hours earlier. It was true: he'd always had a natural aptitude for the study of the Conflagration, and one he'd still never been able to properly explain.

After the incident on the *Pride of the Expanse*, things had moved quickly for Caymus. Far too quickly, in fact. The fire had been determined to be an accident in the end: the pitch-pot had been set up too close to the ship. Since there's been so much still-drying pitch between the seams of the *Pride's* decks, the vessel had burned quickly. All anyone had been able to talk about, however, was how the hull master's son had come flying out of the hull like an arrow just before the scaffolding had collapsed. He'd apparently had a lot to do with that collapse, in fact, having smashed through three sections of scaffold on his way to the ground. Miraculously, however, besides some heavy bruises and a slightly fractured wrist, he'd not been hurt.

In fact, only one person had been affected by that fire: his father. Aster Bolwerc hadn't been burned in the flames, but he'd inhaled a lot of smoke while trapped in the ship's bilge. In the end, that smoke had been too much for him. He'd spent two weeks convalescing at home in Woodsea, struggling for every breath, before his body had finally given out.

Those two weeks had been hard for Caymus and his mother, but they'd been eased somewhat by the fact that only three days after the fire, a priest from the nearby Temple of the Conflagration had knocked on their door. The master had introduced himself as Be'Var.

Be'Var's purpose had been two-fold. First, he'd been told of Aster's condition and had believed he could help ease the man's suffering with his arts. Caymus still didn't know what Be'Var had done for his father that day, but shortly after he'd laid his hands on the man for about ten minutes, the man had been better. He'd still had a great deal of trouble breathing, but the coughing and wheezing had lessened enough that his body wasn't constantly wracked with pain anymore. Caymus had been so grateful for that.

The other thing Be'Var had come for was Caymus. News of his daring escape from the *Pride* had travelled around Krin's Point quickly. Be'Var had taken an interest, having taken particular note of the fact that neither Caymus nor his father appeared to have been burned by the flames that had consumed the ship. The master had claimed that only someone highly attuned to the fire element could possibly have escaped that inferno unscathed, and that such a person would do well as a disciple at his temple.

Caymus had rejected the idea at first, never having had any desire to become a priest. His father, however, had made him promise to go, to try.

"What if it turns out you have an aptitude," he'd said, "but you never found out because you never tried it?"

Caymus had, after a day or two of reflection, agreed to at least make the attempt.

His father had been pleased at his son's decision. He'd died the very next day.

After the funeral, Caymus had spent a couple of weeks helping his mother get the house in order, and then the two of them had spent two days walking to the middle of the Saleri Forest, where the Temple of the Conflagration lay. After a heartfelt goodbye, she'd left him at the building's doors, wishing him all the luck in the world.

Caymus had been a month away from his seventeenth birthday then. He'd thought at the time that he'd be home again by his eighteenth. Instead, he'd found in the Temple of the Conflagration a place where he truly belonged.

From the very first moment, Caymus had taken his discipleship in stride, immersing himself in his lessons and picking up concepts quickly and easily. He found that he loved learning about the Conflagration, that fire was a truly fascinating subject. He rarely studied, rarely practiced his rituals beyond the minimum requirement; he came to his answers through intuition rather than reason, and his natural aptitude meant he'd flown through the First and Second Circles rapidly, landing himself very quickly in Be'Var's class of advanced disciples.

Some of the other disciples, of course, resented his rapid progress through the circles. Many felt that by not studying hard he didn't earn his successes the way they had to. The majority of Be'Var's class, in fact, treated him with a distant sort of respect, acknowledging his achievements while being unwilling to reward him with their actual friendship.

Sannet was the exception, of course. He was another of Be'Var's advanced students, though he was a far more typical student. Sannet studied for hours on end and sought out private tutorials with the various masters at the Temple. He read and he practiced, then he read some more. Like Caymus, he was always able to correctly answer the questions that Be'Var asked of him, though, unlike Caymus, Sannet was always able to explain how he'd arrived at his conclusions, then refer back to some tome or lesson that supported him. Caymus rather envied him that ability.

Caymus sometimes wondered why Sannet never seemed to resent his natural ability. The two of them were often considered to be the strongest of the Temple's Second Circle disciples, though Caymus usually found himself at the head of any competition, if only because he could find his answers more quickly than Sannet. If his bespectacled friend ever felt any anger toward him, though, he never revealed it. It was one of the things Caymus liked most about him, in fact: he never made their implied competition personal.

Rill was, well…was Rill. Though Sannet was a good friend, he was a student first, always putting the interests of the Temple and of his own education before anything else. Rill, on the other hand, was the kind of friend who came through in a pinch, who was always around when Caymus needed help with something. He wasn't a particularly good student, having barely passed his Trial of Devotion, the gateway to the Second Circle, the previous month, but he was loyal and honest, and he was good at judging a situation. If ever Caymus ever found himself in a difficult position and didn't know what to do about it, he could always turn to Rill for a good solution, even if that solution was to simply escape from his problems for a while.

"Anyway, Rill," he said, picking up the threads of their conversation, "I think you're probably worrying about it all too much." He turned his head toward his friend, who was staring off into space in a world of his own. "You never thought you'd get past Devotion, did you? If you can pull that off, why not Courage?"

Rill sighed. "The Trial of Courage's different, Caymus," he said. "You know that. *Really* different."

Caymus was about to answer, but then he was interrupted by the dormitory door flying open and crashing against the inside wall. Caymus flinched at the sudden volume of it, then all three boys turned to see what intruder had caused such a racket.

Standing in the doorway was Ramone, a First Circle disciple who had latched onto the trio since his arrival about six months ago. He had dark features, a lean frame, and an overly-enthusiastic smile that almost never left his face. Caymus frowned at the interruption. Ramone was alright, he supposed, but he was a bit too high-strung to be around for more than a few minutes.

At that particular moment, Ramone was breathing hard with his hands clutching either side of the open doorway. His clothing and hair were in disarray as though he'd been running. "Girls!" he panted, "at the doors!"

Within the space of a second, all three boys had reached their feet.

"What?" said Caymus. "When? Why?"

"Showed up about ten minutes ago!" he said. "Three of 'em, plus a couple o' fellows that look like they could use a dose of civilization, if you know what I mean. Missionaries, they said. Said they're here to get supplies for their mission and drop off the two fellows."

The trio just stood there, too surprised to act, for a few seconds. Ramone looked at them incredulously. "Well?" he said. "Come on, ninth-bell's some time off yet, so if we hurry, we can go help out and get some time with 'em."

Rill was the first to move. "What are we waiting for, then?" he shouted, laughing as he pushed Ramone out of the way of the door.

The spell of inaction was broken, and the four made a mad dash down two flights of stairs, through three chambers and several hallways, and then out the sanctuary doors, much to the surprise of Master Ket and the small group of travelers he'd been talking to just outside the Temple's main doors.

Caymus quickly took stock. There were four women, all wearing the red traveling cloaks that were common among the Temple's missionaries. The eldest of them, a woman with long, silvered hair and kind eyes—she looked to be in her late sixties—had clearly just been speaking to Ket. The other three women were much younger, their ages likely ranging anywhere between fifteen and twenty. They were standing between the older woman and a horse-drawn wagon, watching the boys with curiosity.

There were two men standing behind the wagon, and Caymus immediately understood what Ramone had meant when he'd described them. Their skins were a deep brown color, their heads were shaved, and they carried unfamiliar markings on their bodies. Their dress was simple: breeches, tunics, and leather moccasins, all loose-fitting and travel-worn. One of them carried a satchel that clearly contained something large: the bulges in the leather revealed it was at least the size of a melon and that it was quite heavy. Their faces weren't exactly unfriendly, but they looked as though they were sizing the group of boys up, as though they were making up their minds as to whether Caymus and his friends constituted trouble.

Ket's expression was much easier to read. The always frazzled-looking man looked at the boys and raised a bushy, gray eyebrow at them. He always reminded Caymus of an owl when he did that. "Gentlemen," he said, "can I help you with something?"

Caymus knew his friends well. Rill, he knew, would try to be too charming. Sannet wouldn't be able to speak without spending five minutes considering his words. Even Ramone would trip over his own tongue in his enthusiasm. He therefore quickly took a step forward and took the position of group spokesman.

He cleared his throat. "Master Ket," he said, doing his best to walk the thin line between a sort of playful bravado that would impress the girls and a respectful supplication that would respect the master's authority, "we'd just heard that the Temple had visitors from one of the missions, and we thought we could…" he paused, then eventually settled on, "…that we could lend a hand?"

Caymus had never exactly been the most persuasive of people, and the sharp intake of breath behind him made him briefly fear he'd done it wrong. However, the two adults immediately turned and gave each other a knowing look, and at least two of the three young women were smiling.

"Well, I don't know," said Ket, and Caymus was surprised to hear a distance note of mischief in the man's usually grumbly voice. "Matron Y'selle, what do you think about all this? Do you actually need a hand…" he glanced back at the boys, "…or eight?"

The silver-haired woman beamed with delight; she was clearly enjoying this. "Well, to be honest, Master Ket, there simply isn't all that much that needs to be done tonight." She looked the boys over. "I'm not sure that any assistance is warranted, and I'd hate to put them out with ninth-bell so close. These young disciples surely must have studies to attend to?"

Caymus felt his hope deflate a little. Then, one of the girls stepped forward. She had golden-blonde hair and fair skin. Caymus thought she was rather pretty. "Matron Y'selle," she said, her smile just as wide and just as mischievous as the matron's, "if I may?"

Caymus kept his expression flat, though he couldn't help thinking that the whole situation seemed completely bizarre. He felt like the whole scene was completely false, almost as though everybody was putting on a play, rather than actually talking to one another. He knew that it was just a form of playful teasing, but it made him uncomfortable, nonetheless.

The matron turned, still smiling. "Yes, Gwenna? Do you have a suggestion?"

"Well, Matron," said Gwenna, dragging out the sound of the first word as she spoke it, "I know we've already unloaded the grain sacks, but aren't there also those *heavy* barrels of ore that we need to load up for the trip back?" She turned to the boys. "I know we were going to use the horses to haul them up and into the wagon tomorrow, but if these helpful young men could handle them instead, the poor horses could save their strength for the journey home. I'm sure there's still time."

Rill quietly hissed. "Oh, that's going to hurt," he whispered, just loudly enough for his friends to hear.

Rill was right. Caymus had seen the ore barrels that the matron was talking about. They'd come in from Krin's Point about six months ago, and no less than ten disciples had been involved in unloading them into the storage building that afternoon.

The matron clapped her hands together. "Oh, what an excellent idea," she said. "Girls, if you could show them where we want everything, I'll just finish discussing a few matters with Master Ket here."

Ket turned to the boys. "Well then, hop to it, gentlemen," he said. Then he gave them an approving nod which seemed to Caymus more than just a granting of permission. Ket liked to go on about "the balance" and he was likely quite satisfied with the deal the boys had just struck. They'd got what they came for: some time spent with the girls. They were, however going to pay a hefty price for it, not only shouldering near half a ton of ore and scrap metal, but also trying to do it quickly enough to have time to spare before curfew. Yes, Ket would like that: pleasure mixed with pain. The good came with an equal amount of bad, and thus "the balance" was maintained.

The girl named Gwenna motioned them over. "Come on boys," she said, leading her companions in the direction of the storage building, "let's get to work."

Victorious, yet also rather deflated, the four disciples followed the girls, hoping the upcoming ordeal would be worth it.

~~~

Half an hour later, Caymus and Rill, working together, hauled the last of the hundred-pound barrels outside and heaved it into the back of a creaking wagon. Caymus, tired but also invigorated, wiped his hands on his tunic and looked around at the group. The seven had been chatting while they worked—or rather, while the boys worked—and he'd learned that the girls, Gwenna, Monette, and Bridget, were from Flamehearth Mission in the city of Kepren, a couple of hundred miles to the Southeast. They had spent two weeks traveling across the Tebrian Plains and over the Greatstone Mountains to get here, and they were only planning on staying a night or two before heading back.

One obvious reason for the trip was for the supplies they had just loaded. Apparently, Kepren was experiencing a drought that had lasted for over a year. Crops which had once been fed by rain now relied upon the water from the Silvertooth River. There was no irrigation to speak of in the area, and so, while the Silvertooth's waters were plentiful, the effort of getting it from there to where it was needed had there was a drought in Kepren, one which had lasted long enough that people were starting to worry. birthed a new labor-based economy. The region around Kepren was mineral-poor, and so the ore they were taking back—the masters had purchased it as cast-offs from the shipyards and other industries in Krin's Point, then had extracted the metals themselves—would be a valuable commodity for trade. Caymus could barely wrap his head around the idea that the mission would essentially be buying water with this stuff; it seemed wrong, somehow.

The other reason the missionaries had come had been to escort the two dark-skinned men—their names were Guruk and Fach'un—to the Temple. The men were recent converts. They'd been living and learning at the mission for a couple of months, and now they wanted to spend some time learning about the Conflagration from the masters themselves. Their culture, it seemed, was also one of fire-worship, though it embraced different Aspects than those that Caymus was used to. The Aspect of pulling, for example, was a skill that Caymus was quite familiar with, as it was something he saw the masters perform on a near-daily basis. These people—they called themselves the Falaar—didn't know of pulling, but apparently knew of an Aspect which protected them from being burned or even singed by fire. The girls hadn't known what was in the satchel that
~~~

one of the men carried, though their best guess had been that it was some sort of gift to the Temple or possibly the Conflagration itself.

Caymus smiled a contented smile. He'd never have guessed, when he woke up this morning, that this was how his day would have turned out, and he felt good about helping with the ore, as it meant he was helping the mission, and, by extension, the Conflagration.

"Well, that should do it," said Ramone, sitting down against one of the wagon's large, wooden wheels. He sighed and wiped the sweat from his brow. "Wasn't too hard," he said, puffing out his chest and trying to appear larger than he actually was.

The red-haired girl named Monette immediately sat down next to Ramone. Caymus hadn't quite managed to get a read on Monette. Of the three girls, she seemed the most out-of-place, having a the only non-blonde hair and a slightly fuller figure than the other two. She'd also, it seemed, taken a liking to Ramone, but maybe that was because they seemed roughly the same age.

"Well you're just so strong," she said, reaching out to touch Ramone's arm and putting on a show of being overly demure. "You made it look so easy."

"You think so?" he replied, seeming both nervous and excited at the same time.

Monette nodded, and the two sat staring at each other for a few seconds until she turned away, blushing slightly.

The remaining five shared amused glances, then with tilts of their heads decided that they should quietly make their way someplace else. The opportunity to flirt was a rare thing in the Temple, as it was in the Conflagration's various missions. The two of them should be allowed to do it in private.

The storage building was near the stables at the back of the building, and so the group spent a few minutes making their way around the east wing of the Temple toward the front of the building, their plan being to sit out on the huge lawn which encircled the structure.

A slight breeze blew across the grass, carrying the scents of pine and everwood from the surrounding forest. Caymus quietly removed his cloth-and-leather shoes as they walked so that he might enjoy the cool, tickly feeling of the grass on his bare feet. As the others, encouraged by his example, did the same, he looked up at the dark, late summer sky. Bright stars filled the blackness and a full moon cast a pale light down on everything. It was a fine night to be outside.

He stole a look back at the Temple which had been his home for the last years of his life. Though not exactly a magnificent building, it was a very large one. The edifice stood four stories high and was over two hundred yards from end to end. The large, cylindrical structure that marked the sanctuary divided the east and west wings, themselves rectangular in shape. Many small windows looked out over the lawn where they now stood. Some of the windows revealed the faint glow of firelight as masters and disciples alike prepared for evening curfew, though most were simply tiny squares of black against the moonlit glow of gray brick. Short crenellations ran around the top of the building, telling of the days when this had been a fortress, rather than a place of worship.

The thing which dominated the scene though, and which still caught Caymus's breath in his throat every time he saw it, was the Conduit, the huge pillar of fire that seemed to begin at the roof of the sanctuary and which then extend heavenward for as far as could be seen. Every flame which had ever existed, of course, was tied by a conduit to the vast realm of the Conflagration, but *this* conduit—*The* Conduit—was different. It burned and swirled as it rose ever upward. It had been there as long as anyone could recall. It fed upon nothing. It was the sole reason that the Temple had been built here—in a part of the Saleri Forest that was otherwise the middle of nowhere—in the first place.

Caymus shuddered, partly with the overwhelming majesty of the vision before him, and partly with dread. In the morning, he was due to take his Trial of Courage, that he might prove himself worthy of the Third Circle. Caymus had been preparing for the moment for over a year, but he was still worried about this Trial. He loved the Conflagration and all its wonders, but he knew that a wise man also feared it. He wondered which would be the more appropriate response to intentionally stepping into a raging inferno.

After a moment or two, he decided there was no use worrying about it now and instead returned his attention to the present, and to the small group, now sitting in a rough circle in the grass.

Rill and Sannet seemed to be enjoying themselves, though Sannet was clearly a great deal less comfortable being here than his friends. He obviously wanted to impress these girls, but he found himself stumbling over some of his words. Rill, of course, had just been clowning around and generally being entertaining. Rill was good at making people laugh, a talent for which Caymus was glad. What Caymus was good at was being huge and generally conspicuous, so it was nice to have Rill to take peoples' attentions off him at times.

Of the girls, Gwenna seemed to be the most outspoken. She held herself with easy confidence and seemed to enjoy simple laughter. Her blond hair fell in waves to the small of her back and she had the kind of eyes that smiled along with her mouth.

Bridget was quieter, shyer. She was blond too, but her hair, straight and wispy, only reached her shoulders. It often fell in front of her face and hid her eyes, so she spent a good deal of time brushing it back in a very girlish manner.

"I can't imagine the idea of actually buying water," Rill was saying, his words echoing Caymus's earlier thoughts as the group sat down on the lawn. "Just how bad are things down there in the city?"

Gwenna answered. "Bad," she said. "I mean, it's been over a year since it rained, and people are saying the river is starting to get lower, too. The farms around the city are working harder than ever to keep the crops from drying up, and everyone who keeps a herd has had to move them closer to the Silvertooth, so there are all these little fights breaking out about who gets to keep their animals along the riverbank." She ran her hands through the grass as she spoke. "Nobody's actually starving yet, but that's largely because of the work Flamehearth and other missions are doing." She sighed. "I don't know, though: in a city as big as Kepren, I think it's only a matter of time…"

Bridget, looking down and also touching the grass around her, quietly said, "I have this little girl in one of my classrooms…" She brushed her hair back again. "She has to stay at the mission a lot of nights because her father is watching their herd, three miles downstream." She briefly looked up and made eye contact with Caymus. "They used to graze them just to the north of the city, but it's so much harder for him now."

Gwenna nodded. "There are a lot of people in the same situation these days. That ore's going to help a lot. It's worth a lot in Kepren for some reason, and it'll be good to have something to trade for food and water."

"There's something I don't get," said Sannet, pushing his spectacles back up the bridge of his nose. "If things are as bad as you say, shouldn't any food or water that's available be getting distributed throughout the city? Shouldn't people be pooling their resources." Sannet had been paying particular attention to the talk of the drought. He was from Kepren, and his family was still there.

Bridget said, "The dukes say it's not necessary."

"Dukes?" asked Rill.

Bridget nodded. "It's how the districts are run. The king and Prince Garrin rule Kepren but it's the dukes that run the districts."

"And that means they run the city," glowered Gwenna. "Fact is, right now it's just the farmers and the poor people who are struggling. I think a lot of other people aren't feeling it yet, even though they all know it hasn't rained in a long time."

Caymus noticed that Sannet visibly relaxed when she said that.

"Flaming dukes," continued Gwenna angrily, "and their flaming wells won't give us any flaming help!" She looked about at the surprised faces around her. "They all have personal wells, you know? Deep ones." She dropped her voice a bit. "They set rations and put out policies all the time about when you can and can't farm, how many cattle can be slaughtered in a day, whether washing with anything more than a damp cloth will get you publicly flogged. It's all for the 'common good' but you can be sure the nobility will be the last in the city to starve to death."

Nobody said anything for a while; everyone simply sat quietly with downcast eyes. Caymus found he had difficulty imagining the scenario that Gwenna was describing. He'd grown up in a small, fairly wealthy town by the sea, and the idea of a drought was completely alien to him.

Rill, who had never been particularly comfortable with silence, was the one to break it. "I can't imagine how hard that has to be," he said. "Is the mission getting by okay?"

"Sure," said Gwenna, noncommittally. "We'll be fine; we always are." Then, her lips turned up into a very slight smile. "Don't get me wrong; it's wonderful being there. It's good to be able to help people and teach the children, not to mention bringing people closer to the Conflagration." She sighed. "But I think I'd rather be here, where it's safer." She looked at the three young men and raised her eyebrows. "You boys get to stay here and learn to be priests while the missionaries are out doing the real work."

"Hey," said Rill, mirroring her expression, "it's not all that easy here, you know."

"Oh yeah?" said Gwenna.

Caymus knew Rill was right, of course. He found himself thinking about his upcoming Trial again, considering just how dangerous it was, remembering the stories he'd heard of disciples who'd thought they were ready, but had instead been incinerated.

Rill, however, hadn't been talking about that. "Yeah," he smirked. "Take Caymus here." His tone changed to one of mocking. "The poor thing was forced to do hard, manual labor all evening just because he can't do what he's told!"

The boys all chuckled at that; even Caymus. The girls smiled, though they exchanged confused glances as well.

"Funny," said Gwenna, "you don't strike me as a rebel, somehow."

Caymus grinned. "I just got a bit excited today is all. Pushed a little further than I should have."

"*Pulled*, you mean," said Sannet.

"Oh?" said Gwenna, looking impressed. "I didn't realize you were all in the First Circle."

Caymus shook his head. "We're not," he explained. "I'm just taking my Test of Faith tomorrow."

"And the masters," said Sannet, "decided to give him a preview of what comes afterward."

The girls looked at Caymus with raised eyebrows. "Wow," said

Gwenna, her tone verging on incredulity. "That's…unusual, isn't it? I'm impressed."

Caymus shook his head. "Don't be," he said. "It didn't go very well."

"What do you mean?" asked Bridget.

Caymus didn't really like talking about himself like this, and the fact that he could really feel all the eyes on him in that moment was making him uncomfortable. He was saved from having to explain himself, however, when he heard a sound, faint and familiar, drifting on the wind.

Caymus beamed. Before he even realized what he was doing, he'd gotten to his feet and was facing the tree-line off to the West.

"Something wrong?" asked Bridget.

Caymus looked suddenly back at them, slightly embarrassed to realize he'd momentarily forgotten they were there. He did he best to save himself by turning toward them and giving them a polite bow. "Sorry everyone, forgive my manners, but I need to go."

"What?" said Rill. "Caymus, ninth bell is something like five minutes away! What do you mean, you need to go?"

Caymus gave his friend a wince. "Cover for me tonight, will you, Rill?" He knew he was asking a lot, but he also didn't want to take the time to answer questions about what he was doing and where he was going, so he quickly durned and started jogging across the grass toward the forest.

"Was it something I said?" he heard Bridget say. Other sounds of confusion and curiosity arose in his wake, too. Caymus felt a little bad about that. He made a mental note to make apologies in the morning, not to mention to thank Rill for yet another favor tonight. He hated leaving his friends to make excuses for him, but the night suddenly held such promise of adventure, and with all the stresses of the day weighing on him, he simply couldn't resist the call.

Chapter 2

A cool breeze—not cold, but crisp and invigorating—blew across Caymus's face as he jogged across the well-manicured lawn, suddenly alone with his thoughts. There was something he loved about the night, something the day just couldn't match: the dark hours were calm, serene, and yet also full of mystery and excitement. Sometimes, it seemed like the world itself was pausing for breath in the darkness. Now that man had gone to sleep, the land could be at ease for a while, could rest from the day's exertions under the sun.

Before long, he had traversed the lawn that marked the boundary of land claimed by the Temple and had crossed into the wood of the Saleri Forest. Here he slowed to a brisk walk, as there were roots and vines he didn't want to trip over. Plus, now that he was out of sight of the Temple's windows, he didn't have to worry so much about being noticed breaking curfew.

As he moved, he caught sight of a white bird sitting quietly in a tree not far from him. For a brief moment, he slowed to look. He was surprised to discover that the small, white shape was a hawk. That was strange: he wondered what a day hunter would be doing out here so long after dark. The hawk had seen him too; though it didn't seem particularly disturbed by his presence, it was watching him intently. Caymus smiled, imagining that the bird was just as surprised to see him as he was it, and for the same reason.

That was when he noticed the quiet. With his footfalls no longer disturbing the evening's calm, he could suddenly hear the sounds of the night: owls made their low, mournful calls; the occasional sound of fluttering wings disturbed the stillness of the air; he could just make out the rustling of small creatures scurrying about in the darkness. He also thought he could detect the movement of some larger animal off to the north, too far away to be seen: a deer or elk, perhaps. Each of the sounds played above a melodious cacophony of crickets and cicadas.

With some disappointment, Caymus realized he had to get moving again, so he gave a casual wave to the hawk, then resumed his journey. He knew that he would spend the better part of half an hour trekking through the trees before he arrived at his destination. The path he was following was one he knew well, as he'd forged it himself with a the dozen or so trips he'd taken out this way in the past couple of years. He made sure not to follow in his old footsteps too closely, though: he didn't want to leave too obvious a trail for the masters to find.

Caymus smiled as he breathed in the night air, enjoying the familiarity of the journey. The canopy of leaves and pine needles above let shafts of moonlight through here and there, so he had no trouble picking out the red bush with the yellow flowers, the tree with two trunks, the ring of toadstools, and other markers he had discovered on previous nights that confirmed that he was going the right way.

Before long, he came to the base of the small hill that he'd been aiming for all this time. He stopped briefly at the bottom and looked up the rise in anticipation. The hill wasn't exactly steep, but it was covered in dense foliage, and a thick carpet of tree roots made the ground uneven and treacherous. The pines and everwoods grew closer and closer together the farther up he looked, too. It was no wonder, really, that nobody ever went up there, that he might actually be the only person in the whole of the Temple who regularly ventured all the way to the top.

Grinning, he started climbing, and his breathing quickened and became more labored as he picked his way through the foliage. Halfway up, he paused for a moment to catch his breath, and as the sound of his own rushing blood diminished in his ears, he began to hear ghostly music drifting down to him.

Chuckling quietly to himself, he started toward the sound with renewed vigor. The music, simple and haunting, came from a small wind instrument, though he didn't know whether it was properly called a pipe or a flute. A light breeze was carrying the sound to him through leaves and branches, making it seem soft and far away. It was a wondrous thing to her, though. It sounded to his ears like the night looked to his eyes: peaceful, tranquil, but with a promise of adventure just under the surface.

Suddenly, the foliage gave way and Caymus emerged into a small clearing that was so gray and bereft of trees that it seemed completely at odds with the rest of the forest, as though he'd somehow stepped through the trees into another land. White moonlight lent a ghostly feel to the area, which was an almost perfect circle, about thirty feet wide and ringed by gaunt junipers.

In the center of the clearing was a large rock: a plinth, really. Ten feet high and pockmarked, it had obviously been placed there by human hands a long time ago. It was carved into a squared pillar of dark stone, three or so feet to each side. Its gray hue almost perfectly matched the color of the earth at Caymus's feet.

Atop the plinth sat a man. Caymus wasn't sure of his age, but he'd always assumed him to be somewhere in his mid-twenties. He sat quite serenely, his legs crossed in front of him, his eyes closed. In his hands he held the small instrument from which the music emanated. The thing was a simple affair, being a piece of wood about a foot long which was peppered with a dozen small holes that the man's fingers gently covered and uncovered to create the somber tones. The man's hair was light brown, and it hung down from a blue headband straight to his shoulders where it was evenly cut. He wore loose garments of browns and blues that hung slack from his limbs.

The actually astonishing things about him, however, were his wings. They followed the curves of his arms, and were attached to them at the joints by several cords of leather. Fashioned from the feathers of more birds than Caymus knew the names of, the wings were motley constructs of reds, whites, browns, yellows, blues, and as many other colors as there were winged creatures in the sky. Hundreds of hours must have gone into their creation and more still into keeping them from falling apart from everyday wear. Caymus had seen them at least a dozen times, yet he still couldn't quite believe they were real.

For a moment, Caymus just stood there, watching. Then, he walked to the base of the pillar and sat down with his back against it, listening to the song. He knew he'd heard the tune before, and he was fairly sure it was called "Night's Lament"; he'd have to ask later to be sure. As he drank in the sounds, he glanced up just in time to see another bird glide across the face of the moon on outstretched wings. Maybe it was the same one he'd seen earlier. Caymus laughed quietly at himself. Wouldn't that be odd: some strange, white hawk following him through the trees under the light of a full moon?

He was still thinking about the hawk, his mind toying with the idea of himself being carried off like a mouse or squirrel, when he realized the music had stopped. He looked up from his makeshift seat and saw the man staring down at him.

"Hello Caymus," grinned the man. "What took you so long?"

"Hello Milo," chuckled Caymus. "It's good to see you too, and I came as soon as I heard your whisper".

"I'm sure you did," laughed Milo. He shook a finger at Caymus, still grinning. "Naughty Conflagrationist, out past his bedtime, yet again. I wonder what the masters back at your temple place will have to say about that!" He stood up. "Out of the way! I'm coming down."

Caymus stood and moved a few feet from the base of the pillar. He then watched as Milo spread his arms, and so his wings, and jumped. As he plummeted, feet first, Caymus could first hear, and then feel, the column of air that rose to meet him. About halfway down, his descent gradually slowed to the point that, rather than hitting the earth with a great thud, he was instead deposited lightly upon it.

Caymus shook his head. "I still want to know how you do that," he said, moving toward Milo and extending his arm.

"Sorry, my friend. Wrong religion," said Milo, and he shook the offered hand. His fingers would have seemed pitifully small in Caymus's huge grip had either of them cared to notice.

Caymus shrugged. "I suppose that's fair," he said, letting go of his friend's hand. "How have you been, Milo? I don't think I've seen you for, what, five weeks? Six?"

"Same as usual, really," said Milo, sitting cross-legged upon the ground. "Took a little trip down to Krin's Point to get some extra bowstrings and meet a couple of fletchers. Last one got a little frayed, I'm afraid."

For a moment, Caymus was taken back to the shipyard, to the supply shed, and to the fiery belly of a ship called *Pride of the Expanse*. For a moment, his eyes welled up and his stomach turned with the pain of terrible memories…

Then, the moment was over, and he was standing atop a hill again. What had Milo said? He'd gone to Krin's for supplies, hadn't he?

Caymus nodded. Krin's wasn't exactly far away from here—going southwest through Saleri Forest and crossing the Wandering River would take about a day if somebody was in a hurry about it—but knowing Milo, his arrows took time to make, so a few weeks away made a fair amount of sense.

"Otherwise," continued Milo, "hunting's been good, that rain we've been having finally let up a few days ago, and, for the most part, people from your temple have been staying clear of the woods, so things have been pretty uneventful." He looked around the clearing and into the sky. "There is, however," he said, "this bird that's been following me around ever since I got back."

"A bird?"

"Yeah," said Milo, narrowing his eyes. "Silly little white thing. Keeps landing in a branch next to me and screaming in my ear. I try to tell it I don't know what it's squawking about, but…" He trailed off and shrugged his shoulders. "Weird behavior, really. Can't figure out why it's so interested."

"This bird…" said Caymus, frowning, "…it wouldn't happen to be a hawk, would it?"

"Yes! How did you know that?"

Caymus laughed. "I think I've seen it. I think it followed me here. Almost pure white, yes? Orange beak, with of gray in its tail?"

Milo snapped his fingers and pointed at him. "Ha! Yes, that's the one! So, she's been pestering you too, eh?" He smiled. "Good. Maybe that means she'll leave me alone for a while."

Caymus chuckled. "So, is that what you brought me out here for?" He turned his gaze eastward, the direction from which he'd come, and his eyes found the Conduit. Though he could barely make out the Temple in the soft moonlight, the pillar of fire itself was clearly visible in the darkness. "That 'whispering on the wind' trick you do is neat at all, but sometimes I feel like you do it just to show off." He turned back to his friend and gave him an inquisitive look.

"Only sometimes," said Milo. "Tonight, I whispered with a very specific purpose in mind." His eyes narrowed in a way that made it clear he was up to something. "A little bird told me that those old men at your temple have finally gotten it in their heads to teach you that Aspect thing of yours."

Caymus was about to ask how Milo could possibly have already learned about Caymus's incident. It had happened only hours ago and, as far as Caymus knew, he was the only person from the Temple that Milo had any contact with. He decided not to press the issue, though. "It's called 'pulling'," he said. "Yes, Master Be'Var decided I should give it a try this afternoon." He frowned. "It didn't go very well."

"No?"

"I…got in some trouble for taking things a bit further than I should've," he said. "And," he continued, "to be perfectly honest, I'm not even sure I did it right."

Milo frowned, "Really? Hmm…" He tapped his chin with his finger a couple of times. "But you *were* able to control a flame, weren't you?"

"Well, yes," said Caymus. "Sort of."

"Excellent," said Milo, and his frown vanished. "That's good enough for me." He stood up, rubbing his hands together. "There's something I've been wanting to try ever since you told me you were studying to be one of those fire-master things." There was a positively impish quality to his demeanor. "Now that you're actually starting to do it, I think it might finally be time."

Caymus narrowed his eyes and spoke cautiously. "Okay," he said, "What do you want to try, exactly?"

He watched as Milo moved off to the edge of the clearing and foraged around for a bit. When he returned, he was carrying a piece of dead wood, about the size of his leg, which he brought over and dropped on the ground between them. "Can you start this up from scratch or am I better off using flint and steel?"

Caymus decided to just keep an open mind and go along with this until he saw a reason not to. He trusted Milo—albeit in a wary sort of way—though the air priest did occasionally display a tendency to act without thinking things through. "I can't start it from nothing," he said, "but if you can give me some sparks to work with, I can speed things along."

"Right," said Milo, and he produced a small piece of flint and a hunting knife. He then wandered off again and quickly returned with some pine needles and twigs. Moving quickly, he set the bits of kindling on top of the log and got to work rubbing the knife and flint together to rain showers of sparks down on it.

As Milo worked, Caymus closed his eyes and, as he had done earlier that day, reached out, searching out the sparks that Milo was creating. Each one served as a very small conduit to the Conflagration, and if he could get hold of one, he could manipulate it. He'd have to wait for one of them to land on a pine needle; talented as he was, he was certain he wouldn't be able to hold onto one of the short-lived sparks on its way from the flint to the tinder.

As he waited, he opened his senses to the rest of his surroundings. He could feel Milo's presence easily enough, could feel the air priest's body radiating heat with the effort he was putting into starting the fire. He could also feel every individual spark as each was pulled into existence and rapidly snuffed out. The hardest thing to sense was the tinder itself. The wood, needles, and twigs had all been dead for quite some time, and so the fire element that remained in them felt like echoes, mere shadows of what had existed when the things had been alive. Without that fire, they were barely distinguishable from the ground or even the air that surrounded them.

Still, with some effort, he eventually found what he was looking for, and he managed to latch onto an individual needle. There, he rested his consciousness, waiting for a spark to land in just the right spot. The showering of tiny conduits which resulted from Milo's quick movements meant he shouldn't have to wait long. After just a few seconds, he had his spark. Quickly, he tried to feel out the tiny conduit before it vanished, but to no avail: it died out before he could get a firm grip. A moment later however, another spark landed, and this time Caymus was better prepared. Like a silken thread, the spark's connection to the Conflagration was light and weak, but it was enough. As he had done earlier that day, he focused his will upon it. This time, though, instead of constricting the flow, he worked to draw it open, expanding it so as to allow the spark more volume, to give it greater ability to catch the needles.

His work began to take shape, and he felt the tiny spark begin to gain purchase on the dead material, felt it burn and grow as it enveloped more of its fuel. With concentration and effort, he guided it down through the needles and into the wood. There, it took hold, tentatively at first, then with greater confidence.

After a few more breaths, once he was sure his intervention was no longer needed, he opened his eyes and witnessed the fruits of his labor. He smiled, both pleased and slightly amazed: he'd managed to nurture a spark into a flame. It was a small flame, sure, but it existed independently of him now, and was dancing quietly upon the bark of the log.

Caymus took a moment to be pleased with his progress: if only he'd been able to do this earlier in the day! He was about to say so, but Milo interrupted him. "Wait," the air priest said excitedly, having sat down on the other side of the log. "Don't stop just yet. Can you heat it up some more?"

"I…can," Caymus replied, a little unsure at the wisdom of the idea. "That's where things went wrong today, though. It's probably not safe."

Milo let out an easy chuckle. "Oh, don't worry about that," he said, and closed his eyes. "It couldn't possibly be more dangerous than what *I* have in mind." He briefly reopened one eye and looked pointedly at Caymus. "Please? We're going to need it really, really hot for this to work."

Caymus sighed, then he shut his eyes and focused on the flame once more. Suddenly, he recoiled, finding something he hadn't been expecting. There was something there! Another presence, toying with the elemental nature of the dead wood. The presence stopped, as if waiting. Only then did Caymus realize that it could only have been Milo, performing whatever part it was he was playing in this little experiment. He took a breath, shrugged off the surprising sensation, and pressed on. He did what he'd done earlier in the day, wrapping his conscious self around the stream of fire and narrowing it, though being a bit more cautious about it this time.

His actions took effect quickly. He could hear the flame starting to burn vigorously as it caught more of the wood, could feel the conduit growing larger.

"More, Caymus," came Milo's voice.

Again, Caymus narrowed the stream, holding on to it tightly so as to force greater and greater intensity. He knew that was nearing the point where disaster had struck in classroom earlier that day. This time, of course, he was outside, and so he was fairly certain there would be no trouble with breathing, but he felt panic start to build in him, nonetheless. Maybe he should stop, lest things get out of control in some other way?

Then, he felt Milo's presence in the wood again, but this time the priest was acting, and not only on the burning log. The air in and around the blaze was beginning to act on the flames themselves, to penetrate them, to coax them this way and that. Caymus's natural reaction was to resist this interloper. He tried to somehow strengthen the conduit, to make it more resistant to the invading air.

"Woah, Caymus," came Milo's voice, rising sharply in volume so as to be heard over the roaring fire. "Sorry, but if you don't let me in, this isn't going to work."

Caymus nodded. He exhaled, relaxed his mind, and did his best to let his guard down, allowing Milo's air into his creation, into the conduit itself. He could feel Milo's consciousness doing something nearby, though whatever the action was, it was completely foreign to his understanding. He had the briefest sense of another conduit opening, but to a realm he didn't know, a place unfamiliar and alien.

Milo's voice, when it came again, was ecstatic. "You might want to open your eyes for this!"

Caymus did as he was told, wincing slightly. The flame had now completely engulfed the log and was burning with such a brilliant white light that it was painful to look at.

Then there came what felt like both a massive blow and a release. The sensation was sudden and violent, and Caymus felt as though he should have been knocked over. The searing flame shot out toward the stone column in the center of the clearing, extending out to span the distance in less than a second. He was astonished. A stream of white fire, emanating from the burning timber, was actually beginning to sear through the side of the rock. The clearing was brightly lit now, as if by the sun, and the noise was so furious that he had to cover his ears for fear of being deafened. Within mere seconds, the flame had burned through a giant section of stone and the top of the column was toppling directly at them!

With a shout, Caymus dropped his connection to the conduit and rolled backward out of the way of the falling monolith. The thing crashed heavily between the two friends, shaking the ground and sending night creatures swarming into the air and scurrying into trees.

After the screaming in his mind had died away, Caymus stood up and looked around. It took a few moments for his eyes to readjust to the moonlight, as the fire had been neatly extinguished by the column it had destroyed. "Milo!" he shouted. "Milo, are you okay?" He relaxed when he heard giggling—quiet, but with increasing momentum—coming from the other side of the fallen section of rock. He looked over it and saw his friend rolling with giddy laughter on the ground.

"Milo!" he shouted at him. "Are…are you alright? What *was* that? What did you do?"

Milo managed to restrain himself long enough to look up and speak for a bit. "Wasn't that," he said, and he lapsed into laughter again, "wasn't that the most incredible thing you ever saw, that you ever felt?" He sat up, calming down a little, and held his hands up in front of his face. "Two elements," he said, a look of wonder in his eyes. He then brought his hands together, intertwining his fingers, "Working together to create something new and..." he put his hands down and shrugged his shoulders, "...wonderful." Then he fell back on the ground and started laughing again. "But you should have seen the look on your face," he said, pointing, "when that thing came down!"

Caymus just stared at him. By all rights, he should be furious at him for putting them both in such danger. But, as he watched his friend's ecstatics, he couldn't help laughing too, his heavy, resounding voice offering a stark contrast to Milo's manic giggling.

Nearly a dozen minutes later, their mirth spent, the two of them stood together, staring at the remainder of the once-magnificent column, which now ended in a mass of black char about four feet up. Caymus felt a small sense of loss at the sacrifice, and he wondered if Milo had realized that the force they had created was going to be hot enough to burn through stone.

"Well, I guess my little throne's broken for good," said Milo, his tone mirroring Caymus's own feelings.

"You'll find something else to sit on, Milo." Caymus gazed around the clearing. "But I don't know that it'll be in quite such an ideal place as this."

"Oh, I don't know," said Milo, moving toward the pillar. He grabbed onto the top edge and hoisted himself up into a seated position, spinning himself around so that he was facing Caymus. He swept a finger along the charred stone and examined the black stain it left. "Once another good rain comes along to clean up a little, I think it might still do."

Caymus turned away, facing the Conduit in the distance. "I really can't wait to get back and tell the masters about tonight."

"I'm not so sure about that, you know," said Milo.

Caymus looked back and saw that his friend's expression had turned unusually thoughtful.

"Why? What do you mean?" he said.

"Well," said Milo, looking toward the Temple grounds himself, "Caymus, you know as well as I do that, despite the 'live and let live' policy most have adopted, besides a few haphazard friendships like you and me, the different elemental factions have never really found a good reason to get along. What we just did? Well, you'd think surely somebody's done it before, right? But if so, why haven't we ever heard about it?" He looked back at Caymus. "Right?"

"Yes, that sounds right," admitted Caymus.

"So, just think. This fire-master disciple, not even in the—what do you call it? Third order?"

"Third Circle."

"This 'not even a third circle' disciple walks in and says, 'Masters I was hanging around this air priest the other night and we found out—'." He jumped off the column and brushed the soot off his hands and clothes as he spoke. "I doubt you'd get much further than 'air priest' before being taken into a room for a few days and given a long series of lectures about why people like me can't be trusted."

"Lectures like: 'they'll crush you with giant pieces of rock in the woods'?" said Caymus.

Milo smiled and pointed at him. "See, they even have pretty good reasons," he said.

Caymus nodded with more than a hint of resignation. "So, what do we do? I can't just not ever tell anybody. It was kind of amazing."

"True," said Milo. "I don't know. I'll ask the winds about it. You do whatever it is you do when you're not sure about something and we'll see if we can figure it out between us." He finished dusting himself off. "In the meantime, you take your test tomorrow as planned and get into your new circle thing. I'm sure that's got to be a pretty good start."

"I'll do that," nodded Caymus, seeing the sense in it.

The two stood in silence for a moment, looking out at the forest around them and at the small amount of destruction they'd wrought on the little clearing. After a while, Caymus turned to go. "I'd best be getting back," he said. "If I'm too tired in the morning, Be'Var might start wondering what I've been up to all night." He looked sharply at Milo. "They're not looking for me, are they?"

Milo cocked his head, listening. "Nope," he said after a while. "Only sound coming from that place is snoring. And I," he added, moving to the far side of the ruined plinth, "will be going, too." He picked up a bow and a quiver of arrows he'd apparently stashed behind it, then headed off to the western edge of the clearing. He turned toward Caymus and waved his hand. "Good luck tomorrow." Then he turned and bolted off into the trees. "May the wind be with you!" he shouted, giving the traditional farewell of air worshipers.

"Go with a flame in your heart, my friend," Caymus said softly, giving his element's own version of goodbye. With that, he turned and, using the Conduit as a guide, started the trek back to his temple home.

~~~

Caymus took hurried steps as he made his way back through the forest. He believed what Milo had said, that nobody was awake at the Temple, but it would take him some time to get there and he knew that the
~~~

morning would come sooner than he wanted. And what a morning it was going to be! Tomorrow, he would take his Trial of Courage. Tomorrow, he would become a disciple of the Third Circle and begin the final leg of his journey toward becoming a master of the Conflagration.

As he picked his way through the branches and roots of the forest, he couldn't help trying to reconcile his last years of training with what he had just experienced. His entire life, he'd been taught that the other elements, though just as essential to the creation of the world as his own, were completely separate and foreign from one another, that a priest of one element couldn't hope to work with one of another. The various sects of each religion could find common ground when they shared Aspects, of course: the men that the missionaries had brought with them, for example, apparently knew of an Aspect that prevented flesh from being burned when touched by flame, whereas Conflagrationists stressed the ability to control the fire conduits themselves, that they might manipulate temperatures.

But here, this very night, he had discovered that completely different elements—at least those of fire and air—could work together to create something new, something powerful. In his wildest dreams, he'd never even conceived of that possibility. Though, when he allowed himself to think about it, he had to admit that it made sense. In the years he'd been at the Temple, he had been shown that everything—every plant, every animal, every stone, the stars in the sky, every single thing in existence—was composed of different amounts of the four elements, so why shouldn't they interact easily?

Earth gave things their hardness, their sturdiness. It was primary in the composition of the ground beneath his feet. It made men firm and unbending, stubborn and uncompromising. "Earthy" people were steadfast and dependable, though they were often hard, too.

Air made things light and supple. Though it was most obviously present as an invisible substance that surrounded him and filled his lungs with each breath, it also existed in other, less obvious places. It could be brought out of a pot of water by bringing it to a boil, for instance, or carry ash and smoke up from a burning tree. Air made a person giddy and childlike. People whose bodies were composed of more air than was normal made quick sprinters and graceful dancers.

Water was not only responsible for the moisture of objects, but it made things soft and gentle. Water and air were sometimes referred to as the "soft" elements by earth and fire, as they seemed often to be related to one another: just as air could be coaxed out of cooking water, for instance, rain sometimes fell from the sky in a way that was hard to comprehend. Water was compassion and grace. It was elegance and beauty.

Fire was the heat that made a man's breath warm. It was the volcano that pierced the ground. It was the element of power, of raw emotion, of destruction. A body became warm when pushed to the limits of exhaustion or when in the grips of disease. It also gave a person courage, strength, the will to fight on against even the worst of odds.

Caymus considered these things, wondering what his newly-win experience might mean for him in the near future, when, quite suddenly, a flurry of white flashed before his eyes. Quickly, he brought his arms up to shield his face, but in doing so he lost his balance and, with a thud, fell on his back. A lightning-shot of pain went through him from back to front and the faintest of cries escaped his lips. Hurriedly, he rolled over, reaching for his left shoulder blade with his right hand. He couldn't detect any blood or feel any real wound and. Since the pain was subsiding, he guessed he hadn't really hurt himself too badly. A quick scan of the ground revealed the small rock he'd landed on. It wasn't sharp, but it did protrude from the ground an inch or two. He was lucky, really: that could have been worse.

Caymus got back to his feet, shaking his head. Burn it all, his back would be tender tomorrow and it would probably bruise. He didn't mind the pain, of course, but he didn't want any stiffness giving him away. If he could manage to hide it from the masters, he'd be alright, but he had no talent for lying and if they asked him how it happened, he'd have to face the music.

Sighing, he looked around for the cause of the little incident, and he found it. The cause was still there, sitting in a branch about waist-high, looking at him with its head cocked at a slight angle, as though wondering what he wanted. It was the same white hawk he had seen before. He was almost certain of it.

"Thanks," said Caymus. "What are you, trying to get me in trouble?"

The hawk responded by screeching at him! Then, with incredible swiftness, it spread its wings and took flight, aiming directly for his head!

"Whoa!" Caymus ducked out of the way, then turned to watch the hawk land on another low-hanging branch just a few feet away. It wasn't watching him anymore; instead, it was facing away from him, looking in the other direction.

"What's the matter with you, bird?" Caymus was starting to get frustrated with his small tormentor. "Are you—"

Then, he saw what the hawk was looking at.

The first thing Caymus noticed was a pair of shiny, wet orbs. They looked like they might be onyx, or perhaps smoked glass. Each was about a hand-span in size. They stood at shoulder-level and were a few inches apart.

They looked like eyes.

They couldn't be though, not as big as they were. Still, they were unnerving, glistening in moonlight that penetrated the forest canopy. When the hawk screeched again, Caymus backed away slightly, and he was shocked when the orbs moved to follow him. It was then that he became certain that they were, indeed, eyes. It was then that, for the first time in his life, Caymus knew true fear.

He was face to face with some kind of horrible creature. And it was huge! Caymus thought the thing must easily reach ten feet. Those eyes, deepest black, protruded slightly from a head that appeared covered in the carapace of an insect, bony and reflective in the moonlight. Beneath the eyes was a mouth filled with vicious-looking, sword-like teeth that curved inward at impossible angles. Below the thing's head were almost a dozen legs, arrayed along the evenly spaced sections of its long, centipede-like body and holding it a full two feet off the ground. Each leg, too, was covered in the black, armor-like material; each had what appeared to be tufts of hair at each of three joints; and each ended in a long, sharp claw. Caymus could hear what sounded like breathing coming from the thing, a deep and ghastly rasp. As it breathed, its entire body rose and fell slightly and the teeth in its cavernous mouth wavered menacingly, back and forth.

It just stared at him, like some dead thing. The eyes had no lids, no pupils. The face—if it could be called a face—seemed to regard him as would a freshly-risen corpse, given the chance to confront its killer: accusation emanated from that face, as did loathing and menace. Caymus could feel his heart race, felt his breath quicken, felt a cold shock rush through him. For a moment, his legs felt like they might buckle underneath him, but he swallowed his fear and managed, somehow, to hold onto his nerve. He didn't know what this beast was, had never encountered such a thing in even his darkest nightmares. The only thing he know—and he knew it with absolute certainty—was that he dared not move.

Again, the monster moved toward him with a short, scuttling motion. Caymus, terrified, threw a hand over his mouth, partly to stifle a scream and partly to ward off the smell. The thing carried the foulest of odors, like the reek of dead fish mixed with the stench of a rotting bog. Underneath the foulness was another smell: it sweeter, like burnt sugar, though against the reek of rot and death that now permeated the air it stood no chance.

The thing advanced again. Caymus felt something heavy appear behind him. He had been moving away from the creature without thinking and now he found himself backed up against a tree. Oh no!

The creature stopped too, though not because of anything Caymus had done. Rather, it had reached the branch where the hawk still sat. It shifted its gaze toward the small bird, raising its head slightly so that its eyes were level with the branch. For a few moments, there was no movement, just the rasping sound of heavy breathing as the two just stared at each other. Then, the creature reared its head back, opening its jaw wide. As it did so, each tooth seemed to unfold and extend outward until it actually protruded from the huge mouth. Then, suddenly, the head came forward and snapped. The movement took only a fraction of a second, but the hawk was faster, and by the time the creature had bitten down, its prey had vanished. As massive fangs splintered the branch, the hawk beat its wings hard and flew out above the trees, crying out into the darkness as it vanished into the sky.

Its quarry gone, the creature shook its head back and forth, dislodging the fragments of wood from its maw, and folded back its teeth. Then, it turned its attention back to Caymus, who still hadn't managed to move. He knew he should flee. He knew he should run faster than he had ever run in his life, but his legs wouldn't budge. Why couldn't he run?

The thing scuttled closer. Caymus's breaths each came in ragged, shallow gasps. He was terrified! But somehow he couldn't break free of those eyes, of that dead stare.

The creature stopped. It was right in front of him, close enough that Caymus could feel the moisture of its breath on his face; close enough that he could smell the pine branch it had just bitten through; close enough, surely, to do the same to him. Still, he couldn't move. By the Conflagration! Was he going to die here? Tonight?

Then, with a sickening scream, like a thousand mourners crying out, the monster reared up, lifting its front section off the ground and raising its two forelegs into the air above him. With that huge movement, the spell was broken, and Caymus was freed from his prison. He only just had time to roll out of harm's way before the massive body came crashing down and the legs stabbed into the space where he'd just been standing, embedding themselves deep into the flesh of the tree.

Caymus fled. He ran full with the knowledge the death lurked behind him, that he dared not slow, lest it catch him. He paid no attention to low-hanging branches as they swatted his face or to the rocks and roots that stubbed his toes and threatened to trip him. He stumbled forward and ignored the pain. Again, he heard the creature screaming close behind him—much too close!—as he dodged around another everwood. He didn't dare look back; he knew it wasn't far behind him; he could hear it smashing through the trees as it gave chase. The sounds of cracking branches and splitting tree trunks were evidence that the thing preferred to go through obstacles rather than around them.

What was that thing? Where had it come from? Feeble, helpless sounds escaped Caymus's lips even as he tried to understand, as he poured his strength into pushing himself as fast as possible. The creature was something out of his most horrible nightmares. It was so big, so strong! The memory of how easily it had bitten completely through a half-foot's worth of pine branch kept playing over and over in his mind. Caymus didn't want to die, didn't want to meet those teeth. He had to keep moving, had to keep running, to keep ahead of it somehow. Of flames! How could he possibly outrun it? The scream came again, and he was sure it sounded closer, was certain that the sound of it barreling through the forest was getting louder.

Get to the Temple, get to the Temple, get to the Temple. He played the words over and over again in his mind, a mantra keeping him focused, keeping him sane even as tears came down his cheeks. He visualized his escape, imagined himself getting to the sanctuary doors, slamming and bolting them before the creature could follow. Then the scream came again and the image evaporated. It was so close! He didn't know how far he'd run. His throat was dry, and his lungs ached. His legs were burning with effort, struggling to meet the incredible demands he was putting on them. *Get to the Temple, get to the Temple.*

Then, the unthinkable happened, and Caymus knew without doubt that he was done for. The certainty of it was calming somehow: it allowed his mind to free itself of any thought of escape; for a moment, all his worries disappeared, time slowed down, and he was able to focus completely on what was happening.

The first thing he felt was a kind of hot pressure on the heel of his left foot as it extended out behind him, mid-stride. The pressure was just to the left of center, on the outward side of the foot. In the instant that it happened, he didn't think much of it, but when he brought the foot forward again to take his next step, he planted the heel on the ground and pain shot through his leg like a blade. He might have been able to keep his balance at another time, but he was so tired, had run so fast. As hard as he tried, he couldn't make his leg obey, and it folded under him.

Next, he threw his hands out, bracing himself for a collision with the soft forest floor. Immediately, he noticed a fist-sized stone in front of him, which his right hand would surely connect with. For just a moment, he hesitated, and the moment meant that when he landed, his left elbow was locked but his right wasn't, and he landed awkwardly and unevenly, his left hand scraping across pine needles and moss, his right arm buckling at the elbow when his palm hit the stone. He collapsed toward his right and his shoulder made contact with the obstacle, rolling it over so that a sharp edge, previously hidden, turned face up. Caymus's momentum continued to carry him forward, but the stone caught on an exposed root and he felt it tear into his chest.

Finally, his knees connected with the ground and he rebounded, flipping over the sharp surface, then rolling two times more before landing hard on his back. In an instant, the whole world went askew, and he struggled to get his breath back, to reorient himself. What was probably only seconds felt like years before, finally, the trees swung back into focus.

The monster was over him, shifting its weight this way and that on its spider-like legs. Caymus just lay there. He knew he should get up. His chest was on fire, and there was a dull, throbbing sensation in his heel, but he should at least try to run. He couldn't make himself move though: he'd never been so scared in his life. He found that he was whimpering like a child as the thing looked down at him, its teeth twitching, as if deciding how best to end him. With a sense of immense sadness and regret, Caymus waited for that end to come.

Before the creature could strike, however, a twang and a whooshing noise pierced the night. Caymus couldn't see where the sound had come from, but in the moment the creature turned its head to look, the arrow made purchase, striking it in the head and bouncing off the carapace. By the time Caymus had thought to look for the source of the arrow, he heard another twang of the bowstring and a second missile came sailing out of the darkness. This arrow bounced away just as harmlessly as the first, but the monster lifted its front legs and screamed, regardless.

Caymus's eyes finally found the archer. It was Milo, walking quickly toward them and already nocking another arrow! He turned toward his fallen friend. "Run, Caymus!" he shouted, then he turned his attention back to the creature and loosed another arrow. This one struck inside the creature's mouth, still not penetrating, but making the beast recoil all the same.

Caymus scrabbled backwards as the monster's black eyes regarded the new threat and it started advancing. "Milo! What is—"?

"I said *run*!" Milo shouted again, backing away from the creature and producing yet another arrow.

Caymus didn't wait any longer. His chest still aching madly, his foot shooting pain up his spine, he pushed himself to his feet and managed to stumble into a run.

"Skies above, you're ugly!" Caymus could hear Milo's voice faintly behind him as he burst from the tree line and lurched onto the Temple's lawn. *Almost there*, he thought, but when he glanced up from the ground, all his hope evaporated.

The scene made him sick with horror. He was still a good hundred yards away from the Temple, but he could see that things weren't right there, either. Three more monsters, exactly like the one he'd just escaped, were pacing around the doors to the Sanctuary, while still another scuttled around the far corner of the east wing. He could see movement, too, up on the roof of the building: could he make out the silhouettes of *people* up there?

As the scene washed over his eyes, he drew slowly to a halt. His chest was on fire and his stomach hurt, and so he bent at the waist, put his hands on his knees, and craned his neck to keep looking. Should he continue? Was there any point? He couldn't possibly get through the doors with those things crawling around and he knew the doors to the cellar would be locked and bolted by now. Shouldn't he just turn around and help Milo face the one in the forest rather than try to get past this whole group? Maybe it would be best to just flee the area entirely and ensure his own safety?

No. That would be cowardly, not in the spirit of a fire master at all. Still, he had to do something. He couldn't just stand here. He needed to *act.*

Suddenly, he turned around, puzzled. He couldn't hear the creature's shrieking anymore. What had become of it? What had become of Milo?

As if answering the unspoken thought, his friend came dashing out of the trees, his bow slung over one shoulder, his hair streaming out behind him. He seemed uninjured, though some of the feathers from his left arm where missing. Caymus shouted toward him. "Milo, are you alright?"

"Fine, fine," Milo panted. He stopped next to Caymus and looked toward the Temple, taking things in. "Looks like up on top is where we need to be, eh?" he said, pointing to the moving shapes on the Temple's ramparts. "I don't suppose you know any clever ways of getting up there?"

Caymus shook his head, still breathing hard. "If we can get through the main doors and into the sanctuary, there are stairs to the top, but we'd have to get past those things first." He looked behind them again. "What about the other one?"

"That thing's quick," said Milo, "but I'm faster. Couldn't get an arrow to stick for the life of me, but at least I bought some time. I lost it back there, but if it can track at all, it'll be here before long." He looked at Caymus's foot, where his shoe was becoming soaked with blood. "And with an injury like that, there's no way you'll stay ahead of it. We need to get moving. Come on!"

The pair started toward the Temple at a brisk jog. Caymus realized that he was limping rather badly; he wondered just how bad the wound to his foot really was.

"Are those doors going to be locked?" Milo asked, between breaths.

Caymus winced with pain, and with worry. Beyond the fire in his lungs, he wasn't sure what kind of damage he might be doing to his heel with each excruciating step. Still, he pressed on. "With all those things outside, they probably dropped the portcullis," he said. "Even if they saw us coming, there's no way they'd be able to raise it in time." He looked at his friend. "Milo, what are those things?"

"Absolutely no idea," Milo responded. "All I know is that one back there was about to make a rather hefty meal of you, and I don't suppose those," he pointed to the others, now all gathering around the main doors, "are much friendlier." He looked up at the roof again. "So. If we can't get in through the door, we're going to have to be creative. How good a climber are you, Caymus?"

"What?" Caymus said.

"Climber," repeated Milo, grinning a little as he said it. "Can you climb or can't you?"

"I can, I guess," said Caymus, not sure he liked where this was going, considering his injuries. "But Milo, my chest. My foot. If you think I'm going up the wall—"

"Eh, don't worry about it," Milo said, a wry smile on his face. "I'm going to help you."

Caymus attention was then pierced by an all-too-familiar scream. He turned to see the creature Milo had been shooting at as it erupted from the trees in pursuit of them. The thing's long, sharp legs propelled it along the ground at a distressingly fast pace.

"Time to run," said Milo, and Caymus managed to summon up just a little more strength, to ignore just a little more pain, and run. Milo kept pace, his light, natural quickness helping him keep up with Caymus's long strides. They were now more than halfway from the edge of the forest to the temple walls. If they could keep ahead of the creature, they might just make it—that was, if Milo's 'help' was enough to get them up the wall.

As Caymus wondered about Milo's plan, he saw one of the other four creatures, still gathered around the main doors, glance in their direction, then turn its attention back to the sanctuary's entrance. Whatever they were, whatever the reason they were here, they were currently more interested in getting through those doors than they were in chasing two people dashing across the lawn. One of them tested the heavy oak's integrity by hurling its huge body against it. Caymus could hear wood crack as it struck. The delay between his seeing the action and hearing the sound would normally have summoned some amount of curiosity in him; now, it was just unsettling.

More pressing at the moment was the monstrous thing chasing them. He chanced another look behind; it appeared to him larger than before. It was gaining. "Milo, it's getting closer!"

"Stop looking back!" yelled Milo, himself looking straight ahead. They were about twenty yards from the wall. Caymus could now see that there were more people on the roof than he'd first thought. Not only that, but a lot of them seemed to be gathering along the crenellations to watch them. He could hear shouting and yelling, and he could imagine that his fellow disciples were beckoning him, willing him to make it to the wall before the creature got too close.

Milo was beginning to trail, slightly. From the edge of his vision, Caymus could see that his friend's eyes were closed, that his brow furrowed in concentration and that he was slowing down a little. He tried to slow a little too, that he might match his pace, but Milo wasn't having it. "Keep moving," he said, shooing him further ahead. Caymus considered arguing against leaving him behind, but he stilled his voice when he realized what the air priest was doing. Near the base of the western wall, the grass was being blown about as though by a whirlwind. It blustered about, this way and that, until finally each blade in a semi-circle about ten feet wide was leaning inward as though being pulled toward the building. Specks of dust and small dirt clods shot up the wall, easily clearing the second story. Caymus recognized the intensity of the stream of air now blowing toward the roof: it was the same force he'd seen his friend use countless times to slow a long fall. So, this was Milo's help. He hoped it was enough.

With forty or so yards to go, Caymus started being able to make out the voices yelling down to him. He couldn't distinguish the individual speakers, but they all seemed to be shouting his name. He was also able to feel the air around him being sucked toward the column of wind Milo had created. His injured heel momentarily forgotten, he pushed himself as hard as he could, hoping against reason that he was staying ahead of the creature.

Milo was still behind him. How far, he didn't know, and he didn't dare look.

Finally, he reached the wall. He didn't take time to stop, or even to slow down: he just allowed his body to slam to a stop against the hard surface. The blow was hard, but it was the sudden tumult of noise that was actually disorienting: the shouts of his fellows on the roof, the screams of the monster that was chasing him, and even the sound of his own blood rushing through his head were all drowned out by the incredible din of the wind blowing past him. He desperately wanted to cover his ears, to wrap his arms around his head and block out the deafening noise, but he forced his hands to instead reach out for the rough stone wall of the Temple and find a way to climb. With relief, he discovered that, even with his injuries, the large spaces between blocks of granite and the immense force of the air lifting him up made his ascent easy. After he'd risen a few feet, he looked over his shoulder to make certain that Milo was close behind.

He wasn't. The priest was standing still about a dozen yards away, his arms raised, his hands open, driving the air upward. His mouth was contorted into a savage grimace, his eyes shut tight. Behind him, the creature was still moving, still running with its terrible speed.

"Milo!" Caymus shouted. He considered dropping back down.

"Keep moving." Milo's voice was faint, carried quickly away by the wind, but it was definite, certain, leaving no room for argument.

Caymus climbed, and climbed fast. His heel throbbed whenever he put his weight on it, but the pain was bearable. Mostly, he was finding foot- and handholds in the crevices between the stones of the wall, but the stones themselves also allowed him some traction, their surfaces rough and uneven. He noted, too, that after the first ten feet or so the going became easier as less well-tended masonry afforded him more solid grips. He became suddenly very thankful for those grips when, as he was about halfway up the wall, the wind died away.

Caymus's first sensation was that of falling, but he dug his toes into their purchases and gripped tightly with his hands. His heel threatened to give in to the pain, but he was able to hold on. In the next moment, however, he was overcome with shock and grief. If the wind had stopped, it meant the creature had gotten Milo. It meant his friend was dead. The shock of it stripped his mind away from him, and he found himself pressing his head against the wall and trying not to imagine the scene below, to not think about the sacrifice Milo had just made for him.

Now that the roar of the wind was gone, however, Caymus's ears were telling him a different story. Whoops of amazement flew from the roof. Cries of, "Burn my eyes!" drifted down, as well as, "Look at him go!"

With renewed hope, Caymus quickly turned his head and looked over his shoulder, almost dislodging himself as he did so. From his position it was hard to see but, if he strained, he could just make out Milo bolting with incredible speed toward the wall, the creature mere inches behind him. *Come on, Milo*, he thought as a single whispered word escaped his lips: "Please."

Milo had been right, earlier. He was faster than the creature, if only a little, and by the time he reached the wall, he had managed to pull away, just a couple of feet. More impressive than that, though, were his acrobatics once he got there. A couple of yards from the base of the building, he leapt with delicate grace towards the wall, planted his leading foot firmly, then pushed back off, directly toward the pursuing monster, itself having slowed to avoid a collision with the unyielding stone. Before it could open its jaws to grab him though, he pushed back off its head with his other foot, gaining precious extra height before coming back in contact with the stone surface, a good ten feet up.

Milo's body scrabbled more than it climbed, but he found handholds quickly and he managed to ascend with almost unbelievable speed. As the creature scraped and prodded at the granite, trying to give chase, it screeched in frustration.

The cheering from above was electrifying as Milo made his way up to the spot where Caymus clung. The man was grinning like the whole thing was no big deal. "Hello, Caymus," he said, once they were at eye-level. "My word, what are you doing stuck to a building?"

Caymus couldn't help but grin back at him, but smile turned to grimace as his heel flared into fresh, hot spasms of pain. He couldn't keep weight on it anymore, and he had to dig in even harder with his hands. He could feel the stone cutting into his skin and was almost certain that one of his fingernails was tearing off. The creature was still down there. If he slipped, even just a little, he died. He wasn't out of danger yet.

"Milo," he said between clenched teeth, "I can't move any further. I can barely hold on."

Milo looked up, and with a relieved note to his voice, said, "I think you'll manage," just as a thick cord of rope slapped the wall between them. Caymus looked up, too. He was immensely relieved when he saw Rill waving down to him amongst a dozen other concerned faces.

"Can you tie him off?" Rill yelled down.

Milo nodded, shuffled until he was right alongside Caymus and, using one arm, deftly looped the rope under his arms. "Did you know you can tie a bowline with one hand?" he said, and knotted the rope on to itself, just above Caymus's head. He then signaled to those above, and Caymus felt himself being pulled up. The rope was tight and painful under his armpits, but at least Milo had avoided allowed it to put any pressure on the gash in his chest. Caymus tried to do some of the climbing himself, but there wasn't much strength left in his legs, and so there was nothing to do but hang there and be lifted. After the intensity of fleeing from the monster in the night, it was a relief, really.

Milo climbed alongside, keeping a watchful eye on him. Caymus was amazed at how easily the priest moved, making his way up a sheer stone building as quickly as another man might stroll down a riverbank. Only when he noticed that Milo's hair and wings were being lifted upward did he realize that the air priest was probably using an air column of his own.

The creature was still screaming down below when Caymus was finally hoisted over the rampart's edge, where friendly hands pulled him up and onto the roof. Rill busily untied the knot while the larger boys who had been pulling the rope—there were about a dozen of them—gathered around both their classmate and this stranger who was suddenly among them.

Rill was shaking his head and looking over Caymus's injuries. "You gonna make it?" he asked.

Caymus nodded, closing his eyes. "I think so." He realized he was only just starting to catch his breath.

"Good," said Rill. "Not exactly what I pictured when you said, 'Cover for me'.

Caymus looked up to apologize, but Rill just smiled back, obviously more relieved than upset. "Hmm, I guess we should do something about this blood," he said, regarding the slash on Caymus's chest. He pulled off his own tunic and started measuring it his friend's wound, as though considering using it as a makeshift field dressing. He also glanced at Milo, who was busy taking off Caymus's shoe. "So, uh…who's this?" he asked.

"A friend," said Caymus. He closed his eyes again. The screams of the creature had subsided. Instead, he could hear the repeated slamming of huge, chitinous bodies into the oak of the sanctuary door downstairs. "He saved my life twice tonight."

"That's right," said Milo. Then, he met Rill's look and smiled broadly. "And you've only saved it once, so that puts me in the lead."

Rill laughed, sounding both surprised and relieved. "Yeah, okay," he said.

Milo had removed the shoe and was assessing the injury: a giant gash in the fleshy part of the outside of Caymus's heel. "Wow, Caymus, you nearly cut a chunk right off," he said. "No wonder it hurts." He pulled at the wound a little, and a large flap of skin and flesh dislodged, attached by a very little amount of actual tissue. "I'm pretty sure this is going to want needle and thread, but for the moment…" he looked at Rill again. "Can I have a bit of your bandage?"

Rill shrugged, tore a strip from his tunic, and offered it to Milo. Milo accepted it with a nod of his head and proceeded to start carefully wrapping the foot. "So, what did we miss?" he said as he wrapped. "Any idea where the big bugs came from?" he said as he tied it off.

"Kind of a lot, and no clue," said Rill, tearing up the remainder of the tunic and doing his best to tie it around Caymus's chest. "By the time I knew what was going on, one of them was already inside and somebody had sealed the doors."

Once both bandages were placed, Rill and Milo both tried helping Caymus get to his feet. Caymus stood up on his good food, then gingerly put some weight on the injured heel. He was rewarded with a fresh spasm of pain, but he knew he could bear it for now.

Rill continued, "That one couldn't get through the corridor that leads up to the roof, so everyone who's up here is safe for the time being, but a lot of people are still inside."

Just then, a pair of students was pushed aside as Be'Var came barging through. He pointed a thick finger at Caymus and shouted, "Boy, where have you been!"

Caymus didn't know how to explain things quickly. "Master, I was—"

Be'Var raised a silencing hand. "Never mind. You can tell me later.

Come!"

Caymus thought to ask Be'Var what was happening, but it didn't matter. The old master wasn't listening to him. Rather, he was grabbing him by the arm and hauling him away towards the center of the roof, toward the Conduit. Now that there were no longer a dozen disciples crowding around him, he could see that a few of the masters were standing around the pillar of fire. They were spaced equidistantly, each facing inward, toward the flames. There were Master Fentis, Master Ekka, Master Ket, and Master Valerek. There were probably on the other wide of the Conduit, but Caymus couldn't see them through the flames.

For just a moment, Caymus was struck by the way the Conduit continued to burn, shooting into the heavens as it always had, heedless of the chaos surrounding the building.

"I know at least three of the masters are dead," said Be'Var, shattering Caymus's musings. "Another seven are unaccounted for and are probably doing their best not to be hacked to pieces downstairs. Knives, axes, clubs…nothing anybody's tried has been able to get through that armor, so those of us who are left are going to burn these things to cinders using the Conduit. But we are learning that they don't burn easily, so we need all the minds we can muster."

Caymus started. "You mean you want me to help?"

Be'Var turned on his student, looking as if he was about to yell, but then his face softened, and he put a reassuring hand on the young man's shoulder. "You can do it, Caymus. I know you can. Besides," he looked around the rooftop at the chaotic frenzy of panicked faces, "of all the students who made it up here, you're the only one who knows the slightest thing about how."

Suddenly there was a loud, crashing sound and the roof seemed to shake under Caymus's feet.

"They've broken through!" yelled one of the students from the edge of the building.

"Time's up," said Be'Var. "Come on, boy." They had reached the Conduit. Be'Var stood a few feet from the pillar's edge and motioned Caymus to his side. "Just like I showed you before, Caymus."

"But Master Be'Var, I—"

"Caymus," Be'Var interrupted, his face one of absolute seriousness. "*Just like I showed you.*" He then turned toward the Conduit and closed his eyes, expecting no further argument. "And, Caymus," he added, after a moment.

"Yes, Master?"

Be'Var smiled, but there was no mirth in it. The play of light and shadow upon him made his wrinkled face look positively devilish. "This time, make it as hot as you like."

Caymus nodded and closed his eyes, unsure if he could do what Be'Var was charging him with, and yet unwilling to fail.

For the third time that day, he opened his mind and felt for a connection to the Conflagration, felt for the heat of it, for the majesty, for the absolute power of the realm of fire. When it came, it came with such abruptness, such force, that he nearly recoiled and lost the connection. It wasn't just a conduit he was searching for; it was the most powerful conduit known to exist. The size, the strength of it was overwhelming, and he had to concentrate hard to maintain his focus.

There was something else there, too, another source of power and energy. It appeared to his mind as a band of white light streaming through the Conduit, among it, within it. Intuitively, Caymus understood that this was the combined consciousnesses of the masters already present, and that he needed to join them, that he might add his effort to theirs. As quickly as he dared, he slowed his breathing and gently allowed his mind to join with them, to become part of the collective. He expected it to be difficult, but he felt himself drawn to them, as though they were coaxing him in. In the next moment, he was with them, having become one piece of a whole, part of a thread that stretched between worlds. He relaxed his thoughts and felt for that thread, felt for the connection points: one was anchored in the realm of eternal fire; the other connected to each of the terrible creatures now attacking the Temple.

How he was able to sense the monstrous forms, to perceive them through the stone of the Temple without being able to see them, he didn't know, but he could feel them now, and he shrank away from the sensation. Fire was there, for certain, as were the water, air, and earth that were the primordial building blocks for all life. But there was something else there too: not an element at all, but something different, something alien. It felt dark, sticky, and unclean. If not for the combined wills of the masters, he probably would have released his grip and shied away from the feeling.

Still, he persisted, starting the process of spreading his own consciousness along the Conduit, strengthening it, adding his own will to that of the group. As he did so, still uncomfortable with this new process, he felt a sense of belonging, of acceptance and fellowship, and also of monumental strength. Suddenly, he was able to understand what Be'Var had wanted him to do earlier that day. He could feel the group pulling the power through the Conduit, could feel the raw energy flowing through them and into the creatures below. With effort, he added his strength, or tried to, but as much he understood what his fellows in the stream were doing, as much as he wanted to help, he still couldn't grasp whatever it was that they were pulling on, still couldn't make the power flow through the stream any faster.

Hotter. Hotter. He could hear the thought in his mind, though he didn't recognize the voice. He didn't know if it came from Be'Var or from the masters as a collective, but he obeyed, trying to pull the force of the Conflagration through, making his best effort at igniting the creatures. He felt his pulse throbbing within his body as the power rushed through the group, felt the desperation of the masters' effort, but he could also feel that what they were doing wasn't working. The fire element inside each of the monsters seemed constantly on the verge of catching, but then that strangeness, that unfamiliar substance, quickly quenched any hope of ignition. The thing that frustrated him, though, was the knowledge that *he* wasn't helping, that his efforts were useless and impotent. The thought made him sick to his stomach: his might be that small amount of added power which could finally destroy the attackers, and yet he couldn't provide it!

Caymus, it must be hotter. Only you can do this. This time, there was no mistaking Be'Var's voice. Caymus did his best to obey, to help. He strained and he pulled, but it was useless. Whatever talent it was that the masters had for drawing the flames through the Conduit, it was lost to him.

There was no choice: he'd simply have to do it his way. He'd have to find a way to help without simply adding his own brute force. With a massive effort of will, he pulled himself away from the collective so that he was, once again, watching them from outside. He considered simply making his own separate stream and adding heat that way, but without the masters he was no longer connected to the creatures, and he couldn't see them to form a connection of his own. Instead, he remembered his lesson from that afternoon and took a deep, deep breath. Gathering all his fortitude, he treated the Conduit and the collective filament of the priests as one and the same, and he wrapped his conscious self around both.

The tiny conduit of the small fire earlier that day had seemed like a challenge at the time; Caymus now realized it had been mere child's play. The Conduit strained and stretched under him, within him, bursting with power and energy and threatening to tear the tiny mind that dared to envelop it. Caymus had the sensation of having wrapped his arms and legs around a twenty-foot-long giant squid, and having the audacity to hold on as it bucked and swam against him.

And yet, hold on he did, and after a short time when he felt his entire being seem to stretch, he renewed his concentration and felt his grip on the two streams firm and tighten.

Then, he squeezed, just as he had done twice before, narrowing the Conduit and, in turn, the minds of the masters themselves.

The roar of the fire as it rushed through the Conduit toward the creatures was incredible. He could feel himself tensing, felt his back arching with the severity of it. His breathing was rapid. His heart felt like it would burst out of his chest. The entire world began to darken against the incredible brightness of what he was trying to do. As he fought to stay conscious, he realized what a foolish thing he had done. This was the Conduit, the strongest link to the Conflagration in existence, and he had the audacity to try to manipulate it? He might as well have tried to pull the sun out of the sky!

Still, barely moments passed before his efforts took shape. The latent flame inside the creatures, at first impossible to stir, burst into life! He could hear the screeching of the monsters again, but this time, rather than anger and frustration, this was the sound of panic, of fear. They were burning, dying. He could hear the pop and sizzle of carapace, could feel the creatures cooking inside their own chitinous shells!

Caymus was vaguely aware that he was screaming too, that his eyes were actually bulging from their sockets. Still, he held the connection, narrowed the stream until the very last of the alien substance was burned away from the things' bodies. Then, with a vicious snap, he finally lost his grip on the Conduit and his mind catapulted back into his physical body. He found that he was lying motionless on the roof, racked with pain, his back arched so that only his feet and shoulders were touching the stone beneath him.

He could still hear the cheers of his fellows and the roar of the Conduit as, slowly, peacefully, he drifted into darkness.

Chapter 3

Caymus woke with a start. As soon as his eyes were open, he lifted his head and looked around. Were there any more of the creatures? Was there still danger?

No. He was in a room, in some sort of infirmary, lying on a straw mat on the floor. It was nighttime, and the immediate gloom of the place was oppressive. The few dim torches on the stone walls didn't so much shed light as punctuate the darkness. Through small, square windows, though, the stars were shining. All around the large chamber, cots and mats were arranged in neat, organized rows. Most were empty. Some contained quietly sleeping forms. Others held young men who quietly moaned, writhing in pain.

Then, the smell of the place hit him, and he nearly retched. Mixed into a blanket of decay and rot were the pungent odors of ointments and creams, not to mention the metallic smell of blood. There was also a slight undercurrent of vinegar, and Caymus suddenly realized where he was: one of the storerooms had been converted into a place to care for the injured. He glanced at the cot to his left; it held one of the other students. Caymus didn't know the boy well, but he thought his name was Heron. He slept quietly in his makeshift bed despite the fact that he was missing one of his legs, absent just below the knee. Caymus turned away, suddenly thinking to look himself over. Was he alright? Had he suffered any great atrocity that shock had made him unaware of?

A quick glance down told him he was fine, though he could still feel a dull ache in his heel, which was now wrapped in a cloth bandage. A dressing also covered a large portion of his bare chest.

"Caymus?" a voice said.

He turned and saw Gwenna standing behind him, a bucket in her hands. In the darkness he hadn't noticed her. He gasped. Her clothes, worn and tattered, were covered in blood.

"Gwenna!" he said, staring at it, "are you okay?"

"Never mind me," she said, gently. She knelt down next to him and set the bucket on the floor, "it's not my blood. How are you feeling?" She inspected his bandage, running her hand along its edges to check the tightness.

"Fine, fine," he said, relieved, then he tried getting up. As he did, pain erupted in his chest. A faint cry escaped his lips and he collapsed back to the ground.

"Idiot!" said Gwenna as she laid him back down and began unwrapping his bandages. "If you tore it open again…" Her tone was rebuking, but her worried expression revealed that she was more concerned for his health than with any actual reprimand. She got the bandage off. Caymus regarded his scar as she ran a finger along the raised flesh. It had healed nicely and didn't appear to be bleeding. There wasn't any pain at her touch, either.

Gwenna appeared satisfied that her patient hadn't caused any major damage. She looked him in the eye briefly before re-wrapping the bandage. "You'll be fine," she said. "Just go easy for a couple of days. Master Be'Var said the burning would fix the wound, but that it still needed a day or two before it would be fully healed."

Of course: Master Be'Var. Though the master knew several Aspects of fire, his true talent was as a healer. Caymus had seen the old man use his abilities to close an open wound before, but the healing time that had followed had certainly been more than mere hours. A concern began to form in his mind.

Gwenna was continuing. "It's a wonder you didn't tear it. You boys are all so eager to get yourselves hurt that—"

"Gwenna?" said Caymus, interrupting her. She looked him in face, startled, seeming to have just realized that she'd been talking. "How long has it been?" he asked.

She looked down and shut her eyes. "I'm sorry," she said. "I forgot; you've been unconscious all this time." She looked up and around the room at the prone figures around them. "After it happened, we all stayed to help, took turns taking care of the injured down here. So many didn't wake up. So many just died in their sleep."

"Gwenna?" he said again.

She looked back at him, and her eyes were shimmering. "I'm sorry," she said again, a slight catch in her voice. She suddenly sounded very tired. She wiped her eyes on her sleeve and seemed to regain her composure. "Three days," she said. "You've been sleeping for three days."

Caymus felt he should have been shocked at the news. Somehow, though, he wasn't at all surprised. "Sleeping?" he said.

"That's what Be'Var said," she replied. "He said your body was tired because of something you'd done to fight off the insects and it needed to sleep. He…he never admitted it, but I think he wasn't sure you'd wake up." She met his gaze again and managed a slight smile. "I'm glad you did, though."

Caymus took a deep breath. "So am I," he said, rising to a sitting position, a bit more gingerly this time. He looked around at the other forms scattered about the room. "What happened, Gwenna? The last thing I remember is being up on the roof. I remember burning those...things, but that's all."

Gwenna's face hardened slightly, as though she didn't want to remember. She swallowed, and her eyes took on a faraway look. "Bridget and I were just getting to sleep when we heard the commotion. That monster was already inside, killing people, by the time we were out of our room. We tried to get out, but there were more of them outside and the other one started chasing us." Her voice was getting louder, sharper, more frightened. "We hid in the kitchen, in one of the pantries." Suddenly, she broke out of her trance, and looked around. "We just hid," she said. "We could hear people screaming, dying, in the halls outside, and we just cowered in that room."

Caymus tried to think of something encouraging to say, something that would make her feel better. As a Conflagrationist, she'd have been brought up to value bravery; hiding was probably something she felt ashamed of. He didn't blame her, though. He'd known what it was like to have his life in danger even before that night, and the memories of his own feelings of helplessness at the sight of that…thing…were still fresh in his mind. He could still hear the screams of the monsters as they'd burned.

He opened his mouth to tell her all this, but she held up her hand and frowned. "Don't..." she said. "Don't try to make me feel better about it? You won't." She was obviously upset, but she managed a slight smile, as if to say that, while she had no wish to be comforted, she appreciated his concern.

Heron started to moan restlessly. Gwenna shook herself out of her unpleasant memories and, seemingly without conscious thought, set back to work, wetting a cloth in the nearby bucket, then turning toward the boy and placing it to his forehead. "His fever's not going away," she said, her voice barely loud enough for Caymus to hear. Caymus carefully stood up from his mat as she continued. "After you did...whatever it was you did, you were out cold, and a lot of people were hurt. Those of us that could still walk brought the injured down here. Be'Var fixed up the ones he could, but a lot of them didn't make it. So many of them were dead already…" She turned her head slightly to look at Caymus out of the corner of her eye, then turned back to her patient. "Your friend," she said, "Ramone? He and Monette...we found them together, outside, by the wagon where we left them." She let out a long, staggered breath. "I've known Monette most of my life and I could barely recognize her."

Caymus shuddered. He thought again about the massive jaws of those monsters, thought about their dagger-sharp claws. He didn't want to imagine what his friend had looked like once they had done their grisly work. The thought triggered something in him, and he asked quickly, "Sannet? Rill?"

"They're fine," she said. "And that air priest friend of yours..."

"Milo."

"He's still around somewhere. Said he didn't want to go until you came around. Odd fellow, that one."

Caymus smiled. "Yes, but a good friend."

Heron was getting louder, his moans gaining in both intensity and frequency as he began twisting and writing. Gwenna moved to examine his leg and Caymus, mindful of his own injuries, moved to stand beside her. "Can I help?"

"The wound's bleeding again," she said. She handed him the cloth and, taking his hands in hers, placed them on the wrapping that covered what was left of the leg. "Just try to keep blood from going everywhere while I fetch Master Be'Var," she said. She looked at him seriously. "Can you handle that?"

Caymus nodded, so she stood and hurried out through the room's open doorway, leaving him with a weeping Heron and his own thoughts. He again surveyed the room. Despite the noise, the other occupants were either still asleep or, more likely, trying not to notice the sounds his new charge was making. There were at least a dozen of them, occupying perhaps of a third of the available cots and blankets on the floor. In many of the other spaces, there were dark stains where someone had tried to scrub away blood. Caymus wondered briefly how many of those patients had survived and thought to check his own mat for blood, but when he turned to look, the movement of his hands only served to send Heron into greater fits of pain.

He found he had a good deal of respect for Gwenna, or, for that matter, anyone else who could handle being in a room like this one. Death and pain didn't frighten him so much, but this place was dark and cheerless, oppressive and cold. Caymus suddenly realized that sickness could be far more terrifying than death itself. The thought unnerved him.

Just beyond the crying, Caymus heard someone approaching, and was glad for it. The footsteps turned out to belong to Rill and Milo, who both jogged over to the bedside, seeming at once to be glad to see Caymus and concerned about Heron. "What happened?" said Rill. "We saw Gwenna running out and heard the noise."

"I'd say someone's started leaking again," said Milo, assessing the bloody cloth. "She went to get Be'Var, I take it?"

Caymus nodded. "Yes."

"Then I guess we're stuck waiting," said Milo. "While we do, though, perhaps you," he looked at Rill, "could help me keep him still so he doesn't make things any worse thrashing about?"

Rill nodded, and together they set about holding Heron down. As he changed positions, Rill managed a quick smile for his friend. "Good to see you're up and about, finally," he said.

"Yeah," said Milo. "You gave us a bit of a scare back there, you know. I suppose it's too much to ask you not to do it again?"

Caymus smiled, despite himself. It was good to see Milo was still the same. Here he was, holding down a boy who might be bleeding to death, and he was being funny. "I can't make any promises," he replied.

Rill just looked back and forth between the two of them and shook his head.

A few minutes later, Gwenna came back with Be'Var in tow. The master looked tired. As the old man stooped, to assess his patient, Caymus suddenly wondered just how late into the night it was. Be'Var then took a breath and knelt beside Caymus. "You're going to want to hold him tighter than that," he said to Rill and Milo, then he deftly moved Caymus's hands aside and set to removing the dressing. The others obeyed and Caymus, relieved of his duty, shifted over to assist in keeping the patient still.

Once the bandage was gone, Caymus winced slightly at seeing the place where Heron's leg had been severed. It was a clean slice, and he was forced to wonder if the injury had actually happened that way, or if a surgeon's knife had been used to make it so tidy. The wound was bleeding slightly, expending a steady trickle of red. Caymus couldn't tell where exactly the blood was coming from, but Be'Var took the ruined appendage confidently between his hands and then closed his eyes.

As the master went to work, Caymus reached out with his own mind, trying to get a grasp on what was going on. He'd been the recipient of Be'Var's healing before—results of bad falls and rough-housing with his friends—but he'd never had the benefit of his recent training to help gain more than a surface understanding of the process. When he got a feel for the area around the wound, it seemed at first chaotic and uncontrolled, as though slices of energy were ripping through space in every direction. After a minute or so had passed, however, he realized that just the opposite was true.

Be'Var's mind was moving rapidly, first reaching out to the various blood vessels and capillaries, then checking them for bleeds, and finally adding heat to those that weren't sealed, cauterizing the wounds. What had seemed like random energy was actually the result of the speed with which he was moving from vessel to vessel. He was working on two or three at a time, almost as if he was searching with one part of his mind while he left another part to deal with actually tending to the bleeds.

In less than two minutes, it was over. Heron stopped thrashing about and fell into a fitful sleep. Caymus looked up from the leg to see Be'Var's eyes on him, a questioning look on his face. Then, the master stood up and bent backwards, popping a few vertebrae as he stretched. "That's the third time I've had to stitch him back up," he said. "Something's not right about it." He furrowed his brow, considering, then he shook his head. "Nothing for it. Keep an eye on him, Gwenna, and let me know if it happens again." He then turned to Caymus. "You're out of bed, I see. Feeling well enough to stay that way?"

Caymus shrugged. "I think I'll live."

"Good," said Be'Var. "When you're done here, come and see me in my office." He gave a nod to the group, then he turned and walked out of the room. "Don't take all night," he said as he did so.

"Skies above, that was neat!" said Milo, a huge grin plastered all over his face. "Can all of you do that?"

The priest's good nature was infectious, and everyone smiled back at him. "Afraid not," said Caymus. He shifted his weight gingerly from foot to foot as he spoke, testing out his heel. It felt like he should be able to walk on it, though he'd definitely limp a little for a while. "Healing is a specialty of his. Never seen anybody better."

"I thought he was a blacksmith?" said Milo. "Last couple days, I've been watching him make new metal bands for the broken gate thingee."

"That, too," said Rill. "It's all the same Aspect."

"Aspect?"

"Pulling," said Rill.

Milo's expression showed he clearly didn't understand.

Caymus explained, "It's like a special kind of talent or ability. Pulling is how we describe the ability to heat things up. It's what most of the masters teach us here."

"Some of us," Rill said with a frown.

"So," said Milo, slowly, "he's not a healer, and he's a blacksmith, but he's actually both because he's one of these *puller* things?"

Gwenna, who had by now moved off to check on another patient, gave an exasperated sigh. "He's not a 'puller', that's just what he's good at. If you happened to be good at running, you might be a courier or a scout. You wouldn't call yourself a 'runner' unless you were actually running messages for somebody."

"Ah," said Milo. "So, there are other fire things you can be good at, besides pulling? Other…" he raised an eyebrow, "…Aspects? He just happens to be good at this pulling thing?"

"Yes," said Caymus, "and he's learned to apply it specifically to closing wounds and heating metal. Some people are good at adding heat to things. Some are good at taking it away. There are a couple of masters here that can make fire into different colors."

"There's a healer, somewhere in Kepren," said Gwenna, "who heals by removing the heat. He calls it 'venting'. I've never seen him actually do it, but I've heard he's just as good as Master Be'Var."

Milo shook his head. "You fire-lovers are all so stodgy about everything."

"What do you mean?" said Rill.

"Well, we've got kind of the same thing," said Milo. "There are different things you can do with air. I'm good at moving it around, for instance—making wind and breezes and stuff—but we don't call them 'Aspects' or try to put ourselves in this or that category. We're all just differently talented, and," he shrugged, "you know, that's that." He looked at the walls around them. "Everything's so formal here. Even this building. You wouldn't catch an air priest staying inside like this, all day, every day. Too many rules. Too many people telling you what to do."

Caymus shrugged. "It's that or just cast your education to the winds."

His companions shook their heads. Rill looked pointedly at him. "Don't be funny, Caymus. You're not good at it."

Even a couple of the patients laughed at this, and a lot of the room's tension and gloom seemed to melt away.

"Well, whatever your 'Aspect' is, Caymus," said Milo, "I guess it's working. That was a pretty impressive display the other night. Speaking of which," he continued, "I'm going up to the roof to see if there's anything new to report." He gave Caymus a wink. "Good luck with ol' sourpuss tonight. Hope he doesn't roast you alive or anything!" Then he turned to the others. "See the rest of you…well, just as soon as you fail to avoid me, I guess." He gave a little bow and jogged out of the room through the same entrance Be'Var had used.

"He's a strange one," said Rill, looking after the retreating form, "but I have to admit, it's hard not to like him."

"He seems to be getting along with everyone pretty well," said Caymus. "I'm glad. I wasn't sure he'd be all that welcome here."

"Wasn't at first," said Rill. "But, wow, he's helped out with everything so much over the last couple of days—did you know he can send messages over the *wind*?—that it kind of feels like he lives here now. And we lost so many people too, so I don't think anybody minded having a new face around to cheer them up a bit."

"If you boys don't mind," said Gwenna, walking up to them and wiping her hands on a cloth, "not that I mind the company, but some of my guests are trying to sleep." She offered them a tired smile. "If you're going to stand around talking, could you do it somewhere else?"

They nodded. "Of course," said Caymus. "I need to go see Be'Var, anyway." He looked at the darkness outside again. "Is it early or late?"

"Late," said Gwenna. "About an hour after ninth bell."

"Thanks," he said. "Rill, you coming?"

As the two walked out together, Rill turned to Caymus. "It really is good to see you awake," he said. "Everyone heard the sounds you were making that night, on the roof."

"Sounds?" asked Caymus.

"Yeah!" said Rill, surprised. "You didn't know? Flames, Caymus, you were screaming like somebody was trying to pull your arms off or something." He shuddered. "Then, when I got to the Conduit and saw you on the ground..." He didn't finish the thought. "What exactly did you do up there, Caymus?"

Caymus shrugged. "Helped, I guess, then blacked out. Why?"

"All I know is, one of those things—a smaller one, if there is such a thing—was starting to make its way up the wall. It must have seen you and Milo and decided it could climb up, too. We were scared to death it was going to get us." He took a long breath. "Burn me, Caymus, I don't think I've ever been so scared before. Then, suddenly, it turns red hot and starts smoking and popping. It fell, and it practically exploded when it hit the ground. Then, we could all hear you screaming and then you and the masters all collapsed at once. We didn't know what had happened! Were you asleep? Were you dead? The masters all got right back up, but you..." He shook his head. "Caymus, we shook you and we shouted—Sannet even poked you with a paring knife—but we couldn't wake you up.

"Eventually, ol' Be'Var got his bearings and told us you were asleep and that we should leave you alone. Said you'd done something to start the bugs burning, something the rest of them couldn't. He said your body must be recuperating from the exertion. Seemed pretty sure you'd get up, but he kept checking on you all the time, like he wasn't really sure." He chuckled at a thought. "I don't think he quite knows what you did, either, and now that you're up, I honestly don't know if he's going to be more concerned about your well-being or about getting answers."

Caymus considered this. He didn't remember much of what he'd done up on the roof of the Temple three nights ago. That is, he remembered everything he'd done in vivid detail, but it was all instinctual to him, natural reactions to stimuli. One may as well ask what he remembered about ducking under a particular branch in the woods, or filling a particular pail with water. He was interested to learn that Be'Var was so curious, though. Based on what he'd just seen in the infirmary, he didn't think it possible that the man could be surprised by anything.

"How are they handling what happened, the masters?" he asked.

"Same as everyone else, I guess," said Rill. "At first, people were either sobbing or getting about doing things in a kind of stone-faced way. Be'Var was one of the stone-faced ones; afraid I was one of the sobbers." Rill sighed. "After a day or two, though, I guess we all got used to the idea that nothing would ever be okay again."

Caymus nodded. He knew that feeling. He'd felt it when his father had died, and then again when he'd left home to come and be a disciple at the Temple of the Order of the Conflagration. It was a feeling of the world being wrong, of your life being over despite your heart still beating. And the only thing that could fix it was time: time to get used to the new world, the new life.

"As far as the rest," Rill continued, "at least a dozen masters died that night, and the ones that are left have been sick with the idea that there wouldn't be enough of them around to keep the Temple going, so they've been letting students take their Third Circle trials early."

"What?" Caymus was shocked by the idea.

"Yeah," said Rill, and his eyes turned sad and distant. "Sannet's a Third Circle now. So's Marvek, and so's Talis." He sighed again, making a long, heavy-sounding noise. "They were the lucky ones, though."

"Lucky?"

"They passed."

Caymus understood. The trial that took you from Second Circle disciple to Third Circle was the most treacherous moment in any Conflagrationist's life. Success meant training in the Aspects of the Conflagration, training to become a full master. Failure was nothing less than a death sentence.

"How many?" he asked.

"Two," said Rill. "Gorrik and Felwig. After Felwig, people stopped asking to be tried. It's weird," he said. "Somehow, those two deaths felt worse than everybody we lost that night."

They'd reached the stairwell that led up to the masters' offices, and they paused there. "I suppose," said Caymus, after a brief silence, "it's because they chose to take the risk, even after so many people got killed." He tried to meet Rill's eyes, but his friend was looking away. "It's like the Temple's broken, and everyone's trying to fix it, then these people just go and break it some more before you're even done picking up the other pieces."

Rill dropped his head. "Maybe," he said. After a few seconds, he continued. "I don't know what I'm going to do, Caymus."

"What do you mean?"

Rill lifted his head, looked him in the eyes. He wore a haunted expression, as though all the memories of the past few days were coming back to him at once. "I'm never going to be a master," he said. "Everyone stopped trying after Felwig, but it didn't take two of my friends burning up to convince me. Both of them were better at this than I'll ever be. If *they* couldn't survive the trial, then I've got no hope."

"You've just got to—"

"No!" Rill interrupted loudly, then lowered his voice. "No," he said again. "Caymus, I appreciate your confidence in me—really, I do—but we both know I've never had the talent for any of this." He leaned back against the stone wall. "I've been just going through the motions, treading water, for a long time. That last test was something I'd have to think about eventually, but not now. Well, eventually's here and there's no more sitting in the back row, hoping I won't be called on. It's time I made a decision," he said, and for a moment his gaze lingered on the far wall, "and that decision is that I can't do this anymore."

Caymus didn't know what to say. They'd both spent so much time at the Temple that it was hard for him to imagine a world that didn't involve his best friend. Rill wasn't a fool; in fact, at times, he was quite brilliant. He was always the fastest at solving any of the puzzles or riddles that the masters put in front of them, and he was quick-witted enough that he could talk himself out of almost any amount of trouble. Caymus had always believed that his friend's failures to grasp the Temple's teachings had been a question of motivation, rather than lack of ability.

Still, Rill was his friend, and his friend deserved his respect and support, as much now as any time before. "If not the Temple, then what?" he said.

"Dunno," said Rill, then he smiled a little. "Oh, don't worry, I'll figure something out, I'm sure. Maybe I'll go back to Shorevale and work with my father." He shrugged. "We'll see. Anyway," he said, hitting Caymus on the arm. "Don't keep ol' Be'Var waiting. I'll see you back in the room."

Caymus watched his friend go, then he started up the stairs. Rill was right: during the three days he'd slept, the whole world seemed to have changed. As he ascended, he wondered what other surprises might be in store for him.

~~~

Be'Var sat quietly in his study, writing messages intended for other far away priests. He'd been writing for hours, as there were a lot of messages to send; normally, he'd have reserved such missives solely for other Conflagrationists, but the sudden appearance of Caymus's new friend three days ago had meant he could extend his reach to members of other
~~~

orders and sects, too. Be'Var shook his head in wonder at that thought. Under normal circumstances, he would having one of those flitty, gallivanting air worshipers in the Temple the same way he avoided getting poked in the ribs, but the young man's ability to communicate with his fellows over great distances had proved incredibly useful over the last two days. 'Whispering', the man called it. Well, Be'Var didn't care what it was called; it was helping him send and receive, in hours, messages which would normally have traveled for weeks, and so Milo was very welcome to stay as long as he wished.

It seemed that Milo wasn't the only air priests to suddenly start coming out of the woodwork since that awful night. From what the air priest had been reporting, the Temple hadn't been the only place to suffer an attack that night: the insect creatures had ravaged several populated areas and places of worship. Thousands—maybe tens of thousands--had been slaughtered, and there were entire towns that nobody had heard from yet. Almost overnight, air priests from all around had started talking to each other about it and, within the span of a full day, had established a network of communication that was allowing various leaders and representatives of cities and churches to communicate.

Be'Var was glad for their efforts, but he was still making sure to pen his notes quickly, as he'd known a few air worshipers in his time, and he was certain this network wasn't going to last. Air people just didn't know how to keep their attentions from wandering for very long.

His hand, however, was beginning to cramp, and so he swore and put the quill down. As he rubbed the knuckles of the hand, he also infused the muscles and tendons with warmth and ruminated on the rather obnoxious circumstance of being almost seventy years old in the middle of the world turning on its head.

So much had changed, and in just one hour. All across the land, rumors were flying about what the creatures were, where they'd come from, and what event had set their attacks in motion. Be'Var was doing his best to quash rampant speculation and replace it with knowledge. This wasn't some implausible coincidence of fate, and it wasn't an act of natural destruction like an earthquake or a sandstorm. No, the locations of the incidents revealed there was intent here: some strange, unknown enemy had reared its head and delivered a massive, surprise attack against what seemed to be the entire known world. To Be'Var, it felt like an invasion.

People would dismiss him, he knew, but that wasn't the point. The point was just to get the idea out there to as many people as possible as quickly as possible. That way, when the truth eventually became so obvious that it couldn't be denied, at least nobody would be caught off-guard.

Then there was Caymus. That boy was like an itch in Be'Var's mind. He'd been trying very hard not to leave that itch alone for the past couple of weeks, but he was coming to terms with the idea that he was just going to have to give up and scratch. He was trying very hard to set any expectations for the boy—and for himself, come to think of it—but he had a hunch, and once he had a hunch about something, he found it was nearly impossible for him to let that something develop on its own without his interference.

As if summoned by his thoughts, there came a knock at the door, and Caymus's voice called out. "Master Be'Var?"

Be'Var picked up his quill again. A master of the Conflagration had to look busy, after all. "Come in, Caymus."

When the boy entered, Be'Var indicated a wooden chair in the corner of the room and Caymus sat down, though he was at least two sizes too large for that particular piece of furniture. Be'Var hurriedly scratched out the remainder of his missive and, after quickly opening a conduit, scorched his personal mark into the parchment. Had he been alone, he'd have scolded himself for that: who, besides Milo, was actually going to see this piece of paper and care whether it carried his mark or not?

He then looked up at his pupil, who was still sitting patiently. For a moment, he was struck by the image: Caymus looked like some great warrior king, sitting so quietly and intently with his torso bandaged up. Whatever else one might say about the boy, he had presence.

"How are you feeling, boy?" he said.

"Good," said Caymus, nodding and tiling his head in consideration. "Tired though, which seems a bit strange, considering."

Be'Var nodded. "It happens when someone pushes themselves as hard you did. New disciples think working with the Conflagration is all in the mind. It's not. The whole body's involved in opening conduits and manipulating fire energies. The tissues get soaked with the stuff. Normally, it's fine, but push hard enough and it starts doing damage, and that damage takes time to repair. Do you remember dreaming at all?"

He watched Caymus as he spoke, making sure he was paying attention. He was. The boy's eyes were fixed on his as though they were hunting them. "I…" the boy began. "No, I don't think so."

Be'Var nodded. "I'd imagine," he continued, "that the three days you've been out have mostly been about your body repairing that damage. Now that's over, you can start sleeping properly." He indicated the bandage. "How about your other injuries?"

Caymus made a show of lifting and rotating his shoulders, as though testing them. "They hurt to move," he said, "but that's all."

"They will for a few more days. That girl probably over-did it with the bandaging, really. The body really gets a chance to patch itself up with the kind of deep sleep you've been getting, so you'll have healed more than you normally would have." He decided not to mention the fact that some people never woke up from the state. He'd seen it three times in his years. Two of masters who'd lapsed into the deepest sleep had awoken again within a day or two. The third had never stirred again, and had eventually died of thirst within a week.

Be'Var put down the quill, then he folded his arms in front of him and leaned on his elbows. "It was quite a thing you did, the other night."

Caymus flinched visibly at the memory, as if embarrassed to talk about it. "I…I guess so. I don't really know what happened. I tried to pull with the rest of you, but it wasn't working." His voice trailed off and he ended the sentence by shrugging his shoulders.

"I know, Caymus. I was there. I saw what you did. It confirmed something I'd first thought earlier that day when you were doing your best to suffocate us all."

Caymus had the decency to look slightly ashamed at that, but he was also leaning forward in his seat. Be'Var suppressed a smile. He had the young man's fullest attention.

"You, boy, are a shaper."

Caymus furrowed his brow. "A what?"

Be'Var leaned back in his seat. "It's generally regarded to be a rare sort of thing. I have only, to my knowledge, met one other shaper in my life: he was a master when I first became a disciple at this temple, a long time ago. He was like you. He didn't pull energy from the Conflagration like the rest of us did. Instead, he manipulated the conduit itself, shaped it according to his will. His control over the actual flow of heat wasn't up to par with even the meanest disciple, but his control over the flames themselves was astounding. He could make a flame tall or short, wide or narrow. He could make it dance around the room, untethered to its fuel source. I once even saw him take the flames of a campfire and shape them into a galloping horse."

As he explained, he could see understanding taking place in Caymus's expression. The boy was nodding quietly with slow comprehension. "So," he said, "that explains why I have to keep finding different ways of drawing fire from the Conflagration. What you do by pulling, I'm having to translate into shaping?"

Be'Var nodded. "Exactly."

"And…" Caymus frowned, "…you were hoping I'd do the same thing up on the roof that night, weren't you?"

"Yes." Bright boy. Be'Var wondered if he'd make the other important connection by himself.

"So, rather than adding to the whole, I *amplified* what everyone else was already doing, and that added a lot of extra heat to the creatures, which is what finally got them burning." Caymus's eyes were moving back and forth as though examining the ideas as he talked through them. He then looked up at Be'Var. "It sounds like it could be a very powerful kind of talent."

"It is. The master I knew wasn't the sort of man you would cross."

"But," said Caymus with a sigh, "that master will dead by now, and since we don't know about any other shapers, there's nobody that can teach me how to use this Aspect."

Bright boy, indeed. "So, you see that you have a bit of a problem there."

"I see," Caymus said, also sitting back in his chair and looking defeated. "So, what are you telling me, Master? You're not going to make me leave, are you?"

"No," replied Be'Var, waving the question off, "of course not. What I'm telling you is this: you're a shaper. Whether it's the will of the Conflagration, or a coincidence of nature, you have a gift the rest of us don't have. The upside is that this gift can be as powerful as it is rare; the downside is that you're going to have to learn to use this gift, for the most part, on your own. The various Aspects all rely on the Conflagration, of course, but they work differently, and take different sorts of people with different ways of thinking and acting. I and the other masters can teach shaping; but your mind doesn't know how to grasp it. So, that means once you enter the Third Circle, you're going to be largely under your own initiative." Be'Var paused briefly, considering something for the first time. "You *do* still plan to face your trial?"

"Yes," said Caymus. No hesitation. Good. Be'Var allowed himself a twitch of a smile.

"All right. You'll be doing that first thing in the morning, then. No sense putting it off."

"Yes, Master."

"Once you're marked, you and I will try to figure out some way to structure your studies. I may not know anything about shaping, but I know how quickly a Third Circle should be learning. You'll figure things out, and I'll advise and monitor your progress, and we'll adjust as we go. That sound fair to you?"

"Yes, Master." His student's expression was a mixture of confusion and curiosity, but at least his voice was strong. Be'Var had confidence that Caymus would pass his trial, much more confidence, in fact, than he'd had for the last two students he'd sent into the Conduit…

Felwig.

Gorrik.

Those two names would haunt him for the rest of his days. He'd lost students before, of course—not everybody was ready for the trial that led to the Third Circle—but never before had he allowed testing for any so obviously unprepared. He'd known in his heart that they weren't ready, but in his haste to replace the lost masters as quickly as possible, he'd let himself give in to panic, and had allowed the two of them to try anyway. He'd allowed them to try and the Conduit had taken them. Never would he make that mistake again. Never would he allow himself to be anything less than absolutely certain a disciple was ready before taking that test.

Caymus was ready. Though he was no longer going to be the youngest disciple ever to enter the Third Circle, and while he might not be the most studious of the young men in his charge, his might just be the most innately talented mind Be'Var had ever encountered. He would make a fine master of the Conflagration some day.

That was if "some day" ever came, of course. The thought brought Be'Var around to the other subject he'd wanted to talk to his student about.

"There's one other thing, Caymus," he said. "When we were turning those bugs to ash, did you notice anything unusual about how they felt?"

"I did," said Caymus, whose eyes suddenly seemed to shift to something distant. "They seemed sticky, somehow, like they were coated in something oily. It's like I kept slipping off them when I tried to grab hold, and they didn't want to burn." His eyes focused on Be'Var again. "It felt...wrong."

A good word for it. "It *was* wrong, Caymus. It was very wrong." Be'Var leaned forward again. He corked his ink pot and picked it up, turning it around in his hands as he spoke. "Do you enjoy history, boy?"

Caymus waggled his head, noncommittally "I suppose," he said. "I like to listen to it, listen to the stories, but I sometimes find I don't remember much of it later."

"Well, listen now," Be'Var said, "because this bit of history used to be saved for when a person became a full master." He sighed. "Things are different now, I suppose," he said, and he put the ink pot down. "What elements exist, Caymus?"

"Fire, water, earth, and air," Caymus replied, automatically. "There are a few small cults that say life is some kind of element, but nobody really takes them seriously."

Be'Var nodded. "Do you know why it's those elements? Those four?"

Caymus frowned, surprised by the question. "Because they're what the world is made of?"

"True, yes. But why is the world made of them?"

"Master?"

"Why, Caymus, is the world constructed, in its entirety, of differing mixtures of those four elements?"

Caymus's frown deepened. "Because they're the basic building blocks of the world. They're the smallest pieces, the foundations of nature."

Be'Var smiled. He hadn't quite gotten his point across yet. "But why, Caymus? Why those four? Why isn't 'grass' an element, or 'cloud', or something you've never even heard of before?"

"I..." Caymus was struggling with this. "I don't think I understand."

Be'Var waved a hand. "It's alright, Caymus. Like I said, it's an advanced concept." He looked seriously at his student. "A long time ago, before the great cities were built, before humans ruled the land, before most even kept histories, there were many elements, not just the four you and I know. How many exactly, I don't know, and depending on which master you talk to, or which tome you consult, you'll get a number from a dozen to hundreds. Nobody knows what they all were, what they looked like, what they were called, but you can be sure that you and I wouldn't recognize the world as it looked back then."

Be'Var paused a moment, allowing the idea to sink in. Caymus seemed untroubled by the information, but then it would probably take a while for the full force of such a momentous concept to sink in. "What changed?" he asked.

"War," Be'Var replied. "War among the elements. A war for supremacy, where the penalty for losing was to be cast out of our world forever."

"Cast out?"

"Yes." Be'Var measured his words carefully, trying to make Caymus understand. "Imagine if the four elements of today went through the same thing," he said. "Imagine…let's say that air, water, and earth allied themselves against fire and won out against it."

Caymus nodded. Be'Var continued. "The conduits would be cut, and that would be it. There would be no link between the Conflagration and our world. Fire would cease to exist. There would be no flame, no heat: just cold. Men would not know anger, would not know passion. There would be no such thing as a torch, a campfire, a volcano or even the warmth of the sun. Can you imagine that?"

Caymus shook his head, his brow furrowed. "Not really," he said, eventually. "The more I think about it, the more I realize that it's something I can't even comprehend. I wouldn't even recognize it as being 'the world'. I…I wouldn't even be *me* in the world you're describing."

Be'Var was surprised. He'd been expecting Caymus to say yes, of course he could imagine it, and then to have to tell him all the reasons why that was a foolish thing to think. But the boy was smart. He seemed to be getting the idea right away.

"So," Caymus continued, "you're saying that these other elements were cut off, and that, when that happened, the world changed from something completely unrecognizable into what it is today?"

"Yes," said Be'Var. "That's the basic idea."

"How did we win?"

The question was one Be'Var had asked, himself, when he'd first learned of the elemental war. "I don't know," he said. "From what I can tell, nobody does. There are two tomes on the subject in the masters' library, both copied from originals that have long since turned to dust. Neither of them says much about the actual battles or gives specifics as to tactics or logistics. Mostly, they speak about the conduits and how the realms of the elements and our world are connected. It's where a good deal of our knowledge of the Conflagration comes from. History is written by the victors, Caymus, and the victors in this war didn't care much to write down the hows and wherefores of the vanquished. Indeed, they seemed happy to try to forget about them completely, other than to mention that they were destroyed in the first place."

Caymus wasn't looking at Be'Var. His face was a mask of concentration as he puzzled his way through what he was being told. Be'Var allowed the boy to take his time. He busied himself with shuffling through some papers on his desk, keeping his hands occupied until Caymus eventually asked his next question.

"If this is information," the boy said, "that only masters know about, why are you telling me now?"

Be'Var looked up, and he could see from Caymus's expression that he'd likely already pieced together the answer.

"Because one of the vanquished elements seems to have found its way back into our world," he said. "I don't know what it's called or how it manifests, but whatever it is, those giant insects were flush with it, and it seems to be resistant to fire."

"Which is why it took all of us to burn them," said Caymus.

"Correct."

"...*and* the Conduit."

"Yes."

Caymus sat for a long time, gazing at nothing. Be'Var tried to imagine what was going through his mind. Was he remembering his encounter with those creatures? From what that air priest had said, the boy was one of the very few that had actually come face to face with one of those things and lived to remember it. Coming to terms with the fact that the single scariest thing you'd ever seen in your life was actually more dangerous and alien than your wildest imagination had guessed was probably more than a little taxing. Be'Var had only seen the creatures from a distance, only encountered them through the Conduit as he'd pulled fiery death into their bodies, and even he was a bit shaken by them. Surviving one trying to tear you to pieces...that must take some time to get one's mind around.

Finally, the boy nodded. "What do we do?"

Be'Var smiled. Caymus wasn't the loudest or most riotous of his students. Despite his size, he was calm and even-tempered most of the time, but his manner constantly revealed a kind of courage that few people would ever know, the kind that fully and completely considered and understood the dangers, then put them aside and simply determined what needed to be done. Warrior king, indeed.

"Well," he replied, "I'm going to be letting as many people as I can know what we're up against here." He indicated the papers in front of him. "For as long as I've been around, this has been a largely academic concern, but now that it seems we're under attack again, I can't see any reason to keep it a secret. It could be that this attack was the only one we'll see and the whole thing's over already, but if it's not, people need to know what they're up against. You," he pointed at Caymus, "take your trial in the morning, earn your mark, and start learning about this Aspect of yours. If the happenings of the other night are any indication, we're going to need your talents before this is over."

"I will, Master," Caymus said, simply.

"Good," said Be'Var. "Now, get out of my office. I have work to do." He waved Caymus out and picked up his quill again. "Your trial begins at second bell tomorrow. Be ready."

After Caymus had closed the door behind him, Be'Var put the quill down and rested his head on his hands. In the morning, he'd have another Third Circle disciple to train, and this one gifted with a talent for shaping. After that, he'd have to start thinking about how many of his remaining students actually stood a chance at becoming full masters and how many would best be sent home or assigned to do some other work so as not to draw on the resources of the Temple unnecessarily. He'd never liked triage, and yet here he was performing a version of it yet again. Still, but if there was truly a possibility of some kind of elemental war on the horizon, then he and the other masters would need to seriously consider how best to utilize the resources of the Temple, and they simple couldn't afford any dead weight.

He only hoped they weren't already too late.

Chapter 4

Caymus felt ill.

He stood quietly in the sanctuary, staring at the stark entryway. The Temple's new doors, still only half-built, sat on a workbench a few feet away from the empty arch they were meant to occupy. The portcullis, too, was being repaired, and several heavy lengths of iron rested against an anvil just outside where Be'Var and any other masters who were experienced at shaping metal had been working. Caymus still couldn't quite believe that the creatures had managed to push through so much dense wood and metal; he supposed he was glad the Temple's main entrance had held those teeth and claws at bay as long as it had.

The sanctuary itself was enormous. As was the case with many of the rooms in the Temple, it was circular, the walls forming a large, stone cylinder that stretched high enough to reach the Conduit, which met the building at its roof, several stories up. A dais stood in the center, and two dozen or so benches were arranged in widening circles around it. The masters occasionally gave lectures or sermons from the dais, though it largely went unused. Mostly, it was the place where new arrivals got their first instructions on life at the Temple.

At the northern edge of the floor was the foot of a stairway that spiraled up three times around the chamber, disappeared into a passageway in the ceiling, and then finally ended up on the roof. That passageway had taken a great deal of abuse on the night of the attack, as the creatures had tried very hard to force their way through, that they might get to the still-living people gathered beyond. Caymus had seen the cracks and gouges in the stone with his own eyes, and he was as amazed by the brutality involved. Be'Var had assured him that the roof wasn't in any danger of collapse or anything, though stonemasons would need to be brought in to make repairs at some point.

As the stairs wound their way upward, they passed through three rings that were painted on the walls, each about a foot wide and colored, from bottom to top, orange, red, and white, representing the three circles of discipleship one would pass through in order to become a master of the Order of the Conflagration. That end-goal, represented by the Conduit itself, was visible through a translucent glass ceiling, which both allowed a person in the sanctuary to see the Conduit at all times and also allowed the light from the raging inferno to illuminate the room below.

As he stared, Caymus thought of his own journey along that path. Entering the First Circle had been easy. The Trial of Faith was a simple declaration of your allegiance to the Conflagration and of your willingness to contribute your talents and abilities to the Order. He'd taken his trial the same day as Rill. Indeed, that had been the day the two of them had met. Caymus's mother had brought him to the Temple late in the afternoon. The two of them had said a teary goodbye, and Caymus had walked through the main doors alone while she'd started her way back to Woodsea and the empty house. Rill had already been in the sanctuary, having been dropped off by his father in the morning, and was waiting for one of the masters to get to him. Caymus had been hesitant about this new place and all the new people, but Rill had put him at ease with the simple gesture of offering him some of the lunch his father had packed for him. The two had become fast friends after that.

First Circle disciples spent their time learning about the history of the Order, of how the Temple had been built as a fortified palace for a nobleman, Porindus Veccion, who had wished to keep the majesty of the Conduit all to himself, of how he had befriended Merek Del'Ran, perhaps the greatest master who had ever lived, and had become his first disciple. Porindus's life had become one of study and toil after his conversion, but though he had loved the Conflagration with all his heart, he'd never shown the talent needed to become a master. His greatest contribution, in the end, had been to turn his home into a place of learning for others who wished to know the ways of the fire element. When he'd died, the masters and disciples who'd lived in the building had discovered he'd left the building to them in his will.

So, too, did first circles learn of Maretta, his daughter, who had led the Conflagrationists after Del'Ran's death. Maretta had been a fierce master in her own right, but she chose to give her life over to missionary work, bringing knowledge of the Conflagration to strangers, rather than teaching those who had already declared themselves. It was she who had set up the first missions, and she'd spent the latter part of her life tending to those who asked for an introduction to the Conflagrationists' ways. It was because of her example that women tended not to join the ranks of the disciples, preferring instead to be missionaries themselves. Indeed, the

Temple had consisted entirely of men and boys for over two years. A handful of girls had come through since then—some had even passed into discipleship—but all had been lured away to other callings before their studies had become serious.

The rest of a First Circle's life was spent understanding other aspects of the church itself, how the circles worked, why no single master had controlled the goings-on of temple life since the time of Maretta Veccion—the various egos in such a place would likely destroy each other if there were a position of leadership to contend over—and what was expected of a disciple at the Temple of the Order of the Conflagration. Most passed through these lessons relatively quickly, and the Trial of Devotion, a recitation and verbal examination of a disciple's understanding of what they had learned, was generally a simple affair.

Caymus had spent a single month in the First Circle. Rill had not picked things up so easily though, passing his trial only after six months of studies. Those months had been difficult for him, and while they had marked the first time he'd expressed serious doubts about his abilities, they certainly hadn't been the last.

Caymus's last few years at the Temple had been spent in the Second Circle, along with most of the other boys that constituted the population of the place. Whereas the First Circle was concerned with learning about the church, its procedures and its history, the Second Circle was about understanding the Conflagration itself. Students spent hours upon hours in meditative states, practicing the kind of mental conditioning that was necessary to obtain any kind of mastery over the conduits that bridged the different worlds. They were given long lectures about what fire actually was, how it manifested in the world, and what effects it could have. Many of the lessons were ancient, having been penned by Del'Ran himself centuries ago. The idea was simple: The more time spent in contemplation of fire, of the Conflagration and the conduits that connected it to the world, the better grasp one would have of what it would feel like to try to manipulate those conduits, to force changes in them.

Caymus himself had spent many days sitting cross-legged in front of the Conduit, trying to truly understand, to really feel what it was the masters had told him about, to truly understand what had happened to him that day on the *Pride*. He never really talked about it to anyone, but there was a desire within him—a need, really—to understand why he'd survived that fire, what had made him so special and others not. The lessons about the Conflagration had given him something to pin his hopes on, and so he'd pursued them vigorously, though for the first few months he'd done so with limited success. As much as he'd tried to reach out the flames in the ways the masters had suggested, he'd never really understood their meanings in any helpful way.

Then, one day, he'd felt his mind moving outside of his confines of his body, and he'd suddenly been able to "feel" his surroundings, to see the fire in the objects and people all around him. It had been a glorious afternoon of exploration, and the moment he'd reported the epiphany to the masters, his lessons had changed to focus on that ability, specifically.

That was when he and Sannet had become friends, as they both had shown remarkable aptitude. That was also the point at which Be'Var had come back into the picture. The old man had been the one to initially suggest to Caymus that he join the Temple, but it was only after making that leap of consciousness that the he'd begun taking a special interest in his student's development. For a few weeks, the three of them—Be'Var, Caymus, and Sannet—had spent a good deal of time together, developing the boys' proficiencies at feeling out their environments with their minds. Not long after that, Be'Var had invited a few of the more gifted students to form a sort of special class of Second Circle disciples. The class had become the talk of the building for a while, as they were often apart from the rest of the students, practicing various techniques to make the process easier, more intuitive. They would sometimes spend days out in the wilderness, moving from location to location as Be'Var explained what an elm should feel like, how an ant's body was put together, or how to find the fire component in the very air they breathed.

Caymus had enjoyed those lessons thoroughly, and had gone out by himself on a number of occasions—though it wasn't technically allowed—to study alone. In general, those had been calm and uplifting days, but he would always distinctly remember one particular moment when, sitting alone in a clearing, he had been practicing the ability to reach out into his environment and had suddenly touched upon another person. When he'd opened his eyes, a many-feathered man had been standing in front of him. "Hey, watch where you point that thing," he'd said, and then he'd stuck out his hand. "I'm Milo, by the way. What are you doing out in the woods?"

From that point on, Milo had been another important presence in Caymus's education. For all the harping-on Be'Var and the other masters did about the wonders and the importance of fire, they often neglected to put their lessons in any sort of context. The air priest had helped him to understand the values of the other building blocks of the world, too. Caymus didn't worship the other elements as he did the Conflagration, of course, but he attained a newfound respect for the way they fit into the grand scheme of things. The actual interactions between the elements weren't often spoken about at the Temple—something Milo was more than happy to point out—which was a pity, as there were a lot of interesting facts to consider in that regard. Flames wouldn't burn in a room without air. A little bit of wind would make a fire burn hotter, but too much wind would put the same fire out. Milo had never lectured Caymus; rather, his knowledge of things like that had always seemed like trivia: little bits of information without any kind of formal structure to them. That, of course, was just the way Milo's mind worked.

Caymus had never really figured out what Milo was doing out in the forest. At first, he'd thought the man simply lived out in the woods as a hermit, but then he would say something about "telling the people back home," about some event or other, and that would disabuse Caymus of that notion. On the one occasion he'd actually asked Milo about it, he'd just shrugged and said, "I followed the winds, and the winds brought me out here. They didn't seem to think there was anywhere else I needed to be after that, so I stuck around."

While it was an infuriatingly non-specific answer, it did at least seem honest, and so Caymus had always taken it at face value. The idea of Milo hiding something from him, or of being dishonest in any way at all, seemed so outlandish to Caymus as to be actually funny.

Caymus had spent the better part of two years like that: lessons with Be'Var in the morning, study and practice in the afternoon, letting off steam with Rill and Sannet in the evening, and then the occasional jaunt into the woods to either study alone or visit Milo. It had been a wonderfully peaceful couple of years, and Caymus, who'd first come to the Temple out of such tragedy, finally began to see the place as a kind of home, a place where he belonged. He'd realized then just how much he wanted to be a master, to fully immerse himself in the wonders of the Conflagration, then to teach those wonders to others. What a life that would be.

During one of his long meditations by the Conduit, Caymus had been thinking about such things when, quite suddenly, his hold on the flames had slipped and a small burst of fire had erupted into his startled face. He hadn't understood what had happened, only that he'd seemed to have grasped something—he wasn't even sure what—he'd never even noticed before. Be'Var, who'd seen it happen, had first made sure his student hadn't been scorched too badly, and then had informed Caymus that what he'd done was immerse himself so completely in a conduit that he'd managed to touch the energies of the Conflagration itself; and if he was able to do that, then it was time for him to take his third trial, that of Courage.

It was for this very trial that he was now trying to ready himself.

The Trial of Courage, from what the masters would tell, was the most difficult to prepare for. "You're either ready or you're not," Be'Var had once told his class. "There's no studying. There are rules to follow, or to break. It's not an examination; it's a judgment, a *trial* in the truest sense.

You will sit at the feet of the Lords of the Conflagration and they will test your soul. And the Lords of the Conflagration don't possess things like patience of empathy: you either pass the trial, or you don't come back."

Since coming to the Temple, Caymus had seen three students take the Trial of Courage, had watched with bated breath as each had stepped into the maw of the Conduit. All three had walked back out mere moments later, marked by the Conflagration. The mark was a small one, black like charcoal, burned into the back of the left hand. It was a slim shape, rounded off at the bottom and tapering to a point at the top, surrounded on either side by two semi-circular lines with slight bows and bends in them which gave the impressions of fingers and knuckles. Two hands holding a glowing flame—that was what the masters said it represented. The mark meant you were a disciple of the Third Circle, that you were learning an Aspect under the personal tutelage of one of the masters.

Though it was understood that there was an additional trial for a student to break free from discipleship and become a full-fledged master, Caymus had never seen one, nor had any new masters been made in all the time he'd spent at the Temple. The masters never mentioned that trial and always obfuscated when asked directly. That such a trial existed was only hypothesized among the disciples because the masters carried the same mark as the Third Circles…except the outlines of their flames were red.

Caymus swallowed hard. Having not actually witnessed the trials of the last three days—the ones that had led to the deaths of two students—he wasn't as apprehensive as others in the building about today. The fact that he was standing here, waiting to be summoned for his own trial, proved that much. That didn't mean he wasn't nervous, though. Before today, the thought of a person being burned alive inside the Conduit was only an idea, a scary bedtime story the masters told students to warn against a lack of preparation for important tasks. Now that two students were actually dead, the idea had solidified into something actually possible, and the possibility of death was much more frightening than the idea of death.

"Caymus?"

Master Eavuk's voice echoed throughout the sanctuary and Caymus looked up to see him standing near the top of the stairway, just below the point where it disappeared into the roof.

"We're ready for you."

Caymus nodded, then he made his way to the foot of the stairs and started his way up. Be'Var was right: his wounds didn't hurt nearly as much as they should have with only three days rest. He barely limped at all as he made his way thrice around the chamber before finally reaching

Eavuk.

Master Eavuk was a gangly stick of a man with sunken eyes and a calming smile. About thirty years of age, he had, years ago, been the last disciple to have attained the rank of master and was therefore the one being sent down to fetch the student being tested. Caymus noticed that the man's usually unshakable serenity was tainted slightly with concern. Undoubtedly, he was thinking of the same things as Caymus, of the impending task and, more significantly, of the cost of failure. The master put a hand on Caymus's shoulder, nodded, and then guided him the rest of the way up the stairs and into the passageway.

They emerged into a bright, clear day. Caymus couldn't help noticing how strikingly blue the sky was, how bright the sun, as he looked around. Twelve masters, six to each side and dressed in their formal red robes of station, formed a path from the stairs directly to the Conduit. Just in front of the blaze stood Be'Var, his expression blank. As the master who had taken so much personal responsibility in Caymus's instruction, it was his place to lead the trial, to make sure it was done properly. "Who is this you bring before the Conflagration?" he said in a loud, authoritative voice.

"This is Caymus, disciple of the Second Circle of the Order of the Conflagration," replied Eavuk. "He has come for his trial."

"And will you vouch for him?" said Be'Var.

"I will."

"Very well," said Be'Var, nodding. Eavuk made his way down the left row of masters to stand at the end, just to Be'Var's right.

Master Be'Var addressed Caymus directly. "Caymus, you stand ready for your trial. Are you prepared to face the judgement of the Conflagration?"

Caymus replied in as confident a voice as he could muster. "I am."

"Then step forward, and stand among us."

As Caymus walked between the ranks of the masters, Be'Var continued. "This disciple has earned the respect of one among us. Master Eavuk speaks for him. Are there any here who would speak against Caymus? Does anyone believe him not ready, or not worthy, to face this trial?"

Nobody moved. All was still. A faint breeze tugged at the masters' robes, swishing red fabric and making faint, rustling sounds.

"Very well," said Be'Var. "Caymus, you have progressed as a disciple of two circles and are now ready to be tried a third time. This trial will test your resolve; it will look into the depths of your soul to see what is there, and to determine what is lacking. Only one who is strong at heart, one who sincerely believes he belongs to the Conflagration, can hope to pass, unscathed. Only the most courageous will return to us."

Be'Var looked at Caymus severely, and only in that moment did

Caymus realize how red the master's face was, how creased his forehead. Be'Var wasn't taking this lightly: he was genuinely afraid for him.

Be'Var tilted his head slightly. "So, Caymus, are you prepared to face the Trial of Courage?"

Caymus nodded once and managed not to gulp. "I am."

"Very well," said Be'Var for the third, and final, time. He then melted into the ranks of the masters, opposite Eavuk. "Then step into the Conduit, and be tried."

For a moment, Caymus held his breath. Then, without hesitation and with large, purposeful strides, he walked toward the Conduit. Even as the heat from the blaze threatened to scorch his skin, he didn't let his pace falter. He had to believe he would pass. *Courage.* He repeated the word to himself as Be'Var, once again, began to speak.

"Lords of the Conflagration, we offer you the disciple Caymus to be tested. We ask that you offer him your judgement, and hope that you find him worthy."

With those final words echoing in his mind, Caymus stepped into the Conduit.

~~~

Caymus knew he should be burning. He knew his skin should be sloughing off his bones even as his tongue boiled and his eyes melted. He could feel the heat—such intense heat—licking and biting at his skin. Yet, he didn't burn. His skin didn't scorch. Despite the inferno, he was unburnable, unkillable, defiantly alive.

He was standing in the Conflagration—not the Conduit, but the Conflagration, itself. No matter where he turned his gaze, all he could see were flames. Red, orange, white or yellow, the fire was everywhere. It roiled in every direction at once, giving him no clear way to tell up from down, left from right. There was no ground beneath his feet, no sky above his head. There was no air; with every breath, he inhaled liquid fire.

The noise was deafening. Pummeling his eardrums was an incredible roar, like the fiercest wind of some tumultuous storm. Yet, he could somehow make out the sound of his heartbeat, hear his own breath in his lungs. They both seemed slower than they should be, as if time didn't flow properly here.

"Why are you here?"

The question was his own, yet not his own. He recognized the pitch and timbre of his own voice, but it had come from without, from some other presence.

"I am here to be tested by the Lords of the Conflagration!" He tried to
~~~

scream above the din of the flames, but even with the greatest effort, he could barely hear himself.

His efforts must have been noticed though, as shapes began to coalesce in front of him. At first, the shapes were just yellow orbs, floating in random patterns about him. There were six of them. Their golden color was reminiscent of the flames that surrounded him, yet these were different, somehow. They glowed in a way that fire shouldn't, and they appeared to twinkle. Slowly, they changed direction, moving in a more organized fashion, until all six were arrayed in front of him. Then, they paired up, three sets of two. A moment later, a small black circle appeared in the center of each.

Three sets of eyes. And they were looking at him.

How far away they were, he couldn't tell. Distance was confusing in this place, and even as the vague shapes of men began to appear around the eyes, without a point of reference, he couldn't judge their size.

"Your name?" The voice was raspy and whispered, yet he could tell it was still his own voice addressing him. It came from the center-most of the three figures, though he could detect no moving lips in the form.

"Caymus Bolwerc," said Caymus. As he spoke, the center figure appeared to move toward him, its dimensions still impossible to fathom. The figures were like suggestions of men. He felt as though they appeared the way they did only because he expected to see them that way. They were outlines, their forms filled with the same fiery hues that surrounded them.

When it got close enough, Caymus realized that the figure—in fact, all three of the figures—looked like him, too. Understanding sunk in. Of course, the Lords of the Conflagration were beings of fire. They had no shape, no substance other than flame, and so they were borrowing his likeness in order to communicate. He wondered if that was difficult for them.

When the fiery visage of himself got close enough that he could easily recognize his own face, it spoke again. This time, he could clearly see the movement of a jaw. "What is in your heart, Caymus Bolwerc?"

"Hope." Caymus was startled at his own answer. He didn't know why he'd said it; it was the first thing that had come into his mind. Suddenly, he felt afraid. Had that been the wrong thing to say? Surely, he should have put some thought into an answer given to an elemental lord.

But it was too late to change anything; the figure was already moving closer again. The image loomed larger and larger in his field of view until the yellow eyes seemed inches from his. "Caymus Bolwerc," it said, and there was some menace to the voice now, "you will give your life to the Conflagration today." Caymus could clearly see the roiling lips now. "One way," it continued, "or another."

Then, with incredible speed, all three figures rushed toward him, passed into his body. As the third set of eyes made contact with his, he saw a bright flash that blinded him entirely.

When the light faded away and he could see again, Caymus found he was, somehow, living inside his own memory. He stood apart, observing his own life. He could feel the Lords of the Conflagration there too, separate consciousnesses within his own, watching, waiting, judging.

He was home. His mother was making dinner, chopping celery, parsley, and rabbit to put into a stew. He was nine years old. Even as a child, Caymus had been large. He sat quietly in front of the cooking fire, mesmerized by the crackling flames. His mother called to him a couple of times to help with the cooking, but the child didn't hear her, and she eventually had to tap him on the head with a wooden spoon to get his attention.

Another flash of light. He saw himself again, sitting on a plank, dangling from a pair of ropes attached to the railing of a dry-docked ship. Caymus felt his eyes well up looking at the memory: he was with his father. The two of them were in the shipyard in Krin's Point. Caymus was older in this memory, but not by much…eleven, perhaps? Aster was checking the seams between the planks—this was back before he'd been made Hull master—that comprised the ship's hull; Caymus was helping by steadying the supplies and rechecking those seams his father had just gone over. It was the first time Caymus had been to the dry dock; his father had taken him with him that week, that he might see what it was he did while he was away from home. It was one of Caymus's favorite memories, and seeing it so vividly was bittersweet. The two of them were so happy, just spending time together on the side of that ship.

A flash. He was out in the woods with his friends, spending the night outdoors, away from nagging parents and writing lessons at the school. Sara, Willet, and Gerud were telling ghost stories while Caymus tended their campfire. He was barely paying his friends any attention at all as he walked out into the darkness to find more fuel wood, lest his creation go out for lack of care. The real problem was the he'd built the fire much too large and it was burning through the logs he'd gathered faster than he could replace them.

Flash. The fire. The ship was on fire. Caymus's father was trapped in the bilge and Caymus had gone in to look for him. He reached the bilge. He stumbled. He found him. Caymus then watched, his eyes desperate to cry, as he picked his father up from the floor. Then the steps collapsed, and the moment came. There was fire everywhere. There was nowhere to run. When a number of flaming planks of wood fell before them, Caymus hesitated for a moment, looked around, then made that fateful decision: better to brave the flames than to die inside the craft. As the memory of Caymus ran through the flames, Caymus, the observer, got to see the thing that he'd only ever heard other people tell him about: the flames parted for him, peeling backward as he passed and flowing around him, less than an inch from his and his father's skins.

Caymus didn't want to see what came next. He knew it all too well. The fall to the ground, through the scaffolding, and they'd both lost consciousness. The dry-dock had closed, the workers sent home. It had been that woman, Yvonne, who'd put them on a cart and taken them back to Woodsea, where his mother had cared for them.

His mother, it turned out, had known Master Be'Var, and had asked him to come and lend his expertise. The old man had arrived within two days.

Caymus turned out to be fine. Be'Var set and mended a broken rib and made sure nothing inside was damaged. He'd also suggested, upon hearing about the parting of the flames, that Caymus should join the Temple as a disciple.

Aster Bolwerc hadn't been as lucky. Sure, Caymus had gotten him out of the wreckage alive, but the man had inhaled several lungfuls of smoke while he'd lain belowdecks, and the damage had been too much for his body to bear. The next few days had been the worst of Caymus's life: he'd had to simply watch, helpless, as the man who'd raised him, who'd taught him everything he knew, provided for his every need, *loved* him…slowly suffocate to death. In the end, Aster had died in the night, gasping for air and holding his wife's hand.

The day before his passing, he'd made Caymus promise him one thing: that he would go to the Temple and find out everything he could about what they had to teach. *You don't have to stay*, he'd said, *but promise me you'll try.*

And now, that promise had let him here, to the Conflagration itself.

Flash. He was at the Temple now, and things were moving quickly. He saw Rill, Sannet, and other friends as he made his way through his classes and went through his exercises. He saw himself sitting before the Conduit, watching it, studying it for hours.

Flash. He was in the small classroom where Be'Var had tried to teach him the Aspect of pulling. Caymus got the distinct impression that the Lords were taking particular interest in this memory. They watched intently as he sat on the ground and reached out to feel his surroundings, all while under Be'Var's watchful eye. They strained as he grasped onto the tiny conduit, and Caymus could sense they were somehow pleased with the effort.

When he shaped the flame, however, when he changed the nature of the flame by shaping the conduit rather than pulling energy through it, something suddenly seemed to go terribly wrong. All at once, he felt rage, anger, passion, jealousy, and fear. The memories of his life evaporated and he was in the Conflagration again. The manifestations of the elemental Lords left his body and began circling around him, making low, moaning sounds which grew louder and louder with each passing second. Caymus covered his ears, trying to block the sound out, but nothing he did silenced the mournful dirge.

Just as the sound was becoming unbearable, the Lords flew into him again, only this time there was no white light, and he was not transported to a place in his memory. Instead, the roaring flames that surrounded him seemed to penetrate his body, to flow through him. He could feel the elemental beings' presence within him now, moving, tearing through his flesh.

As they passed through his skin, through his muscles and organs, the Lords burned him. Some part of his consciousness was aware that they were leaving no trace of damage as they did so, but the feeling was as though somebody was carving through his body with the edge of a dull knife: burning, scraping, and ripping. Caymus screamed just so that he wouldn't pass out, though he wanted nothing more than to collapse onto the ground and cry himself into unconsciousness. But there was no ground in this place, and as much as he hurt, he fought to keep his eyes open, to stay awake, to keep himself in the moment. He didn't know what had gone wrong, but if he was going to meet death in this place, he was going to do it on his terms.

As he struggled against the feeling of his body being torn to shreds, as he put all his effort into keeping his wits, an image flashed before his eyes, like a bolt of lightning in his mind. The image had been a face. It was a man's face, neither young nor old, but weathered and scruffy. As the image drifted into memory, Caymus realized the most striking thing about it was the strange man's expression. He had seemed crushed, as though under the weight of responsibility, and yet there had been joy there, too. Caymus wondered who the man was, and whether the Lords had chosen to show him the face, or if it was just one of their own memories playing through his mind.

Then, without preamble, the pain stopped, and the Lords retreated from Caymus's body and, once again, stood before him. Compared to what he had just been through, the feeling of just standing in the flames of the Conflagration was near-euphoric. He had to fight to keep his mind focused on what was happening, to pay attention to events around him and not simply indulge in the sense of relief.

The center figure spoke again. "Caymus Bolwerc," it said, "We have seen your mind. We have seen your memories. We have judged your intention and we have tested your very flesh." For a moment, the figure paused. Caymus didn't know what to think. When it spoke again, it spoke in a quiet, flat voice, completely void of emotion. "We can find no fault with your heart, Caymus Bolwerc, but there exists an impurity in your flesh, a taint to your soul." Then, the speaker's eyes turned to an orange glow as it said, "You will never be a master."

Once again, the figures rushed toward him. Once again, he felt pain, but this time it was only in his left hand. He brought the hand up before his cringing face, but he could see nothing there.

This was it, then: the moment of his death. The Lords had, for some reason, judged him unworthy and were now going to destroy him. He put his hand down, closed his eyes, and prepared himself. The last thought in his mind, before pain erupted in his chest, was that he missed his mother's rabbit stew.

But he wasn't burning. Rather, the pain he felt was from some tremendous force knocking him backward. He fell. He didn't know how long or how far, but he could hear his heart beating in his ears again as flames rushed past him. Lub-dub. He was falling. Lub-dub. The pain in his hand disappeared. Lub-dub.

Caymus hit the stone roof of the Temple hard, earning himself a nasty crack to the back of the head. He was dizzy, cold, confused, and his eyes didn't seem to want to focus on anything. He could hear the masters all around him, though. To his addled brain, they seemed concerned, or possibly angry. Some of them were whispering. Some were yelling and gesticulating wildly.

"Quiet, all of you!" Be'Var's voice carried over the other masters, giving Caymus's mind something to focus on as colors began to coalesce back into familiar shapes. The sky was still the magnificent blue he'd seen when he'd walked into the Conduit. The Conduit itself still roared with the same eternal fury it always had. Be'Var was kneeling over him, looking at him severely as if he couldn't decide whether or not he was glad to see him. "Are you alright, boy?" he asked.

Caymus got himself to a sitting position, then reached around to the back of his head and turned to look at the roof to see if he might be bleeding. His head felt dry and there was no evidence of blood on the stone. "Seems that way," he said, turning back to Be'Var.

It was then that he noticed Be'Var wasn't looking at him, or rather not at his face, but at his hand. A quick glance around showed that the other masters, too, were staring at his left hand, still held to the back of his head. Before he could look at it himself, Be'Var had snatched his wrist and was turning over it so all could see.

He had been marked.

Only, he hadn't. Where the brand of a Third Circle disciple should have been, there was another mark, still branded into his skin, but entirely different in nature. There was a representation of a flame, rounded at the bottom and tapering off at the top, but where the Third Circle's flame went straight up, his curved to the right as though caught by the wind. Behind it was another figure: a long, diagonal line, crossing behind the flame from bottom right to top left. At the top end of the line was another, shorter line, a crossbar which looked like a hilt, making the lines resemble a sword.

That was it. The shapes were black, like they were supposed to be, but there were no hands coddling a central fire, just this flame and sword design. What was this thing? Every Trial of Courage Caymus had ever heard of had only ended in either the mark of a Third Circle or the death of the student. This was an outcome he hadn't expected. As he looked around at the faces surrounding him, he could tell that nobody else had expected it either. He looked at Be'Var, asking the question with his eyes.

Be'Var shook his head, looking perplexed, angry, and more than a little worried. He offered Caymus his hand to help him to his feet. As Caymus took it and rose, the master said, "Well boy, perhaps you'd better tell us all what happened while you were in there."

Chapter 5

The sanctuary was too still. Be'Var entertained the thought for about the hundredth time as he ascended the stairs toward the roof. A week had passed since those insectoid creatures had attacked, and the Temple of the Conflagration wasn't anywhere near back to its usual routines yet. The last of the young men in the infirmary was either back on his feet or dead, but evening sermons had not yet resumed and classes were only being held haphazardly. He knew he carried his fair share of blame for that, having spent most of his recent time penning communications for Milo to whisper to out into the world, but the deviations bothered him, and he couldn't stop wondering: would thing ever be normal again?

He was about halfway up the staircase when he realized he needed to stop for a moment, as his left knee was aching with each step. Flaming dog-spit! When had he gotten so old? As a younger man, he'd been the adventurous sort, having joined the ranks of the physicians' corps in Kepren once he'd fully appreciated his talent for healing. He'd met a lot of interesting people during those years, and he'd learned a great deal about how the world worked. Those years had kept him fit, and he'd managed to maintain that fitness after leaving the corps...for the most part. Admittedly, his calisthenics had fallen off rather a lot since he'd taken up a life that involved desks and classrooms for the most part.

At least he was better off than most of the other old fossils around here. Most of the Temple's other masters were the bookish sort, rarely having dared to venture more than a mile from their own homes in their lives, much less to other cities or nations. Eavuk was practically a walking skeleton. Porindus had gotten so large over the last decade that it was a wonder his joints hadn't all fallen to pieces already. Be'Var didn't care for the idea of the masters not maintaining their own bodies as much as they did their minds, not least because of the example it set for the disciples.

It was a good thing that the Temple was run by the masters as a group, rather than by some high priest; he liked his fellows, but the thought of having to follow one of them gave him shivers.

Be'Var decided to just sit down on the staircase for a minute. The blacksmithing he'd learned while he was in the corps had kept his arms and chest strong all these years, but damn these stairs!

Caymus. Again, he thought about Caymus. Ever since he'd stepped—no, since he'd been tossed!—out of the Conduit with that strange mark on his hand, the boy hadn't been right. He was quiet, isolated, melancholy. He'd not attended a single class, and whenever Be'Var took the time to go looking for him, he was usually out on one of his long walks in the Saleri Forest. For his part, Be'Var had to admit he hadn't been much help. He and the other masters had been unable to attach logic to why Caymus had received a different mark than any other disciple in the Temple's history, and so he'd been unable to lend the boy any explanation or comfort. He wasn't even sure if the boy could rightly be called a disciple at this point. Burn it all. The whole thing was a mess.

From what Caymus had told him about the events of that morning, everything seemed to have gone generally the same way as his own trial, all those years ago: everything, that was, up to the point that they started galloping around him and then burning him up from the inside. Had the boy come out of that blaze with any sort of normalcy, Be'Var would have thought the story made up, but that strange mark was ironclad evidence that his experience had been unlike any other. The shaping. Caymus said they had gone quite mad when they'd seen him shaping. But that made no sense. Master Alvis, the shaper who had been at the Temple when Be'Var had been a young man, had certainly carried a master's mark. Why, then, would the elemental Lords have some problem with Caymus?

"A taint to your soul," Caymus had said. Well, whatever *that* meant, it seemed it wasn't bad enough for them to actually kill him over, but what the actual significance was, he had no idea. The concept was completely foreign. A taint? Would he ever understand what it meant?

Be'Var sighed heavily, slapped his hands on his knees, got back to his feet, and started up the stairs again. He had to stop thinking that way. Mysterious taint or no, Caymus was the most innately talented student at the Temple and that was that. Be'Var would just have to give the other masters time to get over the fact that they had, here in the Temple, someone who simply wasn't going to fit into any of the established circles. Once they came around, he'd give the boy a good crack over his head with a stick to shake him out of his misery, and a properly education could begin again.

With that issue good and decided, Be'Var emerged onto the roof, looked around, and found who he was looking for. Milo was standing at the northern edge of the east wing, about thirty feet away, facing the forest beyond the Temple's lawn. The old master walked over to stand beside him. Well, maybe not *beside* him: the crenellation wasn't very high at this part of the roof, and the air priest liked to stand suicidally close to the edge. Perhaps a foot or so back would be safer.

As he neared, he could hear the faint sound of Milo whispering into the wind, could see his lips moving as he sent yet another message to some other air-lover in some other place, some crazy number of miles away. Be'Var had admitted to himself that the practice, which had the look of a disturbed individual mumbling to himself, made him a bit edgy, but he was glad for it all the same. Thanks to Milo, he'd been able to communicate with a few other fire masters and get the general idea of how various cities had fared.

There were still some places he hadn't heard from. Albreva and Ni'lag'ren were two in particular he wished to know the fates of, as there were the beginnings of small Conflagrationist schools in each. Milo, however, had told him that he didn't know those places. Apparently, the whispering depended not only on knowing who you wanted to talk to, but also on having a good idea of where they were standing. Be'Var didn't understand the logic, but he took Milo's word for it. He loved a good theological discussion, but lately just never seemed like the right time for one.

As he thought about the far-off cities, he realized that Milo had gone quiet and was now standing with his head cocked to one side, his eyes closed. Be'Var figured he must be listening to somebody else's message to him, though he certainly couldn't hear anything besides the faint breeze blowing across the grass down below.

Then, Milo opened his eyes, slumped his shoulders, and then fell into a deep crouch, his arms resting on his knees.

"Any luck?" said Be'Var.

"Not a bit," said Milo. "Everyone I ask, not one of them knows where they came from." He shook his head as he gazed into the distance. "And everyone's telling the same weird story, too: everywhere those things attacked, it's like…they didn't come from anywhere. People seem to think they just sprung out of the ground."

Be'Var frowned. "Tunnels?"

Milo shook his head. "No, I don't think so. Digging would have left holes behind, and there never seem to be any. I had a look around that first spot where Caymus was attacked, and while there were plenty of broken branches and uprooted trees to prove that the thing had travelled *across* the ground, there was no evidence whatsoever that it had gone *through* it." He sighed. "It's like they don't actually touch anything unless the idea is to destroy it."

Be'Var thought that was an interesting way of putting things. "So, whatever these things are, they seem to be able to travel through the earth element." It was Be'Var's turn to sigh. "For the first time in my life, I wish I had a dirt-lover to talk to about a couple of things."

"That's the other thing," said Milo.

"What is?"

"The mitre. Nobody's heard much of anything about them except for one clan, waaay off to the East. That one was completely wiped out."

Be'Var considered this. The mitre were a race of giants: huge, even to someone like Caymus. Not all earth-worshipers were mitre, but all mitre were earth-worshipers. They were legendary tunnelers who concealed vast underground cities behind shoddy-looking surface encampments. Attacking the mitre was almost the same as attacking the Sect of the Rounded Stone or the Sand Dwellers of Hurahna, so immersed were they in their faith. Why would the creatures attack the giants?

"They seemed to be attacking holy places?" suggested Milo, as if reading Be'Var's thoughts. "Cities, temples, wells, just about anywhere there's any kind of religious presence. Could be that they went after the mitre because of their connection to earth." He shrugged. "Or maybe they just ran into them underground."

"Maybe," said Be'Var. "At this point, not much would surprise me. Anything else?"

Milo shook his head again. "It's been getting quieter and quieter as the days go on. It'd be different if there'd been another, but all this just waiting around to see if they come again…nobody knows what to do." He stood up and turned to Be'Var. "So, how's our golden boy?"

Be'Var chuckled, dryly. "The same, but I'm sure he'll snap out of it. Of course, now that he doesn't have working in the infirmary with Gwenna to distract him anymore, he has more time to brood."

"They're getting quite friendly, those two, aren't they?" Milo smiled.

"Yes," said Be'Var. He'd been a bit irritated about that particular development, but he supposed that he really should have seen it coming. During his time as a physician, he'd often seen situations where nurses and the patients they cared for very quickly developed romantic ties. They almost never worked out, of course. "Pity she'll be going back to Flamehearth in the morning with the rest of them," he said. "I think they're getting supplies together as we speak."

He changed the subject. "Are you going scouting again today?"

Milo nodded. "Yes," he said. "I need to have another look. I just don't believe these things simply popped up out of nowhere. If I can find a tunnel, a track, something, maybe it will help for next time." He looked out to the forest again. "If there's a next time."

"There will be," said Be'Var. "There's not a doubt in my mind."

At that point, Be'Var heard the sudden flapping of wings, and he turned to see a white hawk landing on the edge of the roof, not far from where they were standing. The bird had some manner of large rodent in its mouth: apparently its afternoon kill. It looked at them for a moment or two before it put the thing down, at which point it proceeded to tear its meal into manageable pieces.

"Never saw one of those come so close to people," Be'Var said.

"Just that one," said Milo, who gave it a mistrustful look. "I don't know why, but it's been following me around."

"You don't say?" said Be'Var, intrigued.

"I do," said Milo. "Ever since that night the bugs attacked. Caymus said it tried to warn him about the one in the forest. Said it probably saved his life." Milo looked at Be'Var and shrugged. "I honestly don't know what to do about it."

Be'Var smiled. "Have you given it a name yet?"

"No!" said Milo, looking taken aback. Then he seemed to consider the idea. "I suppose I could…" He turned to the hawk, which had finished gulping down the rodent. "Hey, bird! You want a name?"

The hawk looked up at the noisy man and cocked its head to one side, as though unsure whether this was something it wanted or not. Then it looked behind the two men, puffed out its chest as though startled, then it flapped its wings and flew off to the West.

"Was that a yes or a no?" said Milo.

"Master Be'Var?"

The pair turned to see Caymus, as though summoned by their earlier conversation, emerging from the staircase.

"Ah," said Be'Var, "nice to see you out and about, at last." He glanced at Milo, who was giving the boy a warm smile. "The 'woe is me' bit was getting a little trying for my taste."

Caymus nodded as he walked over to them, though he looked a more-than-usually unsure of himself. Be'Var noticed his right hand was covering the back of his left; it seemed an unconscious action, and he wondered if the boy even knew he was doing it. "There's something I wanted to ask you, Master," he said. "Or rather, something I wanted to tell you."

Be'Var raised an eyebrow. From the timid way the boy was approaching the subject, he wasn't certain this was going to be something he wanted to hear, and when Caymus finally looked up and met his eyes, he realized he had a pretty good guess at what it was the boy had to say. He felt his ire rising of its own accord.

"I'm leaving the Temple," said Caymus. "If they'll have me, I'm going to accompany the missionaries back to Flamehearth in Kepren."

Be'Var could barely contain his indignation. Of all the flaming stupid notions! "Idiot child!" he yelled. "You think that will help things, do you?" He pointed a finger at Caymus. "You find yourself in a hard situation and you think you can fix it by running off with some girl?"

They, Caymus did something surprising: for the first time since Be'Var had known him, Caymus yelled back. "This has nothing to do with Gwenna!"

"Oh really?" shouted Be'Var. Then, he reined in his anger and said more calmly, "What time you've not been spending on brooding and sulking lately, you've been spending with her. Now, she and the rest of them are going back where they came from, and you just happen to want to go along? What, to be a missionary? You want to tell stories about the Temple and send other children here, hoping that at least one of them is as good as you might have been so you don't feel so guilty about leaving?"

Caymus seemed about to say something, but he held it back. He instead looked back and forth between Milo and Be'Var for a movement, then he sighed. "No," he said, "I don't."

"Good," said Be'Var, "because you'll be a damn sight better shaper than you ever will a mission-keeper. You're not going to give up on your education because of some self-deluded sense that you're not up to snuff. You're going to learn to control your Aspect, and that's an end to it."

Caymus looked him square in the eyes. He even let his gaze hang there for a while as if trying to out-stare him. Then he sighed and shook his head. "You'll never be a master," he said. "That's what they said to me, Be'Var. It's not some delusion, and it's not a lack of confidence. The Lords of the Conflagration themselves told me that I won't ever—*ever*—be one of you."

Burn it all, that was actually a good point: simple and irrefutable. Be'Var prepared his response, but upon consideration, he realized he actually didn't have one. What argument could he make? *You'll never be a master.* Why stay? Why bother? What was the point?

But the boy had so much potential! To let it go to waste just because he'd never be able to gain a master's mark was idiotic! "Caymus, you—"

But Caymus held up a hand and cut him off. Be'Var raised his eyebrows, practically stunned. He couldn't decide if whether the move revealed confidence or simply an inordinate amount of cheek.

"I don't want to be a missionary, Master," Caymus said, lowering the hand. "I do want to learn more about shaping—of *course* I do—but you said it yourself: there's nobody who can teach it to me here. And now I've got this mark, this thing…" He looked down at his hand, absently scratching at the sword and flame symbols as though they might come off. "Nobody here knows what it is or why I have it. What should I do? Just wait around here for years and years hoping the answer just falls into my lap?" He looked up again, this time gazing over Be'Var's shoulder into the distance. "No, I think it's pretty clear that if I want answers, I'm going to have to go out into the world and look for them. This just seems like a good opportunity to do that."

He met the master's eyes again, and his gaze was challenging.

Be'Var sighed. Burn it, but he was right. As much as he wanted Caymus to stay on at the Temple under his tutelage, the master knew there wasn't much he could tell the boy about shaping. Plus, he'd been through all the books in the Temple's small library in the past few days, and there wasn't a single clue about the strange mark, not one recorded instance of somebody receiving it in over a thousand years.

He considered the boy's proposal; realizing it had merit. Kepren would actually be a good place for him to start his search. For starters, the king kept a decent royal library. It wasn't generally accessible to the common folk, but given a formal request from a master, the scribes could probably be persuaded to let Caymus in to have a look around. And who could say: maybe, with enough time, he'd run into another shaper down there and have someone to compare himself to, if not learn from?

Or, even better…

"Fine," Be'Var said, scratching his chin. "You're right, staying here isn't going to do you any good, and if you're going to look for explanations for that mark on your hand, I can think of a number of people in Kepren that might be able to point you in the right direction." He briefly glanced toward Milo. "Do you know," he said with a menacing smile, "I've heard that there's a master in Kepren who's adept at healing. I really should go and speak to him and compare notes; maybe see if we can't come up with any ideas on how to deal with this new element." Be'Var could see a look of both confusion and concern crawling across Caymus's face, and the master took great delight in it. "Ket can handle the few classes I'm running for the time being, so it's not as though the Temple really needs me around at the moment." He nodded. "Yes. Yes, I think I'll go as well."

Caymus looked like he wanted to argue, but he must have realized there was no point. He dropped his shoulders in defeat, obviously resigned to the fact that he really didn't get any say about the comings and goings of a master of the Order of the Conflagration.

Milo was choking down laughter. "You didn't think it would be that easy, did you?" he said.

Caymus looked toward the priest and, to his credit, grinned in spite of himself. "I guess not," he finally said.

Be'Var quietly breathed a sigh of relief; it was good to see the boy smile again.

"Good," said Milo, pointing at Be'Var, "because I think you're going to have a bit of trouble getting rid of this one."

Be'Var wasn't sure how he felt about being called 'this one', but he decided not to dwell on it.

Milo put his pointing finger down, then he paused a moment, thinking. Then, he grinned and turned to Be'Var. "Room for one more?"

It was Be'Var's turn to laugh. Caymus just rolled his eyes. "Are we going to be taking the whole Temple with us?" he said.

"Tut-tut," laughed Milo. "Don't lump me in with the rest of your heathen religion!" He spread his arms out, making a grand, sweeping gesture. "I travel wherever the wind blows!" he exclaimed, spinning around. Then he dropped his arms and turned back to Caymus. "And I think it's fairly obvious that the wind is blowing in your direction at the moment." He grinned broadly, showing all his teeth, then turned to Be'Var. "What do you say, oh wisest of fire-masters?" Then he bowed deeply holding his arms wide and spreading his many feathers to either side.

Be'Var grumped. He didn't want to like Milo. It wasn't just that he was an air-worshiper; Be'Var had lived enough years to know that the other religions weren't evil, or even necessarily at odds with his own. No, it was more that the man in front of him seemed the sort that would turn out to be undependable, the kind who would take to being distracted from important issues by butterflies and shiny things in his path. Still, the fact that Milo had been so crucial in letting him know what was going on in the world lately—and had kept on doing so all week, despite all the confusion in the region—spoke volumes about his character. No, he didn't want to like Milo, but despite his preconceptions, the old master had to admit he enjoyed the clown's antics, and that he wouldn't mind having him along.

There was also that the fact that, as clowns go, he was an awfully good shot with that bow of his. That could actually be really useful. With all the chaos in the land, who knew what kind of trouble they might run into on a journey to Tebria's capital? "I think that would be fine, Milo," he said. "What do you think, Caymus?"

Caymus just sighed and shook his head, looking resigned and defeated.

Be'Var couldn't help feeling a little bit sorry for him: the boy had probably been getting quite excited about this great adventure he was going to take, and now the whole endeavor was suddenly getting completely out of his control. "Don't worry boy," he said, "I won't embarrass you in front of the young lady too much." Caymus had the decency to blush slightly at that. "Just remember, you may not have become a Third Circle disciple, but you're still my student. And I may not be able to tell you much about shaping, but if you think you've learned all I have to teach you, you're very much mistaken."

Caymus nodded his understanding, seeming to take the words

seriously. Good. Be'Var had been expecting an argument. "We're going to keep up your instruction," he continued, "just like we'd planned. On the road's as good a place as any, I guess."

Caymus nodded again. "Okay," he said simply.

Be'Var nodded. "Alright," he said. "Well, I suppose you need to go and pack a few things if you're going to be leaving first thing tomorrow?"

"Yeah," said Caymus, who turned to go. "I guess I do."

"Good," said Be'Var, "I'll let Matron Y'selle know that they're going to have company on their return trip, then I'll sort out the supplies with Ket." He turned to Milo. "You don't eat much, do you?"

"I'll get started on my packing," said Caymus, who had reached the stairs. Then he stopped. "Master Be'Var?" he said.

Be'Var turned and saw Caymus looking seriously at him.

"Thanks," he said, then he smiled and went down the stairs.

Be'Var smiled. "That boy's going to do alright."

"Don't you have things to pack, too?" asked Milo.

"Of course," said Be'Var. "But I had to let him get ahead of me by a few minutes first. It wouldn't do for the students to know a master of the Order of the Conflagration was off to do something quite so mundane as *pack*, now would it?"

Milo laughed. "Have it your way," he said.

"Yes," said Be'Var, "well, I suppose I'd better go and be mundane." He started cataloging things in his mind. Smoke and ash, he'd have to take half the Temple with him if he wanted to do this properly. As he shuffled off to begin his project, a thought occurred to him. "Milo?"

"Hmmm?"

"Will you still be able to do that whispering thing while we're traveling?"

Milo shook his head. "Afraid not. I've been around the Temple long enough that my friends know how to find me here, but it takes a while to describe a new area, and there won't be time when we're on the move."

Be'Var frowned. He was fairly certain Milo had just spoken utter nonsense to him. "Describe a new area?"

"It's called 'speaking the place'," said Milo. "It's a bit more involved than whispering and takes most of a day to do. Basically," he continued, "it's like painting a picture of the area in words, being as accurate and vivid as you can. That way, other people get a feel for the place and the whispers can find you."

Be'Var was still confused, and his expression must have revealed that confusion.

"Look," said Milo, grinning, "let's say you want to send a letter to someone. You have to write down who it's for and where they are, right?"

Be'Var nodded. "Okay, I follow that."

"Well," said Milo, "whispering's the same way, only you're not handing a note to some courier who's been to wherever-the-place-is a thousand times and can find it easily. You're directing the message yourself, so if you don't know the place, there's no delivering the message." He paused. "Get it?"

The analogy seemed to make sense. "So, until we get to someplace these friends of yours know, or one you can spend a day describing to them, we're in the dark."

"There, you have it," said Milo, who seemed happy he'd gotten the point across. "I'll be able to send my whispers out on the wind, but expecting a reply is another thing entirely."

"That's a shame," said Be'Var. "Oh well, nothing for it, I suppose. We'll just have to hope the world manages to go on without us."

"It usually does," said Milo. "Well, if there's nothing else you need, I'll be off having a look around."

Be'Var watched with no small amount of wonder as the priest turned, took two big steps, and jumped straight off the south side of the roof. He didn't see Milo land, but he heard the great whoosh of air that signaled he'd used his priestly abilities to protect himself upon reaching the ground. Less than a minute later, he watched the air priest disappear into Saleri Forest. Flames, but he was fast! Be'Var wondered if manipulation of the wind had something to do with that, too.

He didn't have time to wonder long, though. He had a great deal of work to do if he was going to be ready to leave with the others at first light. He'd have to let the missionaries know he was going with them. He'd have to let the other masters know he was absenting himself, too. They'd raise a fuss at his leaving, of course, especially Ket, but the fact was he was needed elsewhere for the time being, so they'd just have to get along without him. They'd be fine. The Temple got along for several centuries before he turned up; it would get along after he left.

He also needed to write some final messages for Milo to whisper before they all departed. As he started back down the stairs, he thought again about how much everything was changing: strange creatures attacking in the night, an air priest feeling right at home in the Temple of Order of the Conflagration, and a remarkable young man receiving a mark from elemental lords that nobody had ever seen before.

Caymus. Be'Var was old and set in his ways. He didn't believe in destiny. Yet, somehow, he felt that a destiny was exactly what Caymus had. He believed there were grand and important things ahead for that boy, and as he made his way back down the stairs, he thought that he'd really like to live long enough to see those things through.

Or, he thought, maybe just long enough to find out why the Conflagration marked him the way it did.

~~~

Caymus yawned again. He'd been up far too late into the night. Not only had he needed to get all of his belongings together—he didn't actually have many belongings, so the task hadn't been difficult—but just as the sun had been going down, Be'Var had come to fetch him to help with all of *his* packing, too.

The old man had sent him searching through shelves of books and dozens of crates for a handful of specific items: a journal he'd written about using the pulling Aspect to fight infections, a bottle of what he'd said was especially good wine, several empty notebooks, an old cooking pan that apparently was necessary for the old man's survival, and a small statue of a horse were just some of the odd things Be'Var had insisted he take with him.

Still, the entire lot had eventually fit nicely into a large trunk, which Be'Var had then warned him against trying to open due to a "surprise," he'd put in the locking mechanism. Caymus hadn't asked questions; he'd just been glad the think was finally closed.

He'd just finished heaving the thing into the wagon, along with some meats and breads from the kitchen that Master Eavuk had insisted they take, and he was investigating whether the creaking he'd heard was anything to worry about. He glanced underneath the wagon, but he couldn't find anything actually broken. With all the supplies they were taking for Flamehearth, however, the thing was riding low on its springs, and Caymus wondered if it would hold together for a trip which would take them right over the Greatstone Mountains and across the Tebrian Desert before finally reaching Kepren; there were still passengers to accommodate, after all.

Having decided there was nothing he could do about the springs, he stood and leaned against the wagon for a moment. His moment of rest, however, was interrupted by a snort, and looked up to see one of the horses staring back at him reproachfully. It nickered at him, as though thoroughly disappointed with the heavy item he'd just added to its burden.

"Sorry," he said, shrugging his shoulders.

"Oh, don't listen to Feston," said Gwenna, walking up behind him. She was carrying another trunk, though this one was much smaller than Be'Var's. "He's always complaining." She gave Caymus a smile and handed him the trunk, which he took and placed next to Be'Var's. She then stood next to him and opened it. She shuffled through some linens as though looking for something. "If you let him, he'll nag you all the way back."
~~~

Caymus smiled. She was standing close, actually leaning on him slightly, and he liked the feeling of her against him.

"There we are," she said, and she pulled out a small pouch which she upended to produce a few small, curved shapes. She offered the shapes to Caymus. "Here, give him these. It's time you got acquainted anyway."

Caymus hadn't seen these things before. They were rigid, but they felt light in his hand. "What is it?"

"It's made from wheat," said Gwenna. "They grind it up, add water, then dry it out." She took his other hand and led him to the horses. "They love it, and it doesn't make them as nippy as sugar. Here, hold your hand out flat, like a plate." She demonstrated, giving some to the other horse, a black gelding named Staven, stroking his mane as she did so. The horse gobbled the treats up greedily. "Keep your fingers together," she said. "If he bites one off by accident, he won't be able to tell you he's sorry."

Caymus wasn't exactly encouraged by that idea, but he did as he was told. Feston looked at him for a moment, as if deciding whether he wanted anything from this strange, too-large boy, then he gave in and took the proffered food. Gwenna stroked his long face. "Good boy," she said, then she gave Caymus a wink. "See? You're going to be good friends."

She handed him a few more of the oddly shaped little treats. Caymus had a hard time holding onto them for more than a moment before Feston grabbed them out of his hand. They laughed, and Feston even let Caymus pat his mane, though the horse was sure to keep an eye on him as he did so.

"I…I'm glad you're coming, Caymus," Gwenna said suddenly. When Caymus looked down, she met his gaze for a moment, and then quickly turned away and went back to stroking Steven's mane.

For a moment, Caymus was overcome. He'd known Gwenna barely a few days. In that time, he'd found her to be resilient and able. There'd been so much awfulness in the past week, but every time somebody had needed her, she'd put on a brave face and gotten on with helping. He wasn't used to her seeming so unsure, so…vulnerable?

He wasn't sure what to say to her. "Me too," was all he could think of.

For another quick moment, she turned to him and shared a quick smile.

"All right, you two!"

They turned to see Matron Y'selle, Bridget, Sannet, Be'Var, and the two converts who'd arrived with the missionaries. Caymus realized he hadn't seen the latter pair very much in the past few days. He knew their names were Guruk and Fach'un, but he didn't actually know which was which. In fact, this was the first time he'd gotten a proper look at them in the light of day: their skin was the color of dark sand, their heads were shaved, and they had sharp features with jutting jawlines and piercing blue eyes that seemed as if they saw everything. He'd heard that they'd been inducted as First Circle disciples soon after they'd arrived; idly, he wondered if they'd made Second Circle yet.

Be'Var, who was carrying some sort of sack over his shoulder, looked cross. Everyone else was grinning.

"If I'm going to have to put up with that kind of thing the whole trip," the master said, "I might as well stay here and keep my sanity."

Caymus looked at Gwenna, who shrugged and winked at him. They then dropped one another's gazes and walked around the wagon to join the rest of the group.

"Has Milo been around?" asked Be'Var as he tossed the sack on top of one of the crates.

"He was here about half an hour ago," said Caymus. "Said he was going on ahead and would meet us down the road a bit."

"Fine," said Be'Var, who then walked off a ways with Matron Y'selle and the converts, leaving the younger people to themselves for a moment.

"I'm surprised Rill's not here," Sannet said.

Caymus shook his head. "We said our goodbyes late last night. I haven't seen him this morning. I guess he's not much of one for seeing people off." In truth, Caymus was a little hurt by Rill's seeming indifference to his leaving the Temple, possibly forever. He'd had a kind of faraway look when they'd spoken about it the previous night, as though not entirely there in the moment. Then, he's just wished Caymus luck on his journey walked out of the room. Caymus didn't know what to make of that; it was odd behavior for Rill. He hoped he was alright.

"I suppose he's not," said Sannet, shrugging. "It's going to be strange not having you around, Caymus," he continued, "for all of us." He looked down at his hands. He was carrying something: a small, wooden box, about four inches to a side, wrapped in wide, yellow ribbon. Caymus couldn't help noticing the Third Circle mark on Sannet's hand, which suddenly reminded of the new symbol on his own skin.

"What do you have there?" he said.

"I was wondering if you could do me a favor, Caymus," he said, then he held the box out. "My parents are in Kepren and I was hoping you could give this to them when you find some time."

Caymus, intrigued, nodded as he took the box.

"It's just a note," said Sannet, "and a trinket they'd be happy to see."

Caymus nodded, happy to do his friend a favor. "Of course," he said. "I'll find them as soon as I can."

"Franklin and Margaret Teldaar," said Sannet, and then he extended his hand, which Caymus took in a firm handshake. "Thank you, Caymus."

Then, he turned and walked back into the Temple by himself.

"He's, um…" said Bridget, brushing some stray hair back over her ear as she watched him go, "he's not exactly overly emotional, is he?"

Caymus smiled. "Sannet? No, I wouldn't say that. It's not that he doesn't want to be friendly or anything," he said. "I think he just sometimes forgets that people expect it is all."

He nearly said more, but Be'Var and the others were coming back.

"You ready to go?" Be'Var said to them. They all nodded. "Good, then we should be off."

Matron Y'selle beckoned the girls over to do a last check of the harnesses while Be'Var hoisted himself up onto the driver's bench, leaving Caymus to make sure all the luggage was secure and to latch the wagon's gate.

He was surprised when the two converts quietly stepped up beside him and began assisting with the straps.

"I am sorry that we did not speak with you," said the taller of the two. His voice was deep and musical, though he had a fierce accent which tended to cut off the words before he had gotten them completely out. Caymus was suddenly struck, too, by the way the two men moved. Their movements seemed overly deliberate, as though they paid a great deal of attention to even the most insignificant of motions. The effect, he realized, was actually a bit intimidating.

"I'm sorry I didn't make more of an effort myself," he said, trying to be pleasant. He hesitated a moment. "Is it…Guruk?"

The man smiled. "No," he said. He indicated his companion. "He is Guruk. I am Fach'un."

Caymus winced. "Sorry."

"It is alright," said Fach'un. "Perhaps we will get a chance to be introduced correctly on a day soon." He put out a hand.

Caymus took it. "I think I'd like that," he said.

Guruk, whose voice was higher in pitch but just as musical as Fach'un's, said, "Where you are going is not far from the land of our people. Perhaps you will go there and be introduced to them as well."

Caymus hesitated again. He wasn't sure if Guruk was chiding him or simply offering a suggestion; he was completely unable to read the two men. "Perhaps," he said, and as he spoke, he realized that he really would quite like to see the place Guruk and Fach'un came from. "Where is it from Kepren?"

Guruk smiled a toothy-white smile. "It is south of Kepren, near the border between Tebria and the place you would call Mael'vek."

Fach'un nodded. "If you seek out the hill in the desert, you will find our home at its feet."

Caymus nodded. "I'll try to remember that."

Fach'un and Guruk smiled, then both stepped backward from the wagon. Caymus closed the wagon's gate and slid the latches closed, thinking that he genuinely was sorry he hadn't made more of an effort to speak to these two.

When he looked up from his musings, the checks on the gear were complete and Y'selle was up in the driver's bench next to Be'Var, taking the reins from him. Once she was situated, the matron called back, "Is anybody not ready to leave?"

When no answer came, she flicked the reigns, and Feston and Staven ambled forward. Caymus glanced back to see Fach'un cupping his hands around his mouth. "Go with a flame in your heart!" he yelled to all of them.

Caymus smiled at the salvation, very glad to hear it, and began walking forward with the others.

Y'selle had asked him to follow along behind the group for the first day of the trip. He was supposed to keep an eye out for things falling out of the bed of their wagon, not to mention anything that might go amiss with wagon itself. Bridget and Gwenna were responsible for the horses; they walked alongside them, watching for limping or any other changes in their gait that would signify something might be wrong.

"How far do you think we'll get today?" Caymus asked of anybody who might be listening.

Be'Var turned slightly to yell back. "Fifteen or so miles, if all goes well. When we hit the Greatstones though, things will slow down."

"Is it going to take long to get across the mountains?"

"Yes," said Be'Var. "We're going to stop at Otvia, the mitre encampment that the women passed on the way up here. Find out what's happened there."

"How long are we staying?" said Caymus.

"I don't know," said Be'Var. "Quit asking questions!"

Caymus sighed. He hoped Be'Var's grumpiness was just due to their late night and that it wasn't going to continue for the whole trip.

A soft breeze blew across his face; the sun was hiding behind some wandering clouds. Despite it being late summer, the day was cool and pleasant, and Caymus found himself elated by the prospect of adventure. As the minutes passed, he found that he kept looking over his shoulder, back at the Temple, so that he could watch it get smaller and smaller in the distance. Just as they were about to hit the tree-line that would mark their entry into Saleri Forest, however, he noticed that there was a figure approaching from behind.

"Someone's coming," he said, and everyone turned to look. Y'selle stopped the horses and suddenly everything was quiet.

The figure turned out to be Rill, running to catch them, a sack over his shoulder, his approaching footfalls the only sounds anybody could hear. When he reached them, he was out of breath and covered with sweat. "Wasn't sure I'd…catch you," he panted. "I'm…coming too."

It was more of a question than a declaration, and from the way Rill was staring at Be'Var, he was obviously looking for the old man's approval. For a tense moment all eyes turned to the old master in anticipation of what he would say.

Be'Var didn't take long to deliberate. He took a deep breath, then turned to face the direction of travel. "Put your things in the wagon," he said, simply.

Rill grinned at Caymus and the others, then he threw his bag in with the rest. As Y'selle got the wagon moving again, he fell in next to Caymus.

"Good luck on the journey, eh?" said Caymus. He wasn't sure if he was glad to see his friend or upset that he hadn't know that this had been his plan.

Rill shrugged. "Honestly, I didn't know I was coming until about ten minutes ago." He glanced over his shoulder at the Temple. "Flames, I probably forgot about dozen things back there."

"Why?" said Caymus.

Rill turned to face the wagon again, a resigned look on his face. "There's nothing for me back at the Temple," he said. "I think that's pretty obvious. I'm terrible at all the things I'm supposed to be good at. I spent forever just getting to the point where I could enter the Second Circle, and it would be a small miracle if I ever got to the Third." He looked straight at Caymus. "Burn me down, but even if the Flame-lords themselves were to tell me I was ready to take that trial, there's no way I'm stepping into the Conduit to be burned alive!"

He nodded, seeming more certain of himself with every world. "I've been hanging around because I didn't know what else to do, but now that they're testing students sooner than ever…" He let the sentence trail off. "I'm a failure as a Conflagrationist. If I keep on at the Temple, I'll just keep on being a failure as a Conflagrationist."

"And," said Be'Var, looking over his shoulder at them, "you're an idiot." He turned around. "Don't worry," he continued, "Kepren's a big place. It's full of idiots. You'll do just fine."

Rill looked a little stunned at that. He didn't seem to understand that Be'Var was, in his own taciturn way, approving of Rill's logic. Caymus grinned, knowing that if the old man had really thought Rill was a waste of time, he'd have sent him back to the Temple to be someone else's problem, no argument allowed. Rill, however, didn't know Be'Var as well as Caymus did, and so he just hung his head, looking crushed.

Caymus grinned and punched Rill in the shoulder. "Idiot," he said, under his breath.

Rill looked up at him, looking even more crestfallen. Then he saw the grin on his friend's face and the breaking smile on his face revealed that he finally saw the joke of it all. Suddenly, his broken expression turned into a relieved-sounding burst of laughter.

Rill's mirth was contagious, and for a few moments, everyone had a good laugh. Caymus was glad. It was a good way to start a journey and he found himself looking forward to his future more than he had in a long time. He didn't know what he would discover in the coming days and weeks—about himself, about the mark on his hand, about anything at all—but he was glad to be sharing an adventure with these people, and he couldn't wait to see what lay around the next corner.

Chapter 6

Caymus narrowed his eyes against the glare of the sun and wiped the sweat from his brow. The steady heat of a late summer day beat down as he, Rill, and Milo rolled an empty, three-wheeled wagon toward a rust-colored boulder a dozen or so feet from the road. Milo rather clumsily held up the corner with the missing wheel, while Rill steered the contraption and Caymus lent his great mass to pushing it along.

Bridget watched bemusedly as she tended to the horses, while Gwenna and Y'selle rifled through the group's belongings, now sitting several feet from the trail, looking for some of the bread and cheese they'd brought with them.

"Not so fast, Caymus!" Despite Milo's natural agility, he was having trouble keeping his feet under him as the trio moved forward. The three remaining wheels supported the weight well enough, but the corner that was missing, being to the front and right, kept wanting to tip forward due to the weight of the bench and harnesses. The small rocks underfoot weren't helping things either.

"Sorry!" said Caymus. He wasn't actually trying to knock Milo over, but he had to keep giving the wagon an extra shove to get the one of the remaining wheels over a large stone, now and again.

They had been on the road south for just over a day, having passed through the thick greenery of the Saleri Forest the previous evening. They were now traversing a rocky plain, dotted here and there with shrubs and grasses, which would eventually become the slopes of the Greatstone Mountains.

The first day's travel had been uneventful, as had their first night sleeping in the wilderness, though Caymus recalled unsettling dreams about being trapped in the smoking hull of a burning ship. This day, too, had been fairly uninteresting until the moment, just after the sun had reached its zenith, when one of the metal bindings that held the wheels together had split with an audible "pang!" and had rolled off ahead of a pair of startled horses. The incident had left the bare wood of the wheel exposed and the group of travelers in a less-than-enthusiastic mood.

The noise had frightened the horses, and only Y'selle's careful handling of the reins and the calming voices of both Bridget and Gwenna had kept them from bolting and dragging the wagon towards almost certain disaster. The wagon had been brought to a halt and Rill had chased the metal band down the road until it had rolled to a halt about a hundred yards away.

Once the horses had been calmed and Rill had returned with the band, Be'Var had given the wheel an appraising look and concluded that it was fine apart than the missing banding. "We could continue on it," he'd said, pursing his lips, "but it won't last. We'd do a lot of damage to it before we get to Otvia and there's no way it's going all the way to Kepren before it splinters to pieces."

They'd decided to stop and have some lunch while Be'Var attempted to repair the broken band of metal. They'd emptied the cart, removed the wheel from the axle, and had left Be'Var to look over his new project while Caymus and his friends rolled the ungainly wagon over to nearby, waist-high boulder with the intent of balancing it there until the repair was complete.

"Okay, stop!" said Milo, once they'd reached the boulder in question. "Let it go!" They did, and the wagon tipped slightly so that the affected corner was resting on the hard stone while the opposite while rose a couple of inches in the air.

Caymus looked back and forth a couple of times between the boulder and the raised wheel. He then looked at Milo, who shrugged. Rill walked back to the raised corner and pushed down on it, rocking the wagon over the two wheels that still touched the ground. "I *think* it'll stay where it is," he said, as if he wasn't sure whether it would be sufficient. He rocked it another couple of times. "Is it moving off the boulder over there?" he said to Milo.

"Only when you touch it," said Milo.

Rill smiled. "Good enough," he said.

Caymus tilted his head toward the spot in the road where Be'Var had knelt down. "Come on," he said, "let's see what else we can do."

When they walked up, Be'Var was holding the band of metal close to his face, perhaps three inches from his eyes. He was staring intently at the broken edges, occasionally flexing them back together as though trying to figure out how they fit. "It's called the 'tyre,'' he said, absently, as they approached. "Ties the wheel together, thus: tyre." He flexed the band again. "Caymus," he said quietly, "would you get—" Then he stopped, frowned, and got to his feet. "Never mind," he said, putting the band down, "I'd better get it." He walked off to the place where they had left their various barrels, trunks, and sacks, rubbing his chin as though deep in thought. Caymus remembered the 'surprise' Be'Var had mentioned having put in his trunk, and he briefly considered following him to get a better look at what the master had meant.

Milo, meanwhile, sat down cross-legged on the ground and produced a leather waterskin. He tipped his head back, took a long drink, then offered the water to Caymus. Caymus decided Milo had the right idea. He accepted the skin as he, too, sat down. Rill, however, was hunched over the tyre, looking over the split in imitation of Be'Var, as though trying to figure out what mysteries the old man could divine in the cold iron. Caymus tried passing the skin to him, but Rill waved it away. "Something interesting in there?" he said, handing it back to Milo instead.

"It looks…torn," said Rill, looking even more closely. He was hunched down with his face barely off the ground in a fairly comical manner.

Caymus leaned over to see what he was talking about. To him, it just looked broken, like so many items in the Temple over the last week. "What do you mean?"

"See there," Rill pointed to one side of the break. Even Milo got a little closer. "There are a lot of little points and it's thinner toward the edges. No," he said, "not torn. More like, stretched, like someone pulled it apart."

Caymus didn't see what Rill was seeing, and the notion seemed just a little absurd. He leaned back and shook his head. "Rill," he said, "I think the sun might be getting to you. You can't stretch metal."

"Of course you can," said Be'Var, who was walking back, carrying two hammers, two pairs of tongs, and a surprisingly small anvil that was barely the size of his foot. "You can do anything to iron you can do to clay or wax or any other earth-heavy material." He knelt and set down his tools. "You just need to heat it first. This part of the band," he motioned toward the break, "was probably weak from the moment the iron was cast. It happens when they don't use enough flux and impurities get in. Here, take these."

He pushed a pair of tongs each at Rill and Caymus, then he motioned for them to kneel on either side of him. "I'm going to need the pair of you to hold the two sides together. You," he indicated Milo, who started getting up, "lift the end so this thing is standing straight up, with the break at the bottom." Milo did as he was told, grabbing the band at one end and holding it up over the ground. Be'Var took Caymus's tongs from him and closed them onto one side of the break. "Hold," he said once he seemed happy with the grip; Caymus grabbed them and held. Be'Var did the same with Rill, who seemed to be watching the procedure rather intently. Be'Var then stood and placed one of the hammers under the inside curve of the hoop, extending the handle away from him for Milo to grab. "It's going to get a bit warm in a minute, so you're not going to want to touch it." Milo nodded and held onto the hammer, letting the tyre hang from it. "It will rest on the anvil and these two will keep it steady, so you just need to keep it from tipping over. Think you can do that?"

Milo nodded.

"Good," said Be'Var, kneeling back down. "If it falls, I'm burning off your feathers."

There was a bit of negotiation as Be'Var repositioned the hoop, placing his six-inch high anvil under it, then moving it again until the two were in contact. "Everybody stay right where you are." He closed his eyes, then he opened them again and looked at Caymus. "Pay attention to this part," he said.

Caymus nodded, closed his eyes, and reached out, feeling for the iron. He was quite well-practiced at this, so finding what he wanted and latching on to it was relatively easy. As he firmed his grip, he thought about how different the metal felt when he held on to it this way, rather than with his hands. To his skin, the metal would have felt cold because his body contained more fire than the iron, but to his incorporeal mind, the sensation of solidity—of density—was most prevalent.

As he considered this, he sensed the presence of Be'Var's mind, and he retreated slightly to watch him work. He could feel the old man brushing over both of the broken edges of the metal; he was surprised to discover, however, that as the master moved, he seemed to leave things behind.

They felt like small tendrils, connections between the master's mind and the piece of metal, left to keep the connection open over several points, rather than just one. How was Be'Var doing that? He wasn't sure how many he was laying down, but after a minute or so had passed, he counted at least a dozen.

When the process was finished, he suddenly felt Be'Var pushing against something—not against him, and not against the metal, but against something else: something he couldn't see. The sensation was strange, as though Be'Var's mind was struggling against an invisible wall, though not a wall. It was more like a membrane of some sort, like the skin over day-old soup, only much, much thicker. As Be'Var continued to exert force, he felt the membrane begin to yield to his efforts. Then, there was a puncturing sensation, and Caymus understood what Be'Var had done. Instead of lighting a flame by hand and drawing energy through the conduit that manifested, he had formed his own conduit, small and completely independent of any existing fire. He'd created a direct connection to the Conflagration, and he was using his creation to feed the majesty of the realm of flame into the metal through the tendrils he'd left behind. The process was fascinating.

Be'Var then pulled energy through the conduit he'd made, just like he would have done with any other flame. Push, then pull…Caymus liked the symmetry of it, and he idly wondered how long Be'Var had spent learning how to do it.

The effect was immediate. Caymus felt the iron growing warm, then warmer, then hot. After a while, he could actually feel the metal reaching the point where it started to lose its solidity. The process took several minutes, and he was certain Be'Var could have heated the tyre faster. Was there a reason for slowing the process down so much?

"Good," whispered Be'Var.

Caymus opened his eyes. The first thing he saw was Rill squinting and looking away. The second thing he saw was that the bottom part of the metal band was now emitting a bright, yellow glow. Caymus had seen Be'Var working with iron before, but he'd never been able to observe this closely. The man's control of the heat was amazing. The hardest thing about pulling was maintaining a constant flow of energy through the conduit so that the affected material didn't burn or cool too quickly; the fluctuation in *this* conduit was so minute that it was barely noticeable.

"Yes, that will do nicely," said Be'Var. "Hold it very still, please." He then set to work with his hammer, lightly tapping on the glowing metal, his eyes still closed. As the master worked, Caymus felt the two pieces of iron beginning to meld into one another, joining together and shaping the broken tyre back into one continuous band.

After several minutes of hammering, the procedure was complete; the tyre was, once again, a complete loop. Be'Var slowly released the tendrils he'd placed upon the metal, as well as the conduit itself, and they all quickly vanished out of existence. Caymus would have to ask him how he'd done that. He'd always known it was possible to create a conduit from nothing, but this was the first time he'd ever had such an intimate view of the process, and he had no idea what it was that the master had been pushing against in order make it happen. The whole thing was fascinating.

Once the metal cooled to the point that it was no longer glowing, Be'Var opened his eyes. "Good," he said. "You can lay it on the ground now."

Caymus and Rill let go with their tongs and Milo lifted the hoop from the anvil, set it on the ground, and let it fall over, catching the top with a leather-booted foot and easing it down so that it didn't strike the hard road.

"Finished?" The voice was Bridget's, who was standing behind Rill and who appeared to have been watching the whole thing. She was carrying some bread and cheese which she then handed out to eager hands and smiling faces. "Come on," she said, and she led them back to the spot where their mix of cargo and personal belongings sat. Several of the larger trunks and boxes had been separated out to make some seats.

Caymus looked back, feeling a little odd about leaving their tyre in the middle of the road, and saying so.

Be'Var brushed off the notion, saying that the metal needed time to cool off before the next step. "Besides," he continued, "if we meet anybody on this road before we cross the Greatstones, I'll quite literally die of shock."

Caymus wasn't so sure about Be'Var's assessment. Earlier in the day, they'd passed the intersection where the path from the Temple itself, little more than a trail, met the main road between Krin's Point and Kepren. Though still rough, it showed signs of frequent use, and Caymus had been on the lookout for other travelers. Considering how widespread the reports of attacks by the insectoid creatures had been, however, he supposed Be'Var might have a point. People would be less likely to travel if the apparition of danger was about.

"What's the next step?" asked Rill, wolfing down a piece of bread. "Of the mending, I mean."

"Chew your food," said Be'Var, cutting a piece of cheese. "Right now," he continued, pointing at the band with his knife, "the inside edge of the tyre is a bit smaller than the outside edge of the wheel. We're going to have to heat it up again to make it fit properly." He turned to Caymus, raising an eyebrow at him. "Did you see what I did back there, boy?"

Caymus nodded. "You were leaving something behind as you went along, like—"

"No, not that," Be'Var said. "The other thing. The conduit."

"Oh," said Caymus. "Yes."

"Did you see how I managed it?"

Caymus frowned, momentarily forgetting about the piece of cheese he'd been chewing on. "It felt like you were putting pressure against… something? I honestly couldn't say what, though."

"Pressure, yes, that's close enough," Be'Var said, and then paused to consider something. "When we heat it up again, I'm going to have you do that part. Need to learn how, sooner or later." Be'Var said it matter-of-factly, leaving no room for argument, then he started on his lunch, obviously content to drop the subject entirely. Caymus looked around at the group. Everyone seemed very interested in the conversation.

"So, how—" he started, but Be'Var cut him off.

"Eat," the master said. "I'll tell you when the time comes."

"I'm sorry," interjected Rill, "but you said that heating the tyre up again will make it fit on the wheel. How does that happen?" Caymus's friend was paying no attention at all to his food, so rapt was his attention. It was an unusual thing to see. Rill was a generally curious person, but he hardly ever showed interest in anything said about the Conflagration itself.

Be'Var must have had the same thought. He gave Rill a long, appraising look before answering, as though deciding whether the boy was worth the effort of an explanation. "I'm going to pretend," he said, "that you've not been a Second Circle disciple for the past three years, Rill, and answer that."

Rill's face began turning decidedly red, which seemed to satisfy the old man.

"Fire makes earth grow," he said. "Right?"

Rill nodded. "Right, okay."

"Alright, so heating the iron up," continued Be'Var, "will expand the hoop, making it just large enough to fit over the wheel." He turned back to his meal. "When it cools down again, it will shrink and make a tight fit over the wood so that it doesn't come off."

Rill looked confused. He looked around and the group, and then down at the ground as though to give up on the subject, but then he changed his mind. "Sorry, I'm confused. I'm sure in one of Eavuk's lessons, he said that fire makes earth shrink?"

Caymus was stunned. He couldn't quite believe the questions that were coming out of his friend's mouth. Even the missionaries, who received far less training than the disciples of the Temple, were looking at Rill with more than a hint of shock. These were fairly basic concepts that most Second Circles picked up in their first year—in their first month, even. Still, there was something about Rill's expression in that moment that Caymus couldn't deny: something completely genuine and sincere. Rill's face was flushed, and he was obviously embarrassed about the entire exchange, but his eyes were intent, focused, interested.

Gwenna spoke up. "Water," she said. "Only water shrinks with heat."

Rill shifted his gaze to her, obviously relieved.

"It's easier to see in reverse," she continued. "If you take heat away from water, it turns into ice and gets bigger, right?"

"Riiight…" said Rill, closing his eyes with concentration, "that's what breaks a lot of the large rocks into smaller ones in the winter, isn't it? It rains, the rain gets into a crevice in the rock, freezes, the water turns to ice, expands, and the rock splits."

He opened his eyes again and addressed his next question to Gwenna directly. "But it doesn't do the same thing to iron?"

"Feawseg, Rill," said Caymus.

Be'Var turned and looked at Caymus with a raised eyebrow. "Didn't know we were still teaching feawseg," he said, taking a bite of bread.

"Some of us even listen," said Caymus, looking pointedly at Rill with a grin.

Rill had closed his eyes and was quietly moving his lips, trying to remember the mnemonic.

"Fire…" he muttered. "Eats air," he continued, then opened his eyes and smiled. "Water shrinks. Earth grows." He looked genuinely proud of himself.

"That's the one," said Caymus. "So, let me get this straight: you memorized it, but never gave a second thought to what it actually meant?"

"For that," said Be'Var, "he'd have had to give it a first thought."

"No offense, Rill," said Bridget, "but for a Second Circle, you don't seem to know a whole lot." She wasn't berating him; it was more of a question than a statement.

Rill had the good sense to look a bit sheepish, then he shrugged his shoulders. "It…just never seemed all that interesting until a few minutes ago."

"Could've saved us a lot of time," said Be'Var, not looking at him, "by mentioning that a few years ago."

Rill let his shoulders drop and leaned forward on his knees. His face took on a thoughtful, pensive look. "You'll get no argument from me," he said with a sigh. Then, he smiled to himself. "You know, I used to sit in the classroom, hearing all these things, all this stuff that you're telling me about right now, and only really thinking about when I was going to get out of the room and be able to do something else. Anything else. Now, here we are, and something's actually broken that requires you know a few things in order to fix it. Suddenly, there's a reason to know the stuff." He shrugged again and looked plaintively at the faces around him. "Suddenly, it's interesting."

"So, what you're saying," said Milo, "is that there aren't enough broken wagons at the Temple for your liking?"

Rill chuckled. "Something like that. I don't know, it's…"

"Context," said Y'selle. They all turned to look at her. She was folding the remains of her lunch into a cloth.

"Ma'am?" asked Rill.

"Sometimes, all we need to understand the lessons taught us," she continued—and she was looking at Be'Var, rather than Rill—"is to wrap it in the right context."

Be'Var grunted.

Y'selle looked at Rill. "You seem like a bright enough boy, Rill. I don't know anything about your studies at the Temple, but I'm guessing you know more than you think you do. A clever mnemonic is all well and good, and the lessons that the masters have to teach are important. But," she continued, "for a lot of people, all the theory in the world doesn't mean a thing…until it's needed to fix a broken wheel."

Rill nodded slowly, suddenly seeming a great deal more content.

Be'Var was looking hard at him. The old man looked as though he wanted to say something, then he appeared to change his mind and instead went back to his cheese. Caymus was wondering what the old master was thinking when he suddenly noticed a streak of white out of the corner of his eye. The hawk, the one he'd first met on the night of the attack and which had been constantly nearby since they'd left the Temple, had landed on the edge of the wagon, several yards away from them. "Milo," he said quietly, keeping his eyes on their small companion.

"I see her," said Milo, who was reaching into a pouch on his belt. He produced a small piece of dried meat and held it up in front of his eyes, looking past it at the hawk and twirling it around to give the bird a good look. The hawk tilted its head slightly to the left, then to the right, then it spread its wings and took flight, heading toward Milo, who threw the morsel into the air as it passed. The hawk swooped downward and caught it with sharp talons, then beat its wings hard to regain altitude as it flew by. Eventually, it dipped down again and disappeared behind a nearby ridge.

"Perra," said Milo, turning away from the retreating figure.

"What?" said Caymus.

"I've decided to call her Perra," he replied.

"Her?" said Gwenna. "The hawk is a she?"

"Yep," said Milo. "I asked a friend of mine, who knows a lot about birds, and described the markings. I caught his answer just before we left. He said she's a Perranus Mouse-Catcher." He looked back to where the hawk had disappeared.

"Perra," said Gwenna, trying it out. She nodded. "I like it."

"Apparently," said Milo, "it's a bit unusual to find them this far south."

A slight breeze picked up. It was cool, and it felt good against Caymus's sweaty skin and clothing. He closed his eyes and raised his head to feel the sensation on his neck.

"That's odd," said Milo. Caymus opened his eyes and saw Milo looking in the direction of the Greatstones, confusion on his face.

"What is?" said Be'Var.

"Sorry?" said Milo, as though seeing him for the first time.

Be'Var sighed. "What's odd, Milo?"

Milo shook his head. "That bit of wind. It was stronger than it should have been, considering where we are."

Matron Y'selle, strands of her gray hair blowing about in the breeze, turned to look in the same direction. "A storm coming?"

Milo shrugged. "Could be." He visibly relaxed and ate some cheese. "Probably not. Just odd, that's all."

Everyone seemed to accept Milo's word. Those who hadn't yet finished their lunch ate in silence for a few minutes while the others began packing things up. Caymus chanced a few looks at Gwenna and kept finding himself smiling when he caught her looking at him, too. After the first couple of times, it became a game, seeing who could turn unexpectedly and catch the other staring. When she shook her head at him and started talking quietly to Bridget, effectively ending the game, he let himself relax for a moment. He thought about what Be'Var had said when he had first announced his intention to leave the Temple, that this was nothing more than an excuse to be near her, and he was forced to wonder if it was true. He liked Gwenna. She was confident, smart, and pretty, and he enjoyed her company. He just wondered how much of his leaving had to do with this new mark on the back of his hand and how much had to do with her. He hoped it was more the former than the latter.

"Where did you learn to be a wheelwright?" said Bridget, breaking the silence.

Be'Var thought for a few moments before answering. "I'm not a wheelwright," he said. "In my younger days, I served in the physicians' corps of the Kepren army." He smiled at the surprised faces looking at him, obviously pleased with himself. "Don't look so shocked," he said. "Not all of the old fossils at the Temple spent the entirety of their lives there. All young men want adventure, and I was no exception." He ate his last mouthful of cheese and began talking around it. "I was a physician, mending the wounds of soldiers so that they could go out and get cut to ribbons again, for five years. You learn a few odds and ends when you're traveling with a large fighting force. Learned how to ride a horse, how to march in formation, how to fight with a sword and shield—"

"How to take orders…" mumbled Milo.

"You can use a sword?" asked Caymus, with greater fervor than he'd intended. "How come I never see you with one?"

Be'Var smirked at him. "Haven't needed it for a very long time." Then he tilted his head, indicating something on the ground. When Caymus followed his gaze, he noticed a cloth bundle lying next to his trunk. The piece of green fabric had been wrapped around something long and thin, then tied off with a cord of leather. He could just make out the gleam of metal. He wondered why he hadn't noticed it before.

"Is that…" said Caymus.

"Yes," said Be'Var.

"Can I—"

"No."

"Anyway," Be'Var continued, "it turned out that with my skill at pulling, I was a bit useful when it came to blacksmithing, so I got to help with some of the repairs: shoeing horses, fixing weapons, and even helping the wheelwrights with the wagons. Speaking of which," he said, looking around at mostly finished lunches, "we'd better get back to it. Rill, go fetch the wheel and roll it over to the tyre, will you?"

Caymus stood up, dusted off his hands, brushed the crumbs off himself, and moved back to the spot where the tyre still lay while Rill went to retrieve the wheel, lying a few yards off. As they all got back to work, Caymus considered what he'd just learned about Be'Var. The master had never before spoken of any military service in his past, and he was fairly certain that none of the other students at the Temple knew anything about it. Perhaps it was only because he and Rill were no longer counted among those the Temple's disciples that Be'Var was telling them of it now? He supposed he was just glad that the old man seemed to be softening on this trip, if just a little.

"Alright, boy," Be'Var said, interrupting Caymus's thoughts, "here's how this is going to work: I'm going to do what I did before, moving around the metal and leaving those little bits of myself all over the place. You are going to follow behind me and open a conduit on each one."

"How do I do that?" Caymus asked. He wasn't any good at pulling, and he wasn't sure if he'd be able to make a conduit by himself. As exciting as the prospect was, he didn't like failing and he felt a little nervous about the possibility of doing so, especially with the others looking on. He knew the feeling was silly, but he felt it all the same.

"First," Be'Var said, "focus on that spot, the point where I place the tendril. Don't focus on the metal, mind you, but the spot, the place. You understand?"

Caymus wasn't sure that he did. He shook his head.

Be'Var sighed. "This tends to be easier after some other exercises that we're skipping. Alright," he said, motioning around them, "we've got this wind blowing around us, right? What's left if the wind goes away?"

"Just air," said Caymus.

"Just?" said Milo, feigning injury.

"Quiet," said Be'Var. "Yes, air, but what if you took that away?"

"If you took the air out of the air?" Caymus had never even considered such a thing. Could it even be done? "I don't know," he said.

"Empty space," said Milo.

"I said quiet," said Be'Var, darting a look at Milo. He turned back to Caymus. "Well boy, is he right?"

Caymus thought about it. He supposed there was a significant difference between empty space and air. "Okay," he said. "I get it. You take air away, you get nothing."

"Not nothing," said Be'Var. He looked to Rill, who was coming up behind him, rolling the wheel. "Put it next to the tyre," he said, then turned back to Caymus. "'Nothing' wouldn't exist. We're talking about empty space here. You can wave your hand through empty space; you can't do anything with nothing."

"Void," said Milo, adding his own perspective. "Some air priests can do exactly what he's saying, take the air out of an area and just leave void."

"I'd quite like to see that," said Rill, laying the wheel down.

"So would I," said Gwenna. "Can you see it happen?"

Be'Var let out a very loud, very deliberate sigh. "Could everyone not learning how to open a conduit to another realm please keep quiet?" He looked around at a few muttered apologies, and then turned his exasperated eyes back to Caymus. "Void, empty space, whatever you want to call it, the point is that even if you take all the elements out of a place, that place still exists. Understand?"

Caymus did, though he was coming to it in stages, as the idea was forcing him to change a couple of basic assumptions. "So, the world isn't exactly made up of elements, but rather it's made of empty space, with the elements filling it up."

Be'Var nodded. "Technically 'the world' is made of elements, and the world fills the empty space, but that's close enough. The idea is to be able to make the distinction, because when you're opening a conduit, you're opening it in the space, not the material."

"Ah," said Caymus, as a big piece of a puzzle fell into place, "so that's what you were pushing against?"

"Exactly," said Be'Var, "but you'll do better to think of it as opening a hole, rather than pushing. You'll have more success that way." He picked up the tyre and held it on top of the wheel. It was obviously too small to fit over the six-spoked piece of wood, and he looked up to make sure everyone noticed that fact. He then put the band down and picked up the two pairs of tongs from the ground, handing one each to Rill and Milo. "You and you," he said, "pick it up by either side and hold it up just above the wheel. When I tell you, drop it and it will slip nicely over the wood." He looked at Caymus again. "Ready?"

"I think so," Caymus said. He still wasn't sure he could do it, but he was very curious to explore this new concept and see what he could accomplish. Be'Var closed his eyes, and he followed suit.

He reached out and felt the iron band, quickly finding Be'Var on one side of it. Within moments, the master had put down one of the strange tendrils. "Go ahead, Caymus," he said.

Caymus felt down the length of the tendril to the very spot where it touched the iron, then started searching for the 'space' that Be'Var had been talking about. He felt around the metal surface of the tyre, seeking it out, but he didn't find anything.

"Not the tyre," said Be'Var. He had to raise his voice slightly, as the wind was starting to pick up. "If you just feel for the tyre, you won't get there. You have to reach beyond it, into the space it's taking up."

Caymus frowned and tried again. He wasn't sure about this. He felt like he was a blind man feeling along a stone wall searching for a tiny crack or drawing that he only knew existed because someone had told him it was there. He didn't even know exactly what he was looking for. Then, for an instant, he felt it, and it was gone. His mind recoiled, but he felt his heart race. For just that fraction of a second, his consciousness had passed beyond the physical existence of the tyre and had felt something else, something much grander but far less tangible. With effort, he calmed his mind and tried feeling for it again; the sensation was elusive, however, almost as though it was taunting him.

Caymus was reminded of a time or two in his life when he'd found himself standing in front of a patterned surface: the bricks in the wall of a building, the boards that made up the hull of a ship, the clay tiles on the floor of somebody's home. Sometimes, when he'd encountered these kinds of surfaces, he'd found that there was some distance at which the regular patterns seemed to merge in on themselves, leaving him unable to tell exactly how far away they were. He would know that he stood several feet from the pattern, for instance, but all the while his vision would tell him he was mere inches away, or vice-versa. He would feel like his eyes were somehow crossed, and that if he could just uncross them, the illusion would be broken, and normalcy restored.

This was very like that sensation. He knew that what he was looking for was there, but he just couldn't quite get himself to—

He found it. Instantly, he felt strange, as though he was now part of the iron, feeling through it to get to this empty space. With some trepidation, he held on.

"Good work," he heard Be'Var say. "Now, open it up."

Caymus did his best to do as he was told, and he discovered that, now that he had a firm hold on the space he was trying to manipulate, this part was actually quite easy. He simply selected a point in space, focused his attention on it, and exerted pressure in two opposite directions simultaneously. Instantly, a conduit—small, fragile, and wholly dependent on his attention for its very existence—appeared.

"Well done, boy," said Be'Var. "Very well done. Now, just follow me around the tyre, and do it a few more times."

As Caymus felt Be'Var moving around the band of metal, he repeated his newly learned skill, opening a conduit wherever the master left behind one of his tendrils. Each time, the process became easier, and it eventually began to feel intuitive. He even had time to wonder how each conduit stayed open after he had moved away from it, or how, as each connection was established, it opened to the realm of fire and not to that of some other, completely unfamiliar place. He wondered these things only casually, though. To think any harder would be to risk ruining the attention he had worked so hard to forge.

He realized he must have been having an effect when he felt heat radiating from the tyre. Be'Var must have been pulling heat through the conduits already!

Once the two of them had finished with the seventh conduit, he opened his eyes. He smiled when he saw the result of his work: the tyre was glowing an intense orange. The tendrils—little bits of the master's concentration—were allowing Be'Var to spread his attention and pull heat into several places in the metal at once. How these tendrils worked and how Be'Var had lain them down in the first place was something Caymus couldn't quite figure out, but he held his curiosity in check, assuming it was something the teacher would explain to the student in due time. He relaxed, knowing that his part of this process was complete, and allowed himself to simply watch the old man work, feeling his clothing getting blown about as he did so. The wind really had started to pick up in the last few. When he spared a moment to look to the sky, he saw that dark, gray clouds had moved in from over the mountains.

"Drop it!" barked Be'Var, and the tongs released the tyre, which slid partially down around the wheel. Be'Var opened his eyes to examine the fit, and Caymus felt all seven conduits instantly evaporate. Then, with great care and fine movement, Be'Var used a small hammer and rod to tap the rapidly cooling piece of metal down onto the smoking wood of the wheel. After a few moments, the band of iron was flush with the edge of the wheel, and Be'Var seemed to have things the way he wanted them. "That will do," he said, sitting back, satisfied. At point, he raised his head and finally appeared to notice the weather. He looked around slowly, his expression of triumph changing rapidly to one of concern.

The weather had worsened dramatically in the time they'd been fixing the wheel. No longer cool and refreshing, the wind was now decidedly cold, and Caymus even considered fetching some of his extra clothing. Above them, darkening clouds gathered strength, looming over the group in a decidedly threatening manner.

Milo was walking slowly into the wind. "This isn't good!" he yelled back. "We should get moving!"

Be'Var gave the clouds a stern look, as though his irritation alone might drive them back. "Give the metal a few more minutes to cool off," he said, "then we can put the wheel back on the wagon and get loaded." He suddenly moved his hand up to his face, then pulled it away and looked at it in disbelief. "Impossible!" he exclaimed.

Caymus was about to ask what Be'Var had meant, but then he felt it too: a cold prick of water on his hand. He brought his other hand up, intending to wipe the raindrop away, when he realized why both Milo and Be'Var had seemed so concerned. Where he had expected to find a drop of water, there was instead a small, delicate flake of white clinging to his skin as though afraid of being blown away by the increasingly icy wind.

"Snow!" breathed Gwenna, her eyes wide.

It wasn't even autumn yet.

~~~

A few hours later, Caymus found himself behind the wagon, pushing hard against it and taking in great lungfuls of icy air as they fought through the worst snowstorm he had ever seen.

The storm had developed so quickly that by the time they had finally secured the wheel to the axle, a few inches of fine, white powder had already gathered upon the ground. Be'Var and Y'selle had argued about whether or not they should turn back and head for the relative safety afforded by the trees, miles behind them. Y'selle had wanted to press on; Be'Var had counseled going back. The matron had been about to give in when Bridget had remembered a cave, near the bottom of the mountain trail, which the missionaries had passed on their way to the Temple.

After some pressing, the other women had remembered it too. The problem was that, other than to agree that it couldn't be any greater distance away than was than the tree-line behind them, none of them were quite sure how far away it was. Reluctantly, Be'Var had agreed that a cave would offer much better shelter than mere branches and leaves, and so they had pushed forward.

Nearly an hour later, after a great deal of effort negotiating the increasingly slippery path, they had finally reached the incline that marked the start of their ascent up the Greatstones. The location of the cave, however, remained a mystery, and the rust-colored rocks, dotted here and there with evergreen trees and covered with powder, didn't seem to be giving away any secrets.

Bridget and Gwenna were walking out front, making sure the horses didn't get spooked and doing their best to keep them on the increasingly snow-covered road. The girls had been forced to put blinders on Feston to keep him calm. He didn't like the whine of the wind or the cold snow in his eyes, but he was allowing himself to be led. Staven, too, was doing better now that he had a lead-line.

Be'Var and Matron Y'selle both sat on the driver's bench, peering ahead through the flurries, trying to locate any dark shadows that might be the entrance to the shelter they sought. Caymus, despite wearing two layers of his thickest wools, could feel the cold clear to his bones, and so had been amazed when he'd noticed that both adults were sitting quietly
~~~

upright, neither hunched over nor shivering. He'd chanced a quick investigation and discovered that they were keeping themselves warm through elemental means, pulling heat into their own bodies. He was surprised to learn that the matron was trained in the pulling Aspect. Did all matrons have such training?

He considered the idea as he gave the wagon another shove, pushing the wheels over another unseen obstacle under the snow. He and Rill had been walking behind the wagon, helping the horses move it through the deepening snow, for what felt like hours. His shoulders were tired and his back was killing him, but at least his legs had stopped hurting, having succumbed to a kind of dead numbness some time ago. Thankfully, he could still feel his toes, and so could be certain he hadn't lost them to frostbite yet. As he trudged through the cold, wet powder, he allowed himself to smile at the thought that that stretching and straining of his muscles was probably the only thing keeping him warm.

Rill, it seemed, wasn't doing as well. Caymus felt as though he was having to shoulder more of the wagon's weight than he had just ten minutes ago, and though he could attribute a lot of that to his own tiring state, he was fairly certain that his friend was fading, now leaning on the wagon's gate more than he was forcing it forward. Rill was hunched over, his head hanging down between his arms, and was convulsing with the occasional spasmodic cough. Caymus was worried about him, becoming more and more certain that they should have turned back hours ago. He panned his gaze around again, looking for any sign of either a cave or of Milo's silhouette amidst the bleak, white backdrop.

Just how long Milo had been gone, Caymus couldn't say. He, too, had an unusual way of dealing with the weather: while he had still appeared to shiver under the cold snow on his skin, he'd seemed completely unaffected by the biting wind that accompanied it. Indeed, Caymus had found it somewhat eerie watching him walking alongside the wagon, his garments—and, in particular, the feathers on his arms—not stirring in the slightest, despite the rabid gusts that occasionally struck out of nowhere and tried to knock the rest of them off their feet. Being so unhindered, the priest had decided he should go on ahead and search for their presumed destination while the rest of them concentrated on keeping the wagon moving.

Caymus hoped nothing had happened to him.

"It…close?" Rill's voice, a scant few inches away, was barely audible. Caymus cringed to hear how weak his friend was becoming; his death-grip on the wagon seeming to be the only strength left in his body. Rill's legs kept wobbling beneath him, causing his head to jolt up and down. On the one occasion that Caymus could make out his face, his eyes had been closed.

"Get in the wagon, Rill," Caymus said.

"No. Have to help. Have to pull my weight," said Rill, his eyes still closed.

"You won't be any help if you freeze to death, Rill. Get in the wagon!"

Rill stubbornly refused, weakly shaking his head back and forth. "Not quitting!" he shouted, and the shouting seemed to open another source of strength to him. His back straightened and he lifted his head, opening his eyes to give Caymus a challenging look. Through chattering teeth, he said, "I'm not done yet, Caymus."

Caymus couldn't help but smile. He nodded, clenched his jaw, and gave the wagon another heave up the slope of the mountain road, glad to see his friend hadn't lost his resolve. Rill always had always been obstinate, though he made up for it with a stubborn kind of courage. 'Foolhardiness' was the word Master Be'Var would probably have used. No matter. They continued on, and whatever well of fortitude it was that Rill was drawing on, it continued to flow for him. He didn't drop his gaze.

Then, Caymus felt something strange, a sensation at the base of his neck that was both numbing and prickly at the same time. He had the sudden urge to look over his shoulder, but when he did so, nothing was there but the same blowing powder that was everywhere else. Shaking his head a moment, he faced forward. Then felt it again, more severe this time, as though somebody had poured ice water down his back. He turned again, and still nothing was there. The sensation then backed off a little, settling into a low prickle at the back of his neck, but it stayed with him. Perhaps there was something out there, in the snow. Perhaps fatigue was catching up with him.

A sudden jerking sensation brought his attention back to the task at hand as the wagon caught on something. He could hear the horses struggling to pull free from the hindrance, and so he put his shoulder against the back end and pushed. As he did so, he heard an alarming cracking sound.

"Wait!" came Rill's voice. "Stop!" Before Caymus had even disengaged himself from the wagon, Rill had shifted around to the side. Rubbing his hands in the hopes of massaging out some of the cramps he was feeling, Caymus followed to see what he was doing. When he rounded the corner, Caymus winced. A large branch was caught in the spokes of the front-left wheel. It had obviously already broken something and would have done more damage if they hadn't stopped trying to force themselves free. Rill was pulling with two hands on the branch, which was easily as long as he was tall and a half-a-foot in diameter at its thickest point. "Help me," he said, and together they dislodged the offender.

After they had disposed of the troublesome branch, Rill knelt by the wheel and inspected the spokes, running his hand along them. "Cracked one along the length," he said, turning his head up to report to Be'Var. "About seven inches long, going halfway through, at least."

Be'Var nodded. "All right," he said. "Good eye, Rill. We'll keep moving. It should last long enough to get us to this cave," he continued, and then looked around. "Wherever it is."

"Hang on," said Rill, then pulled a small length of linen cloth out of a pouch on his belt. Caymus recognized it as a bandage and wondered where he'd gotten it from. He unrolled it to its full length of about two feet and began twirling the ends in opposite directions until the strip of cloth had rolled and tightened to the point that it resembled a length of thin rope, which he tied around the damaged spoke. "To keep it from splitting any more," he said.

Be'Var gave Rill another look, the same one he had given him when they were repairing the tyre, as though sizing the young man up. Finally, he nodded his head. "Good," he said, then he turned quickly, as they all did, to look ahead at a sharp whistle that emerged from the enveloping white.

Milo was running toward them at a lope, a broad smile on his face. "Found it!" he shouted when he got close enough for them to hear him. He reached the point where Caymus and Rill stood, speaking loudly enough for all to hear him. "It's about a hundred yards further up, then another two hundred off the road to the left."

Caymus noticed Rill's expression turn to shock and disbelief. "Flames, but I'm glad he's here," he said. "Two hundred yards off the road? We'd have passed right by it in this weather." He looked about to say something to Milo, but Milo was busy investigating the piece of fabric Rill had just tied to the spoke of their wheel, its loose ends fluttering in the wind like tiny flags.

He looked up from the makeshift bit of rope at Be'Var, mock accusation on his face. "You broke your wagon!" he said. "Again!"

Caymus knew that Be'Var sometimes found Milo amusing, but the old master was just as often exasperated by his friend's antics. It was hard for Caymus to gauge which was the case this time, though Be'Var's blank expression suggested the latter. The old man shook his head and indicated to the girls that they should get the horses moving again.

Milo gave Caymus a wink, then jogged up to Gwenna and Bridget to help guide the horses to their goal. Caymus didn't quite have the strength to laugh out loud as he and Rill took their positions and began pushing again.

~~~
~~~

Ten minutes later, Caymus was ruminating on his tired feet—he couldn't feel most of his toes now—and how much he'd like to prop them up in front of a warm campfire for a while, when the dark shadow of the cave appeared through the driving snow. The entrance was about ten feet high and twice that in width. Caymus hoped as much has he had ever hoped for anything that the shelter was deep and wide enough to keep far from the weather, but either way he counted his blessings. Rill had been right: there was no way they'd have seen this place from the road with the blizzard raging around them. Milo had probably just saved all their lives.

The air priest was the first to pass through the entrance. Moments later, Gwenna and Bridget entered behind him, guiding the horses in. Even with the promise of shelter so close, the animals seemed wary about the dark place. Ears twitched. Feet stamped. Caymus didn't blame them. There was something about this place that bothered him, too. He felt the pinpricks on the back of his neck increase in intensity again, and he was sure the little hairs there must have been standing on end.

He couldn't put a name to the sensation. It was bothersome and uncomfortable, but he couldn't help thinking that it was also familiar. Had he felt this way before? Was it something he'd experience back home in Woodsea?

As the wagon wheels rolled from wet snow to dry dirt, he suddenly realized that it was because he'd felt it before. No, it wasn't at home; it was in Krin's Point, all those years ago on the *Pride of the Expanse*! Yes, he was nearly certain of it! He'd felt the very same thing just a few minutes before the fire had started! He'd been in that fight with those two boys back then, and so at the time he'd attributed it to having just been punched a few times, but the feeling was the same: a kind of deep-seated sense of urgency…not so much that something was wrong, but that something *wasn't right.*

He wanted to look around, to try to find out if there was a reason for what he was feeling, but then the sensation was suddenly replaced by the feeling of immense relief at having finally pushed the wagon past the mouth of the cave and out of the biting snow. They came to a stop a few moments later, and in the sudden silence Caymus realized his teeth were chattering. Flames, he was tired. He was tired, and he was so very cold.

He and Rill took a moment to rest, just leaning against the back of the wagon, their heads drooping, their breaths coming in heavy pants. He could hear the crunch of gravel and dirt as the others moved about the cave floor. Then, he felt the wagon shifting slightly, heard the springs creak.

"Master Be'Var," came Y'selle's voice, "would you kindly start a fire and get some light in here?"

There was some rustling along the side of the wagon and then a torch sputtered to life, illuminating the cave's interior. Caymus lifted his head to see Be'Var standing a few feet from the wagon, holding the torch high and surveying their new surroundings.

The cave was deep. The portion of it that the torchlight made visible opened further to about thirty feet in width, which would leave plenty of room for the group to spread out and stay the night. The floor had a noticeable downward slope, and it seemed to take a slight turn to the right at the edge of the torch's light. Caymus wondered just how far back the cave went, but he didn't think too hard about it. He still felt uneasy and—more to the point—exhausted.

Y'selle was sorting through the group's belongings and producing more torches, which Be'Var was helping her light. "Bridget, Gwenna," she said with a warm smile, "would you dears unhitch the horses and make them comfortable?" Then she turned to Caymus and Rill. "And if you boys could check the supplies and separate out anything that's gotten wet and needs to be dried out, please?"

"Yes, Matron," said Caymus. Rill just nodded, still shivering. Y'selle smiled at them. It didn't appear lost on her that the travelers themselves were among the things that needed to be dried out. "Thank you, boys," she said. "Be'Var and I will start setting up some semblance of a campfire to get everyone warm again." She turned around. "Milo, if—" She peered into the darkness. "Where's Milo?" she said.

"Saw him heading to the back of the cave," said Be'Var, his tone gruff and annoyed, even for him. "I imagine he'll be back soon enough."

They each set to their tasks. As he worked, Caymus felt his breathing slow and becoming less ragged as warmth slowly returned to his core. After a few minutes, he could even feel his fingers and toes again. Though he was working perhaps a half-dozen or so feet inside the opening, he felt no chill; the cave was remarkably well-protected from the wind. He wondered why that was. Was it a freak of circumstance that kept the gale outside from entering this place, or was there some design to it?

Y'selle had given a torch to Rill, who held the light aloft so that Caymus could pick clothing and bedding from the back of the wagon and either set them on the bench or drape them over the sides so they could dry out. As he worked, he gazed about himself, absently examining the walls of their temporary home. He was taken aback when he realized that stone was smooth; at least, the circular walls were smoother than he'd have expected for some random cave in the middle of nowhere. A cave should have been riddled with cracks, crags and protruding rock; instead, the walls were no more coarse or uneven than the bark of a tree. Indeed, the texture of it reminded him of the skin of a mountain pine.

"Think someone used to live here?" said Rill, following his friend's gaze.

"Maybe," said Caymus. "Someone definitely smoothed all of this out at some point."

"And added fixtures," said Rill. "Look," he said, pointing to a spot on the wall behind Caymus.

Caymus turned. Attached to the wall were two small bands of metal, one above the other, forming a torch sconce. "Yes," he said, giving it a hard look. "Yes, I *do* think somebody used to live here."

Rill paused a moment before speaking again. "Think somebody might *still* live here?" he said.

Suddenly, Milo's voice burst out of the darkness. "Storms!" he cried, and then a scream echoed through the chamber, filling the space like a flood. Caymus put his hands to his ears to shield them from the noise but felt panic rising in his throat.

The scream hadn't been Milo's. No, the sound took him back to the night that he'd been chased, terrified, through Saleri Forest. One of those creatures was here.

After several agonizing moments, the scream subsided. Caymus jumped down off the wagon. "Milo!" he yelled into the darkness, not sure what to do other than walk forward. The others also seemed unsure about what to do, though Be'Var moved toward the scream too, just a few steps behind Caymus.

A moment later, Milo's voice came again, closer this time. "I'm okay," he said, and he came briskly jogging out the darkness, looking far less concerned than Caymus had expected him to be. "It's all right," he said to the anxious faces around him, "It's—"

He was cut off by another reverberating cry, though this one wasn't nearly as loud. It also seemed less shrill, less angry, more…scared. Milo squinted his eyes until the noise abated, then continued. "It's all right," he said again, "I don't think there's any danger."

By now, Milo's face was bathed in flickering torchlight as the travelers converged around him. Be'Var stepped up to on his left side and peered into the darkness. The master appeared to have found his sword, too. "What happened?" he said, stealing a look into the darkness. "I know that scream, and I don't exactly see how it could *not* be dangerous."

"Yes," Milo said. "It's one of the creatures," he quickly said, "but it's safe. I think."

"You think?" said Rill.

"Yeahhh…" said Milo, turning to follow Be'Var's gaze into the blackness. As he spoke, there was another cry, but this was no scream of rage. This sound was morose, quiet, the sound of something in pain.

"It's trapped," said Milo, turning back to the group, and Caymus was surprised to see a look of pity in his friend's eyes. "Come on," he said, "and see for yourselves."

If not for that last sound, Caymus didn't think anybody would have followed Milo, but they'd all heard just how pathetic and anguished that cry had been, and so follow they did. As he walked behind his friend, Caymus shook his head at the insanity of what they were doing: knowingly and willingly walking toward those claws, those teeth. But how could they not? How could any of them have heard such a pitiful sound and not felt the need to investigate, maybe even try to help?

But to try to help one of those things, when so many people had died to them. He couldn't quite wrap his mind around it.

Before he could develop the thought any further though, the group rounded the corner at the back of the cave and then stopped abruptly as their torchlight found the thing they sought.

Caymus recognized the claws, the head, the eyes of one of the horrific monsters that had nearly caught him the night of the attack. He immediately understood what Milo had meant, though: there was no danger here.

The creature was trapped in the floor of the cave.

He spent a moment looking for another way to understand what his eyes were telling him, but there really was no other way to see it: the entire back end of the creature appeared to have simply fallen *through* the ground, somehow. There were no furrows in the soil, no piles of dirt, no loose rocks, not even scratch marks on the ground. The creature's head and front claws seemed to have simply risen out of the dirt floor without having dug through it. Its mouth hung open and its front legs twitched and scrabbled as it attempted to free itself, but it could gain no purchase, make no progress. Other than its head and forelegs, it was simply and completely trapped in the earth. After a few moments, it stopped moving, and it made a noise that reminded Caymus of a frightened dog.

How could the creature possibly have arrived at such a state? A cave-in or other collapse was something Caymus could have understood, but this was clearly something else. He'd heard tales of earth priests who could pass through the ground unhindered, but the idea that one of these otherworldly monsters could possess abilities so similar to those of some of the wisest holy men in the world was almost as sickening as it was improbable.

Caymus felt a small hand grip his and he sensed Gwenna standing beside him. "The legs," she said, her words coming out in a whisper as she pointed at the creature's twitching appendages with her free hand. "Look at the legs."

Caymus didn't understand what she'd seen at first, but once he did, he gasped. The creature was slowly clawing at the ground around it, trying to gain enough leverage to pull itself out of its earthen prison. The sharp tips of its claws, however, didn't scratch or till the dirt. Instead, they seemed to pass right through, as though either the claws or the floor had no substance.

"How?" Rill breathed, taking an absent step forward.

Be'Var grabbed Rill's collar, yanking him backward. "Careful, fool," he said. "We don't know how long it's been stuck there, or even if it's really as trapped as it seems."

"You think it's pretending?" asked Y'selle, arching an eyebrow at him.

"How?" Rill said again, this time more loudly. He was pointing at the legs, which were still passing like apparitions through the floor.

Be'Var sighed. "I don't know," he said. "These things are made of an element that hasn't touched this world for longer than most histories remember. We already knew they're all but immune to fire." He then motioned around the creature. "It would appear that this substance, whatever it is, is capable of passing right through the earth element, too."

"Huh," said Milo, putting a crooked finger to his chin, "it would explain why I wasn't able to find any tracks around your Temple." He didn't hang around for a discussion, but rather moved away and began an inspection of the surrounding walls. By the torchlight, Caymus could see that the cave itself didn't extend much farther back. If he considered the area in which they currently stood—everything past the corner they had turned—to be a sort of room, then the creature had come up in the room's center.

"Why here?" said Rill, his eyes following Milo as the priest felt the walls.

"Why not here?" Be'Var said, not really listening. The old man was staring at the creature which, by now, was moving a great deal more slowly, as though losing the will to fight.

"No, really," Rill said, with greater conviction, "if these things are capable of literally moving through earth, why did this one decide to come up here? For that matter," he continued, motioning toward the wall Milo was examining, "aren't the walls of this place made of earth? Aren't the walls of the Temple? If the creatures can pass through the earth element, why didn't they just walk straight through the walls that night and kill us all?"

Caymus didn't much like the implications of what Rill was suggesting.

"Aha!" exclaimed Milo. When Caymus turned to him, he was looking down at something. "Come," he said, waving them over with a vigorous arm, "look at this!"

The group, excepting Bridgett and Y'selle, made their way over to see what the fuss was about. He was standing over what looked like a large stone, about half the size of a grown man, which was cut into rectangular shape and lying on its side on the ground. A large section of it—about a quarter of the total mass—was missing from one side.

"Help me lift it," said Milo, who grabbed hold of the surface with the missing chunk and motioned for someone to do the same. Caymus obliged, and together they stood the stone up on its end.

When they stood back, Caymus wasn't sure what he was looking at. The piece of rock had a bowl shape carved into it the area where the large piece had been cut out. The facet of stone that stood perpendicular to the bowl seemed to have once had some kind of writing etched into it, though he didn't know the language and the words were so worn away with the passage of time that he wasn't sure he would have been able to read them, even if he had.

"It's a light stone," said Be'Var. He pointed to the carved bowl. "They fill this with some kind of flammable oil and set it on fire so they have light to see by."

"Who does?" said Milo.

"Earth worshipers," replied Be'Var, now shifting his gaze to the upper edges of the walls and the ceiling. Without asking, he grabbed Milo's torch and waved it about, trying to get a better look. "Look there," he said, pointing at a black substance that coated the area above and around the stone, "that's from the flames, the burning oil. This used to be a place where dirt-lovers gathered to worship."

Caymus thought about it, thought about their own night of terror. "You think that's why it came here?" he said. "To kill earth worshipers?"

"If it did," Be'Var said, glancing over his shoulder at the now barely moving form, "it's a number of years too late. I don't suppose anyone's worshiped here for centuries, maybe longer."

"What if it's the place," said Gwenna, who was bending down to get a closer look at the faded writing on the stone, "and not the people?"

"The place?" said Caymus.

She nodded, then looked at Milo. "Didn't you tell me that your friends had said the creatures attacked a lot of temples and churches on the same night they came after us?"

Milo nodded. "Cities and places of worship seemed to be their targets."

"Have you heard of any cities that were attacked that didn't have places of worship in them?"

Milo's eyes looked away a moment, considering. "No," he said, looking back at her with a slight smile. "I don't believe I have."

"So," she said, standing up and dusting off her hands, "what if places —the actual *places*—where people worship other elements are the only places they wanted to attack?"

Caymus wasn't sure what to make of the thought. He glanced at

Be'Var, whose leathery face was tight with concentration as he, too, tried to tease apart the threads.

"It's not that they want to attack those places!" said Rill, whose eyes had suddenly gone very wide. "They're the only places they *can* attack!"

There was a moment's pause while everyone waited for Rill to explain. "Come again?" said Be'Var, giving voice to Caymus's own thoughts.

"How is that different to what I said?" said Gwenna, frowning and folding her arms.

"Sorry, Gwenna," said Rill, now speaking very quickly, his eyes still wide. "I mean, what if they can *only* attack places like churches and temples: places of worship? What if they're the only places they can actually *get* to?" He looked around at the confused or doubtful faces around him. "Look," he said, flitting his gaze back and forth between Caymus and Be'Var, "from what I overheard this afternoon, the way you two make fire is to open a kind of doorway into the Conflagration, right?"

Caymus nodded. He wondered if Rill knew how much he talked with his hands when he was excited. "Right," he said.

"Well," Rill continued, "these things have to come from somewhere, right? What if they come through the same way?"

Be'Var was wearing his exasperated look. "Of course they do. They're not from this world, so they'd have to come through a conduit."

Caymus could see his friend's enthusiasm starting to deflate. "Go on, Rill," he said, encouragingly.

"Doesn't it fit, that…" Rill stopped for a moment, gathering his thoughts. He put his hands together to form a square in front of him. "If someone builds a church somewhere," he said, "and people spend years and years there making these conduits and making little doorways into other places like the Conflagration, doesn't it follow that it would be easier for these things to come through in those places? It's like if you take the same path through a clearing, over and over again: eventually, you're going to wear a path where the plants don't grow."

Be'Var opened his mouth to say something, then closed it and seemed to really think about what Rill was saying. "So, what you're suggesting," he said after almost a minute, "is that what we do—the opening of conduits—opens the natural barriers between our world and the elemental realms, and that doing so in one particular place over a long time *wears a path* and makes that spot vulnerable to entry by these creatures. Is that what you mean?"

Rill was nodding slowly, but before he could speak, Bridget's voice broke through. "I think it's dead."

As one, they all turned to look at the creature, which had stopped moving. Caymus noted a new sensation, a sort of emptiness in the room that he couldn't quite put a name to.

It was quite obvious that the creature had died.

"I'll bet," said Rill, quietly "that the stronger a place of worship is, the more people there that practice the kinds of Aspects you practice, the easier it is for these things to get through, wherever it is they come from." He took a deep breath, then continued. "I think this cave used to be one of those places, but it hasn't been used for so long that the way in closed back up, and that's why this one got stuck halfway through."

Nobody said anything for a while. Nobody seemed able to take their eyes off the dead thing before them.

"I think you might be right," Be'Var finally said. "I think you just might be."

Some moments later—Caymus didn't know how many—Y'selle stepped toward the front of the cave. "Come on," she said, "the monster isn't going anywhere, and we have a lot left to do before we can bed down for the night."

The others moved to follow her, but Caymus remained behind, still staring at the creature. He felt torn. The last one of these things he'd seen had tried to rip his flesh from his bones, and only the combined power of a dozen masters, not to mention the use of the Conduit itself, had saved him from a grisly death. This one had been so sad, so pathetic. Chances were that it had been trapped here since the night of the attack, over a week ago. He couldn't even imagine the horror of being so completely trapped for so long.

"It's not the same, is it?" Be'Var had evidently turned back and was now standing next to him.

"I know that it would have killed me if it could," said Caymus.

"But you still feel sorry for it." The old man sighed, blowing out his cheeks. "It's like that when you're fighting for your life." Be'Var was standing with the blade of his sword planted in the ground, his hand resting on the pommel. "When we fought for king and country all those years ago, we followed our orders and we fought ruthlessly." He nodded slowly. "But in the end every single one of use eventually had to come to grips with what we'd done, with the fact that that every man who fell to our swords was loved by somebody, was precious to somebody. Most of us were able to get past the guilt, to find a way to live with it. A lot never did." He shook his head. "Never thought I'd feel sorry for one of these things, though."

Caymus looked at his old mentor, and his gaze shifted to the sword he carried. "I thought you were a physician?" he said.

Be'Var nodded. "That I was, but it doesn't mean I wasn't called on to fight, sometimes. The quartermasters, the engineers, and yes, even the physicians...we all had our jobs to do, but as far as the army was concerned, we were all soldiers first."

"Master Be'Var," Caymus said, "if that thing had gotten loose and tried to attack us, what would you have done? Even the two of us together couldn't have burned it. Not without the Conduit."

Be'Var brought the blade up to eye level as he answered. "I still know how to use this," he said. "I severely doubt that I'd have been able to kill it, but I might have been able to hold it back long enough for the rest of you to escape.

"And what would I have done?" said Caymus.

Be'Var looked at his pupil and cocked an eyebrow. "Is this your ever-so-subtle way of asking me to teach you to use a sword?" he said.

"Yes," said Caymus. "I don't really see what else I might be able to do the next time we run into one of those things."

Be'Var nodded. "I suppose," he said, "it was only a matter of time. Burn it all, but I guess if I'm going to teach you everything I know, it may as well be everything I know. We'll start in the morning." He raised a hand to touch Caymus's shoulder. "Come on," he said, steering him back toward the front of the cave. "If we don't get back to our camp, Y'selle will have us both roasting on spits by night's end."

As Caymus returned to the business of setting up camp, he thought about the day's events, about how strange the last few hours had been. He thought it was strange that nobody had even *mentioned* the blizzard that still raged outside, how it had so suddenly appeared, or what it meant for them. He supposed nobody really wanted to think about it.

He also spent a long time thinking about the dead creature in the back of the cave. He was glad it was hidden around a sharp corner, that they wouldn't have to look at it all night. The idea that Gwenna and Rill had hatched about how it had gotten there had been an interesting one, and possibly very useful. If it was, in fact, true that the creatures could only enter their world at very specific places, then they might be able to effectively plan against attacks in the future. He wondered what planning like that might entail. What kinds of fortifications or weapons would be strong enough to protect the people he cared about against another onslaught? So very little that they had tried been effective against these monsters, so far.

He also noticed that the tingling sensation at the back of his neck had gone away. He was thankful for that.

Milo was standing to the left of the wagon with a roll of twine, doing his best to set up a drying line for their clothing. As Caymus watched him work, he remembered the 'experiment' that the two of them had performed in that clearing atop the hill on the night of the attack. The two of them had created a flame so hot and so forceful that it had melted through a foot of stone in mere seconds. They'd decided on the night that such a cooperative effort between worshipers of different elements might be best kept to themselves, but Caymus was beginning to think that was the wrong way to think about it. As he dropped the last sack of wet clothing down onto the bench, he decided that he would tell Be'Var about what the two of them had done that night; he would just have to hope that the master ended up seeing it the way he did: as a possible weapon against the creatures that had invaded into their world.

Chapter 7

"Keep your shield arm up, fool!" Be'Var yelled out, yet again. On this occasion, he also jumped off the wagon's bench and marched to the point where Caymus and Rill had, until that moment, been sparring.

Gwenna couldn't help but smile. She knew that Master Be'Var wasn't actually angry with the boys, and that they knew it, but she felt a little sorry for them all the same. Be'Var reminded her of her grandfather: stronger than he looked, and just as cross-looking when he was trying to make a point. She wondered if the master had any children—or grandchildren, for that matter—of his own.

"What did they do wrong this time?" said Bridget. She said it just quietly enough that Be'Var couldn't hear, her own grin concealed behind her hand.

"Shh," said Gwenna as Be'Var forcibly grabbed Rill's wooden sword away from him. "I think we're about to find out."

Two days had passed since the blizzard and the dying creature in the forgotten cave. Nobody had slept easily that night knowing they'd been sharing space with that monster, dead though it was. At least they'd awakened to good news: the snow had stopped completely. In fact, it had been as unseasonably warm the following day as it had been cold previously one and most of the snow and ice had quickly melted, leaving a lot of puddles amongst the rocks and brush they now traveled past.

She'd found out the morning after the blizzard that Caymus had asked Be'Var to show him how to use a sword, and that Be'Var had agreed on the condition that Rill learn as well, an idea which neither boy had dreamed of taking issue with.

Since the bargain had been struck however, Gwenna had frequently wondered if they'd had moments to regret their decision.

The heat radiating from the gravel and red stone that surrounded them, not to mention all the sweat and road grit, must have been only barely tolerable, and Be'Var had insisted that they practice—"drilling," he called it—while they moved. So, not only were they swinging their newly made wooden swords and shields at each other all the time, they were having to do so while keeping up with the horses. There'd actually been a frightening moment on the first morning when a startled Staven had nearly bolted free of his harness. The event had taught the boys that they needed to stay well-ahead of the wagon, where the horses could keep an eye on them.

That was how the last day-and-a-half had gone. Be'Var and Y'selle drove the wagon; Gwenna and Bridget walked alongside the horses; Milo disappeared for hours at a time, scouting ahead; and Caymus and Rill spent hour after hour smacking each other's shields, arms, and heads with lengths of hardwood that Be'Var had carved into makeshift weapons.

Gwenna watched with some amusement as Be'Var explained to them —demonstrating with Rill's sword and shield—precisely how they were making a mockery of swordsmanship. It seemed that as each boy was swinging or stabbing forward with his length of wood, they were both unconsciously trying to gain more leverage by pulling their shield arms backward. Be'Var appeared less than satisfied with this behavior, and he was demonstrating to them how they must keep the shields in front of them for protection while they "lunged like idiots" with their blades.

Gwenna gave some thought to the lesson as she observed it, but she didn't really understand what the problem was. Of course you'd want to keep your shield up at all times, especially when taking a swing; that only made sense, didn't it? Only when she mimed the action herself did she discover that she, too, had a tendency to throw her left hand back when she lunged forward when her right.

"Oh my," she said, miming the motion again, "that's going to be awfully hard to un-learn."

Bridget peered past the horses at her. "Going to be a swordsman, too?" she mocked.

Gwenna smiled. "Swords*woman*, thank you." She put her hands down. "And no, just trying to figure out what Be'Var was on about."

Bridget grinned at her, seeming unconvinced.

"Now drill it," Be'Var said as he tossed the wooden implement back to Rill and stormed back to the wagon which, by then, had nearly caught up to the three of them.

Caymus flashed Gwenna a quick glance, a look of quiet surrender on his dirty, sweat-streaked face. She grinned at him and gave him a wink, after which he and Rill jogged another few dozen yards up the road to start a new round of drilling.

"How do they keep going like that?" said Bridgett, notes of disbelief and admiration in her voice. "My arms would be falling off by now."

It was true, Gwenna thought, that they'd been at it for an awfully long time. When they'd camped the night before, the two boys had fallen asleep nearly immediately after the evening meal. The next morning, they'd both been rubbing sore muscles, and Caymus had told her that his right hand—the one holding the sword—had been smacked so many times that he could barely feel his fingers anymore. The fact that they were still at it was, she had to admit, quite impressive—or, she supposed, maybe just a bit thick-headed.

She watched the two of them work through the lesson that Be'Var had just taught them. Even in this simple act, it was easy to see just how different the two of them were. Rill slowly went through the motion of swinging the sword, backing the arm up and moving it forward again, correcting here and there, trying to find and fix mistakes as he made them, as though the motion of swinging the sword was a procedure that he had to learn to execute properly. Caymus, on the other hand, swung the sword over and over again, going through the entire motion at once until, little by little, the problem behavior disappeared. The act was more physical, more kinetic, for him.

She wondered why she was so fascinated by this boy from the Temple. He was so very different—and not just in how tall he was—from the boys she knew in Kepren. Most of those were loud and boisterous and always doing stupid thing to try to impress her, but Caymus just seemed to quietly get on with thing, and he spoke to her not as though he was trying to woo her, but as though they were already friends. Maybe it was just that—the fact that he seemed so comfortable around her—which made her feel so comfortable with him? She wasn't sure, but it was really refreshing.

"Ahem."

Gwenna turned to see Bridgett, who had repositioned herself so that they were both on the same side of the horses, looking at her pointedly.

"You were staring."

"I was not!" said Gwenna, a little louder than she'd meant to.

"Were so!" countered Bridget, grinning at her and pointing. "If you weren't staring, then why are you blushing?"

Gwenna pushed Bridget's hand back down. "Stop it!" she said, doing her best to shush her friend. She was looking around, hoping the others hadn't noticed this little exchange, trying to be as small as possible. Be'Var and Y'selle, sitting mere feet away on the driver's bench, had obviously heard, but the boys both seemed to be too busy with their exercises. Y'selle raised her eyebrows with a little smile; Be'Var just shook his head.

Gwenna was grinning so hard that her face hurt.

"Okay, okay," said Bridget, lowering her voice again and patting

Feston's mane. "I still don't get it," she said, after a while, "I mean, tall is one thing, but he's the size of a house!"

Gwenna just shrugged. "I know," she said. "He's unusual."

Bridget seemed to accept this, and she and Gwenna went back to watching the boys practice, as it was really the only entertainment to be had. By that time, the pair of would-be warriors appeared to have decided that they'd mastered waving the swords around at the air and were going to go back to waving them at each other.

Gwenna wondered about the justification for it all: why the two of them were learning how to swing a sword in the first place. Caymus had told her his reasons, of how he felt that he needed to be able to defend himself—maybe defend all of them—and that the work he and Be'Var had been doing with the Conflagration so far was great, but was of no use against the creatures. She had to admit that seemed like a pretty good reason to learn to use a sword, and she suddenly wished she was learning, too. She wondered if Be'Var would teach her though, or if he'd even be willing to take on any third pupil at this point, now that he already had the other two to keep track of.

Another thought occurred to her: even Be'Var *did* teach her, would she ever have the stomach to actually swing a blade at a living thing?

Then, she thought of Milo, and about his weapon of choice.

"Do you think Milo would teach us how to shoot a bow?" she said, absently.

"What?" said Bridget. "Why would you want to learn that?"

Gwenna turned to her. "For protection," she shrugged.

Bridget seemed genuinely confused by the idea. She motioned to Rill and Caymus, practicing their stances. "Isn't that what we have them for?"

Gwenna sighed. She turned back to the practicing young men, pulling a stray strand of hair out of her face and tucking it behind her ear. "Yes," she said, unwilling to argue, "I suppose so."

So, if she was going to try to convince Milo to teach her, she'd be doing it on her own. Okay, she could do that. She just hoped Milo wouldn't want to strike the same kind of deal Be'Var had made about having a partner.

They walked in silence for a while. Rill and Caymus drilled until the horses had caught up with them, then jogged ahead again. Gwenna, having turned her attention to the subject of Milo's bow, found all kinds of question suddenly appeared in her mind. What kind of wood was a bow made from? How did he get it to curve the way it did? How were the arrowheads made? How did he get the little feathers on the arrows to stay on?

Her mind remained busy with thoughts of bowyery until the group caught up with the boys again. Once again, the pair jogged ahead, and this time they turned a corner, passing a particularly large boulder, and disappeared from view. Gwenna noticed that the sounds of their practicing didn't resume, though. She was about to remark on the sound's absence when the wagon, too, rounded the boulder, and found them standing in front of Milo. Milo was sitting by the side of the road on some dusty, flat rocks.

He didn't look happy.

"Whoa," said Be'Var, bringing the horses and the wagon to a halt. He rested his elbow on his knee and looked at Milo. "Problem?" he asked.

"We're there," Milo replied, standing up and dusting himself off. "The mitre encampment," he continued, pointing at a large rock-face a few hundred yards up the road, "it's just ahead."

"Good," said Be'Var, nodding, "I can't wait to—"

Milo interrupted. "It's not good," he said, shaking his head.

Be'Var looked at him severely. They all understood the unspoken question.

Milo sighed. "There are bodies."

~~~

When they reached the encampment that was the above-ground part of the mitre city of Otvia, Gwenna felt her heart drop.

"Oh, no," she whispered.

Mitre were a quiet, private race. Their huge statures—some of them were over ten feet tall—belied their gentle natures and peaceful countenances. The entire race was comprised of earth worshipers and so they lived nearly exclusively underground in vast networks of caves and tunnels. Gwenna had never been beyond the camp and into Otvia itself and so didn't know how large it actually was, but she'd been told that the city honeycombed the entirety of the mountain range that they'd just spent the last few days climbing.

Mitre didn't invite others into their cities; Gwenna had never met anybody who had claimed to have stepped foot into even one of their tunnels. Some people claimed this was due to a rampant xenophobia that permeated the entire race, but Gwenna didn't believe it. She hadn't met many mitre, but the few she had encountered had made her believe that, as a people, they didn't have the capacity for hate. They simply wished to keep their homes to themselves, and to keep the loud, obtrusive outside world out on the surface.

Mitre accomplished this by building these encampments outside their doors. The camps were meant to make human visitors and traders
~~~

comfortable while also avoiding the need to bring them underground. This one, the Otvia Encampment, had consisted of white-brick structures and canvas-covered meeting areas where mitre and human alike opened small stalls or sold goods off the sides of wagons. The encampment occupied a flat area of ground which resembled a shelf carved out of the side of the mountain, about fifty yards to a side. Gwenna, Bridget, and Y'selle had passed through the encampment on their way to the Temple mere weeks ago. The camp had been a far cry from the bustling metropolis of Kepren, but it had felt alive with color and activity.

This place had been home to nearly a hundred souls when she had last seen it. Humans, mitre, families, children…

They were dead now.

They were all dead.

Be'Var and Y'selle stopped the wagon and climbed out as they all took hesitant steps forward into the camp. Gwenna shook her head as she walked. She couldn't believe what she was seeing. There had been bright, red and yellow-striped tents erected at this, the southern edge of the shelf, the last time she was here. People had drunk their ales and wines here, had talked and laughed into the night. It had been a happy place. Now, the tents lay broken upon the ground, their fabrics shredded. Even the white brick structure that had stood near the trail was barely standing, two of its three walls having been knocked to the ground. The rest of the camp, as far as she could see, was in a similar state.

Then she really looked at them: the bodies. There were so many. Two of them lay directly in front of her, faced down, half-covered by the remains of the tent: a human man and woman. The man's legs were hidden by the canvas, but Gwenna could tell by the way the fabric fell that most of his left leg was missing. The woman had a large tear in what had once been a pretty blouse, and Gwenna guessed that if she were to look underneath, she would find a similar tear in her flesh, extending straight through her torso to her front. Their skins were dry and cracking, and their appendages seemed swollen and distended.

Then there was the smell, a putrid aroma of rotting flesh that mingled with the sounds of swarming flies.

In the past week, she'd become used to tending to the dead and the dying, but this wasn't a hospital. This was a graveyard.

"Flames," said Rill, quietly.

Bridget collapsed to her knees and vomited, and everybody stopped to let her finish. Once she was spent, Gwenna bent down to help her back to her feet, but she couldn't take her eyes off the scene in front of her. The bodies were scattered all over the area. Some were covered by the remains of ruined buildings. Others had simply collapsed in the open.

She had to avert her gaze when she noticed the body of a young woman that had fallen on her back with her head turned toward them. The girl's eyes were missing.

Bridget managed to stand again, but she didn't let go of Gwenna's hand.

The group was silent for what seemed like ages until Caymus spoke. "They're all human," he said. "All of them."

Indeed, when Gwenna looked around, she didn't see any mitre. That was strange. There'd been mitre here when she'd passed through before.

"You're right," said Be'Var, who started moving forward again. "Come on," he said, "let's take a look at the doors. If there's any luck left in this world, maybe they didn't get into the city."

As a group, they moved toward the face of the mountain, stepping gingerly over rubble and the dead alike while shooing flies away from their faces. Bridget was still holding Gwenna's hand, squeezing it tightly, clinging to her as though her survival depended on not letting go.

When they stopped before the rock face, Gwenna realized that couldn't see the entrance, though she knew she must have been looking right at it. The surface they stood before was flat and featureless, as well as perfectly perpendicular to the ground. The smooth, stone surface fanned out for a dozen yards to the left and right, as well as above them, until it abruptly ended and gave way natural, jagged rocks of the mountain. The shelf that the encampment stood upon, when taken together with this flat, up-and-down wall, created the impression of the mountain having been a large cake from which some immense force had carved a piece.

Where were the doors, though? The last time Gwenna had looked upon this wall, a massive pair of stone doors had been here forming an arched entrance that was over a dozen feet high. While she'd never approached them directly, she'd glanced those doors half a dozen times, and they'd always stood at least partially open. Now, they were simply gone.

"The entrance—the doors, they were here before," she said, running her hand along the surface. "I swear they were."

"I'm sure they still are," said Be'Var. He was looking very closely at the stone, his face mere inches from it. "The mitre can do some very impressive things with earth, but I doubt they'd actually make the only way in disappear completely."

"Unless that's how they kept the creatures out," said Caymus.

"Maybe," admitted Be'Var, "but from what I know of the mitre, actually sealing up rock like that takes a little while. If they were fending off the same creatures here that we did at the Temple a week ago, I doubt they'd have had time."

As the rest of the group also felt the stone, the master traced circles upon it with his eyes, obviously looking for something. "My suspicion is that it's just very well crafted, to the point that we just can't see the seam, now that it's closed. Still, there must be a small gap…somewhere. I wonder if someone sensitive enough could find a draft." He turned around, saying, "Milo, could you—" He looked around, as did the others. Milo was nowhere to be seen.

"Slag and Cinder!" said Be'Var, "where's he gone now?"

"Leave him be," said Y'selle, gently, "he's done more than earn his keep, wouldn't you say?"

Be'Var grunted, then turned back to the wall. "Yes," he said, "I suppose." Then, he suddenly turned to Caymus. "Boy, what are you doing?" he said.

Gwenna looked at Caymus. He had his eyes shut, his head cocked to one side, as though listening for something. She looked down at his right hand and saw that his index and middle fingers were twitching. He had a tendency to do that when he was working with the Conflagration.

"Feeling for the entrance," he said. "There has to be less fire in the space between the doors, right?"

Be'Var looked almost pleased, but not quite. "I wouldn't count on it," he said. "I'm not sure how it is they build these places, but—"

"Be'Var!" Milo's voice interrupted, from the other side of the camp. "Be'Var, come here, and quick!"

The group made a mad dash across the encampment, each of them occasionally calling out, trying to locate the air priest. They ran through three sets of broken buildings and tents, trying not to see the bodies on the ground, until they rounded a still-standing wall and found Milo squatting next to a large flap of blue tent canvas that was draped over what was left of some masonry.

"What?" said Be'Var. "What is it?"

Milo motioned for them to come closer, then he lifted up a corner of the canvas. Underneath were three mitre bodies.

Gwenna was struck by the paleness of their skin. The complexions of mitre were always light to begin with—all the time they spent underground and away from the sun left its mark on them—but these people, two men and a woman, were almost white. Their huge, lean bodies were pressed close together on the ground. As was typical of mitre, they had no hair, not even eyebrows, and they wore very little in the way of clothing: leather leggings, cut off at the knees, and a short-cut tunic for the woman. Gwenna was struck by the difference between these bodies and the humans they had seen earlier. The humans all showed evidence of decay and bloating; these mite bodies showed no such signs.

Then, Gwenna realized why Milo had called them over so insistently: very slowly, their chests were rising and falling with barely perceptible breaths.

They were still alive.

"Caymus," said Be'Var, urgently, as he pushed past Milo into the makeshift tent, "get in here."

Caymus did as he was told. For a moment, Gwenna was surprised by how quickly he moved, how little hesitation he showed as he ducked under the canvas.

Gwenna felt a hand on her shoulder and turned to see Y'selle looking past her and Bridget at the scene that was playing out. "Come, ladies," she said to them as she turned around and walked back toward the wagon. "If he manages to revive them, they'll be thirsty."

The three women moved quickly. Gwenna tried not to think about the corpses she was stepping around as she went. She looked over at Bridget, who still looked ill, her face a ghostly shade of white and her eyes wide.

"Bridge?" she said, trying her best to look sympathetic.

Bridget didn't look back, instead keeping her eyes straight ahead as though afraid to see the place through which they were walking. "They're all dead," she said, her voice faint. "All of them. Even that sweet little boy."

Gwenna swallowed hard. "You saw him?" she asked.

Bridget opened her mouth, then shut it again. She just nodded.

Gwenna knew the boy she was talking about. When they'd passed through here on their way north, they'd parked their wagon near a small family who'd recently set up a stall selling small pieces of jewelry that they made from shells and colored stones. The parents, both in their thirties had two children with them, the youngest of whom had been a boy somewhere between five and ten years old. The boy had been quiet, but also bright and inquisitive. Bridget, in particular, had liked him a lot.

Gwenna was immensely grateful she hadn't seen that body. She'd never been more grateful for anything in her whole life.

When they reached the wagon, Matron Y'selle climbed onto the driver's bench and motioned for the girls to lead the horses. Gwenna took hold of Feston's harness, and she and Bridget together started moving the wagon—and the precious water it contained—back toward the mitre.

About halfway there, they reached a point that was too narrow to fit the wagon through. Rather, it was too narrow to navigate without having to drive over a pair of sun-scorched bodies. Gwenna didn't see a way to get past the obstacle without having to drag away the bodies of people she'd talked with—even laughed with—just a week ago. She was thus hugely relieved when Rill and Milo appeared before them and, without being asked, began quietly moving the corpses from their path and tucking them under the folds of fallen tents. Every few yards, they did it again, going about the task with solemn silence.

Gwenna hadn't thought much of Rill when she'd first met him. He clearly wasn't stupid, but he seemed directionless, careless, as though he had no idea what he wanted to do with his life and didn't care to figure it out. Her evaluation of his character changed, however, as he and Milo worked. Every single body he cleared from her path was one more heartache she wouldn't have to suffer. At one point, she caught he gaze, and she mouthed the words "thank you". He didn't say anything in return; he just nodded.

By the time they had stopped the wagon before the tent that covered the three mitre, Caymus had emerged and was walking toward them. "Water?" he said to Y'selle, who turned around and picked up one of the water casks, which she handed down to him. Gwenna recognized the little cask with the long scratch around its middle. She'd filled it herself with packed snow the previous day.

"Thank you," said Caymus, tucking it under his arm. "They're awake," he continued, turning his head to address the group as best he could. "Be'Var says they'll be fine; they're just dehydrated and hungry." Then, he turned to take the water to his new patients.

Gwenna moved to follow him, but Y'selle called for her to stop. "They're probably not quite ready to meet all of us yet," she said, dropping back down off the bench.

"You're…dirty."

It was Bridget who'd spoken. Gwenna turned to her and saw that she was pointing a Milo. He'd gotten dried blood and gore and who-knew-what-else on his beautiful sky-blue tunic. He looked like he'd been working in a butcher's shop.

"He's going to get dirtier, I'm afraid," said the Matron, assessing both him and Rill, who was likewise covered in the remains of the dead. "Come on," she sighed, "our hosts will be up and about eventually." She looked around at the scene around them and sighed. "We should take care of the rest of these poor souls before the sight of them causes any further anguish."

~~~

Several hours later, filthy and exhausted, Gwenna found herself standing before a giant mass of flames as the bodies they had collected, thirty-seven in all, burned themselves out of the world. She stood next to Caymus, leaning on him, her arm crooked around his. He felt solid. He felt warm. She was glad he was there.

The entire group, save Be'Var, stood before the funeral pyre observing the solemnity of the moment. They'd built the pyre at the northern edge
~~~

of the shelf, as far from the road and the camp as possible. Caymus had placed a torch to it just as the last light of the sun had disappeared behind the next mountain peak. Now the only sound was that of the flames turning the dead to ashes, and Gwenna was comforted by the familiarity of it.

She was glad the fire didn't smell worse considering all the bloated, decaying flesh contained within the flames. All she could smell was the tent fabric that the dead had been wrapped in, not to mention her own sweaty skin.

She was glad it didn't smell worse. She didn't think she'd have been able to stand that.

She looked around at the group. Bridget had regained her composure sometime after she'd been given the responsibility for cutting tent fabric into shrouds, and she now stood the closest to the pyre, Y'selle close behind her. Rill sat on the ground, hugging his legs to his chest as he watched the flames do their work. Milo sat cross-legged next to him. He'd mentioned that in the village he came from, people had open-air funerals rather than pyres, but he hadn't complained.

Be'Var, as far as she knew, was still on the other side of the camp talking to the mitre who were, by now, conscious. The master had spent most of his time with his patients that evening, making sure they didn't run into any complications as they drank and rested and slowly recuperated. She wondered how they'd come to be there, the three of them, amongst naught but humans. She wondered about the creatures that had so obviously been here. She wondered about the one trapped in the cave several miles down the road. She wondered why they had to just show up and start killing people. It didn't seem right. It didn't make sense.

She tried to push the thoughts out of her mind as the members of the little group, one by one, turned and walked back in the direction of the wagon and the surviving mitre. Eventually, only she and Caymus remained.

"Why did they do it?" said Caymus. "Why did they attack us?"

Gwenna was surprised to hear her own thoughts passing his lips, but she couldn't find any pleasure in it. "I hate them," was all she said. Then she squeezed his arm. "We should get back."

They turned around and walked in the direction of the others.

When they reached the camp, they saw that a small campfire had been set up near a freshly erected tent. The three mitre all sat on the ground on one side of the tent while the humans sat on boxes, large stones, and other makeshift chairs. One of the mitre men was speaking.

"I had been studying the Ritual," he was saying, speaking mainly to Be'Var but also occasionally turning to include the others as well. "My teacher had been asking me to take my turn, and I had been there for hours with Er'ken and my sister, Muria."

Gwenna had learned earlier in the day that the speaker's name was Merkan. She didn't know what 'the Ritual' was, though since a mitre was the one talking about it, it surely had something to do with the worship of the earth element.

"They came fast," Merkan continued. "There was shouting and screaming, and the call came through the halls to go to the Center."

"The Center?" asked Milo. Gwenna noticed that he was doing something with a piece of leather as he listened.

Merkan paused for a moment. He didn't seem to know what Milo was asking, so Be'Var explained for him. "Think of the Center like the keep in a castle," he said. "It's the most heavily defended place in their city." He darted a look at Milo. "Now hush. Let him speak."

Merkan nodded toward both of them, affording a slight smile for Be'Var. "As we ran for the Center, we saw them, the monsters. They were like giant insects, with swords for claws and skulls for heads, and five of my people were trying to fight one of them off. So frightening." His face grimaced, looking angry at the memory. "I could not believe what my eyes saw. Within moments, they had cut down two of my friends. I told Er'ken to take my sister to the Center and I ran to help the ones that remained."

Gwenna looked over the three mitre while Merkan spoke. They seemed so much taller, now that they were no longer lying down. They were also all fit-looking and well-muscled, and she realized she had trouble imagining them being frightened of anything.

"I brought my blade to bear and I ran at the monster, knocking it over onto the ground." He raised a closed fist and made a stabbing motion. "The blade, though, it could not get through. It was as though the monster wore the thickest armor. I struggled to keep it down, to keep it pinned down to the floor. I yelled at the others to go, but they would not leave me." He shook his head. "They tried to help me, but they had no training in a warrior's arts, and so they did not know how." Then, he lifted an arm up in front of his face, rotating the hand to the left and right. "One of my friends, I saw his fingers were cut off as he tried to hold on to it also." His voice drifted off slightly at that, as though he was lost in the memory. "I do not know what happened to him."

After a moment, he dropped his hand. "When that occurred, I pushed it again, pinned it against the wall." He made the stabbing motion again. "I tried again to pierce the monster's armor." He paused, holding his hand at the bottom of the stabbing arc. "I could not get a good swing, though. All I could do was press into the armor. And as I pressed, the blade began to pass through." He dropped his hands to the ground. "Slow at first, but then quickly, the blade sank to the hilt."

Milo dropped the piece of leather. "You actually got a knife into one of them?" he said, his eyes wide. Be'Var was looking cross again, but Milo pressed on, regardless. "How? I must have fired a dozen arrows at those things, at the weakest points I could see, and they all just bounced off."

Merkan looked at Milo and shook his head. "I do not know," he said. "It was as though the quick motion," he brought his hands up and clapped them together, "could not get through the armor, but the slow press could. I do not understand it."

"What happened after that?" said Be'Var.

Merkan continued. "The monster disengaged from me. I heard a gasp, then it got away from me and it ran," he said. "We did not follow. We ran to the Center, but when we arrived, we found the doors were shut and barred, and many more of the monsters were moving around outside, trying to get in."

Gwenna shuddered. She remembered all-too-well a very similar situation at the Temple.

"So," Merkan continued, "we fled out here, among the dead men and women." At that point, he suddenly dropped his head, putting his hands to his forehead. "I am so sorry that we did not bury them properly, and I ask your forgiveness."

"It's fine," said Be'Var, in a surprisingly gentle voice. "You had other things on your mind."

"Thank you," said Merkan, raising his head again. "Yes, we fled to this place nearly a week ago. We made camp, and we have occasionally returned inside to see if circumstances have changed, but the monsters remain. Our families and neighbors are still locked in the Center." He looked in the direction of the mountain. "We sealed the door so that the monsters would not surprise us as we slept, and we waited."

"Waited for what?" asked Be'Var.

"For circumstance," Merkan replied. "We had no weapons to fight and no way to reach our people. We had to wait for something to change so that we could rescue those who are trapped. The walls of the Center were built in ancient times; they would take many months to be opened, even from within. The Center has food, and water, and ventilation for many, many weeks, but they cannot leave that place without help. The circumstances have prevented us from helping our families, so we have waited for the circumstances to change."

"Earth is a very patient sort of element," Be'Var said in response to questioning looks he was getting from Caymus and Rill.

Merkan nodded, then he raised his eyes, looking at the darkening sky. "Then," he said, "the snow came." He ran a hand over his bald head. "We were not prepared for that."

Gwenna thought she saw the other male mitre shudder at the mention of the snow.

"We made a cover for ourselves as best we could," Merkan continued, "stayed together for warmth." He looked directly at Be'Var. "My next memory is of seeing you, Master Be'Var." Then, he took a deep breath, and his eyes took on a slightly pleading quality. "My family, friends, the entirety of my people are trapped in the Center of Otvia, with monsters I do not know how to fight hunting outside. Do you bring new circumstances? Can you help us?"

Be'Var was quiet, appearing deep in thought.

"We *have* to!" said Caymus. "We have to help!"

The searching look Be'Var gave Caymus perfectly illustrated what Gwenna was sure the rest of them must have been thinking: of course we have to help, but how?

"You have a suggestion?" the master said, his brow furrowing. "We can't burn them down without the Conduit, and aside from what Merkan just told us about his knife, I've never heard of anyone being able to hurt one physically before. If you have an idea about how to take on a dozen of these things at once, I'd be glad to hear it."

Caymus seemed like he was about to say something in return, then he stopped himself and frowned. He turned to Merkan. "Earlier, you said your friends weren't warriors. Does that mean you *are* one?"

Merkan nodded. "I received training in the Mael'vek nation's regular army. I was apprenticed there for seven years." His eyes seemed to glass over slightly, as if remembering something. "I believed I had measured myself in every kind of combat. These creatures though: I have a hard time in describing the way they fight, but I believe that it is only my training that left me alive to speak to you of it now."

"Your relative size probably had a little to do with it as well," said Be'Var, absently.

Merkan nodded again. "Your point is accepted, Master Be'Var."

Gwenna didn't know much about Mael'vek, the empire to the south of Kepren and the Tebrian League. She knew that the two nations, Tebria and Mael'vek, had warred with each other frequently in the last few hundred years or so, and it was widely accepted that Mael'vek's warriors were among the fiercest in the world. The idea that even a mitre, trained by Mael'vekians, wasn't able to defeat one of these things seemed impossible.

For a long while, nobody spoke. The frustration around the campfire was palpable: nobody wanted to just leave hundreds—perhaps tens of thousands—of people to fend for themselves against the most terrible creatures anyone had ever encountered, but nobody knew what to do about it. Even Caymus's expression was a mask of pain and anguish.

Then, of all people, Rill turned to the mitre, his eyes wide with anticipation. "Merkan," he said, excitement creeping into his voice, "you said the creature 'gasped' when you stabbed it, right?"

Merkan seemed unsure what to do with Rill's sudden enthusiasm. His eyes betrayed confusion and suspicion. He spoke in measured tones. "Yes," he replied. "There was no mistaking it. The monster drew a deep breath when my blade found its guts."

Rill nodded quickly, then he turned to Milo. "I once heard a priest in Shorevale say something about 'white air'. I don't remember the specifics, but he said it's just one part of the air, that it's the part that we all inhale when we breathe. He seemed to think that fire uses it, too. Does that sound right?"

Milo had a pondering look on his face, like he was trying to figure out what Rill was up to, but he nodded. "Technically, we inhale the whole of the air, but the white part is what doesn't come back again." He smiled. "It's pretty advanced stuff, and I've never studied it very much so I'm not an expert or anything. I knew a priest who made white air his life's work," he said. "He told me that he could actually see white air enter a person's mouth when he breathed, and that it was gone, replaced by another color, when he exhaled. And yes, he told me that fire did the same thing."

"It does," said Be'Var. "Fire *breathes* much the same way we do." He arched an eyebrow. "You have an idea, Rill?" Gwenna noted that Be'Var's expression was a great deal less incredulous than she would have expected, considering the history between these two.

Rill's expression, on the other hand, was ecstatic. His hands moved rapidly as he spoke. "They breathe!" he exclaimed, looking around at the now curious faces. Nobody understood what he was getting at yet, so he turned to Caymus. "Okay," he said, "before we left the Temple, Wrentyl was telling me about the day you did your first pulling trick—or rather, failed to. He said that you got to the point where you'd made this really nasty flame, and suddenly it was getting hard to breathe in the room. He said that right before the fire finally snuffed itself out, he was literally gasping for air."

Caymus nodded. "I didn't really see it happen at the time, but that's what they told me afterwards."

Be'Var scoffed. "You better believe it happened, boy. That blasted flame of yours had eaten up all the—" Be'Var stopped, and a smile of understanding suddenly crawled over his face. "Burn me," he said. "Burn me, Rill, I think you might actually have something there."

Gwenna couldn't quite believe it when the two of them, Be'Var and Rill, simultaneously turned to Merkan and asked if he could draw a map of the tunnels. Then the pair, obviously just as surprised as she was, turned to each other with wide eyes.

For the first time since she'd met him, Gwenna heard Master Be'Var laugh. She looked at Caymus, who was looking back at her. He shrugged, but he was smiling.

For the next few hours, Gwenna watched as Be'Var, Rill, Caymus, and the three survivors concocted a plan to rescue the mitre who were trapped in the Center of Otvia. It was actually a wonderful thing to behold, and as she listened, she felt her sprits begin to life as a week's worth of anxiety and uncertainty was replaced with possibility and hope.

As the night went on and the plan was hatched, Gwenna paid particular attention to Caymus, trying to make sense of him. She enjoyed his friendship, enjoyed being close to him. He had been a warm, easy presence in her life ever since the moment he'd awakened in her little hospital. Was she attracted to him, though? She honestly didn't know, and she didn't know why she was having so much trouble figuring it out. She'd found herself mooning over boys before of course, but this was different. She really liked Caymus, so why didn't she feel drawn to him?

In the end, she supposed that it wasn't attraction at all that she felt for the boy from the Temple. It was comfort. She wasn't sure she could fall in love with him any more than she could a warm blanket.

Eventually, she noticed that Bridget had noticed her noticing Caymus, and she looked away, feeling embarrassed. Everyone else was trying to figure out what they were going to do about the people trapped in the earth below, and there she was, trying to figure out what she was going to do about a boy.

In the end, all she could do was hope that they would all be careful when this plan of theirs went into motion.

Chapter 8

Rill could scarcely believe where he was, and he wasn't certain if anticipation, fear, or wonder filled the greater part of him in the moment. He was crouched in darkness, in a small hollow in one of the stone walls of Otvia, waiting for a plan that he'd had no small part in creating to take shape and to, perhaps, decide the fates of flames-knew how many mitre.

He'd have laughed if he hadn't been so nervous. The silence in the halls of the underground city seemed as intense as the thrumming that his own heartbeat was making in his ears. Somewhere in the earthen tunnels though, he knew the skittering and shrieking of the dark creatures would hammering on the minds of his friends.

The hollow had been carved from one of the tunnels, and was hidden behind a wide-open stone door, just outside a fairly large chamber. The chamber itself, from what he'd seen of it, was roughly circular, with a mitre-sized stone door on either end. When he'd peered in earlier, he'd seen a small, stone plinth standing in its center. Unfamiliar figures had been carved into the plinth's surface, and it had stood in a small pool of some oily substance that had been burning quietly and peacefully.

The room, its single ornament, and the soft, flickering firelight had been beautiful in their simplicity. Merkan had told him this was the place where he'd been performing the steps of what he'd called 'The Ritual' just before the attack. Rill hadn't understood most of what Merkan had told him about this Ritual, but he'd figured out that it had something to do with the celebration of some long-dead hero of the mitre.

Rill took a deep breath, trying to calm himself, to center his mind and stave off panic. Milo ought to be standing outside the opposite door to the room, waiting to fulfill his part of the plan. Rill wished he could see him, that he could see *anything*. He didn't like sitting in the darkness like this; he wanted to be doing something.

For the time being, though, his only responsibility was to hide behind this door in this little hollow which Merkan himself had created about twenty minutes previously. The mitre had explained to Rill that he wouldn't be visible once the door stood open; Rill, skeptical of the explanation, had asked for a little time to examine said door. He'd soon discovered that the door's hinges jutted out from the stone frame somewhat, allowing the big slab of stone it to lie flush against the wall. He'd then tested the heavy door a couple of times and had concluded that the mitre was right: once opened, the door to the Ritual Room would very effectively hide anything on, or in, the adjacent section of wall.

Merkan had nodded patiently, and had proceeded to create the hollow.

Rill had been amazed by Merkan's abilities. He'd been expecting him to produce tools of some manger, but the giant had simply pressed his hands into the stone of the tunnel and molded it like bread dough, all the while humming and singing quietly with his eyes closed. He'd finished creating the hollow in less than a minute, and once Rill had crawled into the resulting depression, Merkan had opened the door wide, proving decisively that the whole thing could be covered completely.

Satisfied that Rill was well hidden, Merkan and Caymus had quickly jogged off in the direction of the Center.

And so, Rill knelt in his hide, still trying to balance excitement and trepidation, and waiting for the next step in the plan to execute.

Any moment now, Caymus should come running up the underground corridor and into the room with the plinth. The creatures—hopefully, all of them—should be following close behind. Once the last of the huge, insectoid creatures was through, it would be Rill's responsibility to slam the door shut and throw the massive bolt, blocking any exit from this side of the room. On the other side, Milo was supposed to do the same, but only after Caymus had passed him and gotten to safety.

The timing needed to be perfect. If even one of the monsters managed to follow Caymus through that second door, or if Rill slammed his door before all of the creatures had gone through, the plan would fail. There was also, of course, the possibility of Caymus getting trapped in the Ritual Room with the creatures. That was a thought Rill didn't want to linger on.

Be'Var had a part to play in all this too, and should have already been waiting with Milo on the far side of the room. Once the creatures were trapped inside the room, the plan called for him and Caymus to use their abilities to turn the small fire around the plinth into a roaring inferno that would quickly engulf all of Milo's 'white air' and leave the creatures to suffocate and die.

Both Be'Var and Milo had raised concerns about this part of the plan, saying that while Merkan's story had certainly implied that the creatures breathed, there was no guarantee that they breathed the same air as humans and mitre. The debate had lasted for several minutes, but in the end, they had decided that the risk was acceptable and that, at the very least, having the creatures trapped in the room should allow enough time for them to free Otvia's citizens from the Center.

There had also been some discussion about whether the creatures might be able to simply pass through the stone doors. They had arrived here, after all, in one of the holiest cities in the world without passing through the front door, and if Rill's theory about the "worn places" between the realms was right, there was no reason to think the creatures couldn't just pass through solid rock back to their own realm and then return immediately to another spot in this one. They'd considered calling off the entire affair at that point, but then Merkan had raised another point: if the creatures could pass through stone, what had been keeping them out of the Center for the last week?

The group had agreed: the risk was minimal, and so the rescue attempt would move forward.

Matron Y'selle, the girls, and the other two mitre had stayed outside. Gwenna had argued for a minute or two about not being allowed to go, but when the matron had asked her for help getting bandages and poultices together, that they might be able to treat the wounds they were almost definitely going to see in the next few hours, she'd given up her protest. Rill had gotten the impression that she'd actually had her mind changed, that she agreed that nursing was a better use of her skills and that she *wasn't* simply acquiescing to the Matron's orders. That might have been an act, though. Rill wondered about that girl. He knew Caymus had taken a liking to her and that she seemed interested in him, too. Rill just hoped she wouldn't end up being trouble. Girls were so often trouble.

As he waited, Rill rubbed the stone walls of his hiding place with the palms of his hands and was amazed by the smoothness of them. Every surface in the underground city was the same way: looking like sandstone, but feeling almost as smooth as river rocks. From the moment Merkan had revealed the entrance to Otvia—he'd done it in much the same way that he had created this hollow, making the outlines of the huge doors suddenly appear with little more than a touch and a deep, humming sound—every single thing about this place had been fascinating. They'd gone through several small chambers—small by mitre standards; enormous by his own—on their way here, and each chamber had been connected to the whole by a web of corridors and tunnels. How did they keep it all straight in their minds, when every surface looked the same?

Rill wondered if mitre had ever lived in that cave they'd slept in during the snowstorm. The walls there weren't anything like as smooth as they were here, but somebody had clearly cared for them. Rill smiled. It was just another amazing mystery that he was going to have to solve one day.

Rill had been thinking about that a lot, lately, about how despite invasion and the bodies and the horribleness of everything, he couldn't help but think that these had been some of the best days of his life. He felt as though he was actually living, that he was finally really discovering the world he lived in. In just the last few days, he'd learned more about the elements—even that of fire—than he had picked up in two years of cloistered studies.

It had been Milo that had changed his mind, really. The tremendous power that the priest had demonstrated when he'd literally flown Caymus up on to the walls of the Temple, had made Rill realize that he no longer wanted to be a disciple of the Conflagration, that there was so much more to find out about the other elements and the other peoples of the world, and that he would never find those things while trapped behind the Temple's walls.

He considered the quiet dignity of the room over which he now stood guard, considered the carvings on the stone plinth and what they might have to do with the Ritual that Merkan had spoken of. He'd never met a mitre before and he had more questions for the giant than he could count. Why had he become a warrior in the Mael'vekian army? How many mitre were actually down here? Did Otvia keep in contact with the other mitre cities? Just how big was Otvia compared to those cities?

He hoped that this plan of theirs worked, else he might not ever get to ask those questions.

As he pondered, he kept absently running his hands over the surfaces surrounding him, unconsciously expending nervous energy. When his fingers met the open door, he realized that there was a figure carved into the stone, invisible in the near pitch black of the hollow. He could tell the figure was roughly a foot high and half as wide, but he didn't have enough light to make it out properly. He hesitated for a moment, listening for footsteps or yelling, or any other evidence that the plan was already in motion. When he heard only silence, he chanced opening the door about an inch, just enough to let some of the light in from the corridor.

When he saw the image, he gasped and quickly pulled the door back into position.

The figure carved into the doorway was a simple one: a straight line, straight up and down, with another small line crossing perpendicularly along the top. That figure, a simple representation of a weapon, was an incredibly close match for the mark on the back of Caymus's hand. Instead of a master's flame, however, this one stood in front of the outline of a circle. Rill was quite certain that the circle's diameter was exactly the height of the flame that his friend carried upon his skin. The likeness between the two symbols, from the simplicity of the objects to the thickness of each line, was uncanny.

"Flames." Rill had to fight himself to keep his voice to a whisper. "Caymus, you'd better make it out of here in one piece so you can see this."

~~~

Left, left, right, left, right. Caymus repeated the words in his mind again and again, trying to burn them into his memory with repetition. He was crouched behind a low wall, looking down into a giant hall. The hall contained dozens of semi-circular rows of stone benches that cascaded down onto a large, flat area. Merkan had told him that important meetings were held here, that the flat area was a stage from which the leaders of Otvia spoke to their people. Behind the stage, the wall took on a convex shape which stretched up to the ceiling, high above him, and to the left and right several dozen yards. That, Merkan had said, was where the door to the Center lay, closed and hidden as effectively as the entrance to Otvia had been just a few hours ago.

An even dozen of the creatures slowly crawled back and forth along the length of that wall, prodding at it with their sword-like claws, presumably trying to find a way in.

The back of Caymus's neck was burning like fire.

Merkan had just moved off to a darkened area of the chamber. Whereas Caymus stood near the center of the rear of the great hall, very near the mouth of a huge tunnel—the chamber's only entrance—Merkan was about a quarter of the way around to the left, keeping hidden behind the back row of benches, waiting. It would be Merkan's responsibility to get the attentions of any creatures that didn't follow Caymus out of the hall. His part was critical: if they didn't get every last one of the creatures into the Ritual chamber, their plan would likely fail.

Left, left, right, left, right. Caymus had been picked to act as bait for the monsters because, other than the mitre who were all still feeling the effects of dehydration and malnutrition, he had the longest stride and could run the fastest. Caymus had suggested that Milo was actually the fastest among them, but Milo had countered that his usual speed would be greatly affected by the fact that they were in tunnels, that there wasn't enough air to carry him here.

"Plus," Milo had said, "we already know you can outrun one of them." The priest had grinned while delivering the comment, though Caymus hadn't thought it particularly funny at the time.

Left, left, right, left, right.

Caymus had asked Be'Var if he could borrow his sword for this part
~~~

of the plan. Be'Var had told him no, that it would only serve to slow him down, either weighing down one hand or bouncing off his hip. "Besides," he'd said, "not to be cruel, boy, but if there are as many as Merkan says… let's just say that if they do catch up to you, a sword isn't going to make much difference."

Caymus had been forced to concede the point.

Left, left, right, left, right.

They'd left Be'Var and Milo on one side of the Ritual chamber, Rill tucked into a hidden hollow on the other. Merkan was in place. He'd told Caymus to start whenever he was ready.

He was nothing like ready

Left, left, right, left, right

He took a very deep breath, trying to steady his nerves.

Left, left, right, left, right. All right. Here we go.

Caymus was honestly surprised to find himself suddenly standing up and waving his arms with the biggest motions he could manage. "Hey!" he shouted. "Over here!"

The creatures, all of them together, didn't even turn their heads to look at him before they began charging in his direction. Caymus didn't even have time to think about how fast they were moving before he was turning and running in the other direction.

Left. The first turn came almost immediately as the tunnel branched off in three different directions. Not one of them was lit at this point, and so Caymus had a brief flash of fear has he dashed headlong, into a darkened corridor. As he ran, he heard an all-to-familiar scream behind him, only multiplied by a number much bigger than he was comfortable with. The sound reverberated through the hall. He hoped that meant they hadn't entered the tunnel yet.

Left. A relatively small—only ten feet high at most—passage peeled off from the main tunnel. This one was lit on either side by pools of oil that gathered in troughs along the walls. Caymus could feel his legs starting to burn. The first time he had done this, he'd had to run all the way back to the Temple, a marathon to today's sprint. This time there were also no roots and leaves to trip over, and so he could afford reckless speed.

Right. The passage opened into a small chamber with stacks of barrels along the edges and large holes in the walls, up high near the ceiling. On the way to the Center, he'd wanted to ask Merkan about those holes; now, he didn't give them even the slightest thought. Three passages exited out of this room: the one he just entered through, and two more. Caymus hurried through the one on his right.

Left. For a moment, he panicked. The passageway continued straight ahead, but a fairly large tunnel opened up to the right. Did 'left' mean 'straight'? He knew to continue forward, but would this count as his left and make the next turn a right, or did 'straight on' not count in his list of directions, meaning his next turn should be a left?

The sound of falling barrels and skittering claws behind him pushed him forward, regardless. He felt panic pushing its way into his heart: his pursuers were getting much too close and his lungs were staring to ache.

Caymus felt an immense sense of relief when he entered the next chamber. For the last few seconds, he'd been worried about what his next turn would be but, as luck had it, he recognized this room. It was full of small statues and a few dozen blank canvases. More importantly though, he recognized the two troughs of flame that flanked the passage which he knew led to the Ritual Room.

Right.

When he finally reached the doorway of the Ritual Room—the place he'd been heading for all this time—he quickly changed direction, ducking to his right through the portal and hoping Rill was still behind the open door like he was meant to be. As he turned, he chanced a look behind and immediately wished he hadn't. They were *much* too close. Several sets of fangs and black eyes glared back at him, daring him to stop, or even slow. They felt like they were inches away, and as he flew into the room, he could only hope that they'd have some difficulty getting through the doorway with all of them trying to push through at once.

As he moved through the room, he had momentary feeling of dread as he found himself running at the plinth in the center and its surrounding pool of burning oil. He hadn't thought about the fact that he'd have to get around it, and he felt that if he took the time needed to make the small changes in direction, the teeth would be upon him. Summoning what was left of his stamina, he leapt over several feet's worth of dancing flames. He stumbled slightly when he landed on the other side, his foot slipping a few inches across the stone floor, but he managed to catch himself and kept moving toward the exit.

Milo was standing in the doorway, his hands out at his sides and held slightly in front of him. Caymus didn't know what he was doing, but since he didn't feel he had the wherewithal to stop at this point, he just hoped that his friend would get out of his way quickly. His concern was unwarranted however as, with a dancer's grace, Milo jumped back behind the door just as Caymus came barreling through it.

Caymus only had enough stamina left to slow himself a little bit before allowing himself to simply run into the wall across from the door, turning to his side to let his shoulder and ribcage take most of the force of the impact. As he did so, he heard the stone door slam into place behind him. A moment later, the bolt took hold just before the sounds of huge, insectoid bodies slamming into the stone came echoing through the passage.

Gasping for breath, he turned and leaned against the wall just as he heard another door slam home. He realized his eyes were closed, and quickly opened them to see the twin sights of Milo putting his hand on the door, as though feeling for something, and of Be'Var walking quickly toward him.

Before they could start the next step—the burning of all the white air from the Ritual Room—there was the unmistakable sound of Rill shouting, as though in great distress. The sound didn't come from behind the stone door. Rather, it seemed to emanate from a several yards down the passageway. Merkan had mentioned that there was a passage that connected the two doors, but Caymus hadn't considered that the connection would be so direct. Summoning a second wind, and with Be'Var yelling after him, Caymus took off down the passage.

The connection turned out to be simple: the tunnel curved quickly around the circumference of the Ritual Room until it had wrapped around to the other door. When Caymus arrived, he found Rill on his back, scrambling backward, while Merkan grappled with one of the creatures. Caymus had skidded to a halt next to Rill and was helping him to his feet when suddenly he felt a nasty smack to the back of the head.

He turned to see Be'Var standing behind him, a furious look on his face. "You bone-headed fool!" he said, grabbing him by the sleeve and pulling him back down the passage.

Caymus tugged free. "We have to help him!" he yelled, and he started walking toward Merkan and the creature. The giant's limbs were locked with three of the legs of the huge insect as each tried to overpower the other.

When Be'Var grabbed again he wasn't gentle, and Caymus suddenly found himself staring into the master's face. "Boy!" he said through clenched teeth. "You have a job to do!" When Caymus started turning his head around again, Be'Var grabbed him by the chin and turned it back. "He can handle it," he said, looking his pupil intently in the eyes. "I need you now, Caymus. I need you to focus."

Caymus slapped Be'Var's hand away and stared his master in the eye, deciding how he could get the old man off his back long enough to help Merkan. As he did, he heard the sounds of the creatures continuing to slam their bodies against the doors. This time, however, there was a loud snapping sound that accompanied it and Caymus turned to face the door that Rill had been hiding behind.

Where there had been nothing but smooth stone a moment ago, now a tiny crack extended from the center of the top of the door down to the middle of the left edge.

They were going to get through. He really *didn't* have time to help Merkan.

Be'Var must have realized he finally had his student's attention. "Come on!" he yelled, and he turned and ran back down the passageway to the far entrance, Caymus close behind him.

Upon their return, they found Milo leaning bodily against the door. He looked up at them, wide-eyed. "Nice of you to come back!" he said.

Caymus followed Be'Var to the door, where the old man ducked down and peered through a small, square hole near the bottom of the stone slab. Merkan had put the hole in the door just before carving the hollow in which they'd secreted Rill. It was large enough that Be'Var could look inside—he would need to be able to see the flames in order to pull into them—but small enough, according to Milo, not to allow the airflow the creatures would require to survive the burning of white air from the room. They had been lucky in the choice of the Ritual Room for their trap, in fact. Most of the chambers of Otvia were well-ventilated via small holes and capillaries that went all the way to the surface; the mitre burned oil for light and heat after all, so fresh air was essential. This room, however, was intentionally sealed off, a fact which had something to do with the rituals that were performed here.

Be'Var turned to Caymus. "Ready?"

Caymus nodded, then he sat down on the ground and closed his eyes, trying to shut out the sounds of the creatures smashing against the doors and of Merkan's life-or-death struggle, not a dozen yards away.

When he was, at last, able to concentrate, he reached out and found that Be'Var had already pulled a great deal of heat into the oil-fed flames. Caymus could feel them getting fiercer, angrier. He felt for the conduits themselves and found that there were several dozen of them. Be'Var was allowing the flames to spread out along as much of the surface of the pool of oil as possible. With effort, Caymus began working to spread his consciousness out over them.

He encountered a great deal more difficulty than he had been expecting. He tried several times, but he simply couldn't get himself to spread out across so many conduits in so little time. He knew he could probably manage it eventually, but he just hadn't had enough practice. The frustration of it nearly severed his concentration.

"Don't try to use all of them," he heard Be'Var say. "All you need is one. The rest will feed off it."

Caymus understood, felt himself nodding. He disentangled himself from the mess of conduits over which he had been trying to divide himself and focused on a single point instead. This he knew well how to do, and he quickly had his consciousness wrapped tightly around one of them, squeezing as tight as he dared.

Within moments, he could hear as well as feel that the once peacefully burning pool of oil was now an inferno of angry flame. More importantly, the sound was replacing the pounding of carapace against stone.

"Keep it going, boy, as much as you want."

Caymus squeezed even more. He found that he was able to make an even tighter connection into the conduit by wrapping himself around it many times over. He tightened and tightened until he felt he was at the limit of his ability. He was amazed: until that moment, he'd thought that squeezing too hard would eventually cut a conduit completely; such did not appear to be the case.

He thought he heard Be'Var say something, but the voice was swallowed by the tumultuous roaring and hissing sounds coming from the small hole in the door.

Then, suddenly, it stopped. Caymus felt as if he'd broken something, and he flinched backward as though he'd been slapped. The conduits had suddenly vanished. He opened his eyes and saw Be'Var lean back against the wall, exhaling loudly. Caymus wasn't sure what had just occurred but seeing the relief on his master's face made him relax a little, too.

"What happened?" asked Milo in the sudden silence.

"Take a look for yourself," answered Be'Var, tilting his head toward the hole in the door.

Both Caymus and Milo ducked down to peer together. The room was dark, lit only by the tiny amount of light coming in through the hole. Still, it was enough to see: the chamber was empty.

"When the white air was used up," said Be'Var, "the flames went out, and the creatures just seemed to—" he made a digging motion with his hands, "to vanish through the floor and disappear."

Caymus looked at his master intently. "Back where they came from?" he said.

"Let's hope so," Be'Var replied. "I could see them struggling just before the air ran out." The corners of his mouth turned up in a very slight smile. "I guess Rill was right."

Caymus stood quickly. "Rill!" he exclaimed, and took off running again, back to where he'd last seen his friend and the struggling Merkan.

When he reached them, he saw Merkan sitting with his back against the wall of the passageway. He had a large gash on his left thigh to which Rill was applying pressure. The door to the Ritual chamber was open. The room was dark, the ceiling scorched, but there was no sign of the creatures, save the one Merkan had been locked in struggle with: that one lay on the ground a few feet away, not moving.

Caymus jogged over to them, knelt, and fished the bandages out of his pocket that Y'selle had insisted they all carry with them. He handed them to Rill, who added them to his own, and then called for Be'Var.

"You did it," Caymus said, a relieved smile on his face.

Merkan nodded. "As did you," he said. He was trying to assist Rill in putting pressure on the wound, but his enormous hands were just getting in the way.

When Be'Var turned the corner, the old man shooed Rill away and started working to cauterize the wound, as he had done so many times before. As he worked, Merkan continued. "Where are the other monsters?" he asked, peering into the now darkened room.

Caymus answered. "Gone. They passed through the ground." He nodded at Rill. "Just like the one in the cave."

He found himself staring at the body of the creature that Merkan had brought down. It was the first of them that he'd ever seen one defeated by anything other than the power of the elements, and while the image was ghastly, it also gave him hope. The fact that someone had killed one with nothing more than a knife and bare hands made him think they might actually stand a chance against these things.

"They will not return?" said Merkan, who was watching with a surprising amount of detachment as Be'Var pushed the flesh of the foot-long gash back into place with his hands and then knitted it together with fire.

Caymus looked at Rill, then at Milo, who had just arrived. "I don't know," he said, turning back to Merkan. "Wherever they come from, suddenly springing up through the ground is how they seem to get here, so I'm hoping they've just gone back."

"It would seem," said Milo, squatting down to watch Be'Var work and offering Merkan a waterskin, "that if they're able to move through earth whenever they feel like it, they'd have just popped up on the other side of the door."

Merkan accepted the water and took a quick drink before handing it back. Caymus wondered just how much Merkan could drink in a day as the giant replied, "I think you are right. This, to me, feels like it was a retreat."

"It wasn't," said Be'Var, still concentrating on his work. "I saw it happen. They didn't *move* through the floor; they passed through it."

"What," said Milo, "they fell through the ground, you mean?"

"Don't know," said Be'Var, shaking his head. "I couldn't say if they fell, or they were pulled by something else, or if the lack of air in the room somehow shoved them through. They didn't put their heads down and start moving downward though, they just went down, like something else was acting on them."

Caymus frowned. The idea of any "something else" that could act on creatures so terrifying was unnerving. He couldn't think of anything intelligent to say about it though, so he kept his mouth shut.

Be'Var finished closing the wound and started wrapping it with his own supply of bandages. "If you trained in Mael'vek," he said, "I'm sure this isn't the first of these you've had." He indicated the wound, then tied off the bandage. "Just don't go fighting any more monsters for a while and it shouldn't open up again."

Merkan nodded. "Thank you, fire-master," he said, standing up. When he got to his feet, he frowned, "I am afraid we are not yet finished with the creatures, however."

~~~

A few minutes later, the group was in the huge meeting hall, in the same spot where Caymus had been hiding less than half-an-hour earlier.

"Burn me," muttered Be'Var. They were looking down at the stage in the middle of the hall. Two of the creatures were down there. It seemed that those two hadn't joined the group that had chased Caymus. Merkan hadn't been able to get them to follow him, either. The pair were still poking and prodding at the hidden entrance to Otvia's Center, still completely consumed with trying to find a way in. "Somehow, I don't think we're going to get away with the same thing twice."

"I can try to take them myself," said Merkan, staring down at the creatures with resignation in his eyes.

"Trying is all it would be," said Be'Var, shaking his head. "You might get one of them, but not both. Besides," he continued, "I've only just sealed that wound back together, and you'll pass out pretty quickly once you tear it open again."

Caymus felt a tap on his shoulder and turned to see Milo looking at him, tilting his head toward Be'Var, and making some quick motions with his hands that he obviously expected Caymus to understand.

With the feathers dangling from his arms, he looked a bit like a flapping chicken. If not for the immediate danger in the room, Caymus would have laughed out loud. "What, Milo?" he said.

Milo looked a bit frustrated at not being understood. He pointed at Be'Var directly. "Have you told him yet?" he said.

"Told me what?" said Be'Var, who pulled Milo down a little lower so that the creatures wouldn't see him.

Caymus's eyes widened. "About...the trick?" he said.

"Yes!" Milo replied, managing to weave exasperation into a whisper. "Have you told him yet?"

Caymus hadn't, and he wasn't sure this was the time or the place for it. "No," he said, looking between Milo and Be'Var, neither of whom seemed appreciative of the answer. "No, not yet."

"What's this?" said Rill. By now, they were all watching the exchange.
~~~

Be'Var had one eyebrow raised quite high and was looking back and forth between Milo and Caymus, obviously expecting somebody to enlighten him.

Milo took the bait. "We—" he stopped, then briefly raised his head to peer over the stone bench at the remaining creatures. "Come on," he said. He started backing off toward the exit, indicating that they should follow.

Once they had turned a couple of corners and had reached the relative safety of a nearby room, Caymus and Milo started telling the others about the evening of the attack on the Temple: how they had met in a clearing atop a hill nearby, how Milo had talked Caymus into performing 'a little experiment' with him, and how the resulting experiment had resulted in a lance of flame that had cut through over a foot of stone in seconds.

As Milo filled in a few details, Caymus watched Be'Var's face intently. He'd planned on telling Be'Var about this eventually, of course, but he'd been wary about what the old man's reaction to the two of them co-mingling the powers of their respective elements might be. Add to that the fact that Caymus never had quite gotten around to explaining where he'd been on the night of the attack, and he was now having to force the master to accept a lot of things all at once.

Be'Var had, indeed, seemed irritated about the revelation at first. His eyes narrowed and his nostrils flared when they told of Caymus setting a flame in the deadwood. Caymus understood why: only that very afternoon, the master had delivered a scathing rebuke concerning what he considered to be reckless behavior.

When they'd gotten to the part about the stream of fire that had eradicated a section of stone however, the old man's eyes had gone wide. Now that Milo was trying to explain to Be'Var the different colors of air he had coaxed out of his surroundings to make something more flammable than usual, the master's brow was furrowed in concentration, his eyes downcast.

When they'd finished, silence fell over the group. Even Merkan seemed to be waiting for Be'Var to pronounce judgment on the tale. Before the master could speak though, Rill punched Caymus in the arm. "You weren't going to tell *me* about this either?" he said.

A smattering of quiet laughter broke the tension, and Be'Var finally nodded, raised his gaze, and spoke, looking directly at Caymus. "You think this will work against the creatures, boy? This wind-fire concoction?"

Caymus wasn't sure. "I don't know, Master," he said, "but I think it has to be worth a try. If we had your help, the lance might burn even hotter."

"What about the other one?" said Rill.

They turned to look at him. "The other one?" said Be'Var.

"You know," Rill replied, a bit taken aback and pointing in the direction of the hall they'd just left, "the other one." Rill turned to Caymus. "From what I've just heard, you've got a really interesting weapon to use there, but it sounds like it can only hit one of them at a time." He raised his thumb and index finger on his left hand, then covered the thumb with his right. "But what about the other one?" he said, wiggling the remaining finger at them.

Merkan answered. "You must take them as a surprise, when they are separated," he said, "and hope that your fire burns fierce enough to put the first down before the second can close the distance. If need be, I will hold the second back to give you time."

Caymus didn't like the idea of putting Merkan in that much danger again. The giant had already saved Rill's life—probably all of their lives—and had received a deep wound for it. He looked at Be'Var, hoping the old man would have a good reason to tell him no.

Be'Var ran his hand across his scalp and shut his eyes momentarily. When he opened them again, he grunted. "I don't like it," he said, looking at Merkan, then at Caymus. "Not one bit. But I just don't see a better option." He sighed, then said, "We'll need something to burn, then, and all of this rock is out of the question."

Merkan nodded. "There is oil in a nearby chamber," he said. "Come. We will collect it."

As the group made its way down yet another smooth, stone corridor, Caymus thought about what they'd all just agreed to, and he smiled. He knew he shouldn't be smiling, knew this was going to be as dangerous as anything they'd done already, but he couldn't help himself. Up to now, his victories over these huge bug-creatures had relied on luck, on the skill of a warrior with greater size and skill than he would ever have, or on a complete dependence on the Conduit itself. This time, though, they were going to wield a weapon—an actual *weapon*!—against the things, something that they controlled, something that didn't leave anything to chance. If this worked against the two creatures in front of the Center, it could be used to fight others, too.

If it worked...

They walked into a large chamber, about three times the size of the Ritual Room, yet not even half the size of the meeting hall. Caymus recognized it as being one of the rooms he'd run through on his path to their trap, or one very like it. There were a few dozen barrels of varying sizes stacked against one wall, but the rest of the room's perimeter was covered in small holes. Each of the holes was about the size of Caymus's closed fist, cut into the shape of an upside-down triangle, with a small spout jutting out at the bottom. All around the room, what looked like stone guttering ran to or past each of the holes, then turned slowly downward to empty into what appeared to be raised marble bowls, the rims of which were tall enough to reach Caymus's chest.

When he looked more closely, he could see that small droplets of some clear liquid were dripping from each of the holes, one drop every few seconds. The droplets were being caught by the guttering and funneled down into the bowls.

"What is this place?" he said.

"We collect the stone oils here," said Merkan, who walked over the pile of barrels, picked up a small one—it was small by his standards anyway; he needed only one hand to carry it—and brought it to one of the marble bowls to be filled.

"Stone oils?" said Caymus, peeking over the rim of the nearest vessel. He could see it was about half-filled with the liquid and that, when gathered together in a pool, the stuff appeared to have a slightly orange tint.

"It is the oil we burn to see in Otvia," said Merkan, who had filled his barrel. "It coats the torches and fills the troughs in the tunnels and chambers. It burns for many days and makes no smoke."

"I suppose," Milo said, looking around, "smoke would be a bit of a problem down here."

"Why do you call it 'stone oils'?" said Caymus.

Merkan didn't seem to know how to answer the question, and so Be'Var answered for him. "The oil comes out of the stone itself," he said. "No idea how they do it, but the Otvians have been coaxing oil out of stone for as long as I've been around. Probably a lot longer."

Caymus supposed he shouldn't be surprised at anything that the mitre were able to get stone to do, but he didn't think that getting liquid out of it should be possible. He wanted to know more but, for the moment, there wasn't time. He scratched at the back of his neck, which had started itching.

Merkan smiled at Be'Var and nodded graciously, then he indicated the barrel in his hand. "Who will carry this?"

By now, they had all gathered around the bowl which Merkan had used to fill the barrel. All eyes turned to Rill, who sighed. "I suppose that would be my job, wouldn't it?" he said, then he raised his arms. "Give it here, then."

There was a bit of fumbling and catching as Merkan handed a barrel, which he could hold with one hand, to Rill, who needed two, and who still managed to slosh the oil about somewhat.

"I don't think you should make any plans to stay, after this," said Milo, chuckling and indicating the spilled oil at Rill's feet. "The place doesn't seem built for—behind you!"

They all turned to see the two creatures entering the room, one after the other, through the same corridor they had used. The monsters must have followed them here, but why now, all of a sudden? In the flash of a moment that followed, Caymus noted that they were clawing at the ground and rearing up just the slightest bit; they were about to attack. He needed to act fast.

"Rill!" he yelled, "put it down! Now, Rill!"

With greater speed than Caymus would have imaged from his friend, Rill slammed the barrel onto the ground, covering his face and torso in splashing oil as he did so. Then, in the next minute, he was out of the way, diving back behind the bowl.

"Be'Var!" Caymus didn't wait to see if Be'Var had heard him before he closed his eyes and felt for his master's presence in the barrel of stone oil. It wasn't there. A quick scan of the room found that the master of the Conflagration had instead placed his mind into the bowl itself, still almost completely filled with stone oil. A flame was already taking shape within it, already growing in intensity.

Caymus latched on to the flame, skittering atop the pool of oil, which had already cascaded into dozens of conduits into the Conflagration. He chose one at random, wrapped his conscious self around it, and squeezed. He felt the rush of power through him, felt it pour into the oil, heard the fire roar with fury, felt the heat of it on his skin.

Then, Milo was there, and the flame leapt out, streaming at the leftmost creature, striking it like a blazing spear in the face. Caymus's eyes were closed, but he could hear it emanate a scream that could only have been born from the most severe pain.

It was working. It was actually working!

They had not, however, had surprise on their side as they had hoped. While the creature on the left was held back, struggling against the combined power of the three men, the other was advancing quickly—too quickly. Somewhere, past the sound of the flames, Caymus heard a deep voice cry out in pain, followed by the sound of a body falling to the floor, and he knew that Merkan had opened his wound trying to get into the creature's path. Caymus opened his eyes and saw that the awful claws and teeth were going straight for the prone mitre, that they would be digging into him in a mere moment.

Things seemed to move slowly, then. He saw the lance of fire, which seemed to grow like some living thing out of the bowl of oil before striking out at the creature farthest from them. He noticed that it wasn't as arrow-straight as he had thought; rather, it wavered back and forth by perhaps a hand's width on the way to its target. It reminded him of the river that nourished the village where he grew up; it, too, sometimes wavered in its path toward the sea, depending on what the winter snowfall had been like. If the waters were strong enough, it would sometimes even get split in two by a small hill near the coast.

Without making a conscious decision—as instinct!—Caymus shifted his consciousness again. He pulled away from the conduit, but he left a portion his being behind to keep the flame burning. The rest, he placed directly in the path of the lance, turning his own mind into a massive obstacle, into that hill that split the river.

The lance of flame parted around him, and the resulting second stream of fire struck out at the legs of the charging creature, making it stumble, and then forcing it backward. The original portion of the lance, however, veered off to the left, moving away from the creature they had already targeted and instead hitting the wall just below one of the triangular holes. Carefully, Caymus repositioned himself. He felt as though he were trying to keep his balance on a narrow beam, shifting himself, and the resulting streams of fire, again and again until both finally struck true, forcing the creatures backward.

As he watched both monsters slowly backing away, he wrapped the conduit again, squeezing the flow of the Conflagration with all his might. He wasn't certain how long they'd already kept up their effort, so fierce was his concentration, but by now the fiery lances glowed with a brilliant red.

In the next moment, the trial was over. Caymus was amazed to see the creatures seem to crouch, then to suddenly pass bodily through the ground beneath their feet until they were gone. In the next moment, Caymus let go of the conduit and brought his consciousness back to himself. The currents of air that had formed the lances slowly dissipated, and Caymus could feel Be'Var pinching off the conduits one by one, snuffing out the flames.

They were all gasping for breath. "There are vents in the ceiling," said Milo, holding himself up against one of the large bowls, "that should let new air back in, but I'd suggest that Be'Var fixes up Merkan again and we get out of this particular room, eh?"

In short order, Merkan's leg was closed up and the five of them, having caught their breaths, found themselves making their way back to the meeting hall and the Center of Otvia.

"All right," said Be'Var, with more than a hint of exasperation in his voice, "which of you did that thing, splitting the flames up?" He looked back and forth between Caymus and Milo. "I was sure one of you would be bragging about it by now."

Milo burst out laughing. "I thought *you* did that!" he said.

They both turned and looked at Caymus, who smiled self-consciously and shrugged. "It just seemed..." he paused, looking for the right words, "like it needed to be done."

"Ever do that before?" said Be'Var.

Caymus shook his head. "Never."

"Mind telling me how you knew to do it?"

Caymus had been wondering the same thing, but he hadn't yet come up with an explanation that he was really happy with. "There's this river that runs a few miles north of Woodsea, the town where I grew up. It's the same one that goes through the southern part of Saleri Forest. They call it 'The Wandering River' because it sometimes changes course, depending on how strong the water's flowing that year. I was thinking of this little hill that sometimes ends up cutting it right in two and...it just felt right," he eventually said.

Be'Var nodded, and he didn't ask any more questions. The answer, apparently, was satisfactory.

When they reached the circular wall that the creatures had been trying to get into, Merkan asked the others to stand back, then he closed his eyes and pounded with his fist three times against the stone surface. A moment later, Caymus was amazed to hear a tone, like a long, sad note played by a lonely violin, emanate from the rock itself. As the note played, a square doorway that was a few heads taller than Merkan appeared before them. Merkan pulled at a large handle that had formed in the structure, and the door opened wide.

Caymus looked in and gasped. He had been expecting that their task had been to rescue a few dozen, maybe a hundred, trapped mitre. Instead, inside the huge, well-lit chamber, the weary, frightened faces of at least a thousand souls looked back at them.

Be'Var clapped a hand on Caymus's shoulder. "You did good today, boy."

Caymus pushed a smile past the disbelief on his face. It was the single nicest thing the master had ever said to him.

Chapter 9

Gwenna could feel the tension collecting in her neck and jaw as she watched the velox down below. The large, mountain creature reminded her of a goat, but it was half again as large and had three curved horns growing out of its head: one on either side, the other in the center, and all three curving forward to dangerous-looking points. It was a great, shaggy thing with brown fur that was long enough to reach the ground in some places. As it approached the edge of the water, she forced her jaw to unclench and took a slow, steadying breath, all the while holding the nock of the arrow against the bowstring at her waist.

Milo leaned forward and whispered behind her ear. "Don't draw yet," he said. "Wait until it starts drinking. It won't be able to hear as well with all the sloshing."

Gwenna nodded her understanding. She and Milo had been watching the small pool of water—it was shallow and barely three feet across—that they'd found tucked away in a small ravine above the Otvian encampment for what felt like hours. Milo had said that velox made their homes in this rocky terrain, and that if they waited long enough, one of them was bound to turn up here. Now, here one stood, approaching the pool.

A small amount of frustration took hold in Gwenna's gut as the velox stopped, still several feet from the edge of the water, and looked about. It didn't seem frightened or tense though, and the eyes didn't linger in their direction, and so she remained still, kept quiet, waited.

As she waited, Gwenna gently tested her bowstring, drawing it back ever so slightly to feel the tension in the weapon. The bow had belonged to a mitre child who had not survived the assault of the last week. Gwenna had recently acted on her impulse to ask Milo to teach her the bow, and when the child's father had learned that one of their saviors wanted to learn to shoot, he had presented it to her in thanks for all she and her friends had done.

Indeed, there had been so very much to do in the two days since the men had enacted their mad scheme to drive off the insects. The boys had mostly helped with rebuilding parts of the city. She, Bridget and the matron had spent long hours tending to the sick, while Be'Var dealt with their wounds. Dozens of mitre had been injured by fangs and claws in the attack, and many of the wounds had begun to fester, so they'd had no lack of patients in the last forty-eight hours.

In the end, she'd found the occupation all-too-familiar, and when Milo had found her this morning, tired and depressed, he had insisted she come hunting with him, both to give her a chance to practice her archer skills, and just to give her a break from it all. She'd been grateful for both the respite and for the instruction, short though it was: the two of them had spent barely an hour taking practice shots before they'd come out to watch the pool.

Gwenna realized that she'd been holding her breath, and she exhaled quietly. The velox was moving again. As the animal dropped its head to drink, she looked to Milo, who nodded slowly. Moving as quietly as she could, she raised the bow to shoulder-level, took aim, and pulled her bowstring tight, bringing the tip of her index finger to the corner of her mouth as she'd been taught. Milo had said that the heart was usually the best place to land an arrow but that velox had unusually thick ribs and so her best target was the neck. When she believed her aim correct, allowing just enough extra height for the arrow's descent, she let her fingers fall open, loosing her arrow. She also winced slightly as the bowstring scraped past her forearm.

The arrow flew in the right direction, but it struck the ground considerably short of her target. Gwenna watched with frustration—and some amusement—as the velox raised its head to watch the projectile as it skittered across the ground, passed underneath its shaggy belly, and landed in a clump of dry-looking brush. The beast tensed its legs, preparing to run, but before it could move Milo had already loosed a second arrow which plunged into the creature's neck.

Eyes wide, the velox reared up and, with a bleating, gurgling sound, ran in the other direction. Faster than Gwenna could believe, Milo was up, dashing down the rocky slope to give chase. Gwenna considered following after him, but she wasn't nearly so sure-footed as he. Instead, she followed the along the edge of the ravine, hoping she'd be able to keep up that way instead.

As she ran, Gwenna rubbed her forearm, cursing aloud. Milo had told her a number of times that it was important to rotate her left arm slightly inward when taking aim, lest the joint of the elbow find itself in the path of the bowstring. She wondered just how much the mistake had cost her in terms of accuracy.

She scurried as fast as she dared across the rocky landscape, trying to avoid the stones that looked as though they might shift or skid under her feet and picking her way past small bushes whose sharp-looking thorns warned of certain injury should she fail to avoid them. When she looked up from her feet, she could just see Milo dashing across the landscape, jumping over rocks and bushes alike about ten yards below and several dozen yards ahead of her. His blue clothing stood out against the reddish-brown of the Greatstones, flying over the landscape as though it wasn't even tethered to the ground.

She wondered if Bridget would have been able to keep up with him. Bridget was lither than she, had longer legs, and had always beaten her in their little races around Flamehearth Mission. Gwenna frowned, thinking of her. The two of them had argued that morning, just before she'd left with Milo. Her friend seemed to think that she was treating Caymus unfairly, that she was leading him to believe she wanted to be with him, despite the fact that she didn't seem to really have those kinds of feelings. "I know you like him, Gwen," she'd said, angrily, "but you don't like him *that* way, and it's not fair for you to make him think you do. You can't do that to men. Do you want to end up a lonely spinster when you're old?"

It had been that word, "spinster," that had bothered Gwenna, though she couldn't explain why. She did like Caymus, liked his rich, full voice, the broadness of his arms and the pleasing contours of his face, even though that face sometimes only displayed frustration and contemplation for hours on end. She liked the intensity of his eyes after he'd decided on some dangerous course of action. She really wasn't sure that she didn't have romantic feelings for him; she just didn't feel like she wanted the relationship between the two of them to develop any further than the flirty playfulness they now enjoyed.

Bridget didn't understand. She saw the world through the eyes of a maiden, measuring each boy she met as a possible future husband. Gwenna just didn't see things the same way. She'd become a permanent fixture of Flamehearth Mission on her thirteenth year, and this was the first real adventure, the first real freedom she'd experienced in a very long time. She didn't want to think so hard about the future when she was just starting to really enjoy the present. She was hunting velox with an air priest at the top of the Greatstone Mountains! What other wonders might be in store for her?

Still, maybe Bridget was right. Maybe she should let Caymus be closer to her, or perhaps put him at arm's length, if only so as to avoid hurting him, or giving him the wrong idea.

Flames, but why had the word "spinster" upset her so?

She was still thinking about Bridget and her hurtful words when she crossed a short ridge and saw Milo kneeling over the red-stained velox, about fifteen feet below her. The way down to him was steep, but she thought she could manage it if she chose her footing carefully, so she slung her bow over her shoulder and started down.

She kept one eye on Milo as she picked her way downward. His bow lay next to him on the ground. He was bent over the velox, his hand resting on its neck. She could see from the occasional twitch of muscle that the animal was still barely alive. As she reached the bottom of the ravine, she saw that Milo's eyes were closed and that his lips were moving, whispering some soft words she couldn't hear. The sight intrigued her: Milo usually exhibited such a light and carefree attitude to everything, so this solemn moment seemed out of character. She considered saying as much, but then she decided against it and instead sat down on a nearby rock and waited for him to acknowledge her.

After a few minutes, when the velox's breast no longer rose and fell, Milo raised his eyes. "Your stance was good," he said, "and you remembered to hold the string with three fingers instead of two, but I think we'll need to work on your aim a little."

Gwenna smiled. "I'm sorry," she said. "I forgot to move my arm, like you said."

Milo's dismissed the thought with a small wave of his hand. "Don't worry about that," he said, then he leaned back and shifted from a kneeling to a sitting position. "The most that's going to happen there is that your arm is going to sting for a while." He looked pointedly at her, so she lifted her left hand to show him the red patch that was developing on her forearm. He smiled. "Smarts, doesn't it?"

Gwenna nodded, then put her arm down. "It didn't ruin the shot?" she asked.

"Nope," said Milo, "just need to spend some time working on your distances, learning just how much to raise the tip of the arrow," he illustrated by putting his hand out flat, fingers together, before him, angling it up and down slightly, "depending on how far away your target is." He put the hand away. "You'll get the hang of it." He got that impish look on his face. "And I've found that string-against-the-elbow mistake is one that people don't usually make more than once. Maybe twice."

Gwenna nodded. She could believe that; her arm still felt as though it had been slapped, and hard. "Thank you, Milo," she said, "for teaching me."

Milo beamed. "Of course!" he said, standing up and brushing himself off. "Thanks for asking! I never could get Caymus interested in the bow." He cocked an eyebrow, "and with the weight he could pull, that's a real shame."

Gwenna tilted her head. "Weight?" she asked.
Milo answered, though he was looking at the ground around them, distractedly. "Each bow has a certain weight to it, which is how much the wood resists being bent. The same arm that can lift, say fifty pounds of something off the ground can fully draw a fifty-pound bow. It's all a question of how strong you have to be to use the thing, and of how much power the arrow's going to have when it leaves the string. I'd say the one you've got there is about a twenty-five or thirty pounder. Twenty-five pounds isn't really enough to do a lot of damage to be honest, so you'll want to get a heavier bow sooner or later."
Gwenna nodded understanding, then asked, "So how many pounds is your bow, then?"
Milo stopped looking around and winked at her. "I'll never tell."
Gwenna smiled. As she stood, she asked, "Milo, what was it you were doing when I got here? You were whispering something."
Milo looked down at the fallen animal. "Saying sorry," he said. "I was apologizing for stealing all of its remaining days, for taking its last breaths so that we might have more of our own."
Gwenna thought about this, frowning. "I didn't think an air-priest could be so...melancholy."
Milo looked up at her with a knowing, and slightly sad-looking smile. "We're not, as a rule. It's something my mother taught me."
Before Gwenna could pursue that statement, Milo began his hunt for something on the ground again. "Come on," he said, "we need to find a long stick or a branch or something if we're going to get this thing back to Otvia again before the others start wondering about us."
Gwenna glanced around the immediate area. The only things she saw were rocks, dirt, and the occasional shrub or very small tree. She considered telling Milo what she thought about the chances of finding a branch around here, but instead just shrugged, smiled, and got on with it. One of the nice things about spending time with Milo was that she could feel free to just go along with the insanity. Earnestly, she began her search for the impossible object.
"That reminds me," said Milo, looking at her out of the corner of his eye, "you didn't happen to pick up the arrow you fired on your way here, did you?"
"Umm," Gwenna said, an apologetic look forming on her face. She couldn't believe she hadn't thought to retrieve it from the bush it had landed in.
Milo laughed aloud. "Don't worry about it," he said. "I guess I was always going to need to teach you how to make them yourself eventually."
Gwenna smiled, feeling better than she had in weeks. Adventure, indeed! And should couldn't think of better people to be having it with.

~~~

Caymus, wooden sword in one hand, wooden shield in the other, stood his ground under the warmth of the noon sun, prepared for a blow that he was sure was coming any moment.

"Stronger," said Merkan, not quite yelling. "Hit me stronger."

Caymus considered his situation. Merkan was trying to teach him something about swordplay, something the mitre warrior obviously felt was important, but Caymus couldn't quite understand the point he was trying to convey. Earlier, he'd seen Caymus practicing his drills while waiting for someone to give him something to do, and so had decided he would show him something of the Mael'vekian style of combat. The giant now had his own wooden sword, about twice the size of Caymus's, held horizontally so that the entire length of the faux blade faced outward, the grip held with both hands. And he wanted Caymus to hit him.

Caymus steeled himself. The only thing Caymus had figured out so far was that Mael'vekians tended not to use shields, and yet they still seemed to be able to effectively defend themselves against attacks.

With a grunt, he swung out at Merkan's side. The mitre brought his sword down and, in one fluid motion, blocked the attack and then carried the swing overhead to create his own offensive motion. Caymus brought his shield up fast and the blade bounced off of it.

Merkan held up a hand, indicating a pause. "You have not understood," he said, putting the point of his sword in the ground and leaning on it slightly. His wounded leg was healing nicely, but he still favored it somewhat. "You see attack and defend as different things, yes? Attack is the sword, defend is the shield?"

Caymus nodded, keeping the shield up in front of him, protectively. "Yes," he said. "I guess that sounds about right."

"That is a Tebrian idea," he said, "A Kepren idea. Kepren soldiers strike out with the sword, then hide behind the shield, believing it makes them safe." He lifted his sword again and stepped back a couple of paces. "Mael'vekian soldiers do both at once." He took a swing at the air. "Each movement is for both defense and attack." As he swung the sword, he pivoted it, turning the attack into an obvious block, then spun on the ball of one foot, weaving the result into another swing. To Caymus, it seemed like a dance: a single, graceful motion from which the blade occasionally emerged. He thought the motion of it was beautiful.

When Merkan stopped, he pointed at Caymus's shield. "Kepren
~~~

soldiers believe shields will save them. This is not the case. A shield is good for thwarting a rock thrown by a child, but it will not save you from a Mael'vek sword."

Caymus frowned. "Sure, you move quickly, but if I manage to block just as quickly it defends just fine."

Merkan smiled. "You think so?" The smile held not even the smallest measure of malice or mockery; Merkan was obviously trying hard to help Caymus understand this point of his. "Come," he said, stepping forward again, "I will show you." He brought his sword up, holding it parallel to the ground, pointing at Caymus. "Ready?"

Caymus brought his shield up, brought his sword hand to his side. "Ready."

Merkan made a side-swing at Caymus, which he blocked easily, though the force of the hit jarred the bones of his hand. Then, Merkan swung overhead. Again, Caymus easily blocked it, but Merkan was using more of his strength than before and Caymus could already feel his shield arm getting numb.

Three more times, Merkan attacked, and Caymus realized that the giant wasn't even trying to get past his defense but was aiming deliberately for the shield. Each time, the smack of wood against wood rattled the bones of his arm until he couldn't feel his hand. Caymus had known the mitre had been holding back from his full strength before, but he hadn't realized just how much. He wanted to parry, or even to return a strike, but there simply wasn't enough time between Merkan's attacks for him to mount a counter.

The sixth swing, which came within a moment of the first, connected directly with the very center of Caymus's shield and was so powerful that it actually knocked him back off his feet. When Caymus had shaken the stars from his eyes and was able to get his bearings again, he found he was face up on the ground with Merkan's sword at his heart. Merkan's gaze met his eyes and he nodded slightly. "Understand now?" he said.

Caymus let his body go limp, and he laughed. "My shield won't save me," he said. "I understand."

Merkan smiled, then he reached down to pull Caymus back to his feet. "Good," he said. "Shields are good for arrows and good against those who do not know how to fight properly, but if you learn to use your sword for defense also you will live longer." He then motioned to Caymus's sword, now lying on the ground a couple of feet from him. "You may want to try a larger weapon also, considering your mitre blood."

Caymus, who had been reaching for the sword, stopped short. He turned sharply to Merkan. "My what?"

Merkan gave him a quizzical look. "Your mitre blood. The blood of the mitre that runs in your veins."

Caymus picked up the sword very slowly, dragging the point through the dirt as he lifted it. "What makes you think I have mitre blood?" he finally asked.

"You...are large for a human," said Merkan, his head cocked slightly. "You have large arms and a strong face. We all," he motioned all around him, as though to indicate all of Otvia, "assumed that you have mitre in your ancestry, at least in small amount." He gave Caymus a strange look, as though he didn't understand the confusion. "Did these come from another source?"

Caymus was dumbstruck by the thought. Merkan was right, of course, that he'd always been exceptionally large, even as an infant. His mother and father had not been overly tall and so people had always questioned his parentage, but he'd never had any doubt that he was anything but a regular human man, albeit a very big one. Could Merkan be right? Now that he thought about it, ever since he'd arrived here, he'd found something familiar in the faces of the mitre. Could it be that the familiarity had something to do with recognition of his own features? Could some fraction of himself actually consist of mitre blood?

The thought was too strange for him to pursue further, at least for now. He changed the subject, trying his best to pick up the thread of the previous conversation. "Do all Mael'vekian soldiers fight the way you do?" he asked.

Merkan exhaled slightly, as though glad the exchange was over. He was leaning on his sword again. "Not all," he said, "but many. Mael'vek's way of war is stronger, fiercer than Kepren's. It takes longer to learn, though. Kepren's soldiers are more numerous, but not as well trained. Mael'vek soldiers are more capable, but there will never be as many of them."

Caymus's knowledge of the two cities was not great. He knew they had been in a de-facto state of war for a long time, that their last great battle had been for a city that stood between them. He didn't know how large the battle had been, nor even the name of the city. Mael'vek had won the fight, but had been unable to press any further, so now the boundary between the nations was drawn just north of that battlefield. From what he'd heard from Gwenna and Bridget, modern Kepren was home to many refugees of that city, which had never properly recovered from the conflict.

The idea of an Otvian mitre—any mitre, for that matter—fighting for the nation of Mael'vek seemed strange to him. He didn't know much about standing armies, but he knew they were generally comprised of citizens of the nation the army protected. His mind turned back to a mitre named Kormen, whom he'd known growing up in his hometown of Woodsea. Kormen, the first mitre Caymus had ever met, had appeared in town about the same time as Caymus had been learning about the shipyards of Krin's Point. After Kormen had found somebody willing to take him on, he had become an apprentice at his father's drydock.

Kormen and Caymus hadn't been close by any stretch of the imagination, but they'd always been on good terms and so Kormen had been happy to explain to him what he was doing there. That was the first time Caymus had learned about the mitre way of apprenticing in foreign lands.

Most mitre never left their underground tunnels and caverns, preferring their lives of quiet isolation, but there were some who had wanderlust in their hearts and who received permission to leave their cities for a time. Those who did so were asked by their people to learn some skill, trade, or other ability that he or she might bring back to the city at the journey's end, be it something practical like carpentry or something more artistic like glassblowing. The relationship usually benefited both parties. The mitre benefited from the knowledge brought back to them and most humans were eager to have someone the size and temperament of a mitre to assist them in whatever trade they picked.

Merkan had chosen to learn a warrior's arts, that he might be able to teach his brethren how to fight when he returned. The story he'd told Caymus was that he'd entered the city of Mael'vek he'd simply wandered into the first soldiers' barracks he could find and offered his services. The commander of that particular garrison had been more than happy to have a 'man of his size' on their side.

Thinking back to his time with Kormen, Caymus considered the particular trade he'd been apprenticed to, and he frowned. Knowing what he did now about the homes of the mitre, he couldn't imagine there would ever be much call for the services of a shipwright several hundred feet underground.

"Hey, you two! If you're through smacking each other for a moment, could you give me a hand?" Rill was calling down to them from some scaffolding where he had been working while they'd sparred for the last half-hour or so. The platform he stood upon was about half again the height of a mitre, and from it he was efforting a repair on a wooden contraption of some description. Caymus didn't know what the contraption was, but Rill had apparently become quite excited when he'd first set eyes on it.

The place where they were standing was several hundred yards from the main entrance to Otvia. Merkan had fetched Caymus that morning with the intent of showing him the outer workings of the city, and also to show him what Rill had been up to all morning. Caymus been quite surprised to discover the path at the edge of the encampment, hidden by fallen masonry, which wound up and around the back side of the peak from which the mitre had carved their home. After several minutes of walking along the path, they'd come to another shelf, much like the area where the encampment was built, only smaller, which was home to a huge garden where potatoes, carrots, several kinds of squash, and a few plants Caymus couldn't identify grew in the sunlight.

Caymus had marveled at it, at this parcel of farmable land the mitre had created out of the side of a mountain. Then he'd looked further up the path and found that he could see several more like it. Merkan had explained that the same abilities they used to extract oil from stone allowed them to turn barren rock into something that could sustain the planting. The only thing they needed was water, and that was where the contraption came in.

The machine consisted of a substantial length of rope, a number of gears, pulleys, and what Caymus had learned were the bladders of some goat-like creatures that lived in these mountains. The rope, which he believed to be tied into a continuous loop, emerged out of a hole in the ground that was about the same diameter as his own waist. Connected to the rope at lengths of about two feet were the bladders, which were all empty. There were a handful of gears and pulleys embedded into the rock also, but Caymus couldn't divine their purpose, not without seeing them in action.

Rill was currently holding onto one of these gears while he motioned for the two of them to come over to the scaffolding. "This thing's not all that steady," he said, "and I could really use some hands holding it in place while I knock the rest of the pegs in."

Caymus turned to Merkan, who nodded, and they both put their practice weapons down and walked to the scaffolding. "Is that all you need?" Caymus yelled up.

"I've dropped three pegs already just trying to keep my balance up here, and they keep going down the chute. If I drop any more, I'm going to have to go down and ask Ventu for another set."

Ventu was the most affable mitre Caymus had met. He spoke quickly and smiled a lot. He'd been here when Caymus and Merkan had arrived, showing Rill what he'd needed done to the mechanism at the top of the scaffolding, then he'd gone back inside, purportedly to see how the machine was looking at the other end. The machinery had been damaged during the attack; getting it fixed quickly was a priority for the residents of Otvia.

Caymus and Merkan, standing on opposite sides of the scaffolding, placed their hands on it to hold it steady. The beams were just bunches of thin wood which were tied together with twine into thick bundles and lashed into the structure before them by slightly thicker cords of rope. When Caymus put his hands to a couple of the lengths of wood, he heard them creak and felt the whole thing flex. Rill was right: it wasn't steady at all.

"Got it?" Rill shouted down at them.

"Got it," Caymus said, hoping it was true.

Rill nodded down at them and got to work. Caymus watched bemusedly as he started connecting the gears together with their anchor points in the wall next to him. Rill's hands moved quickly as he fed the rope through the pulleys and small protrusions, knocking them into place with small, wooden pegs. Caymus wondered if the holes in the ground had been created using the same method Merkan had employed in creating the hollow that had hidden Rill during the rescue attempt. Another hole, this one large enough that he could probably climb through it, existed in the wall near his shoulder. Merkan had told him it was a chute that they used to send the food they gathered up here down to cold storerooms below.

Caymus looked up at Rill. "Are you sure you know what you're doing up there?" he said, in a playful tone.

"Yeah, yeah," replied Rill. "Ventu showed me what to do. Just keep it steady is all. I'm just about done." Caymus was a little surprised at how quickly Rill's fingers moved as he put the pieces of the watering machine back together. His friend seemed confident and relaxed as he worked, and there was no suggestion of hesitation or indecision in the placing of parts. He just seemed to know where they went. He even had a smile on his face.

"You're enjoying this," Caymus said, "aren't you?"

Rill's grin broadened. He kneeled and began fishing for something in a small pail at his feet. "You know, between learning the various ways to light things on fire, fighting nearly indestructible monsters, and fixing a broken machine, I'll take the machine any day." He found whatever it was he was looking for and stood up again. "The rest of it, you can keep."

"You mean it's less dangerous?" Caymus asked.

"Ha!" Rill was keeping one side of the rope taught with one hand and holding one of the gears tight to it with the other. "You've got your hands on this platform. Does it feel safe to you?"

Caymus shrugged. "Fair enough."

"It is," Rill continued, now anchoring the gear into the wall by banging a couple of pegs into small holes, "a whole lot more interesting though. You should see the other gardens. They all use risers like this one." He indicated the mechanical contraption he was working on. "There are four gardens in all, and they all get water from the same source, and the machine slowly turns all day to make sure it gets distributed evenly." He looked down at Caymus, his eyes wide with a mixture of excitement and wonder. "They only have to wind the mechanism once a week to keep it running. Ventu built it, and he keeps the whole system running by himself!" He shook his head with wide-eyed wonder, then he turned back to his work and started hammering again.

Caymus was enjoying the look in his friend's eyes. Too often during scores of lessons and practices he'd known Rill to be quiet and sullen, to be constantly trying to find something to occupy his mind that didn't concern the ways of the Conflagration and almost always getting in trouble for it. "Well," he shouted up, "you certainly seem to have a knack for it."

Rill was fitting another gear in place. "Ventu told me that Kepren has a corps of engineers that travels with the army, keeping the catapults and such working. That's where he did his apprenticeship, where he learned to do this stuff." He looked down at Caymus again with a sly grin. "I was thinking I might ask him for a recommendation before we leave."

Caymus wondered at the idea. He considered what he knew about his friend, about the way he fit in with organized groups such as a circle of disciples. He had to admit, he was skeptical. "You think you'd be alright in the army?" he said.

"Corps of Engineers!" Rill shouted back, with no small amount of triumph in his voice. He then got back to work, carefully aligning the various pieces in just the right way. Caymus didn't know much about such things, but the machinery looked as though it was more or less together at this point, and he wondered how much more there could be to do.

As he watched, he heard a slight fluttering sound behind him and felt a small presence. He turned to see Perra standing near the edge of the shelf. The area was ringed with large stones, all about waist high to Caymus, and she stood quietly at the apex of one of them. "Hello, Perra," he said, more to himself than anyone else.

Merkan looked at him quizzically. "This animal is your friend?" he asked.

Caymus laughed. "I suppose so," he said, "though Perra's more like a friend of a friend." He turned and looked over his shoulder at the path that led down to the entrance to Otvia. "Speaking of which, if she's around then he can't be far behind."

As though summoned by his words, Milo came meandering around the corner, waving when he saw that Caymus had noticed him. He had something lifted up on his shoulder, and when he turned to navigate a curve in the path Caymus could see that he and Gwenna were carrying the body of some animal, suspended by its feet from a large stick or branch between them. It seemed that Gwenna's first outing as a hunter had been successful. Caymus enjoyed a feeling of satisfaction at the thought.

A few steps behind them came a mitre whom Caymus hadn't met

before. He was old, with weathered, wrinkled skin—the top of his head resembled a white walnut—and a slight hunch in his gait. Merkan had told him that Otvia's leadership consisted of a council of elders. Caymus wondered if this might be one of them.

"Hello, Caymus," said Milo, when he got within a few paces of him. "Gu'ruk told us to bring the beast up this way," he indicated the old mitre that was following them, "but he didn't mention you were up here, too." The three of them stopped, looking up the length of the wobbly scaffolding and its lone occupant.

"What's Rill doing?" said Gwenna, rather matter-of-factly.

"He's fixing the water-raising machine," said Caymus, looking up too. "At least, he thinks he is."

"Ha, ha," said Rill, testing the tension on the rope. "Let's see you do it." In response, Caymus gave the scaffolding a bit of a shake. "Hey!" yelled Rill, his eyes wide as he crouched down to keep his balance. When Caymus stopped, he looked over the side at him.

"Not funny?" said Caymus.

Rill made a show of putting on a big sigh, then stood up and got back to what he was doing. "Not so much," he said.

They all grinned at each other. The old mitre that Milo had referred to as Gu'ruk tapped Milo on the shoulder. "Over here," he said. He motioned Milo and Gwenna over to the large hole in the rock wall next to Caymus's shoulder. His voice was gravelly, but it was deep and rich with a baritone sound that Caymus found he liked. "Just place the velox in there."

Milo blinked at him. "What, just..." he nodded in the direction of the void in the wall, "just dump it in the hole?"

Gu'ruk smiled. It was a warm smile that held no malice or mocking, and it made some of the creases in his face disappear. "Yes, my friend. Just dump it in the hole."

Milo looked back at Gwenna, who shrugged, and the two of them moved forward to stand in front of the chute. They then put the animal —a velox, Gu'ruk had said—down and untied it from their improvised carrier. Upon closer inspection, Caymus could see that it wasn't one large stick but rather a bundle of small sticks tied together, the same as those that constituted the bones of the scaffold he was holding steady for Rill. Once the velox was untied, they lifted it together and placed it, headfirst, in the hole.

The interior wall of the chute was nearly as smooth as glass, and before any of them knew it, the beast was gone, sliding down to some chamber below where, presumably, it would be stored or prepared by someone waiting on that end.

"That felt weird," said Milo, scrunching his face up and looking around at everyone.

Caymus nodded. "It looked a bit weird," he said.

"Good," said Milo, "not just me, then. I get worried when it's just me." He looked up at Rill, who was hammering away at something. "Does he know what he's doing?"

"He seems to think so," Caymus said, following his glance. "I asked the same thing not five minutes ago, funny enough." He turned to Gwenna, who was picking up the sticks they had used to carry the velox. "It looks like you did well today," he said.

Gwenna smiled and shook her head. "Milo got it," she said. "I took the first shot, but I didn't even come close." She glanced over at Milo, then back at Caymus. "I've got a lot of practicing to do."

Milo put a hand on her shoulder. "Early days, yet," he said.

Caymus was delighted that Gwenna was learning to shoot. It, of course, meant that she would be able to hunt with Milo for food for the group when necessary, even to protect herself at a distance; more than that, however, he liked the idea of her being able to take care of herself. He couldn't quite explain to himself why, but it made her more attractive, as though the mere act of learning the new skill had added something physically beautiful to her.

As he stood there, considering Gwenna, he felt a large hand on his shoulder. He turned his head slightly to see the old mitre whom Milo had called Gu'ruk. "You are Caymus, yes? Be'Var's student?"

Caymus frowned slightly, but he nodded. "I am," he said. He inclined his head, "Gu'ruk, right?"

Gu'ruk seemed pleased that Caymus knew his name. His face split into a satisfied grin. "Yes!" he proclaimed. "Yes I am."

For a moment, the old mitre just stood there, smiling at Caymus and looking him up and down, appraisingly. Caymus felt a little uncomfortable, as though he were a horse being considered for purchase. Eventually, Gu'ruk leaned in conspiratorially. "I do not suppose," he said, his voice lowered considerably, "that I could see that mark that is on your hand?"

If Caymus had felt uncomfortable before, now he was becoming suspicious. This mitre, whom he didn't remember meeting before now, either wanted something from him or knew something that he hadn't shared yet. Still, he couldn't see any reason to actually distrust the old man, and so, keeping his left hand steady on the scaffold so as to prevent Rill's untimely demise, he offered the right one up to Gu'ruk.

Gu'ruk leaned down and examined the mark of the flame and the sword, squinting his eyes and pursing his lips for several moments, after which he abruptly straightened and gave a curt nod. "Thank you," was all he said before he turned around and walked back down the path to the main entrance.

Caymus watched Gu'ruk as he left, and once the hunched figure had turned a corner and vanished from sight, he put his hand back on the scaffold and looked to the others, who seemed as confused by the encounter as he was. "What was that all about?" he said.

Merkan smiled a broad smile. "Gu'ruk is our Relic Keeper," he said. "I saw that he was speaking with Be'Var earlier this day." He shrugged. "Be'Var must have told him about your mark."

"Do you think he knows something about it?" said Caymus.

Merkan shrugged. "I do not know." He looked to the point where the old mitre had disappeared. "Relic Keepers spend much time alone. They are solitary for most of their lives. Their thoughts are hard to know."

Caymus thought about the interaction. He wondered if he should have said something while Gu'ruk had been inspecting the mark. Between this encounter and the one the previous day when Rill had shown him the symbol on the door to the Ritual Room, he felt suddenly like there was an awful lot that people weren't telling him. He was beginning to get a bit frustrated about that.

"Is Rill nearly ready up there?" For a moment, Caymus didn't know where the voice had come from. It seemed faint, as though from a great distance. When it asked the question again, he realized it was coming from the holes in the ground. Caymus figured it was probably Ventu, the mitre engineer, checking on the progress of his new student, though he had to admit he didn't know the mitre's voice well enough to be sure.

Rill shouted down. "Tell him I just need another minute!"

Caymus relayed the message, though he felt a bit foolish yelling down a hole at someone he couldn't see. When he raised his eyes again, everyone was looking at him as though having the same thought. Their mitre companion didn't seem to think there was anything strange going on, but Gwenna was hiding a grin with her hand and Caymus recognized Milo's face as the one he wore when he was trying very hard to keep from laughing.

Rill was as good as his word. Within a few moments he put his tools down. "Done!" he exclaimed, a look of immense satisfaction on his face. He turned down to look at the group below him, singling out Caymus. "Tell him to test it?" he asked.

Caymus shouted the request down the hole. He wondered just how loud he had to yell to be heard at the bottom; he didn't even know how deep the hole went, which probably had something to do with why he felt silly doing it. "All right!" the voice replied. "Stand back!"

With that, a slight clattering sound emanated up the hole and the rope began moving. Caymus watched as the bladders slowly rose up, were fed by gears and pulleys through a few twists and turns, and then descended again. The purpose of the twists and turns escaped him until about a minute later when bladders started emerging with actual water in them. When the full bladders went through the system, they were handled in such a way that they got upended, just before they reached the very top, into yet another hole that Caymus hadn't noticed before. This hole was only a few inches in diameter, and it was only the complicated way in which the rope moved the bladders that caused them to be completely emptied before they passed the opening. Then his eye caught a slight shimmer by his feet, and he looked down to see that water was seeping out of the wall through well-hidden channels in the stone and being carried along the ground in shallow grooves to be distributed among the plants.

Caymus was surprised by the artfulness of it all. The machine that raised the water was rickety and clanky and anything but subtle, but the actual channels and grooves in the ground were so slight that he hadn't even noticed them until that moment. Still, the whole machination was so effective that not a single drop of liquid appeared to be wasted. As much as Caymus had always been impressed by what Be'Var and the other masters could do with flame, he was just as impressed by what the mitre could do with stone and earth.

Caymus felt the scaffold shaking and looked up to see Rill climbing down. When his friend was a few feet off the ground, he jumped the rest of the way and dusted off his hands. He wore a look of absolute triumph on his face. "Perfect!" he said, looking at both Caymus and Merkan. "Thanks for the help."

They each let go of the scaffolding. "Any time, Rill," said Caymus, looking up at the still-churning contraption. "Glad it worked out in the end."

Rill turned to address the assembled group. "That's all Ventu wanted me to do up here," he said. "Shall we head back down?"

Caymus looked to Merkan. "Are we done?"

Merkan nodded. "We are."

"Great," said Milo. "I'm starving!" The air priest took off at a jog down the trail, leading the way as usual.

"He makes a good point," said Gwenna, who hooked her arm around Caymus's waist, and began pulling him down the path. Caymus was all-too-happy to follow along. Since the trail was only wide enough for two humans—or a single mitre—Rill, and then Merkan, followed behind them.

"Hey, Caymus," Rill said, "did Be'Var ever find you today?"

Caymus looked over his shoulder. "No, was he looking for me?"

"Yeah," said Rill, "something about that weapon and circle symbol on that door. He didn't say it was really important or anything, but he was wondering if I'd seen you."

"Thanks. I'll keep an eye out for him." Caymus thought again about that symbol, and about what it might mean. He'd never imagined he'd find any answers in Otvia, but if Be'Var had found something out, he wanted to know what it was. He frowned, wondering where in the vast network of tunnels and caverns of Otvia the master might be at that moment.

As it turned out, Caymus didn't have to search. When they reached the encampment, they found Be'Var and Matron Y'selle both sitting on some broken masonry near the main entrance. Caymus was amazed at how much cleaner the place seemed considering how badly destroyed it had been just a couple of days ago. Besides the bodies they had burned, most of the debris had now been cleaned away, too. There were no bloodstains on the ground, nor was there any other evidence that so many people had died here. No new buildings or tents had gone up yet, though. From what Caymus understood of conversations he'd overheard, the mitre of Otvia weren't planning on putting up any new structures unless people actually moved into the encampment and asked for them.

As they approached the master and matron, Caymus noticed Y'selle was holding one of Be'Var's hands in hers, and that she appeared to be saying something to him. He'd seen the two of them sitting like this more than once over the last few days, and he'd even heard Be'Var refer to the matron as "'Sella" at one point. It was becoming apparent to him that the two of them had some history before her arrival at the Temple. He wondered how far back that history went, and how they'd first met.

His ponderings were cut short, however, when Be'Var saw them coming. In a flash, he'd stood and was marching over to the approaching group. His expression displayed an unusual intensity. He wasn't angry—an angry Be'Var was a familiar sight, and it didn't look like this—but Caymus was beginning to wish the master had found him earlier in the day after all.

"Boy!" he said when they were in earshot. "Where have you been all day?"

Caymus removed his arm from Gwenna's shoulder to put his hands in front of him in a surrendering posture. "I was up at the first shelf, up there," he said, pointing behind them. "I didn't know you were looking for me until a few minutes ago."

Be'Var seemed about to say something, but before he could, Merkan stepped forward and offered him a small bow, his hand on his chest. "I am sorry, Master Be'Var," he said, "I asked Caymus to spar with me, that I might teach him Mael'vekian sword arts."

Caymus detected a glare in his master's gaze at the mention of Mael'vek, but it only appeared for an instant. After that, Be'Var's eyes softened, and he rubbed his fingers on his chin and nodded. "Yes," he said. "I suppose that probably is a good use of his time." He put his hand to his chest and bowed back to the mitre. "Thank you, Merkan. You'll probably end up having saved his life on some future occasion."

Merkan seemed pleased by this, but before he could say anything else, Be'Var strode up, grabbed Caymus by the elbow, and started hauling him toward the entrance to Otvia. "Come on," he said as he grabbed, "things to show and tell you, boy."

Caymus looked back at Gwenna as he let himself be pulled away, an apologetic look in his eyes and a shrug on his shoulders. She smiled back at him and mouthed the words, "Good luck."

"The mitre of Otvia," began Be'Var, letting go of Caymus's arm, but still leading him, "in addition to learning all kinds of skills from the world around them, also are collectors of information and artifacts. One of their number is always assigned to keep watch over these items. This mitre spends most of his time trying to understand them."

"Gu'ruk," said Caymus. They were passing through the mountain entrance into Otvia now. "The Relic Keeper?"

Be'Var turned to Caymus, surprised. "You know him?"

Caymus nodded. "I met him less than an hour ago. He wanted to see the mark on my hand."

Be'Var stopped abruptly, putting out an arm to stop Caymus also. He was wearing that intense look again. "And what did he say?"

Caymus shook his head. "Nothing. He just thanked me and walked away."

"Hmmm," said Be'Var, who began walking again. "I'm guessing he knows something very interesting indeed." He slapped Caymus on the shoulder. "Come on," he said, "let's go find Gu'ruk. This time of day, I expect he'll be near the Center, eating with everyone else."

Caymus got moving, thinking that he hadn't remembered to eat breakfast that morning and that a meal sounded good. After a moment, however, it was his turn to stop. "Master Be'Var," he said, "I was sparring with Merkan..." He grinned. "Actually, I was getting knocked to the ground by Merkan when he casually mentioned he thinks I might be part mitre."

Be'Var seemed to consider this. He stepped back, folded his arms, and scratched his chin while he looked Caymus up and down. "Hmph," he said. "Yes, I suppose it's possible. Hadn't considered it before, but it would explain a couple of things." He took his finger from his chin and pointed it at Caymus. "You remember, during your trial, when the Lords of the Conflagration told you that you wouldn't be a master?"

Caymus nodded. "Kind of hard to forget that."

"Do you remember the reason they gave?"

"Yes," Caymus said, "something about a taint to my soul. I didn't—" He stopped, his eyes widening. "You don't think—"

"It's possible," said Be'Var again, in a more thoughtful voice. "Mitre are earth worshipers, without exception. It would make sense that the Lords would have a bit of a problem with you if you had a drop or two of dirt-lover in you." Then, Be'Var reached forward, put a hand on Caymus's shoulder, and looked him in the eye with a slight smile. "Let's find out what Gu'ruk has to say about it, shall we?"

Caymus, not quite sure what to do next, considering the fact that his world was spinning around him, just nodded and allowed himself to be led.

~~~

Several hours later, after a hearty meal of potatoes, carrots, and velox meat, Caymus found himself walking down a long, steep corridor in what he imagined could only be the very bowels of Otvia, following a path down which Gu'ruk had been leading both him and Be'Var for over an hour.

Their first destination had been the Center, which had amazed Caymus even more than it had the first time he'd lain eyes on it. There wasn't anything special about the stone archways, domes, or vestibules of the Center, nor were the stone-crafted workshops, merchant areas, or gathering places that littered the edges of the great hall any more interesting than any of the other structures in city. It was the light that was so amazing. Somehow, the Otvians had channeled sunlight all the way from the surface of the mountain down to this huge chamber. The light wasn't particularly bright, would never burn one's skin on a hot day, but in the dark realm of the mitre, it seemed as though the sun itself had taken an interest and had wandered underground for a visit. A few small trees, dotting the ground here and there, testified as to just how much light actually made its way down.

They had then taken some tunnels through several storerooms. They'd even gone past a room that was pierced from floor to ceiling by a machine very like the one on which Rill had been working all day, though Caymus didn't know if it was the same one. Sometime after passing that room, they had started down a single, long tunnel that spiraled at a steep angle, farther and farther downward.

"Otvia is unique among the clans of mitre people," Gu'ruk was saying as he led them down the passage, a softly glowing torch in his hand. Caymus realized, for the first time, that the old mitre wore more clothing
~~~

than his brethren. Long, dark sleeves and a tattered, blue gown were draped over his limbs. A blackish-red cape dropped down the length of his back from his neck. "We are the ones that keep the relics. We are the ones that learn from them and keep them safe." Caymus couldn't see Gu'ruk's face, but he heard a great sigh emanate from it. "We used to, at least. When I was young, we had several Relic Keepers among us, but now there is only me."

The passage took the occasional sharp turn, left or right. There was something odd about the way Gu'ruk took those turns, something unusual about his stance, but Caymus couldn't put words to it. "Did something happen to the others?" he asked.

Gu'ruk waved a hand at him. "No, no," he said, "nothing like that. The young ones simply have no interest in the relics anymore. They would rather build machines or play with swords, like Ventu and Merkan." He sighed again. "I fear I am becoming a relic myself."

"Children!" said Be'Var, his tone both annoyed and a little playful. "They have no appreciation for the ways of their elders."

Gu'ruk chuckled, his voice echoing through the passage. "It is the way of things to change," he said, "and the way of the young to change with them." He paused for a moment, though he didn't break his stride. "Though I fear that when I am gone there will nobody left to care for the relics, to know them and their histories. I have had to spend many hours of late, therefore, cataloging their uses."

Caymus was starting to like Gu'ruk. He had a better grasp of the language of humans than most other mitre, and was able to speak more complicated sentences, and that made him easier to understand. The three of them had eaten together, and Caymus had asked many questions of him, a fact which Be'Var had seemed to approve of.

He had learned, for instance, that Gu'ruk knew exactly what the mark on the back of his hand was, but that he hadn't wanted to tell him at the time, insisting that he wanted to show him, and that the showing would necessitate this trip into the dark underbelly of Otvia. He'd told them that the room he was taking them to Otvia's Vault, though it didn't have the guards and locks that such a name generally signified. The Vault held many items, not the least of which were books and scrolls that kept a historical record of the mitre. Caymus had been genuinely interested in seeing the contents of such a room; this had delighted Gu'ruk greatly.

There had also been the subject of Caymus's ancestry. Once he'd told Gu'ruk what Merkan had said earlier that day about his having mitre blood, the wrinkled face had burst into a wide grin. "Of *course* you do," he'd said. "I'm half blind, and I can see that much!"

Caymus wasn't sure about what to make of the revelation. He had no idea how it could be, that part—even a small part—of his ancestry could be mitre. Considering how obvious his lineage seemed to the people of Otvia, he thought that the ratio must be fairly high: one eighth, at least, if not one quarter. Again and again, he kept thinking back to his childhood, trying to remember any detail that might shed some light on the mystery. Could his father have not been his real father, or his mother not his real mother? Neither of them seemed large enough to possibly carry such a heritage.

One day, he would be home again; on that day, he hoped he would find some answers.

Thinking of home, of his mother, alone in the house that his parents had once shared, made him sad. He wondered when he would get a chance to see her again. He'd thought he might return to Woodsea for a visit once he'd past his final trial, but that obviously hadn't happened. Events seemed to be conspiring to keep him from home for as long as possible. And those events, he knew, were likely to continue on for quite some time.

At least they seemed to be making progress. They had learned a great deal in the past week, not the least of which was the fact that the creatures they were fighting had some ability to pass through the element of earth and that the ability seemed contingent on there being some strong place of worship nearby. It still didn't make sense, though. He thought back to the moment when he had forked his and Milo's lance of fire in two, thought of the way that the insect creatures had managed to pass through the stone of the floor to safety. If they had been able to pass through the earthen floor, why hadn't they used the same ability to pass through the rest of the walls of Otvia, or to capture and kill the mitre behind the door to the Center?

Perhaps Be'Var was right. Maybe the creatures vanishing through the ground wasn't something they were consciously choosing but rather something that was being forced upon them? Could that be some outside agency working on them? Maybe that was just how that particular element worked?

He was glad, either way, that they finally had a way to fight the creatures, should they encounter more of them. He knew they'd been lucky this time, though. There was no doubt in his mind that it had been the density of the stone oil—the fact that only a small amount of it could sustain a flame for hours at a time—that had allowed them to create a lance of sufficient heat to drive the creatures back. Future uses of the flame-lance would depend on having a similarly potent source of fuel. Merkan had said he would give them a few small barrels of the stuff to take with them, just in case the need arose again while they travelled.

He still could barely believe that he had split the flame lance the way he had, that he had so instinctively known what to do. Part of him was frustrated by the fact that he had no idea what he'd actually put in the flame's path in order to divide it so perfectly. He'd asked Be'Var about it, but the only thing the master had told him was, "That's what a shaper does: he shapes the flames."

The explanation had been of little help. He had so much more to learn, and he wondered just how much time he would have to learn it.

Rill had told him it was the most awesome thing he'd ever seen.

Caymus smiled at the memory of Rill staring at him, his mouth hanging open, after the flames had died out. His friend had asked questions about it well into that evening. Caymus couldn't believe the way Rill's curiosity had so suddenly been ignited by the events of the last week. He was even asking really specific questions about the ways of heat and fire, something he'd ignored with a vengeance while an actual disciple at the Temple. Caymus wondered what the catalyst had been for his friend's recent change in outlook. Had it been that first near-death encounter with the creatures? The decision to leave the Temple? Or had something else entirely suddenly made his friend so curious about the world?

Whatever the reason, he was awfully pleased that Rill was taking such interest, and he marveled at the thought of him joining the Corps of Engineers at Kepren. The skills he'd demonstrated just that afternoon proved he had the requisite talent. Caymus just hoped his friend was able to maintain his enthusiasm long enough to see the plan through to its end.

"Nearly there," said Gu'ruk, breaking Caymus's concentration. They were coming to a point in the passage where the walls narrowed slightly, forcing the old mitre to turn sideways and duck to make his way through. As he did so, Caymus figured out what it was that was different about Gu'ruk's movements: the ancient mitre seemed to be particularly careful about the walls, as though he didn't want to touch them. Caymus wondered why that was as he and Be'Var followed after him.

The passage continued for a few yards before it abruptly came to a dead end. Caymus would have been a little concerned about this only two days ago, but now he knew of a few of Otvia's tricks, and so he simply waited.

Gu'ruk made quite a show of clearing his throat as he passed his torch to his off-hand and reached out to touch the wall they had just come to. After a moment or two, he made a low, rumbling sound, deep in his throat. The noise echoed up the passage behind them, reverberating like the hollow cry of some dead thing when it returned to them. The effect sent shivers running up Caymus's spine. When the sound finally died away, however, the wall before them seemed to just melt away, revealing a room beyond.

Caymus had to blink several times to get his eyes to adjust to the light in the room. Like the Center, this place was brightly lit, though when he looked about to find the source of the light, he could find none.

"Behold the Vault!" Gu'ruk swung his arm wide and spoke in a sort of mocking grandeur. He turned to them for a moment with a proud smile before he turned back and stepped inside.

The Vault wasn't a particularly large room. Much smaller than the meeting hall where the creatures had roamed for so many days, it was about the size of the chamber where the stone oil was collected. The walls were covered in extruded shelves, most of which supported books and scrolls. Here and there, however, were pieces of armor, weapons, and bits of jewelry. Some of the artifacts seemed covered in dust and grime, though others gleamed in the strange light.

In the middle of the room was a single table. It was square, with four chairs around it, one to each side. Four sets of parchment, inkpots, and quill pens sat in the middle of the table. It was also clearly sized for a mitre. Caymus thought he could probably stretch into it, but he didn't think Be'Var would find it terribly comfortable.

"Have a seat," Gu'ruk said, indicating the table and chairs. "I must find the one we need."

Caymus walked over and sat in one of the chairs, then scooted it forward. Be'Var grumbled and t'sked a little, but he did the same thing. Once sat down, though, the master's eyes could barely see above the plane of the table, and Caymus had to bite his lip to keep from laughing.

Before Caymus could spend much time looking at the contents of the desk, Gu'ruk was back, two books in his arms. One of the books was thin, barely a few dozen pages long, and protected by a covering of stiff leather. The other was nearly a foot thick and was bound with sturdy-looking, wooden covers. "This one," said Gu'ruk, indicating the thinner tome, "is the one I wanted to show you. This one," he said, passing the other, thicker book to Be'Var, "is for you, Sir."

Be'Var opened the book and flipped through it for a moment. "This looks like some sort of notebook."

"Oh," said Gu'ruk. "Sorry, it is not for your eyes. It is for your, uh," he paused, waving his hand at the chair, "posterior?"

Caymus couldn't help himself. A moment of laughter escaped him in a snort.

Be'Var looked at each of them in turn, then he gave a resigned sigh. He clambered off the chair, placed the book on the seat, and then climbed up onto both. Finally, his head and shoulders stood above the table. "All right," he said, "what's the other book?"

Gu'ruk sat down too, and he opened the tome. "This," he said, with a twinge of excitement, "contains the story of the Earthwarden."

Caymus squinted his eyes, recalling something Rill had told him. "He's the one that the Ritual Room is for, isn't he?"

Gu'ruk smiled. "You have it right," he said. He flipped a couple of pages, then he dragged his finger down one of them as he paraphrased. "Back before the world was as it is now," he said, "there was a war among the elements. Many, many of those elements existed in our world at the time, fighting each other to live, to be a part of the world we inhabit."

Caymus nodded. "Be'Var told me about this. He said the four elements we know—earth, air, fire, and water—banded together to defeat the rest."

Gu'ruk looked up at them, his eyes widened slightly, obviously impressed. "You have the right of it," he said again. "The way the elements went about their war was a little bit different for each. I do not know how every one of them did it, but some chose champions. These champions were paragons of the elemental realms. Each contained the power of their element within his or her skin, representing it in all ways and fighting tirelessly to keep that element from being destroyed and vanishing from this world forever." Gu'ruk looked briefly at each of them in turn, satisfying himself that he had their attention. "These champions were given a title of honor and virtue, one which hasn't existed in our world since the war ended. They were called 'knights'."

Be'Var spoke up. "The Earthwarden was one of these knights, I take it?"

Gu'ruk nodded. He turned to another page. "There were two brothers, sons of a king. One was named Cra'veth, the other Morogin." He turned the book around and pushed it forward. "Cra'veth was the knight chosen by the realm of earth. He was called Earthwarden. This," he tapped a finger on the page before them, "was his mark."

Caymus looked down to see the same mark Rill had shown him on the door to the Ritual Room.

"The sword and circle symbol," he said.

"Sword?" said Gu'ruk. "Oh dear no." He pointed at the sword-like object. "See how the shorter line isn't near the end of the longer one, as yours is, but is instead right at the tip? It is no sword, but a hammer."

"Ah," said Be'Var, nodding sagely. "That makes a bit more sense."

There was also, on the opposite page, a portrait of a man with a thick jaw and close-cropped hair. There was something familiar about him, but he couldn't decide what it was. He put his finger on the portrait. "This is him?"

"That is him," Gu'ruk replied. He then gave Caymus a long gaze. "His brother, Morogin, was chosen by your lords of fire. They called him, simply, 'Knight of the Flame'. This..." he turned the page, "...was *his* mark."

Caymus felt sure his heart skipped a beat. On the page to the left was the sword and flame symbol. He brought his left hand up, holding it next to the page to check the resemblance. It was exactly the same. When his eyes drifted to the right, however, to the face portrayed on the next page, he felt pins and needles all over his skin. The face closely resembled the one on the previous set of pages, but it was thinner and had longer hair, cut to the shoulders.

"Flames!" he said. "Be'Var, that's the face, the one I saw in the Conduit!" He stabbed a finger at the portrait. "That's him!"

Be'Var nodded, then exhaled. "Well, that's one mystery less, I suppose. I'd been wondering what that had been about. Morogin, is it? So, they showed you the face of the Knight of the Flame." He looked up at Gu'ruk's intent eyes. "What happened to them, after the war?"

Gu'ruk turned the book around again. "As I said, they were brothers, and sons to a king. When the war was over, after they had won, they went back to their lives as princes. Morogin was older, and so was destined to rule after their father. Cra'veth turned his attentions to ministering people in the ways of earth. He came to the mitre, who had dwelled above the ground back then, and taught them of the joys of his element. It was he who brought us underground and showed us how to call to the rocks and the stone and the soil." Gu'ruk frowned, still turning pages. "Cra'veth died at one hundred and three years of age. He fathered no children." He looked up at Caymus. "There is scant little information about Morogin in these pages, I fear, but I assume that his line continued."

"Why is that?" Caymus asked.

"The surname of Cra'veth and Morogin was Tebran."

"Tebran?" said Caymus. "As in 'Tebria'?"

Gu'ruk nodded. "I believe so."

Caymus swallowed hard. If the information was true, and he had no reason to doubt it at this time, then the area they lived in was named after these men. He'd grown up in Woodsea, in a quiet place that didn't need to think much of the geography of the world, but he'd always known that the greater region he lived in, from the eastern plains of Kepren, to the seas of Shorevale, all the way north to the Saleri Forest where the Temple of the Conflagration sat, was often referred to as "The Tebrian League" or, more simply, "Tebria".

As Caymus sat there, trying to understand the significance of it all, Be'Var spoke up. "Does it say anything else interesting?"

Gu'ruk shook his head. "No," he said, "not about the brothers Tebran. However, there is an appendix at the end, a catalog of the other elements which they fought during the war." He turned to the back pages. "This element that we face, I already know that it can pass through earth at times. That narrows the choices considerably." He looked up at them. "Do you know how it reacts to fire?"

Be'Var nodded. "It doesn't. It's nearly impossible to burn those things when they show up."

Caymus watched as Gu'ruk slid his finger down the page. The appendix was written in a language he didn't understand, but it had the look of a ledger: several columns, the first of which always contained a word while the others sometimes contained a check, a single letter, or nothing at all. Gu'ruk looked up at them. "Kreal," he said.

Be'Var squinted his eyes. "Kreal?"

"That is the name of the element," replied Gu'ruk. "Or, at least," he continued, "the name that our elements gave to it while the war raged on." He consulted the page again. "You will find that Kreal reacts to air in much the same way that everything else in our world does. Water, however, is an antagonist."

"How do you mean, an antagonist?" Be'Var asked.

Gu'ruk shrugged. "I do not know," he said. "That is all the appendix says on the matter." Gently, he closed the tome and put it on the table before them. "It may mean that the two explode when they meet or, perhaps, that they cannot touch at all. It may even simply mean that they make each other angry." He frowned. "I am sorry, Master Be'Var. I would tell you more, that I could."

Be'Var nodded, appreciatively. "Thank you, Relic Keeper. You've been a big help to us."

Gu'ruk beamed at him. "I am glad to be of service."

Caymus, still sitting there quietly, looked over the back of his hand again. He felt a surge of hope building in him. Finally, he was getting answers. Finally, he knew what he was meant to do. "Knight of the Flame," he said, just loud enough for the others to hear.

As he spoke, Be'Var and Gu'ruk both turned to look at him. "Burn me," said Be'Var. "There'll be no shutting him up now."

Chapter 10

Caymus squirmed uncomfortably on the floor, his ears under assault by the total silence of the small chamber. He lay on his back on a thin mat, hands behind and supporting his head, clothes still on, staring at the ceiling of the sleeping area that the mitre had assigned him.

He didn't like this room.

Barely a few hours had passed since he, Be'Var, and Gu'ruk had returned from their discussions in the Vault, and by the time they had emerged from those deep tunnels the evening had long since given over to night. Caymus had gone to his assigned room, latched the stone door behind him, lit a single candle, and lain down on the mat to consult with his own thoughts for a while.

He didn't know how long he'd been lying there, eyes scanning the ceiling, ears listening for the faintest hint of sound. He'd learned so much this day: about the ancient war, about the mark on his hand, about himself. He felt he should be happy, should be excited about the knowledge, but in that moment he just felt alone. He'd realized that, prior to arriving at Otvia, he hadn't actually slept completely by himself for a long time, not since he'd left his home to join the Conflagrationist's temple. For years, there had always been another body in the room, other people nearby. Even in the last week or so of travel, he'd known that others, people he cared about, were close at hand.

He'd slept in this same small chamber the previous night and had felt the same discomfort, though he hadn't been able to explain why back then. He understood now, but the knowing wasn't helping him get to sleep. With a heavy sigh, he sat up, reached for a pack that contained some of his belongings, and retrieved another candle. The candle was new, and since the one that he'd already lit wasn't yet half consumed, he felt a little guilty about using it, for wasting its light when his need wasn't really that great, but he also felt he couldn't stand the gloom anymore.

Quietly, he placed the small cylinder of wax on the ground to his left, as far away from him as the one to his right. Then, he sat back, closed his eyes, and reached out to it. When he found it with his mind, he quickly opened a small conduit, the way Be'Var had taught him. Within moments, a timid flame was born upon the wick.

Caymus smiled at his achievement. Opening conduits was getting easier. As he lay back, once again supporting his head on his arms, he idly wondered if he'd ever be as good as Be'Var.

The extra light helped a little. He knew that the room also held a small pool of stone oil in a shelf that ran along the walls, up near the ceiling, but he felt he would be foolish to use it. Lighting a second candle felt wasteful enough; lighting an entire ring of stone oil just to brighten his mood would just make him feel even guiltier.

He thought about the room itself, about its purpose. It was small, barely two of his arm-spans across, and generally round in shape, with walls that arced out from the floor to the ceiling in smooth lines except for the oil shelf. Merkan had told him it was, in fact, a room where people were meant to sleep. He was glad that he had found it empty, glad that it appeared to be meant for guests and that it hadn't recently been made vacant as a result of the krealite attack.

"Krealite." He said the word aloud, listening to the sound of it on his lips. Of all the information he'd gained in the Vault, he was surprised to find that this was that word that had given him the most comfort, that the creatures invading his world were of a specific element, and that the element had a name: kreal. It sounded right somehow, dark and sickly. He was relieved to have that knowledge. He'd grown tired of simply referring to the things as 'the creatures'; something about putting a name to his enemy made them seem more real, more substantial, less like something out of a nightmare. He didn't know how to defeat a nightmare.

Be'Var was worried about the 'antagonistic' effects that kreal was supposed to have on water. He'd apparently already had concerns that the drought that was affecting the grasslands around Kepren and the strange blizzard that had assaulted them only a few days ago might have had something to do with the introduction of this new element into the world. Caymus had seen flashes of desperation in the old man's eyes as he'd spoken of it. He was worried about the implications, worried that their enemy might be able to win this new war by simply affecting the weather. What if they could just stop the rain…forever? What could anybody do against such power?

Caymus had asked more questions of Gu'ruk than the Relic Keeper had been able to provide answers for. They'd learned of the Earthwarden and the Knight of the Flame, but did the elements of water and air have champions, also? Gu'ruk had said that he didn't know, that the book in question was more concerned with the Earthwarden than anything else, but that it had referred to such champions in the plural. He'd admitted that he'd long suspected that water and air, sometimes referred to as the 'soft' elements, tended to place their power in many champions, rather than just one. "Though the elements we know chose to fight together," he'd said, "it doesn't mean they are the same. They did—and continue to do—things very differently from one another."

Be'Var had asked if there had been anything in the book about Morogin being a shaper. Gu'ruk, however, hadn't known the term. When Be'Var had explained the differences between pulling and shaping, the Relic Keeper had mentioned that the Earthwarden's talents had been more suited to battle than anything else: that he, as a knight, had been charged with protection above all. He'd carried a huge battle-hammer in his life, an item that he'd left behind when he'd died. Gu'ruk said that only the Relic-Keepers of the Otvian cities knew the location of the hammer today, but that if a new Earthwarden were to be chosen, he would be drawn to it.

He hadn't known if the Conflagration's champion had carried a similar weapon.

That idea had ignited Caymus's imagination. Might there be some weapon, or some other item once carried by an ancient warrior, that he would be drawn to? He hoped so. Even as he lay there, he experimentally reached out, feeling around him to see if he was 'drawn' anywhere.

He wasn't.

There had been one more thing that had grabbed his attention in that book. When Be'Var had been asking his questions about shaping, Caymus had turned back to the pages with the symbol and portrait of Morogin. He'd been fascinated and a little frightened at the expression on the man's face. Behind the weariness, behind the responsibility, there had been an undercurrent of naked aggression, and Caymus had wondered if he could ever find himself quite that attuned to the element of fire. His concern, however, wasn't really about the portrait, but rather the symbol on the opposite page. As he thought about the sword and flame he'd seen there, he brought his own hand up in front of him. At first, he'd thought the two images exactly the same, but he'd later realized there had been a very slight difference between them, and the difference had him concerned.

As he lay there considering, his mind still freely wandering about the small chamber, he began to feel a presence coming toward his door. Moments later, there was a timid knock.

Caymus wasn't sure what time it was, only that it was late. He sat up. "Come in?" he said just loud enough for someone on the other side to hear.

The latch unhooked, the door swung open just a little, and Gwenna appeared in the doorway. "Are you still awake?" she said, whispering.

Caymus smiled. It was good to see her. "Come in," he said, waving her toward him.

She did so, closing the door gently behind her, keeping hold of the latch as it moved so that it wouldn't make noise clicking into place. When she was satisfied it wouldn't open again, she turned and sat down in front of him on the mat. "Milo told me you went down with Be'Var so some kind of storage room."

"The Vault," Caymus nodded. "We did." Caymus was glad to have some company, especially hers. The night had been far too quiet for him. "It was quite a place. Books and scrolls everywhere!"

Gwenna sat cross-legged, her hands held gently in her lap. She brought her gaze up to his face, meeting his eyes and tilting her head ever so slightly. "Find out anything interesting?"

Caymus laughed. "You could say that." He wondered where to start. "The creatures? The ones we seem to keep running into?"

Gwenna nodded, her eyes narrowing.

"Apparently, the element they're made of is called kreal."

"Kreal..." Gwenna seemed to be testing out the word, much the same way Caymus had only moments before. "Does that mean we know what to call the creatures?"

Caymus shrugged. "Be'Var just called them krealites. I suppose that's as good a word as any."

"Krealites." Gwenna's eyes had become unfocused, looking at something Caymus couldn't see. Gwenna had pretty eyes. Absently, she shifted her gaze, her attention moving down Caymus's arm. She reached out and took his left hand in both of hers, bringing it in front of her. He marveled at how much smaller her hands were than his, how much slimmer each finger was, how much smoother her skin. Gently, she turned the hand over and began tracing the outline of the flame symbol. The touch made his heart flutter. "What about this?" she asked.

Caymus had to concentrate to keep his voice steady. "There was a book," he said. "Gu'ruk said it was about a man called the Earthwarden. He was some kind of champion, a knight for the earth element in the old war Be'Var talked about."

She looked up at him again. "A night? What's night got to do with any of it?"

He smiled. "Knight. With a 'k'. I don't know what it means, but it's what some of the elements call their champions. Knights are supposed to be warriors, protecting the elements themselves. You remember that symbol on the door to the Ritual Room? The one that Rill showed us?"

She nodded. Her eyes seemed to be watching his lips, but they darted occasionally to his eyes.

"Well," he continued, "that symbol was the symbol of the Earthwarden."

Gwenna looked down again at his hand, now stroking the back of it with her thumb. "What about yours?"

Caymus took a deep breath. "He had a brother, another knight, but he was a knight for the Conflagration, the Knight of the Flame. Apparently, that symbol was his." He placed his right hand on his left wrist, close to her fingers. He wasn't sure if he should touch her or not. "Well," he said, "almost."

Gwenna looked up again, her eyes questioning, searching. "Almost?"

"Yes," he said, holding her gaze, then looking back to the symbol. He traced the sword symbol with his right hand. "On his symbol, this part is the same." He then traced the outline of the flame symbol behind it. "But in the book, this part was red."

She was looking down, following his finger. Her voice was quiet, almost silent. He could barely make out her features in the candlelight. "Like the masters' marks then."

"Yes," Caymus replied.

"What do you think that means for you?"

He shrugged. "I don't know."

When she looked up again, her eyes were mischievous, her smile wide. As she spoke, she squeezed his hand. "What do you want it to mean?"

"I don't..." he let the sentence trail off and leaned forward, his face inches from hers. She didn't move away. He could feel her breath on his lips. He leaned forward some more, tilting his head slightly, and closed his eyes. Their lips touched.

In the next moment, Gwenna was standing, smoothing down her dress. "I'm sorry," she said, not looking at him and speaking quickly. "I don't...I don't want to make any trouble for you."

Caymus was startled. He was just getting his breathing under control again. "Gwenna, it's no—"

"I'm sorry," she said again. She moved quickly toward the door, grabbing the latch with both hands. "It's late and I need to sleep." As she lifted the latch and began opening the door, she paused. She turned her head toward him slightly, looking at the ground. "Goodnight, Caymus," she said, a sad but gentle tone to her voice. "I'll see you in the morning."

With a flurry of motion, she was gone, the latch of the door clicking into place behind her.

Caymus sat there, stunned, confused, staring at the door. He wasn't sure what had happened, but he felt certain it had been his fault. He'd thought she'd wanted him to kiss her, but maybe he'd been wrong.

With a heavy sigh, he fell back on his mat. A moment ago, he'd been happy not to be by himself. Now, the room felt even lonelier than it had before she'd come. He reached out with his mind to extinguish the candles, but he found that he couldn't concentrate and ended up having to just blow them out.

As he lay there, by himself in the dark, he wondered what it was that had gone wrong. Gwenna seemed to like him, but then why had she run away? Should he have done something differently? Should he have gone after her? Absently, he wondered if he'd have had a better idea of what to do if he hadn't been cloistered with other men and boys for the last few years of his life.

Another thought came, unbidden, to his mind, and he found himself fighting off a choking feeling in the back of his throat. Most young men had their fathers to ask about things like this. He'd never missed his as much as he was missing him now.

Confused and alone, Caymus lay on his mat in the darkness, trying not to think about his father, about home, until he finally fell asleep.

Chapter 11

Be'Var frowned at the stones and dust as the springs of the wagon's bench squeaked under him. They had finished crossing the Greatstone mountain range four days ago and had been traveling in a generally southeasterly direction through the Tebrian Desert ever since. By his reckoning, they should be about three days from the city of Kepren and ought to have been passing into grassland by now. He didn't like the fact that they were still surrounded by nothing but sand, rocks, and the occasional shrub. It meant that the drought that the missionaries had spoken of was worse than he'd feared.

Plus, there was Caymus, and his incessant questions. He and Rill were practicing their swordplay up ahead of the wagon, as usual, but Be'Var could tell from the glances he kept getting that more questions were about to spring forth from his lips. Be'Var suppressed a moan. He knew many masters who maintained great delight and wonder at the curiosity of youth, but he knew better than that. The curiosity of youth be burned, it was no end of aggravation.

"Here comes another round," he grumbled, under his breath.

Y'selle looked over at him and managed a faint smile. "Be nice to him, Be'Var. He means well."

Be'Var glowered. "He means to drive me mad."

As Caymus and Rill neared, he turned, looking behind to see if Gwenna was about. She was not. Since they'd left Otvia, she'd been off with Milo more often than not, scurrying about somewhere or other and learning to use that new bow of hers. How the two of them could remain unseen in the middle of a flat desert, he had no idea. Bridget was still there, walking alone behind and off the right of the wagon, and she gave a him a small smile. Before he could frown at her, which he knew she'd take the wrong way, he turned around again and gave the reigns a purposeless flick, hoping the action would somehow quell youthful curiosity.

Something had happened between Caymus and Gwenna in Otvia. He wasn't sure what it was, though he had his suspicions. Whatever it was, she'd been avoiding the boy as though he had a contagion. Still, the upside was that Caymus had been focusing on his swordsmanship with greater determination, although Be'Var was less than thrilled to see that the Mael'vekian style Merkan had introduced him to was appearing more and more often in his forms. He was forced to admit, though: the style seemed to suit him. Be'Var was even considering fashioning a two-handed practice weapon for him, just to see how well he did with it. A small smile tugged at the corner of his mouth when he realized that he actually felt a bit sorry for Rill. The youngster had a few good clobbering coming in the days ahead, for sure.

The master had been puzzling over the information they'd gained in the Vault ever since the night Gu'ruk had revealed it to them, mulling it over with every waking hour that wasn't otherwise occupied with the tasks of travel. He was glad to know a bit more about this element, this kreal; the more they knew about their enemy, the better their chances of survival, should they ever run into one of the krealites again.

There was so much to learn, however, and he just didn't have time for it all. The Temple's historical and academic volumes, as an example, contained almost no information about the earth, air, and water elements, and so he'd been amazed to find that the Vault contained an actual archive naming the elements that fought in the ancient war. He'd asked Gu'ruk to tell him more about them, and the Relic Keeper had obliged, but after a half hour of description, they had all begun to blur together in his mind.

The kreal was the important thing, anyhow. Unless there was an invasion of yet another alien substance into their world, it was the only one of the old enemies they needed to concern themselves with for the time being.

Gu'ruk had confirmed one other thing for him, too. At least, he'd supported a theory. Ever since learning that the intrusion into their world was of an actual foreign element, Be'Var had been trying to piece together the implications. What, basically, happens when you take the fundamental makeup of everything around you and then add something to it? Does everything not of the new element just carry on the way it was, careless of the intruder's actions until it comes along to destroy? That theory was all well and good, but then one had to consider what 'destroy' would really mean in that situation. If a man were killed by a krealite, his bones should return to the ground to be consumed by, and distributed back into, the four elements. But how would the new element be accounted for in that scenario? No, if the world had been made of countless elements before, then had been reduced to four, there had to have been a transition, a time between the two states when the defeated elements slowly vanished out of existence. That suggested that in this case, now that the krealites had brought their element into the world, the world must be in a new transition, that even now, everything around him was changing to incorporate the new building block. Their own transition into beings of five elements should only be a matter of time.

Gu'ruk had agreed that this was likely the case.

He'd been sure to let his companions know of his theory, hoping to impart some greater sense of urgency to their collective efforts. His actions had slightly more than the desired effect, though; he didn't think any of them had slept at all the first night after the revelation.

At least Caymus was feeling better about himself after their trip to Otvia's Vault. Be'Var had known very little of this Knight of the Flame, which was to say he'd known practically nothing at all. There had been a single reference to some champion of the Conflagration in an old scroll he'd been hanging onto for what seemed like ages, but the text was so vague and generally unhelpful that he hadn't even bothered to bring it with him on this journey. The boy was hanging onto the idea with a death-grip though, and Be'Var wasn't entirely sure that was a good thing.

As though illustrating his previous thoughts, Rill was knocked down again just as the wagon came abreast of the two combatants. Staven flicked his ears and snorted with distaste at it all; Be'Var found something comforting in that. After Caymus helped his friend to his feet, the two of them began walking alongside the horses, catching their breath. Then, Caymus turned his head in Be'Var's direction—yet again—and spoke.

"Master Be'Var, do you think the krealites have a champion?"

Be'Var let out a long breath, not having realized he'd been holding it. "I don't know, Caymus," he finally said. He shifted the reigns to hold them in one hand, using the other to rub the few, short tufts of gray on his head. "Gu'ruk didn't say anything about it."

Rill spoke up next, talking between breaths. "They must be one of the ones that used a group, like water and air."

They all turned to look at him. "I mean, there have been all these krealite things attacking us, right? If they picked a champion, wouldn't we have seen some evidence of it by now? Somebody commanding the creatures? Or some kind of emissary, maybe?"

All eyes shifted to Be'Var. Be'Var noticed that even Bridget had jogged a little so she could catch up and listen to the conversation. "No," he said, with barely more than a mutter, "I highly doubt it."

"What do you mean?" said Caymus.

Be'Var was tired of questions. He glanced over at Y'selle with a plaintive look, trying his best to emote great fatigue.

She smiled that little quarter-smile he knew so well—the turn of her mouth was so faint that most probably wouldn't have noticed it—and saved him. "What I wonder," she said, leaning over, "is why you'd assume that this new element would do things the way we do them. Fire, water, earth, air; groups or champions; why would they be like any of us?"

Be'Var managed to hold back his smile. Sella had always had a patient way of getting to the heart of things.

She seemed as though she was about to say something else, but Rill spoke first. "So," he said, then he paused a moment to gather his thoughts. "So, how do you think they'd do it: divide their power among all their worshipers equally?"

Bridget, who had been very quiet since Gwenna had started disappearing for hours at a time, said, "Maybe they don't give power to anyone at all?"

Y'selle nodded. "Neither case would surprise me. Isn't it interesting though, that we haven't actually met any kreal worshipers?" She turned her eyes forward, looking to the horizon as she continued. "I sometimes wonder if there is any more to this element than those monsters, if there are any human worshipers at all. It could be that those who rule the kreal realm have no use for people."

They all quietly pondered the thought for a few moments. Be'Var was glad for the silence. He noted the crunching noise the wagon's wheels made as they trundled over small stones in their path and felt some of the tension leave his bones. He'd always liked that sound. On nights when, as a younger man, he'd traveled alongside an army, he'd usually done so atop a cart or a wagon or some kind of war machine. The wheels were sometimes wooden, sometimes tied with leather or iron, but they'd nearly always been traveling south, through what was now the Mael'vekian desert, and so the sound was always the same. Crunch, crunch, scuff, pop. Be'Var had never considered himself a sentimental man, but in that moment, he really wanted those days back.

It was Rill—of course it was Rill—who broke the silence. "Why isn't there more kreal around?" When Be'Var turned his tired gaze to what was probably the most troublesome youth he'd ever known, he saw Rill's wide eyes searching, full of energy, from face to face. "If the stuff is here," he continued when nobody answered, "—and it has to be here, if these bugs are here, right?—then why isn't the world starting to be made of it? I'm not saying your theory," he tilted his head at Be'Var, "is wrong or anything, but shouldn't we be seeing more evidence of the kreal by now?"

Be'Var had wondered for the past couple of years whether accepting Rill into the Temple as a disciple had been a huge mistake. He clearly remembered that the boy had been filled with wonder when he'd first arrived, but that the enthusiasm hadn't lasted but a few months. After that, according to every instructor he'd ever had, coaxing attention out of Rill had been like coaxing a bear into a thimble: as pointless as it was unlikely to occur. Now that the boy had extricated himself from the building though, now that he was no longer being spoon-fed on a disciple's lessons and was having to think for himself, Rill was turning out to have a rather first-rate mind. For the past week or so, Be'Var had found himself torn between immense pride at the boy's achievements and exceptional aggravation at the fact that it had taken so long for him to start using his brain for more than just eating, sleeping, and finding a place to go to the bathroom.

"I don't know," he finally said, squinting in thought. "I think it might have something to do with the fact that it's entering an established, balanced world, so it's taking a while to spread."

"Spread…" Y'selle's voice was quiet, hesitant. "I don't even want to think of what that would mean."

Nobody responded to that. The idea that this strange element might somehow seep into their world, into their bodies, was sickening, the stuff of nightmares. Be'Var found himself entertaining thoughts of a sickly, black substance slowly growing into his bones. He looked at the young faces about him and hoped none of them would have to contend with such a thing.

They traveled in silence for some time. Only the wind spoke, picking up some force, gusting dry air and sand into their faces and occasionally rattling the horses' tack. Be'Var spent most of the next hour hunched over, shielding his face with his hands or squinting to keep the worst of the dust from his eyes. When the wind died down and he finally looked up, he noticed that they'd final encountered a change in the landscape. Desert shrubs were giving way to short grasses, coarse sand to hard-packed soil. The soil was dry, the grasses diminutive and mostly brown, but he felt relieved to be finally passing into the Tebrian Plains. Not only did it mean that the drought wasn't quite as bad as his imagination had feared, but it also meant they were getting close to their destination, to the city of Kepren.

"What's that?" Bridget, who was walking next to the horses again, was pointing out ahead of them.

Be'Var shook himself from his thoughts. He followed her arm, squinting into the distance, trying to see what she was pointing at. The sun was about half-an-hour from setting, and in the failing light he could only make out a fairly large boulder, about the size of one of the horses, by the side of the road. There didn't seem to be anything special about it. "Just a rock," he said, happy to put the thought out of his mind.

"No," she said, pointing with greater urgency and now tilting her head at the shape. "Next to the rock. Is that a person?"

Be'Var looked again, tinges of frustration nagging their way into his thoughts. He'd always had sharp eyes, even at his advancing age, but he couldn't see what she was talking about.

"I see him," said Rill. "I think you're right. Somebody's there, sitting up against the boulder."

Be'Var squinted his eyes still further. The evening sun was setting behind them, casting its shadows across the landscape. If there was a person there, it was hiding in one of those shadows.

Then he saw it, the faintest hint of color against the dark browns of the rock. He couldn't make out any details, but the faint outlines he could see were obviously those of a man, lying down, his head and shoulders propped up against the rock. "Burn me," he said, under his breath. He gave the reigns a sharp flick to urge the horses to move a little bit faster.

As they moved closer, more detail came out. The man's simple clothing was of a dark brown, which was why it had blended into the boulder he lay against. A small pack, the size of a messenger's satchel, lay at his side. His features were sharp and gaunt, his skin ashen. He didn't look well.

He did appear to be conscious, at least. He turned his head toward the group as it approached. When they were close enough to speak, he offered them a small wave and a bit of a smile. Be'Var 'whoaed' at the horses and brought the wagon to a stop at the point where the road passed him, about five yards from the boulder. He didn't want to get too close just yet. He'd seen far too many bandits lay traps like this during his days with the army.

"Hello," said the man. His voice was weak and raspy. From this distance, Be'Var could see that his face was sunburned, with small patches of skin peeling off his nose and ears. Likely not a bandit, then. Highwaymen might play the wounded bird sometimes, but he doubted any of them were quite so skilled with stage makeup. "I don't suppose," the man continued, "that you could spare some water?"

~~~

Caymus was getting frustrated.

As he sat quietly amidst the dry grass, he stared out across the twilight plain, listening, feeling for something that he wasn't sure was there.

When the group had found the man, who'd called himself Callun, by the side of the road, they had quickly realized that he was beyond his own help and had offered him some of their water. He had gratefully accepted, drinking down two entire waterskins worth, but his arms had shaken as he'd done so, and when he'd tried to stand, he'd barely gotten
~~~

to his knees before collapsing to the ground again. Be'Var had said the man showed signs of severe dehydration and that it would be a while before he would be fit to travel. Y'selle had suggested that, though they would normally continue for an hour past dark, they go ahead and stop here for the night so they could see to the man's immediate physical needs.

Caymus hadn't liked the situation. To begin with, he'd taken an immediate dislike to Callun. He knew the feeling was, at best, uncharitable, considering the stranger's condition, but something about the man had struck him as 'off' from the moment he'd smiled and waved at them. Perhaps it was just the stress of travel catching up with him.

Strangers on the road be damned, though; the more immediate concern was that he'd been experiencing that familiar prickling sensation on the back of his neck ever since they'd stopped. He couldn't find the source of it, though. He'd mentioned the feeling, which usually heralded the appearance of krealites, to Be'Var, and also to Milo when he and Gwenna had finally shown up, but neither had been able to offer him much he didn't already know. The flat ground around here made it unlikely that there were krealites hiding anywhere. For all he knew, though, they were waiting, lurking, buried in the earth.

Caymus probed, both with his eyes and with his mind, at the dry grassland around him. The occasional short tree or small collection of rocks dotted the landscape, but they were all that he could distinguish. He'd been maintaining his watch for a while, and his instincts told him that if there was a krealite out there, it would have attacked by now. His instincts could not, however, account for the warning his body was giving him.

He felt Milo's approach before he heard it, his friend's warm core being easy to pick out against the cooling evening. Making almost no noise at all with his footfalls, the man stopped, stood at Caymus's shoulder, and took a few deep breaths. "See anything out there?" he said.

Caymus sighed. "Not a thing." Before he realized it, he discovered his hand rubbing his neck again.

Milo noticed. "Still buzzing at you, is it?"

Caymus wasn't sure he cared for the term 'buzzing', but he nodded as Milo took a half-step forward so they could see each other's faces.

The priest of the air furrowed his brow with concern and, Caymus expected, more than a little frustration of his own. "I don't know what to tell you, Caymus," he said. "You're probably right that the only way they're going to sneak up on us is if they're passing through the ground again." He indicated the area around them with a wave of his hand. "I searched about pretty thoroughly. If there's an old worship spot around here, I can't find any evidence of it."

Caymus spoke into the middle distance. "We don't know for sure that it's only worship sites where they can just pop out of the ground like that, you know."

Milo nodded and shrugged at the same time. "You're right," he said. He turned to Caymus and put a hand on his shoulder. "Think you want to come back to the fire? Stew's on." He smiled. "Ever eat snake meat before?"

Caymus started, the twilight's spell on him broken, and he looked at Milo with raised eyebrows. "Snake?" he said. "Really?"

Milo smiled his easy smile at him. "I showed Gwenna how to catch them. She's got quick hands." He clapped Caymus's shoulder a couple of times, attempting to turn him around. "That Callun fellow had a small sack of beans in that satchel of his, so they're making a stew out of it. Come on."

Caymus took one more pensive look at the land around him. The sun had disappeared in the West, and the night had nearly completely taken over from the day. He realized he was very hungry. "Yeah," he said, "okay."

The two of them walked, side-by-side, back to the evening campfire a couple of hundred yards away. Caymus could see the flickers of flame playing amongst the shadows of his friends, could see the glow of warm light on the rock where they'd found the stranger. "I don't like him," he said, quietly.

"Callun?" said Milo. "Why not?"

Caymus had been struggling with the question for hours now, and he hadn't come to any useful conclusions. "I'm not sure," he said. "Something about him just sets my teeth on edge."

Milo looked sideways at him. "It's just a sunburn, Caymus. Haven't you ever worked outside too long on a hot day?"

Caymus wasn't sure if Milo was making fun, but he wasn't interested in sparring with him. "It's not that," he said. "Something about the way he looks at everybody." He shook his head. "I know we had to help him—I'd want somebody to help me if I was dying of thirst out here—but I wish we'd just given him what he needed and been on our way."

"You sure it's not just the prickles on your neck making you a little distrustful?"

Caymus was forced to concede the point, but he was unconvinced. "Maybe," was all he said.

He decided to change the subject. "How's Gwenna doing with her new toy?" he asked.

Milo brought his hand up and waggled it. "She's kind of starting to be able to hit what she's aiming at pretty much most of the time now, so..." He paused, his eyes scanning the sky for words. "She'll never be as good as me," he said after a moment, then he gave Caymus a grin, "but she's a whole lot better than you."

"Ha!" Caymus smiled. It felt good to laugh after the stress of the last few hours. "We didn't even see you two most of the day. How far away were you?"

Milo gave a shrug, the feathers on his arms rustling with the movement. "Distances are odd in places like this. They'll play tricks on you. It's why people like Callun suddenly find themselves dying of thirst right next to a road. I'm not entirely sure, but I don't think we were ever more than half a mile away, at the most."

Caymus thought about the stranger again, about his sunken eyes, his skin that seemed to have just a slightly grayish tint. He had black hair that he slicked back with some manner of oil or grease, too. Caymus suppressed a shudder. The man gave him the creeps.

When the pair reached the light of the campfire, Gwenna waved him over and proffered a tin bowl containing a spoon and some steaming, dark substance—the firelight didn't reach past the rim—which he supposed was the stew Milo had described. She smiled at him when he took it and sat down next to her, which he was happy to see. She'd seemed not to want much to do with him in the days since Otvia, but since she and Milo had made their appearance around sunset, she'd appeared to have reverted to being herself again. Caymus wondered if Milo had anything to do with that.

He considered the bowl in his hands, then leaned over to whisper to Gwenna. "Snake?"

She leaned back to him with a grin. "It's good," she said. "Try it."

He'd hoped she was going to tell him that Milo had been kidding. As he sat there, adjusting his worldview to include the idea of eating things that slither, he glanced up and saw Be'Var looking at him. The old man raised his eyebrows in a silent question, then he reached up and tapped the back of his neck.

Caymus nodded, indicating that yes, he was still feeling the sensation. Be'Var scowled, then went back to spooning his own bowl of stew into his mouth.

"Welcome back, Caymus," Y'selle said. The matron was stirring their fire with a metal rod, letting the wood breathe. Her expression was the complete opposite to Be'Var's. He wore concern on his face; she wore contentment. "Our new friend was just telling us about how he came to be here."

Caymus turned his attention to Callun, who was sitting directly across the campfire from him. The man's dark, sunken eyes were on him again. Trying not to be unfriendly, Caymus forced a look of interest. "Really?" he said. "Where are you from, Callun?"

Callun seemed as though he stared a bit too long before he answered, but when he finally did, his expression brightened and he looked about, speaking to them all in turn. "I set out, many months ago, from Golentah." He turned to look at the faces around him. "Perhaps you've heard of it?" The man's voice was as slick as his hair, and it did nothing to aid Caymus's trust of him.

Caymus turned his eyes to Be'Var who, in turn, was looking at Milo. Both where shaking their heads.

"I'm unsurprised," said Callun. "My home is far, far to the South, and I traveled a long time to get here." A distant smile came to his face and he turned his eyes skyward. "You've stars here I've never seen before. They're quite fascinating."

Caymus considered the words themselves. The stranger's voice did carry a slight accent that he was unfamiliar with. Some words that should be pronounced separately ran together, and others seemed to have extra vowels. "I'm" became "Iyam", and "a long" became "along". He seemed to cut some words off before they were completely out of his mouth, too. The town Caymus had grown up in was highly regarded for its shipwrights, and so people from many far-off places had often arrived there in search of expertise. Caymus had never heard any of them speak the way this man did. He seemed to have an awfully good grasp of the language though, for someone so far away. Could it be that their people shared a native tongue?

"Is your home far beyond Mael'vek, then?" he asked, bringing a spoonful of stew to his mouth. He remembered what it was he was eating only as he brought the spoon away; after a moment's considered chewing, he decided he quite liked snake meat.

For a moment, the man seemed confused at the question, and Caymus thought he saw a split-second's worth of fear in his face, but then the moment was over and Callun's face was smiling a broad smile at them all. "Mael'vek," he said. "I have heard of the place, but I didn't pass through on my way here." He shrugged. "I'm afraid I don't know the answer to your question."

Caymus frowned. By all accounts, the nation of Mael'vek was a vast empire. Its lands bordered the entire southern edge of Tebria and, as far as he knew, extended from the western shore all the way to the end of the world. Could this Callun be lying? Misinformed? Or could there really be a place where one might sneak past the Mael'vckians on his way north.

"So, Callun," said Y'selle, "what brings you so far north, so far from your home?"

The smile appeared again. "I'm exploring. I seek to find out more about the places far away from us. My people are not travelers, and we do not know much of the lands beyond our own, so I decided to travel and find out what's here." He looked around at the darkness around them. "I was doing quite well, and had thought to continue to the North, but I'm afraid I underestimated your desert, which is why you found me here."

"Do you think you'll continue north after this?" she asked.

"It seems I'm not prepared to make this particular crossing," he replied. "I should probably rest somewhere nearby for a while before I set out and try again."

"Well," said Y'selle, "you're welcome to travel with us to Kepren. I'm sure you'll find everything you need there, and I can even offer you a bed at Flamehearth for a few days, assuming there's space when we get there."

Callun tilted his head and raised his eyebrows. "What is this Flamehearth?" He said it with equal parts curiosity and excitement.

Bridget answered first, her face beaming. "Flamehearth is the Conflagrationists' mission in Kepren. We have a small school and a hospital there. Many people come from all over to learn about the Conflagration. There are always a few extra beds." Caymus was surprised to see Bridget so enthusiastic, especially considering how quiet she'd been over the last few days. He wondered if he was finally getting a glimpse of her real personality, one which only appeared when she talked about the mission.

Upon hearing a scraping sound, Caymus looked down to find the source and was surprised to discover that he'd nearly finished his stew. Between the attention he'd been giving to Callun's odd way of speaking and the annoyance of the enduring prickling on his neck, he hadn't noticed how fast he'd been eating. With a small sigh meant only for himself, he rubbed his neck again.

"You keep a hospital?" asked Callun, a look of concern on his face. "Are there many sick at this Flamehearth?"

"It's not quite like that," said Y'selle. "We have a couple of people at the mission who have knowledge of treating injuries and illness, so people who get themselves sick or hurt and who have nowhere else to turn often end up in one of our beds." She looked away for a moment, then said, "Occasionally, we do have people who seem to be sick for no good reason—the drought, especially, has seen to that lately—but there is no danger that you'll catch anything." She looked back to Callun with her gentlest face. "If that's what you're worried about."

Callun smiled back at her. "That is good to know. I think I will be happy to stay at this Flamehearth for a time." He gave her a small nod. "Thank you."

A thought occurred to Caymus. "Matron Y'selle, what kinds of things do you teach at the school?"

She turned to him and frowned, slightly. "Just short lessons about the Conflagration—things you learned at your first year at the Temple—and some reading and writing for the children."

Bridget chimed in. "I teach most of the reading. At the moment, we have about half-a-dozen children. They love the classes."

Caymus gave a half-hearted smile. "That's too bad."

They both frowned at him.

"No, no," he said, realizing what he'd said, "I mean it's good that you're teaching them reading and writing, but I'm supposed to be finding someone to teach me this shaping Aspect, and...I had been hoping..." He trailed off.

He got a couple of sympathetic smiles, but Y'selle and Bridget just shook their heads at him. Gwenna gave him a smack on the arm, then scooted closer, leaning against him. He shrugged sheepishly and cast his eyes downward. "Sorry." He rubbed his neck.

When he looked up again, Callun was staring at him again, and Caymus was finally able to put words to the thing he didn't trust about the man: his eyes didn't seem right. They seemed dead, as though there was no mind, no soul behind them. Those eyes made him nervous, like death itself was peering into him from across the fire.

The dead eyes moved down the length of him, then passed beyond him and fell onto the wooden sword lying next to him on the ground. Callun motioned to it with his chin. "You know how to use that?"

Caymus tried to look friendly when he answered, but he didn't think he succeeded. He put his bowl down as he spoke. "Only a little. I just started learning," he said. "I think I'm getting better."

"I don't know about that," said Rill, raising his eyebrows at him. "Do you have any idea how many times you rapped me on the knuckles today?"

Caymus put his fingers to his chin and looked up in mock-thoughtfulness. "I'd say," he replied, "about as many times as you didn't bring your shield up." He looked back at Rill. "Is that about right?"

Be'Var, at least, seemed to think that was funny.

Rill shook his head and pointed a finger. "I'm going to get you tomorrow, you just wait."

Caymus picked up the wooden sword, pretending to examine the blade. "I and my sword eagerly await you and your swollen knuckles."

That got a chuckle out of everybody. Rill gave him a sour look, then he couldn't hold back his grin any longer. With a shake of his head, he went back to eating his stew.

Caymus put the sword down. He could feel Callun's eyes on him again; he tried not to look at the man as he talked to Be'Var. "Really, Master Be'Var, what am I going to do about learning to shape, once we get to Kepren?"

Be'Var seemed to think about this for a few moments while he chewed. "I've got a few ideas about that," he said, "but I don't want to get ahead of myself. Suffice it to say there are a handful of old acquaintances I want to talk to, but I don't know if any of them will actually be able to assist." He put his own bowl down and wiped his chin with the back of his hand while he looked up at Caymus from under his eyebrows. "You just worry about your drills for now. Let me worry about what we do once we hit Kepren."

Caymus accepted this with a single nod. He hoped that Be'Var would be able to find the help they needed—the help *he* needed—once they reached the city. The moment in Otvia when he'd split the flame-lance in two was the first time he'd done anything that he'd really thought of as shaping a flame, and that had been done more as a reflex than as anything intentional. He wondered how long it would take before he could control it better, how much there actually was to learn.

He wondered why there was no red in the flame on the back of his hand.

"Speaking of your drills," Be'Var said, standing up, "I think it's time you and Rill traded up." He walked the few steps over to the wagon, reached in, and withdrew a long bundle. As he walked back to the fire, he unwrapped gray cloth to reveal two longswords, their blades gleaming in the orange firelight. "Wood for steel," he said, and handed them each a sword, hilt-first.

Rill stood up at once and accepted his sword with a huge grin. Gwenna lifted herself from Caymus's side so that he could do that same. Caymus rose slowly, patting the dust from his legs. He was surprised, and more than a little bewildered. "Are you sure?" he said. The idea of having a real sword filled him with excitement and anticipation, but also with apprehension. He didn't reach for the hilt yet. "I mean, we've only been learning for a couple of weeks now."

Be'Var nodded. "Sure enough," he said, his face serious, but not stern. "You need to start using the real thing sooner or later, if only to get a feel for the balance, which wood can never get right." He proffered the sword to Caymus again. This time, Caymus reached out and took it. "They're from Merkan," he said. "Apparently, he has a small collection of the things."

The weapons thus dispensed, Be'Var folded his arms in front of him and gave them each a long look. "They're not sharpened yet," he said, when he was sure he had both boys' attentions. "When the knuckle-rapping stops, I'll put an edge to them. Agreed?"

Rill nodded vigorously, a serious look on his face.

"Agreed," said Caymus.

As the three of them sat down, Gwenna leaned against him once more. Caymus was glad she seemed to be talking to him again. As he soaked in the feeling of the pressure of her on his arm, he examined the sword he'd just been given. It was simple enough, with a leather-and-wire-wrapped grip and a small, iron sphere for the pommel. Rill could probably hold it in two hands for extra leverage, but Caymus could only fit a single set of fingers around the grip. The cross-guard was angled at a traditional ninety degrees from the hilt, with no decoration or embellishment. The blade was simple, the two edges running straight and parallel until they came together at a point at the very tip.

It looked a lot like Be'Var's sword. Caymus wondered absently if it might be some kind of standard issue for soldiers of Kepren, and how a Mael'vekian soldier like Merkan might have come across it, if it were. He decided he'd never ask that particular question.

Gwenna made a small grunt, which got the group's collective attention, as she stirred from Caymus's arm, slid down, and lay on the ground beside him, reaching back into the darkness to pull a blanket over herself.

"I think," said Y'selle, "she has the right idea."

"Indeed," said Be'Var, standing up. "We lost a lot of daylight today. We'll have to start early to make it up."

Everybody wandered off to find mats and blankets so they could turn in for the night. Caymus still felt the prickling of danger on the back of his neck, still listened to the darkness, hoping to find an explanation for the 'buzzing' sensation.

Twice more, Caymus noticed the stranger watching him with those soulless eyes. Once, he caught him looking at the sword.

That night, Caymus had dreams about being trapped in some sort of sticky, black tar, unable to claw or burn his way out.

Chapter 12

Caymus could scarcely believe the size of Kepren. He stared in wonderment at the thick, wooden gates as he passed through them, at the portcullis raised over their heads, and at the several guards in chain mail and faded green livery standing about the entrance to the city. He had expected Kepren to be a big place, but the true immensity of it threatened to overwhelm his senses.

They had first glimpsed Kepren the previous evening, just before the sun had gone down, two days after they had encountered Callun and decided to bring him with them. Caymus had been practicing drills with Rill—thuds and clacks had been replaced with the ring of steel against steel—when Gwenna had pointed out the shapes out on the horizon. Even at that distance, only able to make out the silhouette of the place, Caymus had been amazed at the hulking mass before him, which stretched to cover what must have been miles and miles. He'd always thought Krin's Point was big, but it was nothing compared to the capital.

There had been some talk of continuing on in the dark, of trying to reach the city that same day, but Y'selle hadn't been sure if the gates would still be open to them if they arrived late, so they'd decided instead to travel only another hour, and then to complete the rest of the journey in the light of the morning.

The early trek had passed slowly, and the sun was now just past its zenith. Caymus had been surprised at how dry the air felt considering the area around the city was mostly grassland: normally, he would have expected grass to lend some cooling moisture to the landscape. There wasn't even a single cloud in the sky. He was finally beginning to understand the extent of the drought that Bridget and Gwenna had told him of.

The buildings around him were mostly stone, though some wooden structures stood amongst them, too. The majority were only a single story high and there were none with more than two floors.

The structures seemed simple to him, and yet there was something unusual about them. As he passed by one facade, the purpose of which he couldn't guess, he noticed that the light gray blocks in the walls didn't appear to have any mortar between them. There didn't even seem to be an order or pattern to the way the stones were arranged, as the separations between them ran every which way. Still, those separations were so small that he had to look twice to be sure they were there. Whomever had built these places, they had cut the rocks so perfectly that he imagined they fit together better than a sword in its scabbard.

The buildings looked new; rather, not one of them looked to be old. The surfaces were clean, untarnished by stain or moss. There were no cracks or fading colors anywhere. Perhaps they were just kept in good condition by their occupants. He remarked on it to Gwenna.

"This is the Grass District," she said, waving her arm to indicate the city around her. "Most of the buildings here are only a handful of decades old."

"Grass District?" he said.

Gwenna nodded. "This whole section of the city was only built about a hundred years ago, back when the Laivusians came from the South looking for a place to stay."

"Who are the Laivusians?"

"Laivus is a city—*was* a city—about halfway between Kepren and Mael'vek. It used to be independent, but during one of the big battles, Mael'vek invaded it and set a huge fire. A lot of Laivusians died, but most of those who didn't fled north to Kepren."

Caymus frowned. He'd remembered hearing of the city that used to separate Kepren and Mael'vek, but he hadn't known what it was called before. He stared at the mass of people in the street. There were a lot of them about, some walking or riding horses, some shouting to each other, some just hurrying in pursuit of some unknown errand. The noise was such that he had to raise his voice to be heard. "So, the rest of the city is older than this?"

She pointed in a generally easterly direction. "That way is the Reed District," she moved her arm slightly, pointing northeast, "and over there is the Guard District, where the castle is." She lowered her arm and kept looking ahead as she continued. "The Guard District is the oldest part of the city. It's where the king lives. The Reed District was given to the people of Shorevale after one of the wars with Mael'vek, and then they built the Grass District after Laivus fell."

Caymus frowned. He was beginning to realize there was a lot about Kepren he didn't know. He knew that Shorevale lay to the West, at the sea's edge, and he'd heard stories about the ferocity of their navy, but he hadn't known that they had anything to do with Kepren itself. He considered asking more about Shorevale and what war she was talking about but, considering the din, he decided on a simpler question. "Why is it called the Grass District?"

She turned to him and smiled. "I'm not really sure," she said, "but I'd guess it's got something to do with the fact that this was all just grassland before the Laivusians showed up."

Caymus nodded. That made enough sense for him. "So, Laivusians are in the Grass District, Shorevalians are in the Reed District, and there's the Guard District, which is what Kepren used to be before the other two came along. It sounds like it's really three cities, not just one."

Gwenna shrugged. "It kind of is. Each district is a little different, and each one is governed by a duke. The king has the final say over everything, but from what I understand, he kind of stays out of their decisions, for the most part." Her face turned a little sour. "They're the ones who are holding back from sharing from their wells. I don't know why the king doesn't put a stop to it."

Caymus took a deep breath, considering what he'd just learned. He'd always thought of Kepren as just the capital city of Tebria, and nothing more. Apparently, the politics of the Tebrian region were a bit more complicated than that. "So," he said, "Flamehearth...that's in the Guard District then, in the old Kepren?"

Gwenna shook her head. "It's here, in the Grass. We're almost there, actually."

Caymus frowned at her, his eyes betraying his surprise. Gwenna smiled at him. "It's a mission, you dope. You don't build missions in the heart of your own city! Flamehearth was originally built along with the rest of the Grass, when the Laivusian refugees first started coming here a century ago. It was one of the only buildings there at the time."

Caymus nodded slowly, thinking it over as they walked. He wondered why, if the point of a mission had been to help educate and take care of refugees, it was still here. The city around him, after all, didn't appear to be populated by refugees, but by citizens who seemed to be doing well. He considered giving voice to the question, but figured he'd learned enough for the moment. He'd have to remember to ask later.

His neck had started tingling again. It had never stopped, really, not since the night they'd met Callun, but it seemed a little bit worse now. With a worried frown, he looked around at the buildings and people that surrounded him. A sudden attack among all this activity would be more trouble than they could deal with. He took a quick look behind him too, looking at the wagon and at Callun, who sat in the back with their belongings. The man had hardly spoken a dozen words in the two days he'd been with them, but Caymus had constantly felt those eyes watching him. He had a suspicion that Callun himself was the cause of his aggravation, but he couldn't figure out why that would be. Anyway, what was he going to do: casually announce to everybody that they'd accidentally picked up a krealite on their journey, and that it just happened to look like a person that he didn't like very much? Caymus turned his eyes back to the wide street in front of him. He needed to find out more about this stranger that had suddenly become part of his life.

After only a few more minutes of travel, Gwenna pointed toward a low, wide edifice off to their right. "Flamehearth!" she said with a growing smile. The building was as simple as the others around it, with the same perfect stonework comprising its walls. It was a single-storied, with a shingled roof of deep red and more red paint trimming the doors and windows. He didn't think it a particularly large place—Caymus had spent the last several years of his life at the Conflagrationist Temple, after all—but he suspected that it must extend back quite a way.

The mission had a good few yards between itself and its neighbors, more than existed between most of the other buildings in the area, and Gwenna led them all down the right side, where they came upon a small yard and a stable. Once Be'Var and Y'selle stopped the wagon, Bridget and Gwenna hurriedly got to the business of freeing the horses from their harnesses and brushing them down so that they could be put into their pens to rest. Y'selle asked the boys to help unload some of the gear, particularly the iron ore that they had carried across the Greatstones. Even Milo got pressed into service, a fact which he seemed to enjoy.

At least they didn't have to move things very far. The girls brought most of the group's belongings inside through a single, red, wooden door, but the ore itself was destined for a large shed which was pressed up next to the wall of the mission. After a short while hauling the barrels and crates, Caymus found himself enjoying the work, taking pleasure in having something useful and mundane to do. The fact that they'd finally arrived at their destination lessened the effort of it, too.

As he and Rill reached for the last of the ore, Caymus wondered where Callun had gotten to. He looked around to find him, but the stranger had disappeared. He sighed. The man was probably inside with the others. He wondered if Callun would stay at Flamehearth, and for how long. This, of course, got him to wondering just how long his own stay at the mission would be.

"Are the three of you nearly done?" Caymus, placing the last of the barrels, glanced over to see Be'Var leaning against the door's frame, looking at them with mock-frustration. Caymus beamed, as it seemed his old master was in a good mood, a rarity as far as he was concerned.

"I don't know," said Milo, "you got any more of these things we don't know about?"

"Something filled with bricks, maybe?" chimed Rill. Everyone seemed to be cheerful today.

Be'Var gave a short laugh, took his weight off the frame, and waved them in. "Come on," he said, "there are a couple of people I want you to meet."

Caymus exchanged glances with his friends, who shrugged, and the three of them followed Be'Var inside.

The interior of the building was startling, as it didn't appear to match the outside at all. The outer walls—those that Caymus had seen—had been bare, gray rock, without a hint of decoration but for the red trimmings. Every inch of the inside walls, however, was painted, and not in a uniform color. The first room they walked through, which Caymus could only guess was some sort of office because of the two desks on opposite sides, was covered in a heavy lavender, with wavy green lines dancing along the top. The hallway they then passed through was painted a light, beige color, with small symbols that looked like little flames dotting the bottom, just above the floor. As they passed by other doors, Caymus looked into the various rooms and discovered that they were all decorated in these severe patterns and colors. He wondered if there was any logic to it at all.

Milo seemed to be wondering the same thing. "Did they keep running out of paint?" he said, his head swiveling around the same as Caymus's.

Caymus couldn't see Be'Var's face, but he imagined it wore a grin. "The children," he explained. "The last time I was here, it wasn't anything like this, but it seems the new mission-keeper lets them run wild with the stuff."

As though summoned by the words, a pair of boys—Caymus didn't imagine they were older than five or six years—dashed out of a doorway in front of them, nearly crashed into Be'Var, and then skidded into another open door. Be'Var cursed under his breath, but otherwise paid them no mind. When Caymus passed by the room the children had scurried into, he took a quick glance in and saw Bridget kneeling down and giving the first one a hug.

She noticed him looking in and gave him a smile. She seemed happier than he'd ever seen her.

They passed a few more rooms, some of which were occupied with people, a few of whom looked up and waved before getting back to what they were doing. Most were women in their thirties of forties, though there were a couple of men, too. They all seemed friendly enough, happy to see new faces. It was quite a contrast to the serious tone that generally permeated the Temple.

A couple of the rooms that he passed, always on his right, afforded views into a small patch of yellow-brown grass that was ringed by columns and paving stones. After having taken a couple of right turns, Caymus decided that Flamehearth must be arranged in a square, and that the center of that square held a small courtyard.

He was just beginning to wonder how big the courtyard was, how green the grass would have been were it not strangled with drought, when Be'Var turned through a doorway on his left and led the three of them into what appeared to be a small dining room. The floor was about a dozen paces across in each direction and the walls had a somber-looking, brownish-orange tint to them. A pair of sideboards lined the two walls to his left and right, one standing next to a closed door. A couple of cabinets, displaying a few simple bowls and dishes, stood against the far wall. A long, wooden dining table filled the center of the room and a pair of plain-looking benches ran down its length.

Sitting on the benches were Gwenna, Y'selle, and two people whom Caymus didn't know. The first was an older woman. She reminded him of a slightly plumper version of Matron Y'selle. Her thin, gray hair was cut to about the same length as the matron's. She wore the same red clothing, though the quality of hers was finer: the material itself seemed brighter, the hems neater, and golden threads wound their way up and down the seams. Despite the surface similarities, however, Caymus didn't believe the two women were related, as when this woman's face smiled up at them it didn't have nearly the same kindness in it as Y'selle's. Instead, she gave the impression of curiosity, of impish inquisitiveness. Her eyes were a pale blue color. They were so pale, in fact, that they appeared nearly white. If she hadn't been looking directly at them, glancing between Caymus, Rill, and Milo in turn, he'd have wondered if she might be blind.

The table's other occupant had dark skin, reminding Caymus of Guruk and Fach'un, the two men that he'd met just before he'd left the Temple. He appeared to be several years younger than those two—he was probably at least a year Caymus's elder—though Caymus had trouble judging age in those foreign features. He wore simple breeches and a plain, brown tunic that covered a lean, well-muscled torso. His head was shaved. He wore a pleasant smile. With some apprehension, Caymus noticed the smile was aimed across the table at Gwenna.

He felt his stomach tighten when he noticed that Gwenna was smiling back.

"Be'Var!" The unfamiliar woman stood, quickly stepped up to Be'Var, and embraced him in a friendly hug. The woman had a weathered, husky voice which, while showing some of the rough edges that came with her age, had no trouble in filling the room.

Caymus was surprised to see Be'Var hug her in return. He'd never known the man to be the hugging type. "How are you, Elia?" he asked, once they'd parted. His smile was as warm as any Caymus had ever seen on him. "It's been far too long." Raising an eyebrow, the master took stock of the woman's accouterment. "Sella didn't tell me you'd taken up the mission-keeper's robe."

Elia immediately turned to Y'selle, still sitting at the table. "And what else haven't you told him?" she said with a playful tone.

The familiarity of the scene made Caymus happy, though he was beginning to feel a bit uncomfortable. He, Rill, and Milo were obviously observing a reunion of old friends, and he couldn't help, standing as he was just inside the doorway, feeling like a bit of an intruder. There was also the fact that Gwenna and the dark-skinned fellow were still sharing a very long look. Did they know each other? Was there some kind of history between them? He didn't know, but he was starting to think he'd really like to leave.

Just as he was considering the best way of politely excusing himself, the woman looked past Be'Var's shoulder at the three young men. "And tell me about these gentlemen, Be'Var! Your manners are still as atrocious as ever."

Be'Var seemed to take a moment to consider his next words, then waved his hand toward them. "This pain-in-the-neck is Rill." Rill smiled and nodded a little uncomfortably when Elia's eyes focused on him. "He recently gave up life at the Temple, so he's technically no longer a part of the Order of Conflagrationists. However," Be'Var narrowed his eyes, "he's smarter than he looks, so I'd ask if you could afford him a bed, or maybe a spot in the corner, for the time being."

The woman moved to stand in front of Rill. Her expression changed from one of delighted happiness to a polite sort of friendliness. "How are you, Rill?" she said. "I'm Matron Elia, Keeper of the Mission, and you're welcome to a bed at Flamehearth for as long as you need one."

Rill's face was turning red, but he managed to stammer out, "Thank you, Matron Elia. I'm in your debt."

Matron Elia's smile extended as though he'd just shared a secret joke with her, then she moved along to stand in front of the next of the arrivals.

Be'Var continued. "That's Milo," he said. "He's the air priest who helped us send those messages from the Temple recently." Be'Var shook his head. "Burn me, but I've started depending on this one."

Milo was beaming. Elia reached out and took one of his hands in both of hers. "Milo," she said. "From what I gather, you and your friends, most of whom I've yet to meet, have been a blessing to us all since the attacks. I don't know if you've a place to stay in Kepren, but you're very welcome to stay with us." She leaned forward, conspiratorially. "I really like your feathers."

Milo's smile somehow got even wider. "Thank you!" he said. "I may just take you up on that!"

Elia nodded and then moved to stand in front of Caymus. She looked up at him to meet his eyes. Caymus was suddenly very aware of his height.

"And that," said Be'Var, his voice assuming a slightly more serious tone, "would be Caymus. He's the shaper I mentioned before we left."

Matron Elia reached up and put a hand on his arm. "Hello, Caymus," she said. Her face was a mix of wonder and curiosity. "It's been quite a while since I met a shaper. I hope you'll stay with us for a time. I feel we could learn a great deal from each other."

Caymus, feeling a bit out of place, nodded. "Thank you, Keeper—uh, Matron Elia. I think I'd like that."

The Keeper of Flamehearth Mission gave him a warm smile. "Good," she said, and gave his arm a squeeze. Then, she turned to Be'Var. "Sit, sit, tell me about the trip. Oh!" she exclaimed. "My manners are getting as bad as yours, Be'Var." She pointed to the dark-skinned youth sitting at the table. "This is Tavrin, one of the Falaar who came up from Terrek recently. He's been with us for a couple of weeks now and he's been amazingly useful."

Tavrin, who had finally stopped staring at Gwenna, stood and gave them a short bow. Caymus noted the slow, graceful way Tavrin moved, the way every motion seemed so deliberate. He'd seen Merkan move like that and so he wondered if Tavrin, too, was some sort of warrior. He suddenly had a lot of questions about the Falaar.

In a few minutes, they were all sitting at the table and Be'Var was telling Elia about their journey. He told them about the strange blizzard, about the Krealite they'd found in the floor of the cave, even about the broken wagon wheel they'd had to fix. Matron Elia asked probing questions, and nodded with each new detail, clearly affording man all of her attention.

Caymus, on the other hand, was paying more mind to Tavrin and the attention that he was giving Gwenna. The two weren't locked in a mutual gaze anymore, but his eyes were certainly still lingering. For her part, Gwenna wasn't openly flirting or anything, but Caymus got the impression that she might have been if he hadn't been there.

Just as Be'Var was getting to the part where they were entering the caves of Otvia, Caymus felt a kick to his shin. Looking up, he saw it was Rill, sitting across the table from him, who was trying to get his attention. Rill was making little head jerks and moving his eyes in the direction of the door, making less-than subtle suggestions that they find a reason to leave.

Caymus did rather like the idea of getting out of the room, but he thought it would be a bit rude to just ask to leave without having a good reason. Then, he remembered a little package that he had received just before he left the Temple.

"Excuse me," he said, once there was a pause in the conversation. "I'm sorry, but do any of you know where Sannet's parents live?"

~~~

The late afternoon sun was beginning to wane in the sky, its friendly warmth beginning to abate, as Caymus and Rill stepped quickly through a busy street, drinking in the sights and sounds of Kepren. Matron Y'selle had spent nearly an hour searching their belongings to find the package that Sannet had given to Caymus, having eventually discovered it tucked in amongst some bedding. As soon as they'd had the small bundle in hand, the two had raced out the mission's front entrance, following directions that, they were assured, would take them to the home of Sannet's parents.

They had already gotten lost a couple of times due to how spectacularly unfamiliar they were with the city. One of Y'selle's directions, for instance, had been to take a right at a particular linen shop; a hurried decision that a linen shop and a shop that sold window dressings must constitute the same thing had resulted in a good ten minutes of backtracking. For now, however, Caymus believed they were on the right trail.

Sannet's parents apparently lived in the Guard District—Y'selle had called it simply "The Guard"—the oldest of Kepren's three districts, so the pair had needed to pass through the large gate in the wall that separated the Grass from the Guard District. Caymus had noticed that the wall hadn't been made of the same perfectly interlocking stones as he'd seen when he'd first entered Kepren. Rather, it was constructed of familiar stone and mortar, much like the outer walls of Krin's.

He was surprised, in fact, with just how different the two districts looked from each other. The Grass was clean, precise, looking as though it had been built with expert hands. The Guard, on the other hand, carried the wear of many centuries. The mortar between the reddish-brown bricks of many of the buildings was chipped and worn, and the cobblestone streets dipped and rose under the pressure of tree roots or unstable ground. Most of the buildings he passed were two or three stories tall, and he occasionally spied one that had begun leaning on its foundation, necessitating complex webs of scaffolding, buttresses, and the hands of dozens of workmen.

Even the people seemed different. Horses pulled carts and carriages in
~~~

these streets, whereas most people in the Grass District had either ridden their horses or had walked with sacks or packs over their shoulders. The overall pace seemed slower, yet here there was a sort of tension in the air he hadn't noticed earlier. He'd seen people smiling eagerly at one another in the Grass. Few people even made eye contact with him here.

The wall hadn't seemed wide enough, somehow. He felt as though there should have been a much broader physical separation between the two places, one which would make a clearer delineation between the people that lived on either side.

"You feel like we just fell into a different world or something?" said Rill, his eyes making wide sweeps of the Guard District. Caymus only then realized that the two of them had stopped in the middle of a tree-lined street, irritating a few impatient pedestrians.

He smiled as he grabbed Rill's sleeve and dragged him to the side of the avenue. "I wonder what the Reed District looks like," he said, once the two were standing safely out of traffic.

Rill reached up and clapped him on the shoulder. "That's the one they gave to Shorevale, right? Gotta be full of ships and pirates, don'tcha think?"

Caymus grinned at his friend. "Something like that."

A few dozen yards into the Guard, Caymus saw a large square where several roads met and formed a circle around a large fountain. Caymus pulled Rill over to it, wanting a better look. A low, circular wall, with a few pipes jutting out from the edges, enclosed a smooth floor of fancy brickwork, but the whole thing was bone dry.

Atop a small pedestal in the middle of the dry fountain was the statue of a man. The smooth, gray surface had subtle veins of pink running through it here and there; Caymus thought that meant it was marble. The depicted figure wore what looked to be fine clothing: calf-high boots rose up over ballooning pants that were tied off with a wide belt. A loose-fitting coat appeared caught by some non-existent breeze. The man, whose wavy hair fell to his shoulders, was holding one of the coat's lapels with one hand as he appeared to gaze off into the distance.

Upon the pedestal was carved the name "Faivun". Caymus felt a small smile at play on his face. While Matron Y'selle had been going through packs and crates, looking for Sannet's package, she had given Caymus a short history lesson which had included this man.

Kepren had started as a small keep out here in the Tebrian plains hundreds—if not thousands—of years ago. Long before the advent of the districts and the duchies, Kepren had stood by itself as a city-state which, while laying claim to much of the land around it, had held very little political power.

It had been the many wars with Mael'vek, their aggressive neighbor to the South, which had forced change. During one of those wars, the Mael'vekians had thought to conquer Kepren through attrition, not only sending troops directly at them from the South, but also launching a small armada of ships up the western coast, delivering troops that would cut off trade at the mouth of the Silvertooth River and eventually force the Keprenites to either open their gates or starve.

The beginnings of what would eventually become the Tebrian League were forged from that conflict, and it started with an accord with the seaside city of Shorevale. Up to that point, Shorevale had generally kept to its own affairs. The people were great seafarers and traders, but they preferred not to meddle in the political affairs of others and their sizable navy had generally prevented others from meddling in theirs. However, once they'd been convinced that, should Kepren fall, the Mael'vekians would come after them next, Shorevale had brought hundreds of ships to bear against the Mael'vekian blockade, keeping the trade routes open so that the people of Kepren could continue their city's defense.

In the end, the war had been won, and a powerful alliance had been forged. To honor the tremendous assistance given during the war, fully half of Kepren, most of which lay along the banks of the Silvertooth River, had been given to the people of Shorevale to rule over. Caymus had balked at the thought, but Y'selle had explained that many Shorevalians had already been living and working in that part of Kepren at the time, so the sacrifice wasn't nearly as great as it sounded.

In the following centuries, the wars between Mael'vek and Kepren had continued, erupting every few decades and lasting at least a handful of years. It seemed that every generation of Keprenites had a war with their southern neighbor to call their own. In the previous century, Mael'vek had launched an attack which had succeeded in expanding its borders, swallowing and nearly completely destroying the city of Laivus, which had lain between the two warring nations. The Laivusians, as Caymus had already learned from Gwenna, had fled north in droves, seeking sanctuary within Kepren's walls until they could return home. Kepren's forces had eventually halted their foe's march northward, but by then the damage had been too great. Laivus had been razed, and so the refugees began to simply rebuild outside the walls of their new home.

It was during that conflict that the kings of Kepren and Shorevale, as well as the remaining leaders of Laivus's government, had been called to a meeting by the man this statue represented, a merchant politician named Faivun. The meeting, held on the deck of a ship anchored in the Silvertooth, was now known as Faivun's Council, and the direct consequences of it were that the Keprenite and Shorevalian areas of the city were officially renamed the Guard and Reed Districts, respectively. In addition, the Laivusians were given their own district: the walls of Kepren were built out to encompass several square miles of grassland, giving the refugees land to build on that was protected by citizens of both Kepren and Shorevale. The area had been called the Laivus Section originally, but it had eventually come to be called the Grass District.

Each of the three districts was ruled by a duke, with the king himself representing the needs of city as a whole. Each faction brought something important to the union: the Guard District provided the knowledge and resources of Kepren's standing army, with centuries of experience in repelling Mael'vekian attacks; the Reed District was home to no small amount of the Shorevalian navy; the Grass District brought with it ingenuity in engineering and craftsmanship, as the Laivusians were renowned artisans, evidenced by the way they put their buildings together without the need for mortar.

The three peoples, coming together as a single city, created not only a new vision of Kepren, but also the greater idea of Tebria. Caymus had marveled at the concept. He'd never really understood whether Tebria—or it's other name, the Tebrian League—was an actual nation or just a region on a map. In truth it was neither, but rather it was an understanding between three cultures that should one come under attack, the others would spring to its defense. There were no borders to the Tebrian League: they weren't needed. If a Shorevalian village needed aid, the aid would be provided, no matter if the village lay a yard from Kepren's outer wall or several miles north of the Greatstone Mountains.

Most of Tebria's duties still consisted of fighting back the advances of Mael'vek every few dozen years, but the combined force also repelled pirates from the coast, built structures for new settlements, and generally kept the peace in the region.

Caymus wondered what kind of man Faivun had really been, what kind of personality it had taken to weave three cities into one, to convince the King of Kepren that giving up two thirds of his city was to his own benefit. He idly scratched the back of his hand and wondered if he could ever be that kind of man.

"Hey!"

Caymus turned to see that Rill, now several strides ahead, had just realized that he wasn't following. "Are you coming?"

Caymus waved his friend over and motioned to the statue with his chin. "Do you know much about him?"

Rill shrugged. "Just the usual stuff, that he's why Kepren's split up the way it is."

Caymus shook his head in wonder. "Where did he come from? Do you know?"

Rill furrowed his brow at Caymus. "Come from?"

"Yeah, was he from Kepren originally, or Shorevale?"

Rill looked up at the statue. "I think he was from Laivus; he ran north with all the rest of them."

"Really?" Caymus's eyes went wide.

Rill looked at him again, suspicion on his face. "Yeah, why?" he said.

Caymus took a moment, trying to put words to what he was thinking. "He came from a place that had just been destroyed," he said, "and he convinced the king of another land to give up an awful lot of his city." He shook his head in disbelief. "How did he do that?"

Rill tilted his head and looked at nothing in particular as he considered. "Well, the king still has the final say about anything that happens in Kepren, so he didn't technically lose any power." He gave a small wince. "Or, at least, he used to have the final say."

Caymus finally took his eyes off the statue. "Used to?"

Rill nodded. "I heard some of the kids chattering back at the mission. It seems the king isn't doing very well lately. I don't know what's wrong with him, but he's been sick for a long time."

Caymus thought about the idea of a monarch not being well enough to govern his own realm. It didn't sit well with him. "So, if he's too sick to make decisions, how does anything get done?"

"The prince," Rill said. "His son, Prince Garrin. He's been in charge of the Kepren army for a good while, and I guess he'll be needing to make decisions about governing the city now, too."

"Don't the dukes have a problem with that?"

"What, you mean with someone other than the king having the power to overrule them?"

Caymus nodded.

Rill shrugged. "Maybe? I dunno. Who can understand the way nobility thinks?"

They stood there a moment longer. Caymus looked up at the statue again, considered the strangeness of this place. Rill waited impatiently for Caymus to be done looking.

Finally, Rill tapped Caymus on the shoulder and indicated their next turn. "You ready?"

Caymus smiled and nodded. "Of course. Sorry."

As they walked down the streets of the Guard, dodging the occasional horse or other pedestrian, Rill changed the subject. "Boy, did you see Gwenna with that Tavrin fellow?"

Caymus was caught off-guard by the question. He wasn't sure if he was angry or just upset by it. He tried to keep the dark tone out of his voice, but he wasn't entirely successful. "I did."

Rill gave Caymus his most supportive look. "Don't worry about it, Caymus. I'm sure he's just a fancy distraction. She'll have forgotten all about him in a day or two."

Caymus wasn't sure about that. She'd never looked at *him* like that. "Do you know who he is? Was he here before Gwenna left and so they already knew each other?"

Rill shook his head. "Just got here a couple of weeks ago, the matron said, which would have meant Gwenna, Bridget and Y'selle would have already been on their way north. I think he came to see those other two, the ones we left at the Temple, but he didn't know they'd left already." He shrugged his shoulders. "I don't know why he's still here."

Caymus frowned. "Great."

Rill elbowed him gently in the ribs. "Don't worry about it," he said again. "I'm sure she'll come around in the end."

Caymus had been keeping his eyes open for a particular sign among those hanging outside the buildings they were passing. Among the various representations, including an anvil, a candle, and an angry-looking chicken, he noticed a picture of a pig that was divided into front and back halves. "I think we're here," he said, pointing up at it.

Rill followed his arm and grinned. "I think you're right! You've got the thing, yeah?"

Caymus reached around to a pouch on his belt and withdrew the box Sannet had given him. "I've got it."

The two of them opened the door and walked inside. Caymus was immediately met by the smells of stale blood and carved flesh: the smells of a butcher's shop. He took a deep breath of the stuff, surprised that he didn't find it unpleasant.

The interior of the place was larger than he'd expected. Along the walls, both left and right, a half-dozen square tables stood with simple, wooden chairs about them. All were empty, though he could tell from the dirty glasses and plates here and there that they'd been used recently.

Along the back wall was a plain but sturdy-looking wooden counter, anchored to the left wall and extending almost all the way to the right. Several cuts of meat, some sitting by themselves, others stacked half a dozen or so high, sat upon the counter while a thin man with graying hair worked at cleaning up. As the boys walked in, the man looked up with a smile. His head was thick with hair that had obviously been changing from brown to gray for a few years while a full, neatly-trimmed beard followed suit. He peered at them over a pair of spectacles whose rims were just a little bit thinner than his waist seemed to be.

The man wiped a knife on his apron and smiled politely to the boys. "How can I help you young gentlemen today?" he said. He waved a hand to indicate the counter. "I was just starting to close up, but I have a few cuts left that need to go out my door soon, so I can give you a good price on them. Mmm?"

Caymus felt a little guilty. He felt an immediate fondness for the man's gentle manner, and it seemed a bit duplicitous to have come in without intending to make a purchase. "Sorry," he said, affecting a wince, "we're not here to buy anything. Are you Mister Teldaar?"

The man almost took a step back, then he raised an eyebrow with what could have been either suspicion or mock suspicion; Caymus didn't know the eyebrow's owner well enough to tell which.

"Hmmm," the man said, folding the hand with the knife under the arm of the other hand, which tickled at his beard. He looked over each of them, in turn. "Well, you both seem a bit young to be collecting for the banker." He wagged a finger at them, thoughtfully, "but I suppose you could be looking for something else from me, eh?" He pondered at them a moment longer, then put the knife down and placed his hands on his hips. "Alright, let's say that I tell you I am Mister Teldaar. What would you say to that?"

Caymus exchanged a glance with Rill, who seemed to be liking this game. Caymus put a hand to his chest. "I'd say that I'm Caymus," he said, "and this is Rill. We just arrived from the Temple, up north? We're friends of Sannet?"

The man's entire demeanor changed instantly. His eyes widened until their whites were showing, and a grin appeared on his face that easily erased ten years from him. "Friends of Sannet!" he said, wiping his hands and quickly stepping to the end of the counter. "Why didn't you say so?" As he made his way to their side of the cutting board, he yelled over his shoulder to a partially open door that Caymus hadn't noticed before. "Maggie, make some tea, will you? Sannet has sent us some guests!" When he reached the two of them, he took each of their hands earnestly in both of his. "You will stay awhile, yes? Have some tea?"

Caymus nodded, returning the man's smile. "Yes, sir, thank you."

The man waved a hand dismissively and moved to the front door, where he threw the latch. "Please, please, I am Franklin, and my wife is Margaret. I'll have none of this 'sir' business with friends of my son." He led them around the counter and toward the door that stood in the wall behind it. "Come, you can sit down with us and tell us how our Sannet is doing."

When they passed through the doorway, Caymus was a bit surprised at the complete change in décor. The public room out front was sparse, with bare, only lightly varnished wooden furniture and not a single piece of ornamentation or decoration on the walls. Beyond the door, however, they entered a hallway adorned with wooden paneling that was dark and rich, upon which hung small paintings of flowers and landscapes.

After a moment, Franklin had turned them to the left and into a big kitchen with two stoves against the wall and a large cutting board in the center. Off to one side of the room stood a cozy dining table with four chairs arrayed around it. The kitchen opened up, further on, into what seemed to be a comfortable-looking sitting room with padded chairs and a large fireplace. A set of stairs stood at the far end, leading up to a second floor.

At the nearest of the two stoves stood a woman who was easily as wiry as Franklin, but whose long hair, tied in a neat ponytail, was only just beginning to go gray. She wore spectacles too, and she looked up at them with what seemed a mixture of curiosity and delight as she finished lighting a small fire under the kettle. "Hello," she said. "Has my husband offered you anything to eat?"

Caymus was a little bit hungry, but things were moving just a little too quickly for him. Rill spoke up. "We're not hungry ma'am," he said, "but thank you."

"Bah!" she said, assisting her husband in leading them to the dining table, "who is this 'ma'am'?"

Franklin laughed. "I told you," he said, wagging a finger at them. "I am Franklin, and this is Margaret." He turned to his wife, "My wife, these are Caymus and Rill and they tell me they just came from the Temple."

Margaret's eyes widened a little. "You only just arrived in Kepren and you come to see us first?" she said. "You must be very good friends of our son, indeed."

"They won't miss us at the mission for a while," said Rill, "and, to be honest, it gave us a chance to see the city a little bit."

"Plus," said Caymus, placing the little box he'd been holding all this time on the table, "Sannet asked me to give you this when we got here, and I thought the sooner, the better."

As Caymus slid the box to them, the couple each put a hand to it, tentatively, as though it might bite them, and gave each other a look that Caymus couldn't quite read. It was the kind of look he'd seen his father and mother give each other a handful of times, usually when he'd done something either very right or very wrong. Caymus had always suspected that they'd been exchanging hundreds of words with those looks, and he'd frequently wondered if it was something that only married people—or maybe parents—could do.

Sannet's father was the first to turn back, his hand still gingerly touching the box. "How is Sannet, then? Is he well?"

Caymus nodded. "He's very well. He's probably the best disciple there."

"I'll say," said Rill. "Between the two of you, it's nearly impossible for anyone else to compete."

Both parents smiled. "So," said Margaret, "he is doing well in the," she paused a moment, trying to remember, "it's the Second Circle, isn't it?"

"Third, actually," Caymus said. "He took his trial just a short time ago."

Both of them looked at Caymus with shocked faces. "Third Circle?" Franklin finally said. "Isn't he young to be in the Third Circle already?"

"I think," said Rill, looking to Caymus for confirmation, "he's the youngest to ever pass the last test, isn't he?"

Caymus considered arguing the point. Technically, it was true that Sannet was the youngest to ever take the final trial and pass it, though Caymus would have been, had it not been for that terrible night with the krealites. It was an altogether murky subject, and though he appreciated Rill's raised eyebrows offering him the opportunity to say something, he really didn't want to get into it. Why would Sannet's parents want to hear about it, anyway?

"I think so," was all he said.

Both parents nodded with disbelieving smiles, and Margaret quietly opened the box with one hand. When the lid lifted, she gasped as the smallest hint of faint, yellow light escaped the box and reflected off the skin of her hand. The couple shared that look again, and Caymus saw a small tear escape down Margaret's check. "He did it," said Franklin, softly, squeezing her hand. "He actually did it."

Margaret nodded and wiped the tear away, then looked back to the box. "Oh," she said through a voice that was flooded with emotion, "there's a letter, too." She reached in and pulled out a square of paper which she unfolded and began reading, quietly, to herself.

As his wife read, Franklin reached into the box and withdrew a small stone, barely the size of his thumb, which was the source of the light. Caymus looked upon the gently glowing object in the man's thin hands and was astonished to think that he could have brought it all the way from the Temple and not known it was there.

Sannet's father must have seen the look of wonder on his face. He held it up and looked at the boys with a proud smile. "You know what it is?" he said, arching an eyebrow. "Did Sannet tell you?"

Caymus and Rill just shook their heads.

Franklin smiled, putting it gently on the table between them. "It belonged to my great-grandfather," he said, "and to many of his ancestors before that." He tilted his head toward the stone. "*He* was able to make it glow like that, my great-grandfather, as was his father and his father before him." He sighed. "My father, however, never could, and neither could I. We never knew why, but it seemed that for two generations the Teldaars lost something special." He put a finger in the air. "But my boy," he said, pride choking his words, "my boy brought it back, didn't he?"

Caymus was delighted. Sannet had never told him anything about the stone, but he understood the significance of it. Not everyone was born with the ability to open conduits, to bend and manipulate the elements, but it was often passed down from parent to child. For the Aspects to have skipped two whole generations would have been of great concern to a family used to counting priests among their line; for the abilities to suddenly surface after having been absent so long was quite a cause for celebration.

As he sat there, watching Franklin stare at the glowing stone, Caymus noticed movement out of the corner of his eye. He looked up and saw a boy, maybe twelve or thirteen years old, sitting about halfway up the stairs, staring at the group at the table with a dark frown. He hadn't noticed the boy arrive, and he wondered when he'd gotten there. Did Sannet have a brother? The boy didn't much resemble Sannet or his parents, having a rounder face, smaller eyes, and a fair amount of weight on his bones.

Franklin looked up, following Caymus's eyes, then raised a hand and beckoned the boy over. "Roland," he said, "come meet these two gentlemen. They're friends of Sannet."

With a look that Caymus could only call contempt, the boy stood, quickly descended the stairs, and ran past them through another door in the sitting room. Caymus winced slightly as he heard one door, and then another, slam, shaking the walls of the building slightly. The silence of the next few moments was only broken by the sound of the kettle on the stove coming to a boil.

Sannet's mother, having put the letter down, slid it over to Franklin and stood, making her way to the stove and removing the kettle. "I'm sorry about Roland," she said. "He's such an angry boy."

Caymus, after checking with Rill and finding him equally confused, said, "Is he Sannet's brother?"

Franklin, who was reading the letter now, nodded. "He is," he said, "but you'd hardly know it, the two of them are so different."

"It's our fault, really," said Margaret, pouring hot water and straining tea leaves. "We gave so much to Sannet. When he was born, we saved for a long time, worked a lot of long hours so that he could be educated properly and go to the Temple. We found him tutors, bought him books, gave him every possible chance." She smiled wistfully and brought the four cups over. "He's done so well, and we're so proud of him, but when Roland came along…" She set the cups down on the table. "There just wasn't much left in the cupboard for him, I'm afraid, and I think he understands that."

"We make certain he doesn't want for anything," said Franklin, a frown on his face as he continued reading. "We even started serving drinks and sandwiches out front, becoming a small restaurant as well as a butcher's shop, to meet the extra need."

Margaret nodded. "I think he just feels that Sannet got more of our love than he does."

"Nonsense," said Franklin, putting the letter down. He looked up at Caymus and Rill, seriousness in his eyes, "Those beasts," he said, "those insect-things, they were at the Temple, too?"

Caymus nodded. "It…wasn't a good night."

Rill groaned, not looking at anybody. "Worst *I* ever had. I could go my whole life without seeing another krealite and die happy."

Sannet's father looked at Rill questioningly. "Krealite?"

Caymus and Rill spent some time telling them about the past two weeks, about the night the creatures attacked, about how Be'Var had told them that they were intruders into their world from the realm of an alien element and how they only seemed to attack places where people worshiped. They told them, too, about the time they'd spent at Otvia and how they'd learned there that the element in question was called "kreal", making the creatures themselves "krealites".

They didn't go into any detail about the Knight of the Flame or the mark upon Caymus's left hand. Caymus saw it as being personal and Rill didn't seem to want to explain any more than necessary.

"I saw them in the street that night," said Sannet's father as he gazed at a spot on the wall. "They were terrible things to behold."

"How many of them were there?" asked Caymus, taking a sip of his tea and noting, with no small amount of delight, that it tasted of oranges.

"I saw three of them, dashing through the streets, killing everybody they came across." Franklin gave a small shudder as he recalled the night. "They didn't seem to want anything, just to kill people." He turned to his wife. "Who was that man with thick eyebrows, the one who sold the candles?"

"Wiclef," said Margaret, not looking up from her cup.

"Wiclef, yes. He was braver than most," he said. "He ran out with a torch to try to scare them away, as though they were common animals that feared a simple bit of fire on a stick." He made a quick, side-to-side motion with his hand. "They cut him in half, like he was just an annoyance." He pointed to a shelf off to the side of the stove. Caymus turned and saw it was covered with dishes, but also with a black candle in the shape of three towers on rock, a wick for each tower. "He made the most interesting candles," he continued. "His son runs the store now," he waved his hand dismissively, "but he doesn't have the talent. I'm going to miss that man."

"It was good," said Margaret, finally looking up, "that the soldiers came when they did."

"Ah," said Franklin, tapping a finger on the table, "the prince!" He leaned forward, whispering conspiratorially. "I saw Prince Garrin himself fighting them," he pointed toward the front room, "just outside there."

He made hacking and slashing motions with his hands as he continued. "At first, they couldn't do anything, just wailed on the armor. It did nothing! At last, though, the bigger men managed to grab onto a leg, here and there, and they were able to hold it still for just a moment." He smiled, triumphantly. "The prince took the Black Sword and put it through one of them, drove it straight through the middle!"

Caymus frowned. "He got a sword through the armor?"

Franklin waggled a finger. "Not just a sword," he said. "The Black Sword of the Prince!" He made a stabbing motion in the air. "I don't know what power is in the Black Sword, but it pierced the monster right through the heart when nothing else could." He leaned back and took a sip of his tea. "When the first died, the other two just seemed to sink right through the ground, like it was water. Strangest thing I ever saw, that. The prince and his men stayed for a while longer, waiting to see if they would come back." He shrugged, "But they never did."

Caymus was amazed. Merkan had told him of his success in slowly forcing a blade through the armor of a krealite, but this was the first time he'd heard of anybody managing to pierce through with an actual sword. He'd never heard of this prince before today, or of his sword, but he was beginning to develop a great deal of respect for both. Anyone who'd stood face-to-face with a krealite and had lived to talk about it was someone Caymus held in high regard.

Caymus thought about the number of krealites that had attacked the Temple. "Do you know how many there were?" he asked. "Aside from the three you saw, I mean."

Sannet's parents looked at each other. Margaret shrugged, stood up, and began collecting empty cups while her husband answered. "From what I heard," he said, "they just showed up in all the districts at once. I'd say," he winced in thought, "more than twenty, less than fifty."

Caymus nearly gasped, thinking of what fifty of those things, fifty sets of ravaging claws and teeth, could do to a city. "Incredible," was all he could say.

Franklin smiled at him. "Well boys," he said, pushing his chair back and standing. "It is time for me to clean up my shop and go and find my little brat of a son. If you hope to be back to your mission before nightfall, you had better get yourselves moving."

Caymus and Rill stood, intending to thank Franklin and Margaret for their hospitality. Before they knew it, however, offered handshakes turned into hugs and they found themselves hurrying out the door with fond wishes and five thick cuts of steak.

The aging couple had been right: night was falling quickly, and lamplighters were already making their rounds, providing illumination for the streets and alleys. As Caymus looked around at the city of Kepren, marveling again at this amazing place, his eyes were drawn to small figure, standing atop one of the roofs.

He recognized the figure as Roland. Why would Sannet's little brother be staring at them like that, and from such a strange place? He was about to say something about it, but Rill interrupted his train of thought: "Race you back!"

~~~

Ten minutes later, Caymus and Rill found themselves alternately jogging or running through the city on the way back to the mission, both hot with sweat. Sannet's parents had given the boys a satchel in which to carry the cuts of meat back to the mission. It wore a bit uncomfortably on Caymus, as the thing was meant for someone of a more average size and so it rode a bit too high on his hip, bouncing and jostling with each step. Caymus had enjoyed visiting with the Teldaars, but he was really wishing they'd left a bit earlier.

By the time the pair reached the Grass District again, the sun had disappeared beneath the high western wall of the city. The dry twilight, however, wasn't yet dark enough for the streetlamps to offer any useful light to passersby. Rill had asked Caymus, between pants, how he thought they kept the lamps burning, as each device was little more than a box lantern held aloft by an iron pole, none of which appeared to contain any significant reservoir of oil. Caymus hadn't known, but he'd suspected that it had something to do with the oil itself, suggesting that perhaps Kepren did some significant trade with Otvia.

The two slowed to a walk once Flamehearth was in sight, allowing themselves to catch their breaths a bit before they reached the front entrance to the mission. Rill opened the door and held it, genuflecting as Caymus walked through as though making way for the lord of the manor.

Caymus's laughter at his friend's antics was cut short when he noticed that several faces inside had turned to look at him. As Rill stepped up beside him, equally surprised to discover that they had walked in on some kind of gathering, Caymus decided that in the future they should use the side door when entering the building.

The front room of Flamehearth was large enough that the missionaries could have meetings among themselves or entertain guests who might have business there. A handful of padded chairs sat against the walls, and a large, circular conference table, complete with hard-looking chairs, took up a full quadrant of the floorspace. Standing about the table, the chairs pushed off to one side, were Be'Var and Matron Elia, as well as two other
~~~

people, a man and a woman, whom Caymus hadn't met before.

The man had the look of a soldier. When Caymus and Rill had made their rather awkward entrance, he'd had his foot up on one of the chairs, his elbow leaning against his raised knee, but he smiled and stood up straight when he saw them. He seemed several years older than Caymus, perhaps thirty or so years of age, having brown hair which was trimmed just short enough to stay out of his eyes. He wore light armor of leather and padding, covered here and there with small plates of circular metal. A sword in a leather scabbard hung from a sash around his waist.

The woman nearly took Caymus's breath away. He wasn't sure of her age, but she couldn't have been more than a year or two his senior. Her light skin was accentuated by brown eyes and dark brows. Her features were sharp, almost as though they'd actually been sculpted from her face. Black hair, wavy and full, fell to the middle of her back and obscured her shoulders. The dress she wore seemed, at the same time, both simple and radiant. The fabric was light blue, the color of the afternoon sky, and was gathered with white stitching and lace as it cascaded down the length of her to the floor. She wasn't smiling. Her eyes were hard, as though they had seen more than her age should have allowed, but they also moved over the two boys standing in the doorway with curiosity, as though she was searching for something.

Caymus thought she might be the most beautiful woman he'd ever seen.

"Have a good run, boys?" Be'Var said, arching an eyebrow at the two of them.

Caymus was keenly aware of the sweat dripping from his chin and was certain the front of his tunic was drenched. "Sorry," he said. He found himself making a small bow. "We didn't mean to interrupt." He grabbed Rill by the shoulder and started leading him off. "We'll just get out of your way."

"No, no, no," Be'Var said. "Come here, both of you. Our guests have been waiting for you to turn up. It's about time you made an appearance..." He cast a disapproving eye over them, "...presentable or not."

The man, an easy smile on his face, walked toward the two of them, his hand extended. "Master Be'Var here said I wouldn't have trouble figuring out which was which." He took each of their hands in turn, shaking them firmly. Caymus felt awkward with the satchel full of meat still hanging around him; he wondered if he should take it off.

"Caymus," Be'Var continued, "Rill, meet Prince Garrin, heir to the throne and Champion Protector of Kepren." He said the last with a slight chuckle and a shake of his head, as though he thought the title absurd.

Caymus was stunned. He didn't have a clue what he was supposed to do. He'd already tried bowing, and he suddenly found himself doing it again. "Your…Highness?"

The Prince gave a short laugh and slapped him on the shoulder. "Please," he said, "oh please, no bowing. I get enough of that kind of thing at the Keep. I make Be'Var call me by my proper name and that demand extends to his friends." He gave the two of them a meaningful look. "Any more 'your highness' business and I'll have you hung."

Caymus was frozen for a moment, but he noticed Rill chuckling quietly out of the corner of his eye and so decided the prince was probably joking. The prince's—Garrin's—broad smirk lent credence to the conclusion.

"Do not be cruel, Garrin," said the girl in the blue dress, shaking her head at him and frowning. In those few words, Caymus detected the hint of an accent, though it was one he didn't recognize.

"Indeed," said Be'Var, shifting one of the chairs over and sitting down at the table. "However much I like a good hanging, these two have had an eventful couple of weeks and probably don't need you threatening them, too."

Prince Garrin, still looking at Caymus and Rill, nodded in acquiescence. "He's right, of course." He nodded to them. "My apologies. It's very good to meet you both." Then, to Caymus, he said with a wink, "Be'Var speaks very highly of his new flame-shaper."

Caymus felt like he was finally getting the hang of this conversation. He'd been caught off-guard, but he decided he liked the prince's easy-going attitude. He was, however, finding it hard to reconcile with the story he'd just heard of the man's bravery during the attack on Kepren. "It's good to meet you, also." He pointed back and forth between Be'Var and the prince. "The two of you know each other, I take it?"

Garrin waved them over to the table, pulling over a couple of the displaced chairs, and indicated that they should sit down. As he spoke, he also pulled out a chair for his companion. "Indeed. Ol' Master Be'Var saved my life once, a very long time ago."

Be'Var waved off the comment. "Not that long ago," he said, "and I stitched up a wound was all."

"You *saved my life*," Garrin said, enunciating every word. He turned to Caymus and Rill, who were, by now, seated. "It was during one of my father's campaigns—must have been at least a dozen years ago. We were holding back a small Mael'vekian raid into our camp." He paused and, for a moment, appeared to gaze into his own memory. "Never did figure out where they all came from, or how they got so far behind our lines." He shrugged, looking back at the faces around the table. "Anyway, my men and I held them back in the end, but I wound up with a sword in my gut for my troubles."

Caymus winced as the prince indicated, with two fingers, a spot just below his sternum and off to one side, where his liver should be. "I was done for," he said, "crying out—for my nanny, would you believe!—as I waited for the life to bleed out of me. Then this cranky old physician marches out of nowhere, kneels down next to me, and says, 'Hold still and shut up, or I'll really make you cry'." He looked over at Master Be'Var, who had his hand over his eyes. "Wasn't even sure, at that point, if he was on our side!"

"You were still laid up," said Be'Var, "for several weeks as I recall, so try not to oversell it, would you?"

Garrin ignored him. "I shouldn't have made it through that night." He flashed Be'Var a wide grin. "Master Be'Var's been my favorite physician ever since."

Be'Var shook his head. "Worst mistake I ever made! I never could get any proper work done after that, what with you and your father always making sure I was near the command tents."

Garrin nodded, then looked at Caymus, pointing at Be'Var with his thumb. "You know, he actually quit the army just to get away from me?"

Caymus, and everyone else at the table, looked at Be'Var. "I did no such thing," was all he said.

"Your manners," said Matron Elia, who had been sitting quietly with her arms folded up to now, looked to each of the men in turn, "are truly awful. Do you know that?"

Caymus was a little stunned at the accusation, but Elia continued before he could ask what she meant. She held out a hand, indicating the girl in the blue dress. "Caymus, Rill, this is Aiella. She's the daughter of Brocke, the ambassador from Creveya, the Summit, and is staying at the Keep with her father."

Caymus quickly rose to his feet, managing to knock the chair out from under him as he did so. "I'm so sorry," he said, his face flushing. He felt all eyes on him, but he wasn't quite sure what to do next. In the end, he gave the most gracious bow he could, with the table in the way. "It's wonderful to meet you, Miss."

Rill, too, stood up and gave her a small bow, though not with anything like the intensity Caymus had shown. As Caymus stepped back to pick his chair up, he looked back and thought he saw the faintest hint of a smile touch her lips.

As he sat down again, he addressed Flamehearth's guests. "So, can I ask why you're both here? You can't really have come just to meet us." As Caymus began adjusting his chair under him, he noticed for the first time that Callun was also in the room, though he sat apart from everyone else in a padded chair in the corner. Callun's eyes were on him and so he gave the man a friendly nod, which he didn't return. Caymus turned back to the table, and as he idly scratched the back of his neck, he tried to shake the uncomfortable feeling that the man engendered in him.

It was Matron Elia who spoke next. "Ambassador Brocke, Aiella's father, is in the courtyard investigating our broken, old water pump. He brought Aiella along because I've been wanting to meet her for some time." She glanced at Aiella, who gave her a small smile.

"You're saying," said Rill, narrowing his eyes, "that an ambassador is here to mend a pump?"

"No, no," said Elia, waving a hand, "not mend it. He's just helping us determine whether there is any water under it."

"My father," said Aiella, straightening a bit in her seat, "he has been helping the crown to locate new sources of underground water since the drought, it began." Caymus suspected, based on the way that only the occasional word carried an unfamiliar accent, that Aiella must have spent some time learning to suppress it.

"The good ambassador," said Garrin, addressing Rill, but looking at Aiella, "has been helping Kepren a great deal over the past few months. It's more than his position requires of him. The man is a credit to the Summit." He gave Aiella quick smile, which she did not return, and then turned back to the rest of the table. "If it weren't for his dowsing, a lot of the farmland along the Silvertooth would have dried up months ago."

Caymus briefly wondered what the Summit was as the Keeper picked up the thread of conversation. "I told him a few weeks back," she said, "that we had an old well pump in our courtyard. It's been disused for as long as I've been here, but he told me he'd like to take a look at it when chance allowed." She turned to face the prince. "What *you're* doing here, I'm actually not certain."

Garrin's smile disappeared, his eyes followed his finger as it traced the woodgrain of the table. "To be quite honest with you, I needed to get out of the Keep for a time," he said. When he raised his eyes to look at Be'Var, some of the smile came back. "And when I heard that my favorite healer was coming back to Kepren, I had the guards keep an eye out for him.

Be'Var frowned at him. "Don't you have more important things to be doing than coming down here among us mortals and, more to the point, bothering me?"

"It's good to see you too, old man."

Be'Var scoffed, but Caymus noticed a very slight smile finding purchase on the old man's face.

Garrin turned back to Caymus. "So, Caymus, Be'Var tells me he's been teaching you the sword and shield. Are you any good?"

Caymus shrugged. "I don't know, to be honest. Rill's the only one I've had to practice with, and he's just learning too."

Garrin nodded. "I see. I may need to have you brought to the Keep for a sparring session sometime, then."

Caymus blinked. "Really?"

"Absolutely," said Garrin. He pulled the sword at his hip a few inches free of its scabbard, revealing a blade that was as black as the midnight sky. "Don't worry, I won't use this thing."

"Just watch your knuckles," said Rill, sighing and rubbing his hands.

Caymus scowled at him, and then turned back to Prince Garrin. "I don't think I'd be much good for sparring, Your—Garrin, but I'll happily come to learn."

"Good," said Garrin, slamming the sword back into the scabbard. "I'll have it arranged for some time in the next couple of days."

A quiet, dry voice drifted out of the corner where Callun sat. "Do you think he will be great?"

Everyone turned to him. He was staring at Caymus with those lifeless eyes of his, but his face wore what looked like a smirk.

"Great?" said Garrin, who then turned to look Caymus up and down. He shrugged, with a curious smile. "Perhaps."

Be'Var's eyes flitted between Caymus and the prince, a look of intense curiosity on his face. After a moment, though, he sighed, mostly to himself, and changed the subject. "Miss Aiella," he said, looking across the table at her, "do you know how long your father's been out there?"

Aiella looked over her shoulder, her long hair bouncing across her frame as her head turned. "It has been a while," she said. "I check on him."

"Would you mind taking Caymus with you?" Be'Var said, rising as she did.

Caymus, standing also, gave Be'Var a questioning look. Be'Var shifted his eyes to him, but then nodded in the direction of the courtyard. "Keep your mouth shut and you might just learn something."

Caymus turned to Aiella, who stood as though considering. "Come along," she finally said, motioning with a small movement of her hand for him to follow.

After sparing a moment to give the satchel of meat to the mission-keeper—she seemed genuinely delighted to receive it—Caymus did as he was asked. He followed Aiella out the door, then he shuffled forward a bit to walk next to her. He felt more than a little uncomfortable being so close to this girl. Even walking directly beside her, he felt as though her eyes were still on him, judging, looking for some form of weakness. He really hoped they wouldn't have to speak before reaching the courtyard.

"Caymus," she said, dashing his hopes, "Be'Var, he speaks of you a great deal." There was no warmth in her tone, and she kept her gaze locked straight ahead. "You are a priest, then?"

"No," he said, surprised that he hadn't properly considered his answer before speaking. "I was studying to be a master, but that's not going to happen anymore."

"You have failed in your training?"

"No," he said, "not exactly." He paused a moment, wondering how to explain it all. He thought it a personal matter and wasn't sure he liked the idea of telling the whole story to a complete stranger.

"How does one do this, to 'not exactly' fail?" she asked. This time, she turned to look at him, her eyes probing.

Caymus sighed. He decided that he might as well just tell her. "I stepped into the Conduit for my final test just after the krealites attacked. When I did, I was taken into the Conflagration and the Lords there told me that I was 'impure' and that I'd never be a master."

When he finished, her eyes moved away from him and she finally turned to face forward again. "Krealites?" she said. "This is what you have named the monsters that attacked?"

Caymus nodded. "Yes, the element they're made of: it's called kreal."

"You seem to know much about them."

"More than I ever wanted to."

She halted her questioning for a moment as they made their way down the corridor. As they turned into one of the rooms that held a door to the courtyard—this room appeared to be a small library, with deep blue paint and little suns painted on the walls that weren't covered in books—she spoke again. "I met a girl earlier, named Gwenna, who seemed to know you well. She is your woman, yes?"

Caymus nearly broke his stride in surprise. "No!" he said, with greater volume than he'd intended. More quietly, he began, "At least…" but then couldn't seem to think of a way to put it succinctly. "No," he finally said, "she's not my woman."

"You appear uncertain in the matter," she said. "It seems a strange thing of which to be uncertain."

Caymus didn't have an answer for that.

They stepped through a large double-door into the small, square courtyard at Flamehearth. The only light was the soft glow of a half-moon, and the only sounds were those played by a handful of crickets, a number of which halted their songs the moment the two figures intruded into their space. A narrow, stone path encircled the perimeter of the grassy area along with small, stone benches, flower beds, and a few dry rose bushes.

Off to one side, a round-looking man was bent over on the ground, his hands and his forehead pressed into the dying grass. He wore a blue alb, the same color as Aiella's dress, and a darker-blue stole over his shoulders. Both were covered in bits of dead plant matter.

"Sit or stand, I do not care," came the man's voice, "but cease your moving." Caymus could hear Aiella's manner of speech much more strongly in him, and now that he was getting a full dose of it, he realized that it wasn't so much an accent—though that was there, too—but rather a different way of putting sentences together. He couldn't quite get a handle on the exact difference, though.

Aiella grabbed Caymus and pulled him over to sit next to her on one of the benches. Caymus leaned over to whisper to her, "I didn't mean to break his concentration."

She regarded him with a frown, as though he wasn't understanding something obvious. She spoke without whispering. "The question, it is not one of concentration. My father, he searches of water, and our bodies, they are filled with it. When we are moving about, the finding of other sources, it is more difficult."

Caymus nodded. He hadn't considered that. He knew that the blood in their bodies was largely composed of water, but he hadn't thought of it as something the man would have to intentionally ignore.

"You do not spend much time with non-fire worshipers. Am I right?" Aiella cocked an eyebrow at him, as though accusing him of something.

She had a point. Caymus had felt a little backward on more than one occasion since he'd arrived in Kepren. "You're right," he said. "I suppose I am a little out of my element." He grinned at the pun, not having intended it. Aiella ignored the comment and looked back toward her father.

Caymus remembered something Matron Elia had said. "Where is the Summit?" he asked. "The Keeper said you were from there. I hadn't heard of it before tonight."

She paused before answering, as though deciding the worthiness of the question. "Creveya, it lies in the eastern arms of the Greatstone Mountains." She glanced over at him. "You know where the Greatstones are, yes?"

Caymus nodded. "We crossed them to get here. Is the Summit part of Creveya, then?"

"Creveya is a lake," she said. "It is a holy place for those that live on and around its shores. Creveya, the Summit, it covers the western shore, rising to the Gavran's Peak. On the eastern side is Creveya, the Tower. It is filled with people who wish nothing more than to destroy the Summit, and to entirely claim Creveya for themselves."

"Destroy?" Caymus said, his face knotting in confusion. "I don't understand, what is it about this tower that makes the people in it want to destroy you?"

Aiella, her gaze narrowing, turned to give him a long, hard look, as though trying to decide whether he was foolish, ignorant, or simply mocking her. Her eyes were oceans of deep browns, flecked with islands of hazel.

Finally, she looked away again. "The city, it is so named for the ruin of a tower that once stood there, just as Creveya, the Summit was named for the view of the lake that Gavran's Peak once offered. The Tower and the Summit, they have always been enemies that fight for control of Creveya." She tilted her head toward the man in the courtyard. "My father, he is the ambassador for the Summit. Somewhere in this city is the Tower's representative."

Caymus considered her words. He had difficulty imagining the place she was describing: two cities, on either side of a lake, which were at constant war over that lake. It seemed preposterous. "And you fight over the lake?" he asked. "Why?"

Aiella sniffed. "As I have said, it is a holy place for all that live there." She paused, reaching up to pull a strand of hair out of her eyes and brush it away. "There has not been much true fighting for many years now, but there are none who believe the peace will last. Sooner or later, one side will attack the other, and the Tower and the Summit will war again." Her voice sounded sad as she said it and Caymus felt, for the first time since he'd met her, that there might be a beating heart under the young woman's hard exterior.

"It sounds like a hard place to live," he said, not knowing what else to say.

Aiella seemed to consider this, though didn't address the thought. "The Tower's ambassador, he also has been helping to find water in Kepren in the last months, trying to earn more favor for his people than my father earns for ours," she smiled, "but he is not nearly as good. My father is stronger at pulling water than anyone else in the Summit, certainly in the Tower."

"Pulling?" Caymus was intrigued by the word. On the few occasions he'd spoken to Milo about the way he summoned gusts of wind, he'd discovered that while the things fire and air priests did to work in their respective elements seemed, on the surface, to be similar, they used a completely different vocabulary which made it hard to make real comparisons. The idea that water priests might 'pull' their element in the same way a master of the Conflagration would pull fire was very interesting indeed.

Caymus reached out with his mind, probing the area around the ambassador and trying to get a feel for what he might be doing. With some surprise, he found that he could, indeed, feel something opening, very like a conduit, but very different also. Where he was used to opening conduits that extended from his world to the Conflagration, this one seemed to have both ends anchored nearby.

Very suddenly, Caymus's concentration was broken when Aiella smacked his face. "What is the matter with you!" she yelled. "You have no decency!"

Caymus's cheek stung and his head rattled from the slap. He rubbed his cheek with the back of his hand, confused as to what had brought her ire down upon him. Before he could give voice to his confusion, though, the ambassador spoke. "Leave him, daughter," the man said, turning his head to level a gaze at Caymus. "The boy, he is a fool."

Caymus, still a little stunned, watched as Aiella rose and walked off to go and sit on a bench that was closer to her father. He wasn't sure what had just happened.

"I am very nearly done, anyway," said Brocke. "Aiella, please would you pump the handle of the apparatus a few times?"

Aiella did as she was asked, getting up and grabbing the iron handle, then raising and lowering it a handful of times.

"Continue," said Brocke, his head still pressed to the ground. Aiella obediently complied, pumping the handle another dozen times or so until a small trickle of water dripped down from the spout.

"Good," said Brocke, rising to his knees, "you may stop. Thank you, dearest." The ambassador finished, pushed himself up to his feet, and then turned his gaze upon Caymus. With a stern look on his face, the man walked right up to him, and Caymus could see a look of hot anger in the man's eyes. His round face and short stature did nothing to diminish the menace in his countenance. Caymus felt the need to stand as Brocke place himself directly in front of him and stared, menacingly, into his eyes. He seemed about to say something harsh and angry, but then his face softened, if only a little.

"You are Caymus, yes? You are Be'Var's student?"

Caymus nodded, trying to keep the apprehension out of his voice. "Yes."

Brocke nodded and sighed deeply. "You, I believe are new to your ability and to this culture, so I will forgive your transgression this night." He raised a finger, pointing it at Caymus's chest. "You should know, however, that had you intruded on a man's mind like that in the place I come from, one of us would now be lying broken upon the ground." He put the finger away. "We understand one another, yes?"

Caymus nodded in the affirmative. Brocke then reached up, clapped him on the chest, nodded without a hint of a smile, and walked out of the courtyard. As he passed through the doorway, he brought a small box out of a pocket, drew something Caymus couldn't see out of it, brought it to each nostril, and sniffed.

Before she followed her father out, Aiella stood in the doorway and gave Caymus a long, cold look, as though she were trying to decide on what method she would use to torture him later. When he didn't speak, but only reached up to smooth his stinging cheek again, she turned and walked out.

"I'm afraid that was my fault." Caymus turned to see Be'Var standing in one of the several doorways that led into the courtyard.

Caymus eyed him suspiciously. "Have you been there long?"

"Long enough," said Be'Var, stepping over the dead grass with his hands clasped behind his back. He motioned at Caymus's hand, still rubbing his face, with a small smile. "The girl didn't hit you too hard, did she?"

"I'll live," Caymus said as he dropped the hand down to his side and stared at the doorway by which the girl in question had left. "What happened there, anyway?"

Be'Var motioned that he should sit, and then sat on the bench next to him. He leaned forward, resting his elbows on his knees, and clasped his hands together. "Well," he began, exhaling the word, "in the Temple, especially when training a new disciple, we make a lot of allowances for the co-mingling of minds for instructive purposes. It's not like that out in much of the rest of the world."

Caymus kept up his suspicious gaze. "What do you mean?" he said.

"It's a boundary that most people don't cross," Be'Var said, a near-apologetic tone in his voice. "Reaching out and touching someone else's mind," he sighed, "in some cultures, such as that of the people of Creveya, it's considered a rather intimate way to touch someone."

"Oh." Caymus could feel his face turning red. "You don't mean I—"

"Just made an advance on Kepren's ambassador from Creveya, the Summit?" Be'Var smiled and put a hand on Caymus's shoulder. "No, not exactly, but if I were you, I wouldn't go poking around anywhere near Ambassador Brocke again without his inviting you to."

Caymus looked about the courtyard in thought, trying to make sense of this new city, with all of these strange, new people. "I think Aiella was more upset about it than he was."

"I met Brocke once, many years ago," Be'Var said, in response. "He's a good man but, like any Creveyan, his head is full of prejudice and suspicion. Having your worst enemy in the world living just the other side of a lake—albeit a rather large lake—does that to a person. He tends to rub people the wrong way." Taking his hand from Caymus's shoulder, he leaned back against the wall behind the bench. "Tonight was my first time meeting his daughter. For the brief time they were here before you and Rill came stumbling in, I got the impression that she's a bit protective of him." He gave a long, tired sigh. "If she's not careful, she's going to end up just like him."

Caymus looked back at him. "What do you mean?

Be'Var closed his eyes, looking very much as though their long days of travel had finally caught up with him. "Creveyans have been fighting about that over-sized pond for centuries. It's only in the last decade or two that there hasn't been actual open war between the Tower and the Summit. Brocke's generation, and all the generations before his, know only hate for the people across the lake." He shook his head, slowly, as he continued. "Aiella and the other youngsters have never known actual fighting, but it wouldn't take much for someone to ignite the spark of war again."

"What's so special about the lake?" asked Caymus. It had been the only thing he hadn't yet figured out about the situation.

Be'Var opened his eyes and turned to look at his student. "It's a lot like the Conduit," he said, "as far as I'm aware. You know the Temple started as a fortress, claiming dominion over our link to the Conflagration, right?"

Caymus nodded. "I remember."

"It's much the same with Creveya. It has something to do with the worship of the water element, and it's important to both the peoples of the Tower and the Summit that they have access to it. Don't understand it myself, but then I'm not a water worshiper." He leaned his head back again. "One day, it will all be settled, and I'm sure it will be a lot like the Conduit is today but, for now, the battle for control goes on. I just hope they can keep the peace a little while longer. Hopefully the krealites helped with that a bit."

Caymus didn't like Be'Var ascribing any kind of positive qualities to the creatures they'd been fighting, but if the Summit and the Tower really hated each other as much as it seemed, then he supposed that their having a common enemy might, in fact, have its advantages. Something Be'Var said struck him, though. "Why just a little longer? Is something going to happen soon?"

Be'Var straightened at the question, then the physically reached out and turned Caymus toward him so as to look him in the eyes. He had a serious expression on his face, though his voice was gentle, "Caymus, I want you to keep this next part to yourself. Do you think you can do that? If you don't think you can do that, I'd rather not burden you with the responsibility."

Caymus nodded. He was better than most at keeping secrets, though he wondered what could possibly be so sensitive as to be kept from everybody, but common enough that Be'Var would trust him with it. "I can," he said. "I will."

"Good," said Be'Var. He leaned back again, though the tiredness was gone from his face. "While we were traveling, those friends of Milo's, the ones that were passing messages back and forth, kept on talking to each other. Have you heard of Albreva or Madd's Hollow?"

Caymus had heard the names before. He vaguely remembered his father mentioning a ship in the yards that was destined for a place called Albreva. "I've heard of them," he said, "but I don't know where they are. North, I think."

Be'Var nodded. "Albreva is a long way north of the Greatstone Mountains, farther out that most Tebrians will ever travel. Madd's Hollow is even farther north than that, and I don't know anyone, other than one or two of Milo's friends, who's ever been there." Be'Var shifted a bit and smoothed out his robes. "Just after we left the Temple, Madd's Hollow went silent. Nobody's heard from it since."

Caymus considered the news. "Couldn't it just be that the priest that was sending messages from there left?"

"That's what they thought at first," said Be'Var, "but yesterday, the priest in Albreva stopped talking, too." He paused a long time before continuing. "The last thing he said was that the city was being choked in dust and that there was a mass of blackness coming from the North."

Caymus frowned. Dust? Blackness? "What does that mean?" he asked. He noticed he was rubbing the back of his hand again.

"I served in the Kepren physicians' corps for a long time," said Be'Var, who had shifted his gaze to the stars above the city. "The only things I know of that cause that kind of choking dust—blackness or no—are a sandstorm or a marching army." He paused. "Albreva isn't in a desert."

"And the blackness?" said Caymus, becoming concerned. "You think it's kreal, don't you?"

Be'Var squinted as he spoke, as though trying to pick out a particular star. "An army would definitely look like a giant mass from a distance. Considering the enemy we face, I would expect that the force to be made in large part, if not entirely, of kreal."

Caymus looked at the ground. "And they're still coming south." It wasn't a question.

Be'Var nodded. "That's the thinking." He sighed and looked back at his student. "It's what the prince is thinking, anyway. You were right that he didn't come tonight just to say hello to an old man."

Caymus managed a small smile and looked sideways at Master Be'Var. "Did you really save his life?"

Be'Var nodded, though there was no smile in it. "That I did."

His brow knitting together, Caymus sat up straighter. "Why tell me all of this?" he said. "Why make me keep it a secret?"

Be'Var met Caymus's eyes, looking at him a long time with a blank expression. Caymus could see the master's eyes darting slightly to the left and right as he stared. Finally, the old man reached down and took his left hand, then turned it over, palm down. He pointed to the mark upon his flesh. "That's why," he said. He let the hand drop. "I don't yet understand why, but the Lords of the Conflagration are telling us you're important. Therefore, I need you to know what's going on, even if we don't understand it all yet."

Caymus brought the hand up again, staring at the sword and flame on his skin. "But why the secret?" he said. "If there's an army coming, why not tell people so they can prepare?"

"Some people would prepare," said Be'Var. "Many more would just panic. If it were just a handful of people panicking, that would be one thing, but a whole city?" Be'Var shook his head. "We'd be dead before the army even got here." He looked at Caymus severely. "You understand?" The words were spoken with as much authority as Caymus had ever heard from the man.

He closed his eyes, dropped his head, and nodded. "I understand."

"Good." With that, Be'Var stood and stretched. "Well," he said, "I'd better see if our guests are still here and make sure Brocke isn't too furious with you."

Caymus affected a slight, embarrassed smile. "I'll have to apologize to him when I get a chance," he said. "And to Aiella."

Be'Var, who had been stepping away, turned and looked at him. "I know you won't listen, but I'd recommend keeping your distance from the two of them. They're both the dangerous sort, and I think the prince has particular interests in Brocke's daughter, if you didn't catch on to that earlier." Be'Var smiled. "Garrin's an honorable man, but don't think he won't challenge you to a duel if he thinks you have the same intentions."

"Don't worry," said Caymus, putting his hands up in supplication, "I don't. She's a bit icy, to be honest. I'll stay away."

With that, the old man turned and walked away. Caymus wondered briefly if the two Creveyans were still inside. He hoped Be'Var would have a chance to make things right between him and them. He really should go find Gwenna and say hello. He'd lost track of time and didn't know how long it had been since he'd gotten back to the mission, but he was fairly certain that she should still be awake.

As he stood to leave, he caught sight of the small hand pump out of which Aiella and Brocke had just coaxed a few drops of water. As he stepped over to it, he thought to reach out and see if there was anything left of what it was Brocke had been doing. As he let his mind wander, he searched for the conduit-like sensation he'd felt before, but nothing was there. Pity. He had been hoping that there would be at least some manner of residue or other leftover evidence of power in the ground, but the dirt and the grass beneath his feet continued to feel resolutely normal.

Disappointed, he squatted down next to the pump. The device was comprised of a large cylinder, with a small spout and a long handle on the top which curved down the opposite side. He grabbed the handle the same way Aiella had and pumped it a few times, experimentally. A trickle of water came out, though not nearly as much as he'd expected.

As he splashed the small handful of water on his face to wipe the day's grime and sweat from his skin, he wondered if Brocke's efforts had been worth such a small gain. He thought that his interference in the process might have caused it not to work as well as it had. He felt a bit guilty about that.

As he pulled a dry part of his tunic up to mop his face, he felt the tingling on the back of his neck again. It was stronger now, uncomfortable, where it had only been a nagging sensation in the last couple of days. Expecting he might have some trouble, he turned around and stood.

In the darkness before him stood Callun, staring at him with an intensity that made him take an uneasy step back. "Callun?" he said, trying to keep the tension out of his voice. "Can I help you?"

Something that was partway between a sneer and a smile played across Callun's face. His dead eyes, at long last, had come to life, staring at Caymus with a ferocity that seemed to bore into his soul. He quickly took a step forward, and then another. "Mrowvain, actually," he said. In those two words, Caymus detected that the accent he'd been hearing for the last two days had suddenly vanished completely. "My name is Mrowvain, not Callun."

The dark eyes registered disappointment when they realized that Caymus didn't recognize the name.

Caymus only just caught the glint of the knife, the blade turned up in a tight fist, before the hand holding it quickly rose to strike him, aiming for his gut. Caymus reacted without thinking, turning to the side and reaching out a level arm to block Callun's forearm before the knife could make contact. He fended off the attack, but before he could move again, his attacker drew his arm back and the double-sided blade sliced across his wrist.

Caymus grunted. He didn't think the cut could be very deep, but the knife seemed to burn his flesh. His entire arm, in fact, suddenly felt like it was going numb. Before the knife could come around for another attack, Caymus stepped off his back foot and threw it forward, planting a hard kick in his attacker's sternum. Callun—Mrowvain, if what the man had just said could be believed—would probably have been knocked from his feet, but he'd already been stepping backward in retreat. Instead, he stumbled back a few steps, then turned to run through one of the courtyard doors.

Caymus moved to follow, but when he brought his foot down, the leg buckled under him, and he fell on his side. The arm that had been cut was now completely lifeless to him. He realized he was bellowing in shock and pain. What was wrong with him? He couldn't bring his arm up to see the wound; he was certain it couldn't have been that deep!

With a grunt of frustration, he tried to stand. With great effort, he got as far as he knees, but he didn't have the strength to rise any further. His vision was starting to spin before him. His ears were ringing. Callun—Mrowvain—was gone. Caymus, looking at the doorway he'd escaped through—the same doorway through which Brocke and Aiella had left—tried to yell for help, but he wasn't sure if any sound came out. He couldn't understand why he couldn't hear, why his arms were both dead, useless weights to him.

Hardly able to think, he managed to use what remained of his strength to fall to his side, rather than on his face. As he lay on the ground, struggling to breathe, he noticed a knife on the ground. It was the one that had just been used to cut him. The knife—a dagger, really—wasn't unusual-looking; it was constructed with a wire-wrapped hilt and a narrow guard, having the general shape of a boot-knife. The blade, though, was a deep gray color, so dark as to be nearly black. It didn't look like metal. He thought, with childlike wonder, that it looked a lot like the armor of the krealites.

Caymus knew that people were near him, yelling at him, and that hands were turning him on his back. He couldn't understand what they were saying.

He wondered what they were so angry about as he felt himself take leave of his body and depart the world he had just been getting to know.

Chapter 13

Be'Var held his head in his hands, breathing deeply, trying to keep calm, to keep his thoughts from turning dark and getting away from him. He was actually frightened for the first time in what must have been decades. And tired. Flames, but he was so tired. He felt a great weariness in his bones, felt the tension of the last few weeks pulling at his tendons. How he was able to think straight lately, much less bend his mind to working with the Conflagration, was beyond his ability to comprehend.

When he finally let out a long breath and looked up, he noticed that the one of the candles, sitting alone on the little table on his right, just to the left of his patient's head, had gone out, its wax having spilled out over the little brass candlestick that had held it for the last few hours. The room looked the way he felt: dark and dreary. Without thinking about it consciously, he reached into the table's drawer and pulled out another little wax cylinder. He'd conjured a conduit to light the wick before he'd even placed it in the brass holder.

Burn him, but he didn't know how to help!

He replayed the scene in his mind. Brocke and his daughter had left moments earlier, as had Garrin a short while before that. He and Elia had still been in the front room, discussing the evening's events and trying to decide what they should try to accomplish the following day, when Callun had burst like a thunderclap through the interior door, nearly knocking both of them down, after which he'd disappeared out the front entrance. Be'Var might have followed after him if not for the screaming from a voice he knew all-too-well. The two had followed the sounds to the courtyard where Rill and Gwenna had been kneeling over Caymus's prone form, a dark blade lying in the dead grass at his side.

After first checking that he was still breathing, and that he didn't appear to have any obviously mortal wounds, the four of them, working together, had carried him through to this small, dark room and into this bed. Be'Var had spent the time since then by his young friend's side, trying to figure out what had happened to him and, more to the point, what to do about it.

He'd been optimistic at first. The first thing his healer's eye had noticed was a deep, clean cut across the side of the boy's right wrist which hadn't seemed a serious injury at all. The area around the cut, however, had been so red and inflamed that if he hadn't known better, he'd have assumed that it carried some deadly infection. Even the worst case of gangrene took more than a few minutes to set in like that, though. Confused, and not knowing what else to do about it, he'd simply closed the wound and bandaged it.

Rill had been the one to bring in the dagger. The dagger, of course, had been the problem. Be'Var had recognized the color of kreal on it, though a bit of wiping and scratching had revealed it to actually be a just normal, steel blade with only a light coating of the sickly substance on its surface.

What had that cursed element done to the boy?

Be'Var held Caymus's wrist again. His pulse was weak, his breathing slow. His eyes didn't flutter under their lids, which meant he wasn't simply in some kind of deep sleep. Most alarming was his temperature: the boy's skin was cold to the touch, colder even than Be'Var would have expected from a corpse. The old master had spent a good deal of time gently coaxing the fire element into Caymus's body, trying to raise the warmth in his core, but the effort had been to no avail.

Be'Var had been a healer for years, had come across every affliction or malady that had ever come upon a soldier and knew how to deal with every last one of them. At least, that's what he used to think. This new element changed everything. It wasn't a part of their world, part of their bodies' makeup. He had no idea what kreal rampaging through a person's body would do to the flesh and organs, had no idea how to counter its effects.

So far, at least, the substance appeared to have reached the limit of the damage it could do; either that, or Caymus was just incredibly strong-willed. Be'Var allowed himself a small smile; he wasn't sure which option he most wanted to be true.

Flames, but what was he going to do?

"Is he any better?"

Be'Var turned to see Gwenna standing in the doorway, a stack of folded towels and blankets in her arms. Be'Var was glad to see that, unlike Bridget, she wasn't crying: Gwenna was generally a sweet girl, but when it came to taking care of the sick and injured, she was all business.

This, of course, wasn't the first time she'd seen Caymus laid up like this, either.

"I don't think so," he replied. "Come in, please," he said, waving her in. "Let's get those blankets over him."

The two of them worked quietly, piling the soft materials over their patient. He'd already been covered with both his own travel blanket and the rug that had previously lain on this room's floor, so by the time they were finished, he appeared as though enveloped in some kind of cocoon.

"Master Be'Var, what's wrong with him?" Gwenna asked as she placed the last item, a rather threadbare-looking towel, over the boy's chest.

Be'Var looked down at him with a scowl. "I wish I knew. It has something to do with this flame-cursed kreal." Heaving a big sigh, he rubbed the top of his head as he looked about the room. "We know that it can pass through earth, that it barely reacts to fire, and that it has some kind of negative effect with water," he said, "but a body is a complicated thing with a mix of all four elements. Those four, the ones that are supposed to be there, are trying to deal with a fifth, that isn't. I can only imagine the havoc it's wreaking."

Gwenna, standing on the other side of the bed, looked toward the door and smiled. Be'Var turned to see Tavrin, the Falaar boy, standing in the doorway, holding his own stack of sundries. He was smiling, too.

Be'Var managed to suppress a sigh. Young people were always so willing to be the causes of their own trouble. He was sure Caymus had noticed those two making eyes at each other when the boys had met the Keeper, earlier that day. The stares between the pair of them had only become more pronounced after he and Rill had left. He still didn't know —didn't *want* to know—what was happening between Caymus and Gwenna, but he knew trouble brewing when he saw it.

"The Keeper found these," Tavrin said, holding up the bundle to Be'Var. "Are they needed?"

Be'Var waved toward a corner of the room. "Put them there for now," he said. "We just put another handful of layers on him. I want to see if they have any effect before we go suffocating him any further."

As Tavrin obediently placed the linens on the floor, Be'Var reached under the sheets to feel Caymus's arm. It was still cold. Flaming dog-spit, but he didn't seem to be making any difference.

"Is there more I can do now?" said Tavrin, looking at Caymus's still form.

"No!" said Be'Var. He tried to keep the anger out of his voice but—confound it—he was angry! "No," he said again, more gently this time, then he looked at the boy out of the corner of his eye. "Thank you, Tavrin."

"What about me?" said Gwenna. She knelt down next to the bed. "I'll stay up with you, if you like."

Be'Var looked up at her and saw the concern in her face. The girl did, at least, have the makings of a good nurse, and he had to admit he wouldn't mind the company. "A little while, yes, thank you Gwenna," he said. "If this doesn't improve soon, we'll have to start watching him in shifts but, for now, it wouldn't be a bad idea to keep two pairs of eyes on him."

Gwenna nodded, a serious look on her face, and stood, grabbing a stool that had been placed against the wall. As she moved, she looked toward the doorway. "I'll see you later, Tavrin?"

Be'Var didn't see the boy leave, but assumed he'd nodded in agreement. Gwenna smiled just the smallest amount, then drew the stool up and sat on the other side of the bed from Be'Var. She turned her face down to look at Caymus, but then shifted slightly to look up at Be'Var. "Caymus saw it, you know? He told Milo that he didn't like him."

Be'Var nodded. He wasn't surprised to hear it. He, too, had held concerns about Callun from the start, especially when Caymus had started complaining about that odd sensation on his neck. Burn him, but why hadn't he just listened to those concerns and gotten that man as far away from Flamehearth as possible? Why hadn't they just left the dead-eyed creep to die out in the desert?

Idly, he wondered if Caymus's neck had reacted to the man himself or to the dagger he carried. Could the bastard's haggard look have had something to do with some amount of kreal in his makeup?

"We couldn't have just left him out there though, could we?" said Gwenna, interrupting his thoughts. "I mean, we had to give him the benefit of the doubt, didn't we?"

Be'Var groaned. "We didn't, but that's what we chose to do. Ninety-five times in a hundred, it would have been the right decision."

"And five times in a hundred, it gets Caymus killed." She barely choked out the last word. Be'Var looked up at Gwenna to see an unacknowledged tear running down her cheek.

"He's not dead yet, Gwenna." He tried to manage a look of optimism. "And my instinct tells me that if he were going to die, he would have done so by now."

Gwenna didn't respond to that. Be'Var didn't blame her. Why had he been so careless with that man? Now that he'd seen Callun's true character, he wondered who he really was, whether he had actually been dying out in the desert and happened upon them, or whether the whole thing had been staged, a trap for Caymus from the beginning.

He also wondered if the man was entirely human. If he was infected with kreal somehow, would the word 'human' even apply anymore?

And now, Caymus was out of commission, unable to learn more about the Aspect of shaping, to spar with the prince, or even to get angry about

Tavrin. He found himself thinking again about Gwenna's feelings for the boy. In his long years, he'd known women who were careless with their emotions; she'd never struck him as one of those. He hoped those two were being careful with one another.

He wondered, too about Brocke's daughter, Aiella. He'd noticed her taking a greater-than-usual interest in Caymus when he'd walked in the door. Caymus had seemed surprised when he'd warned him about staying away from her. That made Be'Var smile. Bless the boy and his oft-oblivious nature. Then, the smile vanished. Obliviousness might just have been the thing that had gotten them here.

He tried to imagine how much time it would take, how long he would have to wait by this bed, before he would finally find out if this young man who was becoming like a son to him—okay, maybe a grandson—stood a chance of ever waking up. He'd seen Caymus out cold before, had even forced him into the situation that had put him there, but he'd known what to do in the days after the attack on the Temple. This wasn't the same at all.

He took another deep breath. The helpless feeling was rising in him again. Between the news from Madd's Hollow and Albreva, and now Caymus, the feeling of loss was becoming unbearable.

"Flames," Be'Var exclaimed, startling Gwenna, "how am I going to get my research done if he stays like this?"

Gwenna wiped her cheek. "Research?" she said. "About Caymus?"

Be'Var nodded. "About shaping, yes." He knew that finding out more about the ancient elemental war—the mitre Gu'ruk had referred to it as the Old War—about shaping, about this new enemy of theirs, was tremendously important. He also knew that if Caymus continued this way, his own plans of dredging through Kepren's various libraries were likely to be impossible. He considered the problem a long moment. "I'm going to have to find someone to do the research for me, I suppose."

~~~

Caymus was alone.

He didn't remember waking up, didn't remember anything between the moment he'd fallen to the ground and the moment he'd suddenly found himself here, in this strange place. Although, maybe it wasn't so strange: the trees around him had a ring of familiarity about them, as did the night sky above him. He'd been here before, but when?

Rising to his hands and knees, he put fingers to his forehead, trying to clear his mind. He felt as though there was some impairment to his vision
~~~

that was stopping him from seeing the place clearly, but that the impairment had nothing to do with his eyes. He felt as disoriented as if he'd been driven from a sound sleep.

He held himself still, trying to focus on the stone in the middle of the clearing, trying to clear the fog from his mind. He knew that stone, reaching high up into the sky, but there was something wrong about it, something that didn't make sense. If only he could figure out where he was.

With the severity of a hammer strike, the realization hit him. He was in Milo's clearing! He looked around, remembering each tree, each rock and encircling blade of grass. Every piece seemed to have a strange way of falling into place the moment he remembered the way it should look, as though he were creating the place with his own recollections. He couldn't shake the feeling, however, that he was missing something; even the smell of the grass was right, but there was still something wrong with this picture.

When he took another glance at the stone plinth, he had it: the plinth was whole. He and Milo had ruined it with their lance of fire, hadn't they? He wasn't sure. He had the strangest sensation that he was somehow out of his own time, that it wasn't that somebody had repaired the plinth, but that he had returned to a time before he had destroyed it. Did that make sense?

He closed his eyes, focused on his breathing, tried to bring the thoughts in his head into some kind of order. Finally, he pushed the thoughts away, treating them as distractions, and just tried to think about breathing in and out. After a moment, he noticed the feel of the dirt under his hands, the way it felt cool against his palms. His mind was coming back to him, though slowly and in pieces. The clearing was coming into better focus in his mind.

He was cold. As the world around him came back into order, he realized he was shivering. Cautiously, he opened his eyes, looked at the branches and leaves of the vegetation about the edge of the clearing, checked for evidence of the biting wind that must be sapping the warmth from his body. There was no movement in the trees, though, no sound at all. Whatever was making him so cold, it wasn't wind.

The most startling thing happened when he looked up. He discovered there were no stars in the sky, that no moon hung over his head in the night. Above the tree line, there was only an endless blackness.

"Do not let fear take you, Caymus."

Caymus's head whirled around, looking for the source of the voice. At the same time his eyes widened and his pulse raced. He knew that voice, knew the last time he had heard it: it was his own, and he had heard it when he'd stepped into the Conduit. He expected at any moment to see the glowing eyes of the Lords of the Conflagration float into view before him. After what seemed like ages of waiting, however, they failed to appear.

"Where are you?" he yelled.

"We are always here," replied his own voice. It was calm, thoughtful, as though telling him a story.

"Here?" said Caymus. His feeling of being displaced in time was evaporating with each moment, and he was becoming quite certain he wasn't actually in Milo's clearing at all. "Where is here?"

"Your body is dying, Caymus," said the voice. It seemed to be coming from no particular direction, yet it was definitely emanating from somewhere outside his own head. "We have brought you here in order to save it."

Caymus shuddered. He remembered the knife now, remembered the icy chill of its bite into his flesh. He lifted his arm up to examine it, but the wound wasn't there. Where was the cut? Why was he so cold? "What do you mean, 'my body'?" he asked, knowing he was sounding defensive. "I'm right here! I'm cold, but I'm not dying!" He kept turning around, hoping to catch a glimpse of the speaker that was using his voice. "Where are you!" he shouted again into the blackness.

An eternity seemed to pass as Caymus stood there, his eyes drifting over the edges of the clearing, waiting for someone to answer him. Then, he caught sight of movement: something was coming through the trees, something that made no noise.

Caymus took a couple of steps backward, reflexively. He reached for the sword at his belt and discovered it wasn't there. He fought off the feeling of panic as a figure finally emerged from the trees of the Saleri Forest and strode into the clearing.

Caymus gasped. He had been expecting an image of himself, but it was Milo that strode up to him. At least, it was almost Milo. The light blue clothing was there, the bow and quiver were at his back, even the feathery wings hung from his arms. Milo's ready smile, though, was absent. In its place was a stony demeanor that betrayed no hint of expression or emotion. The effect was ghastly.

"Who are you?" Caymus asked the image of his friend.

"We are those who tested you." The voice was still Caymus's. The effect of Milo speaking with his own voice was disquieting. "We are those who marked you." The image of Milo gestured toward his hand. Caymus found the familiar sword and flame mark there. "We are those who must now depend on you." As the figure spoke, its expression turned from a complete lack of emotion to that of resolute determination and seriousness.

"Depend on me?" Caymus, confused and freezing, was getting

frustrated, feeling like he'd been placed in the middle of some kind of game, and that he didn't know the rules. "What is going on?" he said, angrily. "Where am I?"

The serious look on the image's face turned to one of sympathy, and it inhaled deeply before speaking again. "You'd probably better sit down, Caymus." The voice was now Milo's, the expressions and mannerisms becoming more like the real Milo by the second. The figure indicated the space between the two of them.

Caymus considered arguing, but after another shudder racked his shoulders, he decided against it and dropped to sit, cross-legged, on the ground. After the image of Milo did the same, its expression turned serious again, almost somber. "You're dying, Caymus," he said. "You were stabbed with a kreal-covered blade by one through whom the kreal works. The element is coursing through your body as we speak. Do you remember the knife?"

Caymus, feelings of suspicion rising, nodded slowly. "I remember," he said. "The man we picked up in the desert, Callun—no, he called himself Mrowvain just before he tried to stab me!" He looked at unbroken flesh of his arm again. "So how did I get here?"

"You didn't," said Milo. "Or, at least, your body didn't. Your body lies in the Quatrain, fighting the invasion of the kreal, but losing." Milo's lips pulled to one side. "Your body is dying a very slow death."

Caymus, about to balk at this, was stilled when Milo held his hand up, begging silence while he continued. "We brought you here, to the Conflagration, partly so as to slow the battle raging in your blood, and partly to give you what you will need to learn to win that battle."

Caymus looked around at the all-too-familiar clearing. "I stepped through the Conduit once," he said. "I've been to the Conflagration. This is not it."

Milo smiled. He'd picked up a small stick and had begun spinning it with the fingers of one hand. It was almost like having the real Milo there. Caymus wondered if he might just be confused, whether this *was* the real Milo. "What you call 'The Conduit' is a direct path from the Quatrain into the Conflagration. It is the only such path that exists." He waved an arm about them, indicating the clearing. "This is the Conflagration, but the fact that we had to bring you here without the benefit of the Conduit means that you're coming to see it slowly."

Caymus looked around again, trying to make sense of it in his mind. "Last time I was here," he said, "my whole body was here." His eyes turned to fix on the image of Milo. "You're saying that's not the case this time, that my body is still...where I left it?"

The image nodded. "It takes power and effort you cannot begin to understand to bring you here the way we did, but we couldn't bring you completely, not without the Conduit. If you had been here completely, we would have been able to remove the kreal from your blood ourselves." The image frowned. "But that wasn't possible."

"So, it's...what? My mind? My spirit that's here instead?"

The thing wearing Milo's face smiled and tilted his head. "In a sense, yes. You know that part of you that you send beyond yourself in order to sense the elements around you?"

Caymus nodded. The image was even starting to talk like Milo now.

"It's the same thing. It's the part of you that exists without your body, lives independently of the flesh." Milo broke the stick in his hands and held one half of it up before him. "That's the part we brought here."

Caymus blinked at the piece of stick. "Why?"

Milo put the stick down, heaved a huge sigh, and placed his hands on his knees. "Because you must live." His eyes took on a serious, almost angry countenance, much more severe than any expression the real Milo would ever have worn. "We don't know how the denizens of the Sograve, the realm of kreal, found a way into the Quatrain, but they are pressing their attack and they are gaining ground. The alliance of the Quatrain, the one that ended the Old War and formed your world into what it is now, prevents us from taking direct action, and so we must choose new champions to act on our behalf."

"Knights," said Caymus.

The figure betrayed a small smile, but then gazed off into the distance, as though reliving some ancient memory. "In the Old War, there were two: The Knight of the Stone, called the Earthwarden by his companions, and the Knight of the Flame. They were the true champions of their realms, beings that were born with the ability to channel the power of their element into martial weapons like no others. It was through their efforts, and the efforts of the other members of the Quatrain, that the war was won. Their posts have been vacant, unneeded, for millennia."

Caymus considered the figure's words. What he was saying seemed consistent with what he'd learned amongst the relics of Otvia. He had so many questions, though. "The Quatrain," he said. "That's your name for our world?"

Milo's image picked at the small stones around him as it spoke. "The Quatrain is the name of the alliance between our realm and those of earth, air, and water. It is also the name of the result of that alliance, the world that you know." The figure brought its hands together, intertwining its fingers. "The two are intimately linked, the alliance and your world. We give you substance. In return, you give us life."

Caymus frowned. He could understand the first part, that the elemental realms gave the world its form. The second part, though, that his world gave life to the elemental Lords, was more of a mystery. Obviously, there had to be some reason that the kreal element was so bent on getting a foothold into his world, but how could something that wasn't alive in the first place actively seek life out? He considered pressing the issue, but he had a strong suspicion that he wouldn't understand, that the concept of life for a being from an elemental realm was completely different from his own.

He watched Milo's fingers as they separated and began picking at a little tuft of grass that grew in the clearing. After he tore off each individual blade, he raised it slightly then released it, then watched as it flitted back down to the earth. Milo had frequently done the same thing when the two of them had been here before. As Caymus pondered his next question, he began to wonder how it was that this Lord of the Conflagration knew Milo so well as to ape his mannerisms, as well as his voice and image.

"Why me?" he said. The image of Milo raised its eyebrows at him. "I don't mean to sound ungrateful," he continued, realizing the question might carry some hint of resentment, "but there must be a lot of people who could carry the responsibilities you're talking about. Surely there are others who could have filled a knight's post?"

The eyes turned away from him. Caymus was surprised at the anguish he saw in them. "Three," Milo's image said. "There were three of you before. Three shapers. Three young people once lived in the Quatrain who had the innate talent necessary to take on the mantle of knighthood." The stolen eyes looked back, narrowing. "One drowned when she was still a little girl, many years ago, a victim of tragic circumstance. The second was murdered while he slept by an agent of the kreal, in a fashion that you would likely find quite familiar. That was only a few weeks ago."

Milo's eyes softened. "That just leaves you, Caymus. You must live to be the champion of the Conflagration. It is not because you are the strongest of all shapers, nor is it because you hold special favor with us." The eyes closed. "It is because you are the only one left who can do it."

"What of what you told me before?" asked Caymus. "What about the 'impurity' that you said I had? Was it something to do with my being partly mitre?"

Milo nodded, his eyes open again. "Only a human can be a master of the Conflagration. It is not a question of preference or of prejudice; it is simply the way that the masteries work." He picked up another few blades of grass, placing them in the air as he continued. "A knight, however, has no such restrictions."

Caymus squinted. "Why?" He couldn't make sense of what he was hearing at all.

Milo's eyes darted back from the grass, as though surprised to see Caymus there. His hand hung in mid-air as he answered. "Humans are a part of the Quatrain. They began there, are as much a result of the alliance as is the world you live in. As such, they represent a balance of all the elements that exist in the Quatrain. As such, they are able to properly affect a conduit and manipulate it with the necessary skill to be considered masters."

"What about mitre?" Caymus said. He couldn't help feeling the image of Milo was holding something back. "Aren't they part of the Quatrain too? Shouldn't they be able to do the same thing?"

Milo shook his head. "No," he said. "The mitre are a part of the Quatrain, but they did not begin there. The beginnings of the mitre race, many millennia ago, were conceived within the realm of elemental earth; each member of the race carries within a small portion of that realm. It is why they have such affinity for that element, are able to shape it to their will so completely and effortlessly."

Caymus tried to comprehend the implications in what he was hearing. Did that mean that he, too, had a piece of an earth elemental in him? What would that mean, if it did?

Milo put his hand down. "The first Knight of the Flame, your predecessor, was human. He could have been a master, had he wished, but his mind also contained the Aspect of shaping, which is what is needed for a knight to perform his duty. That Aspect is the only qualification, and you," Milo was pointing with an insistent finger, "are now the only living thing left in the world that is capable of it."

Caymus didn't say anything for a while. He thought about the other two shapers, people whom he'd never known but whose lives had apparently been inextricably linked with his. His mind then made a small leap of logic, though he didn't really want to confirm it. Hesitantly, he asked the difficult question. "So, if one of these other two shapers had still been alive, you'd have left me to die today?"

Milo's face was unreadable. "We, the beings that live in this place—what you call 'the Conflagration'—have almost no power in your realm. It is nearly impossible to convey the effort, the centuries' worth of accumulated energy, that it took to bring you here. It is unlikely, now, that we will have the power left to take another such action before the coming war is ultimately decided." He paused, looking at Caymus with eyes that seemed almost accusatory. When he spoke again, it was paired with a long exhale. "Yes, if we'd had another option, we likely wouldn't have brought you here, and you would now be dead."

Caymus sat in the silence, listening to the sound of his own breath, trying to understand what had just happened to him, or even to figure out how he felt about it. He'd been excited about this Knight of the Flame business up to now, but it was feeling more and more like duty, a responsibility, than a gift.

Trying to calm his mind a bit, he attempted to shield his emotions with a more mundane question. "Why do you look like Milo?" he asked. "He's not even a fire-worshiper."

The figure seemed almost to laugh. "We don't know who this Milo is," he said, looking at the unbroken stone plinth in the center of the clearing, "but he must have something to do with this place." The eyes turned back to him. "Is that right?"

Caymus nodded. "This is where I first met him, years ago."

The image nodded. "The Conduit brought you directly to us, showed you our realm as it is. The process by which we brought you here, without the Conduit, is slower. You are having to fill in a lot of the details yourself."

Caymus was confused. "So, this isn't actually the Conflagration? This is just a memory?"

The figure before him spread its arms wide and slowly spun to take in the entirety of the setting. "A traveler must feel safe in this place. It is not often that one from the Quatrain is brought here, but when it happens, the mind seems to wrap itself in a cocoon of familiarity, somewhere it feels comfortable and able to cope."

Caymus followed the image's gaze. That made some degree of sense, at least. He thought about the small house he'd grown up in and about the drafty dormitory he'd shared with Rill and Sannet, wondering why he wasn't in one of those places instead if he was supposed to be somewhere he considered safe. He had to admit, though, that Milo's clearing was probably the single calmest, quietest place he could think of, a place where he'd always felt at peace.

"So," he said, "I'm not actually in the clearing, but in the Conflagration."

Milo's image raised a finger and pointed it at Caymus's head. "Is your mind clear yet? Are the cobwebs gone?"

Caymus had been asking himself the same question for the past few minutes; or, at least, what had felt like minutes. He'd been hard-pressed to maintain clarity considering the fog that had clouded his mind when he'd first awakened, not to mention the shock of finally figuring out where he was. He felt clear now, though, and said so.

"Good." The image leapt to its feet in a very Milo-like way. "Then the instruction can begin." The image of Caymus's friend then turned and began walking out of the clearing, fading as he approached the tree line.

Caymus rose quickly. "Wait, where are you going?" he shouted after him. "What instruction?" The frustration of it all was making him angry. Here he was again, thrust into a situation not of his choosing. He hadn't asked to be here, to be whisked away from his world, and now this thing that was wearing his friend's face said there was going to be instruction?

"There are things you will need to know, to understand. You were to have the time to learn these things in your own world, in your own time. Now, you must learn them here," said Milo's voice. As the image reached the trees that ringed the clearing, it drifted into nothingness, seeming to evaporate into the air. As it did, the voice stopped emanating from any particular spot and seemed to come from all around him again. "You will need to understand your enemy if you are to defeat it in the Quatrain. Indeed, you will need to know how to defeat the kreal if you are to survive even a single moment when you are returned to your home."

Caymus was turning, casting around for a face, a pair of eyes, anything that would help him get his bearings and free him from the torment of this disembodied voice. As he turned, he felt the heat of flames dance across his side, and he spun to see the plinth erupt into fire, bursting into a wall of flame that leapt up the stone surface. When he brought his hand back down from shielding his face, he found himself staring at the blaze, momentarily caught up in the beauty of the orange tendrils that rose up the length of it in burning waves.

As he watched, he noticed small pieces of stone and ash falling away from the plinth, to the ground. He had only a moment to wonder what was happening before large chunks of rock were cracking away from the top of the object, falling through fire into the surrounding area. Quicker than should have been possible, the plinth seemed to crumble away in the heat, first from the top, then the sides, until the entire edifice seemed to simply break away into nothingness.

In its place was a sword, its blade piercing the ground. It seemed familiar to him somehow, though he knew he'd never seen its like before. The grip was wrapped in red leather that spiraled from a V-shaped pommel to a large, heavy cross-guard that was ended on each side with another V-shaped protrusion, though these points seemed to fade backward toward the pommel as though mimicking the flames of candles reaching up to the sky. He couldn't determine the blade's length, buried as it was in the dirt, but its edges ran in parallel lines all the way from the cross-guard to the ashes below, with a slight furrow between them.

"Take it, Caymus," said a new voice. It was no longer the voice of his friend, but one that was deeper, richer than any he'd ever heard.

Caymus stepped toward the sword, extended his hand, but he hesitated before touching the hilt. What was he doing? Was it wise to do what the voice said? Would he really ever be able to go home again?

For a moment, he entertained the notion that he might be losing his mind. Absently, he noticed that he didn't feel cold anymore.

"Take," said the voice, this time with a harder edge to it, "your sword."

His sword.

It was in that moment, in the frustration and confusion of everything, when his very notions of reality were being tested that Caymus made a decision. As his hand wavered inches from the grip, he considered everything he'd learned of the krealites, of the fear and death they had caused, of the mark on the back of his hand, of the very idea of a knight.

He would do what the Lords of the Conflagration told him to do. If they would offer him instruction, he would accept it. He'd already effectively promised his life, his very soul, to the Conflagration on the day he'd first stepped into the Conduit. Even though that had been another life, another set of circumstances—he'd wanted to be a master then—he would honor that promise.

For the first time, Caymus consciously accepted the post, the duties of the Knight of the Flame. He didn't even know what those duties might entail, but whatever he didn't know, he would learn, and he would achieve. He would make Be'Var proud, make his father proud, make himself proud.

He reached out, wrapped his fingers around the grip of the weapon, and pulled it from the ground. As the blade slid free of the soil, he accepted the authority of the Lords of the Conflagration, these beings that had brought him here from the brink of death to teach him how to survive. As he turned the sword around, raising the blade in an arc in front of him, he tightened the fingers of both hands around the leather grip. It would have been a two-hander in most men's hands; in his, it was a hand-and-a-half.

Feeling the leather under his fingers, and the hard iron beneath it, he closed his eyes and steeled himself, breathing deeply, preparing to accept whatever these beings might send his way.

His hands gripping his sword tightly, his mind clear and ready, Caymus opened his eyes.

The clearing burned away in a flash, and he found himself, at last, standing amidst the roiling flames of the Conflagration.

~~~

Rill frowned and sat back on his haunches, staring hard at the machinery before him, trying to get a better understanding of its workings.

The hand-pump in the courtyard of Flamehearth Mission had become a problem, one that he very much wanted to solve. Nearly a month had passed since that blue-dress-wearing diplomat Brocke had first come here
~~~

and, presumably, brought groundwater to a level that the pump's well could reach. Barely a trickle had resulted from pumping the handle at the time though, and even that trickle had lasted only a couple of days. Now, no water emanated from the device at all, regardless of how hard or how fast one pumped the handle.

Rill supposed he shouldn't be so hard on Brocke. The man had come back the next week, after all, when he'd learned that the pump had failed to produce water so soon after his visit. Rill didn't know just how busy an ambassador's day generally was, but he figured that coming to the mission twice in as many weeks was a bit out of the ordinary. He was fairly certain, though, that the man had only returned as soon as he had due to his daughter's insistence.

Be'Var had forged some working relationship with Aiella since that first night. Rill didn't know the details of it all, but she seemed to have been running errands for him, something Rill would have thought was probably a bit beneath the social standing of a diplomat's daughter. Whatever it was that she was doing for the master, she was frequently in and around Flamehearth, and Rill didn't much care for that. He wasn't particularly fond of the girl; she seemed to think she was better than him, than everybody really.

She did frequently ask after Caymus's health, though. Rill liked that much about her.

Flames, but he wished Caymus would wake up. He wished that the city guards had caught that Callun fellow so that Rill could have the singular pleasure of watching the man burned at the stake for the attempted murder—possibly the *actual* murder—of his best friend. He missed his friend, missed his company. The fact that he was only a few yards away, lying in a bed that was too small for him and unable to speak or even open his eyes, just made things worse.

Rill shook himself, trying to dislodge his depressing thoughts, and directed his mind back to the task at hand. What did he know? Brocke had told the matrons, after a bit crawling around on his hands and knees, that the water was definitely in a place where the pump's well should be able to reach it. Okay, so assuming the man had been telling the truth and wasn't just trying to avoid admitting to them that he'd failed the first time, the logical conclusion was that something was wrong with the pump. Rill had never seen one disassembled and so didn't know how it was supposed to work, but he was starting, with no small amount of enjoyment, to piece things together.

He was in a bit of a hurry. The Keeper had made an official request of the Royal Engineers to come out and have a look at the device, and one of their number was due to arrive today. This, then, would be Rill's last chance to get a good look at the mechanics of it, and maybe to learn something before all the mystery went out of it, peeled away by the expertise of another.

He'd begun early that morning knowing only that when the handle was pumped, no water came out of the spout, just a faint gurgling sound. The obvious conclusion was that the machinery was broken, internally. He also knew, however, from what Ambassador Brocke, Aiella, and a couple of the children had told him, that it *had* worked, pumping out small dribbles of water, for those first couple of days after Brocke had pulled the water. Rill had a suspicion that the children themselves might have had something to do with the damage, but he was trying not to let that affect his thinking.

That was something Ventu, the mitre engineer, had told him to always bear in mind when fixing machinery: act on facts, validate assumptions, ignore suspicions. Rill had liked the way Ventu's mind worked.

He'd first started with the most obvious things he could think of. He'd checked for blockages in the spout itself, finding nothing. He'd checked the bearings that connected the top of the handle to the rod that delved into the cast-iron cylinder, wondering if perhaps the rod might not have been moving the way it should. From the outside, everything looked like it was working properly.

Now, Rill was sitting back and thinking about the problem, trying to picture the way the internal machinery must function without actually taking it apart. Something had to be happening inside that cylinder, but he hadn't figured out what the process might be. He knew that the purpose of it was to draw water out of a hole in the ground, so there must be some suction involved, but he didn't know how pumping an iron rod up and down could lead to such a thing.

He tried to think of an analogous process and pictured how his own mouth must appear on the inside when he'd drunk water straight out of the stream near the Temple, or when his parents had let him use those fancy, glass drinking straws. How did he do that, create the suction? It seemed to him that he was basically opening more space at the back of his mouth, and since there were no air holes in that closed system, the water was obligated to rise and fill the resulting void. Could the pump before him work the same way? It certainly didn't seem like the cylinder had a way of getting any larger.

Rill smiled. He liked this part of solving a problem, of trying to couch an unfamiliar problem in terms he could understand until he reached the point where inspiration could finally strike.

He'd had a fair amount of practice, lately, to be fair. Be'Var had been busy taking care of Caymus ever since they'd first arrived, so the responsibility of the needed repairs and maintenance to their wagon had been delegated to Rill. He'd begun by replacing the spoke that had cracked, but while he'd been working on that, he'd noticed that the connection between the axle and the wheel they'd replaced was so loose that it had been a wonder they'd made it all the way to the mission without the whole thing falling apart.

With a bit of help and instruction from Be'Var, Rill had gotten that repaired, too. It had been fun, and he'd enjoyed the feeling of being genuinely useful.

He thought some more about the way he drank water from a stream. He supposed that, in the analogy, it was his head, rather than his mouth, that took the place of the cylinder, as that didn't actually expand or contract, either. If the analogy held, then it wasn't the cylinder that was expanding, but rather some internal part of it. Perhaps that was what the rod was for, to move some mechanism that changed the shape of some internal structure in the cylinder?

His face a mask of concentration, he got up and examined the top of the cylinder, where the rod entered it, again. It wasn't a tight seal; air could easily get in and out through the space between the two pieces of iron. In that case, if the internal shape changed, creating suction inside the cylinder, wouldn't it just fill with air from the top?

Rill reasoned that there must be another set of seals, internal to the cylinder, that created a closed system, and that gave him an idea. Slowly, carefully, he began working his way around the cast iron, looking for any cracks or splits or holes or any other way that air might be getting inside the device.

"Do you think you should be fooling with that?"

Rill looked up to see Gwenna, arms folded, staring down at him. She was wearing those earth-colored trousers and tunic that she put on whenever she went out into the grasslands to practice her archery, either with Milo or Tavrin. The dried wildflowers in her hair told him that on this particular morning, she'd been with the latter.

He turned back to the pump. "Does it look like I'm fooling with it?" he said. "I'm looking. That's all." He ran his finger around the bottom edge of the cylinder, looking for anything that might account for a lack of suction.

"One of the engineers is supposed to come around today," she continued. Rill wasn't looking at Gwenna, but he assumed she was wearing her 'know-it-all' face, the one that made it painfully obvious to its recipient that she thought he was being an idiot.

"Yes, Gwenna," he said. He smiled in spite of his rising irritation with her. Of all the things she could decide to bother him about. "I know. I'm just taking a look at it. It's not like I can make it any worse."

She was getting irritated too. He could hear it in her voice. "You don't know that. What if he comes around and—"

Rill stood and glared at her. "Just shut your mouth and leave me alone, will you!" He was surprised and a bit delighted at the look of shock on her face. "I'm not going to make it worse," he said. He pointed a finger at it. "It does. Not. Work. At all. It can't get any worse than that, can it?" She seemed about to answer, but he cut her off. "And I've been out here looking at it for a couple of hours, but you wouldn't know that because just showed up to bother me about it, didn't you?"

Gwenna's face reddened. She unfolded her arms and pointed at herself. "I only just got back, you flaming idiot!"

"Oh," said Rill, in mock surprise, "only just gotten back, have you? Been out with Tavrin again, have you? All morning? Gosh well that's an awful lot of time you've been spending together lately, isn't it? In fact," he put his hand to his chin and rolled his eyes skyward as though thinking about something, "...in fact that's pretty much every day since we got here that you've spent with him."

Some of the heat went out of Gwenna's eyes. She didn't respond, though. He knew that she knew what he was talking about. He'd been avoiding saying anything for weeks now, but he just couldn't stand it anymore, couldn't stand how cold she was. "My best friend, lying in bed, at death's door for weeks, and you're off playing with Tavrin. Have you even checked on him since the night he was almost murdered?"

She looked at him indignantly. "Of course I have," she said, just loud enough for him to hear.

"Well, that's good!" he yelled. "I'd hate for Caymus to wake up—if he *ever* wakes up—and find that you'd completely abandoned him for someone else. Good to know that you're at least keeping up appearances for him. Good to know that if he doesn't *die*, he won't be completely crushed by what you've been doing, you miserable harpy!"

Gwenna stared at him in disbelief for a moment before she spoke. "We aren't—" she said, the sentence choked off. "We weren't—" She didn't seem know what to say. Rill noticed her hands were trembling at her sides and that a tear was making its way down her cheek. In that moment, he felt a bit guilty for yelling at her.

He looked down at the ground between them and lowered his voice. "How about you stay out of my business Gwen, and I'll stay out of yours?"

"Excuse me?" The unfamiliar voice came from one of the doors to the courtyard.

A young man stood in the doorway. He was fair of complexion, with a short fringe of orange hair atop his head and light freckles on his face. He carried a number of pouches and tools on a thick belt around his waist. The blue tunic he wore, one of the uniforms of the Kepren military, carried a small symbol, a gear embroidered in gold thread, upon the left breast.

The newcomer looked between the two of them with a bit of apprehension. "Am I...interrupting anything?"

Gwenna, who had been holding her gaze on Rill, turned to him and wiped her cheek with the back of her hand. "No," she said, "not at all." She briskly stepped away and brushed past him on her way back inside.

The man stared after her for a moment, then he turned back to Rill, an eyebrow cocked in suspicion. "Should I come back another time?" he said.

Rill shook his head. His gaze traced the frame of the door Gwenna had just gone through. "No, no," he said, "it's not a problem. Just a bit of an argument, that's all." He smiled and met the man's eyes. "You're here about the pump?"

The man smiled in return. "About the pump, yes," he said, and he stepped forward toward Rill and the pump. He walked with a slight hunch and what would have been a limp if it were only a bit more pronounced. He was odd. He wasn't an ugly man by any means, but Rill got the distinct impression he wasn't quite put together properly, as though his waist was thicker than his chest, or perhaps his joints were too large. Still, the smile he wore was genuine as he reached out to shake Rill's hand. "Daniel," he said, "of the Royal Engineers."

Rill took the proffered hand and shook it firmly. "Good to meet you, Daniel. My name's Rill."

Daniel leaned forward, conspiratorially. "Don't worry, Rill," he said, "I'm sure she'll come around." He gave Rill a wink, then squatted down and began examining the pump.

"Oh no," said Rill, squatting also, "we're not together or anything." He frowned, trying to figure out how to summarize the state of things. "This friend of mine is sick, and she's been spending an awful lot of time making eyes at another man."

Daniel nodded without looking up. "Ah," he said as he pumped the handle a few times, "that's a shame. Married, are they?"

Rill's frown deepened. "No," he said, "they're not married."

Daniel nodded again, now poking a finger into the spigot in much the same way Rill had done a few minutes previously. "Engaged, then?"

Rill smiled at the thought of Caymus being engaged to anybody. "No, no," he said, "nothing like that. Flames," he continued, "they've only actually known each other for month or so."

It was Daniel's turn to frown. He turned his head up to look at Rill. "Betrothed?"

Rill shook his head. He was feeling a bit confused by the questions.

Daniel stared at him, his freckled face contorted into a mixture of confusion and suspicion. "So, if they're not promised to each other, what's the problem with her spending time with another man?"

Rill was actually a bit stunned by the question, by the way that this stranger had put it so very logically. He felt that twinge of guilt starting to grow. "I suppose it's not really a problem, as such," he said. "They were just spending a lot of time together before my friend got sick, and it just feels like she should show him just a little more loyalty."

Daniel grinned. His fingers were running along the iron cylinder of the pump body. "Ought to be sitting by his bedside weeping, eh?"

Rill couldn't help but smile at the engineer's easy-going demeanor. "Yeah, I guess you're right, when you put it that way," he said. Daniel didn't seem to be but a few years older than he was. Rill wondered if it was age and experience that had him making so much sense, or if his clarity was just about having an outsider's view of things. He turned his head toward the doorway by which Gwenna had left. "I guess I owe her an apology."

Daniel turned his attention back to the pump. "I'm guessin' if she's as worried about your friend as you are, she'll understand." He leaned back and manipulated his legs until he was sitting cross-legged on the grass, his knees on either side of the pump. "So," he said, giving Rill a questioning look and tilting his head toward the device, "what do you think's wrong with it?"

"Me?" Rill was surprised. He'd been expecting the professional engineer to want to be left alone with his work at any moment.

"Sure," he said. "You were poking around at it earlier, weren't you? Can't poke around at something and not learn something, so what do you think's wrong with it?"

Rill appraised the young man, trying to decide if he was seriously asking his opinion or if he was just mocking him. There seemed to be no malintent in his eyes. "Well," he said, looking down at the machine, "there's no blockage in the spigot, the bearings appear to be connecting everything together properly, and I can't find any cracks that would be letting air in." He squinted at the mechanism. "It worked for a day or two, but not very well, so I have to assume there's something on the inside that was almost completely worn away before, then gave out after the first few pumps."

He looked up at Daniel, who was nodding. "Go on," he said.

Rill pointed at the main body of the pump. "I don't really know what's in here," he said, "but I think that the piston," he indicated the rod that went in the top, "moves some sort of plunger up and down that changes that internal dimensions." He closed his eyes, considering the problem in his head, constructing a mental picture of the imagined workings. "The piston has to have a tight seal against the inside of the shaft, and I suppose that could have worn away..." He paused, thinking about it, then shook his head, "but still, you'd get some water, even if the seal wasn't perfect."

"So," he heard Daniel say, prompting him for more, "some part of it that failed to the point that it doesn't pull up any water at all anymore?"

Rill snapped his fingers and opened his eyes, beaming. "The gurgling sound!" He pointed to the very bottom of the pump. "There has to be something down here that keeps the water from going back down once the suction brings it up. If it was broken, the water would all just drain away again. I can hear the water coming up initially, so that must be it." He looked back Daniel, who was grinning and holding a wrench out to him.

"The premise seems sound," he said. "Go ahead and take the body off and let's see if you're right."

Rill hesitated before taking the wrench. "You sure?"

"Yeah," said Daniel, shrugging with a great deal of enthusiasm. "Let's see what you've got."

Rill eagerly took the proffered wrench and felt around the bottom of the pump, looking for the spot where it connected to the well pipe, underground. After he dug a bit of dirt out of the way, he found the large nut holding the two sections together and secured the wrench to it. He looked up at the engineer, wincing a little. "Which way do I turn it?"

"Ha!" Daniel exclaimed. He pointed to his right—Rill's left—indicating a counter-clockwise motion. Rill did as instructed, though he found he needed to exert quite a lot of force before the thing budged. After a minute or so of turning, however, the pump body came loose of the pipe in the ground. Rill was careful not to let any dirt get into that pipe.

"Alright," said Daniel, handing Rill another wrench from his belt, "now take the bottom off it."

Rill had to fumble a bit with the now-freed pump body and the two wrenches before he could get the leverage he needed. In the end, he sat on the ground, holding the pump with his knees, while he pulled the wrenches in opposite directions to remove the bottom section, about half-an-inch's worth of metal cylinder, from the device.

When the bottom came free, he put the wrenches down and spun it in his fingers, examining it. The section contained a small chamber of its own: it had one hole in the bottom, which would have led to the pipe, and another in the top, leading to the body of the pump. Between the two holes, in the chamber, a piece of leather was flopping around. Rill picked and pulled at it until it came out, then took a closer look. It was circular, with a slightly conical shape, and it had a giant tear in the center.

Rill held the flap of leather up triumphantly, poking a finger through the tear. "That's it, isn't it?"

Daniel nodded at him. He reached out and Rill handed it over. "That's it," he said, "the valve." He then reached into one of the pouches at his belt and pulled out another, holding them up for comparison. They were exactly the same, except for the obvious wear and tear on the one that had just come out of the pump. "With the thing out of service so long, it likely dried out, and the pressure of those first few uses would have been too much." He shrugged, then handed the new valve over. "It happens. Would you mind replacing it?"

Rill took the proffered piece of leather and started working it into the mechanism. Daniel talked as he did so. "Never opened one of these up before, eh?"

Rill shook his head. "No."

Daniel nodded. "Ever study them? Known anybody who did?"

Rill smiled. "Nope. Just got to thinking about it this morning, trying to figure out how it worked."

"Well, then," said Daniel, idly scratching at his cheek, "I'd say you have a mind for machines."

Rill smiled, getting the leather in place. "That's what Ventu said."

Daniel raised his eyebrows. "Ventu?" he said, as though shocked by the word. "You mean the mitre, Ventu?"

Rill looked up, screwing the valve section back onto the pump. "Yeah," he said. "You know him?"

"I know *of* him," said Daniel, shaking his head in wonderment. "A mitre serving in Kepren's the kind of thing folks tend to talk about. I never met him myself, but I know he and our captain used to be friends before he left to go back to Otvia." He folded his arms. "When did you see Ventu?"

Rill, now using the wrenches again to get the valve chamber on good and tight, thought about it a moment. "A few weeks ago," he said. "My friends and I passed through Otvia on our way to Kepren." He put the wrenches down, satisfied with the fit. "I helped him fix a couple of things while we were there and he said just what you did, that I have mind for it." He chuckled and gazed at the machinery in his hands. "Even gave me a letter recommending me to the Engineering Corps. I'd nearly forgotten about that."

"Letter, eh?" asked Daniel as Rill went about screwing the pump back onto the well pipe. "For a few weeks? Not really interested, then?"

"It's not that," Rill said as he tightened the fit and pushed some of the dislodged dirt back against the pipe. He stopped for a moment, looking in the direction of the room where he knew Caymus still lay. "I've just had other things on my mind since then, that's all."

"Your friend?"

Rill looked back at Daniel. "Yeah."

They didn't say anything for a few moments. Daniel seemed to be considering something. "So," he said, finally, "does it work?"

Rill shook himself out of his thoughts, stood, and pumped the handle. After a few up and down motions, a steady rush of water came streaming out of the spigot.

"Blast," said Daniel, smiling to himself and not even looking at the pump. He unfolded a piece of dirty-looking paper and what looked to be a charcoal pencil. "I'll tell you what, Rill," he said as he wrote, "lots of folks don't like working with machines and even fewer actually understand them. With all the trouble that sounds like is coming for us in a short time, the captain's told us we're going to need all the help we can get."

Rill looked at Daniel sharply. "Trouble?"

Daniel ignored the question and handed him the piece of paper. Rill took it and examined the writing. It contained a list of tools, from the simple to the complex: hammers, wrenches, calipers, magnifying glasses, and other contraptions he didn't recognize. He looked up from the list. "What's this?"

"That," said Daniel, picking his wrenches up from the ground, putting them back into his belt, and getting to his feet, "is a list of some basic tools you'll want if you're going to join up."

Rill looked at him quizzically, but a small smile was gathering on his lips.

Daniel continued. "Look," he said, "the captain is a good man, but he's not that easily impressed. If you come to him with just a letter, even one from an old friend of his, he's going to politely show you the door. But," he waggled a finger at him, "if you show up with that letter and a complete set of tools, you'll be set. You have access to a forge?"

Rill cocked an eyebrow. "A forge?"

Daniel grinned and tapped a finger at the paper in his hands. "Some of these, you can buy. The rest, you're going to have to make with the ones you can buy."

Rill nodded in understanding. "So, it's not having the tools, it's making them that's the impressive part." He thought of Be'Var's forging abilities. He supposed that the old master might make time to help him with the making of new tools, especially if it got him out of the mission and into a division of the Royal Army. "Yeah," he said, then he looked up at Daniel with a mischievous grin. "It's Flamehearth Mission. Of *course* we have a forge."

Daniel returned the grin. "I'll tell the boss to keep an eye out for you, then?"

Rill nodded enthusiastically. "Definitely." Then, he remembered the other thing the engineer had said. "Seriously though, Daniel, what's the trouble you're talking about? Does it have anything to do with the krealites?"

The word 'krealites' had become part of the local vernacular in the last month. Rill suspected that the prince himself had something to do with the spreading of the term. Daniel had seemed ready to ignore the question again until he heard the word uttered. When he did, his face took on a somber quality and his eyes turned away from Rill until he was looking northward. "I don't really know, to be perfectly honest with you," he said. "It's all just rumors and speculation, but what I'm hearing is that there's an army out there somewhere, way up to the North. It's got men and horses and those krealite things in it, and it's coming our way."

Rill followed Daniel's gaze. "Do they know when?"

Daniel shrugged. "Wish I could say. Like I said, it's all just whispers of hearsay, so I don't even know how much of it's true." He paused for a moment, closing his eyes and wincing, as though remembering some unpleasant thought. "But after what those things did to us that night, I'd believe 'em capable of pretty much anything."

Rill thought about his own encounters with the krealites, about the bloody night when they'd attacked the Temple of the Conflagration, and about the group of monsters they'd trapped in a little room in the caverns of Otvia. The beasts had attacked without mercy. They didn't seem to burn. They could vanish straight through the floor as though it weren't there. Daniel was right: they did seem capable of almost anything.

"I'll get to work on this list, then," he said. As Daniel turned and nodded a friendly smile, Rill looked back at the piece of paper. "What do you think," he said, "a couple of weeks to get it together?"

"Ha!" Daniel exclaimed, shaking his head in delight. "I'll tell you what, Rill," he clapped a hand on Rill's shoulder, "if you manage to get these together in two weeks, you'll have *two* letters of recommendation to present to the captain!"

Rill smiled in appreciation, though he gave the young engineer a curious look. "Why do this?" he asked. "I mean, you must run into people all the time who want to be in the Engineering Corps." He shrugged. "Why me?"

Daniel removed his hand and adjusted his belt. "My friend, I don't run into nearly enough people who want to be in the corps." Satisfied with the fit of his belt, he brushed his fingers through his hair. "And of those, almost none of them could have figured out what was wrong with a broken hand pump without even opening it up." He gave a low chuckle. "Blast it, but most of them couldn't have figured it out with the thing's component parts arrayed out in front of them!"

He cocked an orange eyebrow at Rill. "It could be that you're been mucking me about and you've replaced a hundred pump valves before, but even if that's the case, I think the Royal Engineers could probably use you." He shrugged back at Rill. "Someone's got to keep the catapults running, and I'd much rather it be a smart man than one who doesn't know which end of a wrench to put to a nut.

"Now," he continued, "if you'll pardon me, I have other appointments this afternoon." He reached out and took Rill's hand again. "I have a feeling I'll be seeing you soon, Rill."

Rill shook the hand appreciatively, then watched the young, freckled engineer go. He looked down at the list in his hand with some bewilderment. He couldn't believe how much his life had changed in so short a time. Mere months ago, he'd been miserable, unable to fathom the mysteries of the Conflagration and unwilling to care about them. He'd thought of his leaving of the Temple as a humiliating admission of defeat, yet now here he was, learning that he wasn't nearly as stupid as everybody had assumed and finding the one thing he'd never realized had been missing in his life: purpose.

With a grin, he tucked the piece of paper into a pocket and strode off to Caymus's room so he could ask Be'Var about helping him with the forging of his new set of tools.

Once he'd passed through one of the small offices that served as buffers between the courtyard and the rest of Flamehearth, Rill rounded a corner and passed into the wide hallway that connected the building's rooms. He was so excited about what had just happened to him that he literally bounced a little with each step. He tried to think of the best way to ask Be'Var for his assistance. The old master had been a great deal more receptive to him ever since they'd crossed the Greatstones, but Rill still didn't quite feel like he knew how to talk to the man.

Just after he'd walked past the open doorway to the building's main entrance, however, a young voice interrupted his thoughts of the task at hand.

"Hey, you!" the voice called out.

~~~

Rill actually missed a step and had to recover from the beginnings of a fall, he was so surprised. Once he'd righted himself again, he turned around and tilted his head, listening. The voice—a boy's voice—had to belong to one of the children that lived in the mission, but it had sounded just a little bit too old. It had come from the entrance hall. Slowly, Rill made his way to the open door he'd just passed.

When he poked his head around the corner, he was met with a surprising sight: the boy who had been introduced to him as Sannet's brother a few weeks ago was sitting in one of the chairs, his elbows
~~~

resting on his knees. His face was dirty and his shirt and trousers, obviously made of finer-than-average cloth, were covered in smudges and patches, as though he were some sort of vagabond. The boy's face, too, seemed just as dour as it had the last time Rill had seen him, and the glare in those eyes made him more than a little uncomfortable. He couldn't quite remember the boy's name, either. Reginald? Robert?

"It took you long enough," the boy said, slapping his hands on his knees and standing up. He was taller than Rill remembered him being. Maybe that had something to do with the fact that Caymus had been present the first time the two had met; everyone seemed small when Caymus was around. "I've been waiting here for an hour for someone to come." The face wasn't smiling. He wasn't making a joke.

Rill found himself a little annoyed by the attitude confronting him. Not only taller, the boy appeared slightly older than he'd seemed when Rill had last laid eyes on him. He'd thought the boy twelve or thirteen back then, and now he seemed two or three years older than that. Rill was willing to forgive a selfish attitude in a child; someone this boy's age should know better.

He also remembered the boy as having a chubbier-looking face. Maybe it was a loss of weight that made him look older? Not very much time had passed since then; he couldn't have lost that much weight, could he?

"Sorry," Rill said, finally. What in the flames was his name? "I can find the mission-keeper for you, if you like. Or were you here to see somebody in particular?"

Somehow, the petulant face managed to look even more annoyed with him. "I'm here for you, stupid!" he said. "And that other one. The big one. The one that gave my parents that dumb stone!"

Rill had a distinct recollection of having felt sorry for this boy when he'd seen him before. Any remaining sympathy he might have had, however, was evaporating with every word the little brat uttered. Stupid, indeed! He kept his composure though, despite his growing annoyance. "Well, you can talk to me if you like," he said, "but Caymus—the big one—is out of the question. He's ill."

"Don't lie to me!" the boy said, though there was a slight pause before he said it, like he'd been momentarily confused by the information. Rill felt the muscles of his jaw beginning to tighten. "I've been watching this place, so I know my brother's not here. He's probably still at that stupid church. But you and that other one that's trying to ruin my life are definitely both here!" The boy's face was going a little bit red; his hands were clenched into fists. "I want to talk to him. Now!"

"I told you," Rill said. His voice was rising in pitch and intensity just the smallest amount. "He's not well."

"Liar!"

Rill couldn't believe what he was hearing. He was really getting angry, now. What was wrong with this boy? How could he possibly be related to Sannet, the calmest person Rill had ever known? "You don't believe me?" he said, raising his eyebrows as high as they could go. "Fine, we'll just go see him then, shall we?"

With that, Rill turned and marched out of the room, resuming his path toward his original destination. He half-hoped the little monster wouldn't follow, but the sounds of footsteps behind him suggested that he was half-hoping for too much. Rill sighed. As annoyed as he was with this little fool, he was even more annoyed with himself. He'd been in such a good mood less than two minutes ago; why was he letting this little twerp change that?

As he approached the open door to Caymus's room, Rill could hear a discussion of some sort taking place within. He considered the soundness of what he was doing and nearly stopped right there. Not only was he leading this child, who didn't seem to have a particularly favorable estimation of Caymus, into the room where his friend's helpless body lay, he was probably going to interrupt something important while he was at it.

The first voice belonged to Be'Var. "But what I'm asking," he was saying, "is whether the word originally came from Kepren or the Falaar."

"I cannot say," came the second voice. Rill believed it was Aiella's. Who else would be in that room these days, after all?

Once Rill turned into the open door and stepped a couple of feet into the room, he took stock of the situation, trying to decide if it would be better to just turn around and lead his little tormentor right back out. His surprise at what he saw inside, however, momentarily made him forget his frustration.

All four of the room's regular occupants were present. Caymus, of course, lay on his back in the bed he'd occupied for so many weeks now. Somebody had placed a small table at the foot of the bed's frame and covered it with a handful of cushions, which was nice to see: Caymus really was far too large for the normal-sized piece of furniture, and his feet had been dangling off the end of it all this time, so he looked a bit more comfortable now. His treatment appeared to be different today, too. Rill was used to seeing his friend submerged in blankets, but today he was stripped down to his smallclothes with little, damp-looking towels laid out over his chest, abdomen, and legs.

Gwenna was there also, standing on the opposite side of the bed. It was she who was applying the towels, first dipping them in a large, clay jug on a little side table, then wringing them out before placing them on his skin. She was just applying one to Caymus's left arm when Rill entered. When she glanced up at him, she gave a look that wasn't quite fierce enough to be a glare.

Rill noticed how red her eyes and cheeks were; she'd obviously been crying. He was reminded of the things he'd said to her, earlier. He wanted to offer that apology, but this didn't seem like the right time for it.

Also in the room were Be'Var and Aiella, the former in his red master's robes, the latter in her customary dress of blue, though this particular dress seemed a deeper shade than was usual. Both of them hovered over open books, which was normal for them these days. Rill still wasn't sure why Be'Var had asked Aiella of all people to help him with his research for the last couple of weeks, but since he had, the ambassador's daughter had become a frequent guest of Flamehearth Mission, constantly bringing books back and forth and having long discussions with Be'Var about shaping, about the elemental wars, and about what it really meant to be a knight.

"Well, when was it written down?" Be'Var said. "What's the context in the one you've got there?"

The thing that had so surprised Rill, though, was the sheer number of tomes that currently filled the room. When he'd last stepped foot in this chamber, no more than two days ago, a single stack of books about a foot tall had stood in the far corner. Now there were over two dozen such stacks, and not one was piled less than two feet high. The two researchers had even pushed a couple of stacks together to form a sort of makeshift table. It was this creation which they currently stood over, each looking down at a volume.

"That thing which I am trying to say," Aiella said, pushing her hair back over her shoulder with one hand so she could look up at Be'Var, and holding her place in a small tome with the other, "is that there is no mention of any context here. I understand that your book mentions that shapers were prevalent in this region during a certain time of the war—"

"Corat," Be'Var interrupted, holding his own place in a much larger volume, "it says they were a lot of them around when they pushed an element called 'corat' out." The old man was looking back and forth between the books, obviously agitated.

"Yes," replied Aiella in that frustratingly calm way of hers, "but there is no mention of such a thing here. It tells of a shaper that lived among the Falaar, but it does not say when the shaper's time was, nor does it describe any major event that occurred during his lifetime."

"And the Falaar have been around a very long time," Be'Var exhaled. The old master stabbed his finger at the book. "Burn me, they've probably been living in that same place since the Old War."

Rill turned back to Gwenna, who had shifted her gaze to a point just behind Rill and to his right. Ah, yes. The brat. Rill considered introducing him to those in the room, but he had a much bigger concern at that moment.

"How is he?" he asked, in his gentlest voice.

Gwenna opened her mouth as though to answer, but no sound came out and she closed it again.

"He got hot today," said Be'Var, still looking down at the two books. He obviously didn't know he had just rescued Gwenna from having to speak to Rill. "About an hour ago. I've given up trying to figure out why." The old man looked up at that point and glanced quickly between Rill and his smaller companion, not making any particular sign of acknowledgment. He darted his eyes toward Caymus. "We're seeing if the towels can't help cool him down a bit," he continued. "Not a great deal more we can do, besides that."

"You don't seem very worried about it," Rill said. He carefully emphasized the words so they came out as a question, rather than an accusation.

Be'Var shrugged. Rill noticed just how tired the old man looked. He wondered how much sleep the master had been getting during his constant vigil. "He's lasted this long," he said, after a moment. "I'm coming to believe that whatever in blazes is going on in that body of his, the outcome's up to him, not us. Best we can do is try to make him comfortable and make some effort to stabilize his temperature when it gets too far from normal to ignore."

Rill considered the thought. He supposed Be'Var was right. After all, people who ended up in bed as long as Caymus tended not to look as healthy as Caymus looked. His skin wasn't even pale from lack of sunlight. Whatever was keeping his friend unconscious for so long, it wasn't any sort of disease or malady. Rill had decided a while back that there was something happening to Caymus that they just couldn't see.

A thought struck him. "Does Milo know about it?" he asked.

"Come again?" Be'Var said, cocking an eyebrow at him.

"I mean," Rill explained, "I know pulling can only heat things up, but if anybody might have a way of cooling him down, it would probably be Milo." He shrugged. "A stiff breeze in the room, maybe?"

Be'Var looked away, toward the ceiling, then both tilted and nodded his head. "Yes," he said, "I suppose that's not the worst idea you've ever had."

"Who's your friend?" said Gwenna, finally. Rill turned to see her smiling and looking at the smaller figure who had, by now, stepped around him and entered the room.

Rill smiled, having just remembered the name he'd been searching for. "This," said Rill, extending a hand and managing to keep the sigh out of his voice, "is Roland. He's Sannet's little brother."

"Younger brother," said Roland, as much bile in his demeanor as ever.

He stepped away from Rill and walked around the foot of the bed, keeping his eyes locked on Caymus's prone form as he circled. When he stopped, he was standing beside Gwenna, separated from her by the little table that held the water jug. "What's wrong with him?" he said, tilting his head up a little. He spoke the words as though he was accusing the sleeping form of something.

"We don't know, really," Gwenna replied, adjusting one of the squares of cloth on her patient's chest. Her voice held a distant sadness, as though a part of her had given up hope that he would ever wake up. In that moment, Rill realized something about her, that she probably felt as conflicted about her feelings for Caymus as Rill had expected her to feel, and that the one person she really needed to talk to about it wasn't able to speak. The revelation put a knot in Rill's stomach, and he felt worse than ever about what he'd said.

Her eyes were welling up again, so Rill took over the explanation. "It was some kind of poison," he said, "one we don't know how to treat. He's been like this for weeks now, and there's no way to know when he's going to wake up."

"*If* he's going to wake up…" Gwenna said. Rill got the feeling she hadn't meant to say the words aloud.

"When," Rill corrected, a bit more forcefully than he'd intended. He understood something about how Gwenna was feeling now, but he felt very strongly that it wasn't any reason to give up hope. Caymus, as broken as he might seem in that moment, was still one of the strongest, most resolute people Rill had ever met. The idea that he might not wake up from this long slumber wasn't something he could even imagine.

In the next moment, Rill found himself wondering if he had actually just seen a little smile flit across Roland's face. No, he must have imagined it. Sannet's little brother couldn't really be that callous, could he?

Rill didn't notice that Gwenna was actually shaking until Aiella moved to stand next to her and placed a steadying hand on her arm. She wasn't crying, didn't seem angry or sad, but she was obviously just barely hanging onto her composure. Aiella spoke quietly to her in a voice that Rill couldn't hear, and Gwenna whispered something back. Rill took a deep breath. He didn't like that he'd had anything to do with this.

"So, Rill," Be'Var said. The old man was stretching when Rill turned to face him. "You must have come in here for a reason."

Rill, glad for the change of subject, smiled a little and covered the three steps to the book-pile desk. "I wanted to ask for your help, actually," he said. "I need to make a few tools."

Be'Var froze mid-stretch and looked at him suspiciously. "Tools?" he said. "What kinds of tools, and what do you need them for?"

Rill grinned. He'd found himself starting to like Be'Var's gruff exterior lately, now that it wasn't actually in charge of his studies anymore. "I just had a talk with a member of the Royal Engineers," he said. He hiked a thumb over his shoulder. "I helped him a bit with fixing the water pump in the courtyard and he said that if I could get a handful of tools together, he'd help me get in."

"Hmmm," Be'Var said. Without looking down, he put his hand on one of the open books and tapped a finger on it. "So, you're looking for my help as a blacksmith, then."

"I don't want you to make them for me," Rill said quickly, fearing he was being misunderstood, "I've just never done it before, and might need a bit of help. I doubt," he continued, smiling, "I could do better than having a human forge helping me figure out the process."

Be'Var just stared at Rill for a few moments, as though weighing his words, or possibly weighing how much he believed their genuineness. "Can it wait?" he finally said.

"It can," Rill admitted. He felt a little deflated at the thought.

"Good," said the old man, turning his attention back to the book. "There's still a lot left to do here, and I..."

The words trailed off as they both turned to see Gwenna, who had by now pulled away from Aiella's hand, quickly striding around the bed and heading for the door. "I'm going to see if I can find Milo," she said. Rill suspected she just needed to get out of the room. He couldn't see her face clearly, but her voice seemed to be on the verge of breaking.

He'd go and find her later and really apologize.

When he looked back, he saw Aiella staring at him, her expression a mixture of curiosity and disapproval. The look didn't have much effect on Rill, seeing as he already felt about as bad as he could about Gwenna, but he did end up locking eyes with the dark-haired girl for a moment. He found himself wondering why it was she was so interested in helping Be'Var with his research. She was Creveyan, after all—one would struggle to find more a devout worshiper of water than a Creveyan—so what was her motivation for assisting with research into things related to fire?

His thought was interrupted by the sound of breaking pottery. When he pulled his eyes away, he saw that Roland, who had just knocked the water jug over, was backing away from the bed, an alarmed look on his face. He had a right to be alarmed, too: the jug itself wasn't likely of much value, but the water it had contained was in the process of soaking into at least two of the piles of books that sat near the foot of the bed.

"Flaming dog-spit, idiot child!" Be'Var yelled. The old man quickly stepped around the pile of books before him, reaching for Roland with an outstretched hand.

Roland, however, was moving much too fast. "I'm sorry, I'm sorry!" he exclaimed as he quickly dodged around Caymus's prone form and ran out of the room. Rill, too, tried to catch hold of him, but the boy ducked and spun as he passed, denying a good grip, even on his filthy shirt. He chased Roland as far as the doorway, then stopped, his hands out against the frame, having decided against following any further. The horrible little child was heading toward the building's exit anyway, exactly where Rill wanted him to go, and there wouldn't be much point in catching him, anyway. What would he do, make him un-spill the jug?

As he stood there, watching Roland turn a corner and disappear, Rill gave brief consideration to running, too. He was, after all, the one who'd brought Roland into the room in the first place. Wouldn't Be'Var blame him just as much as he did the boy? Would the master have any inclination at all to help him forge engineering tools now that he'd brought ruination to a number of the cherished books? He didn't like the odds of a favorable outcome to the day.

He was, therefore, quite surprised at how little anger the master's next words contained. "Burn me," he said in a tone that sounded positively beguiled.

Rill turned to see what it was that had the man's attention, but found he had to step back into the room, since he could only make out the tops of both Be'Var's and Aiella's heads. The two of them were crouched down on the other side of the bed. As he rounded the little table that held up Caymus's feet, he thought to grab one of the towels from his leg. Maybe he could wring it out and use it to mop up some of the water.

When he was finally standing beside the old man and getting a good look at what was happening, Rill immediately understood what Be'Var had been so excited about. Aiella, kneeling on the stone floor before them, had placed each of her hands atop one of the drenched piles of books. She was letting her head hang down and allowing her hair to spill over her face, so Rill couldn't see if her eyes were open or closed, but the hunch of her shoulders gave the impression that she was concentrating hard.

The thing she was concentrating on, it seemed, was the act of literally pulling the water out of the books.

The effect was subtle, at first. Little drops of clear liquid began to appear on the covers, bindings, and even the pages of the books, as though they were somehow sweating. The drops then moved together, collecting into tiny rivulets, and made their way down the stacks toward a single point on the stone floor. Some of the streams of water ran all the way to the floor before moving to that point; others seemed to drip diagonally toward it before getting that far. The impression Rill got was that the water had its own separate source of gravity that was causing each drop of liquid to slowly fall into that single spot where it collected in a growing puddle.

After about a minute, it appeared that there wasn't much left to sweat out of the books. The water had pooled outward and upward until it was about the size and shape of a large, upended bowl. Whatever Aiella was doing to pull the liquid from the books, she was also causing it to collect in this highly unnatural shape. Rill realized at that point that the moisture would still need to be collected once Aiella broke her concentration and the force that was holding the aqueous shape together dissipated. Moving quickly, he grabbed four more of the towels and took them to the room's single open window, where he held them outside and wrung them out.

He was just coming back with the slightly drier rectangles of cloth when Aiella spoke. "The towels, please," she said, and lifted one of her hands to Rill. He gave the collection to her, and she placed them over the top of the little semi-sphere of liquid. Rill had thought she would need more cloth to soak up that much water, but she must have been having an effect there also, as the small collection of material appeared able to absorb the lot.

The dark-haired girl then took the towels in both hands, stepped past Rill toward the window, and wrung them, spilling the entirety of their contents onto the ground outside. She let out a deep breath as she did so, as though she was putting down some huge weight. The feat she had just performed must have taken some significant effort.

"That was quite an impressive display, young lady," Be'Var said, getting to his feet. His tone was both amused and guarded at the same time. "I wasn't aware you took after your father so much."

Aiella, who had by now returned to the side of the bed and was replacing the towels to Caymus's skin, kept her face placid. "My father, he is not aware either," she said. She looked up, her eyes moving back and forth between Be'Var and Rill. "I would be grateful if you would not tell him."

Rill smiled. He knew how important it could be to have things to keep to yourself, especially where family was concerned. "It'll be our secret," he said. When he looked over at Be'Var, he realized that the master might not have been convinced, so he decided to risk over-stepping his bounds. "We won't tell anybody about it, will we Be'Var?"

Be'Var looked as though he was about to rebuke him, then the weathered face seemed to acquiesce to the idea. "Oh, all right," he said. He turned back to Aiella. "Just make sure you tell him yourself, and sometime in the very near future. He'd be cross with me if he found out I was keeping something like this from him."

Aiella actually smiled at that. "Thank you," she said.

"Clumsy fool," Be'Var said, turning toward the door. He looked at Rill again. "You say he's Sannet's brother?"

"I know," Rill said. "Wouldn't have believed it myself if his parents hadn't told me."

"He was not clumsy," Aiella interrupted. Rill and Be'Var both turned to look at her.

"What do you mean?" Rill said.

"I believe he spilled the water with purpose," she said, turning her eyes back to Caymus's sleeping form.

"You saw him tip it over?" Be'Var said.

"No," she said, "I was distracted at the time, but he appeared to react to the drop before the jug began moving, as though he knew already that it was going to happen."

Nobody said anything for a few moments. Be'Var bent down and picked up a couple of the books that had so recently been doused. Rill wondered if Roland could actually have spilled the water intentionally. Aiella's judgment of Roland's reaction to the spill wasn't much to go on really, but Rill was beginning to think that she was a genuinely intelligent person, and so, despite the ice in her veins, he put some stock in what she said.

"Well, well," Be'Var said, slowly leafing through a battered, red-covered tome with yellowing pages. "I was sure this one was done for, but you actually saved the ink."

"That is good," Aiella replied. When she had placed the last of the towels back in its original place upon Caymus's flesh, she looked up at Be'Var, patting her slightly damp hands on her dress as she did so. "I believe," she said, "that I will go back to the Reed Library now, to see if I can find more information on your shaper reference."

Be'Var nodded, still skimming pages. Rill could tell he was only half-listening to her; he wondered if the old man was still checking the ink or if he was already getting lost in the content. "Fine, fine," was all he said in return.

Aiella either didn't feel slighted by the master's distracted tone or, if she did, didn't register it on her face. Instead, she simply picked up a small stack of books from the corner of the room. "You are finished with these?" she asked.

"Yes, yes," Be'Var said, though whether he'd actually heard and understood the question was impossible to say. Rill found himself holding back a chuckle. He'd never seen Be'Var operating in this particular mode before. The distracted scholar before him was a stark contrast to the rough taskmaster he was familiar with.

Aiella nodded, took the books in her arms, and walked to the door. Just before she reached it, however, Be'Var lifted his head. "Did you have any luck with the Royal Collection, by the way?"

Aiella turned around. Only her face was visible above the stack of books she held. "I did not," she said. "I have asked Prince Garrin for permission to enter, but he insists that only the king is able to grant it."

"And the king hasn't been in much shape to grant anything for quite some time," Be'Var said, finishing the thought. He closed the red-bound book and sighed. "Pity. I'm sure there's a lot of useful information in those particular books, but I suppose there's no use complaining about it until we've exhausted the other sources." His wrinkly face managed a smile. "Thank you, Aiella. Your help has been invaluable these past weeks."

Aiella nodded. "You are welcome, Master Be'Var," she said, then she turned and walked out the door.

Rill was suddenly keenly aware of the quiet in the chamber. Now that the others had left the room, he could actually hear the sound of Caymus breathing. He hadn't realized just how much noise four or five people could make. As Be'Var opened the book in his other hand and started flipping through it, Rill found himself walking over to the head of the bed.

He missed Caymus, missed him badly. Kepren was such a huge, interesting place, full of new experiences. Rill had planned to have so many adventures when he'd first walked through the city's gates, but he'd found himself putting them off for the simple reason of having nobody to share them with. He hadn't practiced his sword drills in weeks, either. Very soon after Caymus had first found himself in this bed, Rill had decided that drilling could wait until his friend woke up again, that he couldn't possibly be without his sparring partner for very long. Now, after so many weeks had passed without change, he didn't really know what to do about practicing his swordplay. Milo didn't use a sword; he'd just try to teach him the bow, like he'd done with Gwenna. He'd thought about asking Tavrin, the young Falaar that Gwenna had become so close to lately, if he would be willing to spar with him, but the subject of Caymus and Gwenna was sure to come up eventually, and that wasn't really something he wanted to discuss with him. Tavrin seemed nice enough, but Rill didn't know him well enough to say if he had a temper or not.

"Well," said Be'Var, closing the book and walking up beside him, "I suppose since everybody else has gone, and since there's not much more useful reading I can do before Aiella comes back, perhaps you should tell me more about these tools you need."

Rill smiled. Even with the guilt he still felt over what he'd said to Gwenna, and despite the fact that he'd managed to let Sannet's horrible little brother spill water all over Be'Var's books, it seemed he might just be able to salvage this day yet.

As he pulled the list of supplies from his pocket, he only wished he had his best friend around so he could share his good news.

Wake up soon, Caymus, he thought. *I don't know what you're doing in there, but life out here's a lot more boring without you.*

Chapter 14

Caymus stood quietly amongst the flames of the Conflagration, staring at the wall before him. The wall wasn't very long, being barely a handful of yards across; nor was it high, rising to only a few inches above his brow. It was only a shade lighter than pitch black, the same color as the krealites he'd encountered, which made him wary. He gripped the sword tight in his hand as he continued to watch the dark surface, waiting for it to do something awful to him.

The truly unsettling thing about the wall was the way it seemed to be less than solid. It undulated a little under his gaze, bending slowly toward and away from him. It also rippled slightly, as though it were a standing pool of water with some invisible force acting against it.

A sweet smell hung in the air, like burnt sugar but not nearly so strong. The smell hadn't been there before the wall shown up. Had they appeared at the same time? Did the black wall really smell like burnt sugar?

Caymus got that uncomfortable feeling in the pit of his stomach again, or, at least, in a projection of the pit of his stomach. His actual stomach, he knew, was back in his own world in what the Lords of the Conflagration called the Quatrain, along with the rest of his body. He'd grown comfortable with the idea after some time here, had begun to understand himself in the context of the elemental realm.

He was the only living thing here. He could feel it the same way he could sense the presence of a person or animal in his own world. The being he'd met here, the one that had worn Milo's face like a disguise, was sentient and intelligent, but it wasn't alive, not in the same way he was.

When was it he'd met that being? He felt like it had been mere moments ago, but it might have been years. There was no time here. Beings of fire that weren't alive didn't need time, so the very concept had been stripped away from him when his consciousness had entered this place.

He wished he knew how long he'd been standing there, how long it had been since this accursed wall had quietly appeared before him. He didn't know why the wall had shown up, but he felt instinctively that it was dangerous, that it wasn't supposed to be there. Idly, he flexed his fingers against the hilt of the sword the Lords had given him, then he reached up with his index finger to rub the symbol on the cross-guard. The same sword and flame design that adorned the back of his hand hadn't been there at first, but it had materialized, etched lightly into the metal, sometime after he'd first picked it up.

Caymus smiled, feeling reassured by the steel in his hand. The sword felt more real than anything else in this place. He knew it wasn't real of course, but it *felt* real, and as he held on to the weapon, he also held on to his sanity.

Still, he stood there, waiting. The Lords of the Conflagration had brought him here, placed him before this strange, sweet-smelling wall, but why? Was he supposed to do something to it? Was there something to learn here?

He chewed his bottom lip as he thought about his predicament, trying to carve his next move out of the jumble of thoughts in his head. Glaring at the wall, he decided it was his first priority. The fire Lords wanted him to do something with it, but he needed to understand the thing better before he was going to go any nearer.

He considered reaching out with his consciousness to try to learn more, but he frowned at the idea. Would that work? After all, for the time being he *was* his consciousness. Would the act of trying to project out from his own projection be a mistake? Could it be dangerous?

He pressed his lips together in uncertainty, then decided to try. Reaching out was unlikely to actually hurt him, and it was certainly worth an attempt. He took a steadying breath, closed his eyes, and reached.

Before he'd really made the conscious effort, he was touching the wall with his mind. The suddenness of it actually jarred him physically, breaking the connection and giving him pause. What had happened? With a slight shake of his head, he regathered his thoughts and tried again. Again, he found that he was immediately touching the wall, but that he had no recollection of having crossed the space between him and it. The sensation was strange, like being on the other side of a room the moment after having decided to cross it, not having taken a single step.

He decided that something about being separated from his physical form must be making the act of projecting his consciousness easier, faster. He couldn't believe how intuitive it seemed. Whereas reaching out to something had always required intense concentration before, the same action here was suddenly second nature.

Now that he had his bearings, he ran himself along the edges of the wall, feeling for anything that might betray some clue as to the thing's construction, all the time reveling in the effortlessness of the act. Despite the ease with which he was exploring the wall's boundaries however, he wasn't finding much, though he did discover that in addition to the relatively small height and width, it was also barely an inch thick. Still, there wasn't even the faintest suggestion of air, water, or earth in its makeup, not to mention fire.

Curious, he shifted his thoughts from the edge of the wall to the full measure of the side that faced him. He could sense the movement of the material more clearly now, as though he were now floating on the ripples, rather than hovering above them. Tentatively, he reached out and pressed himself against the surface, trying to move beyond it and into the interior.

He felt himself jerk back violently, like a hand retreating from a hot surface, and he broke the connection. He wasn't sure what he'd expected to find within the dark shape, but he certainly hadn't thought to find another consciousness there! He tensed at the memory of the sensation. He didn't know who or what, but something—a presence that existed on the other side of the wall, but not within the Conflagration itself—had noticed him there.

He also got the distinct impression that the something was coming to investigate.

"Flames," Caymus whispered to himself. He took a few steps backward and brought the blade of his sword up in front of him, holding the grip with both hands. "What *was* that?" As he still had no sense of time, he didn't know how long he waited, but he felt as though he'd taken about a dozen breaths before a dark figure stepped out of the black mass before him.

The figure was human-looking, yet at the same time it was as far from human as his imagination could comprehend. It was the height of a human. It had two arms, two legs, and a head. The arms and legs, however, ended in forms that lacked fingers or toes. Instead, forearms tapered down to black, sharp-looking points and the feet, lacking any sort of definition to separate heel from toe, appeared as shapeless globs of a black, undulating material.

The figure had no face. The head presented only a smooth, black surface, yet Caymus could tell it was looking at him, its awareness of him as obvious as the sickly, sweet smell that emanated from it.

Caymus's neck itched. He knew what that meant: this thing was a krealite. He wondered if the wall itself was made of the stuff, but, if so, why hadn't his skin prickled before the shape had stepped through it?

Caymus's thought was cut short as the figure slowly put one foot forward and then charged at him.

The thing hated him. He knew it with certainty, the same way he'd known that the blank face had been staring at him. He tried to keep his wits as he felt his muscles tense. Could he use that hatred, take advantage of that rage? As the figure neared, he decided to try, and so shifted his right foot outward a few inches, raising his sword up, point held high, toward his left shoulder. Just as the thing was about to reach him, he pushed off the extended foot, spinning his body to the right, and brought the pommel of the sword down the back of his attacker's head.

The krealite stumbled a couple of paces and Caymus took the opportunity to take a step toward it and bring his blade down on the exposed back.

The might of his blow knocked the dark shape to the ground. His enemy was sprawled out on its hands and knees, but not wounded: he'd failed to penetrate the thing's skin. Caymus grimaced with frustration and backed off a few steps. For all he'd accomplished, he might as well have just shouted at it.

Slowly, with great deliberateness, the creature rose from the ground. It didn't appear to be injured in any way at all, but it did seem as though it was considering Caymus with greater wariness now. As the blank face turned toward him again, Caymus raised the sword defensively, waiting for it to make its next move. How did it get here? If it was a krealite, what was it doing in the Conflagration?

His thoughts were interrupted by another charge. Caymus didn't think he could get away with the same move twice, but his muscles seemed to disagree and, before he knew what he was doing, he was repeating his previous motion, letting the creature get close, then spinning and knocking it down. This time, however, he struck out with his blade, rather than the pommel, on the first hit.

As the action was repeated, so was the result. Again, he failed to wound the creature. Again, it was merely battered to the ground. This time, however, he took several strong swings at the thing as it lay there, even taking the time to reverse his grip and thrust the sword's point down into its neck. Still, his blade failed to make purchase, only managing to deliver concussive force.

As he moved away again, he cursed under his breath. The krealite was getting up again, just as deliberately as before, and turning to face him.

Again and again the creature charged. Caymus tried a few variations on his defense, sometimes tripping his opponent, sometimes just driving it to the ground with brute force. His lessons with Rill and Be'Var must have stuck with him, because he always managed to bring the creature down.

But it always got up again.

After what felt like the tenth time going through the pattern of attack and defense, Caymus began to lose his temper and actually shouted at the thing. "What is this!" he yelled between panting breaths. "What do you want?" He was getting frustrated by the creature's failure to stay down, to yield. As he slid a foot backward, preparing for another charge, he marveled at his own luck that the thing wasn't smarter, that it didn't seem to learn from its previous mistakes.

This time, however, when the creature rose from the ground, it didn't immediately charge. Instead, it stood tall, facing him, its arms at its sides. As Caymus watched, he saw the pointed hands of the creature change before his eyes, growing in length, flattening out until the black shape appeared as though it had two short sword blades attached to the ends of its arms.

Apparently, it was more adaptable than he'd thought.

The new weapons, though, didn't affect him nearly as much as the long, deep sigh that escaped the thing's dark, lipless face. Caymus didn't know why it had done that, but he had an eerie feeling that the sound was some attempt at communication.

Before he could give voice to his thoughts, however, the creature stepped forward and charged again.

Caymus was amazed at the ferocity of the pins and needles in his neck as he fought with all his might to defend himself.

~~~

Garrin slammed his fist on the table, knocking over a glass that subsequently dribbled wine onto some scattered documents. The prince thought angrily that the fools at the table must not have believed the papers nearly as important as they had claimed, or at least one of them would be scrabbling to rescue them from the spill.

He stood, pressing open hands against the varnished wood, letting his head fall limp, and closing his eyes as he tried to puzzle a way out of this mess. It was late. The candles in the room had been replaced twice already, and these ridiculous men were no closer to agreement than they'd been when they'd entered that afternoon. He wondered how many of the servants were even still awake at this point, knowing that at least one or two of them would be nearby, waiting to see if the important people needed anything.

He could hear the patter of dust and sand against the single window in the drafty war room, and the sound squeezed his heart. Kepren wasn't accustomed to sandstorms; the dark cloud outside was hardly more than a large dust-devil, but it was stark evidence of just how dry the city had become in recent months. The noise seemed to echo against the bare
~~~

stone walls and ceiling. Garrin had been in this room more times that he could count but, until recently, only as a soldier—a commander of course, due to the royal blood in his veins, but a soldier nonetheless—advising his king. Now, here he stood at the head of the table, in his father's place.

He hated the head of the table.

The three dukes of Kepren, as well as the two ambassadors from Creveya, had been here for hours as the prince had tried to explain to them the dreadful seriousness of what they were up against. Aiella was there too; Brocke always tried to keep her close by, a fact which Garrin didn't mind at all. Not only was she as clever as she was beautiful, but she was probably the only true ally he had in the room.

He opened his eyes again, letting them drift over the same reports, received from either foreign messengers or from the network of air priests that had cropped up since the first krealite attack, that he'd been looking over all day. They were matters of crucial importance and sources of great frustration. Those messages that were hand-carried by couriers, many of whom had ridden several horses to get here quickly, were generally considered to be the more reliable than those carried on the wind, but they weren't nearly so timely. Quite often the sealed letters contained information that was weeks old, at best. Garrin was immensely thankful for the air priests.

Every once in a while, one message would contradict another, making comprehension of what was happening up north difficult but, for the most part, they were in agreement. A large army calling itself "Black Moon" was on a southerly march. Nobody knew where they had come from or what they wanted, but they were moving steadily and would, sooner or later, reach Kepren.

And they were killing people: a *lot* of people.

Garrin took a deep breath, thinking about the city of Albreva. He'd been there once when he was just becoming a man. He'd been sent as part of an envoy to sign pacts and treaties designed to keep the Albrevans from warring with the people of the Tebrian League for the next several centuries. His memories were of men in glinting plate armor, with pikes and swords sharpened to incredible degrees through processes his own blacksmiths didn't understand. They'd had horses and siege engines, and even a moat around a large portion of Albreva—a moat!

Madd's Hollow and Caranaar, too, were said to be the home of some of the fiercest warriors imaginable. Caranaar's bladewhirls were the very hands of death on the battlefield. He'd never been to Madd's Hollow, but he'd heard stories that their warriors were strong enough to tear a man in two with naught but bare hands.

All of them—Madd's Hollow, Albreva, and now Caranaar—had fallen to this Black Moon Army. How such mighty peoples had fallen to this foe he couldn't understand, but the reports from those who had actually witnessed the last days of each city were all the same. Black Moon arrived, camped outside the city walls for the night, and then, by the next day, nobody inside those walls was heard from again.

They didn't even ask for surrender first.

He didn't know how he was going to do it yet, but somehow he was going to spare Kepren from the same fate that had befallen the northern cities. He looked up from the table, regarded the people sitting around it, and tried not to grimace. He had been a soldier all his life and was a gifted commander of men. In the field he was without peer, but these games of politics were something he just didn't have talent for.

Korwinder, Duke of the Guard District, his bushy white mustache a stark contrast to his bald head, cleared his throat and picked up his goblet. "My dear Prince," he said in that condescending tone of his, "I understand that you are concerned for our city. We are all concerned for our city, but evidence of our need to rally a force of such a magnitude as you describe is just not here." He tipped his head at the reports on the table. Garrin hated Korwinder more than any of them. He was an ancient, exasperating know-it-all, sure, but worst of all Garrin suspected that the man wasn't even being devious in his protestations, that he actually believed the words coming out of his mouth.

"He's right."

Garrin turned to find that Duke Chenswig was still playing with that wooden quill of his. "The evidence just isn't there, highness, just isn't there." Garrin was less-than-surprised at this response, too. The young man had become duke of the Grass District barely a year ago, after his father had died of some sudden affliction. He seemed to have no sense of his own responsibilities and generally chose to a parrot Korwinder rather than form his own opinions.

Garrin turned to Duke Fel of the Reed District. "Well, Your Grace," he said, expecting the worst, "what do you say?"

"Well, uh, your highness." Fel's jowls shook as he looked around the room at anything but the sets of eyes that were on him. His shrill voice stretched the words out as though it was uncomfortable speaking them. "I think that it's quite a risk, your highness, yes, quite a risk," his fingers spun a circle in front of him, as though searching for the words, "...uh, to be taking when there's this drought about. New troops cost money. There's training them, housing them, feeding them. Uh, until this drought is over, I think it would be foolish to take such a risk."

Garrin's heart would have sunk had he not been expecting exactly that. Fel was a businessman above anything else, and he was losing money to the drought. Men like him were always averse to any action that didn't positively affect the gold in their treasuries.

Garrin gave a quick glance to Ambassadors Brocke and Cull, of the Summit and the Tower, respectively. They sat a few feet from the table; as foreign dignitaries, they had no say in the matters of Tebrian rule. If Garrin asked them a direct question about Creveya, they would answer, otherwise, they politely kept their mouths shut.

"My good dukes," he said, as calmly as he could manage, "the evidence sits before you." He picked up a handful of paper and threw it down in the middle of the table, giving them a good spin so that they would scatter across its surface. "Reports given to us from the air priests—"

"Air priests!" scoffed Korwinder, picking at his mustache

"The reports from the air priests," Garrin repeated, his voice rising in volume and intensity, "are corroborated by those arriving from the cities themselves!" He leaned on his fists, looking at each of the three in turn. "If that isn't evidence enough that we need to take action to defend our alliance, then I don't know what is!"

"Your highness," said Korwinder, now smoothing the white puff of hair under his lip, "There may be some matter that affected these places, but there's no way to be certain it's coming toward us."

Garrin was about to respond, but Fel spoke first. "And anyway, uh, your highness, all these reports tell us," he indicated the scattered papers with the same, circular motion of his fingers, "is that these Black Moon folk arrived, and the messages stopped coming. There is, uh, no reason to believe that any actual harm came to them."

"Exactly," said Chenswig, still playing with that quill. "There's no way to know what happened over there."

Garrin couldn't decide if he was more dumbfounded or incensed by the three of them. He tried to appeal to them with his own expertise. "Dukes," he said, lowering his tone, "I can accept that we do not have reports of the aftermath of these events. I can accept that you don't have a firm understanding of what happened there." He pushed himself off the table, standing up straight. "I am the commander of the Royal Army of Kepren," he said, "and I say that this represents a threat. Not only that," he said, as he straightened the black sword at his hip, "I say that this threat is coming our way and that we need to raise more troops to have even a hope of dealing with it."

"My dear prince," said Korwinder, not even giving Garrin's words time to sink in. "I know that you worry for the kingdom's safety and we," he indicated the three of them, "are sure you're doing what you think is best." He reached up for his mustache again, twisting one end into a point. "If the king were here to command it to be so, we would obviously all oblige him, but since he is not, we can assume he believes we represent the city's best interests and can act accordingly."

Garrin could have run the man through on the spot. It was another of his political games. Indeed, King Lysandus, Garrin's father, wasn't here. Legally, only he had the right to countermand the dukes' wishes and order them to war, but he simply was not present to do so.

Of course, everyone in the room knew that the king had been sick for nearly half a year, that he currently lay in his bed, wasting away, and that Garrin had been forced to take the reins of leadership in his absence. They also knew that this meant Garrin had not been crowned king himself, that the authority to order them was not yet officially his to wield.

Garrin, keeping his rage at the man's impudence bottled up inside him, looked to the other two dukes, who were both nodding in agreement. He leaned on his fists and hung his head again. "I see," he said.

"Gentlemen," he continued after a moment, not even bothering to look up, "I think you all know the way out of the Keep."

It wasn't a question. The three men stood as one, muttered good-nights to his highness, and headed for the door. Behind them, Brocke, Aiella, and Cull also stood, bowed, and followed.

"Ambassadors," Garrin said before everyone vacated the room, "might I ask you to stay behind a moment?" It was Brocke and Aiella that he really wanted to talk to, but to invite them to stay behind and not allow the Tower ambassador also would show a kind of favoritism he didn't want to acknowledge. "And Miss Aiella, would you stay also?"

If the dukes were perturbed by the request, it didn't register on their faces. They turned and left as the others nodded and walked back toward the table. Garrin motioned that they should sit in the dukes' vacated seats.

After the three men—three men that might cost all of them their freedom, if not their lives, as far as Garrin was concerned—had shut the door behind them, Garrin fell back into his chair and heaved a huge sigh. "I'm sorry to detain you further," he said with an apologetic smile, "but I wanted to ask your thoughts about all of this." He motioned toward the closed door. "Just, without those three hearing about it."

The two men, envoys from lands that had hated each other for centuries, exchanged glances that the prince found quite interesting. There was no malice in their expressions; rather they seemed to be like children with an unpleasant secret between them, unsure if they should divulge it to a parent. Whatever it was the two of them knew, it seemed to weigh heavily on them.

Brocke spoke first, addressing the other ambassador. "Would you like to tell him?"

Ambassador Cull, a wizened-looking fellow whose frame never seemed solid enough to carry the thick blue robes and gold chains of his office, seemed to consider this a moment, then he let out a small breath and turned to the Prince. "It seems that the leaders of Creveya—both the Tower and Summit—are seeing eye-to-eye on matters for the first time since anyone can remember."

Garrin sat up straighter in his chair. "What do you mean?"

"Well," said Cull, "we both have received word from our respective peoples in the last few days that our sovereigns, they have declared that there is an official end to fighting."

Garrin frowned at the man. "I didn't know there had been open war between you."

"No, no," said Cull, waving the thought off with a stick-like arm, "there has not been anything like this for over a decade now, but that is not the point." He leaned forward, his elbows on the table. "There, of course, has always been disagreement between the Tower and the Summit over the matter of Creveya. Though there never is an actual declaration of war, small skirmishes, here and there, occur with regularity." He raised an eyebrow. "You are aware of this, I'm sure."

Garrin nodded. "You're saying these 'skirmishes' have stopped?"

Cull nodded. "It would appear so."

Garrin turned to Brocke, who was staring at Cull with a mixture of confusion and frustration. "So, you've received the same news from the Summit?"

Brocke turned to Garrin and nodded. "I have. It seems that the declarations, they occurred simultaneously, though my messenger only arrived to give me the news today."

Garrin looked back and forth between the two men, who both seemed as confused about the matter as he. He stole a look at Aiella, who appeared to share the sentiment. He decided to ask the obvious question. "Black Moon?"

Brocke answered him. "We do not know, Highness. It has not been made clear to us why the orders have been given, but it seems that things, they have gone so far as to allow our respective priests and priestesses to meet in the waters of Creveya to discuss a permanent peace."

Garrin's eyes widened. He was beginning to understand the consternation in the people before him. Not only was the idea that the Tower and the Summit might find a peace between them nearly unfathomable, the prospect changed the dynamic between these two men considerably. For years, they'd been rivals, had plotted against and hated each other. Now it seemed that, nearly overnight, their rulers had informed them that they were to end all hostilities.

Garrin had to hold back a smile. The ideas that Ambassadors Brocke and Cull might have to be allies, not to mention the obvious discomfort that they were having with the concept, were so bizarre as to be funny. He looked between them again, trying to address both at once. "Do you think it will last?"

The two men, staring at each other with equal measures of disbelief and shock, seemed lost for words. Each drew breath as though to speak, and then said nothing.

Aiella spoke for them. "It would appear, Prince Garrin, that the impetus for this peace, it came from the high priests themselves, not the sovereigns."

Garrin nodded in understanding. The hostilities between Creveya, the Tower and Creveya, the Summit had always been religious in nature, having something to do with the lake between them. Garrin had never understood the subtleties of their disagreement, but he believed that Lake Creveya functioned as some kind of door between worlds, much the same as that pillar of fire at the Temple of the Conflagrationists that Be'Var was so proud of. He imagined the feud had something to do with control of that portal.

If the religious leaders, and not the secular sovereigns, were the force behind the truce, then the proposed peace had real teeth, and thus stood a very good chance of lasting a long time indeed.

Garrin leaned back in his chair again, bridging his fingertips before him and considering the implications of this news. The people of the two nations of Creveya, situated north of the Tebrian grasslands, had long wished to become part of the Tebrian League, the formal alliance between Kepren, Shorevale, and the broken city of Laivus. They had always been denied entry, however, due to the schism between their two factions. A people that could not cooperate with each other, after all, could hardly be expected to cooperate with a greater alliance. If the rift between the Tower and the Summit could truly be mended, though, then their addition to the League was all but guaranteed.

Indeed, the soldiers of Creveya would be a great addition to the forces of Kepren. Besides their battle prowess, many of their people were skilled, in one way or another, in the Aspects of water. Their devotion to that lake demanded an amount of religious study that was uncommon in other cities. Garrin had once heard of the people of the Tower defeating a Mael'vekian excursionary force by pulling an inland sea into the battlefield, drowning nearly half the enemy number. He'd always though the story embellished, but it was a fascinating concept, nonetheless.

The question was one of timing. If he were to count Creveyans among his soldiers against the Black Moon Army, they would have to join the Tebrian League very soon. If these discussions of peace took too long, then there simply wouldn't be time to formally ally with Creveya before Black Moon was knocking at Kepren's doors.

He looked up at the two ambassadors, who were patiently waiting for him to address them. "I suppose," he said, with a plaintive smile, "it's too much to ask to know when this lasting peace might arrive?"

The two men shook their heads with grim expressions. "I am afraid not," said Brocke. He motioned to the other man. "We are still trying to understand the situation better ourselves. Messages take many days to arrive here from Creveya; for all we know, the peace may exist already."

Nothing was said about the possibility that the peace could also have already disintegrated into open war.

Garrin put his hands on the table. "Do you think," he said, "that—should the peace exist—I could count on a united Creveya for assistance against this force from the North?"

"I have already communicated this need to the Summit," said Brocke.

"As have I, to the Tower," said Cull.

The two men glanced at each other with a hint of surprise. It seemed they hadn't communicated that bit of information to each other yet. Garrin wondered if they would ever really be able to work together.

Wearing a smile that he liked not having to force, Garrin stood. "That is all I could ask of you," he said. "Thank you, Ambassadors, for your time."

The two men politely stood, bowed slightly, and turned to leave the room. Aiella followed after her father, but Garrin reached out and gently grabbed her arm.

"A moment?" he said, when she turned. She nodded, but her eyes, those wonderful, brown eyes of hers, didn't betray whether or not she was happy about it. Garrin supposed that being the daughter of an ambassador had something to do with that. "Walk with me?"

They left through the opposite door to the room. The sand had stopped its percussive notes against the window, and so Garrin planned a stroll along the Keep's ramparts. He led her down the main corridor that led toward the stairwell.

"I haven't seen much of you lately," he said, one hand clenched into a fist behind his back, the other holding his sword steady as he walked.

"I have been spending much time in the libraries lately," she replied to the implied question. She kept her eyes straight ahead, not looking at him, as she spoke. Garrin always wondered at the way she did that. Every other young woman in the Keep—in the entire city—would be looking up at him through her lashes in that moment, but Aiella was different. "Master Be'Var, he has asked me to help him with his research."

"Really?" he said, genuinely intrigued. "Research of what sort?"

"Of many sorts," she said. "Many of the books I have found for him are of military history, some are religious texts, but he greatly wishes to discover information of a 'war that came before'."

Garrin looked down at her face, but her dark locks hid all but her nose from him. "Which war?" he asked. "One of those with Mael'vek?"

"No," she said, "it is a much older war. It was concerned with the elements themselves." Her voice took on an uncertain tone, unusual for her. "I am not able to tell, specifically, from what I have read, but it seems that this war, it may have had something to do with the shaping of the world."

Garrin frowned, once again looking ahead. This, then, was why she'd asked for access to the Royal Library. He hoped that his earlier decision to follow protocol, rather than bend the rules and just let her in, wouldn't turn out to have been a mistake. He considered what the consequences of reversing that decision would be as he opened the door to the stairwell for her and they both took the two flights of spiraling steps up to the main rampart.

Remains of dust and sand stood here and there among the smoothed stones of the rampart, but the wind had stopped completely. The dusty smell still hung in the air though, and the evening felt unusually warm. Garrin leaned against the wall and looked out over the city of Kepren. Lamps burned dimly in the main streets and many windows still boasted their own light as people went about the evening's business.

He felt, more than saw, Aiella follow suit, leaning her elbows on the stone wall next to him, though she wasn't close enough that they were actually touching.

"I don't suppose," he said into the air, "old Be'Var would mind you telling me all this?"

She shook her head. "I think he would come and tell you himself, were he not so busy tending to Caymus."

"Right," said Garrin, "Caymus." He'd been to Flamehearth only once since that first time when Be'Var and his party had first arrived in Kepren, but he'd seen Caymus while he was there. The young man's huge body had been lain across a bed that was about three feet too small for him, with Be'Var keeping a watchful eye.

He'd liked Caymus's unassuming attitude when they'd met. Garrin wondered if he'd ever get that chance to spar with the young man. "How has he been? Have you seen him lately?"

"Nearly every day, when I am meeting with Master Be'Var." For the first time, she looked up at him, a frown creasing her forehead. "He is alive, but his body is sometimes hot and sometimes cold." She looked away again, turning her gaze out over the city. "The strange thing is that you would expect someone who is bedridden for so long to have lost muscle, to have begun wasting away."

"And he isn't doing that?"

"No," she said. "In fact, I would swear that he grows stronger by the day. It is a mystery. I do not understand it."

Raised voices came up to them from below, interrupting the

conversation. Garrin looked down to see a pair of guards on one of the lower ramparts arguing about something. They were too far away and their voices too muffled to tell what the disagreement was about, but they carried on for several minutes. Garrin was considering going down there when suddenly the raised voices evaporated into raucous laughter. Garrin smiled. He knew well the frustration of guard duty, as well as the joys of camaraderie that came with it.

"Master Be'Var tells me," Aiella said, picking up the thread of conversation, "that he believes something is happening to Caymus that we cannot see, that we may never understand."

Garrin nodded, more to himself than in any kind of agreement. "I hope the boy recovers soon, Aiella. I really do."

"I do also," Aiella replied, a thoughtful tone to her voice. "Be'Var says he is important."

Garrin had heard Be'Var say that very thing once before, though he still didn't know what the old man meant by it. "Do you agree with him?" he said, still staring out into the dark night.

For a few moments, Aiella said nothing. When Garrin turned to look, he saw that she was slowly nodding her head. "Yes," she eventually said, "I do."

~~~

Caymus reeled, taking several steps backward and bringing his sword up in front of him in a defensive posture. The creature was moving slowly, tracing in a large circle around him, so he took a moment to feel his shoulder. There was no wound, no tear in the flesh, but he felt as though ice had been sewn beneath the skin where the kreal weapon had touched him.

All over his body, there were similar injuries, places where the krealite's hand-blades had snuck past his guard, torn through his clothing, and touched the surface of his body. Each strike had felt, when the blade had hit home, as though it had opened his skin, but none had left any actual holes in him. Each, however, carried either the sensation of freezing or of burning, with no seeming pattern to which he would feel at any given hit.

Gripping the sword with both hands, he joined the thing in the circular movement, watching its feet more than any other part of it, searching for some twitch of motion that would betray its next action.

He felt that he should be tired. He had no idea how long he had sparred with the creature, but he counted their clashes in the hundreds, if
~~~

not thousands. Sometimes his legs or his eyes felt heavy, and yet when the time came to use them in battle, he found himself both quick and strong. He didn't know why the disparity existed. When he'd spared the time to think about it, he'd decided that, outside of his body like this, he might only be as tired as he thought he was.

A small rotation of his enemy's right foot announced another impending attack. The krealite spun into him, both blades extended in a sweeping motion that he easily backed away from. Before he could counter, however, it reversed direction, lunged forward, and thrust with both blades.

Caymus felt a smile cross his face; he knew what to do with this. Quick as he dared, he turned his sword, dropping the point to the ground, then he lifted the blade up and took a simultaneous step forward. In that one motion, he both deflected both the creature's blades—up and to one side of him—and positioned himself to strike with his pommel. Taking an additional step forward, he pressed the counterattack, slamming the heavy butt of his weapon into his opponent's throat.

The creature stumbled backward slightly. Caymus took the opportunity to bring his back foot up and land a solid kick to the exposed mid-section. As the krealite fell backward, he rotated his sword and brought the blade down onto its shoulder, forcing it completely to the ground.

Caymus wasn't sure at exactly what point the smile had left his lips, but as he stepped backward again, preparing for the next onslaught, he noted its absence. This victory, like all the others, would be short-lived.

The krealite was just starting to get to its knees, so he had some time to give his shoulder more careful consideration. He turned his head to get a good look, noting that the fabric of his tunic was torn away, but that the skin of the shoulder was not. He frowned, both in incomprehension of the wound and at his own clumsiness. By his own estimation, he'd become quite skilled at sparring with his opponent. He still had not managed to bring it down in any permanent fashion, but the strike to his shoulder was the first attack it had landed in dozens of attempts. He felt foolish for having left himself exposed, but his mind had been occupied with the feel of a strike of his own, which he'd just landed to the creature's thigh.

He looked back at the dark, faceless form. It was on its knees, preparing to rise. He still had the luxury of several moments to think.

He'd learned something in that last interaction, something he'd been intuiting for some time, but which he was only just beginning to really understand. The creature before him looked more or less human, but it differed from him in more ways that just the absence of a face and regular appendages. There was something about its anatomy, about the construction of it, the feel of it, which was altogether alien to him.

He had already learned, during a moment when he'd gained leverage for a throw by grabbing the creature under its right arm, that the surface there had seemed softer than the rest of the black form's skin. At the time, he'd thought he'd been imagining it, but then he'd discovered a similar sensation when he'd struck the creature at the point where the neck met the back of the head. That time, of course, the strike had been with his sword and not with his hand, but he'd felt his blade make contact so many times now that he was able to sense the differences through the steel: it had made a different sound when it had struck, had vibrated at a slightly lower frequency.

His opponent was on its feet now, though it hadn't turned to face him. He had time yet.

The sensation, that unique ring to the blade that filled the air, had been the same when he'd struck the creature's left thigh. Caymus's momentary fixation on that sound was the thing that had earned him a freezing shoulder. He wondered what it all meant, why a being such as this would have these "soft spots" in such unusual places on its body.

The krealite turned its attention on him. The tingling sensation at the back of his neck intensified slightly. That was something else he'd noticed during this extended battle, here in belly of the Conflagration: the sensation on his neck seemed to have to do with the presence of some agent working on kreal's behalf, rather than that of the kreal itself. The feeling always intensified when that eyeless gaze fixed on him. Standing there, looking back into that gaze, he found he was surprised at having not made that connection before.

He thought about how strong the feeling had been during the rescue of the mitre in Otvia, how much of a distraction it had seemed. Now, the tingling, buzzing sensation seemed no more unusual than any other sensory organ, no more foreign feeling than his own hands. The thought of Otvia made him remember Merkan, the mitre who had managed to defeat two krealites in hand-to-hand combat, much as Caymus was trying to do now.

The memory was hazy; it seemed like such a long time ago. He had to reach deep into himself to bring it forward. What was it that Merkan had said? How had he described it?

The krealite began circling again as he tried to remember what it was that his friend had said to him. It had something to do with the skin, with the impenetrable surface of the things. Could it have had something to do with these soft spots? The memory was rebuilding in his mind slowly, much as Milo's clearing had done when he'd first arrived in this place.

The krealite had no concern for his memories. It lunged forward, this time reaching out with a single blade, the other arm swinging back to give the attack added momentum. Caymus didn't think too hard about his defense; he knew how to guard against this and, besides, his mind was occupied with other things. With a pair of side-steps and a wide swing of his sword, he cleared the attack away and moved himself to the rear of his opponent, at which point he kicked out, again driving the thing down to the ground.

As the krealite was falling, Caymus remembered. Merkan had said that a strike of his blade had been unable to pierce through the creature's chitinous armor, but when he had instead placed the blade and then slowly applied force to it, the weapon had found its mark and had sunk into the black surface.

Caymus slowly tried to feel out the concept as the krealite once again rose to its knees. It didn't make sense to him. How could a blade moving slowly take hold of an enemy when the same blade, moving quickly, could not? He could think of nothing he knew, no parallel in the world, which would react in that way to an outside force.

The kreal, he had to remember, was not of his world, not of the Quatrain. It was of another realm altogether, called the Sograve by the Lords of the Conflagration. He reminded himself that he shouldn't expect such an alien element to react to his blade in a predictable way.

The krealite was making the transition from a kneeling position again, getting to its feet. Caymus didn't wait for it to rise. Instead, he took three steps forward, reversing the grip on his sword as he advanced. He kicked at the back of one straightened leg, dropping the creature back to its knees. Once it was down, he put the sword point to the creature's neck, at that soft place where the dark flesh met the base of its skull. The motion was awkward: his arm was accustomed to large, coarse swings, not this delicate, precise kind of motion. Within the space of half a second, however, he had positioned his blade right where he wanted it.

Instead of raising the blade again and stabbing, he simply pushed.

The result, despite what he had been expecting, was profound. He found, as he applied force, that the cutting edge met with a great deal of resistance. His first impulse was to push harder, but he controlled himself, managed to force his arms to hold back, to instead reduce the pressure. The blade began to sink, surprising Caymus despite his own hopes and expectations. His muscles weren't used to this kind of attack, and a great deal of his effort was required in order to control the pressure. As the blade slid into the blackness, however, he did find that the further he drove the steel, the more pressure he could exert upon it, and the faster it sank.

In the space of a moment, before he could fully come to terms with how he had done it, he had buried his blade a full foot into the neck of his enemy. When he felt that he could attain no additional result, he withdrew the weapon. It came free easily, as though he had pulled it from a lake rather than a body. As soon as the entire length was removed, he reflexively stepped back, preparing for another attack.

He looked down at the krealite. There was no blood. There was not even the appearance of a wound. As he watched the body lose tension and slump forward, he heard what sounded like a heavy exhale of breath coupled with a muffled scream. He was nearly certain that the sound came entirely from within his own mind.

He could scarcely believe the accomplishment. As he watched the fallen body crumble to dust before him, he reveled in what he had done. He felt as though he had been fighting the thing for years—decades, even!—but he had finally prevailed over it. A wicked grin played over Caymus's face as the dust that had been the body of the krealite dispersed, catching on a non-existent wind and blowing away and into the wall of kreal from whence it had come.

Suddenly, Caymus was not the least bit tired. Suddenly, he was eager to succeed in battle again, to use what he had learned, to hone his skills.

Without consciously thinking about what he was doing, acting solely on the purest instinct, he prepared to reach out to the wall of kreal again, to summon a new opponent from its inky depths.

~~~

Be'Var looked up from his book when he heard the knock at the door. A quick glance out the window told him the hour was later than he'd thought, and the dwindling supply of candles at Caymus's bedside came as a bit of a shock. He could have sworn there were an even dozen of them a mere hour ago. Now, they numbered only five.

Stifling a yawn and scratching at his face, he looked to the door. "Yes," he said. "Come in."

The door opened just a few inches and Milo's headbanded face popped through, a tired-looking smile on it. "Any change?" he asked.

Be'Var smiled. He liked the way that Milo always inquired after Caymus first, rather than him. Y'selle and Aiella would always begin by asking if he was busy or how his reading was going, but Milo always came straight to the point. In the three months since they'd arrived in Kepren, Be'Var had really come to appreciate the man's honest and simple outlook.

He turned his eyes to Caymus, who was still resting quietly on the bed. Be'Var had spent today just like every other day of the last few months, working to either raise or reduce the boy's temperature, depending on the need. After all this time, he'd still not been able to figure out what was happening to him, why he could be so cold one minute and so hot the
~~~

next. There even appeared to be days when one part of his body seemed colder than the rest: feet or fingers he could understand, but a rib or shoulder? It made no sense.

Today had been a fairly uneventful day. In fact, and he'd gotten quite a lot of reading done.

"No change," he said, looking back to the door. "Come in, come in," he said, clearing some books off a nearby chair. "Tell me about life outside this room."

Milo grinned at him and entered. He grabbed the back of the chair that Be'Var had cleared and turned it around so he could straddle it, leaning his arms on the backrest. As he did so, he reached into a pocket and brought out a few small pieces of paper. He pushed them toward Be'Var. "From Master Ket," he said.

Be'Var started at him, then reached out and took the folded messages. "Ket?" he said. "This is from the Temple?" He gave Milo a questioning look. "How is that possible? Who sent them?"

Milo smiled and held his arms up in a supplicating gesture. "It wasn't one of mine!" he said. "It arrived by regular messenger. Sorry, I guess I should've said."

Be'Var rolled his eyes at himself. "Of course, of course. That was stupid of me, wasn't it?" Just because Milo was the one that brought him a message from the Temple, it didn't mean that it had arrived through the air priest's network of wind-whispers. As he opened the messages, he noted the tears at the edges of the paper and the slight smudges of dirt that betrayed this message had, indeed, been carried to Kepren by hand.

As Be'Var read over the text, Milo produced a pair of apples from a pouch at his waist. He silently offered one to Be'Var as he crunched into the other. Be'Var waved it away, so he instead put it on top of one of the stacks of books.

Milo ate in silence for a time, allowing Be'Var to quickly scan both notes. Only when he'd finished with the second sheet of paper, and was going over the first again, did the air priest open his mouth again, talking around the piece of fruit. "Anything good in there?"

Be'Var had lost himself in his thoughts for a moment, and so was a bit surprised when he looked up and discovered there was someone else in the room. He shook off the feeling. What was wrong with him lately? Was it just being cooped up in here that was driving him to such distraction?

He took a deep breath. "The Falaar boys are doing well, it seems," he said. "One of them, Fach'un, is a master now."

Milo looked away for a moment, considering. "That's pretty fast, isn't it?"

Be'Var nodded, looking over the message again. "It is. Less than six months. Although it must be said that they had quite a bit of experience with their own fire Aspect before they arrived, so I'm sure they had an advantage over the rest of them."

Milo squinted at him. "What is their Aspect anyway, the Falaar?"

Be'Var looked up from the papers again. "They call it 'Unburning'."

"Unburning?"

Be'Var snorted. "Tacky, isn't it? It means they're able to walk through fire without getting scorched."

Milo tilted his head as he chewed on another bite of apple. "Unburning…" he said, then he smiled. "I like it. Doesn't beat around the bush. You can't be burned, so," he snapped his fingers, "you're Unburning."

"I still say it's the kind of word a simpleton would use," said Be'Var.

"Unlike 'pulling' you mean?" said Milo, arching a grinning eyebrow at him.

"However," Be'Var continued, ignoring the eyebrow, "it seems that the Knight of the Flame—the first one, from the Old War—was a friend of the Falaar." He looked around at the stacks of books, trying to remember which one he was thinking of. "Bah," he said, after a moment, "I don't remember which of these said it, but there was a passage about him 'knowing their tricks and secrets'."

Milo had a look of curiosity on his face. "It mentioned the Falaar by name? I didn't think they'd have been around long enough to show up in an old book."

Be'Var managed a small smile. "It seems," he said, "that cities have risen and fallen since the Old War. The Falaar, however, have been a constant. I think it might be a good idea for one of us to go down there and see what we can learn about them before much more time passes."

Milo waggled his head, noncommittally. "What's the other note say?"

Be'Var looked down at the other piece of paper, considering it. "You remember I asked Ket to take a look in the library for any reference to kreal, or knights, or anything about the Old War?" He held the paper up, then surveyed the three dozen or so books piled around the room. "He's coming up with the same kinds of references I've been seeing."

"About the weapon?"

Be'Var nodded, searching for the quote on the message. When he found it, he read aloud. "The knight is his weapon. The weapon makes the knight. The knight seeks his wisdom within his weapon's grip. Without it, he is but a man."

Milo had stopped eating. "You found those exact words in one of the other libraries, didn't you?"

"Yes," said Be'Var, "or Aiella did, in any case. And it wasn't word-for-word, but it was similar."

Milo held the half-finished apple absently in his hand. He was looking at Caymus. "What do you think it means?"

Be'Var, too, looked toward the motionless young man. He'd asked himself the same question a dozen times since Aiella had brought him the moth-eaten scroll that had referenced the knight and his weapon. He sighed. "I wish I could figure out if it means that a knight needs a weapon," he said, "or if he needs a particular weapon."

Milo raised both eyebrows. "You mean a particular kind of weapon?"

Be'Var shook his head. "I don't think so. I think the flaming thing means that," he waved his arm in a big arc, "somewhere out there, there's a very specific weapon that we need to get our hands on, one that's going to have a very special significance for Caymus. Gu'ruk told us that the Earthwarden had a hammer that he's keeping safe until the rock-knight returns, so it stands to reason the Knight of the Flame had his own special weapon, too."

Milo frowned. "Anything I should be looking out for?"

Be'Var barked a laugh. He indicated the mark on Caymus's hand. "I suppose if you happen to come across something with one of those on it, you might be on the right track."

Milo smiled a sad smile, though he didn't laugh.

Silence filled the room for a long moment as they both looked at their sleeping friend. "It was his birthday yesterday," said Be'Var, his voice barely more than a whisper. "Did you know that?"

Milo's eyes flitted to him for a brief moment. "I didn't," he said. "I'd have gotten him something."

"It's really happening, isn't it, Milo?" Be'Var asked, breaking the quiet that followed. "There's actually an army of worshipers of some flaming-bizarre element marching down at us right at this moment, isn't there?"

Milo nodded, then looked at his hand, seeming to remember the apple. He took a bite and talked around it again. "Afraid so," he said. Then, his eyes went wide, and he motioned toward Be'Var. "Did you hear," he asked, "that the Tower and the Summit finally signed the treaty?"

Be'Var allowed himself a small smile. "I knew they'd been talking peace for a while," he said. "You're saying they're actually sticking with it now?"

Milo nodded emphatically. "Heard the message myself," he said. "With Black Moon marching south the way they are, they can either come through Falmoor's Pass or go around the Greatstones altogether. Nobody knows which it's going to be, so I suppose it was just a matter of time."

Be'Var nodded. Falmoor's Pass was the obvious way to cut through the Greatstone Mountains from the northern cities, but the way was narrow enough that an army might have trouble moving through it. Creveya was located at the eastern end of the Greatstones, so if the army decided to go around the mountains, rather than through them, the Tower and the Summit, rather than Kepren, would be the next civilization under the sword.

"They still haven't figured out which way Black Moon will turn, then?" he asked, absently.

Milo shook his head. "Not yet," he said. "They still haven't come south far enough."

Be'Var was watching the gentle rise and fall of Caymus's chest. The boy didn't seem to need to eat or drink as he lay there; yet, for reasons Be'Var couldn't fathom, he still appeared to need to draw breath. The gash, that black wound on his forearm, still hadn't healed, and Be'Var was convinced that Caymus wouldn't come out of this apparent deep sleep until he had found a way to remove the kreal from his body.

"There's still time, then," he said, more to himself than to Milo. "Come on, boy, come back to us." He paused. "While there's still time."

~~~

Caymus spun as he stepped forward, letting his blade race out to its target. As soon as the point of his sword touched the skin of the krealite in front of him, he twisted his arms in the other direction to halt the weapon's momentum, then started the pressure of the actual attack.

He didn't know how long he'd been fighting, only that it had been too long.

His attempt to pull another creature from the wall, all that time ago, had been successful, earning him another adversary, another chance to learn how to kill krealites. He didn't know how many times he'd repeated the process since that first time.

He had found, after having been in so many battles, that it was possible to combine elements from what he had previously learned of swordsmanship with the set-and-push motion that was necessary in order to actually pierce the skins of these creatures. He had spent a long time retraining his muscles, combining the two concepts. Now, after hundreds and hundreds of battles, his completely new style of swordplay had become graceful and deadly, and he had luxuriated in the thrill of it every time he applied his blade to another opponent.

He had also discovered that different opponents had different "soft spots" along their surfaces, but that he didn't necessarily need to find them in order to exploit the weakness. The remains of four krealites, turning to dust at his feet, were proof of that. The soft places were merely areas where he could apply more force than usual, where he could
~~~

pierce the skin without having to be quite so careful and measured in the pressure he afforded his blade. In the case of this krealite, he had chosen not to search for one of these spots, but had simply gone for the easy target of the chest.

His flesh felt heavy, the pain of dozens of small, icy wounds biting into it. As he plunged the blade into his opponent's torso, his eyes drifted over the hands holding the hilt. They seemed worn, grizzled, calloused, the hands of an old veteran. How long had he been here, in this place? Hadn't there been another place before this one? The creatures came from another place, didn't they? Surely there were other places.

Tearing his sword away from the body of his foe, he turned once again to the wall. There was almost nothing left of the boy that had first arrived here. There was only so much battle. Sneering with the intense anger of that thought, of the years—the life!—he'd lost to this fighting, he once again reached out to the mass of kreal, searching for the attention of another of the beings from the other side, probing so as to catch either their curiosity or their hate.

Instead, for the first time, he felt fear.

The fear wasn't his own. It emanated from the beings behind the wall. They had become afraid of him. He smiled with pleasure at the thought, again sensing the freezing battle scars all over his body, remembering how he'd earned each one, as though they were badges of pride. The krealites wouldn't come through anymore, wouldn't offer him any more pain.

He was struck dumb by the realization. He was a warrior. That was his role, and this was his battlefield. What was he to do if there was no opponent, nobody to fight? Again, he reached out, placing his mind into the wall itself, trying as hard has he could to make his presence known on the other side so that somebody might take note of his brashness and accept the implied challenge of it.

Nothing occurred. There was only the fear.

Caymus realized his breathing had become heavy. Why wouldn't they come? He had to fight them. There was nothing else. He fell to one knee, confused. He gazed about at the flames of the Conflagration, letting the fire lick at his legs and arms. What was he to do?

He looked, once again, at the wall, watching it intensely. If they wouldn't come to him…

With a sudden burst of furious energy, he rose to his feet and ran with all his strength at the dark wall before him. As he made contact with it, he felt the icy grip of the kreal over his body, felt it threaten to overwhelm his senses, if not completely tear him apart.

He felt he was in another place. He tried to get his bearings, but the difficulty of it was great. He could not see the inhabitants of this realm. His eyes saw only black, but he knew the beings were there. With desperate fervor, he reached out to find them with his thoughts, latching on to a particular presence that seemed about to scurry away. Before it could take two steps away from him, he had his sword buried in its torso.

Another presence was nearby. He added the withdrawal of his blade from his first victim to the attack against the second, making a single, graceful motion. The bodies of his foes didn't crumble into dust in this place. Instead, they slumped to the floor as he felt what seemed like sprays of blood on his face and arms. He felt rage, a warrior's rage, as he reached out for another and took its head off.

He knew his opponents too well. They didn't stand a chance against his blinding speed and his practiced movements. Before he had time to think about the motions his body was making, he had felled three more.

As he drove his sword into the last of these, he felt a firm tug on his shoulder that pulled him backward. "Enough!" yelled a voice that he knew too well. The voice was his own, speaking to him in the way the Lords of the Conflagration often communicated their wants. Caymus felt the sensation of falling through the darkness, then he was plunging, headfirst, out of the wall of kreal, and onto his back. Again, he was surrounded by the flames of the realm of fire.

He felt at once afraid and ashamed. As he listened to his own voice shout at him, he rose from the ground, taking to one knee in supplication.

"You are not here to wage war on the insignificant specks that inhabit the spaces between the realms!" the voice said. Caymus tentatively lifted his gaze, looking about for the speaker. The flames around him seemed to be burning with greater intensity than before, but the source of the voice was nowhere to be seen.

He was embarrassed at his actions. A part of him had known, when he had jumped through the wall of kreal, that he had been taking the attack too far. He was considering utterance to some kind of apology when the voice spoke again.

"You are here to learn, Caymus! You are here to understand how to defeat the kreal that is destroying your own world! Your own body! Have you done that?"

Caymus let his eyes sink to the ground again. There was no doubt that he had learned everything he could about the krealites that had been sent against him. He felt like he'd been studying them for years, that he knew more about fighting krealites than he did any other single subject. Placing the sword on the ground in front of him, he said so.

Then, as he gazed into the flames littering the ground around him, the words sunk into his fogged and addled mind: his own world. He had come from another world before. He had come from a place where there was more than just fire, more than just battle. He had a home, a family, and friends that cared out him.

He remembered that they needed his help.

How could he have forgotten? Was the experience of the Conflagration so intense that it had made him forget? Perhaps it had been the fact that he'd lived for so long outside of his body, outside of the shell the held his memories? A tiny smile found a place on his lips as he remembered Be'Var, Milo, Rill, Gwenna. They were the precious things in a life that were not just battle. How could he have possibly forgotten them?

How long had he been here?

As he stared into his own memory, the sword before him vanished as though the flames themselves had stolen it away. "This is not your sword," the voice said, much calmer now, as though instructing rather than scolding. "Your sword exists in the Quatrain," it continued, "and you must find it if you are to truly discover the skills you will require, to become the champion that we so desperately need."

Caymus looked up again and his eyes scanned the flames around him. He understood. The sword of the Knight of the Flame, a sword much like the one he had been using through so much battle, was infused with the power, with the will of the post. He had to find that sword, and he hoped he would remember that fact; he knew he would forget some things when he left this place, much as he had forgotten things about his home when he had arrived. "How will I find it?" he asked.

Instead of receiving an answer, he found that that the edges of his vision were going black, that his mind was becoming foggy again. He briefly considered allowing panic to take him, but he was too weary for that. Somehow, he knew that he was going home, that his consciousness, once pulled away from the Quatrain, was being allowed to pass through the void that separated the realms and find its way home.

He thought of how glad he was going to be to see everybody, how much he had missed them, even though so much time had passed? Would they still recognize him? How would he ever explain what had happened to him here?

As he considered what he would tell Rill about his adventure, pain gripped him, taking hold in his forearm and radiating throughout his nerves and blood vessels, constricting his heart. He did not panic. The pain was one of intense cold, and he knew it well: he had been touched by kreal, and he must defeat it.

Where the challenge would once have been too great, it was no large thing now. As he felt breath fill his lungs, heard a groan emanate from his throat, he reached out to feel for the kreal in his body. The majority of it, a residue that had coated the poisonous knife, was still in the wound in his arm, though there were pieces of it throughout his body's vessels.

He wondered if he was alone. He thought he could hear voices.

Exhaling, then taking another deep breath and calming his mind further still, he used the skill he had learned over the past—weeks? months? decades?—and reached out to feel for the soft spots in the kreal. Even the smallest grain of material had such spots: it was part of the makeup of the element, as intrinsic to it as the fact that fire burned upward or that water felt cool against the skin.

Once he had located the spots he was looking for, began to carefully heat them, opening tiny conduits into those places in order to apply heat to exactly the right points. These elements of kreal were so small that no blade would pierce them, and so he had only his shaping ability to lean on. He guided the minuscule flames through the residue of kreal, shaping them so as to gain entry into the soft places, then using them to burn the tiny poisonous elements from the inside out.

The process took several hours. He found a soft spot, he shaped his flames, he destroyed a fragment of kreal, he moved on. As he burned more of the element away, he became more aware of his surroundings. He heard Be'Var's voice, as well as Milo's. There were also two other voices that he recognized, but which he could not place.

He wondered where Rill was.

When the battle was over, the final trace of kreal eliminated from his body, Caymus took a deep, glorious breath and opened his eyes.

Milo was there, his face hovering only a few inches above his own. Caymus could hear the rustle of the feathers on his arms, and the sound was so comforting that he could almost cry.

His friend, lost to him for so long, smiled that huge, friendly smile of his.

When Caymus returned the smile, Milo turned to look over his shoulder. "He's awake!" he said to whomever else was in the room, ecstatic joy in his voice. He turned back to Caymus and then, in a lower voice, said, "You *are* awake, right? You're not just putting me on?"

Caymus, despite the weariness in his bones, couldn't help but chuckle. "I'm awake," he said.

He turned to see another pair of faces in the small, candle-lit room. Brocke, the ambassador from that city up north, was there, his fleshy face affording a smile warmer than Caymus had thought him capable of. Present also was Prince Garrin, who was beaming and clapping Milo on the back.

Caymus wondered what the prince of Kepren was doing in the room. Based on the voices he'd heard while he'd been ridding himself of the kreal, he didn't think that he could have been there for very long. Perhaps he had come when Caymus had begun to properly wake? Would someone have summoned the prince for such a thing?

One more person was in the room. Sitting on a chair next to the bed amidst several small piles of books was a tired-looking Master Be'Var. The old man seemed pale, and the flesh of his face seemed to sag more than Caymus remembered, especially under his eyes. Still, Caymus's old master afforded him a small, relieved smile.

"Welcome back, boy," he said. "I think you may be just in time."

Chapter 15

Caymus took a good look at his opponent as he deflected yet another clumsy attack. The young man couldn't have been any older than he and was probably at least a couple of years his junior. His blonde hair looked as though it hadn't seen a comb in weeks, and a small wisp of a mustache hung over his lip. He and his two friends were all very thin. Their clothes were all threadbare and their skins were pallid, as though they hadn't eaten in a while.

None of them seemed to know how to handle their weapons, either. The attacker in front of Caymus was the only one with a proper sword. The other two, a lanky lad who couldn't have been far into his teens and another equally young boy with red welts and scabs all over his face, had come at them with a scythe and a hatchet, respectively.

Caymus had decided to take a shield with him on their journey south, and so was having no difficulty in blocking his opponent's ineffectual swings. He took a moment to glance at his companions, to see how they were faring. Milo had shoved his attacker, the one with the hatchet, back a few feet and now both he and Gwenna stood facing him, arrows leveled at him and bows drawn. Tavrin, the Falaar who was leading the party, was doing much the same as Caymus, blocking the swings of his attacker with his barak sticks, but not pressing any attack of his own.

Caymus, despite his unfavorable feelings about Tavrin, had to admit he appreciated the man's martial skills. The barak sticks, a pair of short, wooden rods each about two feet in length and recently capped with iron, moved too fast for Caymus's eyes to follow sometimes. The footwork that the man used, too, was impressive. He seemed nearly to dance with his opponent, rather than fight him. The blonde teenager appeared to get increasingly frustrated each time he swung with his scythe and discovered his target had moved somewhere else entirely.

After Caymus's young opponent had taken a few more wild swings against him—he got the impression that the boy was actually aiming for the shield, rather than past it—he decided he'd had about enough. At the same moment that Tavrin swept the scythe-wielder's legs out from under him, Caymus took an opportunity to lunge forward and bash his foe with his shield. He aimed for the major mass of the chest, rather than the face; he didn't really want to hurt these boys.

The young man fell backward with a shriek, his sword flying out behind him. Caymus took a step back to allow him some room to recover and get his wits back, but when he saw that the kid chose instead to scrabble back toward his sword, he stepped forward again and kicked him over on to his back.

"Hey!" Caymus yelled, leveling his shortsword at the prone figure. The boy looked up at him, his eyes fixed on the sword point. There was genuine fear and panic in those eyes. "Perhaps," he continued in a level tone, "you should look around and see how you're doing."

The boy seemed momentarily surprised at the idea, but he eventually pulled his gaze from the sword's tip and turned his head to look at his fellows. Tavrin had his foot on the neck of one of them, the boy's scythe in his hand, and was looking down at him with a stony countenance. The other boy was on his knees, his arms held out wide, with both Milo's and Gwenna's bows, arrows draw, leveled at his chest.

Caymus took a deep breath as the boy finally pulled his gaze back to him. He was amazed at his own restraint. A few days ago, he knew he would have gutted the boy already, his mind still consumed with endless thoughts of the battles of the Conflagration. "I think you should go," he said, in a steady voice. "Don't you?"

The boy nodded quickly. Caymus dropped his sword point as the frightened adolescent scrabbled backward, picked up his own weapon, and joined the other two in making a quick dash away from the party they'd just attacked. They shouted insults at each other as they stumbled over small rocks and shrubs and otherwise made their way through the desert to a destination only they knew.

Caymus took a long look at the sand and dust around him as he placed his sword in the sheath at his hip and strapped his shield on his back. He'd been told that in the space of three months—the same period of time he'd lain in that bed, his consciousness trapped in the Conflagration—most of the Tebrian grasslands had begun to look like this. When he and the others had first made their way into Kepren, there had been at least some semblance of green scattered about. Now it was all gone, the withered stalks having crumbled to powder. Apparently, there was some hope that runoff from the Greatstones might keep some of the northern grasslands alive, but it was clear that this, the Great Tebrian Desert, was expanding every day.

He watched as Milo, his bow already shouldered, inspected the saddlebags of their two horses. Caymus shook his head, absently. He couldn't quite believe the boys had summoned the nerve to attack them.

People seemed to be getting more desperate every day. The party had seen two other groups like this, small bands of boys who had decided to try their hands at banditry, since they'd departed Kepren's South Gate two days ago. Most were smart enough to back off after observing Caymus's sizable form, not to mention the fact that all four members of their party were armed in one fashion or another. These had been the first to actually come at them.

Caymus knew, of course, that it was more than just his size that made people afraid of him these days. Since he'd awakened in that room in Flamehearth two weeks ago, several people had remarked that there was something different about him now, something in his eyes that spoke of experiences beyond his years. There had been a polished mirror in one of the common rooms of the mission, and Caymus had spent hours staring into it, taking stock of his reflection, trying to see what others saw, but to no avail.

His hands had been another story entirely. For the first few hours that he'd been awake, he hadn't believed that his hands were his own. The hands were too young; they should have been old, should have carried scars and weather-beaten skin. He'd spent a long time wondering if he was in some nightmare where he was living in another person's skin!

Eventually, he'd had to hide the flesh from his eyes by covering them with leather gloves. He still hadn't taken those gloves off.

"They must be desperate," said Gwenna. Caymus looked over to see her shouldering her bow and placing the unfired arrow back into the quiver at her waist. He'd had an opportunity to be quite impressed by the skill she'd attained with that bow: when a particularly nasty-looking sand viper had surprised him on their first day out of Kepren, seeming to have simply appeared next to his shoe, Gwenna had put an arrow through it before he'd even thought to back away.

Tavrin, tucking his barak sticks behind his belt, walked up to her and put a hand on her shoulder. "We will encounter fewer of them, the farther south we go."

Caymus nodded, hoping it was true. "Is everybody alright?" he asked.

"He cut the leather!" Milo exclaimed, running his finger across a great gash in one of the saddlebags.

"Which one?" asked Caymus.

"The clumsy one with the hand axe," said Milo. "He took a swing at me and nearly hit the horse!"

"I can't say I'm surprised," said Gwenna, inspecting the other animal.

"They didn't really seem to know what they were doing, did they?"

Tavrin came up behind her and also inspected their baggage. "I would say that they had not attempted such robbery before."

Caymus smiled. "That," he said, "or we're the first that ever put up a fight." As he spoke, he noticed Gwenna turning to Tavrin and looking into his eyes with that adoration he'd been getting so used to. Not for the first time, he wondered at the wisdom of this trip.

He'd learned the details about the blossoming relationship between Gwenna and Tavrin from his closest friend soon after he had awakened. Unfortunately, Rill had been unable to get away from his duties as a royal engineer until two days after hearing the news that his friend was finally on his feet. Caymus had been awfully glad to see him when he'd finally showed up; he'd also marveled at his new engineer's uniform.

Rill's main concern, in fact, had been how Caymus was handling the burgeoning relationship. Caymus had considered the matter for a while before finally having to admit that he didn't really know what to think. He and Gwenna had obviously been friendly and flirtatious before he'd been attacked, but they'd hardly been anything more than that. The fact that she was so openly enamored with Tavrin now did bother him a little, but the feeling had less to do with any sense of possession he had about Gwenna—he'd completely forgotten about such things in the Conflagration—and more to do with the fact that the relationship was evidence of just how much the world had gone on without him. It planted a very lonely feeling right in his gut.

He was genuinely starting to enjoy Tavrin's company, anyway. This trip marked the only time the two of them had experienced any real contact with each other, and Caymus found the young Falaar to be quiet, contemplative, and friendly: all traits that he could identify with. Plus, there was no denying both his respect and affection for Gwenna. He took any excuse to be near her, yet he didn't coddle her. Even now, they were standing in front each other, foreheads touching, hands on one another's arms, each checking that the other was alright.

Caymus nodded to himself. Though there was a small amount of regret in him also, mostly seeing the two of them together like that was one of the few things that could make him smile, lately.

Tavrin turned to Milo, concern on his face. "The seed?"

"It's fine," Milo said, waving the question off. "The kid made a good gash in the leather, but the sacks are still intact."

Tavrin was visibly relieved. There were several reasons that the group was making this trip to the village of Terrek, and one of them was so that he could bring home a few bags of planting seeds, that he might see if he could make them grow in the desert. The Falaar knew of agriculture, but Tavrin had explained that Kepren's crops seemed to him to be hardier varieties than those in Terrek. The idea of losing any of the precious seeds due to the clumsiness of some foolish boy would not have been a pleasant one for him.

Caymus was glad the horses hadn't bolted. He didn't know these two drab gray mares, and he found that he missed Feston and Staven. The mission's two horses had been pressed into some manner of official service in Kepren during his long sleep.

In short order, Milo had adjusted the baggage on the packhorse to account for the torn leather and Gwenna had checked the straps on the other animal. Satisfied that they were ready to move again, Tavrin pointed south with his chin. "Let us continue," he said. "We can travel several miles by the end of today."

Caymus regarded the afternoon sun, still high in the cloudless sky, and agreed. He let Gwenna and Tavrin walk in front with the first horse, and he took the lead of the other. He and Milo walked together, several yards behind the others. Gwenna's position, out in front and holding the lead of her horse, reminded Caymus of their journey from the Temple to Kepren.

"You alright?" said Milo. Caymus turned to see his friend looking sideways at him. "You've been about a hundred miles away all day."

Caymus attempted to present a reassuring smile that he didn't really feel. "I'm fine," he said, "just remembering something." Nearly four months had passed since they'd taken that trip, but to Caymus it might as well have been years. He returned his eyes forward and tilted his head. "When did she cut her hair?" Gwenna's hair had been nearly long enough to reach her hips when he'd been attacked. It was much shorter now, chopped so that it only hung as low as the bottoms of her ears, with a few extra inches at the back that covered her neck.

"A couple of months back," Milo said, "after she really started learning the bow." In answer to Caymus's questioning look, he said, "Long hair gets in the way when you shoot. It either gets in your eyes and distracts you, or it gets caught between the string and the arrow nock and gets ripped out on the draw." He grinned. "It's why I wear this thing," he said, indicating his headband.

Caymus nodded. A small smile of comprehension touched his lips, but it only stayed a moment or two and then quickly vanished. "So much has changed," he said. "It's strange, it was like I lived a whole life while I was in that bed. I know it was only a few months, but it seemed so much longer in the Conflagration."

"Does time not work the same there?" Milo asked, wearing a look of genuine curiosity.

Caymus shrugged. "I don't know," he said. "No," he continued, "it's more like there's no *sense* of time." He paused, considering the idea. "I wouldn't be surprised, actually, if there *is* no time in the Conflagration."

Milo screwed up his face. "No time?" he said, "what's to keep everything from happening at once, then?"

Caymus almost smiled. "I'm not sure," he said, "but I don't think the Lords of the Conflagration need time." He raised his eyebrows at Milo. "They're not—strictly speaking—alive, you know."

Milo's eyes widened at this. "What?"

Caymus tried to think of how to explain it. He'd grasped the concept while in the Conflagration, though he hadn't really internalized the idea and understood its implications until after his return. "The Lords, the beings that live in the Conflagration," he said. "They're not alive."

Milo's eyes danced about the landscape as he considered the idea. "So they're…what, ghosts? Figments of your imagination?"

"Nothing like that," Caymus said, shaking his head. "They're sentient beings. They think, they communicate, they have influence, but they're not alive: not like you and me."

Milo looked at him questioningly. "How exactly do you know this?"

For the first time in days, Caymus laughed. "*You* told me, actually."

"I don't," replied Milo, his eyes searching, "remember doing that."

"It was one of the Lords," Caymus admitted. "But he sure looked like you while he was doing it."

"He looked like me?" Milo said, his voice sounding a little disappointed. "Nobody looks like me!"

Caymus smiled. "This one did. He wanted to make the transition into their realm easier for me, so he took an appearance he thought I'd be comfortable with."

"And he chose me?"

"Yes, he did," Caymus said. "I remember him telling me it was all something my own mind was doing as it tried to get used to being in the Conflagration, but I'm certain it would have happened another way if he'd wanted it to."

Milo's eyes squinted into the distance. "So, if a Lord can have that kind of..." he groped the air with his hand, searching for the word, "...that kind of empathy, then how is it that they're not alive?"

Caymus considered the best way to get his point across. "When I was in the Conflagration," he said, "I was there as my consciousness, as a collection of thoughts and feelings. My living body was still here in this realm, but it—my body—was the thing that was alive, not my thoughts. I think the Lords are the same way, only they don't have living bodies here."

Milo was obviously confounded, but also intrigued, by the idea. "How do you suppose something can be sentient, but not alive?"

Caymus smiled slightly. It was a question he'd asked himself several times already, never having come to a satisfactory conclusion. "I'm not sure," he admitted, "but it's true. There's something about this place," he passed his hand over the sand before them, "what they call the Quatrain, that is intimately tied with life, with living. There isn't any life in the Conflagration, and I suspect," he said, holding up a finger, "that it's the same with the other elemental realms."

Milo nodded. "I guess that would explain why the bad guys are so interested in being here."

Caymus had reached the same conclusion. He didn't understand how it all worked, but something about having a presence here, in this world, imbued life to an element that wouldn't otherwise possess it. The beings of kreal wanted to live. That's why they were invading.

Milo gave Caymus a sideways look. "You did tell Be'Var all this, right?"

Caymus chuckled. "Are you kidding? He wouldn't give me a moment's peace until I'd told him absolutely everything that happened, from the second that knife got me 'til the very instant I opened my eyes again."

They walked in silence for a few moments, then Milo said, "I tracked him, you know."

Caymus raised an eyebrow. "Be'Var?"

"No," Milo said, shaking his head. "Callun. The one who attacked you." He looked at Caymus. "You said he told you his name was actually something else, didn't you?"

Caymus nodded slowly. "Mrowvain."

"Mrowvain," Milo said, testing the word on his tongue. "I wonder why he felt the need to hide that."

"Must have thought we'd recognize it," said Caymus.

"Maybe." Milo obviously wasn't sold on that theory just yet. "After he stabbed you, after I showed up and saw that Be'Var already had you well in hand, I tracked him for a while."

Caymus was surprised. He'd been told that there had been a search for the man with the dead eyes, but nobody had mentioned that Milo had been part of that search. "I didn't know that," he said. "Did you find anything?"

"I tracked him for almost a day," Milo replied. "I followed him out the front door of Flamehearth, then down a few streets, into the Guard District, and then out the North Gate." He scratched at his shoulder as he recalled. "He went north," he said, "directly north, didn't even follow a road, just took a straight path up to the Greatstones."

Caymus nodded. "He was heading for Black Moon."

Milo inclined his head. "That was what I thought. He must have been a scout for the army."

Caymus turned to look at his friend. "Or an assassin."

"I suppose a man could be both."

Caymus nodded. "How far did you track him?"

Milo exhaled. "All the way to the point his tracks just up and disappeared, exactly like the krealites." He stroked the horse's mane as they walked. "Do you think he was actually made of the same stuff?" he asked. "Or was he human, like us?"

Caymus shrugged. "I'm sure he was at least partially krealite," he said. "I could feel it in him."

Milo nodded. "That thing with your neck?"

Caymus smiled. "That thing with my neck." He let the smile fade as he walked. "I just wish I'd known what it meant at the time."

Milo dropped his hand to his side. "Me too."

They walked on in silence for a few minutes, so Caymus changed the subject. "So, how long are you going to need, once we get to Terrek?"

Milo visibly brightened. "Most of a day," he said. "It will go faster if the weather cooperates." He turned his eyes to the blue sky. "I don't think there's much chance of rain, but I'm wary of a sandstorm down here."

Another reason they were going to the Falaar village was so that Milo could 'speak the place', doing whatever it was that air priests did that allowed them to send their wind whispers there. Tavrin had agreed to either be the one to listen for these whispers or to find somebody else who could be trusted with the task. The Falaar didn't count air priests among them—they were fire-worshipers, after all—and so couldn't whisper back, but Milo could at least let these neighbors to the south know of any immediate danger heading their way.

Caymus had of the sandstorms that sometimes occurred in the desert. Tavrin had said they could turn a bright day to pitch black, and that they could flay the flesh from a man's bones. Caymus turned to his friend. "Is there anything I can do to help you?"

Milo grinned. "What, a fire-lover like you?"

Caymus shook his head, returning the grin.

"No," said Milo, shaking his head, "I've got to do it on my own. Anyway," he continued, "aren't you going to have your own thing to worry about?"

Caymus wasn't at all sure about how long his particular task would take. He wasn't even sure if he would be allowed to try.

When he'd come out of his months-long slumber, Be'Var had spent a good deal of time explaining what he'd learned whilst sitting by his bed. It seemed that he'd enlisted the help of Aiella, Ambassador Brocke's daughter, to find books and scrolls from several private libraries around the city while he'd tended to the body of his pupil.

What Caymus had been most surprised to learn was that there was an ancient link between the Knight of the Flame and the Falaar. Be'Var hadn't been able to provide details of that relationship, as it seemed to have been largely personal in nature and so not much of it had been recorded. However, one important fact that the man had gleaned from a particularly old-looking tome was that the Falaar were the ones who had taught the Knight of the Flame the particular Aspect of flame-walking—what the Falaar themselves referred to as Unburning.

Be'Var had insisted that Caymus go with the group to see the Falaar, to ask if they would show him this Aspect, help him learn to use it. For some reason, this Unburning seemed important—crucial, even—to the Knight of the Flame. The master was certain that Caymus would need to learn it if he ever hoped to properly fill the position.

Caymus had no idea how he was going to convince a people he'd never met before to teach him a skill that was very uniquely theirs. Why would they do such a thing? It seemed like an invasion of their privacy, or at least of their culture.

"I don't know," he said, finally. "I spoke with Tavrin about it before we left, asked him if they'd even be willing to teach me."

Milo tilted his head. "And?"

"And he seemed fairly certain that I'd be able to persuade them, but he wouldn't tell me how. Didn't say what might be involved or how long it would take." He frowned and shrugged at his friend. "For all I know, I could spend months learn this Unburning thing."

"It will not take so long as that," the Falaar yelled, looking over his shoulder at them.

Caymus nearly lost a step. He hadn't thought Tavrin or Gwenna could hear them. Had he said anything he might not have wanted them to overhear?

While he was thus distracted, Milo asked the obvious question. "Do you know how long, then? Should we be ready to leave Caymus there when it's time to go back?"

Tavrin chuckled, then he and Gwenna slowed so that they could talk without shouting. "I myself have not learned the Unburning," he said, "but those who have, they learn how over the course of two, sometimes three, days."

Caymus exhaled, relieved to hear the news. The latest sightings of Black Moon still put them north of the Greatstones, but just how far north they were at that moment was anybody's guess. He just did not have time for another months-long bout of instruction.

The four continued walking together, and as Milo started asking Tavrin questions about the area around his village, Caymus turned his gaze out across the desert. The village of Terrek, Tavrin's home, lay south of the border between Kepren and Mael'vek, which meant they would be crossing into the lands of a hostile nation sometime today, though Caymus didn't believe they had done so yet.

The Falaar were not Mael'vekian, nor were they allied with any of the larger nations around them. Tavrin had told him that the land around his home had been claimed by the people of Kepren or Mael'vek many times in the last few centuries, and so they had learned to not pay much attention to the wars of these foreigners. Caymus had marveled that these people had managed to stay out of such conflicts so successfully for so long. He did not, however, like the idea of having to cross into the realm of Mael'vek in order to reach Terrek.

Two more days of travel, he thought, and they would be there. He just hoped they didn't run into too much more opposition on the way.

~~~

The night was a fabric of darkness laid down over the sands by a new moon. The desert was so dark, in fact, that Caymus found he was able to smell the village of Terrek before he saw it. The scent was hard to define, but he could clearly detect new moisture in the air, a stark contract to the dryness that had permeated him since leaving Kepren.

He also noticed an absence of stars in the lowest portion of the southern sky, suggesting that they were approaching a remote hill or small mountain. The village, he'd been told, lay around the bottom of such a hill.

"The Watchman," Tavrin said, motioning toward the great form. "Its eyes have kept our people safe for more centuries than are remembered."

Caymus considered the idea, wondering if Tavrin meant it as anything more than a metaphor. The top of the cliff would certainly make for a great vantage from which to spot oncoming invaders.

As the ghostly shapes of mud and brick huts began to appear before him, he wondered why nobody had come to meet them yet. The village, with its back against the hill, was obviously positioned to be easily defendable, yet they had encountered no guard, no sentry.

Perhaps it was too late in the day. He wondered what time it was, knowing only that it was long past ninth bell. They had pushed hard that evening, having decided they would rather arrive late this day than early the next.

"Don't you keep lookouts?" asked Milo, echoing Caymus's thoughts.

Tavrin smiled at the air priest. "We do," he said, "but we will not see them." He turned to face his home, and his smile widened. "We are expected, so there is no need to challenge our approach."

Caymus was surprised to hear this. "Expected?" he said. "How could they expect us? We only decided to take the trip a day or so before we left."
~~~

"Tavrin's brother," said Gwenna, looking around at the buildings as they got closer. "Elon. He arrived in Kepren the day after you woke up. After we decided to come here, he ran on ahead to carry the news."

Caymus felt conflicting emotions within himself upon hearing the information. On the one hand, he now wouldn't have to be the one to announce to the chieftain of Terrek that he wanted to learn their closely guarded secrets. On the other, it meant that somebody else—somebody he didn't even know—had now set an expectation for his behavior. He didn't like the idea of somebody else speaking for him, especially about something as important as this.

He kept his misgivings to himself, however, as they passed the first line of huts. The dwellings were small, mostly just single rooms, though a few seemed as though they could contain two or three chambers within. There were windows, though those contained no glass or casements. Doors were mere strips of leather or cloth; Caymus supposed that was because wood was hard to come by in this place. There seemed to be no order to the placement of the buildings, which seemed strange; perhaps they'd simply been built as need had arisen, with no sense of planning for streets or walkways. The haphazard nature of it reminded him of some of the older parts of the Guard District, which had grown in a similarly organic fashion.

He tried to estimate how many people might live in the village. More than a hundred, he thought, but less than a thousand. He would have a better idea, of course, when the sun came up again.

As they passed another line of structure, he heard snoring coming from a few of them. He winced. They must have arrived even later than he'd thought. Flames, would anybody be awake at all here, or would his very first act upon arriving be to rouse someone from peaceful slumber? He couldn't afford to anger the Falaar. Unless Be'Var had been very mistaken, he needed them.

His worries turned out to be unfounded. As they reached the steep face of the Watchman itself, they came upon a figure sitting on a small, stone block in front of one of the larger huts.

The man was big. He wasn't as tall as Caymus, but he was even more solidly built, with thick arms and legs that told of a person who used his entire body as a tool. His thick, gray hair, hanging in a long ponytail down his back, suggested that he was in his late fifties, or perhaps sixties. He wore no shirt. His leggings consisted of hides. His weathered skin was as dark as the leather bracers on his wrists.

When he looked up, Caymus was taken aback by the intensity of the man's glare. He didn't seem to be angry, but Caymus had the distinct impression that he and his friends were being judged.

"Chieftain," said Tavrin, leaving Gwenna with the horse and taking a step forward. As the big man turned his gaze on him, Tavrin dropped his head slightly and brought a hand up in front of his eyes. He held the hand there for a moment, then dropped it.

A moment later, the chieftain did the same thing, first bringing one hand up on front of his eyes, then dropping it again.

"May I bring these friends into our home?" Tavrin said.

The chieftain looked at the other three again, then nodded his head once. In the movement, Caymus noticed that the man was wearing a headband, and that a small, yellow gem sat in the center of it.

"You may stay with us for a time," the chieftain said. He then stood up and crossed the few steps to the hut in front of which he'd been sitting. He extended a hand and pulled back the cloth curtain in the doorway. "You will stay here," he said.

Caymus was about to say thank you, but the chieftain interrupted him. "You and you," he pointed to Caymus and to Tavrin, "will come with me now." The man's tone, as intense as his glare, made it clear that he expected no argument. Before anybody could speak, he strode off into the darkness.

Tavrin motioned for Caymus to follow, then started after his chief. Caymus, still holding the horse's lead, held it plaintively out to Milo. Milo took it from him, an amused expression on his face. Caymus barely had time to catch up with the two retreating figures before they disappeared into the darkness.

Nobody said a word as they walked a path that followed the cliff wall, past several identical-looking huts. The chieftain kept an impressive pace, and Caymus had no doubt that he was serious.

After they had walked for a couple of minutes, passing a few dozen huts—Caymus now revisited his estimation of the population to possibly over a thousand—the chieftain pushed past a leather flap of a door and into a hut that seemed, if anything, smaller than the others.

Caymus followed Tavrin into the building, needing to duck to fit through the door. When he got inside, he found himself in a small, circular room ringed with stone benches upon which Tavrin and the Chieftain were sitting down. The interior wall was covered in brightly colored sheets of cloth and even a small tapestry which seemed to depict a setting sun. A shaft of wood was anchored into middle of the dirt floor, and lashed to the top of it was a small glass bowl that contained a few inches of some clear liquid.

Caymus had been about to close the leather flap, but the chieftain shook his head and motioned for him to sit. Caymus did so, then he sat in silence as the man produced a small, wooden box from under his seat and then opened it to retrieve a flint and striker. Placing the open box on the bench next to him, he stood and struck the flint over the bowl. The liquid, obviously some manner of oil, lit under the curtain of sparks, producing a small flame which burned tall, if not fiercely.

As the chieftain replaced the implements to the box, then the box to its place under the seat, he nodded toward Caymus, then to the door. Caymus rose and closed the flap so that only the small flame, and no starlight, lit the inside of the hut.

Once Caymus was sitting again, the chieftain turned his glare to Tavrin. "Tell me of this one, Tavrin," he said, indicating Caymus. "Tell me why he should be allowed to learn the oldest secrets of our people."

Caymus noticed immediately that the chieftain of this isolated tribe spoke the common language of Tebria with almost no inflection or accent. He was surprised. Tavrin and the two Falaar that Caymus had met at the Temple, Guruk and Fach'un, all spoke with obvious hesitations which betrayed the fact that their first language was their own, and not that of Tebria.

Tavrin nodded without smiling. "I have only begun to know this Caymus in the four days we have traveled here," he said. "Most of what I know of him, I know from his friends, Gwenna and Milo."

The chieftain's eyes narrowed very slightly at this, but he did not speak.

"They have told me," Tavrin continued, "that he is calm, that he is courageous, that he is considerate of the needs of others, and that he thinks before he acts. Friends of Caymus have a strong opinion of him. They say he can be trusted."

The chieftain nodded. "What do you know of this man," he said, "that is not the repeated words of others?"

Tavrin betrayed a vague hint of a smile. "This Caymus was attacked with a poison that should have killed him," he said. "He was strong enough to survive the poison and is wiser for the battle."

Tavrin turned his eyes to Caymus as he continued. "I can also tell that our group was attacked as it made its way here," he said. He turned back to the chieftain. "The fight was not difficult, and it was easily won, but when Caymus had beaten his opponent, he did not kill him, and instead offered him back his life."

The chieftain's face registered this information more than it had any other, his eyes noticeably widening and darting to Caymus for the briefest moment.

When it was clear that Tavrin had no more to say, the Chieftain nodded. "Thank you, Tavrin," he said. Then, his face broke into a smile that was as warm as his glare had been intense. He stood, opened his hand, and placed his palm upon his heart.

Tavrin, also smiling, stood and mirrored the gesture. He had barely put his hand to his chest when the big man reached out and grabbed him in a bear hug. "Welcome home, Tavrin," he said, smacking the younger man's back. "The fields have missed your touch," he said as he let him go.

"Thank you, Kavuu," Tavrin said, his smile as broad as the chieftain's. "It is good to be home."

"Good," said Kavuu. He inclined his head to Caymus, who was still sitting on his bench. "Leave me with him, please."

Tavrin nodded, then he turned and walked out, giving Caymus a surreptitious nod and smile as he went.

When Tavrin was gone, the door flap standing closed behind him, the chieftain sat back down on his bench and returned his gaze to Caymus. The man's countenance was much softer than it had been at first, though it still wasn't what Caymus would describe as friendly. The yellow stone upon his forehead seemed to glow brighter than the faint firelight should have allowed.

"Tavrin is a strange man," the chieftain said, directing his gaze briefly to the tent flap. "When he was a boy, he would tend to growing things while others his age were fighting with the barak. When the other boys hunted the sands for game, he walked alone through the village, seeing stones." He leaned in slightly, as though sharing a secret. "Some do not understand his ways," he said, "but I know that he has the ability to see into the heart of a place, of a situation," he pointed a thick finger at Caymus, "even a man."

The chieftain leaned back, pressing what looked to be a silk curtain against the mud-brick surface behind him. "Tavrin's words tell me that he is confident you are a good man," he nodded, "and so I am confident." He then leaned forward again, further than he had previously. "I wonder, though," he said, "if you are worthy to learn what you would ask us to teach you."

With that, he stood again, stepped to the bowl and the burning oil within, and placed his forearm in the flame. "The Falaar have known the Unburning for many generations. It has been practiced by our ancestors for so long that it has become our birthright. It increases our resilience against those who would seek to rule us. It makes our warriors strong."

Caymus stifled a wince as he watched the man's arm hanging in the fire. It did not burn, nor did it even change color. He had expected, at least, to have the smell of burning hair filling the small room, but even that part of Kavuu appeared to be immune to the flames.

"You are from the Temple in the Forest," he continued, still not moving, "is that right?"

Caymus decided Kavuu must have been talking about Saleri Forest. "I am."

"Then you are the first true representative of these Conflagrationists that I have encountered." Caymus met the man's eyes, surprised at the statement. "There have been missionaries from your Flamehearth, of course," he explained, "and a few of my people have traveled north, but not one of those from the Temple itself has ever come to my village in my lifetime."

Caymus was now even more wary of the position he found himself in. Not only did he wish to ask this man to teach him what had always been a secret of his people, but now he was also the embodied representation of all the masters at the Temple, speaking and acting on their behalves. In the silence, he wondered if he should say something, but he felt that the chieftain wasn't finished yet.

"I am told," the big man finally said, staring at his arm, "that the Conflagrationists understand the flames also, that you have power as we do, that you bend not to the nations of mankind, but to the fury of the flame." He looked back to Caymus and arched an eyebrow. "This is what I can do, what my allegiance allows me," he said, his eyes darting to his arm, still held in the fire. "What power do you have?"

Caymus considered the question, considered how best to answer it. He considered telling the man that most of the masters of the Temple were skilled at the Aspect of pulling, or that his talent was for shaping the flames and the conduits that created them.

Instead, he decided to let action, rather than words, speak for him. He reached out with his mind to touch the flames that enveloped the chieftain's arm. With quiet concentration, he felt out the conduit that connected it to the Conflagration, letting himself drift around it until he enveloped it completely.

Then, with the speed of a thought, he tightened down on the space in which the conduit existed, breaking the connection to the Conflagration. In that moment, the small room was plunged into darkness.

Caymus sat still, waiting. He had thought that showing the man that he, too, had a way of dealing with a dangerous flame was something that might impress him. For several long moments, however, all he heard was silence.

Then, as though he were a spirit summoned out of the darkness, Kavuu, the chieftain of the Falaar, began to bellow with a deep laughter. Caymus could hear surprise and satisfaction in that laugh, and he sagged slightly with relief.

A moment later, still laughing, though more quietly, Kavuu sparked the flint again and brought firelight back to the room. As the man once again replaced the flint box back to its place underneath the bench, he let his mirth fade. By the time he was seated, his elbows on his thighs, his fingers intertwined before his eyes, the Falaar chieftain had become silent again. He was looking hard at Caymus, considering, judging.

"I suppose you are worthy, indeed," he finally said. "I had always expected that those who called themselves Conflagrationists might be trying to trick my people into giving up their secrets, that they might have no secrets of their own to share, nothing to trade in kind." He nodded to himself. "It is good to see that, at the very least, we both have lessons we might teach each other."

Caymus smiled, thinking of the two men at the Temple. "I imagine Guruk and Fach'un have likely learned how to accomplish what I have just done by now," he said, "and probably a good deal more. Opening and closing the small conduits to the Conflagration is something they would have been taught by now."

Kavuu seemed satisfied with this, having visibly brightened at the mention of his fellows' names. He leaned forward again, and his voice assumed a thoughtful tone. "So," he said, "I believe that you are a good man, that you will use anything we might teach you for reasons you believe to be noble. I also believe that you are worthy of the knowledge, that you and the people that you represent have worthwhile knowledge to pass to us in return. What I do not know," he said, his face losing all expression, "is why."

Caymus frowned at the implied question. "I'm sorry?"

"Why are you here now, Caymus?" the chieftain asked. "I have spoken with the Conflagrationists' missionaries for many years. They have always been interested in the Unburning, but never before has one ever asked me to teach it, much less one from the Temple itself. I want to know why you are here now, what force it is that drives you to seek this knowledge. The reason," he said, pointing a finger at Caymus, "is as important as the intention."

Caymus thought about the question, thought about the last few months of his life, about the krealites that had attacked that first night, about the mark on his hand that named him as a possible knight, about the three months he'd spent battling in another world. He wasn't sure if he could explain it all and do the story justice.

"Have you heard of the Knight of the Flame?" he eventually said.

"Hm," said Kavuu, putting his chin in his hands. "What is this, a knight?"

Caymus smiled. "I'm not all that sure, to be honest," he said. "It is a title that I learned from an old book in the bowels of Otvia."

"The mitre home?" Kavuu raised an eyebrow.

Caymus nodded. "From what I understand, a knight is a champion, one who fights for a particular element, a warrior whose allegiance is to a church, rather than a nation." He raised his hand up to the light so that Kavuu could get a good look at the sword and flame. "I received this," he said, "when I entered the Conflagration for the first time."

Kavuu reached out and grabbed Caymus's wrist, firmly turning and twisting it, getting a good look. Caymus continued. "My desire had been to take my next step in becoming a master, but the Conflagration had other plans, it seems."

Kavuu let the wrist go. "They want you to be this knight, then."

Caymus nodded. "The realms of the elements all hold a place in our world. They've done so since they won that place in a long-dead war. Another element called kreal, which comes from a realm that the beings of the Conflagration refer to as the Sograve, has attacked and is trying to claim a part of our world."

The chieftain was looking at Caymus seriously, weighing his words, measuring his intent. "The insects," he said. It wasn't a question.

Caymus simply nodded

"You are this Knight of the Flame, then?"

"No," Caymus said. "Not yet, anyway. My teacher, Master Be'Var, has learned that the last time the Conflagration called a knight to defend our world, many thousands of years ago, the man that filled the post knew the Falaar well. It seems he learned the Unburning from your people."

Kavuu's expression changed to one of surprise and no small amount of incredulity.

Caymus pressed on. "There is something about the Unburning that is important to becoming this Knight of the Flame. From what I and Master Be'Var have learned, I would need to learn this skill in order to claim the title." He paused, considering whether he should go on, but he decided there was no point in holding anything back. "I also must find a sword, one which the previous Knight of the Flame held."

"A sword, you say?" said Kavuu.

Caymus nodded.

"And when you find these things," said Kavuu, his countenance turning suspicious, "you will be this warrior, this Knight of the Flame?"

Caymus shrugged, his arms wide in a plaintive gesture. "I don't know," he said. "There may be more to it, there may not. I only know what I've been told and what I've discovered so far." He managed a faint smile. "I'm having to learn as I go, I'm afraid."

Kavuu reflected Caymus's smile momentarily, and then his eyes took on a countenance of deep thought. He sat there, staring into the fire, for a long moment. "When I was young," he said, finally, "my father was slain, protecting the people of this village, by soldiers of Kepren."

Caymus kept his eyes fixed on Kavuu, wondering where this was going.

The older man continued. "Both Kepren and Mael'vek have claimed dominion over this land in the past. One or the other has alternately—sometimes at the same time, even—claimed that our lands are theirs. The landscape of their politics is ever-changing. Today, Mael'vek says that we are Mael'vekian."

He turned his gaze to Caymus. "I do not hate these nations for what they have done, for the trouble they bring to my people," he said, "but I will not join with anyone who proposes to rule me, not if I can prevent it with my sweat or my blood."

Caymus nodded his understanding. "The Flamehearth Mission is in Kepren, but it is just that: a mission. Those who live and teach there owe their allegiance to the Conflagration, to the Temple where the Conduit reaches into our world, not to the city, not to the Tebrian League."

He took a deep breath and adjusted himself in his seat. "I do not propose to rule you, Sir. I am asking for your help in defeating an enemy that would see the end of life in our world as we know it. The beings of the Sograve exist in their own realm for now, but they have reached their claws into this one, and they've hurt us. If they establish a firm footing, the very nature of this place…" he looked around to signify the land about them. "We don't know for certain, but we think it will change to the point that we won't even recognize it as home."

Pausing, he stared into the flames between them, remembering his time in the Conflagration. "I spent a *very long time* in a world that was not my own, Chieftain Kavuu. It was an experience that I wouldn't wish to repeat, that I wouldn't wish for anybody." He turned his gaze back to Kavuu. "If I can prevent that by taking up the mantle of this Knight of the Flame, then that is what I will do."

The two men stared at each other a long time. Caymus hoped he had convinced the man, but he was unable to read the Kavuu's face. The man was just looking at him, as though assessing his eyes, rather than his words.

For a moment, he had hold himself back from laughing at the absurdity of it all. Here he was, asking a man he didn't know to tell him a secret that he'd never told anybody, that none of his ancestors had likely ever shared with an outsider—save the previous Knight of the Flame—and he didn't even really know what was so important about the secret.

Why was it so important that the Knight of the Flame understand this Aspect? Wasn't shaping enough? What were the chances of ever being burned by a fire if he was able to control it in the first place?

Kavuu interrupted his thoughts by standing up, then indicating that Caymus should do that same.

"This man you speak of," the chieftain said, a far-off look in his eyes. "This *knight*. He sounds like the Paladin."

Caymus felt his face light up. "The Paladin?" he said. "Who is the Paladin?"

Kavuu smiled a sad smile. "The Paladin was a hero from our legends, a traveler who came to our people in a time of strife, who protected us from unknowable dangers. In exchange, we taught him to protect himself from the fires that burned through this land." He shook his head slowly as he continued. "It…is a story which we tell our children, but which I had not thought about in many years."

Caymus felt his pulse racing. He didn't know for sure they were both referring to the same man, but if they were, then Be'Var's theory about the Knight's ties to the Falaar had just been confirmed.

Before Caymus could ask any more questions, however, the big man shook himself from his reverie and became serious again. "I will think on your words tonight, Caymus of the Temple," he said. He offered his hand, which Caymus took in a firm handshake. Kavuu looked to the door. "Your air friend," he said, "the one with the feathers?"

"Milo," Caymus said, smiling. Milo's feathers were often the first things people noticed about him.

"Milo," said Kavuu. "He will be doing what he must so that we can receive words from your people tomorrow, yes?"

"I believe so," Caymus nodded. Kavuu was still gripping his hand. "He told me it will take most of a day."

"Good," Kavuu said. "While he does, I would suggest you spend some time in contemplation upon the brow of the Watchman."

Caymus narrowed his eyes, curious about the phrase, but decided to keep his mouth closed. He needed this man to trust him, so he would follow his suggestions. "I will do that, then," he replied.

The chieftain's lip turned up in a wry grin. "Good," he said again, then he gave Caymus's hand a final, firm shake and let it go. "I now say good night to you." He tilted his head to the door. "Can you find your way back to the structure where I met you?"

Caymus nodded. "I can." He had counted the buildings on the way here, just in case.

Kavuu gave him a single nod, and so he turned and made his way back out into the chilly, night air.

Moments after he'd begun making his way back, he discovered Milo at his shoulder. "How did it go?" Milo asked.

"Well, I think," Caymus said, not mentioning Milo's sudden appearance. "He said that he would think about it."

"You think that means it went well?" Milo asked, incredulously. "I don't know about you, but when I tell someone I'll think about it, I'm not usually planning on giving them good news later."

Caymus smiled. He raised his chin to indicate the hill beside them, rising as a sheer cliff face. "I think he said I should spend some time up there tomorrow, while you're speaking the place. He called it 'the brow of the Watchman'."

Milo frowned at the cliff. "I see." He shrugged his shoulders. "I suppose there must be a good reason for it," he said. "I'd do what he says."

"My thoughts exactly," Caymus replied, stifling a sudden yawn. "For now, though, I just want to get to sleep and not have to think about it."

Milo cringed. "You might want to sleep under the stars tonight," he said. "Right after I left the hut, Gwenna and Tavrin started making kissy noises in there."

Caymus sighed. "Thanks for the warning," he mumbled.

Milo clapped him on the shoulder. "Don't mention it," he said. "I left your pack outside, just in case you decided to make a quick getaway."

"Thank you, Milo," Caymus said with an appreciative smile. "Once again, you've saved my life."

Milo grinned at the gratitude, if not the hyperbole.

"Where are you sleeping?" Caymus asked.

"Don't know yet," Milo said, looking around at the squat buildings of Terrek. "I'm not tired. I'm going to do a little exploring before I settle in."

"Don't explore too long," Caymus said. "It's late enough as it is."

"I make no promises," Milo said. He clapped Caymus on the shoulder again. "Goodnight Caymus," he said, then he jogged briskly into the darkness.

"Goodnight, Milo," Caymus said quietly, as his friend disappeared. He'd lost a lot of himself when he'd spent all that time in the Conflagration, but traveling with Milo was helping him regain some of his good humor, at least. "May the winds guide you."

Milo had been as good as his word. When Caymus arrived at the hut, he found the horses tied and bedded down and his own pack propped up near the doorway to their hut. When he reached down to pick it up, he heard the distinctive sound of Gwenna giggling inside.

Caymus rolled his eyes, then slung his pack over his shoulder and walked along the cliff wall, a little annoyed at the behavior of the two lovebirds, but also glad for them, that they were getting some time to themselves. He realized he didn't feel any anger or jealousy about the matter, and decided he was happy about that.

After a few minutes of walking, he'd moved beyond the buildings to a point where the cliff wall didn't reach as high: two stories, maybe? Only a few more minutes of travel, he realized, and he would likely find a place where he could begin the climb up in the morning. This spot, then, would be an ideal place to bed down for now.

Taking deep lungfuls of the cold night air, Caymus unrolled his mat and blankets and lay down to a sleep more peaceful than any he'd known in weeks.

~~~
~~~

Caymus took another drink from the waterskin at his pouch. The late autumnal air was cold, but it was also dry, and he was surprised by how often he was thirsty.

He was nearing the top of the hill, following the contour of the cliff-face that overlooked the village of Terrek. He wasn't sure how much sleep he'd gotten, but he'd awakened before the sun had fully appeared in the sky and had felt awake enough to start the day. Now that the sun was cresting the horizon, he was feeling invigorated, eager to meet the day.

Before he'd begun his ascent, he'd had encountered Milo, who, accompanied by Tavrin's younger brother Elon, had just been starting his process of "speaking the place".

Elon had been designated as the primary recipient of Milo's, and later other air priests', messages. He was a serious-looking young man, and he'd apparently asked to be involved in the initial process so that he could better understand things, hoping that it would make him a better recipient of the messages in the future.

Milo had explained to Caymus that the process of speaking a place, of becoming intimately familiar with a location, was both lengthy and arduous. Once finished, however, it would be relatively easy for him to communicate the relevant details to others so that they, too, could send their whispers to Elon. He'd explained that it had something to do with the language of the winds, that the difficult part was translating a description of the place into that language; once translated, communicating the translation to somebody already fluent was fairly simple.

The procedure had looked strange to Caymus. Milo had begun by slowly wandering around and around a point in the center of the village, making ever-expanding circles. He would then pause every few steps, turn in a seemingly random direction, point at something, speak quietly to himself for a few moments, and then continue walking. The whole process seemed highly ritualized and quite un-Milo-like.

When he'd left, a few dozen Falaar had already gathered to watch the air priest, fascinated by his strange movements. Elon had been busying himself with making sure nobody got in Milo's way.

Caymus smiled as he climbed, thinking about the group of children who'd been mimicking Milo's actions. He was remembering how much bumping into each other the children had been doing when he realized that he was approaching the top of the ridge, and that there was something green up there.

It was a tree, a healthy-looking conifer, brimming with thick bunches of dark green needles and standing at about three times his own height.

Caymus was momentarily dumbstruck by the sight. A tree like this had no business growing here, out in the middle of the desert.

When he reached the tree, he gingerly put his hand to it, part of him certain that it must be an illusion. He felt the bark, pulled some needles through his fingers. It was real. What was it doing up here?

Quietly reeling at the discovery, he turned around to discover that he was, indeed, at the highest point of the cliff face. The tree was growing about two yards from the edge. There was no doubt in his mind that this must be the brow of the Watchman. This was where Kavuu had told him he should be.

He began to sit, but he first gave the tree a sidelong glance. He'd been thinking that 'the Watchman' was a name given to the hill, but might it refer to the tree instead? He tried to recall how the word had been used the previous night, but he couldn't remember the exact phrasing. He mused on the idea that, had they not arrived so late at night, he might have been able to see the tree growing up here; maybe then he'd have asked for clarification.

He turned, deciding to leave the question of the anachronistic plant for another time, and sat cross-legged on the ground, about a foot from the edge of the cliff.

He winced. The ground beneath him was hard stone covered by a sprinkling of fine sand. It felt cold against his legs and he briefly wished he'd brought his blanket to sit on.

Taking a deep breath, he allowed the cool, morning air to soak into him and invigorate his senses. As he did so, he allowed his gaze to drift over the vista before him.

He could see quite a lot from up here. Tebrian desert—no, the *Mael'vekian* desert—stretched out before him: a flat, endless plain of sand and dry shrubs. To the west, he could see what looked to be plots of farmland, though nothing appeared to be growing there. Tavrin had been right: the Falaar clearly knew a bit about agriculture, but they couldn't properly be called famers. Caymus wasn't an expert either of course, but he knew the landscape back in Woodsea, and this was the time of year when the summer crops had been harvested and the fall vegetables were just beginning to sprout; there was just far too much fallow land down there, even if the Falaar were using a three-field system.

His eyes caught some movement down there, but it was too far away for him to make out any detail. He tried to imagine that the shapes were Tavrin and Gwenna, planting the seeds they had brought with them.

He'd briefly encountered the two of them on their way to see Milo's speaking. Gwenna had adopted some of the style of dress of these people, wearing leather leggings and an overshirt of a light, brown material. She'd even been sporting the leather moccasins that the Falaar wore, rather than the boots she'd travelled here in. The change had been surprising, even striking: if not for her blonde hair and fair skin, anyone could have mistaken her for one of the Falaar.

"You seem pretty comfortable in those," Caymus had said.

Gwenna had smiled. "Thank you," she'd replied. "I am." She'd turned to gaze at the village, at the huts, at the children chasing each other between the buildings. "It's a wonderful place, isn't it?"

Caymus had agreed. It was quite true.

He briefly wondered where the Falaar got the leather they used in so many of their materials. He hadn't seen any cows or goats anywhere, and he couldn't imagine there was much hunting to be had out in the sands. For that matter, if the Falaar weren't experienced farmers, then where did food for all these people come from?

He looked across the village itself. Now that he could see the entirety of it, he estimated between four and five hundred of the small buildings rested in the shadow of the hill. If most of those held families, then the population of this place could very well be in the thousands.

Something picked at the corners of his attention as he gazed across the village…something unusual, but which his conscious mind wasn't registering. He frowned, trying to puzzle it out.

He could see Milo down there, still walking in circles in the middle of everything. A fair-sized crowed had gathered around him by now, which was amusing, but which didn't seem particularly strange. No, whatever his subconscious had noticed, he was fairly sure it wasn't about the people. It must have been the buildings, then. He was too far away to make out any real detail in the mud and clay huts though, so what could he possibly have seen?

Realization dawned on him. It wasn't the buildings he was seeing, but rather their arrangement, the way they were laid out. Until now, he'd thought the layout of the village to be random; but no, there was some kind of pattern there.

After some more consideration, he saw that the buildings were arranged in crooked lines that fanned out from the cliff face, starting from a point directly below where he was sitting, and ending out in the desert, beyond the boundaries of the village. It wasn't even the buildings themselves forming these lines; it was the spaces between them, which was why it had been hard to make out in the first place.

Caymus closed his eyes, taking his eyes off the pattern before him, and considered it through the filter of memory. Were the lines even really there? Might his imagination simply be trying to force order out of a random process? As he thought about it, about the sand between the structures, he noticed the feel of the sun on his face. The air around him still held a morning chill, but he could sense the heat against his skin.

He sat there, his hands on his knees, his face turned up to the sky, reveling in the sun, in the cool, in the desert all around him. He hadn't so peaceful, so calm, since the last time he'd sat before the Conduit and just *felt*. Gwenna had been absolutely right: Terrek really was a wonderful place.

Caymus felt, more than heard, the presence approaching from behind. "I have always loved this spot," the presence said. The voice was Kavuu's, his tone embracing the serenity of the moment.

Caymus didn't reply, choosing instead to remain as he was. He heard the rustle of clothing behind him, heard the scraping of sand over stone. He suspected that the chieftain of the Falaar was also sitting down, taking a spot under the branches of the strange tree.

A few minutes after the rustling stopped, Kavuu spoke again. "There is a power here that few understand, an energy in the land itself." He paused a moment. "Are your eyes open?"

Caymus tilted his head down and opened his eyes. "They are."

"Do you see the paths?"

Caymus nodded, again looking at the strange arrangement of the small buildings below him, and now he noticed something new: before, he'd thought of the spaces as beginning from the hill and fanning out into the desert, but now he intuited that the opposite was true. "They all seem to lead here," he said.

Kavuu was silent a long moment. "You are perceptive, Conflagrationist," he finally said. "The power, the fire, it burns throughout this land. The sun pounds upon on the sand, baking the soil, turning it to clay, making it hard by infusing it with flame."

Caymus let his mind drift across the words as they were spoken. He'd never before considered the idea of the land itself containing the fire element. As far as the masters had ever explained, the land was of earth and nothing else, the only exception being soil, which contained water, too. He wasn't sure of the reality of what Kavuu was describing, but he did like the idea of the Conflagration having a foothold, an actual home, in the desert.

"My people, the Falaar," Kavuu continued, "discovered this power many generations ago. In the beginning, we did not know how to use it, how to harness it, how to turn it to our need. Over time, however, our ancestors learned that the power could be shaped, could be channeled, gathered into a place.

"That is the pattern you see. Our homes, built of the land itself, bear the power of the sun to a point, here, at the Watchman's brow."

He stopped again, letting the words sing into Caymus's mind. Caymus gazed out at the village. He could see the logic of it, now. If he though of the desert as a sea, then the huts were placed in a such way that the waters would be channeled to the point directly beneath him.

"That power—the power of the sun coursing through the desert—it nourishes us, feeds our people. It is why this tree grows here. It is why we come here to meditate, to learn."

Another long pause. "You must find this power, Conflagrationist. You must feel and understand it. You must allow it to flow into you here, in this place, if you are to learn the thing you wish me to teach."

Caymus closed his eyes, wondering how Kavuu expected him to do that. Of course, he only knew of one way, and so he reached out with his consciousness and tried to gain a sense of his surroundings.

He felt the ground under his legs. It was still cold, lacking the element of fire almost completely. He felt the area behind him, in front of him, and to either side. There was no significant heat there, no trace of the Conflagration's fury.

He reached backward to feel the tree. There, he discovered a strange thing: the tree was quite warm. The exterior bark had the same, unsurprising feel that his fingers had touched earlier, but the core of the wood, just below the surface, was as hot as if a fire burned inside.

Caymus reveled in the sensation. The tree felt vibrant, so unbelievably *alive!* And it was more than just heat he was feeling: it was an actual manifestation of the fire element, as though the thing was somehow filled with the Conflagration's energy.

The sensation was breathtaking. Caymus felt himself inhale sharply as he gained a small glimmer of understanding of the power that Kavuu had described.

Curious and elated, Caymus moved his conscious attention to the base of the tree, to the point where it met the ground. There, he felt the same force, the same energy, trickling up into the living wood from the rock and sand. The fire didn't emanate from the tree; it flowed from without, from below the tree, then up into its trunk.

He let his attention drift further downward, tracing the flow of power backward, down the cliff face and into the earth at its base. He was following the path of energy the same way he traced a conduit back to the Conflagration, following a stream of the fire element back to its source.

Far below, the power split into multiple streams, into the various channels the followed the pattern of the village. Opening his eyes, Caymus let his attention wander across the ground, let himself travel between the streams of energy. He felt the way that they fanned out, backward, each becoming less and less distinct until they dispersed into a slow, steady hum that permeated the desert.

Elated, he travelled back toward the Watchmen, and there as he reached the cliff face, he discovered yet another sensation. Beyond the streams of the sun's power, beyond the fire of the desert itself, there was something else, something grand in the earth and stone beneath him, something which collected that power and then absorbed it as though it were nourishment, then sent it up the cliff face to the tree.

He'd never known that such a power existed right below his feet. He began to wonder if the Conflagration manifested in this way in other places: in Kepren, in Krin's Point, or even in the Saleri Forest that surrounded the Temple.

For the first time since he'd awakened from his long slumber, Caymus knew pure joy. "I have it," he said. "I feel it." As he spoke, he was unable to keep the rapture out of his voice.

"Good," said Kavuu, his voice sounding more distant than before. "Now, you must take that power into yourself. You must let the power of the land flow into you, let it make you strong. You must accept it into yourself as you would accept the love of a companion or the pride of a parent."

Closing his eyes again, Caymus brought his mind back to the brow of the Watchman. He felt, once again, for the stream of energy that flowed into the tree. When he found it, he held it carefully, probing its edges and its limits until he had a complete sense of it.

Using the same intuition he'd relied upon when he'd first shaped a conduit, he attempted to move the flow of power, to redirect it from the tree to himself.

Nothing happened. The stream of energy did not waver.

"No," came Kavuu's distant voice. "You cannot force it to come to you any more than you could force the affections of a lover. You must open yourself to it, be a receptacle for it."

Caymus released his grip on the stream, though he kept his attention on it, making sure not to lose the thread. He tried to understand what the chieftain was saying. How could he be a "receptacle" for the flames?

He considered the tree, considered the energy flowing into it. Why did the power flow there, why to that spot? Why did it not simply continue into another place, or even dissipate completely? The only answer Caymus could think of was that the tree was a living thing and that the energy, concentrated as it was, somehow sought out living things.

Okay, then why enter the tree? He and Kavuu were both here, too: why not enter them? What made the tree special?

Caymus considered the nature of the tree. It was a plant, of course, and plants had a special relationship with the sun, seeming to actually absorb the very light of day in order to grow. Kavuu said this power originated with the sun, so might this be the same process? Might the power flow into the tree because the tree was so ready receive it?

How, then, could he shift the flow of energy from the tree to himself?

Was it as simple as Kavuu said: let himself be open; make himself a willing receptacle? Could he possibly be more receptive of the sun's energy than a tree?

He could only try.

Caymus let his attention stray from the energy flowing through rock and brought it back to himself. He thought on Kavuu's words, one how he had compared the flow of the power to the affections of a lover. The idea was confounding, and yet it gave him a place to start. Experimentally, he tried to shift his thoughts, tried to imagine the power flowing through the land as someone he loved, tried to accept that power as he would the affections of such a person.

Nothing happened. Clearly, he was doing something wrong, but what? Perhaps it wasn't surprising. After all, he'd never been in love before. Sure, there was Gwenna, but he had no difficulty admitting to himself that he'd never actually loved her, that any attraction between them had never been anything more than friendship.

He'd seen how Tavrin was with her in the last few days. When Gwenna and Tavrin looked at each other, he could see the feeling—the love, he had to admit—between them. There was something special about those looks, something intense, and yet completely trusting.

That trust, he thought, might be the thing. They left themselves open, vulnerable to one another.

Caymus tried to imagine the feeling, the sensation, of making himself completely vulnerable, totally defenseless, to another person. How would it feel to trust somebody so much that he could leave himself totally open, so love so deeply as to expose that love as a raw nerve, and to feel no fear?

As his mind considered such a feeling, his body responded in kind. He felt his throat tighten, felt his back arch slightly, as a wave of emotion crested over him. And as the wave hit, he felt a slight tremor in the path of the energy: the flickering of a candles flame in a breath of wind.

He intensified his effort. He tried to let his imagination conjure up a love he'd never felt, a look that could make him tremble. He dug deep into the core of himself as he let his own defenses, the barriers to his heart, crumble away, and tried to let himself, for the first time he could ever remember, to be completely open.

Without intent or forethought, and as a complete surprise, a figure appeared in Caymus's thoughts. The image was indistinct, though he could make out dark hair, dark eyes, and a flowing blue dress.

In that moment, the entire world seemed to hold its breath.

The rush of the power into his body was sudden, intense, excruciating. Caymus felt himself gasp aloud for air. He'd briefly sensed that the stream of power was moving from the tree to him, but he'd not expected it to be so fierce as it entered his body.

"Good." Kavuu's voice was stronger now, more insistent. "Hold it, Caymus. Do not let it go!"

Caymus tried to do as he was told, but it was difficult: his sense of the power was tangled up with a sudden burst of raw emotion that he was trying desperately to get under control. Though he wasn't crying, he could feel wetness on his cheeks. His breathing was fast and shallow, as though in a panic.

"Hold it, Caymus," said Kavuu again, "You must hold it!"

The power coursing through his body was almost more than he could bear. He could feel it coming up out of the ground, crossing into his legs, and then flooding through his torso and searing through his arms, neck, and head as though he were sitting in the mouth of an erupting volcano. As he attempted to hold onto the power, to even get his bearings, he opened his eyes.

The view that greeted him was shocking. For a moment, he thought the sun was still in the sky, the light around him was so bright. He took only a moment, however, to realize that day had passed, and that night had taken its place. *He* was the source of the light! A sheen of yellow and orange stood between his eyes and the vista before him.

He was on fire.

"Close your eyes!" Kavuu shouted, now standing a few feet to Caymus's left.

Caymus quickly slammed his eyes shut, trying not to think of what he'd just seen. Had he imagined it? Could he really be burning?

"Don't let go, Conflagrationist!" Kavuu was shouting in Caymus's ear now. "You listen to me now. You must hold on to the flame, accept it as part of you, love it as you would your heart's desire, or you will not survive this day!"

Caymus struggled to keep fear and panic out of his thoughts, fought to keep his emotions in check. He understood what the chieftain was trying to tell him. He had called the fire to him by accepting it into himself. The only way to prevent it from killing him was to make that acceptance complete and unconditional.

He let the power into his heart, let it burn its way through his body. He could feel the flames underneath his flesh as intensely as he could feel them licking at his skin. The Lords of the Conflagration had tested him in a similar fashion; this was less painful than his trial had been, and yet it was somehow much more frightening. Still, he didn't fight, didn't flinch from the sensation. After more time than he could bear, he began to relax, to allow the energy to become a part of him.

"Good," Kavuu said, his voice now a great deal calmer. "Now," he continued, the sound barely more than a whisper, "let it go."

Caymus didn't quite know what Kavuu had meant by that, but he made an attempt, regardless. With slow, gentle countenance, he attempted to disengage himself from the flames, not so much letting the power go as decreasing his desire for it and allowing it to leave of its own accord.

The result came sooner than he'd expected. Without preamble or fanfare, the power of the sun quietly shifted from his body and drifted back to the tree behind him.

He felt his entire body sag with relief. He opened his eyes. The sky was still dark, but there was no longer any glowing fire consuming him. He smiled with the thought of what had just happened, then he noticed Kavuu standing just to his left, his big arms folded across his huge chest, a wide grin on his face.

Without even thinking about the consequences, Caymus jumped up and gave the man an enormous hug, laughing joyously all the while. If Kavuu was surprised by the sudden outburst, he didn't show it. He slapped Caymus on the back a few times, then held him out at arm's length.

"You did well," he said, his eyes glowing with pride.

"That was it, then?" Caymus said, excited, but not quite able to keep the reverence out of his voice. "That was the Unburning?"

"It was," Kavuu said, disengaging. "You controlled yourself well. Most spend more than a single day on the Watchman's brow." He looked down at the village below. "Some never succeed in calling the flames. Some call it, but are then unable to keep it from consuming them." He looked back at Caymus and clapped him on the shoulder. "You did both. I understand what your Master Be'Var sees in you."

Caymus thought about Be'Var, thought about how he would enjoy telling the old man about this. "I hope he gets to meet you, someday."

"That would be good," Kavuu said, grinning. "Come," he said, grabbing Caymus's shoulder and spinning him around, "we must return."

The trip back down the slope of the Watchman didn't seem to Caymus to take as long as had the trip up. His mind was dancing, his heart soaring. He was so consumed by what he had just learned that before he knew it the minutes had flown by and he was back among the huts of the village.

He was among Terrek's people too, and each face he saw split into a wide grin when it saw him passing. Every one of them then covered his or her eyes with one hand, then reached out to touch his arm or slap his shoulder. By the time the two men had arrived at a central area of the village, where stone blocks and benches sat arrayed in circles, they must have met a good three dozen people, each of whom repeated the same gesture.

"Kavuu," Caymus said, after two teenage boys had made deliberate efforts to touch him, "I don't understand why they cover their eyes."

"It is our custom," Kavuu said, leaning over and speaking softly, "I believe your people shake hands when they meet, yes? For a man to cover his eyes when he meets you means that you are trusted, that he feels he can take his gaze from you while you stand a sword's length away."

Caymus nodded. He liked the idea. "I thought I saw Tavrin touch his chest too," he said. "Why don't they do that?"

Kavuu laughed aloud. "To touch one's heart means that we are of one people, one heart, that we share the same blood." He arched an eyebrow at Caymus. "Everyone saw the spectacle of your Unburning this night, and so they all know that you are trusted among us, but you are a very long way from being one of us."

When they reached the gathering place, a few dozen people were there. Mostly, they were young men and women, though a few children played in the shadows, too. A few of the oil-filled bowls shed light here and there, but there was no central fire pit. What, indeed, was there to burn around here?

He smiled when he saw Gwenna and Tavrin approach him, walking hand in hand. Tavrin's smile wasn't as wide or as toothy as those of the other Falaar Caymus had encountered, but he seemed genuinely happy to see him. Caymus reflected the smile, and when Tavrin reached up and covered his eyes, he reflected the gesture.

He was about to do the same with Gwenna, but she beat him to the punch by throwing her arms around him in a tight hug. "I knew you'd do it," she whispered in his ear. Caymus gave her a quick squeeze in return before she pulled back to hold Tavrin's hand again. "He wasn't sure you'd be able to on the first night," she said, grinning and tilting her head at Tavrin, "but I told him, 'Oh, you don't know Caymus!'"

"I am glad to be mistaken," Tavrin said, glancing at Gwenna before taking Caymus's hand in a firm shake.

Caymus suddenly felt a real sense of belonging, of kinship, and it made him glad. Beyond what he'd just accomplished at the top of the cliff face, he felt surrounded by friends who cared about him and whom he cared about.

"Thanks," he said, "both of you." He shook his head in wonder and looked up at the Watchman. "I suppose it must have been quite a sight."

"You lit the whole village!" Gwenna said. "Somebody could have seen you miles away!" She dropped her voice a little and looked around, secretively. "You don't want to tell me how you did that, do you?"

They all laughed, including her, at the joke, and she stepped back towards Tavrin, who put his arm around her. Caymus had never seen her look so happy. It was only then that he noticed that she was dressed completely as one of the Falaar now, that she even had a barak stick in her belt. They hadn't been there long enough for her to have come to need these clothes; she was making a conscious effort to blend in.

He didn't take long to realize the significance of it: Gwenna wasn't planning on returning to Kepren with them.

He discovered that he was incredibly happy for his friend, but also sad for himself. He wondered if he'd ever see her again.

"Nice trick."

Caymus turned to see Milo and Elon walking up behind him. He was about to offer his thanks when he noticed the worried, haggard look on Milo's face. Seeing Milo in anything less than the most carefree of spirits could only mean trouble.

"Milo?" said Gwenna before Caymus could speak, concern etched into her voice. "What's happened? Are you alright?"

"It didn't work, did it?" Kavuu said, "this speaking you have been doing."

Milo looked at each of them in turn. "No, it worked fine," he exhaled, sharing a look with Elon. Elon, who was about fifteen years old, was slowly shrinking away from the conversation as though he didn't want to be noticed. Milo looked to Caymus, "But I'm afraid we have to go," he said. "Now."

"Nonsense!" said Kavuu, spreading out his arms. "This man has taken the Unburning upon himself this night. There must be celebration for it."

Milo shook his head. "I'm sorry," he said, "but there's no time. We have to go tonight."

"What is it, Milo?" Caymus said.

Milo looked over his shoulder. "I finished speaking the place nearly an hour ago," he said, then he turned back to the group. "Only moments after I whispered Terrek to my friends, the message came through." He looked directly at Caymus, and the corner of his lip turned up in an apologetic smile.

"Black Moon is on the move," he said. "They're about to cross the Greatstones."

Chapter 16

"You're sure you know what you're doing?"

Rill gave his fellow engineer a withering look, then set back to the task at hand. Daniel had asked him that very question at least half a dozen times in the last hour, and it was getting a bit grating. Why did people always ask him that? "Could you let a bit more light in here?" he replied, finally.

Daniel sighed, stepped over to the Gearhouse's single, small window, and opened the shutters wide. Sunlight streamed in, revealing the various piles of mechanical debris strewn that made this place look less like a military building and more like a large, unkempt shack.

Barrels stood in disorganized rows around the walls of the Gearhouse. Some of the barrels were filled with screws and bolts of various design; some contained more chemically oriented materials like iron filings or graysilt; and still others were empty, tossed gracelessly into a huge pile in one corner. Also arrayed around the edges of the building were groupings of springs, small piles of wood or sawdust, hand tools, rods, and dowels. There was even a giant gear sitting on top of one plain-looking crate; Rill had wondered on other days whether it might be the building's namesake.

In the center of the Gearhouse, covered with various small boxes, glass containers, grinding stones, and several types of tools, stood a long workbench that stretched the entire length of the room. The bench was crafted of sections of granite, hardwood, and even glass, the idea being that not all chemicals reacted well with a standard wooden table, and so options were required in the experimentation area.

Rill had been sitting at the workbench for two hours. He was using one of the glass jars, stirring the liquid contents inside it with a thin, wooden rod. He'd had some concerns, initially, that the rod might not agree very well with the process he was trying to sustain. In the end, however, he hadn't been able to come up with any better solutions.

"How's that?" said Daniel.

"It'll do," said Rill.

"You sure?" said Daniel. "I mean I could knock a couple of holes in the wall if that would make it any easier."

Rill rolled his eyes and smiled. He knew that the young man, who'd gotten him accepted into the Corps of Royal Engineers two months ago, and who'd since become a fast friend and helpful co-conspirator, wasn't actually in any way upset about his little project. Rather, he was just a little bit concerned about the possible consequences, should it not go well. "It's fine, Daniel," Rill said. "Thank you."

"Sure." Daniel stepped back to the workbench and leaned on it with his elbows, watching Rill as he stirred. "No smoke yet," he said. "That's got to be a good sign, right?"

Rill shook his head. "Not sure," he said. "I think I mixed it too quickly last time." He revisited the problem in his head again as he stirred the jar's components. "I also think we tried to make too much at once, like the ingredients have to mix slowly for some reason."

Rill wished he could be sure about any of it, as he needed to understand what was happening. He was glad there was no smoke yet, though. He'd bungled this same process the previous day: he'd combined these same ingredients and the entire batch had suddenly burned away, leaving black smoke to billow out of the jar and fill the Gearhouse with darkness and soot. The fact that nobody important had caught wind of that particular result had been a small miracle—one which didn't seem likely to happen again—so the idea of the same smoke not making a repeat appearance today was foremost in both of their minds.

"Well," Daniel said, offering a distracted shrug and a sigh, "don't mix it too slowly." He looked in the direction of the yard. "They're going to call drills any minute now."

Rill kept his thoughts about getting got drills on time to himself, party to aid in his own concentration, but mostly so as not to upset Daniel. The Gearhouse, once used for the completion of large and secret royal projects, was mostly a storage area these days. Some private experimentation was still allowed, however, so if the captain could be convinced that the experimenter wasn't likely to actually blow up or set fire to anything, the more experienced professionals were occasionally allowed access to this building and its materials. Daniel's constant recommendations were the reason that Rill, a neophyte engineer, had been given that particular access, and so he owned the guy a lot. Yes, Daniel could be a bit of a worry-wort about punctuality and following the rules, but with all the help he'd volunteered in the last few weeks, Rill was quite happy to let a bit of worrying go.

Even though the two were both royal engineers in the same corps, learning the same lessons from the same lieutenants, their styles were quite different. Daniel was more concerned with procedures and "doing things properly" than Rill was. He wore his uniform nearly all the time, taking it off only to have it washed. Rill rarely walked around in more than his blue trousers and an undershirt. At that moment, he wasn't even wearing his boots, having left them by the door.

Rill pulled the rod out of the jar and examined the consistency of the black goop that clung to its surface. With some frustration, he noted the various flecks of graysilt still present in the mixture. He sighed again. He'd need to add some more of the new substance if he wanted the stuff to burn properly.

"Another couple ounces of the white stuff?" he said.

As Daniel reached out for another jar and measured out a small amount of the white, pasty material, Rill considered all the effort he'd put into this project already, hoping that it wouldn't all turn out to have been wasted time.

He'd had the idea on the very first day he'd joined the Royal Engineers. Daniel had been walking him around the courtyard that the corps used for a lot of their day-to-day activity, pointing out the workings of a half-dozen or so catapults they'd had lined up against the outer wall. Rill had been particularly curious about the barrels of graysilt that were housed in a locked shed nearby. Daniel had explained that adding some graysilt into the cup of a catapult and lighting it at the moment the machine launched its projectile created the impression of a weapon that launched balls of flame instead of boulders, especially during a siege at night. The effect was just an illusion, but the sight of it could be highly demoralizing to an enemy.

At the time, Rill had asked why they didn't just cover the balls themselves with the quick-burning powder, or something very like it, and hurl *actual* fireballs at their target. Daniel had told him that the graysilt burned too fast, and that it would be impossible to stick it to the projectiles anyway.

A couple of weeks later, when he'd been receiving his formal training in the uses of graysilt as a demolition tool—mostly it was used in the quarrying process for splitting large stones into smaller ones—Rill had realized a connection between what the engineers were teaching him and the lessons he'd attended at the Temple of the Conflagration for so many years.

In that moment, Rill had realized that he held in a unique position within the Royal Engineers, having been instructed, at least partially, as a priest of fire before being subsequently trained as an engineer. He recognized the constituents of graysilt: coal, sulfur, and saltpeter. All three were earth-heavy substances that also contained vast amounts of fire within them. He could use those materials to create the substance he wanted: something that could sustain a flame, but which could also stick to a projectile. He already had earth and fire; what he needed to do was find a way to add the water element to the mixture.

The water material would likely need to contain at least some of the fire element also, else it would simply douse the flame. This, it had turned out, was the most difficult thing about the entire process: fire and water were generally at odds with each other, not combining well except under very specific circumstances.

He'd spent the month since then experimenting with different mixtures of various materials. He'd tried lamp oil at first, believing that such an obvious mixture of fire and water would be ideal for his needs, and had spent many afternoons, here in the Gearhouse, trying to make the substance fit the mixture. Some of his results wouldn't ignite at all; others burned away too quickly.

In the end, he'd decided that lamp oil wasn't going to be his perfect ingredient, at least not on its own. The problem seemed to be that the flecks of graysilt never quite dissolved in the oil, and that left a layer of explosive material at the bottom of the mixture. He'd needed to find a way of homogenizing the material somehow, and the hours he'd spent searching the shelves of alchemists and herbalists hadn't gotten him anywhere.

Ten days ago, however, he'd happened upon a possible solution while walking past the furnaces at the northern edge of the city where a handful of small smelters turned coal into coke. The process was a relatively new one, and it was an important step in the production of the hard-iron weapons that were becoming more common by the day. Rill had been learning about smelting when one of the furnace workers had introduced him to a by-product of their coking process: a white substance he'd called naphthalene. They'd been collecting the stuff over several months of production, but they hadn't been sure what to do with it.

Rill had taken some naphthalene back to the Gearhouse, where he'd quickly discovered that the white substance was exactly what he'd been looking for: it broke up the specks of graysilt better than anything else he'd come across. The material wasn't particularly viscous, and so some oil had still been needed in order to add enough of the water element, but he was becoming increasingly certain that he was on the right track.

"Here you go," Daniel said, handing Rill the small spoon containing the naphthalene. He held it back a little when Rill reached out for it. "Try to remember," he said, "that we don't exactly have unlimited quantities of this stuff."

Rill nodded. Daniel was right. The coke workers had collected two small barrels of naphthalene altogether; his experiments had already consumed about a tenth of the total. He took the spoon and slowly introduced its contents into the jar, first scraping a little bit from the spoon onto the stirring stick, and only then adding it to the mixture.

"Any idea how long we actually have?" he said, as he stirred the last remnants of the spoonful into the jar.

Daniel shook his head. "I have to admit, I kind of lose track of time in here."

"I know what you mean," said Rill, grinning at him. "It's great, isn't it?"

Daniel smiled. "It is, rather."

Rill held the stirring rod up to inspect it. He had to hold the jar close underneath it, as the stuff really wanted to ooze off of the piece of wood and onto the table. He was delighted to find, however, that he'd achieved his goal: the flecks of graysilt no longer showed up in the mixture.

He looked at Daniel, trying to make himself appear slightly mad. "It's time," he said, with a wicked grin.

Daniel reached out behind him and picked up a large piece of scrap iron about half an inch thick, which he then placed on the workbench. Rill took the jar and spread his new concoction over it. The stuff had the consistency of molasses on a hot day, and so it was easy to cover the plate without having any drip over the sides onto the wooden surface of the bench.

"If you don't mind," Daniel said, edging toward the door, "I'm going to watch from over here."

Rill was about to say something sarcastic, but then he shrugged and decided not to. In the end, he couldn't really blame his friend for being overly cautious, especially considering the mess they'd made the last time he'd tried this. There were still smoke stains across most of the ceiling of the Gearhouse, after all.

Reaching into a pocket, he produced his flint-stick: a small contraption, about the size of his thumb, which held a piece of flint against a wheel of pitted metal. He held the flint-stick with one hand while he spun the wheel with the heel of the other palm. He used the resultant sparks to light a small oil lamp: Rill had learned early on that sparks weren't enough to light the mixture, that a steady flame was needed in order to get a reaction.

Slowly, being careful not to spill any oil from the lamp, Rill edged the small flame towards the metal plate. He nearly laughed aloud when eh realized he was moving turning his face away as he did so.

After he'd held the flame steady against the mixture for a couple of moments, the entire plate sputtered into a steady fire. Rill took a couple of steps back and blew out the lamp in his hand.

He was surprised. He'd been expecting a slightly more explosive, or at least intense, reaction but the metal plate was burning quite peacefully, a tiny plane of fire lazily floating about an inch off its surface.

"Did you do it?" Rill turned to see Daniel, who was standing behind him and looking at the fire over his shoulder, seeming just as uncertain and skeptical about the result as he was.

"I think so?" Rill said, taking a couple of steps forward.

When he got within a foot of the plate, he suddenly encountered an intense heat. Shielding his face from it, he quickly stepped back again.

"What's wrong?" Daniel asked.

"It's hot!" Rill exclaimed, looking briefly over his shoulder. "*Really* hot."

Daniel stepped up beside Rill and reached out toward the workbench. He quickly pulled the hand back again, inspecting his fingers as though they might not be there anymore. "How can it not have burned out yet?" he said. "If it's burning *that* hot, surely it would have used up all the fire element by now, right?"

Rill had thought the same thing, but apparently there was something more going on here. Somehow, the flames were putting off this incredible heat and yet, at the same time, were also burning at such a low intensity that they lingered, not putting themselves out.

Was it the naphthalene? Did the stuff have *that* much fire element in it?

His face broke into a huge smile. Whatever the reason, it was exactly what he needed.

At that moment, the assembly horn called out, announcing that it was time for the day's martial training.

"Flames," Rill swore under his breath. "Come on," he said, "let's put this out and get out there."

Daniel nodded and the two of them bent down under a nearby shelf to pick up what was essentially an over-sized, elongated pot. It was made of cast iron and it was designed to be placed over the metal plate so that it could snuff out anything flammable upon it.

Despite some hesitation about getting too close to the heat again, they quickly got the pot flipped upside-down and placed over the plate.

The horn blew again, its bright assembly call grating on Rill's nerves. He pulled on his boots and coat while they waited the requisite time for the flames to extinguish. They shared a frustrated look; they were probably going to be late again.

As Rill finished tying his boot lace, Daniel picked up one edge of the flame-douser to check that the fire had, in fact, gone out entirely. "Oh my," he said, and he pulled the pot completely off the plate.

"What is it?" Rill said.

"Come and see," Daniel replied, pointing at the plate.

Rill stood and followed Daniel's finger. He gasped. There was little to no sign of the oil mixture they'd just been burning, but the plate, a thing made of cast iron, had little ruts and grooves etched into its surface where the metal had actually melted. Indeed, there was one spot, off toward one corner of the plate, where it seemed the mixture had stood a chance of actually burning completely through it.

Rill, his eyes wide in surprise, looked at Daniel, whose own expression was a mix of shock and horror. Before either could say anything about it, however, Daniel turned and was suddenly running out the Gearhouse's door. Rill didn't hesitate; he followed close at his friend's heels. Engineers were given five minutes to assemble after the first horn was blown, and he figured they had about a minute left. Poor Daniel. He'd never been the type to get in trouble before Rill showed up.

Rill didn't like drilling. He understood that as a member of Kepren's army each of the Royal Engineers was also a soldier, and that soldiers needed time to practice the fine art of butchering people, but he felt that there was far too much emphasis placed on swordsmanship for people whose primary responsibilities were keeping the engines of war functioning properly during a battle.

"Can't they let it go for just one day?" Rill panted, catching up to Daniel. "Don't engineers have other things to think about?"

"The captain wouldn't drill us if it wasn't necessary," Daniel replied between breaths. He gave Rill a sidelong glance. "Anyway," he said, "if those glazed looks of yours are any indication, I'd say you spend just as much time thinking about the machines during drills as you do any other time of day."

Rill had to admit his friend was right. He'd found, lately, that it didn't matter what he was doing, his mind was always working out some kind of problem.

He did wonder if perhaps Daniel had a bit too much blind faith in the way things worked around here. The orange-haired man was a few years older than Rill, and was clearly a talented engineer, but Rill always thought he was just a little bit too dedicated to the status quo, never quite willing enough to make his own decisions, to come to his own conclusions about things.

He also thought the lieutenants may have felt the same way. Daniel had been a member of the Royal Engineers for a year and a half, but he'd only risen to the rank of second-stationer. Rill had attained the same rank in a single month.

He wondered if the net effect the two of them were having on each other was positive or negative.

As they rounded the corner of the inner keep wall, they entered the marshaling yard, where most of the corps was already lined up in preparation for drills.

They were passing the space where most of the catapults were kept when not in use, and Rill kept an eye out for the broken one. He'd heard that one of the engines had been rendered inoperable overnight; a rumor was going around that there might be a saboteur operating in the city, possibly within the Keep itself.

His eyes went wide when he saw what had happened: the throwing arm of the number two catapult was on the ground, having been completely sawn through! He was amazed. How somebody could have done that kind of damage, could have spent that much time sawing at a piece of foot-thick wood, and not been caught was beyond his ability to understand.

That was it, then: there was no other explanation for something like that; a saboteur was operating inside Kepren. And he'd thought the corps had challenges enough already.

He wondered what the captain would do with the saboteur once he was eventually found. There had been rumors of things going missing over the last few weeks, but a destroyed catapult was another thing entirely. Mere theft was a crime; sabotage was either an act of war or treason. Both offenses, Rill knew, were usually solved with the hangman's noose.

Just as the final horn was blowing, announcing that anybody who hadn't reported already was officially late, Rill and Daniel skidded into place in one of the two dozen lines of men and women. Knowing they were likely under scrutiny, both immediately came to attention and awaited their orders.

The lines of engineers fanned out from a common center. In that center, standing atop a large, granite stone, stood Captain Draya, his eyes taking in the people under his care. Rill inhaled sharply when he saw the captain's eyes flit briefly in his direction, acknowledging his arrival, though not chastising it.

Draya was a tall, stout man in his late thirties or early forties with short-cropped, brown hair and eyes that saw everything. By all reports, he was an incredible engineer: a prodigy, even. There was a story that the veteran engineers liked to tell the new recruits about how the man single-handedly rebuilt the big clock in the Reed District, which had previously been broken for decades. He'd done it without permission from the Duke or even the local alderman. He'd spent two months fabricating the gears, springs, and other parts he'd known he would need for the repair, then he'd simply scurried up the tower with a sack over his shoulder one night and, by morning the following day, had the clock keeping perfect time again. Also, he'd been nine years old at the time.

Rill didn't fell as though he'd figured the man out yet. The only time he'd actually met his captain was when he'd initially been up for consideration as a Royal Engineer, and that meeting had lasted less than a minute. Draya had looked him up and down and asked him why he wanted to be an engineer.

"I think I would be good at it," Rill had said.

It seemed to have been a good answer, as evidenced by the fact that Rill was standing there, awaiting the man's orders.

He appreciated the man's style of leadership, at least. He didn't shout and he didn't scold. Even in that moment, Draya's eyes looked over the gathered crowd before him, but they didn't seem to be looking for any fault with which to take issue. Rather, they wore the same look that had graced the faces of many fathers when they'd dropped their boys off at the Temple. The look was stern, yet it was also awash with concern for the wellbeing of his engineers.

Rill could extremely glad that his captain seemed to take a genuine interest in the welfare of the people he commanded. Too many of the lieutenants clearly didn't share the same point of view.

"I wanted to personally thank you all for being here," Draya said. He didn't raise his voice, yet Rill could hear him easily, even from his position in the back. "I don't believe I need to tell you how important the coming days are." His eyes scanned the faces before him as though he was looking for something. "I know many of you have work to get back to," he continued, "and make no mistake: that work is going to help every member of this company, every member of the king's army, and every single person in this city. Nobody else can do the things that the men and women before me can do. Don't think for a moment I don't know that.

"I also know," he continued, "that there is some resistance to the drills we do every day, that many of you think such things are unimportant to people whose primary asset is intellect."

Rill held his breath for a moment. Flames, had Draya read his mind or something?

Draya nodded. "For the most part, I agree with you, but take a moment to consider what happens if our enemy breaches the gates."

He paused then, and so Rill considered. He was surprised to realize he'd never actually thought about that before. To him, the gates were an impregnable barrier, a bulwark against invasion: if the gates fell, then Kepren fell, simple as that.

But that wasn't really true, was it? If whatever this Black Moon Army was were to actually break through, say, the North Gate…well, there would be fighting in the streets, wouldn't there? The army's soldiers couldn't effectively form lines in the city, so it might actually be every citizen for him or herself. Flames, that sounded terrible.

"Now," said Draya, "I want you to look at the man or woman to your left, then at the man or woman to your right."

Rill did. He knew the man to his left, who was in his mid-twenties, was named Edmun and that he'd just come back from a week's leave because his wife had just given birth to their second child. The woman to his right was named Scia. She was about forty years old and was generally assumed to be next in line for the position of quartermaster in a year or two. The three nodded recognition when they made eye contact, as did everybody else.

"Imagine," continued Draya, "that the three of you are on the same catapult team. You're firing on a ballista that's positioned just outside the wall and that has been firing into the city for the past ten minutes. Imagine that you've finally got the range locked in and you're about to fire, but then an enemy soldier finds you and runs at you with a sword."

Rill took a deep breath, now understanding what his captain was trying to say.

"There are two general outcomes," said Draya, gazing around at his people, "to such a scenario. In the first, the attacker cuts you all down or chases you from your engine, the shot is interrupted, and the ballista goes on to kill five or six hundred more people throughout the course of the battle. In the second, one of you charges to meet the attacker—because in this scenario you all know how to fight hand-to-hand—while the other two take the shot. You might not win the day, but you protect each other —you keep one another alive—and you get to keep doing your jobs as long as possible."

Rill looked at Edmun and Scia again, imagined the two of them dying because he didn't know how to fight. Flames, Edmun *just* had a child! He didn't like that thought. It gnawed at something deep within him.

"I think," said Draya, turning around to take everybody in, "you all get the idea. I hope that will be the end of the grumbling about physical training. You can go back to your important work shortly. For now, though, we will drill as though our lives depended on it. Because, for all you know, they might. Yes?"

"Yes!" they all shouted in response.

Draya nodded. "Good," he said. "I thank you."

He turned to one of the lieutenants at his side—Rill didn't know her name—and nodded. The lieutenant was a tall woman, not to mention rail thin, but her voice was strong as she replaced the captain on the stone and yelled out, "Alright, everyone, get your swords! Pair off! You know what to do!"

In front of each of the lines of men and women were barrels full of short swords. The orderly columns became queues as engineers, one by one, armed themselves, found a partner, and grabbed a space in the marshaling yard to practice their sword-work.

By the time he'd grabbed a sword and was walking off with Daniel to a spot near the inner wall of the yard, Rill's mind had begun wandering. He was thinking about Caymus, about the last time the two of them had done this very same thing. He'd been using a longsword and shield back then and so the movements were quite different, but the feeling was the same: parry, thrust, block, retreat, advance...repeat.

Caymus had seemed so different after he'd awakened from his long slumber. All the time he'd been asleep, Rill had been so afraid that he was going to lose his friend forever. Then, when Caymus had finally awakened, he'd had that stern, faraway look in his eyes and that voice that seemed to come from such a great distance. Caymus seemed older now, sadder, as though burdened with some great heaviness. Rill didn't understand what had happened, but he'd thought at the time that his worst fears had come true.

Be'Var had suggested that Rill give his friend some time, that Caymus was shouldering some big changes and immense responsibility. Given time to assess his new situation and to adapt, some of his old self should start showing through again.

Rill hoped that was true. He'd been so eager to tell Caymus about the engineering corps when he'd arrived at Flamehearth, but when he'd seen his friend's face, the eagerness had evaporated and left in its place concern and worry.

Caymus hadn't wanted to talk to him about what had happened to him, what he'd been through while he slept. "I'll tell you eventually, Rill," he'd said with those faraway eyes, "just as soon as I figure it all out for myself."

That, at least, had sounded like the Caymus he knew.

Rill was suddenly shocked out of his memories with a smack from the flat of a sword against the top of his head.

"Hey," Daniel said, "pay attention, will you?"

Rill was about to protest the rather stark reminder, but he knew Daniel was right. He hadn't been hit all that hard, but he rubbed his head anyway and he gave Daniel a sheepish look. "Sorry."

Daniel acknowledged with a slight tilt of his head, so Rill brought his sword up and continued the drill, thrusting forward three times while Daniel parried.

"What was it this time, anyway?" Daniel asked, parroting the same thrusts back at Rill.

"That friend of mine," Rill said, parrying the thrusts. "Caymus. He spent a long—months, I mean—time unconscious after being nearly killed by someone we really shouldn't have trusted." After the third parry, Rill stepped forward with three slashes, aimed low, middle, then high.

"Funny you should mention him," Daniel said, blocking each swing with one of his own. "I heard one of the lancers the other day talking about someone called 'The Sleeping Giant'. I didn't catch most of what they said, but it sounded like he was supposed to save the day or something when woke up. It was like a fairy tale, but do you think they could have been talking about your friend?"

Rill had heard someone mention that name in passing, too, though he'd never made the connection before. "Huh," he said, unsure what to think of it, "well, he's something like seven feet tall, so yeah, I guess that's possible."

"How long has he been asleep now?" Daniel said, repeating the same three slashes.

"It was a little more than three months," Rill said, performing the requisite blocks, "but he's awake now."

"Really?" said Daniel, taking a moment to brace himself for the next attacks. "The giant awakens, huh? Good for him."

"Yeah," Rill said, stealing a quick moment between drills. "I'm a little worried about him. I don't think he's totally back with us yet. I went to the mission to say hi yesterday, and I found out he's just left the city on some mission or other. I don't even know why."

He prepared for the next drill, which involved three overhead swings which Daniel was meant to dodge or side-step. Instead, he was interrupted by the piercing sound of the yard-master's whistle alerting them that sword drills were over.

Rill was surprised to hear the whistle. It meant they'd been drilling for a full twenty minutes; it had seemed more like five. The first time he'd drilled like this, his arm had been so sore he'd though it might actually fall off. It all seemed so easy now, so effortless. He supposed that meant that the drills were actually paying off, and that even if he never became a better swordsman, he was at least building up some strength and stamina.

The pairs melded back into a single group. Each engineer deposited his or her sword into the same barrels from whence they'd come, then they started running, following a circuit that took them up the stairs of the wall of the Keep, across several dozen yards of rampart, then down another set of stairs. This second section of the training would last another twenty minutes, after which they would work on hand-to-hand combat for a final twenty.

As he made his way around the circuit, Rill marveled at how light and springy his legs felt. He'd run this path several times a day, every day, for over a month now, and he was beginning to realize how fit these drills were making him. When he'd first begun this daily training, he'd barely been able to breathe after one ascent up the wall. Now, he found that he was effortlessly passing others. It was a great feeling.

He remembered how much Milo seemed to like to run; did he feel like this all the time? Rill smiled to himself. He was actually looking forward to the next twenty minutes.

Before he'd made a complete circuit, however, the horn blew, causing a great deal of consternation among the runners: the whistle should have marked the switch back to combat, not the horn. When he looked down to the yard again, he saw that the lieutenants were waving everyone to come back to the assembly area and that Draya was, once again, standing on the stone.

Rill nearly gasped in surprise when he saw that the captain was leaning down so that somebody could speak into his ear, and that the somebody was the prince!

Rill was among the first to arrive back at the stone, and so he took a spot near the head of one of the columns, stood to attention, and waiting for one of the men to speak. By the time the rest of the company had assembled, however, the prince had finished saying whatever it was he'd had to say and was striding away.

The lieutenants nodded to their captain, signaling that the entire company was present. Draya nodded, then simply looked quietly out over the assembly for a long moment. At this distance, Rill could discern the look of unease on the man's face. Rill felt his pulse quicken at that. That the corps had been called in after the prince had spoken to the captain was cause for concern; that something could actually make Captain Draya uneasy was actually alarming

He was relieved, then, when the faintest smile touched the captain's face. "I think it was less than half an hour ago that I told you all how important the coming days are going to be," he said. The smile faded. "It seems they're going to be even more important than we thought. I've just been informed that Black Moon has been spotted at the Greatstones. They're going through, not around."

Rill could actually hear the silence that erupted. His ears had expected that such news should be met with cries of anguish or nervous whispers but, of course, Draya's engineers were too well-trained for that.

The silence, however, was still as nerve-wracking as any scream. Rill felt a chill rise up his spine as he just stood there, waiting.

"The sighting took place this morning, at the northern edge of the range," Draya continued, "which means that they are either about to cross the mountains or that they're doing so already."

Rill quickly did the math in his head. He didn't know what Black Moon's composition was like, but if any of it at all was infantry, it meant they could do a maximum of forty miles per day. Taking into account the breadth of the Greatstones—they had to be traveling through Falmoor's Pass, didn't they?—and the remaining distance from the Greatstones to Kepren, they would be knocking at the gates, at the earliest, in about a week.

"There is already some snow in the pass," said Draya, "which will slow them, but be certain that they will be here in, at the most, ten days." He raised an eyebrow at the gathered crowd. "We, however, are the king's engineers, and we do not assume incompetence in our adversary. We will assume it will take them five."

Five days. Rill wondered just how ready they could be. His mind was drawn back to the supposed saboteur in their midst. How much damage would such a person do to their preparations?

"It seems that those who like to grumble about drills," Draya said, the smile returning to his lips, "are in luck. Drills are canceled for today and for the remainder of the time between now and the day Black Moon arrives at our doorstep. You all know your jobs; you all know the preparation you must do. I will let you get to it. Dismissed!"

With that, the entire company came alive in a flurry of activity. Lieutenants barked orders, people shouted to each other, and men and women of all ranks ran this way and that, all seeing to their respective tasks.

Only Rill stood still amid the sea of movement. He was watching Draya, who was still standing on the stone watching his engineers tend to their work. He tried to get the full measure of the man. He had something he needed to say to his captain, but he didn't know if the man would listen to him.

"Come on, Rill," Daniel had his hand on Rill's shoulder, "they need us to help on the chain squad."

Rill didn't hear his friend. His attention was focused on the man before him and on the decision he had to make. He supposed he could try bringing his thoughts to one of the lieutenants, but he was certain that the two officers whom he actually knew wouldn't spare him even a moment's thought. He suspected, hoped, that Draya might.

"Rill?" Daniel's voice carried concern and irritation in equal parts as Rill stepped away from him and the hand slid from his shoulder.

A lump had risen in Rill's throat and was now so large that it was beginning to choke him. He could physically feel the pulse of blood through his veins, his heart was beating so fiercely. He thought about everything he knew about the krealites, about what he'd experienced himself and about what Caymus and Be'Var had told him. Fire had a hard time burning through the krealites' chitinous exteriors, but a flame of sufficient magnitude, one that could burn through solid rock, could hurt them. Of sufficient magnitude…

He knew there was no reason for anyone to listen to a newly minted second-station engineer's ideas, but this was too important to keep to himself just because he was afraid of being reprimanded. In his center,

Rill had the sudden feeling that he might be experiencing the single most important moment of his life. He hoped Draya was the kind of man he thought he was.

When he reached the stone, the captain noticed him and turned to look down. His eyes narrowed for a moment, then opened again. "Rill, isn't it?" he finally said.

"Yes, Sir," Rill said. He was surprised at how steady his voice sounded. He hoped it stayed that way. This wasn't just about his pride; people's lives could very well depend on what he said in the next few seconds.

Much to his relief, Draya's mouth turned up in an easy smile, though he did raise his eyebrows in small admission of surprise. "What can I do for you, then, Engineer Rill?"

Engineer Rill. He never got tired of hearing that. "If you get a chance today, Sir…if you can spare a few moments at some point, there's something in the Gearhouse that I think you need to see."

Lieutenant Bakkat, a thick-necked bulldog of a man with no sense of humor, stepped forward and grabbed Rill by the shoulder. "Get out of it!" the man said. "The captain ain't got time fer your rubbish. Ain't you just heard there's an army coming at us?"

Before the big man could drag Rill away, however, Draya raised a hand. "Wait a moment, Bakkat." When the lieutenant stopped and turned to face his captain, Draya narrowed his eyes again. "Engineer Rill, would this have anything to do with the naphthalene that Engineer Daniel received from the foundries this week?"

Rill supposed he shouldn't have been surprised. One of the constants regarding Draya was that the man did, in fact, seem to know everything that happened in his corps. "Yes, Sir," he said, "exactly that."

Draya nodded his head and stepped down off the chunk of granite. "I suppose you'd better show me what you've done, then. Come," he said, taking Rill by the elbow and spinning him, "we'll go right now."

~~~

The only thing that Be'Var really couldn't stand about hospitals was the smell.

This, however, was no hospital. It was, at best, a makeshift infirmary set up in a building that, as far as he could tell, hadn't been used in years. The smell was getting worse, though. Besides the usual olfactory awfulness that came with pus, blood, and everything else that came out of a person, a fair number of people were concealing injuries, and some of those wounds were beginning to fester.

There were so many of them. The people of Kepren were no
~~~

strangers to taking care of those whose homes had been lost: the exodus of the Laivusians had seen to that a hundred years ago. The news that the Black Moon Army had been sighted at the northern edge of the Greatstones, however, had heralded a sudden, massive influx of the tired, the weak, the sick, and the wounded, and those who knew how to treat them were reaching their capacity.

Be'Var imagined that in the last day over a thousand of them had filtered into the city, and small areas like this—disused warehouses, abandoned homes, and any other spaces where there was room—had been set up as infirmaries at the northern edges of the Guard District to try to cope with them all. The old blacksmith, healer, and master of the Order of the Conflagration had offered his services in two of the huge clusters of tents so far, but he was barely making a dent in the need for aid, and there were at least two other camps like this that he hadn't been able to get to yet.

These people had endured such hardship. Each and every one of them was from a city or village to the north of the Greatstones, and so each and every one had needed to cross the mountain range to get here. Falmoor's Pass, the only direct route when crossing from north to south at that longitude, was long and treacherous, even in the summer; now that winter was baring its teeth, the snows were beginning to fall, and snow made everything worse.

The refugees wouldn't talk to him about the pass, but he had overheard enough conversations to know that scores of frozen bodies now littered the Greatstones.

Not that the weather was behaving predictably, of course. There still hadn't been a hint of rain in Kepren in all the time he'd been here. The last time he'd seen precipitation of any sort was during that huge blizzard he'd run into when they'd crossed the mountains all those months ago, and he didn't imagine the Greatstones had seen much more weather than that since. Even the temperature wasn't right: autumn had been and gone, so why wasn't it colder?

Be'Var, who had been treating patients all morning, stopped for a moment on his rounds to examine his surroundings. He suspected the building he was in had probably started life as an old guard post. The rotting sections of wood against the stone walls looked as though they had probably once kept arrays of swords and polearms. At least the walls seemed to be in no immediate danger of crumbling away.

Getting back to work, he crouched down next to a man who'd propped himself up against one of those walls, right underneath an old, dusty shelf. He quickly passed his healer's eye over him, assessing his patient's condition.

The man seemed to be in about his mid-forties. He was thin, though not dangerously so, and would probably be tall were he to stand up. His eyes were closed, but the ragged movements of his chest were evidence that he was alive. Strips of dirty cloth were tied around his chest, probably concealing some manner of grievous wound, likely on the left, considering how tense that side of his body seemed to be. The thing that was of greatest concern, however, was how deathly pale his face was.

Gently, Be'Var reached out and touched the man's shoulder. Instantly, though without any sign of shock or surprise, dark blue eyes snapped open and looked at him.

"I'm a healer," Be'Var said. He indicated the man's paltry bandages. "Can I help?"

The man heaved a big sigh. "Please," he said. His voice held no hint of gratitude, nor of pleading, or even fear. Be'Var might have been offering him a glass of water for all of the emotion that voice conveyed.

Be'Var didn't like hearing voices like that. They usually meant the patient had given up.

As gently as he could, he untied the strips of cloth. He didn't actually need to see the wound in order to heal it, but getting a view of it would help him determine what, besides the stitching of flesh, the man might need from him.

When he found the gashes, long and red, on the man's chest, Be'Var had to keep himself from shrinking back. Whatever had made those wounds had managed to miss any vital organs, but the angry, crimson skin was already turning black in some places. However successful Be'Var's efforts at piecing the flesh back together might be, he didn't think there was much chance that this man would survive the week.

"Where are you from?" he asked as he reached out, opened a conduit, and brought the cauterizing heat to bear on the wound.

The man didn't look at him. "Miragor," he said, distantly. He then turned his head and smiled at Be'Var. "Heard of it?"

Be'Var shook his head.

The man nodded. "It isn't surprising," he said. "We're not on most maps, just a small town along the Deradin River." His expression changed slightly. "We *were* a small town, anyway," he said. "I don't suppose there's much left of it now."

Be'Var didn't say anything. He'd heard this story, or others very much like it, several times in just the last hour. If the man wanted to tell him more, he would. If not, Be'Var wouldn't pressure him by trying to awaken memories that were best left alone.

"There were so many of them," the man continued, gazing off into space. "The horizon was a sea of black as they approached. It was a long while before you could tell the men from the bugs."

That was something else he'd learned recently. The Black Moon Army was largely comprised of actual human beings, though many of them had dark, ashen skins, as though some part of them had been taken by the kreal. Based on the descriptions, most of the humans seemed to be foot soldiers, though there were some cavalry among them: riders of the insects.

Be'Var wondered if any of the men in that army had dead eyes, the way Caymus's attacker had.

Of course, there were also the krealites, those giant insect-like monsters that had become so prominent in Be'Var's life. Estimates of their numbers ranged from the dozens to the thousands, so he still wasn't sure how many of the things they would eventually have to deal with.

"That thing that led them, though," the man's face took on a darker visage, as though terror was slowly finding a home there, "I can't believe such a thing is allowed to exist." He reached out and grabbed Be'Var's arm. "It was enormous!" he said. "Black as the darkest night, it stood at the height of three men and was twice that big from side to side!"

The man paused for a moment, waiting until Be'Var looked up and met his eyes before he continued. "The walls around our village have kept out intruders for centuries," he said, "but this man, this…*thing*! It just reached up and pulled the wall down like it was paper, and the bugs came flooding in and started killing everybody."

Be'Var only nodded, not letting himself react to his patient's disquiet. To feed the man's anguish over whatever horrible scenes he was remembering would only drive him to further madness.

This "leader," a dark figure that stood at the head of the Black Moon Army, was another problem entirely. Be'Var had heard seven accounts of him—it—so far, and the descriptions ranged from something the size and shape of a man to that of a huge, quivering mass of arms and spikes with the dimensions of a small building. The blackness of him though, that was what all the stories had in common. They all agreed on the utter blackness of him.

As Be'Var finished burning away as the flesh that was too infected to be saved, and then sealing up the last of the skin that would never close up on its own, the man looked away, dropped his arm, and calmed down. "The smell, though," he said, closing his eyes. "It was like all the flowers in the meadow bloomed at once. So sweet." He settled himself back against the wall. "If it hadn't been for all the killing, it might have been pleasant."

Be'Var sighed as he took the strips of cloth that had been holding the man's chest together and replaced them with a bandage that, he hoped, would let the dying flesh heal itself properly. He didn't think it would, though. He'd seen enough wounds to know that this one would eventually turn completely black and kill its host. He could almost feel life's vital energy draining from the man by the second.

He stood, pushing the bloody, rank strips of cloth into a sack filled with such things. Caymus had told him about the sweet smell, too. He'd personally never noticed that kind of odor from the krealites before, but then he'd never been that close to one that wasn't on the brink of death, nor encountered so many of them at once.

"Sir?"

Be'Var, who had been walking away, stopped and turned. The man's eyes were riveted upon him. "What are they?"

Be'Var frowned, shook his head, and looked away. "They're the end of everything we know, my friend," he said. "I just hope we can stop them before everything we know is gone completely."

When he looked back, the man was nodding, his eyes closed. Be'Var sighed, wondering if hope was something he should even be considering.

A low moan brought the master out of his thoughts, and he quickly stepped a few paces and crouched beside his next patient, a woman who had curled herself up into a dark and musty corner.

She was hardly more than a girl, at most in her early twenties. Her short, black hair was matted against her head and her arms were covered in dirt to the point that it was hard to make out her skin tone.

She hid her face in her hands, but Be'Var could see that she was visibly shaking. He suspected that she was trying to hold back tears. "Miss?" he said, trying to make the word come out gently. He said it again when she didn't respond.

Eventually, he had to reach out and touch her arm to get her attention. The moment he made contact with her skin, however, she bolted away as though struck by lightning, scurried backward, and tried to push herself as far into the corner as possible.

Be'Var lifted his hands away, holding them up for her to see. "I'm not going to hurt you, child," he said. Before he could ask if she was hurt, however, she started wailing and shouting in a language he didn't understand. Her face was a mess. Pink streaks, where tears had cleaned some of the dirt away, covered her cheeks and red spots dotted her chin and forehead.

She was hysterical, in obvious despair, and he couldn't understand her. He thought he recognized the language, though he couldn't quite place it.

When she stopped wailing, put her hand over her mouth, and started simply crying, he spoke again. "I'm sorry, child," he said, "I don't understand you." He heaved a big sigh. "I don't suppose you speak my language, do you?"

"It is the Tower's language," a voice said from over his shoulder. Be'Var turned to see Aiella, her familiar blue dress replaced by a man's tunic and trousers, her hair tied back in a thick tail. She knelt down next to Be'Var. "Rather, it is a dialect that is spoken in villages far from Creveya, the Tower, far from the lake itself. Many of the people who live there do not speak any language that is not their own."

Be'Var was going to ask her if she could speak the young woman's language, but by the time he'd opened his mouth, she was already doing so, pointing at herself and Be'Var, in turn, by way of introduction. As Aiella pronounced the foreign words, the filthy girl looked up at her in seeming disbelief, wiping her cheeks with the palms of her hands. Sudden hope erupted in her eyes. Be'Var had never been so glad to see Brocke's daughter. He wondered how it was she'd come to be here, among the sick and the dying.

When Aiella finished speaking, the woman responded and the two carried some manner of conversation for nearly a minute, the woman speaking quickly and gesticulating wildly; Aiella taking a calmer, more measured tone. Be'Var thought the language a pretty one. It was filled with hard 'A's and many consonant sounds, but it seemed to flow easily, as though each word was intimately connected with the next. As he watched, he noticed the young woman occasionally put her hand to her belly and he got an inkling of what it might be that had her so frightened.

Aiella turned back to him. "She says she is uninjured," she said, "but she says she is with child, that she is worried for the baby inside her."

Be'Var nodded slowly. He kept his eyes fixed on the girl, trying to muster as much tenderness as he could. "Will she let me check?"

Aiella spoke to the girl again, presumably translating the question. The tear-streaked face nodded quickly, desperately, and she shuffled a couple of inches closer to him.

Be'Var gave the girl a small, reassuring smile. Slowly, deliberately, so as not to surprise her, he reached out a hand and placed it on her belly. "Did she say what happened?" he said, turning his eyes to Aiella.

"She says that she fell from a horse during an attack," Aiella responded. "She says it was some time ago, before she came through the pass."

Be'Var nodded, trying to keep the grimness out of his face. 'Some time ago,' wasn't good news. Briefly, he wondered what the Towerian girl had been doing north of the Greatstones in the first place.

As he closed his eyes and reached out into the woman's body with his mind, he wondered how Aiella must have been feeling about this interaction. Until very recently, the peoples of Creveya, the Summit and Creveya, the Tower, had been mortal enemies; now, here she was lending her abilities to the task of helping this girl.

He did a quick survey of the girl's organs, looking for any flows of fire energy that were out of place and which might signify an internal injury. Her liver, kidneys, and heart all appeared to be well. Her pulse was pounding, but that was to be expected.

He then shifted his consciousness to the womb, seeking out the child, looking for the telltale signs of a separate life. The fire element took a slightly different manifestation in almost every person—the flow of the Conflagration's tendrils into a body created textures and hues that could be perceived by the mind as easily as the eyes could pick out an individual face—and even a barely-conceived child had its own unique texture, distinct from that of its mother.

As he worked, Be'Var felt his heart sink. He searched again, but it was of no use. There was no fire there, no energy, no pulse. Whatever had happened to this young woman, the event had taken the life of the child inside her, likely long before Kepren had been a smudge on her horizon.

When he opened his eyes, he could barely stand the look of expectancy on the girl's face. A minute earlier, he had given her hope; now he was going to tear it away again.

"I'm sorry," he said, taking his hand away and shaking his head.

Aiella didn't need to translate the words. The young woman simply melted into excruciating wails before them, her hands balled into fists that she pounded into the ground. Be'Var, in all his years, even as a healer for an army, had only ever heard that level of pain, that unbelievable grief, once before: *she* had been a mother too, searching the remains of a dark, deserted battlefield for whatever was left of her boy.

In the next moment, before he could react, she was holding tight to Aiella, crying against her shoulder and trying to speak through painful sobs. Be'Var could see that Aiella wasn't comfortable with the young woman being so close to her, and yet she didn't pull away. Instead, she held the girl to her breast and spoke kind, reassuring words in that pretty language.

What a thing is war, Be'Var thought, *to elicit such sympathy between mortal foes.*

Marveling at the absurdity of it all, Be'Var turned around, both to check that the girl's cries hadn't upset any of the other patients too grievously and also to see if anybody needed his immediate attention.

He was startled for a moment. He hadn't expected to see the familiar shape of Caymus before him.

He wasn't sure, at first, that it actually *was* Caymus. The man towering over him was filthy with the same dust and grime that covered the rest of these people, and the look in his eyes was one of absolute seriousness. Caymus's face should hold a bit more of a smile.

No, the huge stature, the sword and shield, and the mark on the back of the left hand were dead giveaways. Caymus had returned to Kepren. Be'Var put his hands to his knees and pushed himself up to his feet. "Boy," he said, "you're filthy. Did you just get back?"

Caymus was looking at Aiella and the woman she was comforting. He didn't look away from them as he spoke. "Milo and I ran as fast as we could as we heard the news."

Be'Var's spirits lifted just a little bit. "So, Milo's trick worked then? He heard the message?"

Caymus only nodded.

"Good," Be'Var continued. "All I heard about it was that you were coming back." He looked Caymus up and down. He couldn't believe how serious the boy looked. "And you?" he asked. "Did you have any luck with the Falaar?"

"I did," Caymus said, his voice barely more than a whisper. Finally, he tore his eyes away from the two women and gave Be'Var a small smile. Be'Var's heart sang inside his chest to see that. It had been far too long since he'd seen Caymus smile. "I'll tell you about it on the way," he said.

"On the way?" Be'Var cocked an eyebrow at him.

Caymus nodded. "A page met us at Flamehearth." He shrugged. "I guess they knew we'd arrived. He said that the prince is having some sort of meeting in the Keep and that he wanted us to be there."

"Both of us, eh?" Be'Var knew that the prince was aware that Caymus was important, but he was surprised to hear that the boy had actually been invited to an official meeting.

"And Milo, too," Caymus said. "Matron Y'selle told me where to find you, so I told the page I'd spare him the trouble."

Be'Var nodded absently, then he turned to Aiella and the girl who had become her charge. He wasn't entirely comfortable leaving the two of them in such close proximity. Their peoples were at peace—well, they weren't actively killing each other, anyway—for the first time in his memory, sure, but generations of hate had a way of resurfacing when one least expected it.

Aiella, who'd been watching the exchange over her shoulder, must have understood his concern. "Go," she said, a small amount of irritation in her voice, "we will be fine." She then lowered her head to look at Be'Var from under her eyebrows. "I am not likely to hold a grudge against this woman, whom I have only now met, when the world, it is in great peril."

Be'Var couldn't help but smile. The girl was a constant surprise to him.

"And, Caymus?" she said, just before they turned to go. The faintest hint of brightness touched her features. "Welcome back."

Be'Var couldn't be certain, but the boy seemed a bit surprised that she had addressed him directly.

The two of them turned and walked out of the old building. After they had stepped out into the sunlight, Caymus asked, "Master Be'Var? That girl? That one who was crying? Will she be alright?"

Be'Var didn't look at his pupil. "No, boy," he said, "I'm not sure she'll ever be alright again."

"What happened to her?"

Be'Var let out a long sigh, thinking about the girl's wails, remembering old battlefields, monuments to so very much loss. In that moment, life seemed so tenuous, so fragile. "She lost everything, Caymus," he said. "She lost her entire world."

And she won't be the last.

Chapter 17

"Mind your manners while we're in there, boy," Be'Var said, adjusting his robes on his shoulders. "Considering the people who are going to be in that room, things are likely to get a little heated, and I don't need you adding to the general confusion."

Caymus smiled to himself. He hadn't heard Be'Var mention the general confusion in a long time, and he hadn't realized he'd missed it.

Absently, he scratched at the back of his hand. He wished he'd had a chance to bathe before he and Be'Var had been summoned to the prince's meeting, considering how caked with dirt and sweat he was. Instead, they'd passed by one of the fountains in the Guard District on their way to the Keep—one of the few that still had any water in it—and Caymus had done the best job he could at wiping down his arms and face.

Still, he felt woefully out of place.

They were standing in front of a heavy, wooden door at the end of a long, stone hallway. A guard—a young man, resplendent in his band-and-mail armor and long tabard—stood to one side of the door, somehow watching the two of them without casting his eyes in their direction.

In short order, the door opened inward, revealing a gathering of men standing around a table. At the head of the table was Prince Garrin, who looked up and impatiently waved them in.

Caymus felt a bit out of his depth when he saw who else was arrayed around the table. Standing to the left of the prince was Brocke, looking as serious as ever. To the prince's right was a man Caymus recognized only by rank: the Keep-Marshal. Caymus had never met the man before, but he wore the silver medallion of station that marked him as the primary protector of the Keep itself. *The King protects the doors to Kepren*, the saying went. *The Marshal protects the doors to the King.*

Also standing about the raised, wooden surface, which was strewn with maps of various sizes and many other bits of paper, were three men whom Caymus assumed were the three dukes of Kepren. He'd not met any of them before either, but he'd heard their descriptions: the old one, the young one, and the fat one. They each seemed uninterested in whatever was going on, and not one of them acknowledged him or Be'Var as they walked in.

Caymus was relieved to see that Milo was there too, though it seemed that his friend hadn't been quite so concerned with cleaning up as he had been. The air priest's face was still covered with grime. His teeth stood out like diamonds when he smiled.

The last man stood just behind and to the left of Brocke. Caymus didn't know who he was, but he seemed to be in his late twenties and lean. Brown hair that hung down past his shoulders and also collected on his face in a thick, unkempt beard. He didn't meet anybody else's gaze and his posture showed extreme deference to Brocke. Caymus would have thought him some manner of servant if not for the beard.

"Be'Var!" The man Caymus recognized as the Keep-Marshal smiled warmly and walked toward them, his expression one of delighted surprise. He extended an enthusiastic hand to Be'Var as two men met at the near end of the table. "Garrin didn't tell me you were coming to this thing! How long have you been in Kepren?"

Be'Var took the offered hand, then he clapped the marshal on the shoulder. He seemed genuinely glad to see the man. "Hello, Tanner," he said. "I've been here a few months, I'm afraid." He looked over at Caymus. "I've been a little busy."

The marshal looked up at Caymus and extended his hand to him, also. "You, then, must be Caymus," he said, a big grin on his face, "the Sleeping Giant himself!"

Caymus had heard the moniker a couple of times since he'd awakened and didn't know whether he liked it or not, but he smiled and graciously took the hand anyway. "I suppose I am," he said.

The marshal let go and gave him a hearty, good-natured laugh. "Be'Var isn't giving you too much trouble, is he?" he said, looking back at the old man. "I know he can be pretty tiresome, sometimes."

Caymus looked back and forth between the two men. "You know each other, then?"

"I was a healer," Be'Var said. "The marshal here was a soldier. We were bound to meet eventually."

"Ha!" the marshal laughed. He held up his right hand before Caymus's eyes. "'Meet,' he says! If it weren't for this man, I'd have had to retire as a sergeant!"

Caymus immediately saw what the man meant. Each of the fingers of the hand before him carried a thick band of scar tissue, all lining up in a neat row just above the palm. They had obviously been cleaved off at some point. Caymus raised an eyebrow at Be'Var. He hadn't known the man could actually reattach missing digits. Be'Var, however, just shrugged off the implied question.

"Can we get on with this, then?" came a voice from the table. The marshal stepped aside, revealing the oldest of the three dukes, the one with the thick mustache, as the speaker. "If you're all finished reminiscing, of course."

The marshal seemed about to retort, but instead he just nodded, and the three quietly found places to stand. The Keep-Marshal returned to his previous position at the prince's side. Caymus and Be'Var filled some unoccupied space at the other end of the table

Now that there was a pause, Caymus took a moment to get a good look around. The rectangular room they were standing in wasn't large. The space it occupied was perhaps a little bit greater than that of the central courtyard in Flamehearth Mission. The place was a great deal more splendid, however, with large tapestries and portraits covering the walls, leaving very little bare stone between them. The tapestries depicted what appeared to be scenes of battle. The portraits, all of well-dressed men of varying ages, didn't have nameplates, but Caymus assumed they depicted former leaders of Kepren. A large, unlit fireplace took up nearly half of one of the longer walls and a single, small window let in some of the afternoon's yellow light.

There was also a bowl of water—a font, really—standing about waist high on a narrow column a few steps behind the prince. It seemed out of place in a room that was so obviously designated for the discussion and planning of affairs of state.

"Thank you both for coming," the prince finally said, nodding at each of the newcomers in turn. Prince Garrin was dressed in an embroidered leather jacket, dotted with metal studs, which seemed only a breath away from being actual armor. He also wore the ever-present black sword at his hip. Between his manner of dress and the grim expression on his face, he seemed already prepared, at any moment, to jump into battle.

"Now that everyone's here," he continued, "we can get to it." He took a deep breath and placed his hands on the polished wood in front of him. "You all know that Black Moon was sighted preparing to cross the Greatstones two days ago." He looked around the table, as though verifying this. "Since then, we've had more information. Some of it comes from scouts we've sent into the enemy's path. Some of it comes straight from the lips of the civilians trying to keep out of their way."

Caymus thought back to the building where he'd found Be'Var less than an hour ago, about the people who had littered the floor there, some of them barely alive. Had any of them been among the prince's informants?

Garrin slid some papers around before continuing, as though checking a few facts. Caymus idly noticed that Brocke, standing quietly just beside the prince, had that little box of his open and was taking a sniff of whatever was contained within.

"This gentleman," Garrin finally said, indicating the man standing behind Brocke, "is one of those sources of information." He looked at the faces around the table again as he spoke. "He's brought some interesting facts to light. I've asked you all here so that you can hear those facts directly from him."

Caymus thought that the prince's gaze seemed to hover over the three dukes longer than it did anyone else, though the moment was so short and was over so quickly that he couldn't be sure. "Ambassador Brocke," he said, "would you, please?"

The ambassador was caught off-guard by the request. He fumbled the little box closed and secreted it into a little pocket before addressing the group. Caymus wondered why the prince would ask Brocke, rather than the man behind him, who was presumably the one who had actually seen Black Moon, to speak.

He also wondered what was in that little box.

"The Army of the Black Moon," Brocke made a point of pronouncing the words 'black' and 'moon' separately, "it is not, it seems, as large as we had originally thought. We—"

"What do you mean?" interrupted the duke with the mustache. "Just how large is—"

"If you will let the man speak," the prince interjected, leaning across the table at the old man, "I'm sure the ambassador will be more than happy to tell you, Duke Korwinder."

Caymus didn't know what had previously transpired between these two, but it was obvious that the prince had no patience for Korwinder. The way Garrin's eyes seemed to drag across all three of the dukes at once, in fact, made him suspect that the relationships between the most powerful men in Kepren was altogether unstable.

Korwinder's mustache twitched as he glared at the prince, but he nodded an apology. "Of course," he said, then turned to Brocke. "Please, Ambassador, continue."

Brocke merely nodded in response to the apology. "Some mercenary groups, thieves, and other small bands of men, they have apparently decided to toss their fates in with the Black Moon, and this has increased their numbers. However, the core of their army, it seems it is a group of infantry only about two thousand strong."

Caymus, far from an expert on matters of military tactics, was intentionally keeping his eyes off of Brocke and instead watching the faces of the other men around the table, trying to use their reactions to gauge his own understanding of the situation. Each face registered some degree of surprise upon hearing the figure.

Brocke continued. "They also are counting among their numbers those same creatures that attacked this city—many cities—several months ago." He nodded to Be'Var. "What Master Be'Var, he calls 'krealites'. Some of them, they are even being used as a sort of cavalry, carrying one or more soldiers on their backs."

"You said that mercenaries bolster their numbers." The prince said. "By how much, would you say?"

"Between one and two thousand men," said Brocke, "currently travel with Black Moon, though other, smaller groups, they have been sighted trailing behind the main force, and so this number is likely to grow."

The faces around the table seemed confused and agitated, as though Brocke's words didn't make sense. By his own estimation, Caymus didn't think that an army of four thousand men sounded like that much of a threat to the city, though he knew that discounting the krealites would be a mistake.

"If I may?" Duke Korwinder asked. Brocke nodded. "What siege engines do they bring with them?"

"None," said Brocke.

Korwinder seemed dissatisfied with the answer. "None?" He turned his gaze to the prince. "Your Highness," he said, his tone rising slightly, "a group of only a few thousand men and a few of these overgrown insects march toward us. Half of them are hired thugs, they have no siege engines, and we're meant to be concerned?" He waved his hand around the table. "Three times that many soldiers stand ready to defend Kepren!"

"Do not underestimate this foe, Duke Korwinder," Brocke said in an even tone. "The mercenaries, I will grant you, they are of little concern, but these two thousand man—the core of the army—they have already crushed several cities the nearly the size of this one."

"How?" said Korwinder, shaking his head. "They're just men, aren't they?"

"No," said Brocke, his eyes seeming to lose focus on Korwinder. "My Duke, they are not."

Nobody said a word for a moment.

"Perhaps," the prince said, looking to Brocke, "your man should show us."

Brocke nodded, then he leaned back and whispered something to the figure behind him. The man nodded, then he walked over to the font. Brocke followed. The prince then motioned at group that they should gather around the small pool of water.

Ambassador Brocke took out his little box again and took another sniff of whatever was in it, then he and the other man both closed their eyes and placed a single finger into the water at the font's edge.

"This man," Prince Garrin said in a quiet voice, indicating the long-haired stranger, "is a scout for the Summitian army. He was there when Albreva, one of the major cities north the Greatstones, fell." He indicated the water, which Caymus was surprised to discover was turning white, as though a bottle of paint had been spilled into it. "The ambassador is assisting him in placing his memory of the event into the water, so that we may all see and understand."

Caymus, pressed around the small font along with everybody else, heard Be'Var grunt next to him. Caymus looked over at the old man, but the master shook his head to dismiss the unspoken question.

When he turned his attention back to the water, he was astonished by what he saw. A dark, moving picture seemed to emerge out of the scout's finger and into the water, emanating like ripples from his skin. The image was unintelligible at first, merely a clash of black and orange. After a moment, however, the colors took actual forms and the scene in the water was depicting a place on fire, as seen from a distance of a mile or so.

The picture seemed to shift violently, left and right, every few seconds; Caymus wondered why that might be until the image changed to that of a hand reaching down into a bag on the ground. Caymus stole a quick look at the scout, looking at the color of his sleeves and at the satchel over his shoulder. It was his hand and his bag. The people in the room were seeing the burning of this city as this man's own eyes had seen it.

"The Creveyans call it 'reflecting'." Be'Var was leaning over and whispering in his ear, though not taking his own eyes off the font. "Only the people from the Summit know how to do it, and only a very few of them."

Caymus wanted to ask more about it, but the scene was changing again as the hand in the water reached up and held a spyglass up to the scout's eye.

In a moment, the horror of what was happening to the people in the city was magnified in parity with the image. Men in black clothing with ashen faces and withered-looking hands were hacking people to pieces. Some of the city's citizens were trying to run. Some were trying to fight. Some had given up and lay sobbing on the ground. Some were already dead. Swords and axes swung and fell, spraying blood indiscriminately.

A handful of the people—men in bloodied armor—tried to stave off the attack, tried to defend their friends and neighbors, but even when their swords were able to strike home against their tormentors, the blades simply deflected or bounced off their flesh in a way that Caymus found all too familiar. The dark figures simply laughed and let their own weapons taste the flesh of the defenders as legs buckled and eyes went wide with surprise and terror.

The scout's memory flitted the spyglass back and forth as though trying to take in as much of the battle as possible. Caymus wondered if he might have been trying to count the attackers.

He saw the krealites too. They were eviscerating walls and buildings almost as easily as they were the citizenry. One of them carried two of the ash-skinned men on its back, each of whom stabbed down at people —the ones the beast hadn't managed to kill yet—with spears, spilling blood with every strike. Caymus watched as two crossbow bolts bounced uselessly off the back of the rearmost rider even as he gleefully stabbed an old man through the neck. The rider just laughed harder, then pointed the krealite below him in the direction of the crossbowmen.

Caymus felt anger, pity, and revulsion building up in him. The krealites were bad enough, but now someho these men had become tainted by the kreal as well and had inherited its property of invulnerability to sharpened weapons. He understood now why the Black Moon Army had been so successful, why every city they had sacked had fallen so easily. To the people they had attacked, they were simply invincible.

If only they knew what he knew. If only he could help these people. He closed his eyes. This image was a memory. These people were already dead. There was nothing anybody could do for them.

When he opened his eyes again, he started. There, amidst the death and the confusion, he caught the briefest glimpse of a familiar face.

"I think that's enough," the prince said gently to the two Summitians.

The two men then each let out a deep breath and slowly opened their eyes, seeming surprised to find themselves in this room with these people. Caymus wondered just how much effort this 'reflecting' had required of the two men.

When the tight knot of bodies around the font loosened, the three dukes moved off to one side of the room, near the fireplace. They then proceeded with some manner of private conversation that involved a lot of head shaking.

Prince Garrin stepped around Brocke and put an arm on the scout's shoulder. "Thank you," he said.

The man's eyes were downcast, but the prince kept looking at him until he brought them up and met his gaze, at which point, he quickly lowered them again.

"Yes, your highness," he said to the floor.

Garrin gave the man a warm smile, even though he couldn't see it, then he moved back to the table and started looking over the documents that lay there. Everyone else—minus the dukes, who continued their quiet conversation, and the scout, who retreated to a corner of the room—

followed him and clustered around that end of the table.

"Two thousand men," the Prince said, "and they're going to raze the city unless we find a way to stop them."

"Two thousand *invincible* men," the Keep-Marshal said, his eyes staring at the documents. He looked up at Be'Var. "Tell me you know something, old man," he said. "Tell me you know how to beat them or why those swords just bounce off."

"It's an alien element," Be'Var said. "It doesn't work like anything we know in our world." He sighed. "Why it reacts the way it does, I don't know, but..." He met the marshal's gaze with obvious distress. "No, I don't know how to beat them."

"Blood and bones!" the marshal said, pounding his fist on the table. "I've studied tactics and logistics my entire life, Be'Var! I like to think I'm an expert in this kind of thing. I know weapons, I know artillery, and I know soldiers. I've defended the city against overwhelming forces and pressed successful sieges on impenetrable fortresses. I've beaten back forces three times my size just because I knew what ground to fight from." He placed both hands on the table and hung his head. "But what I can't do is beat back an army when I can't even stick a sword in 'em!"

"They're not invincible," Caymus heard himself say. "Getting past the kreal is hard, but it's possible."

When the marshal lifted his head, the hot gaze he leveled at Caymus made him wish he'd kept his mouth shut. "What do you mean?" he said.

Caymus cleared his throat to buy himself a couple of moments to choose his words. He was talking to the Keep-Marshal after all, and he wasn't sure that assuming he knew something that the protector of the Kepren fortress didn't was entirely wise.

"The kreal," he said. He raised his hands in front of him, holding one out flat and extending two fingers of the other. "If you try to smash your way through it," he stabbed the one hand with the fingers of the other, "you can't get in. But if you make contact," he placed the fingers on the hand this time, "then push," he looked up and met the Keep-Marshal's gaze as he passed the fingers of one hand between those of the other, "it is possible to get a blade through."

The marshal stared at Caymus a long while, then turned to Be'Var. "Tell me, old man, does the kid know what he's talking about?"

Be'Var considered a moment before speaking, giving Caymus a considering look. "While Sleeping Giant here was sleeping," he finally said, still looking at his pupil, "while his body was lying in that room in Flamehearth, the Lords of the Conflagration took his consciousness away to teach him how to fight the krealites. They showed him things I can't begin to imagine." He finally looked back at the marshal. "It's possible—likely, even—that Caymus knows more about fighting kreal than anybody else in the entire world, Tanner."

Caymus was more than a little stunned to hear those words from Be'Var's mouth, though more surprising to him was the realization that the old man was right: besides a single mitre warrior in Otvia, he probably was the only person in the world who knew how to fight the krealites.

When Keep-Marshal Tanner looked at him again, Caymus was nearly crushed by the glimmer of hope in his eyes. He knew what the next question was going to be, and he knew that it would be impossible.

"Can you teach my men?"

Caymus sighed. "Keep-Marshal, I spent three months away from this world, but it felt like a lifetime." He paused to let the thought sink in. "It took me a *lifetime* to learn what I know," he said, "and I had the benefit of krealites to practice on."

The marshal nodded understanding as the hope burned out. "And we have maybe a week." He shook his head. "With all the other preparations we have yet to make..." He gave Caymus a smile and a tilt of his head. "You're right. There just isn't time." He paused. "Still," he said, "stick around once we're done here? I'd like to hear a bit more about this."

Caymus nodded and reflected the smile. Tanner seemed a good, intelligent, responsible man. His face seemed carved from sunbaked leather, but his eyes were fierce, penetrating orbs of the whitest blue. He reminded Caymus of an old friend of his father's whom he'd met dozens of times growing up. For the life of him, Caymus couldn't remember the man's name in that moment.

"That's it!" All in the room turned to look at the prince, who was stabbing his finger at a map on the table.

"Sir?" said Tanner when Garrin raised his head with a look of supreme triumph.

"Falmoor's Pass," exclaimed the prince, stabbing at the map again. "We can get them at the canyon!"

Curiosity grabbed the room and everyone, the dukes included, gathered around the map. Brocke even motioned for the Creveyan scout to approach, presumably in case the prince had questions for him.

Caymus looked down. The map was largely topographical, and it portrayed a section of the Greatstone Mountains. The section was one that contained Falmoor's Pass, the path through the mountains that, presumably, the Black Moon Army was taking at that very moment.

The prince, however, was indicating a spot at the very bottom of that pass, a point about a mile south of where the mountains could be said to end, but which presented a canyon—more of a large gully, really—that one had to get through in order to reach the plains of Tebria.

"You're saying we attack them there, Sire?" said Korwinder. "What good would that do?"

"No," said Garrin, shaking his head. "We don't need to fight them. We take a small group of men and a few casks of graysilt, we wait for them to show up, then we bury them in a landslide."

The room went silent for a few moments while everyone considered the idea. Caymus wasn't an expert at reading these sorts of maps, the ones which showed the relative elevations of things, but it didn't seem to him that the sides of this gully were steep enough to cause an actual wall of earth to fall atop the invading army.

Others around the room seemed skeptical also. "Do you really think that will work?" asked Tanner. "I've been through that place a number of times, and I don't know that it's big enough to hold the whole lot of 'em."

"Doesn't have to be the whole lot," Garrin said, still looking at the map. "Just has to be enough to thin their ranks a bit." The young prince's eye twitched a couple of times. "Maybe a lot."

"But, Sire," said Korwinder, his mustache twitching, "if blades and arrows can't defeat these men, why would stones and dirt harm them?"

Before the Prince could respond, Tanner looked up. "Caymus?" he said, "Would it hurt them?"

Caymus considered the thought, not noticing all the eyes on him. He thought about the way that kreal had felt under his blade, against his hilt, under the heel of his boot, and wondered if a landslide could actually hurt it. "I don't think it would really hurt them," he said, "but, I suppose, you could manage to bury them under it?"

"They breathe," said Be'Var.

"Right, of course," Caymus nodded, still looking at the map. He thought back to the Ritual Room in Otvia. "Even if the landslide doesn't cause them any direct harm, it just might suffocate them."

Tanner considered the thought. "I suppose, if nothing else, it could buy us some more time," he said, turning to the Prince.

"Even if it doesn't kill the Black Moon men, themselves," the Prince said, looking up at the Keep-Marshal, "we could at least take out the mercenaries."

Heads around the table nodded, though none of those heads belonged to the three dukes. "Your Highness," said Korwinder, plaintively, "it's just such a stretch, such a risky undertaking." He squinted his eyes. "I don't know that I would want to commit our forces to such a thing."

Prince Garrin looked a dagger at the duke, but he held his tongue. "You don't have to," he said, eventually. "I'll go."

All at once, half a dozen voices were nearly shouting: Brocke, Tanner, and Be'Var were expressing their concern; the dukes were expressing outrage. Garrin held up a hand to silence them.

"I'll take my personal guard with me," he said. "That way, I won't be pulling any resources from the regular army." He looked around the table.

"Even if it doesn't hurt the bastards too much," he continued, "at least I won't be hurting the city's defense."

"My prince!" Duke Korwinder's face was red with agitation, the color standing out behind his white whiskers. "You simply cannot go gallivanting off into the mountains on a whim!" he shouted. "You must be here! You must aid in the city's defense! You are the Protector-Champion of Kepren, and you will be needed!"

"My dear Duke," said Garrin, carefully controlling his tone, "you have argued with me at every turn about the need to protect this city. When I made it clear that we needed more men, you fought me. When we needed more supplies for the men we do have, you fought me. This time, I will brook no argument."

"You cannot go!" Korwinder yelled. "You are needed here!"

Caymus was physically flinching back from the confrontation, the air was so thick with tension and anger. Garrin seemed about to launch into a tirade when a tiny voice broke through the momentary pause. "Where are you going, Son?"

Caymus, along with everyone else around the table, turned to the spot from which the voice had come. Standing behind the font at the end of the room was a frail-looking old man in a stained, white nightshirt. The man was hunched over as though suffering from rheumatism. His white, wispy hair and beard were long and scraggly. His skin was pale white. His legs shook with the effort of standing.

Judging by the smell in the room, Caymus thought the stains on the nightshirt were likely the result of the man's own incontinence.

All in the room were silent. The anger in Prince Garrin's face evaporated instantly, turning instead to concern and a kind of incredible sadness as he slowly stepped toward the old man. "Nowhere, Father," he said, gently. "I'm staying right here." He took the man by his brittle-looking arms and slowly walked him back out the door.

The man had appeared so suddenly, so startlingly, that it was several moments before Caymus put the pieces together. The frail-looking man had been Lysandus, King of Kepren! The thought was sobering. Caymus had heard rumors that the king was ill, that Garrin was largely ruling Kepren on his behalf, but he couldn't have imagined that such a powerful man could look so ragged, so tired, so old.

The room remained silent for some time. Nobody seemed willing to speak or even look at the other faces in the room. Nobody had been prepared to see the king that way. Caymus marveled at the strength Garrin must have had to bear what was happening to his father, much less his city.

Eventually, after several minutes of quiet, the door opened again and Garrin returned. Caymus was surprised at how different he seemed now.

His eyes were sad, yet resolute. His mouth was set in a firm line, betraying nothing other than the will to control his emotions. Merely a few minutes ago, Garrin had been the mighty, young prince, filled with claims to greatness and the promise of glory; now, in the prince's place, Caymus saw a king, a leader of a nation with the weight of an entire city upon him.

The Prince's eyes stared at nothing. They weren't vacant, rather they seemed filled with thoughts and emotions that he dared not speak of or act upon. His breathing was slow, deliberate, measured, as though he was using his own breath to steady himself, to try to maintain a grip over deep wells of feeling. Caymus could see why people liked having Prince Garrin as the Champion-Protector of Kepren. Despite the man's occasionally lax-seeming and playful attitude, this was a man who could maintain control in even the most desperate situations.

"I'm faced with the real possibility of losing my kingdom, of getting the people under my care murdered by otherworldly forces," he finally said. With that, the prince finally focused his eyes on the others in the room, moving his gaze from face to face until he finally settled it on Korwinder. "I'm not going to lose," he said, with not a hint of agitation, "without having first done everything I possibly could to save it."

"My prince—" Korwinder began to speak, but Garrin halted him with an upturned hand.

The young ruler turned his head slightly as though not quite willing to look over his shoulder. "My father is not the man he once was," he said, then he turned his gaze back to the dukes. "But while he yet lives, he is still the king, and I am still the Champion-Protector. That makes me ultimately responsible for the defense of this city. My men and I are going to get this done." One side of his mouth turned up in a dark smile. "So, we'd better figure out what you're all going to do if I don't come back."

Korwinder said nothing. He knew the argument was over. Caymus watched on in fascination as the men around him, the decision having been made by the figure who was ultimately their monarch, put their heads together and began to erect plans for the defense of the city.

It was quickly agreed that a large number of the buildings outside the high city walls would need to be evacuated, that the people who lived and worked there would be found lodgings inside one of the three districts.

There were also some places in the outer wall that had been weakened by previous attacks—whether by krealites, a few months ago, or Mael'vekians, decades ago—and so plans were made to fortify and support those areas. Fel, the rotund duke of the Reed District, had raised concerns that most of those sections were in the southern wall, and that the fortifications might be a waste of time and resources, considering the fact that Black Moon was coming from the North. Even Caymus had realized, before it was said aloud, that the concern was foolish, that just because an army approaches a city from one direction, there is no guarantee that it will attack from there.

The farmlands on either side of the Silvertooth River had not been as productive as they had been in previous years, but plans were made for anything harvestable to be collected in the next few days, and for the rest to be burned so that, in the case of a protracted siege, the people of Kepren didn't end up feeding their attackers. There was some discussion of actually salting the earth, but it was agreed that such an action would be unnecessary. Even if the siege lasted for a year—nobody believed it would—it was unlikely that the invading army would actually begin farming.

When the prince questioned Tanner about the readiness of the engineers—the Royal Engineers were stationed within the walls of the Keep itself and were thus under his direct leadership—the man's face lit up with excitement.

"Ah yes," he said, then he crouched down, reaching for something under the table. "One of Draya's boys made something new for us."

When Tanner stood and set the small, clay jar on the table, Caymus felt Be'Var's hand clamp down on his shoulder. He understood why, too. Even from several feet away, he could feel that the vessel contained more of the fire element than anything he'd ever experienced outside of the Conflagration itself.

"Burn me to the ground!" Be'Var exclaimed, staring at the jar, and then at Tanner. "You're not planning on lighting that in here, are you?"

Tanner gave the master a mischievous grin. "That obvious, is it?"

Be'Var shook his head. "That," he said, pointing at it, "shouldn't even be indoors, Tanner. It shouldn't even exist!" He gave the Keep-Marshal an incredulous look. "How in the four elements did you manage it?"

The Prince, who had been looking back and forth between the men, cleared his throat. "Does one of you want to tell the rest of us what this is?"

Tanner turned his smile toward the prince. He lifted the lid of the jar so that the prince could get a look inside. "It's, for lack of a better word, a kind of sludge," he said, "and it's made, in large part, from graysilt."

"Graysilt?" the prince said, looking up from the jar. "It's flammable, then?"

"Ha!" Tanner replied. "You wouldn't believe how hot the stuff burns, but to give you an idea…" He, once again, reached under the table. When he stood, he produced what looked like some kind of black metal plate; it was scorched and pockmarked and had several holes in it. He threw it onto the table, where it landed with a clatter. "That," he said, pointing, "used to be a half-inch plate of solid iron. The kid who made this stuff used one spoonful of the sludge," he pointed at the jar again, "to get it looking that way."

There were faint sounds of astonishment around the room, and Caymus heard Milo give a low whistle. After a moment, the prince turned to Be'Var. "Those creatures," he said, "the krealites. I've been told they're hard to set on fire, but that it's not impossible." He tilted his head at the little pot. "Could that do the trick?"

Be'Var scratched his chin and wrinkled his brow in thought for a moment. "It might," he said, then he turned to Caymus. "What do you think, boy?"

Caymus regarded the little pot again, still amazed at the contents inside. He met the prince's eyes. "Whatever is in that pot," he said, "it has more fire in it than anything I've ever seen before. If anything can burn through a krealite's armor," he nodded at the pot, "that will be it."

"I don't want any qualifiers, Caymus," the prince replied. "Can it burn the bastards, or not?"

Caymus thought about what the Prince was asking. He thought about the times he'd managed to burn through a krealite before, thought about how much heat it had taken, then he compared it with what he was feeling from inside the little container.

He thought back to the vision he'd just seen in the memory of the scout, of the gray-skinned men who had attacked the citizens of that foreign city. He wasn't sure how, but he knew those men weren't as well armored as the creatures. The huge insectoid monsters were beings far removed from the Quatrain. In fact, they might have even begun their existences in the Sograve. The men, on the other hand, seemed as though they'd started out as human and were under the effects of some kind of transformation. They looked as though kreal had seeped into their skins, not replaced them.

He looked up again. "As far as the krealites go," he said, "yes, there's enough fire in that jar to burn through a krealite shell. It's just a question of how quickly it can be applied. I believe you could burn one of the things, but you'd have to drench them in the stuff."

The prince nodded, his face grim.

"But the men," Caymus continued, "those gray-skinned men that the bolts couldn't penetrate?" Caymus nodded at his own conclusion. "Whatever this is that the engineers have made, it will burn through one of them easy."

The prince let a slow, cautious smile creep onto his face. "What are the engineers calling this stuff, Tanner?" he asked. "And how much do we have?"

"Draya had some fancy, long-winded word for the concoction—you know how the engineers are," Tanner said, "but the boys are calling it 'Rill's sludge' for the time being."

Caymus nearly burst out laughing when he heard the new compound's name. Milo, never one to stand on formality, actually did laugh, and everyone turned to look at the sudden outburst.

"Rill's Sludge?" Milo said, an extremely pleased grin on his face. "*Rill* made this stuff?"

"That's the kid's name, so I'm told," Tanner said through arched eyebrows. "You know him?"

Milo, Caymus, and Be'Var shared a knowing and somewhat astounded look between them, much to the dissatisfaction of everyone else. "The boy was studying to be a master at the Temple," Be'Var finally explained. "He came here with the rest of us a few months ago." The old man shook his head in wonderment. "I figured there was a brain in his head somewhere, but I never thought it was sharp enough for something like this."

Caymus was beaming. He'd only seen his friend the one time since he'd come out of his long sleep. Hearing that the one-time failure had accomplished something so impressive was, by far, the best news he'd heard in a long time.

"The supply," Tanner said, trying to pick up the thread of conversation, "is another story, I'm afraid. So far, this one engineer is the only one who is able to make it properly," he let out a sigh as he spoke. "And one of the ingredients is hard to come by. Honestly, I don't know how much they'll be able to make before Black Moon is knocking on our door."

The prince's eyes were intense as he replied. "Make it a priority, Tanner," he said.

"I will, Sir," Tanner said.

"I mean it," Garrin said, making sure the marshal saw the seriousness in his face. "You tell Draya to pour as much effort as they can into making more of this stuff, and you make sure this Rill character is teaching the rest of them how to make it by the end of the day." He looked down at the jar, then over to Be'Var and Caymus. "Our Conflagrationist friends say this 'Rill's sludge' can burn through our enemies." He looked back at Tanner. "That means if my men and I aren't successful, it might just end up being only weapon you have."

Nobody could argue with the prince's logic. Tanner had brought the jar of sludge into the meeting to show it off, to give the prince an idea of what the engineers had been up to. Caymus didn't think the Keep-Marshal had realized that he'd been holding the city's best chance for survival.

"It will be done, Your Highness," Tanner said, his scowl matching the

Prince's. Then his eyes brightened a little, as though remembering something. "Draya did have a request that he asked me to pass along."

Garrin nodded. "Anything he needs," he said. "What is it?"

"It's for My Lord Dukes, actually," Tanner said, turning to the three men. The three of them, so different in appearance and yet so similar in attitude, raised their eyebrows in curiosity. Caymus realized that they'd all kept quiet throughout the previous discussions, but that they now appeared involved—suddenly present in the moment—and taking a serious interest in matters. Whatever the situation between the dukes and the prince, Garrin's refusal to let them sway him from riding north seemed to have affected their demeanor.

"What can we do for the captain of the engineers?" asked Korwinder.

"He needs an inquisitor," said Tanner. "There have been four reported acts of sabotage in the yard in the last few days. Damage to the catapults, supplies going missing, that sort of thing." He gave Korwinder a slight smile and a shrug. "Draya would rather police his own people, of course," he said, "but given the current state of things, he just doesn't have time."

Korwinder gave the marshal a sincere nod. "Of course," he said, then looked to the other two dukes. "We will make sure an inquisitor is stationed at the yard as soon as possible."

"Thank you," Tanner said. "I know the captain will appreciate it." His smile seemed to Caymus to be genuine, as did Korwinder's, and he briefly wondered why. Had the dukes' collective outlooks really changed so much in just a few minutes, or did they simply enjoy a better relationship with the marshal than with the prince?

All eyes turned back to Garrin. "Is there anything else you need, Tanner?" he asked once he saw that they were all waiting for him to speak.

Tanner shook his head.

"Anybody?" The prince looked around at all those gathered. "Is there anything any of you needs from me so you can prepare for this invasion?"

The people in the room looked at each other expectantly, but nobody said anything.

"Good," Garrin said. "I will be taking my guard with me to the Greatstones tomorrow night. With the progress Black Moon is making..." he looked at Milo. "What's the latest?"

Milo grinned, his arms folded across his chest. "This sunrise," he said, "the bulk of the regular army was several miles in already, but they seemed to be waiting for the mercenary groups to catch up."

The prince nodded. "In other words, they're moving slowly enough that we'll have just enough time to set our trap." He looked at the faces around the table. Caymus was moved by the sincerity of this man, the leadership he seemed to exude without expending any noticeable effort. He found this Garrin hard to reconcile with the easy-going young man he'd first met at Flamehearth a few months ago. "When I'm gone," he continued, "it will be up to all of you to make sure the city is ready to defend itself. I don't need to tell you," he nodded to the scout, still standing next to Brocke, "the cost of failure."

Caymus, replaying the scene of the burning city in his mind, knew the cost all too well.

~~~

The streets were too quiet.

The sun still hovered over the rooftops in the Grass District, yet Caymus passed very few people as he made his way back to Flamehearth Mission. A few dozen citizens made their through the major arteries of the city, but most of the vendors' stalls, which had been so prevalent when he'd first arrived, were now missing and the sounds of yelled conversations, of hawkers, of the footfalls of horses, appeared to have followed after them.

To Caymus, it seemed as though the city itself was holding its breath.

He only gave the silence a passing thought, however. His mind was filled with thoughts of the prince's meeting, of the things he had learned there. Tanner, the Keep-Marshal of Kepren, had held him back for nearly half-an-hour afterwards, asking him to recount, in as much detail as possible, his battles in the Conflagration. Caymus felt bad for the man. He wanted to defend his city, to find a way to teach his men how to beat back this enemy that would fall upon them so very soon.

When he'd finally left, Caymus had the feeling that Tanner hadn't gotten what he wanted. He'd explained what he could about pressing into the krealites, rather than striking at them, and he'd hoped that relaying that much to the soldiers would help them stay alive, but he wasn't optimistic about it. He wished there was more he could tell the marshal about fighting the krealites, but his own instruction had involved no lessons, no manuals, only experience, and that was one thing he couldn't pass on.

He could imagine the visions that must have been haunting the marshal's mind. As he made the last turn and headed down the street that housed the mission, he saw them too: the dying people of a burning city. There had been so much fire in the scout's memories, so much chaotic, horrifying destruction. Caymus had always been fascinated by flames, had been drawn into them somehow; the images he'd been shown this day
~~~

made him ashamed of those feelings.

And he'd thought he'd seen Mrowvain, the man who had called himself Callun, and who'd been the one to cut him with a krealite blade, in those images. At least, in the brief instant he'd seen that face, he'd thought he'd recognized it as Mrowvain's. The face had been walking through fire. The man that had worn it also wore skin that had seemed darker, more ashen than that of the man Caymus remembered, but the clothes were the same, as were the hollow, soulless eyes.

What could actually be done about that image, about the fact that he'd seen the man who had nearly killed him, Caymus wasn't sure, but the memory was stuck in his mind like the haunting recollection of some vivid nightmare. He supposed that the conclusion was obvious, really: if it was, in fact, Mrowvain that he had seen, then the man was marching with Black Moon and would be at the gates of the city in a matter of days. He wondered if they would meet again, whether the man who had so grievously wounded him, had nearly killed him, would get another chance to finish his work.

He also wondered at the merit of the prince's plan, whether it stood any chance of succeeding. Could he really prevent the bulk of Black Moon from reaching Kepren? Or would he simply die in the attempt?

Caymus found that his estimation of the prince of Kepren had risen a great deal in the last hour. When he'd first met Prince Garrin, he'd seemed charming and good-natured, but he hadn't seemed like a man ready to lead people in a war. This afternoon, Caymus had seen the other side of him: his resilience, his pride in his people, his willingness to die for them. He felt drawn by the man's presence, ready to follow him into any danger. He understood why his people looked up to him, despite his young age.

Still, the prince obviously faced other challenges. When Caymus had first entered the city, he'd had some difficulty understanding the order of things in Kepren, and his grasp of the politics of this place still wasn't complete. He knew, for instance, that the three districts of Kepren were each ruled in their entirety by the three dukes: Chenswig, Fel, and Korwinder. The king himself rightfully claimed only the Keep itself, which occupied a relatively small space inside the Guard District. The king was given responsibility for, and dominion over, the army, but it was the dukes who were in charge of raising the troops, and the prince—the Champion-Protector—was the man ultimately in command of leading the city's forces.

Caymus often wondered at the seeming madness of it. In theory, the king had the authority to overrule the dukes; in practice, he didn't seem to wield any real power outside his own castle. These days, Garrin was king in all but name, but he still retained his leadership of the army. It would likely have been easy for the dukes, for the Keep-Marshal, for anybody in a position of authority to claim that he was no longer the Champion-Protector, and to demand that he be officially crowned the king of Kepren and thus have the leadership of the army taken from him and given to a new Champion-Protector.

The fact that nobody challenged Garrin's rule seemed more evidence of just how well-respected the prince was among his subjects. How did a man become so strong, so respected, and at such a young age? Caymus knew he would have to find a way to learn from him.

As he passed through the front door of Flamehearth, he decided he would ask the prince to allow him to join in his mission, to help him strike the first blow against their enemy.

Something about having made the decision lifted his spirits.

The moment he closed the door behind him, he realized that the silence of the city had been broken. His eyes went wide when he heard the distinctive sounds of steel on steel. He turned his head. The sound was coming from the courtyard. There was fighting in the mission!

Quickly, he drew his sword and ran through the front room and the corridors, heading for one of the rooms with an entrance into the courtyard. He placed his weight carefully, keeping his footfalls quiet. If there were attackers out there, he might be able to surprise them.

When he stepped onto the dry grass, however, he was momentarily confused by what he saw. Aiella was there, standing amongst the small group of children that lived at the mission. She and one of the girls were attacking each other with rapiers, and he wondered what could possibly have possessed the woman to attack children.

When he noticed the smiles on the faces of the two combatants, though, he realized what was really happening. Obviously, she was teaching them something of fencing. She must have believed there was some merit in instructing the youngsters in how to fight. He found that he couldn't argue with the idea.

Rather than sheathe his sword, Caymus let it hang loosely in his fingers as he leaned against the courtyard wall. The attentions of the six children were riveted on the two combatants, and so none of them had noticed him yet. He was impressed by Aiella's opponent—he believed the young girl's name was Tesh—who was stepping quickly backward and forward in response to Aiella's movements.

Aiella, too, was quite impressive. Her arm moved quickly, and she didn't waver when she stepped or lunged, the motions revealing a practiced, balanced form. Caymus found himself captivated by her black hair, tied back with a simple kerchief, and the way it waved and spilled, roughly a half-second behind the rest of her.

There came a pause in the swordplay, a breath in the conversation, during which one of the boys noticed him standing there. The children of Flamehearth didn't know Caymus, as he'd spent most of his time in Kepren in a bed in one of the rooms, but they all knew about the Sleeping Giant, and so the boy smiled and waved enthusiastically at him. After that, the dominoes fell and the entire group, Aiella included, was suddenly looking in his direction.

"You have been standing there long, Caymus?" Aiella said, lowering her sword and motioning for the girl to do the same. She was wearing her usual, unreadable demeanor.

"Just arrived," he replied, then he smiled at the group as a whole. "I didn't know Flamehearth had opened a fencing school."

The children giggled, and even Aiella let a small smile break through. "Children," she said, glancing around her and then pointing at Caymus, "what do you think about that sword Caymus has?"

"It's too big!" the children shouted, almost as one. The younger ones laughed with the proclamation.

Caymus raised his eyebrows. He was still carrying the shortsword he'd brought with him when he'd left for Terrek. A shortsword? Big? He raised the blade before his eyes to look it over. "You think so?" he said. "It's been working pretty well so far." He didn't say anything about the fact that his muscles sometimes screamed for a much larger weapon when he swung this one.

Aiella stared at him a moment before answering. "Let us find out," she said. There was an air of playful menace in her voice, and Caymus tilted his head, curious at her meaning.

"Come," she said, motioning him over, "we will duel to see which is the greater blade." She waved her arm around her. "Children, you must stand against the wall please, and allow us space."

Caymus didn't step forward, though. He wasn't convinced that what she was proposing was a good idea. He'd sparred with Rill on several occasions, and so he felt comfortable with the general idea of dueling, but ever since he'd been young, he'd always been larger than anybody else; he'd learned early on, sometimes the hard way, to be on constant guard so as not to hurt people accidentally. He certainly didn't want to hurt Aiella. "Are you sure about this?" he said.

She smiled a suddenly wicked smile at him. "Do not worry, sir," she said, "I will not be too hard on you."

He wasn't sure how he felt about being called 'sir', especially by her, but the thought was fleeting.

"Do it, Giant!" a few of the children yelled. "Duel!" said others. Caymus stared at the bloodthirsty group in some disbelief, then he looked back at Aiella. She was standing there with one hand on her hip and her eyebrows raised at him, daring him to accept her challenge.

He shrugged his shield and a satchel's worth of belongings off his shoulders and placed them on the ground. "All right," he said, cautiously, as he stepped forward. Briefly, he wondered if Be'Var had returned to Flamehearth yet. If something went wrong here, Aiella might require his healer's arts.

The two duelists stood nearly three yards apart, facing each other. Aiella brought her rapier up, signaling her readiness, and Caymus did the same. He still wasn't certain he should be doing this, but when he met her eyes, he saw an intensity there, a deep concentration that made him think that maybe he'd misjudged the odds in this fight.

In an instant, she was moving, and he knew he hadn't been ready for it. He parried a couple of her swings, barely getting his blade in the way of hers before it struck home. When he moved to make a thrust of his own, however, he suddenly found she had her rapier at his throat.

She grinned at him. "Again?"

He nodded. He wasn't sure what had just happened, but he wanted to see if she could get past his guard a second time.

The two of them backed off, reset, and signaled readiness. Again, within moments, Caymus found himself on the defense, narrowly deflecting her quick-moving blade with his. He managed to get a swing in this time, but it was parried and, in the next instant, the rapier was at his throat a second time.

"Again?"

Caymus glanced around at the children before he nodded. Each of them was grinning at him.

Time and again, they reset their positions, and time and again, Caymus found the narrow blade at his neck. Each time, as the children gasped, he looked up and found Aiella's dark eyes grinning at him. "Again?"

After the seventh or eighth bout—he wasn't sure which—he found himself becoming aware of his emotions, of a rising sense of his own state of mind. A large part of him was becoming frustrated and angry at his constant failure and her mocking smiles. Another part of him, however, was intrigued, curious about what kept happening, how she was beating him. What other tricks this girl might have in store?

He found himself wondering how long she'd trained, how many years she must have spent studying fencing in her youth.

Again, he stood with his sword out to his side, a thin length of steel against his jugular. Aiella must have been on her toes, because her face felt like it was mere inches from his. Her dark eyes narrowed. "Again?"

"Miss Aiella?"

The two of them turned to see a man standing in the same doorway through which Caymus had entered, his head down and his hands behind his back. Caymus recognized the man: he was the Creveyan scout whose

memories Brocke had played out in a pool of water less than an hour ago.
As quickly as she'd advanced on him, Aiella pulled away and placed her blade in its scabbard. "Yes, Keegan," she said, her voice a monument to control, "what is it?"
Caymus quietly sheathed his own sword as the scout approached Aiella and handed her a folded and sealed piece of parchment. After turning it once in her hands, Aiella broke the seal, unfolded the sheet, and spent some time reading. Caymus didn't quite know what to do with himself in the silence, and he considered picking up his gear and going to his room, but the note must have been very short, as Aiella looked up again within moments.
"Thank you, Keegan," she said, giving the sheet back. "Say to him that I will return shortly?"
Keegan nodded and bowed very slightly. "I will, Miss Aiella," he said, then he turned and quietly walked away.
After he was gone, Aiella turned in a circle to address the children, who were still watching the exchange with great anticipation. "No more lessons today, children," she said to them. The children collectively voiced their disappointment, but they wasted no time in running back into the building, presumably to start up little duels of their own.
Caymus walked back to his shield and satchel, picked them up, and secured them over his shoulders again. Aiella followed him. "You are quick," she said.
Caymus looked back at her in surprise. "Not quick enough, it seems," he said. "You got past my guard every time. I don't know how you did that."
She looked away with a distant smile. "I began learning this weapon," she touched the rapier on her hip, "when I was four years old. If I were not quick, I would be a disappointment." She looked back to Caymus, a curious expression in her eyes. "You must not try to be quicker than me," she said.
Caymus wasn't sure what she meant by that. "I'm sorry?"
She seemed to smile in spite of herself. "I," she placed a hand against her chest, "am quick. Many people who have studied the rapier as long as I have are quick. It is my strength, my advantage." A strand of dark hair fell in her face, which she pulled back and tucked into her kerchief. "*Your* strength," she continued, pointing at him, "is not in quickness, but in power. You must not try to be as quick as me."
"Ah," he said, "you mean I should be playing to my size, rather than trying to match your speed?"
She nodded with a small smile. "One who is wielding a quick weapon, a narrow blade," she said, "she must often land many strikes in order to best her opponent. So long as you protect your face, neck, and heart," she

pointed to all three places on him, "you are safe enough. But my blade is small and light. If a strong opponent were to bring his weapon down with all his might, there would be little a quick person could do against it." She held up a finger. "A powerful person, he needs only one strike."

"Of course," Caymus said, after thinking about it, "a quick person might just dodge out of the way and quickly stab me back."

She smiled. It was the first genuinely pleased smile he could remember ever seeing from her. "That is possible, also," she said.

Caymus realized he was enjoying himself, enjoying this simple moment. He'd had some time traveling with Milo in the last two days, of course, but there had been so much to do, and they'd spent so much time rushing. This was the first time since waking up in a candlelit room that he'd had the chance to just appreciate the company of another human being. He was surprised to discover it was this girl—she'd been so cold to him when they'd first met!—who was allowing him such a reprieve from the seriousness of the world. "Thank you for the lesson, Aiella," he said.

She nodded, then the smile vanished, and she turned to look to the North. "I must return to the Keep," she said, then she turned back to him. "Will you walk with me?"

Caymus was surprised, but he didn't see any reason why he shouldn't. "Give me a moment to put my things away?"

"Of course."

Within a few minutes, Caymus had put his bag and his shield—everything except his shortsword—on the bed in his room, and the two of them were walking up the street, back in the direction from which Caymus had just come.

The streets seemed even quieter, now. The sun was beginning to disappear behind some of the houses and merchant buildings, and the lamplighters, boys of about nine or ten who carried long, thin torches, were starting their rounds, setting aglow the various lamps and lanterns that dotted the roads of Kepren. The sun was taking its warmth with it as it vanished, and so a chill was forming in the air around them. Caymus hadn't noticed it before, but autumn had entered its final days as he'd slept, and now winter was beginning to wake.

"You must have become a person who is important," Aiella said as they walked, "if you are being invited to the council of the prince."

Caymus couldn't tell if she was mocking him or genuinely inquiring about his station. "It was just the one meeting," he said, shrugging, "and I'm not sure why I was invited. I think Master Be'Var must have told the prince that I would be useful."

She turned to glance at him. "And were you?"

Caymus waggled his head. He thought about the moment when the prince had asked whether the Rill's sludge could burn the krealites. Master

Be'Var had actually deferred to him. He hadn't thought about it at that time, but he realized now that the moment had been a milestone, a turning point in their relationship. "I suppose I was," he said.

"That is good," she said, hugging herself against the cold. "Garrin, then, he is fortunate to have your assistance."

Caymus shook his head in slight disbelief upon hearing someone say that a prince, the commander of an entire army, was lucky to have his help. "I think it might be the other way around," he said. "I didn't know what a good leader he was until today."

"Garrin is a good leader, yes," she said. Her voice had taken on a more subdued, less brash tone than was usual. "I wish him not but happiness."

Caymus thought it an odd thing to say. He didn't mention the fact, but she must have picked up on his confusion. "My father," she said, "he brought me here, to Kepren, so that the prince might court me," she said. She looked at Caymus pointedly. "You were not aware of this?"

Caymus shook his head. "I wasn't." He'd picked up that there might be something more than friendship between the two of them, and Be'Var had alluded to a sort of understanding between the prince and the ambassador's daughter, but he'd not speculated on the details.

She faced forward again. Caymus looked over and saw an unusually distant look on her face. She suddenly seemed vulnerable, a fact that surprised him more than her rapier at his neck had done. "He is a good man," she said, "a strong warrior, and a good leader as you say, but I have no wish to be married into royalty, especially royalty of a nation that is not my own."

They walked in silence for a time. Caymus didn't know what to say, so he tried to think of something else to talk about. "I saw the king today," he said. "Do you know what's wrong with him?"

Instantly, the vulnerable look faded away, and Aiella shrugged into a deep sigh. "I have been told I should not speak of it," she said, "but it is probably best that you are aware." She looked around them, checking for eavesdroppers. There were barely half a dozen people to be seen, and none of them seemed interested in what the two of them were talking about.

"The king's mind, it is gone," she said, turning to Caymus as though to make sure she had his attention. "From what I have been told, his condition, it began upon at the death of his wife, almost ten years ago." She stared at the ground as she continued. "I feel pity for this man, to lose the person most important to him while he is sacrificing his own happiness attending to the actions of his father."

"The king's father?" Caymus asked. "What do you mean?"

She turned and raised an eyebrow at him. "You are Tebrian, are you not? Can you be ignorant of this fact?"

Caymus shrugged. "I suppose I am, though the place where I grew up is on the borders of Tebria. It's a town called Woodsea. It's about a dozen miles north of Krin's Point, and so that's the place we have the most contact with." He glanced at her as he realized his conclusion. "It's not that we didn't like Kepren. We just never had any a lot of communication with anywhere south of the Greatstones, and so we never had much use for Tebria."

Aiella seemed astonished at hearing this, but she continued, regardless. "The old king—the father of the current king—made constant war with the nation of Mael'vek." She regarded Caymus again. "You know of Mael'vek, yes?"

"Yes," Caymus groaned. "I'm not *that* out of touch."

She nodded in satisfaction. "The old king, he brought his wife, the queen, with him on every campaign, and so his son, King Lysandus, was born in a tent during a battle."

"The king was born on a battlefield?" Caymus's eyes widened at the idea.

"He was," she replied. "What is more important is that he was born on Mael'vekian soil. It is for this reason the emperor of Mael'vek, he believes that King Lysandus is a citizen of his empire, and so Tebria can be claimed as a part of Mael'vek."

Caymus frowned at the idea. "That seems like a bit of a stretch to me."

"It is," Aiella replied, "but it is the excuse for the wars that Mael'vek, it has launched against Tebria. It is the reason for the day that they pushed into Laivus and razed that city. This is why the Grass District had need to be built and why the king, he has spent much of his life defending against an empire that believes that his is a subject of its emperor."

Caymus was baffled by the logic of kings and emperors. He was also amazed at the causality of events, that an accident of birth meant that Lysandus had spent most of his life defending his kingdom from the enemies of his father.

"I wonder what this king is leaving behind for Prince Garrin to deal with," Caymus idly wondered.

"It seems that the king Garrin, he will have new enemies to face," Aiella said. It was a small sound that seemed to be mostly for herself. She frowned. "I wonder if he will wish me to see him before he leaves tonight."

Caymus hadn't realized how quickly they'd moved through the city. He merely noticed the presence of someone else in front of him and looked up to find himself in front of soldiers of the Keep. He smiled to himself. The last time he'd lost his awareness of time, he'd been consumed in flames. This had been an altogether more pleasant experience.

Aiella turned to him with a face that was as unreadable as it ever was.

"I must assist with some of the preparations tonight," she said, "and I am certain that you also are having duties to attend."

Caymus wasn't sure about any actual duties of his own, but he would be glad to finally get a chance to wash the last few days' travel from his skin. He returned the smile and nodded. "I will see you another time then," he said, "Miss Aiella."

"Ha!" she said, closing her eyes momentarily. When she opened them again, she wore a faint smile. "Please do not call me 'Miss' again."

Caymus was particularly surprised when she stepped forward, raised her arm, and placed the palm of her hand gently against his cheek. "I wish you luck in the coming days, Caymus of the Conflagration," she said. Before he could respond, she had stepped through the large, oak door and was gone, leaving two surprised-looking guards in her wake.

Caymus could only offer a shrug to the men, unable to explain what had happened any better than they could, before he turned to leave.

As he walked back through the streets of Kepren, the stone and brick of the city now lit more by lamplight than by sunlight, he wondered about the chance encounter. Aiella's actions were a far cry from those of the woman he'd met when he'd first come to Kepren. He wondered what had changed. He also wondered how much of that change had to do with her and how much with him.

When he finally returned to his room, he spent some time unpacking his belongings, then repacking them again so that he would be ready to travel again at a moment's notice. Aiella had let slip an important bit of information during their conversation; Caymus wasn't sure if she had done so intentionally or not.

As he sat on his bed in the same small room where he'd been so long asleep, he also spent some time sharpening a few of the nicks out of his sword. When he felt a presence in the room, he looked up and saw the girl Aiella had been fencing with, standing in his doorway.

He gave her a friendly smile. "It's Tesh, isn't it?"

The girl nodded, her bright blue eyes following the movement of his whetstone. He couldn't quite judge her age, but he figured she was a little older than ten.

"Well, Tesh," he said, "you seemed to do quite well fencing with Aiella today." He gave her a meaningful look. "Better than I did, anyway."

The girl smiled and looked down at the floor, masking either embarrassment or outright laughter.

Caymus looked back to his blade. "I didn't know she had been giving you all fencing lessons."

Tesh looked up, surprised. "She hasn't," she said. "It was only today."

He narrowed his eyes at the girl. "You mean she specially came out just this one time to show you how to use a sword?"

The girl shook her head and gave him a curious smile. "No, silly," she said, "Miss Aiella comes to the mission sometimes, but she wasn't here to see us today. She said was looking for you."

~~~

Garrin shook his head and rolled his eyes as he lifted the small barrel into the back of the cart, his men laughing all around him. The sound brought an element of cheer to the otherwise dark alleyway.

"Seriously, Garrin, when are you going to stop chasing that poor girl?" Cyrus said, his face a picture of mockery.

Garrin couldn't help chuckling. "Leave Aiella out of it, will you," he said, giving his friend a knowing look, "unless you'd like to discuss the skirts you've been chasing of late. I heard that one of the barmaids at the Three Foals turned up pregnant this week."

"Oh no!" said Big Grant, his thunderous voice booming down the stone walls. "Not another one, Cyrus." Even after all the time they'd spent together over the years, Garrin could never be sure if the big man was being serious or not.

Cyrus pushed his stringy, blonde hair out of his eyes and pointed a finger at Big Grant. "That…particular incident…had nothing to do with me!" He looked around at the other six men. "Still," he said, clearing his throat, "I'd be grateful if my wife didn't find out about it."

"Oh," said Mally, bringing up the last of the small barrels, "I think you're underestimating her again, Cyrus. If your wife isn't already well-aware of the barmaid's predicament, I'd be very surprised."

Cyrus had the good nature to look a bit sheepish at the remark. "Too right," he said. "Still, let's keep it to ourselves for the time being, eh?"

Garrin, dusting his hands off and leaning back against one of the small carts, smiled as he watched his men ribbing each other. They were nearly finished loading their carts with the small barrels of graysilt that they would be bringing to Falmoor's Pass, and he estimated they would be on their way out of the city in a few minutes' time. Considering the danger he was about to put them all in, he was happy to allow some time for levity.

The two Grants were checking the tack on the horses, making sure the carts were secured properly to the beasts. Big Grant wasn't particularly tall. He earned his nickname from the sizable muscle mass he'd gained over the years by lifting heavy stones on a regular basis. Next to him was Bigger Grant. Bigger Grant had only joined the prince's guard a few years ago. While not particularly large of frame, he was a looming six and-a-half feet tall, so a moniker had been needed to differentiate him from Big
~~~

Grant.

Garrin had never used these kinds of carts before, and he was having some misgivings about whether they would be fit-for-purpose. They were two-wheeled contraptions designed to be pulled by a single horse—they actually reminded him of tiny racing chariots—that would carry three of the small casks of graysilt each. The carts looked strong enough, but he was concerned about the stamina of the animals: each horse would not only have to pull a cart, but also bear a rider all the way up the northern road to the mountains.

"Did we pick the right gear?" he asked Mally while the other men continued mocking poor Cyrus.

Mally, standing right beside him, frowned. "Are you talking about the carts again?"

Garrin turned to him. "I am."

Mally sighed. "I don't like the weight either, my friend, but I just don't see another way of getting this many casks up the road that quickly with so few men."

It was Garrin's turn to sigh. "Best bad option, then?"

Mally chuckled. "You know me so well."

Garrin nodded, not quite willing to laugh. "I do."

Mally watched the rest of the men as they fetched the last of the tack from the stables and made themselves ready to travel. He leaned in toward Garrin and spoke softly. "You think he even knows if it's his?" he asked, clearly referring to Cyrus and the pregnant barmaid.

Garrin chuckled. "As much as that man drinks," he said, nodding in Cyrus's direction, "I'd not be too surprised if he's sweating over exactly that question right now." He looked over at Harrison and Bernie, who were checking the group's provisions, and physically flinched. Harrison hadn't pulled one of his pranks in several months now, and there was a good chance he'd want to make up for lost time. He trusted Harrison, of course—he'd frequently trusted each and every one of these men with his life—but he wasn't sure if this particular mission could survive Harrison's particular brand of mischief. He hoped that getting Bernie to keep an eye on him during this mission would turn out to be a wise choice: the two men had contrasting personalities and didn't always get along, but Garrin didn't think they could afford mischief on this trip; and if anybody was well-suited to moderating mischief, it was Bernie.

Six men, his friends and companions, some of whom he'd known for most of his life. The safety of the city was about to depend upon what they were going to be able to accomplish in the next couple of days. The enormity of that idea weighed heavily on Garrin, and yet he found that he was smiling: if he were to live for a thousand years, he could never have asked for better company.

He tilted his head over and whispered, "When did Bigger Grant start growing a beard?" Garrin had noticed the scruffy growth, which was both light and patchy, as soon as the men had started arriving half hour ago, but he hadn't wanted to mention it before now. Against the backdrop of the man's height, the scraggly-looking mass didn't look good at all.

"Ah, yes," said Mally, with an amused grimace, "the beard. It seems he started not shaving a couple of weeks ago, and that mess on his face is the result." Mally, too, lowered his voice. "It's a bit of a sore spot, actually, so I'd give it a day or two before bringing it up."

Garrin shook his head sympathetically. For such a big man—he was nearly as tall as Caymus, in fact—one would think he'd be able to grow some half-decent facial hair.

"Are they ready for this?" the prince asked his longtime friend.

Mally, wearing his usual unflappable demeanor, reached back and tugged on his black ponytail. "What," he said, "you mean this mad, seven-men-against-several-thousand plan of yours? The one where we take the biggest risk any of us can remember, and from which we're unlikely to return?" He looked pointedly at Garrin. "Are they ready for that, you mean?"

Garrin took a deep breath. "Yes."

Mally nodded, smiling that placid smile of his. "They're ready." He looked out over the group again. "We're ready."

Garrin stole a look up at the stars in the night sky. There seemed to be more of them up there than usual tonight. "You'd let me know, wouldn't you," he said, "if I was about to lead us into a needless slaughter?"

Amalwyn—Mally—had been the captain of Garrin's personal guard, of the men before him, for eight years. He had been his best friend for a great deal longer. There was not a single other person in the entire world whom Garrin respected more, or upon whose opinions he was more reliant.

"I would," Mally said. He affected a slight nod. "Don't worry, old friend," he said. "We all known the odds are long on this one, but we also know what's at stake. Three major cities burned to the ground in just a few months, and they don't even take prisoners?" He chuckled. "Slaughter it may be, sure, but not a needless one."

Garrin sighed. "Thanks, Mally."

"That's the last of it," said Bernie, tying down a barrel.

Garrin nodded and looked around at the men. "Good," he said. "Are we ready to go then?"

Nobody said anything, and so everybody mounted their horses. Garrin took a moment to grab his sword, still in its belt and scabbard, which he'd left leaning against a nearby wall as they'd worked. Once he'd belted it on, he put his hand on the pommel and took a deep breath. The Black Sword of the Prince had been passed down through the line of the royal family for more generations than had been recorded. It was as much a family heirloom as it was a functional weapon, but that didn't stop it being incredibly sharp and dangerous. He'd carried it into battle ever since he'd first become the Champion-Protector of Kepren, on the day of his twentieth year. It was completely black from pommel to point, perfectly balanced, and never needed sharpening. It had always felt comfortable in his hand. His father had once told him, before he'd lost so much of himself to sickness, that the sword had looked different in his day, that it had seemed wider and heavier back in the days when it had been Prince Lysandus who'd served as Kepren's Champion-Protector. Garrin had always wondered about that story, whether the weapon could actually mold itself to its wielder, or if the tale had just been the first evidence of the king's decent into madness.

Now, as he got up on his horse, he only hoped he'd somehow get away with not having to use the sword in the next few days.

Quietly and quickly, each man responding fluidly to the movements of the others, the prince and his guard made their way down the alley that would take them to the main thoroughfare of the Guard District, heading for the North Gate. Mally took the lead. Garrin rode close behind him. After him came Bernie, Harrison, Big Grant, and Cyrus. Bigger Grant brought up the rear, as usual. "May'uswell put the tallest felluh' at the back, since he can see everythin'," he liked to say

As the group made its way out of the city, Garrin thought about what Cyrus had said: what *was* he going to do about Aiella? He genuinely cared for the girl, and the two of them got along fine, but he supposed his friend was right. She'd shown absolutely no interest in him romantically, and while the two of them were a good political match, he respected her too much to want to force, or even bring up, the issue of marriage. He should probably stop seeing her so often.

His father wouldn't have approved of that, had he still retained his faculties. He'd have hated the idea of his son being in his thirties and not yet having produced an heir to the throne of Kepren.

Who was he kidding? He wasn't likely to live long enough to sire an heir anyway.

"Who's that?" said Mally.

Garrin, who'd been lost in his own thoughts, looked up and peered ahead. They'd almost reached the North Gate, and someone appeared to be waiting for them there. In the darkness between the lanterns, the figure was hard to make out. Mally was already loosening his sword in its sheath.

When they got a bit closer, Garrin caught himself grinning. The figure was actually two figures. One was a horse. The other was a very tall, very big man. "Stay your swords, gentlemen," he said, then he rode ahead to meet the dark shapes. He pulled his horse and cart up alongside the figure and met his eyes. "You should be careful about lurking in shadows, Caymus," he said. "Someone might mistake you for some kind of highwayman."

Caymus offered up n apologetic smile. "Sorry, your Highness," he said, "I didn't mean to lurk, exactly."

Garrin nodded. "So, want to tell me what you're doing out here, then?"

Caymus's smile faded, his countenance becoming stone serious. "I've decided I'm going with you."

A smattering of muffled laughter rose up from the men behind Garrin. The prince regarded the young man through narrowed eyes. It hadn't been a demand, but it hadn't been a request either. Caymus seemed to have simply stated a fact.

Garrin was about to chide Caymus for taking such liberties, but the intense look on the young man's face stopped him and he found himself considering the idea. He glanced back at the others. Every one of them was a trusted friend. More to the point, they had fought together as a unit for a long time, and so they knew how to get along, how to read one another, both on and off the field of battle. Garrin was aware that Caymus had been taught how to fight, but if he simply dropped him into this group, he might net them more harm than good.

He looked back at Caymus. "Why?" he asked, simply.

"Because," Caymus replied, "I'm not going to just stay here and wait for the enemy to come and kill the people I care about." The look in his eyes intensified, and Garrin could clearly see the fire-worshiper in the face before him. "And if you want a more practical reason, well, I know more about the krealites than any man living. If there's going to be a strike against them, I should be there."

Garrin sat quietly. His horse nickered and stamped at the ground as he considered the words, considered the man before him. Garrin didn't know Caymus all that well, but what he did know, he liked. He had a genuine sort of way about him, a way that engendered a simple kind of trust. Be'Var had also told him that the boy had a quick mind that picked up new ideas quickly.

Then, there was the kreal. Caymus was right about that. Garrin didn't understand this new element, didn't know what it was doing in his world, but the kreal and Caymus seemed, somehow, to be linked, and just having this singular point of view along for the ride might be the single most important reason to take him along.

As he sat there, thinking, Mally rode up next to him and poked him in the ribs. Garrin flinched, but then turned and read the look on his friend's face. The look said, "Don't worry about us. We'll manage either way."

"I don't suppose," Garrin said, turning back to Caymus, "you feel like telling me who let it slip that we were leaving tonight," he narrowed his eyes at him, "and not tomorrow?"

Caymus, who couldn't quite keep a small grin off his face, shook his head. "No, Sir, I don't."

"Fine. Fall in."

As the group rode out of the North Gate and sped up into a trot, Garrin heard Mally and Caymus talking behind him. When the men's voices rose in cheerful laughter, Garrin smiled to himself. Caymus might just fit in, after all.

Chapter 18

"I couldn't believe you were still walking upright, you were so covered in muck!"

The prince gave Harrison a withering look, then he shook his head and smiled. "I suppose I must have looked a bit of a mess."

Caymus looked back and forth between the two men as they rode through the chilly, desert landscape. They'd spent two days riding at a quick pace and were now traveling nearly alongside the Greatstones. For the time being, they'd slowed down a bit to give the horses a break, and so he was being told the story of how Garrin and Amalwyn, the captain of the guard whom everyone called Mally, had met.

Mally was an earth worshiper, though his devotions were completely different from those of the mitre. The mitres' Aspects had all seemed to be about the manipulation of their element. Mally's Aspect, from what Caymus had been able to glean from Garrin's explanation, had more to do with understanding the ways that the earth below them was formed, how it was put together. Caymus hadn't really understood what that had meant, but Mally had just smiled an easy smile and assured him he'd figure it out, eventually.

"A mess?" called out Cyrus, riding behind. "Garrin, the only way I could tell you apart from everyone else was that sword of yours, and only because it was blacker than the mud!"

It seemed that the prince, along with a group of soldiers that had included Cyrus and Harrison, had been traveling through an area of swampland, many miles east of Kepren, in an attempt to come at a Mael'vekian position from an unguarded flank. The swamp, however, had been more than they'd bargained for, and most of the men, along with several of the wagons, had found themselves mired in mud. Mally, who before this time had not served directly under the prince, had used his

Aspect to find a clear path through the swamp and, in doing so, had saved the company from almost certain disaster.

"I remember that," said Harrison. "In fact, I remember we all looked so uniformly muddy that I'd been considering playing the part of the prince for a while."

Knowing smiles and a few chuckles emerged from the men. Caymus couldn't help but join in. He was surprised to find how comfortable he felt here. Despite the fact that he was now traveling with the prince of Kepren and his personal guard, he felt like he was back at the Temple, playing around with his friends. The group around him was easily as diverse as were the boys there.

Mally was the captain of the prince's personal guard and was Garrin's second-in-command on this mission. His long, dark brown hair, when not tied back in a tail, framed a squared-off face and a large, blunt nose. He had an easy-going demeanor and a calm, confident smile. He was thoughtful and considerate, and he always listened to the concerns of the other men, even when they appeared trivial. Mally and Garrin spent a good deal of time conversing privately between themselves, and Caymus got the impression that the two men had known each other, in one capacity or another, for a very long time.

Cyrus was the smallest in the group, though he easily had the biggest, brashest personality. His wispy, blonde hair seemed somehow at odds with the crooked teeth of his smile as though they came from different heads; the smile, however, got used a lot, so one quickly became accustomed to the disparity. He was quick with a joke and, Caymus had discovered on their first full day of travel, was also a bit of a prankster. Caymus wished he had a mirror so he could find out if his teeth were still stained green.

Cyrus was rarely very far from Harrison's side. Harrison was, at the most, three inches taller than Cyrus, and only slightly larger of build. His hair was as black as Cyrus's was blonde. He didn't smile nearly as much, and he didn't say a whole lot, either. Caymus had thought him very serious, but the others had assured him that his outward demeanor was deceptive: he was even more incorrigible than Cyrus, especially when it came to pranks. "Cyrus?" Mally had advised him early on the second day, "Oh, he'll cause you an afternoon's annoyance. When *Harrison* pulls off one of his schemes, it can make a man question reality for a while."

Caymus was certain he didn't want to know what he'd meant by that.

The two Grants were an odd pairing, too. Big Grant wasn't particularly tall, but he was heavily muscled. Bigger Grant wasn't particularly muscular, but he was the tallest man Caymus had ever known—other than himself, of course. They both had hair that was somewhere between brown and red, though Big Grant cut his to stubble atop his head, while

Bigger Grant wore his down to his shoulders. Garrin had said that the two of them had never met each other before entering into his service, which had surprised Caymus: the two were so alike in personality and coloring that they could have been brothers.

Caymus had learned that Big Grant was an avid, though unusual, worshiper of earth, and that he had devised methods of lifting heavy objects to force his muscles to grow bigger and stronger, the goal being to make himself appear more stone-like. There had apparently been some bad blood between him and Garrin a long time ago, though if anybody knew the details of it, they weren't telling Caymus.

Bigger Grant liked to pick the prince up sometimes, which everybody but Garrin found hysterical.

The final man, Bernie, was still a mystery to Caymus. He was the same height and build as the prince and had straight, black hair which fell to about the middle of his back and was kept in a thick braid. He was the only member of the party who didn't use some kind of sword, instead favoring a pair of short spears, which he kept hanging loosely on his back. His sharp, delicate features made him appear more like a foppish dandy than a soldier, but Mally had informed Caymus that Bernie might just have one of the finest strategic minds in military history.

Bernie didn't smile, and he was the only one who hadn't opened up to Caymus in some way. Indeed, his constant glowers made Caymus wonder if he'd done something to offend the man that first night.

Overall, Caymus had been impressed by these men, at how organized they seemed to be. Not counting the evening they'd departed Kepren, they'd spent two nights out of doors, sleeping four hours at a time so as to reach the pass as quickly as possible. The seven men always had camp set up, complete with a cooking fire and a tent for each pair of men, within ten minutes. They took the camp apart even faster. Even more impressive was the fact that they didn't talk while they did it. Each man just seemed to know what every other man was going to do and quietly got on with his own part in the process.

Caymus wondered if the mens' coordination was a consequence of their collective experience at soldiering, or if it had more to do with how much time they'd spent in each other's company.

"I don't think we can be far off now," said Garrin, eyeing the mountains to the north of them.

"I think you're right," nodded Mally. "I expect we'll see Big Grant riding back any second now." Big Grant was acting as the company's scout today, making sure they didn't run into any advance elements of the enemy before they found the pass.

"Once we're there," said Garrin, "how much time do you think you'll need?"

Mally grunted. "How much time can you give me?"

Garrin sighed, thinking. "With the speed the Creveyans said they were moving," he said, "and it's been three days since then..." He waggled his head. "I think we'll have something approaching two days before they come marching out of the mountains at us."

Mally nodded, regarding the peaks and ridges suspiciously. "A day to figure out the plan, then," he said, "and then another to set it all up."

Garrin raised an eyebrow. "A whole day?"

Mally grinned. "The pass is little more than a pair of lines on an old map right now," he said. "It's going to take me a while to figure out the composition, to work out what's sand, what's granite, limestone...what's just loose rocks."

The prince wasn't convinced yet. "Still, a whole day? The idea isn't to enjoy yourself, you know."

Mally's grin subsided. "The longer I've got to figure it out, the better the end result." He hiked a thumb at the graysilt kegs behind him. "Those things will make a pretty good-sized blast, but we don't have very many of them, so we need to make every single one of them count. I can do that, Garrin, but I need time to figure out how."

Garrin nodded slowly. "Alright," he said, then he sighed. "All right, a full day it is."

"Then we'll bury the bastards!" came Cyrus's voice, from behind.

Caymus noticed Mally visibly shudder when the impromptu cheer went up. "You alright?" he said, after nudging his horse a bit closer and lowering his voice.

Mally looked up and gave him a sad smile. "Oh, I'm fine," he said. "It's just that Cyrus is right: we're looking to cause a rock-slide and bury our enemy."

Caymus narrowed his eyes. "And that's a bad thing?"

Mally nodded, his eyes unfocused. "Imagine you hear a big, roaring noise," he said. "Then, you suddenly find yourself being tossed, end over end, around and around, and you get the wind knocked out of you. You have no idea what's happening to you. You don't know which way is up. When you finally have your bearings again, it's pitch black, you can't move, every breath fills your lungs with sand, and you're being crushed by a ton and a half of earth and rock. You can barely get your chest to move so you can breathe, and when you do, all you get is lungfuls of dirt that you can't even cough up." He looked at Caymus severely. "It's a horrible way to go, and that's what we're planning on doing to all of them."

Caymus nodded, finding a strange kind of respect for this person who seemed able to empathize with the monsters who were, at that very moment, on their way to kill him.

"Still," said Mally, "Garrin's in charge, and it's his decision. I just hope we manage to do it right, that's all."

Caymus smiled. "I hope so, too."

He and Mally had fallen behind the others a bit, and Mally urged his horse forward to keep up. Caymus, not in any hurry, hung back, thinking about what Mally had said. He found himself wondering if the act of burying somebody alive might also have some manner of religious significance for the man.

Caymus had also noticed that while Mally had been describing the account of being buried, he'd been rubbing some kind of locket between this thumb and forefinger. He wondered if he should ask about it.

"He's a good man, is Amalwyn Cove."

Caymus looked over to see that the previously silent Bernie had ridden up beside him, his dark brooding eyes scanning the horizon.

Caymus looked ahead at the group. "I think I could say that of any of you."

"No," said Bernie. "Not like Mally. He's the best of us. Always tells the truth, and always listens."

Caymus nodded absently, still looking ahead.

"What are you doing here?" Caymus glanced over and saw Bernie giving him a hard look, a look that held no friendship or curiosity, but rather suspicion and menace. His voice was like sand: rough and irritating to the ears. "And don't give me, that 'I have to do something' nonsense, either. A man doesn't ride out to his death like this unless he's got something immense to gain from it."

Caymus was surprised at the words. "You think we're going to our deaths?"

The eyes before Caymus contained deadly intensity. "Answer the question."

Caymus held the gaze for a moment, then turned to look ahead again. He considered what Bernie was asking him. Why was he here?

What he'd said about needing to help was true, of course, and he did seem to be destined to fight the kreal, but that didn't mean he needed to be a part of this mission. The battle was likely coming anyway—Black Moon would likely be in Kepren within the week—so why did he feel the need to join *these* men on *this* mission?

He picked the prince out from the group, his black sword at his side. There was some kind of pull coming from that man. He'd felt it the first day they'd arrived in Kepren. He hadn't understood it then, and he didn't understand it now, but he was slowly beginning to come to terms with the fact that he felt a compulsion to follow the prince of Kepren, to keep him in sight, to be close at hand. He didn't know where the sensation came from. Was the prince connected to the Conflagration, somehow?

"I need to follow where Garrin leads," he said, tilting his head toward the prince.

"So, it's loyalty then, is it?" said Bernie. "Don't suppose you'll tell me why that is?" Some of the anger, the menace, had gone out of his tone, but not nearly all of it.

"I'm not sure," said Caymus, being as honest as he could. He glanced back at Bernie and gave him a slight shrug. "I promise to tell you when I figure it out, though."

Bernie stared at him a long while. He didn't seem entirely satisfied with the answers he'd gotten, but he didn't ask any further questions. Eventually, he shook his head and nudged his horse to join the others ahead of them.

Caymus wondered if he'd just helped or hurt his relationship with this quiet man who seemed to distrust him so much. He knew it was impossible for a person to get along with everybody, but he felt it was important that he be able to befriend these men, all seven. The fact that even one of them was resisting him was something he'd been worrying over for the past two days.

As he considered the question again, considered that tangible, physical pull he felt coming from the prince of Kepren, he heard cheering coming from the others and rode a bit faster to catch up with the group. When he pulled his horse in next to Mally's, he saw that Big Grant was riding toward them at a leisurely pace, a big smile plastered on his face.

"Well, that's got to be good news," said Cyrus.

"So, did you find anything?" Garrin called out when Big Grant was close enough.

"You bet I did!" said Big Grant as he rejoined the group, turning his horse to walk with the others. The big man looked terribly pleased with himself. "Just a few minutes ride," he said, "and no sign of the bad guys!"

Another subdued round of cheers arose from the men, but Caymus noted that Mally wasn't smiling. Indeed, there was a distinct look of trepidation and distress on his face. "Alright," he said, touching the locket at his neck again. "Let's go have a look, shall we?"

~~~

Captain Draya wiped the sweat from his brow again, surprised to discover how much of it had accumulated on his face. He'd never much cared for the stuffiness of the Gearhouse, and now that so many bodies were working within its confines, the ambient temperature had become uncomfortably warm, despite the chill of the morning outside.

"Slowly," said Rill. He was leaning over Lieutenant Faxon, who was in the process of mixing a small container that held barely a thimble's worth
~~~

of the fire sludge's components. "If you work it too fast, the whole thing will go up."

Part of Draya hated the fact that his men had to work so carefully. He knew it needed to be done, that the process was delicate, but he also knew they were running out of time. Two days had passed since the prince and his small band of soldiers had absented themselves from the Keep, and his engineers had barely made any progress in producing meaningful quantities of the sludge.

Rill reached out and stilled the lieutenant's hand, actively forcing him to slow his movements. Faxon's scowl made it clear he wasn't happy about having a subordinate telling him what to do. The man had always seemed a bit of a bully to Draya though, and in need of some dressing down, so when the lieutenant turned his piggy eyes up to his captain in protest, Draya simply stared at him until he gave up and got back to work.

If he'd been in a better mood, or a cooler building, Draya might have smiled at that. He'd discovered a strange kind of respect for Rill over the past couple of days, and seeing the fearless way he was directing Faxon, not to mention the five others stationed at the workbench, had only increased his regard.

Every new addition to the Royal Engineers had an initial interview with the captain before they were accepted into the ranks, but Draya couldn't honestly say he'd have been able to pick Rill out of a formation a week ago. Now, he found he was coming to rely on the kid as much he did his own hands. This sludge, this fiery weapon that had sprung from Rill's mind, was something truly amazing. Draya had tried, in his younger days, to create something similar, but he hadn't had the necessary knowledge of the fire element to make it work.

Since that fateful day when he'd taken the sludge to the Keep-Marshal and the Keep-Marshal had taken it to the prince, his every waking thought had been about production, about how to create enough of the stuff to make a real difference in the inevitable defense of the city. Draya had heard how hard it was to burn these creatures, these krealites, and so he had concluded that "enough" would mean producing quite a lot of sludge.

Rill, of course, had been in charge of teaching others how to create the substance. Draya handled logistics, providing the people and resources they would need in order to complete the task in its entirety. They'd started by teaching the five lieutenants how to prepare the mixture, three days ago. Since that time, four of the students had graduated to the point that they were able to teach others, and now had been replaced with new faces.

Faxon was the only officer who had so far failed to grasp the concepts involved. Draya was at the point where he was considering finding something more productive for the man to do.

Draya sighed, staring at the clay jug that stood upright in the middle of the long workbench. It was filling at a depressingly slow pace, and he wondered if it would even be full enough to bother with when the guards arrived. The Keep-Marshal had left orders for daily pickups, the idea being to bring the material to a safer, less volatile place for storage until it was actually needed. The guards were due to come and gather today's batch in just a couple of hours.

They'd only filled two other jugs, so far.

"I don't like how slowly this is going, Rill," he said as he watched Faxon work. The lieutenant was making his skin itch, still mixing the material far too quickly.

"I know, Sir," Rill said. He looked up with an expression that was mostly of irritation, but also of some of the same concern that Draya was feeling. "I just don't know of a way to do it faster."

"At this rate," Draya said, "even if everything goes to plan and we get as many trained as we want, we're going to end up with maybe two dozen jugs of sludge by the time Black Moon gets here."

Rill didn't say anything for a moment, instead turning his eyes back to the fumbling hands of the lieutenant. Draya felt a bit sorry for worrying at the lad. He knew Rill was quite aware that things weren't going very well, but the system was set now, the variables accounted for. There wasn't very much either of them could do now to alter the path they were on.

"The process is delicate," Rill said. His tone was matter-of-fact. "If we push the production too hard, we'll just end up burning down the Gearhouse, maybe the whole east wall of the Keep." He turned and raised an eyebrow at Draya. "I think you know that, Captain."

Draya considered reminding Rill whom he was talking to, but he kept his tongue still. He knew the kid was right. He was just frustrated, and his concern for his responsibilities to the prince's army was beginning to take its toll on his patience.

He tried to count the minutes of sleep he'd managed to steal over the last three days. He figured the sum came to somewhere between four and five full hours, with countless interruptions in-between.

As he opened his mouth to offer an apology, he found himself flinching from a short, yet sharp blaze of light in the corner of the room. A moment later, one of the engineers—Draya thought the man's name was Edgar, or possibly Roger—banged his hands on the table and swore out loud.

Draya sighed quietly as he approached. This was the man's third attempt—and third failure—today, and it was about time he was replaced with somebody who wouldn't use up their scarce resources learning how to use them. He was a seasoned engineer, but his hands were clearly better suited to machinery than alchemy. As he stepped closer, the man raised his head, a pained expression on his face.

"I dunno what went wrong, Sir," he said, "honest, I don't." He waved a hand over the ingredients in front of him. "I did it just like Mister Rill told us, put the ingredients in just so, and mixed it together real slow-like." He raised his hands in supplication. "It just keeps going up like that, just before I get to adding that there white stuff."

Draya looked over the man's workspace, looking for obvious faults. He'd had Rill teach him how to make fire sludge on that first day and had succeeded in making a small batch on his first try, so he had a good idea of what could go wrong during the process. He did not, however see any issues with the evidence in front of the man.

He was about to ask the man a few questions about his process when the door to the Gearhouse opened, letting blinding sunlight and a chilly, refreshing breeze into the building. A thin, gravelly voice said, "I am seeking Captain Draya of the Royal Engineers."

Draya, recognizing the official garb, inhaled sharply, trying to mask his frustration. He'd been expecting this visit for three days already. He turned to Rill, who was already standing on the other side of the frustrated engineer. "Figure out what happened here," he said, pointing to the man's workstation.

Rill didn't speak, nod, or otherwise acknowledge the request; he was already picking through the ingredients before the sentence was out. Draya actually got the distinct impression the young man had forgotten his captain was in the room. Almost smiling, he stepped away, leaving the kid to his duties.

It was time to meet the inquisitor.

Judging the man's exact age was difficult: he was somewhere between fifty and one hundred years old. His face seemed to be too wrinkled in some places and too smooth in others. His dark, sunken eyes gave Draya the impression that he hadn't slept in over a month. He wore the long, black cloak of a royal inquisitor, complete with the silver key pendant on the chain around his neck. The key, Draya knew, was meant to symbolize the opening of locks, the dispelling of secrets, the finding of truths. Inquisitors loved stuff like that.

The man had closed the door behind him and who was now standing a foot or so inside, quietly surveying the work going on in the building, his gaze seeming to dart in every direction at once. Draya approached him the way he might approach a wild animal. "You must be the inquisitor I was promised."

The shriveled gaze glanced briefly in Draya's direction, then went back to its inspection of the workings of the engineers. The man's eyes, at least, tired and hollow as they were, also seemed alert and vibrant. "Inquisitor Dalphin," the man said. The voice sounded dry and pinched, as though it had struggled to find its way out of the man's chest. "You are Captain Draya?"

Draya nodded. "I am."

"Good," said Dalphin, still not looking at him. "I have been told that you have a problem to do with sabotage. I am here to correct that problem." The shadowy eyes drifted to the sludge jug. "I am also tasked with collecting whatever amount of the substance your people have produced this day. Is that it over there?"

"It is." Draya already didn't like this man. He'd only encountered one other inquisitor in his life; that experience had been an altogether unpleasant, and this one wasn't shaping up to be any different. The royal inquisitors were employed by the dukes to seek out the truth in various matters, most of which had to do with investigations of criminal acts. The men—and they were *always* men—were soulless, ruthless, and seemed to carry no compassion in their hearts. Draya's previous case had concerned the suspicious death of his superior officer. Draya had been a lieutenant at the time, and his captain had been found dead in the officers' galley. He remembered each of the seven interrogations he'd had to endure under the uncaring eyes of that monster. Inquisitor Stophnos. The man's methods hadn't quite extended to torture, but they had come close.

In the end, the captain's death had been declared accidental, the result of one of the first-stationers having been careless with a vial of powdered seeproot. The vial, left in the kitchen after the engineer had visited a friend there, had somehow gotten mixed into the captain's soup and had stopped his heart. The discovery, however, hadn't undone the hours of intense inquisition Draya had endured.

"It took you quite a while to get around to us," Draya said, using as level a tone as he could muster. "I had requested ducal assistance some days ago."

"The royal inquisitors have many obligations," Dalphin replied. It was not an apology, merely a statement of fact. "It is not always possible to put current concerns aside when new cases come up." He stepped further into the room, inspecting each engineer individually. "However, now that I am on your case, you can be certain you have my full attention." He halted his circuit around the room and began looking at the various tools and mechanical parts strewn about the walls of the Gearhouse. "Please explain your problem with this saboteur, in as much detail as possible."

Draya, inhaled, considered the man before him, exhaled, and then decided to cooperate. Whatever reservations he might have about Dalphin's profession, he would assist him to the best of his ability. The

Keep-Marshal had requested an inquisitor's presence, after all, and on *his* behalf. And so, he leaned on the workbench with both hands and focused his eyes on the woodgrain pattern, doing his best not to actually look at the inquisitor in his Gearhouse, and told the story.

He told Dalphin of the problems they'd had in the recent weeks. It had started when one of the catapults had been rendered useless. The gear system that was used to crank the arms backward had been made inoperable when the catch that kept the system taught had been removed. One of the smiths had needed to fashion a new catch before the engine had been functional again.

Soon afterward, a problem had been found with the Guard-Reed Gate, barely twenty yards south of the marshaling yard. The portcullis simply wouldn't stay open one day, and an investigation had revealed that one of the springs in the machinery that kept the bars raised had broken. Draya had seen the spring himself. It hadn't pulled apart as a result of pressure or age; it had been cut intentionally. Then there was the catapult that had been literally sawn through.

There had been other, less drastic reports of supplies and equipment either malfunctioning or going missing, none of which would, by themselves, normally have given Draya cause for any specific concern. Taken together, however, they suggested the work of someone who wanted to cause interference in the workings of the corps of engineers.

When he looked up again, he saw that the inquisitor's gaze was fixed upon him. The intensity of his eyes gave the impression that he was trying to see more of the story than he was being told. Good. The man did, at least, seem to be paying close attention.

"How difficult," the man asked, "would these acts of sabotage have been?"

Draya narrowed his eyes. "How difficult?"

"Yes," replied Inquisitor Dalphin. "Each of these particular acts, as you've described them to me: how much actual knowledge of the respective devices' inner workings would a person have needed in order to affect them so?"

Draya considered the question. "Not a lot, really," he said, after a moment. "Whoever it was, each time they tried to break something, they picked the quick and easy way to do it."

"So," said Dalphin, "one can assume that this person—this saboteur—does not possess expert knowledge of the workings of your machines?"

Draya nodded. "That would be a safe assumption. If *I* were going to take a catapult out, for instance, I'd just saw the wheels off. It would only take two or three minutes longer than what was actually done, would have made it almost as useless, and it would have been a hundred times harder to repair."

The inquisitor looked away, as though deep in thought. "I would like a list of the equipment that has gone missing, Captain, and where it went missing from, if that is possible."

"I'll have it drawn up and in your hands by the end of the day."

"Good, good." The inquisitor turned and met Draya's eyes again. "You may be certain that your case has my full attention, captain. I will find your saboteur."

Draya once again considered the black-robed figure before him, this time finding some measure of appreciation for the man. He still didn't trust him, didn't like the way the men of his profession went about their work, but he did at least believe the words he'd just heard. At the very least, he trusted their sincerity.

"When you want to catch a devil," his father used to say, "best to send a devil after him."

Draya smiled. He'd never had need of a devil before today.

"Now," said Dalphin, turning back to the working men, "I would like you to tell me more about this 'Rill's sludge'. If I am to be responsible for transporting it, I would have some idea of its nature and what," he waved a hand at the workbench, "your people are doing with it."

Draya took a deep breath. The last thing he wanted to do right now was educate an inquisitor about the nature of the sludge, but he knew the man's concern was valid: a person treated the sludge with much greater care and respect when he knew how difficult the stuff was to make.

He led the man over to where Rill was working with another of the officers, Second Lieutenant Elkin, who had herself been instructing a younger engineer. Rill was performing the steps himself. He was in the second-to-last stage of the process, mixing together some of the base elements that went in before the white material at the end.

Draya explained to Dalphin, in as much detail as he thought the man would comprehend, about the elemental makeups of the various components, about how the main ingredient was graysilt, the same quick-burning powder that was used in several processes throughout the city, from fuse-making to the fashioning of explosives. He also told him about how the fire element was tempered with a few earth element ingredients, and finally mixed with the naphthalene and oil to add the final water element.

As he spoke, he caught Rill grinning at him. He couldn't help but return the smile. They'd each recited this same bit of exposition dozens of times in the past few days. It was becoming a script. Draya wondered if he should just write it down.

"How stable is the finished product?" asked the inquisitor.

"Very," said Draya. "Once you've finished a batch of fire sludge, it's entirely inert until you put a flame to it." He nodded toward the jar Rill was mixing up. "It's only the steps that lead up to it that are a bit finicky."

As if Rill had taken some sort of cue at the word 'finicky', there was a quick, bright flash of light, and the mixture Rill had been working with went up in smoke. There hadn't been much material in the little jar, so nobody was hurt, but everyone in the Gearhouse stopped what they were doing and stared, stunned, for a moment.

"I see," said the inquisitor, his eyes betraying no emotion.

Draya lifted his eyes from the empty jar to Rill, who seemed more surprised than anybody. "What happened?" he said to the young second-stationer.

Rill looked back at him, his mouth open wide. He appeared literally horrified by what had just occurred. "I…" he stammered, "I don't know." He dropped the jar and mixer on the table. "I didn't..."

And then, Rill was gone. At least, his mind was no longer in the room with the rest of them. Instead, he was looking backward and forward at all the ingredients on his table, pointing at them, counting on his fingers, and mumbling under his breath. Draya still didn't know Rill very well, but he'd been working with him long enough to know to leave him alone when he was busy thinking.

Draya turned his attention back to Dalphin. The inquisitor was watching Rill with a curious look on his face. When he noticed Draya's eyes on him, he asked, "What is the concern, Captain? Could the young man have not simply made a mistake?"

Draya nearly laughed out loud. "Hardly, Inquisitor," he said. "It's called 'Rill's sludge', right?"

"That's what I'm told," said Dalphin, raising an eyebrow.

"Well, that," Draya said, pointing, "is Rill."

The inquisitor didn't say anything, so Draya continued. "I've seen him do that a hundred times before, and he's never had a mishap like that."

"Still," Dalphin said, his dark eyes narrowing, "even the greatest of men will make the occasional mistake."

Draya held up a hand. "Of course," he said, "you're right. Still, even if it was just a mistake, Rill's not going to be satisfied until he knows exactly what happened, why it happened, and how it can be prevented from happening again."

Draya nearly flinched a step backward in surprise when he saw the wrinkly face smile. He'd never seen even the smallest hint of emotion on an inquisitor's face before.

"He might make an excellent inquisitor, one day," the face said.

Draya decided not to dwell on that thought.

"I have it!" Rill suddenly burst out. When Draya looked at him, he was holding up a small vial of some kind of crushed material. Rill was looking intently at him, making sure he had his captain's attention. "Fyewig," he said, pointing at the little vial. "Crushed fyewig flowers."

Draya nodded. "Yes, you told me the fyewig is a highly earthen material."

"Right," Rill said, snapping his fingers, then pointing at him. "It holds back the fire element during the mixing process, contains it, stops it from burning out of control while the other ingredients are mixed together."

"Alright?" Draya said.

"Fyewig," Rill continued, tipping a small amount of the powder into the palm of his hand, "has a really bitter taste to it." He reached out his hand, offering the small amount of powder to Draya. "Try."

Draya narrowed his eyes at Rill, but he reached out and led Rill drop the powdered plant into his own hand. He grabbed a small amount between the finger and thumb of his other hand and placed it on his tongue.

The powder was incredibly salty.

Draya spat it out. "That's definitely not fyewig," he said, brushing the remnants from his hands. "What is it?"

Rill shook his head, lifting the vial up to his face to get a closer look at it. "I don't know," he said. "For all I know it might just be colored salt, but whatever it is, it's not supposed to be here."

"Then it would seem," came the inquisitor's faraway voice, "that your saboteur has struck again."

Draya found that he was holding his breath. A broken siege weapon was one thing; contaminating the fire sludge was another matter entirely.

The inquisitor turned, once again, to the jug in the middle of the workbench. "What about that?" he asked. "Is that going to be ruined also?"

"No," Rill said, still spinning the vial before his eyes. "Without the fyewig, it would never survive the mixing process. If it made it as far as the jug, then it's okay. It's the real stuff."

"Very well," said the inquisitor. He reached over and picked up the jug, then cradled it in the crook of his elbow. He turned to Draya. "Captain, I will be requesting guards to be placed around this building at all hours of the day and night so as to prevent this from happening again. I would suggest you take stock of your materials before making any more of the sludge."

Draya nodded. "Thank you, Inquisitor," he said. "We'll do just that."

The inquisitor turned to leave, but stopped and turned his head, speaking over his shoulder. "I am active on your case now, Captain Draya. You can be certain of a swift result."

Draya managed a small smile at the man's repeated affirmation. At least he seemed confident in his abilities. "Thank you, Inquisitor. I would greatly appreciate a result like that."

Dalphin nodded and stepped away faster than Draya imagined his old bones should be able to carry him. In moments, he was out of the Gearhouse door and gone from their lives.

Draya heard a deep sigh from Rill. "I hope the prince and Caymus are having better luck than we are."

Draya found himself nodding. "I hope so too, Rill. I really do."

~~~

For the dozenth time in the past twenty minutes, Caymus scratched the back of his neck and reminded himself to breathe.

The morning light brought with it a slight wind, and the chill was settling into his skin. Caymus had already regretted not bringing warmer clothes with him on this trip, but until now he'd always been busy and active enough that the cold hadn't bothered him.

Still crouching behind the large boulder, he reached back into his belt and pulled out his leather gloves. They were made for protection, not warmth, but they would do. Briefly, he wondered why he couldn't see his breath in the cold air. He supposed he should be grateful for that fact, though.

He was alone, hiding behind a huge rock on the side of what was essentially a big gully. The sides weren't high enough for it to be called a canyon, but they were steep enough that one could put a boulder in motion and expect it to reach the bottom under its own power.

The sensation, that incessant prickling on the back of his neck, was beginning to drive him mad. If he hadn't known better, he'd have thought the skin was actually trying to escape. He wasn't surprised at the reaction, though. He could actually hear the sounds of footfalls on the rocks and sand below: Black Moon was getting close.

When they'd arrived at the pass two days ago, Mally had spent the rest of the afternoon and most of the following night walking around the area, occasionally kneeling and touching the dirt beneath him or just standing still in one spot, his eyes closed, for hours. Just before the sun had risen, he'd reported that they could, in fact, arrange a decent landslide in this place. The company had immediately gotten to work, digging ditches in some locations, building mounds in others. Caymus himself had been given a hand drill and been charged with boring small holes into various boulders and then filling them with graysilt. He hadn't been able to see the method in it all, but Mally had promised that, added together, it was enough to bring the sides of the ravine down on whomever might be in the pass at the time.

They had expected to have a full day to work. They'd only been at it
~~~

for three hours when his neck had started tingling.

Again, Caymus realized he wasn't breathing, and he forced himself to inhale. They weren't ready; they weren't even close to ready. When they'd first realized that Black Moon was arriving so much sooner than they'd thought, there had been hurried discussions about whether then should just set the explosives off and make a run for it, or if they should stick to the plan, wait for the army to enter the ravine, and spring what part of their trap they'd actually managed to build. The former choice might result in a minor blockage of the pass, giving Kepren at most an extra hour or two. The latter might net them a few dozen—maybe a few hundred—enemy dead, but it would risk all their lives.

In the end, Garrin had decided to wait, to try. They were all to find places along the sides of the ravine, wait until the soldiers massed down below them, then see how many they could get. He figured that the tumbling boulders, at the very least, should bring a few of them down.

The prince had known it was a gamble. He'd given everyone the option of leaving. Nobody had taken it.

Caymus felt all his muscles tense as the first of the soldiers came into view, rounding the bend that led out of Falmoor's Pass and the Greatstone Mountains. The figures of the men were still a few hundred yards away, so he couldn't quite make out distinct forms, but he could distinguish easily the darkened, ash-colored skin of Black Moon's main force. Before long, several dozen more of them were making their way into the pass. A couple of them carried banners on long staves above their heads: blood-red, inverted triangles with single black circles in their center. They had to be representative of the black moon that they seemed so proud of.

Caymus was astounded at how quickly the force seemed to move. He was no longer surprised that they had made such quick progress through the pass.

Making sure to stay hidden behind his boulder, Caymus stretched one of his legs out in front of him, trying to keep it loose for the inevitable moment when he would need to run. As he switched his stance to stretch the other leg, he wondered about their plan's chances of success. Their trap wasn't set. Mally had made it very clear that they wouldn't have the impact they had been hoping for. He shifted his gaze. He could still see Mally crouched behind his own boulder about fifty yards to his left. Mally, in turn, was looking to his left, presumably keeping an eye on the prince, waiting for his order to take action.

The army of Black Moon was led by men on foot, though Caymus wouldn't have called them infantry, exactly. They didn't march in lines or columns. In fact, Caymus couldn't make out their formation. He had a sense, however, that they were ordered, that they marched to some sort of organized configuration that was too alien for his eyes to discern.

He could feel the kreal though, stronger now than ever, emanating from each of the figures down below him. He knew that some of the marching men were the same warriors he'd seen in the memories of the Summitian scout. Not all of them were completely taken by the kreal, though: some of them appeared to be normal men, and Caymus assumed these were the mercenaries spoken of in Garrin's reports. The distressing thing, however, was that many of them exhibited lighter or darker skins than others, as though some were in some middle stage in a process of becoming a Black Moon warrior. In fact, just by the feel of them, Caymus guessed that every single man down there was infected with kreal.

He wondered how much the scout's information had changed since it was delivered. How many fewer mercenaries were there now, and how many more ash-skinned killers?

Behind the men, among them in some places, were the krealites, the huge, many-legged insectoid creatures that had already caused so much death. Caymus felt his heart beating hard and loud, as though it suddenly filled his entire chest. He estimated there were at least a hundred of the creatures down there, many more than had been recently reported by scouts. Once more, he forced himself to breathe, hoping as he did so that this was the extent of the monsters, that there weren't more of them at the back of the procession.

Then, without any apparent signal or command, they stopped. They halted as though they were a single unit, man and monster standing still at exactly the same time.

They were still at least a hundred yards short of the kill space, the point where they were meant to be standing when the trap was sprung.

What had happened? What were they doing? Caymus felt his hand touch the hilt of his sword.

A lone figure, black as the darkest heart, came from within the cluster of bodies and began making its way to the front. Each Black Moon warrior stepped aside to let the form pass, then closed ranks behind it. Even from this distance, Caymus could feel that it was of the kreal, that it was constructed of that element as much as the creatures standing still behind it, possibly more. It seemed a good deal taller than the other figures around him, though it wasn't as big as a mitre. It wore black armor that gave the impression of having been fashioned from the chitin of dead krealites. Short, black horns adorned a closed-faced helmet. Caymus could see the outline of a huge sword strapped over the figure's back.

All of Black Moon's eyes watched the figure as it stopped in front of the assembled soldiers and surveyed the area around them. It lifted its head slightly, as though sniffing the air. Back and forth it looked, eyeing the sides of the gully.

Caymus felt his heart stop in his chest when the figure's gaze fell directly upon the boulder he was hiding behind.

Everything had just gone horribly wrong.

The black, horned figure lifted the sword from its back, pointed it at Caymus's hiding spot, and yelled something in an alien tongue.

The soldiers of Black Moon broke their strange formation, screamed awful battle cries, and started scrabbling up the sides of the ravine.

Chapter 19

"Hold your ground!" Even from dozens of yards away, over the sounds of a charging army, the prince's voice rang out clear. Caymus needed no such instruction, however: he stood waiting, allowing the soldiers to get closer to him before acting. He looked around his position, trying to find everybody. He, Garrin, Mally, and Big Grant were on this side of the ravine. He could make out Bigger Grant on the other side, but Cyrus, Harrison, and Bernie were nowhere to be seen.

He wondered what the others must have been thinking about him in that moment. Obviously, whoever this figure at the bottom of the slope was, he'd been able to sense Caymus's presence. Caymus reasoned he must be the leader of Black Moon, the one that varied so much in description. He cursed himself for a fool: he hadn't considered that the enemy might be able to feel him as easily as he could feel them, and that lack of consideration was about to cost them their lives.

Caymus planted his feet solidly onto the ground, making sure he was standing on firm rock, and placed both hands against the side of his boulder. Still, he held, watching and waiting as the soldiers approached. They wielded various implements, from swords and shields, to maces, to scythes, as though each man had simply been plucked out of whatever life he had been leading and thrown into the army on the spot. Most of these men didn't appear to be far along in whatever process it was that converted their flesh to kreal. He supposed it made sense, in a sadistic sort of way, to send in the weakest, the most expendable, first.

The soldiers came close enough that Caymus could make out the expressions on their faces, could read their desire to kill, before Garrin finally gave the order. "Now!"

Caymus shoved hard against the boulder, dislodging it and sending it rolling down the slope toward the attackers. As soon it was moving, he bent down to strike the pommel of his sword against the firing flint at his feet. The resulting sparks ignited a quick-burning fuse that traveled down to the rolling boulder as it made its way down to the advancing forms. The kreal-infected soldiers began diving out of the boulder's way, trying to jump to safety, but just as the huge stone reached their line, the fuse reached the graysilt that nestled in a cavity inside and the mass exploded, pelting the figures with sharp, heavy pieces of rock.

Caymus didn't see the explosion, having turned and run up the slope as soon as he'd hit the flint, but the whooshes and screams behind him told him that the plan was working. A few more explosions and a deep, rumbling sound followed, and he chanced a look over his shoulder to see a large section of the ravine falling down upon his pursuers. The falling rocks and sand wouldn't bury the army as they'd hoped, but at least it would take a few of them out and keep the rest from giving chase for a minute or two.

As he willed his legs to pump harder, to carry him up the slope, he looked back again. Several of the soldiers were still following him, having been above the line of the landslide when it had begun, but the falling sand and stone seemed to be cutting off the pursuit of most of the army. Most importantly, a group of archers near the bottom of the slope, who were even now loosing a volley of arrows, stood directly in the path of several large boulders. They might each get off a shot or two, but no more than that.

As he slammed his boots hard against the ground, Caymus suddenly wished he hadn't left his shield with the horses. He very much wanted to have it hanging on his back in that moment.

Even as he'd formed the thought, two arrows landed in front of him, burying themselves in the dirt just past their points. Despite the tumult of noise near the bottom of the ravine, he was also able to pick out the sounds of a few arrows landing behind him. He was just starting to count himself exceptionally lucky when he felt a heavy thud against the back of his right shoulder and had to reach out to keep himself from stumbling to the ground. He winced. There was no pain—not yet, anyway—but he'd definitely been hit.

When he was near the top of the ridge, he looked up, expecting to see only more sand and rock. Instead, he saw Mally there, beckoning him on. "Come on, Caymus!" he shouted. "Move!" Mally extended a hand as Caymus reached the top, helping to pull him up the last few feet.

Caymus was about to continue on down the other side of the slope, but Mally put a gentle hand against him. "We stand here," he said, an incredible amount of calm in his voice. Caymus, surprised, met the man's gaze as he continued. "You and me," he said. He pointed down the other side of the slope, and Caymus followed the finger to see Garrin and Big

Grant making their way down, heading toward the mounts they'd hidden in the rocks beyond. "We're going to give him time to get to the horses. Any objections?"

Caymus met Mally's eyes again and saw the intensity in them. He expected Caymus to do this, to stand with him against the few soldiers who would make it past the landslide, to give the prince—his friend—time to get away. For a moment, Caymus wondered what Amalwyn might do if he actually said no.

He didn't say no, though. Instead, he smiled, finding himself pleased at the thought of getting to meet the enemy head-on. "No objections," he said, then he turned to watch the men coming up the hill.

Six of them were now closing the distance. Caymus pulled his longsword, the one Be'Var had given him on their journey from the Temple and which was now sharpened, free of its scabbard.

"You've got an arrow in your shoulder," Mally said matter-of-factly, not looking at him.

"Yeah," said Caymus, also keeping his eyes on the oncoming soldiers. "How bad is it?"

In response, Mally reached around behind him and yanked the arrow free. Caymus expected some manner of pain, but none came. "Didn't even get through the strap," Mally said, throwing the arrow down. "You got iron in that thing?"

Caymus nodded, thankful that he hadn't bothered to remove the leather straps that he used keep his shield on his back, which did contain a few metal plates for sturdiness. At least he'd brought that much protection along.

"You ready for this?" Mally's voice was low and controlled, yet forceful. His meaning was clear: this was to protect the prince. If Caymus wasn't ready, then he'd had no business being here in the first place.

"Ready," he replied.

In fact, he found himself preparing for the fight in more ways than he'd experienced before. Not only was he adopting a modified stance, accommodating the fact that he didn't have his shield with him, but he found that his breathing was slowing, that he was becoming intensely focused on the men coming up the hill.

The six men were about ten yards away. They seemed to be moving in slow-motion, and Caymus was surprised at how much detail he was picking out. Not one of them was particularly dark of skin, and thus couldn't have been under the influence of the kreal for very long. Caymus imagined that they might still be as vulnerable to a blade as a normal man, that they might not have built up the impermeability to steel that seemed to be such a large part of the kreal's nature. He was glad for that; it meant that Mally might be able to take one or two of them down.

Two of the men were fitter than the others, not breathing as heavily as they made their way uphill. They seemed to move with greater elegance too, as though they had more experience in battle. Caymus decided to be particularly wary of these two, to cut them down first, if possible.

One of them, the one furthest to the right, had a hitch in his gait. He didn't seem to be injured; rather Caymus suspected that one of his legs was slightly shorter than the other, that he wasn't able to run with the same efficiency of motion as most people. He would likely move in unpredictable ways, and so should be watched closely, also.

The six men, five yards away now, weren't dressed in any sort of uniform, nor did they carry similar weapons. Other than the fact that they all seemed to sport some degree of ash-colored skin, they didn't seem to have very much in common at all. Caymus wondered if the men had even known each other before the Black Moon Army had come into their lives. Had they been part of a mercenary group, perhaps? Had they been ordinary men, pressed into service by an invading element? Their weapons didn't even seem as though they'd been afforded equal levels of care.

That was when he noticed the slight sheen on the edges of the blades. The four swords and the scythe of the first five men, as well as the points of the morningstar of the sixth, all carried the same sickly black color. He'd seen that sheen before; he'd had nearly died because of it.

"Watch the blades," he said, just loud enough for Mally to hear. "They're poisoned."

Mally didn't have time to respond before the men were on them.

Two of the men struck out at Mally. The other four went after Caymus, presumably thinking his great size necessitated extra force. They didn't seem to know how to work together, though: almost immediately, they got in each other's way. One of the men edged another out of position, so eager was he to swing his sword, and the result was that neither of them was able to strike. The third and fourth men, each wielding longswords, thrust out with their tainted blades, trying to score a hit, but neither did so very effectively. Caymus easily stepped away from the first two weapons. He parried the other two with a single arc of his sword, then kicked out at the fourth man, sending him tumbling down the slope.

The krealite men continued to move with incredible slowness, allowing Caymus the initiative in the fight. Before they could react to his defense, he was already attacking, dropping low and spinning so as to put momentum into his swing. The third man's leg fell away below the knee and he, too, fell down into the gully.

The remaining two managed to spread apart a few feet, deliberately disengaging so as to get out of each other's way. Caymus, still crouched, took stock. The one on the left was one of the fitter men; his skin seemed to be just a little bit darker than that of the other. Taking a step forward, the man lunged out in an overhand swing, which Caymus deflected, once again standing to his full height. He then barely avoided the thrust of the second man, having to twist his abdomen so the blade missed him by less than an inch. He cursed himself for forgetting about the unusual ways in which that attacker, the one with the odd gait, might move. Never mind the poisoned blade; if that thrust had been an inch to the left, it would have pierced his liver.

Caymus had a split-second to decide which man to go after: the first man, fitter and darker-skinned, or the second, less predictable one. The second man made the decision easy for him when he left his sword-hand extended an instant too long. Caymus stepped closer to him, grabbed his arm with his off-hand, and then, having his opponent thus restrained, smashed the pommel of his sword into his face with as much force as he could muster. The pommel crushed bone and cartilage and the second man went limp.

The first man, believing Caymus's guard to be down, didn't waste any time in taking another swing. Caymus, using the restrained arm and buried pommel for leverage, spun and tucked himself behind the second man's body, using him as a shield. When the first man pulled his sword free of the second man's flesh, Caymus shoved the lifeless body at him.

Caymus and his remaining foe both backed away a couple of steps, and Caymus used the moment to see how Mally was doing. His ears had been hearing the sounds of steel against steel, but he hadn't had a chance to get a good look before now.

Mally's first opponent was down on the ground, blood seeping into the dirt, but he was currently trading blows with the other.

No. Mally was actually landing blow after blow against his opponent, but the blade wasn't biting. The man—the other "fit" man—seemed to be far along enough in his transformation to not have to worry about swords.

Both opponents, Mally's and Caymus's, seemed, in fact, to have about the same hue of ashen skin, not as dark as those in the scout's vision, but apparently dark enough. Immediately, Caymus changed his stance. This was a krealite opponent, not a human one, and fighting him would require different tactics.

He stood with his sword out in front of him, his feet evenly spaced, facing his enemy. Caymus waited for him to move. The man seemed aware that something in his enemy's perception had changed, however, and he acted more slowly, more cautiously, than he had before.

Caymus waited. He could make a feint, of course, try to throw his opponent off-balance, but he'd have the best chance of defeating this thing quickly if he could respond to its attack, get his blade into the back of its neck and make his sword bite.

Still he waited for the man to make his attack, and as precious seconds passed, he became more anxious. Mally was still fighting, his blows striking true but not taking his opponent down. Mally was obviously the better swordsman, but Caymus knew that part of being a good swordsman was making sure to defeat your opponent before becoming exhausted. Mally wouldn't be used to not being able to take his man down quickly. Sooner or later, he'd tire or make a mistake, and that would be the end of it.

"Come on, burn you!" Caymus heard himself say.

For a moment, the man's eyes went wide. "Burn?" he said, so quietly that Caymus wasn't sure he'd actually heard it or just read the man's lips. Before he could question the reaction, though, the ringing of steel stopped, and he heard a cry escape Mally's lips.

Panic set in. "No!" Caymus heard himself say. He glanced over at Mally, who had a shortsword up to the hilt in his gut and was falling to his knees.

Caymus's opponent took the moment of distraction as an opportunity and pressed his attack. Caymus, ready for the man, brushed the blade away with his own, stepped to the right, past him, then placed the tip of his blade against the back of the man's neck and pushed.

The sharp steel slid home, just as it had in his Conflagration training ground.

The final Black Moon soldier watched Caymus with wide eyes. He desperately put a foot on Mally's chest and pulled his sword free, but it was already too late for him. Caymus was there, finding the soft spot under his left armpit and pressing his blade home.

When the final soldier lay dead at his feet, Caymus took a moment to look for other opponents to battle. His blood was throbbing through his veins and he wanted badly to fight someone, but nobody was coming. Rather, the bulk of the Black Moon Army was regrouping from an onslaught of sand and boulders at the bottom of the ravine. Nobody else was coming any time soon.

Sheathing his sword, he turned his attention to Mally, who was lying on his side, his hand at his abdomen. His breathing was rapid. His eyes were wide with shock, with disorientation, with fear.

Caymus didn't like seeing fear in Mally's eyes. There was something wrong with the world if Amalwyn Cove could be afraid.

He looked at the wound and felt his heart drop into his stomach. He'd thought he might be able to burn the kreal out of Mally's body, as he had his own, but there was too much blood. The blade must have transected a major blood vessel. Be'Var might have been able to stop the bleeding;

Caymus didn't have the talent.

Still, he reached out to Mally with his thoughts. If he couldn't heal the wound, he could at least burn the poisonous kreal out and spare the man the pain that came with it.

He quickly discovered, however, that there was no kreal, no poison in Mally's body. Caymus opened his eyes, startled. He looked to one side and picked up the sword that had pierced Mally, so recently fallen from its owner's hand. Examining the blade, he discovered there was no kreal there, either. What'd he'd thought was a sheen of dark poison had turned out to be a simple coat of black paint. What could that mean? Were the Black Moon soldiers just trying to make their enemies *think* their blades were poisoned? Why would they do that?

Caymus's thoughts were interrupted when he felt a bloody hand grab his wrist. Mally was exhaling hard, as though the simple act of breathing forcefully enough might keep him alive. Caymus dropped the sword. He couldn't believe this was happening. It wasn't fair.

"I'm so sorry, Mally, I can't stop it," he said, holding onto the shoulders of a man whom he'd begun to think of as a friend in the last couple of days, a friend whom he'd just gotten killed by the simple act of being here, of being a lightning rod for Black Moon. He closed his eyes. If only he hadn't come. If he'd just stayed in Kepren, that figure, that horrific leader of the krealite army, wouldn't have known he was there. The trap would have worked, and Mally wouldn't be dying.

He felt arms grabbing at his shirt and shoulders, and he opened his eyes again. Mally's pupils were so large, his face so panicked, that Caymus wouldn't have been surprised to discover that he couldn't see anymore, and yet those eyes were looking right at him. "You have to keep him alive, Caymus!" he shouted, his words hoarse with strain. Rivulets of blood streamed from his lips. "We don't matter. *He's* what matters. You promise me you will keep him alive!"

There was no doubt in Caymus's mind whom Mally was talking about.

"I will, Mally," he said, softly, his hands reaching up to take the ones holding his shirt. "I'll keep Garrin alive."

"On your life!" Mally said, somehow finding the strength to pull himself closer. "Swear it on your life, Caymus!"

Caymus couldn't stand being in that moment. He didn't know Mally, but he knew how his men felt about him. He was a loyal companion, a generous leader…a good man. Now he was going to have to watch him die. He felt his eyes getting wet. "I swear it."

He wasn't sure if Mally actually heard the words. The life went out of his face in that very instant, his hands released their grip, and his body fell back on the ground.

Caymus knelt there awhile—he wasn't sure how long—not sure what to do. Garrin's closest friend was dead, and Caymus had been the one that had gotten him killed. Would the prince ever forgive him? Should he?

He looked over his shoulder at the mass of Black Moon soldiers. They were starting to get organized again. They'd be making their way up the ridge before long.

There wouldn't be time to move the body. He doubted he could take on an entire army at once.

And so, Caymus ran.

He slid his way down the outer slope of the rise, heading toward the red and gray outcroppings of the Greatstones. On this side, the boulders were both huge and densely packed, with spaces in between that would afford him the ability to move around in secret. That had been Mally's plan, to use this place as an escape route should the day not end in their favor.

He felt numb. Every step he took away from the ridge sapped energy from heart. He tried to keep his attention on the uneven ground before him, but he was having trouble concentrating. That terrible moment, when the life had gone out of Mally's eyes, kept playing in his mind over and over again, and the experience of it was sapping his will. Instinct was keeping him going, the instinct to stay alive, to flee from the men who sought to spill his blood. If not for that instinct, he might have simply fallen to the ground, unable to think.

An arm grabbed him as ran, yanking him out of his dark thoughts and behind one of the larger boulders. He spun with his sword, ready to take the arm off, but when he saw Garrin's concerned face looking back at him, he relaxed his muscles.

"Mally?" Garrin's voice didn't hold any hope. He knew already.

Caymus shook he head. "I couldn't stop them in time," was all he could think to say.

He expected to see more emotion in the prince's face, sorrow for a friend whose company he would never enjoy again, or contempt for the one who'd let him die, but Garrin's eyes betrayed no such reaction. Those eyes seemed sharp, alert, focused on the moment. Big Grant was crouched down next to him, his head cocked to one side, his eyes closed, listening for any signs of pursuit.

"We need to get back to the horses," Garrin whispered, addressing both of them. "Black Moon is mostly infantry, so they won't be able to catch up if we can get mounted before they reach us."

Big Grant, his huge arms tense under his leather armor, opened his eyes and chanced a quick look around the boulder. "They haven't crossed the ridge yet," he said when he turned back. "I was hoping we'd have more even ground, but we can hurry through these rocks if we're careful enough."

"Garrin," Caymus said, grabbing the prince's arm, "I can't go with you. I have to go." When Garrin turned to meet Caymus's eyes again, they were angry. "I'm sorry, Your Highness," he said, assuming that it was the familiar form of address that the prince was balking at, "but that soldier out front, the one with the horns, he looked right at me. He knew where I was without looking. If we stay together, he'll find all of us."

"Forget it, Caymus," Garrin replied. "We're in this together, and you're my responsibility. We don't separate. Nobody else is getting left behind."

"But, Your Highness—"

"I said forget it!" Garrin repeated in a forced whisper. "Maybe he knows where you are," he continued, more calmly, "or maybe it was just an obvious hiding place. I don't care. We stick together."

"Mally made me promise to keep you safe, Sire," Caymus said. "The best way I can do that is to stay away."

Garrin's voice softened a bit, his expression lost some of its intensity, and he put a hand on Caymus's shoulder. "All right, Caymus," he said. "I'll tell you what. Right now, we're being chased through unfamiliar territory that we can't hope to hide in forever, which means I'm likely to need that sword of yours far more than I need to be invisible. Once we get to the horses, we'll need to split up anyway, so you can leave us behind then if you're still so inclined. Deal?"

Caymus was about to object again when the unmistakable sound of foot-scrapes started coming toward them. Garrin pulled Caymus against the boulder next to him, and they waited for inevitable confrontation.

Caymus felt his senses intensify again, felt the world slow down a little. He listened carefully to the footfalls, picking out five sets of feet. How had so many of them gotten across the lip of the ravine so quickly? He'd had to traverse the same ground twice that morning, helping Mally set up the trap, and it had taken him at least five minutes each time. He was certain that the fight at the top of the ridge had been less than two minutes ago.

As the steps got closer, the three men tensed, weapons at the ready. Caymus considered his enemy's position: if he were the pursuer, and if he were aware that his quarry was hidden behind this boulder, he'd be sure to split his men up and attack from both sides. Remembering what Mally had made him promise, he kept his attention focused on the side where the prince knelt, preparing to deflect and return the coming attacks.

Just as he was about to leap into action though, he noticed that the footsteps were gathering on only the left side. He paused, thinking it a strange choice of tactic, then realized what it must mean. Quickly, he flattened his back against the boulder again as the five men quickly strode straight past their hiding spot.

Confused, he held still, controlled his breathing, and quietly waited for the men to get out of earshot.

"Couldn't find you after all, eh?" Garrin whispered. Caymus turned to look at him, then sighed in relief when the prince gave him a wink.

"That's good news," he was forced to admit.

"The bad news," said Grant, "is that we've got Black Moon between us and the horses now. That's going to make the going a lot slower." He turned to Garrin. "We could probably sneak up on the ones just passed us, take 'em out without raising the alarm."

Garrin seemed to consider this. "I don't know about our chances of getting away with that." He turned to Caymus. "What do you think?" he asked. "Of the three of us, you're the only one who's actually fought one, so far."

Caymus wished he could be certain of their success against such foes, but he'd already seen enough death today and he dared not take any needless chances with their lives. "Whatever it is the kreal does to their skins," he said, "it hasn't taken fully to all of them yet, so we've got regular soldiers mixed in with the ones that are harder to kill. I wouldn't recommend going after them, though, not if we want to stay hidden. One of them's bound to get away, and that's all it'll take to get the whole mess on us."

Garrin nodded. "All right then," he said. "Looks like we've got some sneaking ahead of us." He turned to look past Big Grant at the southern skyline, just visible between the boulders. "I just hope we get there before we run out of daylight."

The next several hours passed slowly, tortuously, as the three men spent long stretches of time silently making their way through the rocks and gullies of Greatstones' southern flank. They moved at a snail's pace, each man keeping low to the ground, trying to make as little noise as possible. Each time the sounds of footfalls approached, they had to locate and quickly scurry into a small, dark space, wait for the danger to pass, emerge, make a little progress, and repeat the process over again. After a while, the sun reached its zenith, and then began to descend. As the hours passed and the sun descended lower in the sky, the patrols—always groups of five men—became more frequent. The second group they encountered arrived half-an-hour after the first. By the time the sun had set, Black Moon soldiers were appearing every few minutes or so.

An hour or two after dusk had settled into night, Caymus found himself on his belly, hiding under yet another low rock shelf, waiting for yet another patrol to pass. He passed his fingers in front of his face. Though a waxing moon hung in the sky, he could barely see anything in the dark space into which they had secreted themselves. The hollow was tight and cramped. Big Grant, in particular, was having a difficult time squeezing his bulk in.

Caymus hoped the patrol would pass soon. The more time they spent keeping still like this, the greater the chance their tired muscles would start to seize up.

They had to be getting close to their mounts by now. Keeping to the shadows as they were, he was having a hard time making out any of the landmarks he'd noted when they'd left the horses that morning, but his internal sense of direction was telling him they couldn't be far away.

"Alright," whispered Garrin, bringing Caymus back to the present moment, "let's go."

The three men crawled out of the hole they'd been hiding in and slowly crept through darkness, moving toward the same easterly star which had been guiding them for hours now. Caymus, crouched low to conceal himself behind the massive boulders as much as possible, made sure his feet landed squarely, not skidding or scuffing but making perfect contact with the ground so as not to create any unnecessary noise. He held his sheathed sword in his hand, not wanting the scabbard to knock into or dislodge any rocks while riding on his hip. The prince and Big Grant did likewise, though they didn't need to stoop nearly as much.

Caymus had to stop himself from literally tripping over his own feet when he rounded a jagged boulder and met with a sight that made his breath catch in his lungs.

They'd found the clearing they'd been making for all this time. The enemy, however, had found it first. Ahead of them were the corpses of all seven horses, as well as the bodies of two men.

Caymus slowly stepped forward, his heart in his throat, and approached the carnage. He could hear the quickened breathing of the other two men as they, too, rounded the boulder and caught sight of the grizzly scene. The moon illuminated the small patch of sand, shedding ghostly white over the dead. The first body was easy to identify at this distance: Bigger Grant had deep gouges all over him; he lay in the middle of a large, red stain where his blood had soaked into the ground. Harrison was there too, his smaller form a stark contrast to Grant's massive body. He'd been thrown on top of Bigger Grant, as though their enemy had considered him some manner of refuse. One of his hands was missing.

The horses had been butchered. Legs and heads had been chopped or sawed off, then piled together in the center of the clearing. Caymus had to turn away when his eyes caught the brown and white pattern of the gelding he'd brought with him from Flamehearth's stable. Another tumor of guilt took root in his heart. The animal had been quiet and good-natured during the trip, but Caymus hadn't even learned the horse's name before he'd put a saddle on him. The poor thing hadn't asked to be here; he'd forced this kind, gentle animal to come on this trip, and he'd led it to its death.

What kind of monster was he turning in to?

"Caymus." Garrin's voice came from behind, low and gentle. Caymus turned and stared at the prince, unable to speak. "We don't have time. Get whatever supplies you can carry. We need to move quickly." Caymus nearly fell backward in surprise at the prince's coldness. How could he be so calm?

Then, Garrin stepped forward and put a hand on Caymus's shoulder. "It's not your fault, my friend," he said. "Black Moon did this, not you."

Caymus felt a held breath explode, ragged, from his lungs. He nodded, getting control over his emotions again. Garrin stepped past him, slid the hand from his shoulder, and moved among the bodies, his eyes to the ground.

Caymus turned and did as he was told. Finding his gear wasn't difficult: the corpses being all piled together meant everything else—food, water, weapons—lay openly on the ground: bloody, but easy to spot. Swallowing to dislodge the tightness in his throat, he bent down and collected his backpack, opening it to check that his supplies were still there.

He sighed quietly when he saw his shield, splintered and broken, next to the pile of horseflesh. He'd been anxious to get the shield back, anxious to have one more object to place between the prince and the soldiers of Black Moon. Now, there would only be him and his sword.

He hoped it would be enough.

He felt, more than saw, the prince kneel down next to him. "Time to go."

~~~

The night seemed endless.

Caymus kept wishing they could rest as he crouched, waiting in the dark. He wondered just how much time had passed since they'd found the butchered horses and the bodies of Harrison and Grant. The movement of the moon across the sky made him think it must be have been several hours, at least. He kept expecting the sky to start brightening, but it remained resolutely black, as though mocking his petty desires.

Just as they had been leaving the bloody clearing with what remained of their supplies, Bernie and Cyrus had appeared, materializing in the starlight as though they'd been summoned there by magic. There had been a very quick discussion about the bodies of their friends and whether they should bury or burn them and pay their final respects, but the prince had cut the conversation short, declaring in no uncertain terms
~~~

that they didn't have time. The three remaining men of the prince's guard —Cyrus, Bernie, and Big Grant—hadn't liked the idea of leaving their brethren behind, but they'd understood why they'd had to do it.

Since then, they'd spent the night making their way east, generally following the road to Kepren a few hundred yards south, but keeping to the boulders and furrows, that they might stay hidden from the thousands of eyes of Black Moon. They'd managed to remain undetected so far, but they all knew that the road would turn south eventually; sooner or later, they would have to decide whether to keep hiding or make a break for it.

"If it was any other army," Cyrus had said, "we could just steal some horses and get away. Trust us to find ourselves running from the only military in the world that doesn't use regular cavalry."

The words had brought short-lived smiles to the faces of the travelers, with the single exception of Bernie. Bernie's face was set into a seemingly permanent scowl, and Caymus had witnessed several contemptuous stares in his direction over the course of the night. The man obviously blamed him for what had happened to his friends. Caymus couldn't argue the point.

The intensity of the patrols had eased off a little since they'd left the clearing, but they were still appearing, and appearing suddenly, far too often. Caymus couldn't understand why Black Moon was still spending so much effort trying to find them. Surely, the army should have given up on this small band and moved on by now, and instead concentrated on making its way south toward Kepren.

A possible explanation—the obvious one—nagged at him. Somehow, they knew he was in the area but couldn't pinpoint his position. Maybe it was just that single figure, the one who'd stepped out in front of the army and pointed its sword at him, that could tell exactly where he was. That would certainly make the most sense, considering the events of the last dozen hours or so. He only hoped that Black Moon's apparent leader wasn't among the searching patrols.

Garrin still wouldn't let him go, wouldn't let him strike out on his own and lead the Black Moon soldiers away, despite numerous pleas that it was the right thing to do. "Look, Caymus," he'd finally said, "even if that horned bastard is able to find you—and I'm not convinced that he is— you're part of this unit now, and we live and die as a unit. If you want to keep me safe, then do it by using that knowledge of yours. I don't want to hear any more about this 'leave me behind' business. Do you understand me?"

Caymus had stared at the prince a long while before he'd finally acquiesced.

"Good," Garrin had said. "I've lost three very good men today, men I cared about. I'm not losing any more."

Despite his opinion that Garrin, the prince of Kepren, was making the wrong decision, Caymus had to admit that he respected the man's resolve. He found himself wondering again why he felt such kinship with him. He barely knew the prince in any way that mattered, but he believed he would follow the man into the very maw of death.

~~~

Many hours later, in the cool of a fall afternoon, Caymus found himself resting in a hole in the ground with the rest of his companions. They'd managed to sneak past the groups of soldiers, had managed to run under the cover of night from the edges of the Greatstones all the way to the road at the point where it had turned south toward the city. Since then, they'd moved as quickly as possible, alternating between running for twenty paces and walking for ten, trying to get as much distance as possible between themselves and the invading army.

He, Garrin, Big Grant, and Bernie were slouched in what was little more than a ditch about a dozen yards from the road, while Cyrus, keeping his eyes just above ground level, served as a lookout. A small patch of rocks and some scrub brush helped to conceal them, though they also obscured the view in both directions, a fact which kept Cyrus cursing under his breath every once in a while.

Caymus had wondered what the hole, really just a hollow in the dirt that was barely big enough to conceal the men, was doing there in the first place. Grant had suggested that an earlier traveler had carved it out of the ground in some previous year, possibly to stay out of the wind as he slept. The thought had given Caymus a strange sense of history, of connection. The idea that other people might have encountered hardship in this very spot a long time ago, and that those people had left this little sanctuary here for them to use, gave him a feeling of comfort.

"You should all be trying to get some sleep," Garrin said, not looking at any of them, but addressing them all.

"You're one to talk," Grant said, "you've not slept more than any of us has."

"Then I should probably be trying to get some sleep, too," the prince admitted, though he made no move to suggest that was his intention. He lifted his head to look at Bernie. "How long would you say we have?"

Bernie closed his eyes in thought for a moment. "Our pace, minus what they were doing when they came through the pass," his eyebrows bunched as he considered. "I'd say we might have anywhere between twenty minutes and two hours, depending on whether they're still out looking for us or if they just got on with the march."
~~~

Garrin nodded. "Looks like we'll be sleeping with our swords again," he said.

Cyrus chuckled. "I'd rather a good woman, myself."

Nobody laughed, though the prince smiled briefly. "Maybe when we get back," he said.

They all had their weapons out, the prince included. The black blade rested on his outstretched legs, his fingers gingerly touching the hilt. Caymus was fascinated by that sword, by the black hue that permeated the entire length of it, from pommel to point. He was getting his first good look at it since he'd met the prince, and part of him felt he could literally fall into that blackness.

Maybe he was just tired.

"What is that sword made of?" he found himself asking.

Garrin looked up at him, eyebrows raised. For a moment, Caymus thought he'd asked an impertinent question, but the prince didn't rebuke him. Instead, he looked back down at the blade, his fingers still on the grip. "I don't know, to be honest," he said. "It's been in my family for a very long time, passed down from father to son. A lot of people before you have asked that question, and I don't think anyone's ever had a good answer."

"It's always been in your family?" Caymus asked. In the dark corners of his mind, something told him it was an important question, but he was too tired, too exhausted to think very hard about it at that moment.

"I don't know its origins," the prince admitted, "who made it, or when, but the journals I've read don't show that it's ever been in the hands of anyone but the king or the prince."

"The Champion-Protector's blade," said Grant in the moment of silence that followed. "It's given from the king to his son, the prince, as soon as he's old enough to claim the title and start making the defense of Kepren his full-time job." He looked pointedly at Garrin. "One day, when our good prince here has settled down and had a son of his own, he'll pass it down to him." A wry smile played across his lips. "If our good prince ever gets around to finding himself a willing queen, that is."

Garrin smiled, shaking his head. He had just opened his mouth to say something in reply when they all heard Cyrus utter a muffled scream and saw him get suddenly dragged out of the hollow.

Immediately, they all had their swords in their hands, though they dared not stand yet. For all they knew, a volley of arrows was waiting for them to poke their heads above the bushes.

A voice came to them through the dry brush, a voice full of subdued, icy menace. "I think you'd better come on out of there."

Caymus had heard that voice before.

They all looked to the prince, who gave a quick nod and motioned for them to stay their blades. When they stood and walked out of the ditch, they found six figures standing before them, barely a few feet beyond the bushes.

Cyrus lay on the ground, a growing redness beneath his head. His throat had been cut.

Five of the men were strangers to Caymus, though he felt as though he knew their purpose. Each of them exhibited the taint of the kreal, much more so than had the previous soldiers he had encountered. They wore black, leather armor, reinforced here and there with metal plates. The armor seemed to magnify the dark, ashen color of their skins. They looked like they had been covered in soot.

The sixth man, Caymus knew too well. The last time he'd seen the dark figure, it had been standing over him, kreal-tainted knife in hand, while his world had gone dark. Caymus had known him as Callun, though he'd revealed his true name to be Mrowvain.

"Why, hello, Caymus," said the figure, his skin so dark now that it was almost black. "Aren't you supposed to be dead?"

Caymus didn't say anything. What was there to say?

Mrowvain turned his eyes to Garrin. "I'd rather not kill you, Your Highness," he said, affecting a slight bow that showed no measure of deference. "From the time I spent in Kepren, I think I can confidently say that taking your city would be a great deal easier if we had you alive for trade."

Caymus was furious with himself. Why had he not sensed these men coming? Mrowvain, especially, was deep into this dark transformation, so he should have been able to feel his presence from a long way off. How could they have snuck up on him?

"How did you find us?" Garrin said, his voice low and intense.

Mrowvain made a show of inspecting a fingernail, which slightly opened the dark cloak he wore and revealed a short sword that hung from his hip. His eyes were still dead, but they seemed to be enjoying themselves. "The commander has his ways," he said. He looked up at Garrin from under his eyebrows. "He was quite surprised to discover your little band. He's actually is a bit irritated with you." Then, without further explanation Mrowvain stepped forward and drew his sword.

Things started moving very quickly after that.

As if anticipating the move, Grant stepped in front of the prince to intercept the krealite assassin. In response, Mrowvain took a step to the side, spinning his entire body to add momentum to his strike. Grant raised his sword to block the blow, but Mrowvain's sword sliced through the steel as though it were paper, simultaneously slicing halfway through the front half of his torso. Caymus saw the light go out of Big Grant's eyes before any blood appeared at his chest.

"Bastard!" the prince cried. He grabbed Grant's arms, trying to break his fall as collapsed to the ground. In the same moment, Bernie lunged forward, angling a spear toward the men behind Mrowvain. Caymus didn't see much of what happened to him, as he instead shifted his attention to assassin, the man who had almost killed him, who had just taken the life of another of Garrin's friends.

One of the krealite soldiers stepped in his way, blocking him, and he found himself in a sudden struggle against three men in the late stages of the krealite infection. Taking a deep breath, he let the first man, who was swinging his weapon high, come at him. He ducked under the blade, but instead of striking out with his sword, he reached out and grabbed the man's forearm, using his immense strength to swing him into his fellows.

The three men weren't as clumsy as the previous soldiers had been, but they hadn't been expecting such a brash move. The first stumbled into the second, and before they could recover Caymus had neutralized them both, placing the blade at their chests and then thrusting steel into their hearts.

The third man stumbled back a couple of steps, but still managed to place himself between Caymus and Mrowvain. Caymus could make out the fighting between the prince and the spy. He didn't know by what force Mrowvain's blade had been able to cut through Grant's sword, but whatever the power was, the Champion-Protector's weapon seemed immune to it. They traded blows back and forth blade ringing against blade, and seemed to be in a stalemate for the moment.

He couldn't tell how Bernie was doing.

The soldier standing in front of Caymus seemed a few years older than the others had been. The ashen skin made it difficult to say for sure, but he suspected the man had been in his early forties before the kreal had taken hold. His arms were large and strong—almost as strong as Big Grant's had been—and he held his broadsword in both hands. This one was going to be more difficult. Caymus again wished he had his shield.

At least the attacker's blade didn't appear to be coated with kreal—or, more likely, paint. Caymus again wondered why that was. Why would the men he'd fought on the side of the ravine have had painted blades, but not these men? Could it have something to do with how far along they were in their transformations? Was the coloring merely a psychological advantage given to the soldiers who weren't yet actually invulnerable?

He didn't wait for the man to attack. Instead, he stepped forward and struck out first. The soldier brought his blade up at an angle in a parrying move, expecting Caymus to try to cleave him in two. Caymus wasn't aiming for the man's torso, however. He was aiming for the man's hands, anticipating the defensive motion and swinging his sword with all his might at a point in space where there had been nothing a moment before.

His blade struck true, smashing into the man's fingers. He didn't slice the skin, of course, but the concussive force of the blow was enough to make his opponent drop his sword and cry out in shock. Caymus wasted no time. Before the man could recover, he'd put his sword sideways through the man's abdomen and forced him, writhing, to the ground.

Caymus looked up. He could see Bernie locked in combat with the two other soldiers. He was landing blow after blow, but wasn't making any progress. Neither of the soldiers seemed able to hurt him either, at least, such was his skill with his spears.

The prince, too, was trading strikes with his opponent, though neither he nor Mrowvain seemed able to get the upper hand.

You keep him alive, Caymus!

Caymus slowed his thought process and widened his awareness, letting the details of the situation come to him. He measured up the forms of the two men, found the opening he wanted, and stepped forward, taking a swing at Mrowvain's side. He wasn't sure he'd be able to place the blade quite the way he wanted to, but he should at least buy the prince some breathing room.

He was surprised, and somewhat fascinated, by how quickly Mrowvain reacted. As he watched the short blade spinning in his direction, he wondered if the kreal had imparted some measure of unnatural speed to this man or if he'd always been this quick. Mrowvain's counterstrike didn't touch his flesh, but it shattered his sword, breaking the blade into several pieces.

Caymus, surprised, had to take a step back to prevent any of the shards of steel from dropping into his feet. As he did so, he noticed Mrowvain's gaze. The ash-skinned man seemed to be regarding him with a mixture of curiosity and hate.

Garrin, seeing that his opponent's eyes were momentarily watching something else, took his opportunity and slashed out. Mrowvain stepped back at the last second, but the black blade got a piece of him, tearing a gash at least an inch deep through the fabric of his cloak and tunic, and slicing into his chest. Caymus nearly gasped. The Black Sword had cut a krealite!

The look in Mrowvain's eyes was that of murder itself. Caymus was nearly unable to follow the sudden flurry of blows he threw at the prince, his arms spinning and flailing as though he were some manner of killing machine given life.

The prince obviously couldn't follow the blade either. He deflected the first few blows, but then one of them knocked the black blade out of its defensive position.

Garrin seemed surprised to find himself wide open to attack, and Caymus felt a cry leave his own lungs in the same moment Mrowvain sunk the blade, up to the hilt, into the prince's abdomen.

The moment it was done, the spy pulled his blade free and took three steps away from his bested opponent, turning his attention to the fight Bernie was having with his two remaining soldiers. Caymus rushed to Garrin's side, not letting him fall but helping him down onto his back. Garrin was bleeding. He was bleeding far too much. Caymus saw in the Prince's countenance the same wide-eyed expression that had been on Mally's face just before he'd died.

Caymus nearly recoiled in anguish. It couldn't be happening again. Not again!

Garrin's expression was defiant. Though the fire was going out of his eyes, they locked onto Caymus. "Kill the bastard, Caymus," he whispered, blood making the words gurgle. He lifted his weapon up off the ground, picking it up by the blade. Then, with what seemed his last ounce of strength, the prince of Kepren placed the Black Sword into Caymus's hands.

The moment he touched the hilt, fire exploded in Caymus's vision.

Flames seemed to dance before him, as though the entire world had suddenly ignited. A strange awakening began in his soul, and memories of faces he'd never seen, of battles he'd never fought, found their way into his mind. As he reeled from the sensation, he felt the prince's sword changing in his hand, growing, becoming heavier. The black color was melting away, a silver sheen taking its place.

In the next moment, he felt the presence of the Conflagration bursting all around him. Joy, fury, love, despair: all raged through him, found purchase in his heart. The sword's blade and grip lengthened, and the cross-guard widened until he found he was holding a fully two-handed weapon, so long and massive that only the arms of someone as large as Caymus could possibly have lifted it.

The flames in his vision seemed to compress, to coalesce into a point as though trying to contain the might of a burning sun within a space the size of a speck of dust. Then, in the next moment, the power burst forth, filling Caymus's ears with the roar of the Conflagration.

That was when the sword caught fire.

The weapon's entire length was suddenly submerged in orange flames that traveled their way from the pommel to the blade. Immediately, without thinking, Caymus concentrated on the Aspect of the Unburning, forcing himself to embrace the flames as part of himself, not letting them singe his skin.

The sensation was rapture. He couldn't remember ever having felt so alive.

Garrin. Caymus looked down. The prince was still breathing. With a motion that felt like instinct, like need more than desire, he placed the fiery blade against the prince's wound and directed the flames to burn through to the other side, cauterizing the torn flesh, sealing the broken vessels, halting the bleeding.

He didn't know if he'd acted soon enough. Only time would tell him that.

Having done all he could for the prince in that moment, Caymus turned around and rose to his full height. He smiled a vicious smile when he saw Mrowvain, standing as though stunned, abject horror in his usually lifeless eyes. Bernie's battle, too, had subsided as all three combatants were now staring at him with varying degrees of shock and fear.

Caymus could now see Mrowvain with a new perception. He could make out the differences between him and the other two soldiers more clearly now—differences greater than just skin tone. He could actually see the kreal, the smoky, oily substance, running through the man's veins. He could also see all the little weak places in his armor: the inside of the right leg just under the knee, the top of the left shoulder, the right cheek between the mouth and the eye. He knew these weak points, remembered them, not just because of his time in the Conflagration, but because of a thousand other memories of battle, memories of the last Knight of the Flame, a warrior who had fought people like this, people who had served the element of kreal, who'd chosen to take the sickly element into themselves.

He also remembered the word, "Mrowvain". It wasn't a name; it was a title. It meant "fire-killer", and it was bestowed upon the assassin who was charged with ending the threat of the Conflagration to the Sograve.

The shock in Mrowvain's eyes turned to hate. He screamed something that Caymus couldn't understand and charged toward him.

The sword's flames ignited into even greater ferocity.

The fight was over quickly. Mrowvain's intent was obviously to move fast, to strike Caymus in the heart before he could react. What he didn't know, however, was that Caymus was a knight now, that he had a knight's weapon, a two-handed beast nearly seven feet in length. Mrowvain tried to block—or parry, possibly—the mighty swing of that weapon, but it was far too massive and moving much too fast. It swept past his paltry defense and bit into his body at the shoulder, the flames searing through the chitinous kreal as they passed through flesh and bone alike.

Mrowvain fell to the ground, his head and shoulders attached to his torso by only a few inches of muscle and tendon.

The remaining two krealite soldiers fled in panic. Bernie just stared at him, his eyes wide. Caymus said nothing. Instead, he spent the next few moments calming his mind, letting go of his rage, his passion, willing the flames of the sword to dissipate and finally go out. At last, he planted the blade in the ground and turned to the prince, who was, thankfully, still breathing.

The two men, Caymus and Bernie, didn't say anything to one another. Bernie didn't seem to know what to make of what had just happened, but at least he didn't seem to be projecting actual contempt at Caymus anymore. Caymus was glad for that particular respite. Presumably, Bernie would eventually get around to knowing what questions to ask. Caymus hoped that by that time he might actually know how to answer them. Moving quickly and without words, the two of them inspected the prince's wounds, satisfied themselves that he could be moved without causing greater injury, and that he just might last long enough to reach Kepren.

The two men, the ones who were still standing, took the time to bury the ones who were not before they left, gently placing their bodies in their former hiding place and covering them with sand. After that, Bernie gathered up the few supplies that he could salvage and Caymus cut a few pieces of leather and cloth from what was left of Mrowvain's belongings, fashioning a sling for his sword so that he could hang it from his back.

When they were both ready, they nodded to each other. Then, Caymus picked up the prince's body in his arms and they began their long run to Kepren.

Chapter 20

Caymus blinked his eyes, partly because they felt as dry as stones, but also to try to clear the strange images from his vision.

He didn't know what time it was, only that night had fallen again. He and Bernie had been running for hours, nonstop, pushing as hard as they could to reach Kepren quickly. They had a few skins of water remaining, but they had left most of the food behind, trying to keep their burden as light as possible.

About an hour ago, Caymus had started seeing hallucinations.

At least, he thought they were hallucinations. Every once in a while, his eyes would wander off the road and he would see what appeared to be ghostly apparitions of flame dotting the landscape. The fiery, orange shapes had no real form, no physical presence, but he could feel a sense of joy, of approval coming from them, as though the Lords of the Conflagration themselves had come to the Quatrain to lend him their support.

"Stop, Caymus!" Bernie's voice seemed distant in his ears, giving him pause to think that it, too, might be a trick of his mind. Still, he slowed and stopped anyway, just in case. He then turned to see Bernie nearly fifty yards behind, half-jogging, half-stumbling toward him. Caymus understood: the man was badly in need of respite. His own muscles were aching and cramping, and he couldn't remember ever feeling so cold. A rest would be nice right now.

Gingerly, he bent down and placed Garrin on the ground, being careful not to jostle his wound lest the flesh tear and the blood start flowing again. Once he'd inspected the prince's abdomen and satisfied himself that no further damage had been done, he sat cross-legged next to him, resting his elbows on his knees and cupping his head in his hands.

Why was the night so cold?

Bernie arrived and stumbled to a halt. Panting and wheezing, he hunched over, placed his hands on his knees, and hung his head. Caymus thought the man might have vomited if he'd had the liquid to spare. After a moment, he pulled one of the waterskins from his shoulder. "I don't know how you keep all that mass moving, flame-lover," he said in a raspy voice, then he handed him the skin.

Caymus would have laughed, but he was too tired. He wasn't breathing nearly as hard as Bernie, but the non-stop running was still taking its toll. Before taking a drink for himself, he unstopped the skin and reached over to lift Garrin's head. The prince wasn't fully conscious, but he seemed able to swallow, which lifted a huge weight from Caymus's heart. He didn't know much about the water element, but he knew that the man had lost a lot of blood, that blood was of water, and that he would need to drink if he was going to live.

"How is he?" asked Bernie, opening a skin of his own.

Caymus closed his eyes and reached out with his mind to inspect the prince. Garrin's arms and legs seemed colder than they should have been, as though the fire that remained in his body was pooling in his torso, keeping the blood pumping at the expense of the extremities. His heartbeat was slow, but it was strong.

"I think he'll make it," he said, at last. He looked up to meet Bernie's eyes. "I don't think he'll wake up before we get him home, but I think he'll last long enough for us to get him to a proper healer."

Bernie nodded, and Caymus detected what might have been the beginnings of a smile, though it quickly dissipated. "What happened back there?" he eventually asked, sitting down on the other side of the prince.

Caymus considered the question as he put the skin to his lips. Looking back, it all made perfect sense: of course the prince's sword, passed down through the generations of the royal family, had turned out to be the sword of the Knight of the Flame. Gu'ruk's book, buried deep in the bowels of Otvia, had mentioned that Morogin, the original knight, had been the son of a king. It hadn't specified that his kingdom was that of Kepren, but the fact that the Tebrian region was named for him made the revelation unsurprising.

He put the skin down. "You heard about all that time I spent unconscious, right?"

Bernie tilted his head, remembering, "Garrin mentioned it when it was happening. He called you 'The Sleeping Giant'. Made sure everyone in the city knew about it, too." He forced a chuckle. "He thought that was funny."

"My body was asleep," Caymus continued, "but my mind was in the Conflagration, learning to fight the krealites." He looked up to see that Bernie was listening intently. "They were training me to be a knight, the

Knight of the Flame. There was another knight too, a long time ago, and after they trained me, they told me that I would have to find his weapon. It turns out that the knight's sword and the Champion-Protector's sword are one and the same."

Bernie looked down, not saying anything. He seemed to be weighing the words he'd just heard, trying to decide whether he believed them. Caymus didn't blame the man. It was a lot to take in, especially for somebody who wasn't exactly reverent. As he waited for him to speak again, he lifted his left hand up in front of his face to look at the mark there again. He'd only noticed the difference after night had fallen, but he assumed that it had changed the moment his skin had touched the sword.

The outline of the sword was still there, but the flame behind it was no longer a static object. It burned and danced like a living thing on his skin. He'd believed that the mark would change at some point, were he to be successful in his quest, but this had been beyond his expectations. Knight of the Flame indeed!

He held up the hand for Bernie to see, and the man's eyes went wide. "How are you doing that?" he said.

Caymus couldn't help but smile. "Part of the job, it seems," he said.

He'd realized something else as he'd run through the desert and crossed into the dry grassland of the Tebrian plain. All this time, the strange, inexplicable kinship he'd felt with the prince was due not to the charisma of what was obviously a great leader—not that Garrin wasn't a great leader; he was half dead in the desert because he was such a great leader—but rather to the presence of the sword he'd carried. Even in that moment, he could feel that same connection from the sword, still hanging on his back. It was more than a weapon. It was somehow a part of him, an appendage that had been missing from his body until now.

"The knight would be drawn to his weapon," Gu'ruk had said. Caymus was surprised at himself, at his not having put the pieces together sooner.

He put the stopper back in the waterskin, placed it on the ground, and reached over his shoulder to pull the sword free from the makeshift scabbard he'd crafted from Mrowvain's armor. The blade was so long that sitting on the ground meant that it was hanging at a severe angle, the tip buried nearly an inch in the sand. He could hear the steel moving across the earth as he pulled, could feel the tip of the blade traveling through the grit. The moment the sword was firmly in his grip, he could sense a desire to ignite, as though the sword itself wanted to burst into fire again, to revel in the flames. The sword felt like it could be alive. For all he knew, it was.

The sword made him remember things too; or rather it seemed to remove blocks in his mind, allowing him to recall certain events. The events were hazy though, incomplete, as if he were seeing the thoughts and feelings involved in the memories, rather than the images themselves

He remembered the krealites, though not the ones he'd been facing since the attack on the Temple. These krealites were the ones from the first war, the Old War, the war that had decided the fate of the Quatrain. The kreal, like all the other elements that had battled for control back then, had found many supporters, had found many ways to assert its dominance, but the krealites—those huge, armor-plated insects—had been its greatest weapons. There had been so many of them. He remembered the death they had brought to the world. He remembered how terrifying they had seemed, how strong. They had an ability to tunnel through the element of earth to and from the Sograve, the elemental realm of kreal, but only in places where the walls between the Quatrain and the other realms were weak, where pure elemental power could pass through easily. In those days, such places had been everywhere, and the krealites had attacked like nightmares in the dark, appearing suddenly, then vanishing back into the ground.

They'd looked different back then, though the difference was hazy. They'd been smaller, perhaps, and with fewer legs.

He remembered when he'd figured out their weaknesses, the method of piercing their armor slowly, rather than with massive blows. He hadn't figured it out on his own, though. He and the other champions had worked together: the Earthwarden and the Circle of…something. He couldn't see their faces, couldn't remember specifically what they'd done, but he felt the impact they'd had on his life as though they had lived only yesterday.

The Sograve had invested heavily in the insects. Once they'd been hunted down and finished, the worshipers of the dark element had essentially been beaten. They hadn't lasted long after that.

"What is it?"

Caymus looked up to see Bernie staring at him. He was still sitting, waiting. His breathing had slowed but he was tense, as though he expected danger to appear at any moment.

Caymus wondered what the expression on his face must have looked like when memories that weren't his own had been flooding through his mind.

"Nothing," he said. No, that wasn't fair. "The sword," he said, nodding toward the blade. "It's like it's teaching me, showing me what happened last time."

"Last time?" Bernie seemed guarded, but genuinely curious.

"The Old War. The war between dozens of different elements that decided which would make up our world." Caymus found himself smiling, peacefully. The knowledge made him comfortable, somehow. He wasn't sure if the sword itself was remembering these past events, or if it had somehow imprinted the thoughts of the first knight on itself and he was simply accessing them with his touch, but they gave him a sense of calm, a feeling of connection with the first knight.

A flicker caught his eye, and he noticed that the flame on his hand seemed to be dancing more quickly now, more fiercely. It almost seemed a window into the Conflagration itself. He wondered if it was because he was holding the sword.

"And it's teaching you how to beat Black Moon?" Bernie's voice was softer than Caymus ever remembered it being before, but it was still cautious, as though daring him to lie.

Caymus nodded. "I'm a shaper," he said. "I can control flame in a way that is completely different from the way the masters at the Conflagrationist Temple do it." He looked away, admiring the stars that dotted the horizon. There were so many of them tonight. "Because of that ability, the Conflagration chose me to be its champion during this war." He shrugged, then looked down at the sword in his hand. "Don't ask me how, because I don't know, but yes, the sword is showing me the way it happened last time, like it's trying to tell me what to do. It started the moment I touched the hilt."

"And is that what happened to your eyes?"

Caymus snapped his head up, his brow furrowed. "What do you mean?"

Bernie seemed amused by the question. He chuckled, then pulled a knife from his boot, which he spun around and handed to Caymus, handle-first. "See for yourself," he said.

Cautiously, Caymus took the knife and looked at it. The blade obviously didn't see a lot of use; it was polished to a near-mirror shine. He took a quick glance back at Bernie, then brought the blade up in front of his face to look at his reflection.

He could see what Bernie had meant. His irises had changed color, turned to a mix of oranges, reds, and yellows that seemed to slowly swirl around each other, like embers in a coal fire. He could swear that they were also giving off a faint light, illuminating the blade in his hand. Marked, then marked again: any doubt as to who he was, which element he represented, would evaporate for anyone who saw those eyes.

He handed the knife back. Bernie seemed about to say something else, but then Garrin let out a groan of pain, which immediately silenced him.

The two men looked at each other and nodded. Their break was over, and it was time to start running again.

Caymus hoped they were closer to Kepren than he thought they were.

~~~
~~~

Shivering slightly, Rill pulled his coat closed and began buttoning it up. He smiled when he discovered the gear embroidered on his breast. He was still occasionally surprised to find it there.

"You should have been here last year," said Daniel, hugging himself against the chill, obviously uncomfortable. "By this time last year, it had already snowed on us a couple of times."

"Yeah," said Rill, doing up the last button, "I'm sure you took that in stride, too."

Daniel feigned a punch to Rill's shoulder, but didn't follow through with it, as though remembering where they were, and that people might be watching.

They two of them were making their way through the streets of the Guard District, heading to the northern gate. Rill had been assigned the task of checking the fire-sludge defenses that had been set up in several places around the city.

Captain Draya's plan to focus on teaching others how to make the sludge, rather than on raw production, had paid off. Shortly after Inquisitor Dalphin had become part of their lives and had ordered 'round-the-clock protection at the Gearhouse, the engineers' output had increased tenfold, and now several barrels of Rill's fire-sludge sat in various locations around the edges of Kepren, ready for use by the army in their defense of the city. The manufacturing procedure had, in fact, become so efficient now that Rill's own time was better spent out in the city, supervising the use of the material, rather than its creation.

The reason that he was checking the sludge that particular afternoon was that a finished barrel of fire-sludge had been discovered to be inert in the morning. Inquisitor Dalphin had arrived to investigate immediately and had suggested that Rill, the foremost authority on the stuff, make certain that there were no more surprises waiting for the soldiers of the Royal Army. For his own part, the inquisitor had not yet caught their saboteur, but either his actions or possibly just his presence in and around the Gearhouse seemed to have deterred the worst of the interference. Rill didn't know what Dalphin had been doing with his time since they'd first discovered the sabotage in the Gearhouse, but he was glad the man was there—whatever he was up to—and acting on their behalf.

Daniel's presence today had been a surprise. The fact that nobody knew quite how much time they had left before the arrival of the Black Moon Army had made today's inspections that much more important, and Captain Draya had, therefor, assigned Daniel to accompany Rill, acting as his second. Rill had felt a bit uncomfortable with the arrangement so far: not only was Daniel technically his senior in the

Royal Engineers but generally only captains or men of even higher rank ever merited having a second.

He certainly wasn't going to complain about the extra help, though.

For his own part, Daniel seemed quite happy to be acting as Rill's assistant today. The two of them had already spent the morning investigating the defenses that had been placed in the Reed District, and Daniel had been helpful and cheerful throughout. Despite his misgivings about their relative positions today, Rill was glad to have him around. It would have been a much more depressing sort of a day without a friend at his side.

As they walked through the streets, they passed another group of soldiers setting up a barricade on the road. The sounds of hammers upon stone and nails echoed down the streets as the men worked, reminding Rill of just how barren the city seemed today. The only people walking around were soldiers, engineers, and other people of the type who were used to carrying swords. The lonely hammering sounds chilled Rill almost as much as the weather.

"If you'd told me a year ago that I'd ever see the streets of Kepren deserted," Daniel said, "I wouldn't have believed you."

Rill smiled. "They're not deserted," he said, turning to his friend. "We're still here, aren't we?"

The entirety of the Grass District and western half of the Guard District were empty, having been evacuated by royal decree that very morning. Inns, shops, and large homes in the Reed and the eastern Guard were, at that moment, being filled with those citizens who had decided to stay in the city. Many, of course, had chosen to flee instead. The Silvertooth River, which ran through the Reed District, carried a number of vessels upon its surface that afternoon. Between the large ships and the dozens of tiny rowing boats, thousands of people were being carried west, toward the ocean and the presumed safety of Shorevale.

All around Rill, doors hung open and pieces of detritus drifted down the streets on the breeze. A small fire, obviously built to keep somebody warm, still smoldered at the edge of an alley, offering evidence of just how recently the evacuation had been ordered.

"We'll hold onto it, won't we, Daniel?" Rill asked.

"What's that?" Daniel asked.

"The city," Rill said, his voice somber.

"I hope so, Sir," Daniel said. "I really hope so."

"It's just," Rill continued, "I only just got to Kepren, and I was really starting to like it here."

Daniel smiled. "You know, between that sludge of yours and whatever it is the prince got himself up to," he said, "I think we might just be able to beat the bastards."

Rill nodded. "I hope you're right." He turned and arched an eyebrow at his friend. "Did you just call me 'Sir'?"

Daniel gave a short laugh of surprise. "I suppose I did!" He gave Rill a small bow. "Begging your pardon, Sir, but I am your second, after all."

Rill only shook his head. He'd thought their new assignments uncomfortable before; now they just seemed absurd. At least he could laugh at absurd.

When they arrived at the North Gate, they found the area buzzing with activity. Soldiers and engineers were building fortifications, placing arrays of shields and spears at the various barricades, and doing something to the gatehouse, the small building beside the gates that contained some of their mechanisms, that he couldn't fathom. The huge, wooden doors themselves, the northern portal to the city, as well as the portcullis, were open.

Dozens of men and women were working in the area. Rill smiled when he saw one that he recognized.

"Hello Rill!" Milo grinned as he waved the two of them over. He was standing near one of the new barricades, wiping his hands on a piece of cloth. Rill was surprised to see Perra there too, perched atop one of the long, wooden spikes.

Rill extended his hand when he reached the priest, and Milo shook it warmly. "I wasn't expecting to see you here," Rill said. "Did they press you into service?"

Milo put on a show of being hurt. "You make it sound like I'm not naturally helpful!" The expression quickly faded, and he nodded at Daniel. "Who's your friend?"

Before Rill could answer, Daniel was already stepping forward and shaking hands. "Daniel," he said, beaming, "of the Royal Engineers, and you have got to be Milo."

Milo cocked his head. "How'd you know that?"

"Ha!" said Daniel, chuckling. "I think everyone in Kepren knows who you are by now. There must be thousands of refugees who owe you and their friends their lives."

Milo shook his head, still not understanding.

"Come on!" said Daniel, incredulously. "You must know that! Their villages burning, and Black Moon tearing the place up? You're the only reason they knew it was still safe south of the Greatstones!"

The epiphany of just how crucial Milo and the other air priests had been over the past few months struck Rill like a hammer. "You gave them somewhere to run," he said, quietly.

Milo looked between the two of them, a slightly stunned expression on his face. "You know," he said, "I don't think anyone's passed that along to the others yet." He nodded. "I might just do that today."

He cleared his throat. "Still," he said, looking at Daniel, "how did you know that was me?"

"Really?" Daniel chuckled. "With the wings and everything?"

Milo lifted his arms up, inspecting his collection of feathers. "I suppose I do stand out a bit on occasion, don't I?"

"Yeah," said Rill, shaking his head. "On occasion."

Daniel stepped back, then pointed up a ladder to the battlements above the gate. "That should be where they're keeping it," he said. "If you want, I'll go on ahead and get started."

Rill nodded. "Thanks, Daniel," he said. "I'll be there in a minute."

As Daniel walked away and began ascending the nearby ladder, Milo gave Rill a curious look. "'If you want'?" he said. "What, does he work for you or something?"

Rill knew it was hopeless just trying to shrug the question off. "For the time being," he said. "When it comes to Rill's fire-sludge," he continued, "they must think Rill's kind of the expert."

Milo nodded, a genuine smile of pride and approval on his face. "Good for you," he said.

Rill decided to change the subject. "So, what's happening here? I'm seeing a lot of fortifications, but it doesn't look like the gate itself is getting any attention."

"They're leaving it open," Milo said.

"What?" Rill thought he must have been joking.

Milo shrugged. "From what I understand, they don't think much of our chances at actually holding off Black Moon, so what they've decided to do is to try to corral them instead."

Rill thought back to the defenses he'd seen on the streets leading up to here. They made a bit more sense now. He'd seen a lot of barricades and other fortifications that were designed to impede a force's progress, but they were set up along side roads and alleys, rather than across the main thoroughfares. He frowned. "So they're just going to leave the gate open?" He looked at the gate. "Won't that seem a bit, you know, obviously a trap?"

Milo shook his head. "Well, maybe not open, per se," he said, "but they're planning on making it really easy to get into."

Rill let out a long breath. He lowered his voice. "Do you think it's a good idea?"

Milo grinned. "It's that fire-stuff of yours that got them thinking this way."

Rill wasn't sure how he felt about that. He considered the idea, turning it around in his mind, getting a good look at every. He could understand the logic of such a plan. It did make sense to try to force the enemy into specific spaces if the idea was to douse them with flaming sludge, especially considering the fact that there was only so much of the stuff to go around. Still, the risks to the city and to the populace were great, should something go wrong. It wasn't something he would have tried.

"And you thought you'd come and help out?" Rill said, dropping the subject. "I thought they still had you passing messages in the Keep?"

"They did," Milo said. His grin faded a little. "Black Moon's so close at this point, though," he continued, "that asking other people where they are is kind of moot." He turned his gaze to the North. "I can hear them now."

Rill raised his eyebrows. "You can *hear* them?"

Milo nodded, then furrowed his brow in concentration. "The dry air helps. The less water that's in the air, the easier it is for the wind to carry sounds from a long way away." He turned back to Rill, his smile returning. "Plus, an army's a big thing, you know. They make a lot of noise."

Rill shook his head in amazement. Milo, both in his abilities as an air priest and in his constant optimism, was a constant source of wonder to him. "So," he said, cautiously, "can you tell how far away they are?"

Milo looked north again. "I'd wager they'll be here before noon tomorrow."

Rill took a deep breath. He'd known the army was coming, known the entire city was preparing to meet their attack, but actually getting a time for their arrival from a man who could hear their marching feet made things suddenly a great deal more immediate.

Milo turned to the gate again. He seemed about to say something when Perra, the hawk that had been his frequent companion for the last few months, beat her wings and lifted herself into the air, soaring over the wall to the North.

They both watched her go. "I wonder where she's off to," Milo said after she disappeared.

"Well," Rill said, "if Black Moon's going to be here tomorrow, then I'd better get to it."

Milo nodded. "Go on, then." They shook hands again and Rill made his way up the ladder, following Daniel to the battlements of the outer wall.

When he got there, he saw Daniel inserting a small, metal rod into one of the half-dozen barrels that were stored up there. He also saw Aiella, the dark-haired girl who had spent so much time at Flamehearth recently. She was at the edge of the battlements, standing between the crenellations and staring out at the plains. She didn't seem to have noticed him yet.

He knew why she was there, though. "Still no sign of them?" he said.

She slowly shook her head, her dark hair waving in the slight breeze.

Rill still wasn't sure what he thought about Aiella. She'd appeared brusque and conceited when he'd first met her at Flamehearth, though she seemed different—quieter—lately. He'd heard her described as being the prince's woman, yet he'd never seen any evidence of that with his own eyes. In fact, she'd come looking for him twice in the last couple of days, asking if he'd heard any news about the men who'd gone to meet Black Moon, and both times her concern had seemed more for Caymus than for the prince.

He didn't think she and Caymus even knew each other that well. He'd considered trying to find out more, but prying into the affairs of an ambassador's daughter wasn't something he was terribly interested in doing.

He turned his attention back to Daniel. "How does it look?"

Daniel had just placed the rod on the ground and was striking a couple of sparks onto it with a hand-held striker. The oily substance caught, burned for a moment, then went out. The little rods were cut small enough that they wouldn't hold enough of the sludge to burn any longer than that. Rill smiled. He was glad he'd had time to modify the mixture a little, allowing it to be lit by sparks and not always requiring a steady flame.

Daniel turned his face up with a grin. "First one's okay, at least."

Rill nodded, then he pulled his own testing rod and striker from the pouch at his waist. "You check those," he said, indicating the two unchecked barrels closest to Daniel, "and I'll do these two."

Daniel grunted an acknowledgment and Rill set about his work, inserting the testing rod into the first barrel. He was immensely glad that they hadn't found any further evidence of tampering so far. Though Draya's leadership had produced a greater amount of the sludge than anyone had thought possible, it still wasn't as much as Rill would have liked. He'd seen these krealites before, fought them before, knew how nearly-indestructible they were.

They didn't have any weapons, besides these barrels.

As Rill placed the metal rod onto the stone of the wall, a good distance from the barrels themselves, he silently hoped that the prince and his men —not to mention Caymus—had met with some success. He knew in his heart, however, that the fact that Milo could hear Black Moon's approach meant things couldn't have gone well. When he struck his flint, the rod caught the sparks and burned in a satisfactory way. Good. However Caymus was doing out there, at least there was one less barrel to worry about here.

"Do you think the plan will work?" Daniel said, starting another barrel.

Rill realized he'd been miles away. "What?" he said.

"This 'corral the bad guys down one street' plan," Daniel said, nodding towards the men working below. "Do you think it will work?"

Rill raised an eyebrow. "You could hear that from up here?"
Daniel affected a half-smile. "Like the man said, the air's dry today."
Rill, now testing the final barrel, considered the barricades again. He had decided he didn't like the strategy at all. He didn't imagine that an invading horde could be funneled so easily, that a mass of soldiers and krealites would be deterred from making their way down a particular street just because there was a hastily erected barricade in its way.
He couldn't volunteer a better idea, though.
"I hope so," he said. "At least, I'd say it's the best shot we have."
Daniel didn't say anything else. Rill was glad for the silence. He didn't have anything useful to add regarding the city's defenses, and he didn't want the soldiers down below to hear him give voice to any negative comments.
He found himself smiling when the testing rod from the last barrel caught, relieved that nothing further had gone wrong today.
He was brought to his feet quickly, though, when an urgent scream pierced the air.
He turned in a complete circle, looking about for the source of the cry. The noise appeared to be coming from the other side of the high wall, but that couldn't be possible, could it? Only when the sound came again did he realize that he was hearing the piercing cries of a bird, not a person. Was it Perra making that racket? He raised his head, scanned the sky, and found her white shape there.
In the next moment, after a brief sound of rushing wind, Milo was standing next to him. "Perra?" Milo said. Rill turned to see that he, too, was watching the hawk's form, his eyes shaded against the afternoon sun. She was still crying out, as though repeating the same alarm, over and over. "What's wrong with her?"
Rill watched the small, white, shrieking form as it moved against the blue sky. He kept expecting it to get larger, for her to come closer, but she didn't seem to be moving toward them. "Can you see?" he asked Milo.
"She's circling," Milo said, confused. "I don't know why—"
"There!" Aiella yelled, jutting her hand out, pointing out into the distance.
Rill tried to follow her finger, but he couldn't make anything out except the dry grassland about them. "What?" he said, "I don't—"
But Aiella was already making her way down the ladder, a haste to her movements that Rill wasn't used to seeing in people. He turned to Milo. "Do you see what she's talking about?"
Perra was still crying out.
Milo didn't say anything. He, too, was obviously trying to see what Aiella had been pointing at. His face was a mask of confusion as he searched the landscape. Then, the confusion evaporated. "Oh, no," he

said.

Rill was getting anxious. He didn't see what they saw, but his mind was forming a suspicion. "What?" he practically screamed.

"Down there," Milo said, pointing to something Rill still couldn't see. "That can only be Caymus." He turned his attention from the plains to look Rill square in the eye. "And there's only one other person with him."

Rill felt his breath catch in his lungs.

"Weren't there six or seven of them that left before?" said Daniel.

Milo nodded. Below them, Aiella had collected a handful of soldiers and was now leading them at a run out into the plain, along the dusty road that separated fields of dead and dying grass. "Come on," he said.

Rill didn't argue. He jumped down the lower half of the ladder, so great was his hurry, nearly spraining his ankle when he landed. He paid the ankle no mind though, and he burst through the North Gate a moment later. He was several yards behind Aiella and her soldiers, but he made up ground in great strides, his legs conditioned for strength and speed by a month-and-a-half of running up and down the walls of the engineering yard. When he finally caught sight of the two shapes coming toward them, he'd already passed the armored soldiers. Milo, his lithe form dancing across the dust, was still in front of him, but not even the air priest was able to keep pace with Aiella on this occasion.

As they got closer, Rill finally saw what Aiella and Milo had seen: two figures, one smaller than the other. Milo was right that the larger figure couldn't be anybody but Caymus. Rill was relieved by that fact, at least. He wondered who the other shape was, though.

A few moments later, Rill was able to discern that Caymus was carrying a third form. It was then that the reality of the situation, that something terrible must have happened to the prince's party, finally struck him. Eight men, he knew, had ridden out to Falmoor's Pass; only three were coming back, and one of them was having to be carried. Rill tried to will his legs to run even faster—he needed to help Caymus!—but his efforts only caused him to trip and nearly fall headlong into the road, and so he forced himself to slow again.

By the time he was finally close enough to make out the men's faces, Aiella and Milo were already standing before them. Caymus and the man next to him—Rill hadn't met this man before—appeared exhausted, their faces red, their breathing labored. The body Caymus carried was Prince Garrin's. Rill couldn't tell for sure, but it looked as though the prince might be dead. Had Caymus really carried Garrin's body all the way back to Kepren from the Greatstone Mountains?

It was then the Rill saw Caymus's eyes: the colored parts of them seemed to be alight with glowing embers, as though his friend's skull was filled with glowing coals and that his irises were windows into them.

There was also an enormous sword strapped to his back that he'd never seen before. As much as he might want to know where the sword had come from, though, and what had happened to the prince, the only thing Rill could focus on in that moment was his own wonderment at those eyes. What could possibly have happened to do that to Caymus?

"Is he alive?" Milo was saying.

Caymus, his face dirty and sun-scorched, seemed unable to speak. He sank down to one knee, as though a reservoir of strength had finally run dry. His mouth tried to form words around the panting and wheezing.

Aiella turned to the soldiers, who were only just arriving. "Water!" she said, her tone of confident authority unmistakable.

The soldiers produced a pair of flasks that were quickly handed to both Caymus and the other man. Caymus put the flask to the prince's lips before his own, and everyone took a collective sigh of relief when they saw Garrin's throat moving, swallowing the precious liquid. The Champion-Protector of Kepren was alive, and even appeared to be semi-conscious. Even Caymus seemed surprised, which made Rill wonder if his friend had even known whether he'd been carrying a person or a corpse.

Rill was about to ask Caymus what had happened when the third man, the one Rill hadn't met before, collapsed while in the process of raising the flask to his mouth. One of the soldiers—the one who had handed him the flask, in fact—managed to break his fall, and two others rushed in to pick him up, then all three began carrying him back to the gate.

Rill, his concern beginning to outweigh his relief, looked at his friend's face again, trying to get past the orange-red eyes, to see just how tired he might be. "You'd better have a drink too, Caymus," he said. "If we have to carry you the rest of the way, we're going to need a lot more men."

Caymus's attention was still on the prince. Rill wondered if he'd even heard him.

Then, Aiella put a hand to Caymus's cheek. "Caymus?" she said, gently. "Are you with us?" The action surprised Rill. He hadn't known she was capable of such a display of empathy. Her words seemed to break through the fog Caymus was in, though, as he suddenly looked up. For a moment, he seemed confused, as though he was surprised to see all of them there. When the sun-cracked lips parted in a grateful smile though, Rill felt his heart sing. Caymus was still there.

"Hello, everyone," Caymus said, his voice harsh and raspy.

"Have a drink, Caymus," Aiella said.

Caymus looked back down. "The prince," he said. "I need to get him back."

The three remaining soldiers approached him. "We'll take him to the Keep, Sir."

Caymus looked up at the man who had spoken, suspicion in his face. The distrust slowly melted away though, and he nodded. "Be careful," he said. "He's badly wounded." The soldiers gently lifted the prince from his grasp. After two of them had placed Garrin's arms over their shoulders, they, too, slowly made their way back to the city.

"Caymus!" Aiella's voice was more insistent now.

Caymus turned and looked at her. He smiled. "Hello, Aiella."

The dark-haired girl actually smiled back—something else Rill had never before seen—and shook her head at him. She grabbed his hand, the one that still held the water flask, and pressed it toward his face. "Drink," she said, sternly.

Caymus looked at the flask as though noticing it for the first time, then he nodded and emptied it into his mouth. Rill and Milo looked at each other and smiled, glad to see their friend was still alive and apparently healthy, if a bit delirious.

After Caymus took the flask away from his lips and wiped his face with the back of his wrist, he seemed more alert. Aiella let go of his hand, but then was surprised when he briefly took hers. "Thank you," he said, his voice still raspy.

She nodded, and he let go. "You are welcome," she said.

Caymus turned to look at Milo as he got back to his feet. "Do you know where I can find Be'Var?" he said.

"What," Rill said, "don't we get a hello?"

Milo actually laughed out loud. Aiella turned to Rill, her face full of sternness and disapproval, but then the expression quickly melted away.

Caymus just gave a low chuckle as he looked back and forth between his friends. "Hello, Rill," he said. "Hello, Milo."

Milo grinned that impish grin of his. "I think I could track the old man down for you," he said.

"Caymus," Rill finally said, "what happened?"

Caymus's eyes turned solemn. "It didn't work," he said. "They won't be far behind us now." For a moment, he seemed lost in some terrible memory, but then he snapped out of it. He slowly began walking toward the city. Rill, Milo, and Aiella fell in next to him.

"As for the rest of it," Caymus said. He turned to Aiella. "Can you ask your father to meet me?" he asked. "There's a lot to tell, and it looks like I'm the only one left to tell it."

"Better get the dukes together too, then," Milo said, shrugging.

"And the Keep-Marshal," Rill added.

Caymus nodded. "I guess we'd better just go ahead and get everyone."

~~~
~~~

"He will return the sword immediately!"

Be'Var felt like laughing, so ridiculous were the words coming out of Duke Korwinder's mouth. Holding back a sigh, the master looked around the room, trying to gauge the feelings of the others arrayed about him. Only the other two dukes, Fel and Chenswig, seemed to mimic Korwinder's outrage. Everyone else appeared to share his own astonishment.

When Milo had burst into the Reed Ward, a temporary hospital erected to house the sick and injured in the Reed District until the Black Moon threat had either passed or consumed them all, he'd announced that the prince and Caymus were back, that he'd better see them quickly—in that order, too—and that he wasn't going to believe what had happened to Caymus.

He'd certainly been right about the order. Prince Garrin had his own physicians, of course, but the three men knew Be'Var well and had deferred to his particular talents regarding weapon injuries when he'd asked to take a look.

He'd actually cringed when he'd seen the rushed job that Caymus had done closing the wound. The boy had stopped the bleeding, yes, but he'd done it in the fastest, coarsest way possible, not giving any thought whatsoever to the connections of blood vessels, nor the organs that they fed. The first thing Be'Var had needed to do was open up a couple of the more important arteries again, then use his more delicate cauterization abilities to connect them back in their rightful configurations. Yes, Caymus's actions had probably saved the prince's life, but the imprecise way he'd gone about it would eventually have cost the man one of his kidneys and the entirety of his left leg.

Milo had also been right about Caymus. Be'Var had been no less than completely amazed when he'd seen his former pupil again. The sword, the eyes, the actively burning mark on his hand...the boy had somehow become the Knight of the Flame, the champion of the Conflagration, while he hadn't been looking.

Caymus, who'd been the one to call for this meeting of important people, had been reporting on the enemy strength and describing the way that some of the mercenaries were now just as infected by kreal as was the core army. He'd also just been telling them what had transpired on the road back to Kepren, explaining not only why he looked so different and why so few of the prince's party had returned, but why the prince himself was flat on his back in a surgery bed…and why he was without the Black Sword.

Now, Be'Var was going to have to help to defend Caymus's actions from the forces of ignorance and ineptitude. Most of the same people were present, here in the war room, who had been here the last time a meeting had been called. The three dukes were there, of course, as was Keep-Marshal Tanner. Ambassador Brocke stood near the fireplace, though his daughter, Aiella, stood beside him this time. Milo was leaning against one of the room's corners, with Rill and that other engineer, Daniel, next to him. Besides the Summitian scout, the only person who was missing this time was Garrin himself, who was still recovering from his ordeal. Be'Var estimated that the prince could be on his feet again by morning, though it would be weeks before he healed fully.

And now Caymus was actually having to justify himself to the flaming-ignorant dukes of Kepren. Never mind the fact that he'd saved Garrin's life after he'd been run through by a krealite assassin. Never mind that he'd run, non-stop, through the desert plains of Kepren, carrying the prince all the way on practically no sleep, in order to get him to a physician quickly. Never mind that if he hadn't done so, Kepren would now be both without a ruler or even a clear line of succession. The three men actually seemed to think that Caymus might have done something detestable to the prince intentionally. More to the point, Korwinder was suggesting he might have stolen the sword!

"You blustery old meat-sack!" Be'Var heard himself saying. "You'd never have even known it was the same sword if Caymus here hadn't just told you!"

"I beg your pardon!" Korwinder shouted, his face turning beet-red. "I don't care who you are, Sir, you will not address me in such a way!"

"I will address pig-headed stupidity any way I flaming-well please!" Be'Var shouted back. He was surprised. He was usually a bit more tactful than this.

At that moment, the room exploded into noise, into voices all trying to shout over one another. Be'Var rubbed his forehead with his fingertips. He knew this was his fault, that there were better ways of dealing with stupid, useless people than shouting at them.

When he looked around, he could see that almost everyone in the room was yelling at the three dukes, who were, in turn, yelling back at everyone else. The only exceptions were Brocke, Tanner, and Caymus. Brocke wore his usual placid expression, seeming as though he was above all the arguing. The Keep-Marshal seemed to be trying to figure out the other people in the room, like a good tactician.

Caymus, however, didn't seem to be handling the noise as well. From across the room, Be'Var could see the orange of his eyes turning to red, as though a dangerous ferocity was building in him in response to the raised voices. Be'Var wanted to tell everyone to be quiet, to avoid whatever might be coming in the next few moments, but it was useless. Nobody would hear him. All he could do was watch.

Be'Var wasn't sure if the sword on Caymus's back caught fire before or after the hand reached back and pulled it from its sling, but the roaring flames were so loud that they were only overshadowed by Caymus's own voice as he plunged the weapon, blade-first, into the stone floor. "I will have silence!"

The room fell still. All eyes were on Caymus, or perhaps they were on his burning sword. Be'Var now understood, staring at Caymus's grip on that burning hilt, why the knight of the Conflagration needed to know how to not be burned by fire. He smiled, wondering why the thought of it gave him so much pleasure.

The only sound in the room was the slight rumble of the flames as they licked their way up the blade toward Caymus's outstretched arm. Nobody dared speak a word in the face of this strange, new power.

"Black Moon Army," Caymus said, his voice serene, yet loud enough to be heard across the chamber, "is, at best, twelve hours away." He looked to the dukes, and to the Keep-Marshal. "The men and the monsters that are coming are hard to kill, but they are not indestructible. I have instruction that I would give to the soldiers, instruction on how to kill a krealite. Tell your men that I will be giving this instruction in the engineers' marshaling yard in one hour."

He looked at each face in turn. "One hour," he repeated.

Then, he turned, pulled the weapon out from the floor, and as the flames of his sword snuffed themselves out, he walked out of the room.

Nobody said anything for a moment or two, then Tanner cleared this throat. "Master Be'Var," he said, calling across the room. "How is Prince Garrin doing?"

Be'Var, as glad as everyone else that the moment was over, exhaled a long breath. "He'll live," he said, "though he won't be up and about for a while."

Tanner nodded. "Well, then," he said, turning to the dukes, "the king is incapacitated, and so is the prince. That leaves the defense of this city to me, I believe." He raised his brow at them. "Is that under any contestation?"

The three dukes didn't say anything.

"Alright, then," Tanner said. He addressed the rest of the room. "We know now that the enemy strength is greater than it was a day ago, which means our defenses are more important than ever. I'm guessing everyone here has something to be doing?" He didn't wait for acknowledgments. "So, I guess you'd all better get to it." He turned back to the dukes. "I'll be having as many soldiers as I can spare meeting Caymus in the marshaling yard. I'd suggest getting as many men as you can to gather there, too."

The room bustled with activity as people filed out the doors. Be'Var noticed that Duke Korwinder, however, was walking in his direction. He couldn't quite help sighing quietly to himself. He had absolutely no time for the man, but he knew he had to listen to what he might say, just in case something useful emerged from under that stupid mustache.

The duke was talking before he'd even reached Be'Var, and he glowered as he spoke. "Do you really expect me to take the word of some religious zealot, who has self-confessedly just stolen our monarch's birthright?"

Be'Var sighed. He'd really had enough of this fool. "Korwinder," he said, "we're all going to have to fight tomorrow, to fight for our lives. I don't expect you do to anything, but I suggest you shut your mouth and see to your men."

Korwinder seemed about to start yelling again, but then he just sneered, turned away, and led the other two dukes out.

After the three men were gone, Be'Var noticed that only he and Keep-Marshal Tanner remained in the war room. Tanner, his hands clenched behind his back, smiled at Be'Var as he approached. "You really had it in for Korwinder tonight, didn't you, old man?"

"Bah," Be'Var said, "fool doesn't have enough sense to see his best hope standing right in front of him."

Tanner raised an eyebrow at him. "I don't mind telling you, Be'Var, buried somewhere under the anger and the impudence, the man does have a valid point."

"And that would be?"

Tanner chuckled. "You're asking us to put our faith in a man, barely more than a boy, who just carried the near-dead body of our prince into the city and confessed to having taken his sword. Garrin and that guardsman of his are both incapacitated, so there's nobody to back up his version of events. Honestly, if it weren't for your support, I might have had him arrested by now, or at least held and questioned."

Be'Var grimaced. "Well," he said, "maybe I owe the good duke an apology."

"Ha!" Tanner slapped Be'Var on the shoulder. "I don't think I'd go quite that far." His smile faded as he turned to the open door. "I, too, have a few things to get to," he said, "not the least of which is to see whether I can actually spare any men to attend this training Caymus has decided to enlighten us with."

"Spare them," Be'Var said, seriously. "Whatever else you may think of Caymus right now, he's killed more krealites than anyone else in the city, probably in the world."

Tanner nodded. "I'd better get moving, then." He offered Be'Var his hand. Be'Var shook it. "I'll see you soon, old man," he said, then he hurried out of the room.

As the door swung closed behind the Keep-Marshal, Be'Var stood by himself in the cold room, considering the man's words. He was forced to admit that, to somebody who hadn't devoted their life to the Conflagration, to somebody who didn't know the boy as well as he did, Caymus might be a rather frightening character.

But he wasn't a boy anymore, was he? Be'Var hadn't really thought of him that way since he'd awakened from his long sleep, since the good-natured exuberance in his eyes had been replaced with resolve and a kind of longing sadness. Gone was the curious child who had been so interested in flames and conduits. Now, for the first time in thousands of years, there was a knight in this world.

Frowning, Be'Var shook himself from his reverie and strode out of the room. He really didn't have time for all of this navel-gazing; there was so much work left to do, so much preparation to be made before the arrival of Black Moon.

As the old master flew down a stone, spiral staircase and burst through a heavy door to enter the cold night air, he found himself thinking about the people in the hospital he'd visited that afternoon. He wondered how many of the dozens of refugees there would actually survive the coming days, then he decided he needed to think about something else for a while. He took a deep, invigorating breath, then he stopped and looked to the North. The yard Caymus had spoken of—the one where Rill had practically lived for the last several weeks—was nearby. It might be useful to see what he had to show the men who arrived there in the next hour or so.

Smiling and shaking his head at his own boyish exuberance, Be'Var made the decision to attend Caymus's demonstration, and so spun on his heel and marched north, toward the engineers' yard. As he walked, he opened a few, small connections between himself and the Conflagration, letting the warmth of the fire realm soak into his bones. He wondered if Caymus might have learned how to do that yet. He wondered, too, how ready his former pupil really was for the coming battle.

For that matter, how ready was *he*? How ready were any of them?

Rill had appeared in good spirits, at least. Be'Var hoped the captain of the engineers was making good use of Rill. The boy had a fascinating mind: less than useless for studying the Conflagration, but apparently quite adept and learning how to put things together and then blow them apart.

Flamehearth was on his mind, too. Located in the Grass District, the mission had been evacuated earlier that day. The boys and girls were now squeezed into the second floor of a paint warehouse. Other than the fumes, which had given a couple of the children headaches, he knew they were, for the most part, safe. He worried about the building itself, though, worried for Y'selle and, particularly, for Elia. Being the Keeper of the Mission meant holding the responsibility for keeping Flamehearth's every stone safe from harm. She wouldn't do well if the building was damaged in any way, much less if it were completely destroyed by krealites.

As he came within sight of the yard, he noted a dozen or so men that seemed to be milling about. Some wore armor; others appeared to be civilians, as though news of the impending lesson had already spread past the army and into the city's populace. As Be'Var smiled, wondering if the yard would be large enough to hold the crowd that might eventually gather, a small movement caught his eye.

He turned to see three figures standing near a still fountain, all concealed in shadows near the outer wall of the Keep. One of them was definitely Caymus, his big arms crossed in front of him, but he couldn't make out the other two. They stood at the edge of the fountain—a simple, marble affair—neither facing him nor turned away.

Be'Var began walking toward them, curiosity taking hold of his thoughts.

As he approached, he eventually recognized the second and third figures as Ambassador Brocke and the Summitian scout: the same one who had shared his vision of the invading army with the assembled leaders of Kepren a scant few days ago. When Be'Var was close enough to make out Caymus's glowing eyes, he noticed motion in the water of the fountain and realized what was happening. The ambassador and his man were reflecting, playing the memory for Caymus again.

The image of the krealite rider, laughing at the useless actions of two crossbowmen, was playing in the still water when Be'Var got close enough to make out detail. He watched on, sadness in his heart, as the ashen-skinned man turned the krealite toward the two terrified soldiers and charged at them, directing the monster below him to break bones and tear flesh.

Be'Var had learned during his time in Kepren's army that mercy was a luxury that most soldiers couldn't afford, but the cruelty that the Black Moon warriors showed, the absolute barbarity of their actions, was beyond his comprehension. He glanced at Caymus, who flicked his eyes in his direction long enough to acknowledge his presence, but otherwise gazed intently at the images of helpless, dying people.

The scene faded away as the two men lifted their fingers from the water. Brocke, upon opening his eyes, noticed Be'Var standing there for the first time. "Master Be'Var," he said, affecting a small bow. "It is good to see you here."

Be'Var smiled. "And you, Ambassador." He'd decided a long time ago that he liked Brocke's no-nonsense approach to things. The man was hard, incredibly prejudiced against anything that wasn't Summitian, and seemed to have some manner of addiction to whatever it was that he kept in that little box of his, but he was at least dependable and honest.

Brocke smiled. "I am not here," he said, glancing at Caymus. "I am merely doing my daughter's bidding, and now I must see to my household." He bowed slightly, first to Caymus, then to Be'Var. "Good night to both of you," he said, "and good luck."

As the two men walked into the darkness, Be'Var turned his eyes to Caymus. "Doing his daughter's bidding?"

"I needed him to show me what the scout saw again," Caymus said, his voice still, emotionless. "I wanted to know if I could see anything differently with these new eyes of mine. I don't think he wanted do it, but Aiella insisted on my behalf."

"She seems to have taken quite an interest in your welfare, lately," Be'Var remarked.

"She has," Caymus replied, still betraying no emotion.

"And did you?"

Caymus finally pulled his gaze from the retreating forms of the two men, meeting Be'Var's eyes. "Did I?"

Be'Var shook his head. "Did you see anything in the water than you didn't see before?"

Caymus took a deep breath, his arms still folded. "There are only two of them in that memory that have been completely taken by the kreal. One of them was Mrowvain, the assassin that I killed. The other is the one that leads them."

"Their general, then?" Be'Var asked.

"No," said Caymus, arching his brow in thought. "No, more like a chieftain"

"Really?" Be'Var said. "The difference being what?"

Caymus unfolded his arms and looked into the still water again. "A general would just be a military commander," he said, absently. "These men are bonded together by the kreal, like they're all part of the same family, the same tribe. They're not here to win battles; their goal is to wipe out all the other tribes." He looked back at Be'Var. "Chieftain seems more appropriate."

Be'Var folded his arms and gave Caymus a curious look. "How do you know all this, boy?"

A sad smile crossed Caymus's face. "I'm not sure," he said. He reached over his shoulder and pulled the giant sword he carried there. Be'Var still couldn't believe the size of it; the thing was nearly as tall as the man wielding it. This time, at least, it didn't burst into flame.

"The moment I touched it," Caymus said, looking over the weapon as he turned it in his hands, "I could remember things, things I'd never done. It's as though the sword is connecting me to the first knight, showing me what he knew."

Be'Var watched the blade turning, gleaming in the starlight. "Do you think it holds his memories?" he said. "The first knight?"

Caymus shrugged. "Maybe? I'm not sure. I don't remember faces or the exact way things happened, but I..." He looked away, trying to find the words, "...I understand things, the way they happened. I can tell you the way the krealites organized themselves before, but I can't remember their leader's name or what he looked like."

Be'Var nodded. "Is it just the krealites?" he asked. "Do you remember anything about the other champions? Presumably they're out there somewhere. It would be nice to be able to find them, to have their help."

Caymus shook his head. "Nothing specific," he said. Then, he turned the blade around and placed the tip on the ground. "Except Tamrin," he said. "The Circle of Tamrin."

Be'Var glowered. "What's that?"

"I don't know," Caymus admitted. "It has something to do with the air element, but that's all I've been able to remember." He gave Be'Var an amused look. "If 'remember' is the right word for it."

Be'Var nodded, looking across the yard at the people who were slowly trickling in. He would have to spend some time looking up 'Tamrin'. More time spent in the libraries. Assuming, of course, that any libraries were left standing tomorrow night.

"It's why they were able to find me," Caymus said.

Be'Var glanced over, surprised at the hollowness of the sound. He discovered that the face before him was awash with regret. "What?" he said.

"Mrowvain and the krealite chieftain," Caymus replied. "It's because they were so completely taken by the kreal, so engulfed in it, that they were able to pick out my location in the pass." He leaned on the sword's cross-guard with both hands and rested his head there. "Mrowvain probably had a good idea who I was even back when he was calling himself 'Callun'," he said. "I think he spent time traveling with us because he wasn't fully given over to the element yet, so he had to find other ways to be sure he had the right person."

Be'Var remembered something Caymus had said earlier. "You said the word 'Mrowvain' means 'Fire-Killer', didn't you, that he was some kind of assassin?"

Caymus nodded. "Essentially, yes. There are others out there, too: the water-killer, the air-killer, and the earth-killer. There would probably be more if there were other elements to get rid of in the Quatrain."

"Now that he's gone," said Be'Var, rolling the idea around in his head, "will they choose another fire-killer, a new Mrowvain?"

Caymus shrugged, his eyes closing. "Probably," he said. "I don't know for sure."

Be'Var thought back to the dark figure that they'd picked up on the road to Kepren. He still held no small amount of disgust for himself for not realizing sooner than the man was an agent of their enemy.

"I got them killed, Be'Var," Caymus said. "The two Grants, Cyrus, Harrison, Mally..." He looked up to catch Be'Var's eyes. "You'd have liked Amalwyn. He was decent: honest, forthright." He dropped his head to his hands again, letting out a huge sigh. "It was when the chieftain felt my presence out there that the dying started, but I got them all killed the moment I insisted I come with them."

Be'Var had never seen Caymus look so miserable. He hadn't known any of these men himself, but it was obvious that Caymus had discovered some kind of kinship with them in the short time traveled together. "You didn't know, Caymus," he said. "How could you?"

"I'm supposed to be this powerful warrior," Caymus said, now standing to his full height and looking out into the darkness with angry eyes. "I'm supposed to be able to protect people! How am I supposed to protect a whole city when I couldn't even keep a handful of people safe?"

Be'Var had suddenly had enough of this. "Protect?" he said, his voice rising in volume and intensity. "You think you're supposed to *protect* us?"

"Of course I am," Caymus said, still looking away.

"You are *not*!" Be'Var almost yelled.

The intensity broke whatever mood it was that Caymus had been sliding into and he looked, surprised, back at his old master.

"Let me tell you something, Caymus," Be'Var said, using as level a tone as he could muster. "There's a reason that you're not carrying a shield right now, that you're wielding this—" he motioned at the blade, "—this *building* of a sword. There's a reason that you're bigger than any man has a right to be and that you've learned how to hold onto a burning length of steel without getting singed."

He could see he had Caymus's attention. The orange eyes were becoming speckled with red.

"Stone protects," Be'Var said, "or maybe earth can soften a blow. Water soothes. Air can whisk away." He reached out and put a hand to Caymus's forearm. "You are not these elements, boy. You are fire!" He said that last from between clenched teeth. "And fire *burns*."

He could see it in Caymus's eyes now: the rage, the love, the passion, all the things that should fill the heart of a warrior of the Conflagration.

"In the morning," Be'Var said, taking his hand away, "you don't worry about protecting us. You don't worry about keeping this city, or its people, in one piece. You only worry about doing your job and burning those bastards to cinders." He lifted his chin. "Got it?"

Caymus closed his eyes for a moment. When he opened them again, some of the intensity was gone. In its place was pure determination, a clear sense of purpose. Be'Var nearly stumbled backward; he had never seen the like of it.

"Got it," Caymus said. He smiled, warmly. "Thank you, Master Be'Var."

Be'Var gave him a curt nod. "You're welcome." He noticed that a large number of voices seemed to be gathering nearby, and he stepped out of the shadows to see that several hundred men, as well as a number of women and children, had gathered in the engineers' marshaling yard. Tanner, Milo, Rill, and Aiella were all there, too. Flames, even Duke Fel had made decided to make an appearance! Had an hour passed already? "It looks like you've got quite an audience tonight," he said, turning to Caymus, "Sir Knight."

Caymus looked, too. "Good. They need to understand."

"Understand what?" said Be'Var. "What are you planning to show them exactly?"

"The armor," Caymus replied. He nodded to himself as he watched the crowd. "They'll never learn the things I know about fighting krealites in one night, but if somebody can grasp the idea of setting their blade and then pushing through—and not just hacking away at it—it doubles their chances of survival."

"Hm," said Be'Var, stroking his chin. "Good notion. One suggestion?"

Caymus turned to him.

"Call it something simple. I've been a teacher for decades, and I can tell you that people learn a concept more easily when it has a simple name."

Caymus nodded, thinking. "Set the blade, then push it through?"

Be'Var grunted. "How about just, 'set and push'?"

Caymus smiled. "Set and push. That works." He cast his eyes back to the crowd, then took a breath. "Okay," he said, "I'd better get on with it, then."

Be'Var put a hand out, stopping Caymus as he walked by. "Tell me something, Caymus: do you have an actual plan after this?"

Caymus looked out at the gathered people as he spoke. "I know something about carpentry," he said, "so I'm going to help with some of the fortifications tonight. After that, I could really use some sleep."

"And in the morning?"

"I suppose I'll do what I'm good at."

"Add to the general confusion?"

Caymus smiled. "That sounds like a good plan.

Chapter 21

"My father died this morning."

Garrin watched Be'Var turn toward him slightly in acknowledgment. He thought the old man might be about to offer some words of solace, but the fire-master didn't seem particularly moved by the news. "I heard," he said, then he turned away. "Were you there?"

Garrin took a deep breath as the memory surfaced. Only a few hours after he'd regained consciousness, before the sun had even crested the horizon, word had reached him that his father was having convulsions, some sort of fit. He'd come as soon as he'd been able to rise, but there hadn't been anything he could do. The king's mind had given up years ago; this morning, apparently, it had been his body's turn.

"I was," he said. "He didn't last but a few minutes after I got there."

Be'Var nodded solemnly as a stiff breeze grabbed the fabric of his cloak, whipping it up to his shoulders. "He waited for you, then?"

Garrin had wondered the same thing. Had his father, who had managed to recognize his own son only a few times in the past year, actually hung on to life long enough for him to say goodbye? The idea surfaced conflicting feelings in him. On the one hand, it meant that his father might actually have remembered who he was, there, at the very last moment of his life. On the other hand, Garrin wouldn't have wished him all those long hours of suffering, even if it meant getting the chance to let him go, so say goodbye.

"I don't know," he finally said, then he turned his gaze out over the city before them.

The two men stood atop the White Spire, the highest point in the Keep, and also in the city. It had been built centuries ago, before the city of Kepren had grown to include the Grass District, as a lookout point. Standing just a handful of yards taller than any other structure in Kepren, it allowed fair warning to be given, should the armies of Mael'vek suddenly amass to the South. Garrin had never imagined he'd be watching an army approaching from the North from up here

Standing behind the two men—very nearby, as the spire's top was only a couple of yards in diameter—were three boys, not yet old enough to be soldiers, who would serve as runners today, carrying messages from this, the highest authority of the Royal Army of Kepren, to the various commanders down below. The boys had all been trained how to wait patiently for orders, but they were unable to keep still. They could see the encroaching army as well as Garrin could.

Be'Var grunted. "Long live the king, then."

Garrin winced and touched his recently closed wound again. He had enough to worry about today without Be'Var grunting at him. "You're in a mood today, Master Be'Var."

"I am," Be'Var said. He looked down at the city below. "I should be down there, tending to the wounded we're going to have today."

"You know I need you here, Be'Var," Garrin said.

Be'Var spun on him. Garrin had never seen him so angry. "Only because you won't stay in bed and might tear another artery open!" he said in a livid whisper. "You have a man down there who is perfectly capable of leading the defense of this city today. You need to let him do it!"

Garrin inhaled sharply, grimacing at the tightness that the breath caused in his gut. Shortly after his father had passed, he'd briefly met with the marshal, the dukes, and several captains regarding the best way to defend the city. At some point during the meeting—he didn't know when, exactly—he'd managed to undo some of Be'Var's work, and his wound had begun bleeding again, rather heavily.

He knew how lucky he'd been that the master had still been in the Keep.

He also knew that Be'Var was wrong. Yes, Keep-Marshal Tanner was an excellent commander, that he would be an ideal choice to defend the city. But his father was dead; there had been no coronation, but he was now the king. He had to be here, had to lead the people of Kepren—*his* people—against the Black Moon Army.

"I know you don't approve of my decision, Be'Var," he said. In fact, he completely understood why the old man was upset and so kept his voice gentle. "But it's made." He gave the master a knowing look. "You don't have to stay, you know. You could just leave me here."

Another deep grunt rose from Be'Var's throat, and he turned back to the North, casting his eyes upon the black mass outside the walls. "I have half a mind to," he said. "Your Majesty."

Garrin allowed himself a smile at that. Be'Var was frustrated, just like everyone else, but he would stay. The old healer would keep him on his feet. He had to stay on his feet, if only long enough to see the day through.

The dark stain of Black Moon was just outside the northern gate now, collecting around the portal. Everything seemed so quiet, in stark contrast to what his eyes were telling him. Garrin had been told there were between two and three thousand men at the core of that army now, but they looked to be so many more. Somewhere in that mass, too, were the krealite creatures: those huge, many-legged insect things that had seemed so indestructible the last time they had appeared.

Their leader was in there, too. According to Be'Var, Caymus had called him their chieftain. It had apparently been he that had been able to sense their trap in the pass a few days ago, and who had sent the bulk of an invading army after eight men. Garrin suspected the man—the monster, probably—was even more dangerous than he'd already imagined, and he wondered what other tricks a Black Moon chieftain might have in store for the defenders today.

"You still think that sludge Rill made is going to do the trick?" he asked.

Be'Var nodded. "I took another look at it last night. I'm sure." He pinched his face slightly. "I just hope that, between the traps and the bombs, we end up having enough of it."

~~~

Caymus could feel his heart racing, crashing like thunder in his chest as it rushed blood through his veins. He took a deep breath, trying to steady himself. The back of his neck told him that Black Moon's main force was collecting just the other side of the North Gate. The bulk of the army would be massed shortly, and then the inevitable attack would come. A large part of him wished they'd just get on with it. The waiting, the anticipation, was driving him mad.

Still, he did wait, crouched alongside three of Kepren's royal soldiers behind one of the barricades that had been so recently erected a dozen or so yards inside the gate. He didn't like these barricades, didn't like what they meant for the people beside him. They were positioned in such a way so as to coax the enemy to take the easy path down King Street, to force the dark soldiers to pool in a few selected courtyards and junctions. The idea was to gather the dark warriors as tightly as possible so that the fire-sludge could take out as many of them as possible with each strike. Caymus knew the plan was a good one, that it should be effective; he also knew that there would be a cost to trying to control Black Moon in such a
~~~

way, and that the cost would be measured in the lives of soldiers

Nearly a hundred men were currently arrayed around the Gate. Some were quiet, but many of the more experienced men were talking quietly, some even finding the occasional opportunity to laugh. Caymus wondered at those men in particular, who were so used to war and violence that they could just carry on as though a force of killers wasn't standing just outside their door. The low hum of voices was comforting though, and it soothed some of the tension that otherwise filled the air.

The man next to him, Carlson, was still. His steady hands quietly worked a small whetstone against the blade of a boot knife, revealing that his stillness was the result of patience, rather than of paralyzing fear. Caymus admired the man's calm. The two of them had met the previous night and had gotten to talking after Caymus had given his brief 'set and push' demonstration. The man's inability to be rattled had shone through even then.

The presentation itself hadn't gone as well as Caymus had hoped. Not having an actual krealite body to demonstrate on had meant that he'd only been able to mime the technique and give a few pointers on the footwork that was likely to get a person to the point that he or she could use the strategy. Many of the soldiers, young men who had more ambition than sense, hadn't thought much of his effort. Carlson, a soldier in his forties, had asked questions afterward, having known wisdom in battle when he saw it.

"Don't worry about it," Carlson said, his words snapping Caymus back to the present. The ends of the soldier's thin, graying mustache rose when Caymus looked at him. "The attack's going to come, eventually. No sense in willing them to hurry it along. You'll only make yourself crazy."

Caymus nodded, smiled, and turned back to the gate. Carlson was right, of course; he needed to be more patient. He realized he was tapping his foot, and he stilled it. He chuckled to himself. The foot was probably what had prompted the sudden bout of good advice.

He looked to his left at the other two soldiers who were hunkered behind the barricade with him. He didn't know their names. He realized, too, when he looked at the insignias on their arms, that he didn't even know how to properly address them by rank. The organization of Kepren's military was something he was going to have to pay better attention to. He'd ask Carlson about it...assuming they both lived through today.

The two soldiers were perhaps a few years older than he, and the tightness in their jaws signified they were even more anxious. He tried to think of something encouraging to say, but nothing particularly useful came to mind. He just hoped the one furthest from him didn't panic; he was the one in charge of the fuse.

Caymus had hardly managed to get any sleep at all the previous night. He'd done as he'd said he would, having helped with the formation of this particular barricade after the demonstration, but the construction hadn't taken all that long, and he'd found himself with more time to spare than he'd expected. Rather than sleep, however, he'd spent most of the night wandering the deserted streets of Kepren, feeling the silence of the streets, the calm before the storm. He'd barely spent any time in this city at all—not awake, at any rate—but it somehow felt to him like a place he belonged. Perhaps that was because so many of his friends were here. Perhaps it was because he was now so irrevocably committed to destroying the army that was coming to claim it.

Perhaps it was because he now wielded what had once been the sword of the Champion-Protector of Kepren, and that fact made him feel intimately responsible for the city's defense.

He hoped he was ready. He'd never been in a fight like this before.

When the steady hum of voices suddenly turned to silence, Caymus knew the moment was upon them. He tensed his body, gripped his sword in both hands, and waited. When the first, huge clattering sound came, signifying that Black Moon was attempting to bring down the gate, he made sure to turn his face away. The engineers had stripped the gate of most of its supports the previous day, so the act of knocking it down wasn't expected to take very long, and he didn't want to get any dust or wood splinters in his eyes when the massive doors fell.

Captain Draya's boys, it turned out, had been as good as their word. The gate's structure had been weakened to the point that Black Moon only had to hit it one more time to gain entry into the city. As soon as that second strike came, one of the massive wooden structures fell off its hinges and hit the ground with a loud slap that blew a thick wall of air past the barricade. A roar erupted from the invaders, the sound of a thousand voices raised in triumph. When Caymus stood and turned to look, he saw that Black Moon was coming in force. The void left by the gate was wide, wide enough that six or seven men at a time could push their way through at once. The sheer volume of dark armor and ashen faces mixed with bloodied swords and axes was astounding, and more than a little terrifying.

Kepren's first attack would be an important one: it needed to catch the enemy by surprise, to throw them off-balance so that the defenders might start the battle with a favorable morale, and so Caymus held still, kept his composure, and waited for the strike to come. He didn't see the soldier with the spark-striker do his work, but he knew when he had done it when he heard the whoosh of the graysilt fuse as it carried the small, sputtering flame across the street and up the northern wall. Again, he turned his face away, preparing for the explosion of stone and fire that would follow.

But the explosion didn't come.

When he turned around again, everything seemed to be going wrong at once. He saw the astonished faces of soldiers who'd been expecting the same explosion he'd been waiting for. He saw the oncoming storm of Black Moon blades and, behind them, he saw a remainder of unburned graysilt fuse hanging down the inside of the wall. He didn't know what had gone wrong, only that the fuse hadn't carried the flame all the way to the fire-sludge.

The realization struck Caymus in the same moment that the tide of Black Moon soldiers washed up against his fortification. The men on either side of him stood with their pikes at the ready, using them to try to hold back the ashen-skinned warriors, to prevent them from engulfing their defenses. But Caymus could see that the attackers were already making too much progress. Unless something was done about the fuse, and quickly, the barricades would very quickly be overrun.

Caymus looked at the pike at his feet and then back at the hanging fuse. He had only the briefest of moments to decide what to do. Cursing fate for forcing the responsibility of that moment upon him, he ducked down behind the barricade, closed his eyes, and reached out with what he could muster of his concentration. The fuse was dozens of yards away from him. He'd never tried to manipulate anything so far away before—he couldn't even see the fuse from here—but he believed he could do it, could set the fuse alight, from where he was.

As his mind felt the coldness of the stone of the outer wall, he became dimly aware that the soldiers to his left and right were screaming at him. He could feel one of them punching his shoulder, trying to get him to stand with them. They couldn't understand why the Knight of the Flame wasn't fighting, and he had to spend all his willpower to resist the urge to abandon his effort and stand.

So great was his distraction, Caymus was surprised when he finally located the fuse itself. Once found, he wasted no time, though. He quickly grabbed on to the graysilt-laden material, getting as firm a hold as he could manage. As he worked, he felt one of the soldiers next to him dying, felt the fire in his blood suddenly spilling out of his body and onto the ground. He wanted to look, to find out which of his compatriots had already given his life to this fight, but he just didn't have time. Instead, he focused on the space, on the void around the fuse, focused on pulling it apart, on trying to let just some small part of the Conflagration into his world.

There was the briefest instant, after he felt the conduit open, when he allowed himself the joy of success, the utter rapture at the rush of touching the Conflagration itself. He quickly dismissed the sensation, though: he had work to do.

"Kepren, get down!" he screamed, trying as hard as he could to make his voice heard above the din of battle.

The fire he'd coaxed out of the Conflagration traveled up the length of the fuse, and then found the barrels of Rill's sludge that sat above the northern gate. In the next moment, the explosion finally came.

Around each of the barrels of fire-sludge had been placed a few small casks of graysilt. That morning, one of the engineers had explained to him that the design was such that both sludge and silt would catch at the same time, not only igniting the sludge, but also causing an explosion that would shower the deadly concoction in every direction at once.

Caymus smiled. Even with his eyes closed, he could tell the design had been gruesomely effective. As flames burst above the gathered forces of Black Moon, five barrels worth of the fire-sludge rained down on their heads. He could hear some of the material sizzling as it crept down the sides of the wall, setting fire to the very stone as it descended. The rest of it hissed and popped as it came into contact with armor and skin.

The engineers' work was unbelievably precise: the amount of graysilt had been carefully measured so that the spray of death wouldn't quite reach the barricades, and so the krealite warriors—and *only* the krealites—near the gate screamed out in pain as their flesh melted away from their bones. Not a single Kepren soldier was so much as touched by fire.

Those attackers who'd already made their way to the barricades spun around to see what had happened and witnessed their comrades dying in agony. By now, Caymus was standing, looking at them, preparing for the counterattack. He couldn't see the expressions in those dead eyes, turned away as they were, but he imagined that every one of the attackers registered only shock. Presumably, until that very moment they had, to a man, believed themselves invincible.

Caymus didn't wait for the stunned warriors to remember where they were. He drew his sword up before him, and as the blade burst into fiery life, he a thousand memories of battle pour into his heart. Very briefly, he allowed himself a glance at the body next to him. The dead soldier was the one who had held the spark-striker. The death of this man, barely more than a boy, flooded his heart with anger, with rage, with an unquenchable desire for revenge. With a battle-cry forged in fury, he vaulted the barricade and set to cutting his enemies down.

The first two to fall never even knew he'd been there. His sword burned so hot that it seared cleanly through their kreal-infused skin, not to mention their armor and bones. He cleaved the head from the first krealite. He swung his blade down through the torso of the second, starting at the shoulder and not stopping until he hit the sacrum. Only the second man was afforded the luxury of a scream, and as he died, he summoned the attentions of his fellows, all of whom turned as one to discover this new threat.

A few long moments passed as the kreal warriors stared at him, seeming hesitant to approach this huge man with the flaming sword. When they did attack, however, they committed completely, charging as though they were one single-minded entity.

If not for the fact that the barricade had been directly behind him, the dozens of men rushing toward Caymus might have been able to overwhelm him with sheer force of numbers. The fact that he could keep his back against the makeshift wall, however, meant that he couldn't be completely flanked, and so could keep his attention, at least partially, on each and every one of his attackers. Behind the barricade, too, Carlson and the other soldier were still striking out fast with their pikes. Their weapons didn't penetrate the skins of the krealites, but they did force them backward, giving Caymus just a little more room to maneuver.

Caymus struggled not to lose himself in the fury of it all. He was certain that he could take down huge swaths of his opponents with wide swings, but he knew that to fight so recklessly would only be effective so long as he didn't make a mistake. He had to concentrate, had to feel the movements of his opponents, had to move with them, to keep himself alive long enough to kill them all.

Two krealite blades struck out at him at once: one from directly in front, and one from the left. His instinct was to dodge to the right, but he knew that was foolish, would just land him within range of another set of swords. Instead, he stepped to the left, into the path of one of the blades. As he did so, he took his left hand from the grip of his own sword and choked up on it, grabbing the blade about two feet up and allowing himself to fight with the huge weapon in these tight quarters. He lifted the sword just high enough to deflect the leftmost blade over his shoulder, then stabbed his sword, like a spear, through the eye of the blade's owner. The frontmost attacker missed completely, his error overextending him and leaving him open. Caymus pulled his sword, still aligned horizontally, free from the leftmost opponent, and slammed the pommel into the second attacker's skull, knocking him to the ground.

In the next moment, he felt another blade stabbing at him from the right. He still had the prone form of the second attacker on the ground next to him, and that was preventing his feet from moving properly, so he reached out into his sword, took hold of the flames that surrounded it, and shaped them—shaped them!—into a spear of fire that jabbed out into the face of the third attacker. The burst of flame didn't kill the man, didn't even hurt him, but it was enough that it knocked him backward and prevented him from completing his swing.

Again and again, multiple attackers went for him, and again and again, he defended, holding his sword like a spear, barely deflecting the blades that came for him and tearing through the dark flesh of anyone who got too close. Every once in a while, he would find himself in another unfavorable situation where he needed just that split-second more to react, and when he did, he instinctively shaped the flames that engulfed his sword, using them as a weapon and sometimes as a shield, to buy himself those precious extra moments.

He was fighting perfectly, using both his eyes and his mind to perceive his opponents, using his own skill with the sword, the memories that the sword contained, and the power of a shaper to cut down and to burn his enemies. He was the Conflagration's true champion, the Knight of the Flame.

On the other side of the road, he could tell that things weren't going as well. As he jumped, dodged, and sprang, he could hear the crack and splinter of the tearing of wood at one of the barricades. When he chanced a look over the heads of his enemies, he saw that the structure that stood before one of the wider alleyways was collapsing under the weight of its attackers. He wished he could get over there and help, could afford time to seal the gap, but there was no way he could move that quickly, not with all of these blades around him.

"First one's coming!" called a voice from behind him. Caymus knew what the signal meant, had been anxious for the real counterattack to start. He chanced a quick glance over his shoulder to see if he could gauge the projectile's path. The fiery ball appeared to be at the apex of its flight, and he couldn't afford to keep his attention on it long enough to determine where it would land. "Back! Back!" called the voice again, now with an overtone of panic.

The fireball struck directly into the space where the North Gate had been, where a large cluster of Black Moon soldiers now stood. The ball seemed to rupture when it hit and a mass of black, flaming liquid splashed out over the dark soldiers. Two of the krealite creatures, their expressionless, skull-like faces raised up toward the sky, were also caught in the fiery spatter. Caymus was relieved to note that the sludge burned through their carapaces as easily as it did the soldiers. Believing that the fire-sludge would burn hot enough to kill a monster was one thing; seeing the proof with his own eyes was quite another.

His relief didn't last, however. As he cleaved another soldier's legs from his torso, he noticed the shadows of both soldiers and creatures running across the battlements of the wall.

They were getting out of the bottleneck.

~~~
~~~

"Number two, load another!" Despite the clatter of machinery and the din of raised voices, Captain Draya's commands were easy to hear and understand. Rill followed his orders. He and Daniel grabbed another of the small barrels of fire-sludge from beside the wall and started loading it into the cup of catapult number two.

Rill had been glad that Draya had taken his suggestion of using the smaller, five-gallon barrels as ammunition for the catapults, rather than the larger, twenty-gallon affairs. The bigger containers would hold more sludge, yes, but the smaller ones would not only fit more snugly into the catapults themselves, but their lower mass meant they could be fired further and aimed more precisely.

He and Daniel moved as quickly as they dared, but they took their time when it came to actually placing the barrel. The containers, though water-tight, had been relieved of half of their banding, and the remaining bands had been filed down to near their breaking point. They were designed so that that each barrel would break easily upon hitting its target, allowing it to splash its fiery contents over a large area. The design also meant, however, that before actually being fired, the barrels were much more fragile than anybody was particularly comfortable with.

"Number one, aim and brace!" When the barrel had been placed, standing on its end in the catapult's cup, Rill and Daniel each took a step back. Each then turned to look at Draya, then raised his right hand, indicating he was a safe distance from the machinery. Rill chanced a quick glance over at catapult number one, about a dozen yards away, where another team of engineers prepared their shot.

"Number two, douse!" Draya called out, and another engineer, one who had been standing nearby, poured a ladle's worth of fire-sludge over the barrel. He then used a glob of pitch to stick a fuse to the top. The fuse was of the quick-burning variety—though it didn't burn as fast as those currently being used at the gate—and was exactly four feet long.

"Number one, fire when ready!" Rill didn't like the procedure one bit. As the third engineer worked, he turned to watch catapult number one as it loosed its projectile. The arm swung up, lifting the barrel into the air. The projectile sailed upward for about two seconds, then burst into flame. He hated how little time they had between the lighting of the fuse and the firing of the engine. He hated how fragile the barrels were, thinking that even the force of the launch could be enough to break the bands holding them together. If that happened, they'd all be burning within seconds, dead within a minute.

"Number one, reset!" Rill may have disliked the procedure, but he'd not been able to come up with any better ideas, not with the minuscule amount of time they'd had to come up with a solution that would allow them to catapult fire-sludge into the ranks of their enemies.

"Number two, aim and brace!" This was the part Rill hated most. As the four-man team who were responsible for maneuvering the engine made certain it was positioned to deliver its fiery ammunition to the right spot, Rill and Daniel moved to stand shoulder-to shoulder, facing the third barrel-man and holding the fuse between their two bodies. Their job was to keep any stray sparks from landing on the now sludge-covered barrel. Rill felt himself shuddering with thoughts of things that could go wrong in just a split-second.

The two of them raised the arms that weren't holding the fuse—Rill's left, Daniel's right—indicating that they were ready. A moment later, the men behind Rill shouted out that the machine was properly aimed and that they were ready to fire.

This was the really dangerous part.

"Number two!" shouted Captain Draya, "fire when ready!"

At the captain's command, the fuse man held the fuse in one hand and squeezed his striker against it with the other, scraping the piece of flint over the length of steel and sending sparks everywhere. The fuse didn't catch. He squeezed again, and this time it caught, sizzling and popping with life. All at once, the man dropped the fuse, and Rill and Daniel stepped away from each other and dropped their arms, indicating to the watching catapult team that the fuse was lit.

Before Rill could take another step away, the great arm of the catapult was whooshing up past his ear, the sound of the sizzling fuse following right behind it. A moment later, he turned to see the barrel aloft, sailing over the walls and buildings of the Guard District. A moment after that, the fuse reached the pitch and the sludge-covered body of the barrel blossomed into a fiery mass, looking suddenly a great deal more dangerous.

"Number one, load!" Rill wished he could see what actually happened to the barrel when it finally landed at the North Gate. He really hoped the team's aim was true, that it was landing on the enemy and not their own soldiers. He'd never forgive himself if the latter turned out to be the case.

Of course, living to regret it would mean first surviving the day.

"Number two, reset!"

As the catapult team cranked the arm of the machine back into position, Rill wondered how things were going up at the North Gate. Caymus would be there, as well as a few dozen soldiers. He wondered how the strategy of keeping the enemy bottled up there was going, whether the fireballs they were hurling in that direction were even hitting anything besides empty ground. Normally, there would have been a dozen men between catapult and target, using flags to communicate hits and misses. There simply hadn't been time, nor the required number of men, this morning.

"Number one, douse!"

Rill turned his gaze upward, past the wall of the marshaling yard and up to the roofs of the high buildings around the edges of the Guard District, wondering if there might still be a good place to put a man, someone who could at least see farther than any of them could manage at the moment. His breath caught when he noticed dark shadows moving along those roofs. He knew those shapes. Those were krealites: not the men, but the creatures.

When his gaze shifted to the walls closer to him, though, he saw the thing that made his heart stop. At the top of the wall of the Keep, just above the marshaling yard, a hooded, cloaked figure held a bow with a drawn arrow. The end of the arrow was lit, and it was aimed at catapult one.

"Look out!" The words had barely escaped his lips when the arrow was loosed. Rill only just heard the percussive sound of the missile striking wood before the barrel burst and the entire catapult went up in flames.

The two men who had placed the barrel, as well as the four-man aiming team, seemed to have had some benefit from Rill's warning—they must have all been as wary of the dangers the barrels posed to them as he—and were a step or two away from the machine when it started burning. The man who had been placing the fuse, however, was not so fortunate. The barrel burst toward him, spraying him with burning pain.

Not taking the time to consciously think, Rill took the scene in, letting his mind process what was happening and assess what needed to be done. The burning man couldn't be saved, not with as much sludge as was covering him now. He, however, had not been the target. If the hooded figure had wanted to kill the one man, he didn't need to use a flaming arrow to do it. No, the target had been the catapult itself. Remembering back a few seconds, he also recollected that when archer's arm had been exposed, it had appeared as pink, healthy tissue, not at all infected with kreal. The hooded figure wasn't one of the krealite invaders and, therefore, he had to be the same saboteur that had been undoing their defenses for weeks.

Rill looked up again just as the figure melted away, seeming to simply drop down the other side of the wall. All of the other engineers were running toward the blaze that the saboteur had created, trying to save both the catapult and their burning, dying friend. Rill knew he was the only one thinking about the attacker and not the attack. He turned and ran out of the yard. He was going to catch this traitor before he could cause any more trouble.

~~~

"I don't care if you get angry, *Your Majesty*," Be'Var said, irritably, "so long as you keep still!"

Garrin gave the master a few quick nods, holding his side as the man worked to seal up veins and arteries and who-knew-what else. As he worked hard to ignore the pain in his gut, Garrin did his best not to squeal like a child.

He realized how impressed he was with the old man's ability to focus. Despite everything going on down below, the master's hand on his abdomen felt gentle and calm. His eyes were closed in deep concentration. Only Be'Var's gruff words gave him away as being anything but completely serene in that moment.

In spite of having torn his wound open again, Garrin was still managing to stand, to rise over the crenellations of the White Spire and see what was happening in his city. He didn't like what his eyes were telling him. His soldiers seemed to have managed to hold Black Moon at the North Gate for a time, but the enemy was freeing itself from their trap. He'd caught more than a few of the insectoid monsters wandering along the northern wall, and he could see masses of dark soldiers spreading out like a fungus over spoiled food. They were making their way into the Grass District now, many of them coming in from the West Gate.

He gasped as another sharp needle of pain made its way through his middle, and he found himself wondering if it was his injury or the master's work that had caused the sensation. His question was answered when Be'Var opened his eyes and removed his hand. "There," he said, "it will hold for the time being." He gave Garrin a serious look. "Keep very still," he said, enunciating every word, "or that will change."

Garrin nodded, absently. He wasn't really paying much attention to what Be'Var was saying. In the end, he trusted the man to keep him alive, and so he was instead focused on what was happening in the districts. "Thank you, Be'Var."

Be'Var harrumphed in response. The battle for Kepren, far below them, didn't seem to register on his face as he also turned to look over the parapet. Garrin was about to remark on the old man's demeanor when he heard the sounds of small footsteps making their way up the spiral stairs of the spire. He'd sent all three of his runners away with various messages in the last twenty minutes. One of them was finally returning.

He turned to look just as the boy's head emerged from the darkness below. "What is it?" he said, not even waiting for him to get all the way to
~~~

the roof and announce himself.

The boy, panting with the effort of climbing the long, steep staircase, sweat running from his red hair down his pale face, didn't appear to notice his sire's temper. "It's confirmed, Sir," he said, ascending the final three steps, "they lost a catapult." His legs were trembling, and he steadied himself against the wall. "The marshal says it was the saboteur."

"Did they catch him?" Garrin asked.

The boy shook his head, wiping his face as he did so. "They hadn't when I left, Sir."

"Can the catapult be repaired?"

"No, Sir," the boy replied. "They don't believe so."

So, the engineers in the marshaling yard were down to a single catapult, and the man who had sabotaged the other one was still out there, somewhere. Garrin was about strike the stone wall in aggravation, but then he remembered his injury and what Be'Var had said. The incident would be doubly as bad if it caused him to tear his guts open, too.

Instead, he nodded. "Is there anything else?"

"No, Sir," the boy said.

Garrin was no longer the prince of Kepren. He was now the king. That meant the boy should have been calling him 'Majesty' all this time, and not 'Sir'. Garrin almost laughed at the thought of correcting the boy, though. Protocol didn't seem terribly important in the current circumstances.

"Thank you, Charles," he said. "Sit and rest, while you can." The boy registered some surprise in discovering that the king knew his name, but his expression quickly changed to relief at the mention of sitting down.

The king's heart sank as he looked out to the West: much of the Guard District—easily a tenth of it—was burning. He didn't know how that had happened. Elements of Black Moon had made their way through several of the barricades, of course, but they didn't appear to have reached any more of the locations where they might encounter barrels of fire-sludge. He supposed that the invading soldiers might have brought their own fire, resistant to it as they were. He wondered why he hadn't considered that possibility before: they were quite literally fighting fire with fire, and the city was paying the price.

Now, they'd gotten into the Grass District—from his vantage, it appeared that most of the invaders had gathered there, in fact—and elements from both that district and the Guard appeared to be converging on the main portal between them, the Grass-Guard Gate. He didn't want Black Moon controlling that gate; if they captured it, they would control all passage between those two districts. He knew there weren't likely to be enough soldiers in that area to repel the enemy and keep the currently separated elements from joining forces; too many of his men were still concentrated at the North Gate. He sighed and turned to the runner again. "I'm sorry, Charles," he said, "but I'm afraid you're done resting."

To his credit, Charles jumped back to his feet, showing no signs of the fatigue he'd exhibited mere moments ago. Garrin had known Charles for a year now. He'd run many errands and messages for him, both personal and military in nature, and he'd always been reliable and quick. If he ended up as fine a soldier as he was a messenger, he'd probably be a commander, perhaps even a marshal, one day. Garrin had never been prouder of him.

"Tell Tanner," he said, "Black Moon has taken the Guard District. Tell him that he needs to reinforce the Grass-Guard before—"

His words were cut off by a mighty explosion, far below. Garrin winced as he spun around to see where it had come from. His eyes were drawn back to the very spot he'd just been worrying about, the gate between the Grass and Guard Districts. A huge column of black smoke was rising into the air from the point in the wall where that gate should be.

"I don't suppose we did that?" Be'Var said, flatly.

Garrin closed his eyes and held his hand against the wound in his abdomen, trying to calm his breathing. "No," he said, "we didn't. If only we had a way to—" His eyes snapped open and he turned around, once again grabbing his abdomen in pain. He leaned down and put a hand on Charles's shoulder. "Forget what I said before," he said. "Get down to the marshaling yard and grab some signaling flags. I have a different job in mind."

~~~

Milo had to concentrate hard on what he was doing, a task which, even in the best of times, wasn't generally easy for him. Creating a gust of wind was fairly easy. Maintaining a steady flow of air was more difficult. Holding two such flows, starting at the same point and separating out in opposite directions, required all his effort he could muster.

"Run through!" Aiella shouted at the panicked soldiers. "You must run through!"

Milo could understand the mens' hesitation. He was having to pull the air down from above, then force it out in two directions. He was essentially pushing apart the wall of flames that stood between him and the men by creating a vortex in a portion of it. The flames didn't enter the vortex, but they danced around the edges as though they were living
~~~

things, trying to reach in and close ranks again. A person would have to have a great deal of trust in an air priest to believe he could hold the flames apart long enough for them to get through, unburned. These soldiers didn't even know Milo.

Most of them did, however, know Aiella, and seeing her beckoning them, shouting at them to run through the void in the fire, seemed to bolster their courage. The dozen or so soldiers who'd had been cut off from their own forces on the other side of the huge stretch of fire, hesitated again, then ran as fast as they could through the hole that Milo was holding open.

When the last man was safe, Milo let out a breath and relaxed his need. The void in the flames vanished. He smiled. He'd never done anything quite like that before. It had actually been kind of fun.

The soldiers all stopped and looked back at flames they had just avoided, some of them in obvious disbelief. "Thank you, priest," one of them said to Milo. "I think you just saved our lives." His chain-and-band armor was the same as his fellows', but his spaulders and gauntlets were painted red. Milo figured that meant he was in charge.

"Of course," Milo grinned. "What are friends for?"

The man looked at Milo quizzically. An old, white scar on his cheek bunched up as confusion set in. "Are we friends?" he asked.

Milo opened the grin into a broad smile. He liked the man already. "We are now."

Aiella approached the pair of them. "You are a lieutenant, yes?" she asked of Milo's new friend.

He turned to her, seeming glad to have someone else to talk to in that moment. "Yes, Miss Aiella."

Milo turned to look back at the wall of fire. Somebody was there, just on the other side. He couldn't see who it was yet, but he could definitely sense a presence stirring the air, and that presence didn't feel right. No, it didn't feel right at all.

"What are your men doing this far from the gate?" Aiella was asking.

"We were keeping an eye on the West Gate," the lieutenant said. "Our task was to send runners to report when the enemy started trying for the Grass District in force." He paused. "They came so fast, though," he continued. "We all ended up being runners."

"You must get through the Grass-Guard, then," Aiella said, matter-of-factly.

"I'm just glad he was here," the man replied. "At least they won't be able to follow us through the flames."

"I wouldn't count on it," Milo said, over his shoulder. Whoever was on the other side of the flames, he, she, or it was now coming through. He turned to see the astonished looks on the soldiers' faces. "Run!" he yelled.

He didn't turn to look at their pursuers, but he could tell from the faces of the soldiers as they looked past him that that something was there. Relief quickly turned to panic, and each man quickly turned and followed Milo's example. Milo was glad they were all taking his advice. Based on the displacement of air that he felt behind him, he guessed that there were a good three dozen man-sized somethings back there.

The Grass-Guard Gate was a hundred yards, one right-turn, and then another two hundred yards away. All they needed to do was get through that gate before the bad guys caught up. At that point, they should either meet enough of their own forces to hold the enemy back or, at the very least, they should be able to slam the gate shut and cut off pursuit.

He was pretty sure they could make it.

Of course, the gate could be closed already, by now. The way he'd understood things, the plan was to keep the gates open until there was a reason to close them, mostly because opening the locks on the massive doors took a great deal longer than setting them. The people in charge wanted to trap or corral the bad guys if they could but, if not, the idea was to keep the roads open so the good guys could get around more easily. If whoever was watching the gate knew there were already krealites in the Grass District, then they'd probably have locked things up already. He kind of doubted, however, that anybody knew that. *He'd* just found out about it after all, and he was actually standing in the Grass District!

Milo decided that the orientation of the gate's doors was just something he'd have to deal with when the time came.

The group came upon the main thoroughfare through the Grass District, then took the right turn toward the gate. Milo snuck a look behind him. Everyone was keeping up for the most part, though four of the soldiers were lagging a bit, and the few dozen krealite warriors he could see were only about twenty yards behind them.

Acting quickly, Milo glanced around to see what he had to work with. A handful of barrels, remnants of some merchant's stall, sitting at the side of the road looked like his best bet. He hoped the barrels were actually empty as he stopped and summoned a short gust of wind to knock them over. He was in luck: they were empty, and they clattered to the ground just behind the slower soldiers. Of course, the improvised obstacles wouldn't really do much slow their pursuers at this point, but he was fast enough that he could afford the distraction, and every second he could buy for the others would count once they finally reached the gate.

Seeing nothing else he could usefully do for the moment, Milo spun on his heel and started running for the gate again. A steady wind at his back meant he devoured the yards in great strides—he couldn't help giving the astonished soldiers a little wave as he passed them—and by the time he was out in front again, he was able to see the Guard-Grass Gate, just a short distance ahead. They were in luck: one of the massive doors appeared to be opened toward them just a little bit, and the portcullis was raised.

Since there were now barely a couple of hundred feet separating him and the gate, Milo slowed his pace dramatically and turned to jog backwards. He wanted to keep an eye on everybody so he could make sure they all got through the gate before he did. He'd have a much easier time finding another way around than they would, after all. One by one, he waved Aiella and the soldiers past him again. "Almost there! Keep going!"

Fifty feet to go. Milo was running backwards a bit faster than was reasonable, but whenever he felt himself beginning to stumble, he caught himself with a little gust of air and kept going. He was now last in line, a few yards behind the soldiers, and he looked over his shoulder to see that the first of whom was already side-stepping through the gate's narrow opening. He was glad about that. He then looked at his pursuers again, and Milo felt that bubbly, excited-terrified feeling in his chest; the krealites were getting very close! If they'd been normal men, he'd have said he could see the whites of their eyes. As it was, there was no white to be seen, just gray, but he could certainly catch the glint of black on some of their blades. Interestingly, only the least-turned of them, those with the lightest hues to their outsides, seemed to have painted the black substance onto their weapons. Caymus had said something about that too, hadn't he?

He glanced at the gate again, getting his bearings. If it had been just him running between the ten-foot-tall doors, he'd have had no problems getting through in time. The gate, however, was only open by the narrowest amount, and so just one person could get through at a time. Again, he looked at the mob of krealites coming at him, trying to gauge their relative speeds. He didn't like the odds. With the soldiers stepping through the gate single-file like that, he was definitely going to have krealites nipping at his heels by the time it was his turn.

Thirty feet. A few more had made it to the other side of the gate, and now Aiella was stepping through. Besides him, there were still four soldiers on this side. Milo turned his body until he was facing forward again, but he kept a part of his attention on his pursuers. The krealites were close: too close, in fact. He could smell the breath of the nearest one, and that meant he wasn't going to make it. Rather, he might make it, but not with enough time to close the gate behind him before krealite arms and swords were following him through. He was going to have to be clever again.

Good. The moments when he got to be clever were always his favorite! While pushing hard to maintain his pace, he reached behind himself and felt for the disturbed air he was leaving in his wake, especially the stuff that followed behind him as it tried to fill in the empty space he was leaving behind. Once he had a good grasp on it, he felt, deep down, his need to get away. The then used that need to hold on to as much of the trailing air as he could, scooping it up and pulling it along with him. He felt silly doing it: the action was clumsy and not particularly elegant, like a man holding onto great armfuls of silk as he ran down the street. He was in a bit of a hurry, however, so he decided that feeling a bit silly was a price he was willing to pay.

Fifteen feet left. From this distance, he could see that the gap in the gate was barely two feet across. Taking the angles into account, he veered off to the left, adjusting his approach so as to come at the opening straight on. This was going to be *really* close. The last two soldiers were still ahead of him and the krealites were less than two strides behind. He even tried pulling another great wad of air along with him, knowing how narrow his escape was likely to be.

With five feet to go, the last soldier—the lieutenant he'd spoken to earlier, in fact—still hadn't cleared the gate's threshold. Milo had rather been hoping he wouldn't have to use his air-ball in the end, but he didn't have much of a choice now. Holding his breath, Milo bounded with all his strength and threw himself forward. He felt a bit sorry for the lieutenant as he crashed into the man's back, knocking both of them through the opening together. He felt better, however, as the two of them sailed past the threshold and his clever ball of air caught against the open door. He didn't know just how much force he'd been pulling along with him in the end, but it slammed the gate shut with a massive bang, knocking over a cart which had, apparently, been holding it open.

Milo did his best to put both himself and his unfortunate passenger into a roll, trying to soften the landing, but the lieutenant's armor wasn't terribly conducive to gymnastics. Once the two of them had clattered to the ground, he quickly disentangled himself, sprang to his feet, and turned to make sure somebody was keeping the gate closed.

He breathed a sigh of relief when he saw that other soldiers were already throwing the metal bars down across the huge, wooden portal. They were just in time, too: A huge clattering sound and a bucking of the doors that announced that the pursuing Black Moon soldiers were smashing against the now shut portal. Milo smiled, imagining how funny they looked piling up on the other side.

"Back away!" came a voice from the gatehouse, and when the last of the soldiers had stepped back from the gate, the heavy, iron portcullis came crashing down into place.

"That sounded like a close call," came a voice from behind.

Milo turned with a big smile on his face. "Caymus!" he said, "I thought you were up on the north side of this mess." Milo's old friend had changed a great deal in the last few days. The orange eyes, the animated mark on the back of his hand, and the flaming sword were fierce additions to his character, but Milo could still see the young, aspiring fire-priest in that face, and he was glad to see him.

The face nodded, looking very serious. "I was," he said. "We held them off for a good while, but the gate is mostly rubble now, so they've been looking for other ways in."

Aiella, panting after their narrow escape, walked toward him, her hands on her hips. Milo hadn't seen her dressed like this before: the leather tunic and tied-back hair suited her. "And so, you came to this place?" she asked, cocking an eyebrow at him.

Caymus's lip turned up at one end in a half-smile. His right hand was clutching that fiery sword of his, and so he used his left hand to indicate the back of his neck. "I just followed this."

Milo grinned at the revelation. He envied Caymus's ability to sense the krealites, even if the sensing was a bit uncomfortable. Of course, if following the buzzing was what had landed him in this spot, the obvious conclusion was that they were standing right next to the single largest gathering of krealites in the city. "So, now that we're all here," he said, turning to look at the massive gate, "what's the plan?" As he looked at the gate, he wondered why he wasn't hearing more noise from the other side.

"We must hold the gate," Aiella said. Even as she said it, more of Kepren's soldiers started appearing from the streets around the gate. Only a few looked as though they hadn't seen any fighting yet. The rest looked worn down and very tired.

It was Caymus's turn to raise an eyebrow at Aiella. "I'd heard you'd been giving orders, Miss Aiella," he said. "Did somebody promote—"

The massive explosion that cut off the question knocked Milo from his feet. The world tumbled in front of him until he suddenly felt a hard smack against his side. He knew it had been him that had hit the ground, but it sure felt more the other way around.

What felt like an eternity passed while colors swam around in his vision. A muffled ringing sound flooded his ears, and that told Milo that he wasn't dead, at least. He was fairly certain that he wasn't badly injured either, but until he got his bearings again, he knew for sure that he was vulnerable.

He reached out with one hand, felt cobbled stones under his fingers, and managed to determine which way was up. His vision was still swimmy as he pushed himself up to one knee, then both knees. He could make out shapes moving in front of him now, and the ringing was starting to melt away, leaving raised voices in its wake. By the time he was able to stand, the scene before him had solidified back into reality.

The gate itself was gone, reduced to planks and splinters, some of which were still raining down around him. A portion of the wall was still holding the bent, creaking portcullis in place, but dozens of hands and shoulders were shoving against the iron lattice, knocking bricks and mortar loose as they tried to get past. Two of the dark figures were already pushing through one corner; the rest would come at them like a flood the moment the portcullis fell.

There was a fire where the gate used to be, and a thick mass of black smoke rose from it. Whatever Black Moon had used to destroy the gate, the remnants of it were still smoldering. He knew it hadn't been graysilt or Rill's sludge: those smelled different. This smelled…sweet. What kind of explosive smelled sweet?

The krealite soldiers, knowing they were almost impossible to burn, casually stood amongst the flames as they continued pushing against what was left of the Grass-Guard Gate. The blackness of the smoke made the figures seem as though they were shadows given life, emerging from some dark realm of nightmare.

Milo had been thrown a good fifteen feet by the blast. He took a quick look around. Four of the soldiers lay nearby, obviously dead, shards of oak as large as Milo's leg sticking out of their bodies. Most of the rest, including Aiella, were still picking themselves up off the ground, going through the same motions he had gone through mere moments ago.

Caymus, though, was a force unto himself. Milo didn't know how it was that his friend had recovered so quickly, but he was already walking, flaming sword held in both hands, toward the invaders. Milo could feel the intense heat from the air surrounding him.

"Set and push," he heard Aiella say. Milo turned to look at her, and he nodded. She turned to address the rest of the soldiers, most of whom were, by now, back on their feet. "Remember what the knight said!" she shouted at them, pulling her rapier and waving it to get their attention. "If you try to cut, you will die! Set your blade, and push!"

Some of the men nodded understanding, making motions with their swords, practicing the things that Caymus had taught to the willing the previous night. Others just scowled or paid her no mind at all. Milo felt sad for those men; their families would miss them when they died.

Milo regarded his bow, lying on the ground at his feet, apparently having been thrown from his shoulder. One of the tips, meant to hold the bowstring in place, was broken, rendering the weapon useless. He sighed. He'd really liked that bow, had been using it for a good five years now, but it wasn't of much consequence anyway. He'd listened to Caymus last night too. Hard as he'd tried, he hadn't thought of a way to 'push' with an arrow. Instead, borrowed himself a pair of sharp knives from the Keep's kitchens—cooks always kept their knives sharper than soldiers ever did—which he now pulled from his boots.

He hadn't had much chance to practice with them, but how hard could 'set and push' really be?

He was about to find out, and he grinned in anticipation of a new discovery. As the portcullis finally broke free from what was left of the gatehouse and came crashing and clanging down upon the street, he readied himself for the onslaught.

The initial half-dozen krealites never stood a chance. The first thing they met when they poured through the portal was an angry fire knight: Caymus cut them down before they could even ready their weapons. The area they stood in had been designed as an open marketplace, however, so the smarter Black Moon soldiers began giving the big man a wide berth, getting past him so that they could attack—well, just about anybody else.

The first one that found Milo was a brute of a fellow. The man was about a foot taller than him and nearly twice as broad in the waist. His granite-colored face carried all manner of scars and pimples. A thick, brown beard matted his neck and the bottom half of his chin. The head of the large axe he carried had a mean-looking blade that only ended about a third of the way down the shaft. Milo thought it a fitting weapon for the man; he was pretty sure it was called a 'bearded' axe.

Beard-man seemed to have no fear of Milo at all. He made no effort to guard himself as he swung the axe with both hands in a huge arc. Milo took a half-step back and simultaneously pushed against the man with a ball of air, preventing him from achieving his full reach.

Milo took stock of his position. The first thing to do was get that sharp axe away from the nasty man. The grungy face seemed surprised as Milo took a half-step forward, grabbed the weapon's shaft in the crook of his elbow, and placed the tip of a knife against the back of the man's hand. Set and push, Milo thought. He pushed.

He was fairly certain that the yelp the brute gave was more of surprise than actual pain, but he couldn't be sure. As the axe clattered to the ground, one of the man's anvil-like feet took a big step backward. Milo sent a thick gust of air against the retreating foot, making the man just unstable enough that he could be brought down onto his back with a solid kick to the chest.

Milo didn't waste any time or movement. He followed the burly figure down with his knife. He hated this part. While the bearded face was still wondering what it had tripped over, Milo set the tip of his blade against a point just over the man's heart, then he pushed. The man wasn't wearing any armor, so there was only the skin and a bit of crusty-looking fabric to get through.

The sensation of the knife passing through the flesh didn't feel difficult or even strange. Milo supposed the fact that this man's skin was light gray, rather than black, meant that he wasn't all that invulnerable to a blade yet. He wondered if the man had known that. Maybe he'd have worn some armor if he had.

Milo didn't wait to watch the man die. He didn't like to see that kind of thing. Instead, he quickly pulled the blade free and stood just in time to dodge out of the way of a sword point that had been aimed at his chest. As the blade passed before his eyes, he noticed it was covered in fresh blood. Somewhere, nearby, there was a dead soldier belonging to that blood. He closed the distance to the sword's owner before he had time to take another swing, then put one of the knives against his chest.

Set and push.

Another man with an axe—this one seemed much younger—took a swing at him. Milo dodged out of the way, then got inside his swing.

Set and push.

The fighting went on that way for a while before Milo really had a chance to do anything but react to attackers. He didn't know how much time passed; he only knew he'd had to kill a number of krealites—about a dozen—and watch some of the soldiers die—another dozen—before his mind suddenly registered a change in the battlefield.

Two of the krealite monsters had arrived. Caymus was dealing with one of them. The second was attacking a group of three soldiers who seemed like they were managing to keep the sharpest of the claws away from themselves. Aiella was driving her blade down through the neck and torso of another burly-looking krealite; Milo wondered how many men she'd been forced to kill today. Krealite soldiers kept pouring through the opening in the wall, but more of Kepren's warriors also kept arriving. For the moment, they seemed to be fighting to a draw.

The thing that really concerned him was the fire. The flames from the destroyed gate had managed to spread past the edges of the marketplace. Milo took another good look around and noticed that a few of the krealites also carried torches that they were tossing onto the roofs and into the windows of the buildings around them. Kepren had been so dry for so long that materials caught easily. Even the stone buildings contained some wood in their makeup, and almost all of them had flammable furniture inside.

Milo wasn't sure what to do. They were holding back Black Moon for now, but it wouldn't mean much if they lost the city to fire. Caymus was supposedly a fire-shaper, could probably do something about it, but that sword of his was the single greatest reason they were holding this spot, and so they needed him to keep fighting. Milo could try using wind to blow the flames in another direction, but he knew that stood an equal chance of just giving them new life.

"Milo!" Aiella was yelling at him. When he turned to her, she looked over her shoulder at the flames. She'd seen them, too. "Can you keep the soldiers from me?"

Milo wasn't sure what she'd meant, but when she turned and looked at him again, she held a deadly serious look in her dark eyes. "You must keep them from me!"

He was about to ask her why, but she was already moving, running toward one of the buildings that was just beginning to burn. As she passed krealite soldiers, some of them turned to take a swing at her. Her movements, however, were flowing and smooth—as graceful as the water she worshiped—as she dodged or shoved them back, not attacking, but keeping them from pressing in, and then leaving them in her wake.

Milo followed behind. As focused as the krealites were on Aiella, they were easy prey for him. One got a knife in the back of his neck, the other in the left kidney. As he pulled the blade from the second, he watched as Aiella clambered up onto the roof of one of the burning buildings. He wanted to ask what in the winds she thought she was doing, but before he could open his mouth, she nodded at him. Then, suddenly she was closing her eyes and kneeling.

Confused, Milo decided to just go ahead and hope the girl knew what she was about. He turned around and did as she had asked, making sure she was protected from the krealites around her. *Hopefully*, he thought, *she's doing something about the fire.*

His task didn't turn out to be very difficult. Up above the carnage as she was, Aiella didn't catch the attention of many of the attackers. Only two of them actually tried to get past Milo and up on to the roof, and neither counted on the speed of the knives he wielded. The scariest moment was when a krealite crossbowman noticed her and decided to take a shot. Milo saw the leveled crossbow at the last possible moment, barely deflecting the bolt away with a quick, vertical gust. The shooter didn't understand what had happened to throw off his shot so wildly, but Milo closed the distance between them quickly, so he didn't get long to worry about it.

Several minutes passed. Caymus had killed the monster he'd been tangled with, as well as two others that had arrived since. The other insectoid had slain four of the royal soldiers before a few of them had figured out a strategy to take them down: two of them held the huge claws and teeth back with large, metal shields while half-a-dozen others flanked the monsters on both sides, pushing their swords deep into the abdomen.

Another of the buildings was catching fire though, and Milo turned his face up to yell at Aiella. When he looked up, however, he detected a chill in the air, a clammy sort of cold that surrounded her like a second skin.

He could feel the cold somewhere nearby, too. As he ducked out of the path of another sword and sunk a knife into a krealite soldier's heart, he felt excitement rising in his chest. The very air around them was cooling down, if only just a little bit. Aiella was doing something really interesting!

The effect wasn't particularly large or grandiose, but it was effective. Small streams and rivulets of water began appearing out of the ground, as though forced up through the buildings' foundations by some invisible presence. The water seemed to be pouring out of the ground in a large arc around the marketplace, creating a barrier between the buildings that had already caught fire and those that hadn't.

Even as he dodged out of the way of a thrown spear, Milo laughed out loud. She'd found a way. Somehow, she'd pulled enough water out of the ground to keep the flames under control. They would still have to make sure that none of the krealites spread the flames by hand, of course, but now that a small moat of water surrounded their field of battle, there was no danger of the buildings catching each other.

"How long have you been able to do that?" Milo yelled up when Aiella finally opened her eyes again and gulped down some really deep breaths. He'd known her father had some talent for pulling water, but nobody had mentioned that he might have passed the Aspect on to her.

Aiella didn't answer. Instead, she gave him a curious smile and put her finger to her lips. Milo understood: this was a secret for some reason. He wondered if even the ambassador knew the extent of his daughter's talents.

Milo returned his attention to the fight. The stalemate continued, but too many of Kepren's soldiers were dying. Their bodies, either still or writhing in agony, littered the wide street. At least their deaths were counting for something. Every drop of Kepren's blood was spilled holding the line, keeping the forces of Black Moon from advancing any further. He could see it now: something in faces around him, in the ferocity with which the defenders of Kepren were fighting, told him that right here—right in this spot—was where the battle would be decided.

Milo felt himself flinch bodily when the hot air from Caymus's sword passed over his head, taking out the eyes of one of the krealite crawlers. Milo hadn't even realized the thing was there, but he quickly jumped back out of the way of the flailing claws and teeth as Caymus moved in to finish the job. Milo was really glad they had Caymus on their side. The men of Kepren were fighting valiantly, but they would already have been beaten without the Conflagration's champion.

He knew Caymus's very presence was bolstering their courage, too. He knew it because he felt the same thing in himself.

Caymus noticed him watching, and the two of them exchanged knowing nods. The fight could go either way from this point, the tide capable of turning on a single moment of luck or hesitation. For that moment though, they were both still alive; and for that moment, it was enough.

Then, a booming voice shattered the battlefield, bringing both Kepren and Black Moon forces to their knees. The voice called out from somewhere in the Grass District, so loud and so strong that it shattered Milo's vision, making him feel like he'd been knocked backward all over again. It seemed as though it had risen up from the very ground, as though a portion of the world had opened up to let the sound through. Milo thought the voice seemed so angry, so lost, yet it had cried out only a single word.

"KNIGHT!"

~~~

"Stop him!" Rill cried out as he ran. "Burn me, somebody stop him!"

A dozen startled people turned to watch the hooded figure tear past them in the narrow street, but none reached out to halt its progress. Rill cursed again. This part of the Guard District was so crowded with people right now that this villain shouldn't have had anywhere to run, but no matter how thickly people lined the streets, the figure kept making progress.

He supposed it wasn't fair to demand that the people of Kepren worry about a foot chase right now. They could all hear the explosions, the screaming, the intensity of the fighting going on within their own city's walls. They looked terrified, not knowing what to do or where to run. Most of them probably didn't give the billowing cloak or its pursuer a first thought, much less a second.

At least Rill was gaining ground. When he'd first rounded the wall of the Keep, the saboteur had been nearly fifty yards ahead of him. Now, he was within a few strides. Rill wasn't particularly fast; rather the figure had turned out to be quite short, and that was reducing his relative speed. Rill supposed, given this person's stature, that he could be chasing a woman, not a man. He tried to remember if the arm he'd seen had appeared muscular or lean.

When the figure rounded the end of a building and ducked into an alleyway, Rill slowed and nearly skidded as he came to a halt, just before the corner. Whoever this person was, he still had a bow, and he could easily be waiting for his pursuer to turn that corner so he could put an arrow in his chest. Rill weighed his options and sneered at the conclusion he came to. He didn't like his plan much, but he didn't have time to think of anything cleverer.
~~~

Taking a deep breath, he pivoted out into the entrance to the alley. Rather than stop or run after his quarry, however, he continued the pivot until he had his back against the wall on the opposite side. He'd been right to do so. The brief glimpse he'd seen was of a hood with a drawn bow, and of an arrow pointing in his direction.

A second later, the arrow flew out of the alley and cracked against the stone of the opposite wall. Rill seized his moment and ducked into the narrow area between the buildings, moving as quickly as possible in order to catch his assailant before he could nock another arrow.

He heard the clatter of the bow hitting the ground at the same time he saw the cloak billowing out behind the turning, running figure. As he was just a few yards away though, Rill made up the distance before his opponent could pick up speed. When Rill finally grabbed a fleeing shoulder, he also trod upon the cloak, causing both of them to go tumbling down to the ground.

When the alley finally stopped moving, Rill was on top of the saboteur. His knees were on the fabric of the cloak, and that was wrapped around the dark figure so tightly that the man was effectively pinned, helpless. Rill felt immediately relieved: the chase was over. "Gotcha!" he said, and he pulled the hood down.

He nearly gasped when he saw a boy's face looking back at him.

An incredible hatred filled the boy's eyes as he stared up, defiantly, at his captor. Rill couldn't remember ever seeing anybody look so malevolent. What could possibly cause somebody so young to hate so much? Then, as the boy made a useless effort to squirm away, he was struck by a sudden realization.

He knew that face.

"Well done, Engineer Rill." Rill, still a little stunned, turned and saw another dark figure approaching from the alley's entrance. This figure also wore a cloak, though where the boy's was dark gray, this one was pitch black, the hood pulled back to expose an ancient, shriveled face.

"Inquisitor Dalphin?" Rill said. "How did you get here?"

The royal inquisitor's voice emanated from his throat as though under protest as he walked toward the two of them. "I followed you, of course," he said, "from the moment we both saw our enemy's actions."

The boy squirmed again. Rill grabbed him by the back of the shirt and pulled him to his feet. He eyed the inquisitor, suspiciously. "You must be faster than you look."

"I am," was all Dalphin said on the matter. He lowered his gaze to look at the boy's face. "Name?"

The boy said nothing. Instead, he spat on the inquisitor's fine, black clothing.

Rill sighed. "Roland," he said. "His name is Roland Teldaar."

The wrinkled face, unperturbed by the mucus on his cloak, raised its eyes to Rill. "You know the boy?"

"I only met him the once," Rill replied, looking down at his captive. A mixture of sorrow and anger was building within him. "His brother is a friend of mine."

"I see," said Dalphin. He extended a hand. "I will take him now," he said. "I believe you have duties to see to?"

Rill hesitated a moment, wondering how this withered stick of a man intended to keep an angry adolescent under control. Then, he remembered that the stick had somehow kept up with him on a mad dash through the streets of Kepren. The stick was right, too: Rill needed to get back.

Another explosion off to the North underlined the thought, and so Rill pushed Roland toward the inquisitor. The old man only laid one hand on the boy, placing a pair of long fingers around the back of his neck.

Roland's hatred evaporated, suddenly replaced by something between apprehension and terror.

"Thank you, Engineer Rill," Dalphin said. "We—another inquisitor and myself—had suspected this one for the last two days, though we didn't know his identity and could not discover his motivations, and so we were unable to act. Now that he has revealed himself, leaving no room for doubt, to be our saboteur, we can attain our information through inquisition, rather than investigation." He gave Rill a look that seemed genuinely apologetic. "I am sorry we did not capture him sooner, Rill," he said.

Rill wasn't sure what to say to the man, but before he could even open his mouth, Dalphin turned and walked out of the alley. He held the young saboteur—a traitor, Rill had to remind himself—just ahead of him, never more than the two fingers on his neck. When the pair reached the end of the alley, they turned right onto the street. Just before they disappeared from sight, he caught a brief glimpse of Roland's face, which was white as lamb's wool.

In that moment, Rill felt a sudden certainty that he would never see Sannet's little brother again.

As Rill made his way back to the marshaling yard, he tried not to think about what had just happened. He couldn't stop wondering, however, why a boy like that could have turned on his people, on his family. Youthful rebellion was one thing, but to actually kill people? He didn't understand it, and he wasn't even sure he wanted to.

Flames, someone was going to have to tell Sannet, tell his parents. He didn't want Dalphin telling Mister and Misses Teldaar: it was going to break their hearts, and Dalphin wasn't going to notice. Rill was certain about that much. As he jogged back into the marshaling yard, he decided that he would be the one to shoulder the responsibility of delivering that news. Better they hear it from a friend, and from someone who had actually been there.

Of course, he still had to live through today first.

"Rill!"

The voice was Captain Draya's. Rill looked up and realized he was already in the marshaling yard. Had he really been running this whole time?

Draya looked angry as he rapidly approached him. In fact, the captain seemed about to yell at him, but then his eyes softened when they saw Rill's face. "He got away?" he finally said.

Rill shook his head. "No," he said. "The inquisitor has him."

Draya paled visibly, then he nodded. "Back to your post, then."

Rill returned to catapult number two, the only catapult they had left. Daniel, still working as a loader, seemed incredibly relieved when he saw his friend re-take his place at his side, behind the engine. Rill gave him a reassuring smiled. He was, however, surprised to discover that their weapon had been turned nearly ninety degrees to the left.

"What happened?" Rill said, leaning in.

Daniel gave him a triumphant grin. He pointed up, toward the Keep itself. "We have eyes, now."

Rill followed Daniel's finger and saw a boy—he couldn't have been more than thirteen—standing atop one of the Keep's high towers, holding a pair of red flags out to either side of his body.

"Aim and brace!" said Draya, and Rill turned to stand next to Daniel, the fuse held between them. This time, Rill noticed, the engine of war moved a little bit, pivoting a couple of inches left, then a smaller degree right. The massive arm was even cranked down by a further three teeth. Rill had never seen the flags used before, didn't know how to read them, but there had been none of this precision in the aiming of the device before, so it seemed they must be effective.

He braced himself, anticipating the final command to fire, but before it came, he heard a distant voice crying out a single word. The voice seemed, all at once, to be coming from the other side of the Keep and from just other side of the nearby wall. The volume of it hurt his hearing, and he, Daniel, and the fuse-lighter all put their hands to their ears.

"KNIGHT!"

~~~

"They're all converging on that one spot." Garrin frowned as he lowered the spyglass. "It's as though they've lost interest in the city itself. I could
~~~

swear they're going for Caymus."

"Dog spit!" Be'Var cursed, snatching the spyglass from the prince's—no, the king's—hand, and bringing it to his eye. Burn it, but Garrin was right. For the last hour, he'd watched as the battle had spread from the North Gate, past the edges of the Guard District, and then into the Grass. Most of Black Moon's forces had been held at the Guard-Grass Gate for the last half-hour or so, but there had been smaller skirmishes all over both districts. Only the Reed District and the Keep itself had been spared the onslaught.

Then, the explosion had come at the Guard-Grass. The concussion had been so massive that it had shaken the White Spire back and forth a good few feet. When the cry had come up—"KNIGHT!"—every single one of the krealites had started moving toward the rubble of that gate. He wasn't sure just how many of Kepren's soldiers were still alive in what was left of that little market area, but with the glass up to his eye, he could just make out the flaming sword as it spun and whirled about.

No, there wasn't a doubt in his mind: Black Moon was coming for Caymus.

"Flaming dog spit!" Be'Var concluded, putting the glass down.

"I'm not losing this city," Garrin said. Be'Var noted how pale the king's face was. Since the morning, the fool had torn open his injuries three more times and had lost a lot of blood. The fact that he was still conscious was, quite frankly, remarkable. He decided to let that go for the moment, though.

"If we lose Caymus," Be'Var said, handing the spyglass back to the king, "we lose Kepren. I think they've figured that out."

The concern on Garrin's face showed that he understood. "Do you think he can hold them back?"

"What, all of them?" Be'Var wondered if the question had been an inappropriate attempt at humor. "You can bring a bull down with kittens if you have enough of them to throw at the problem," he said. He looked down at the dark growth of battle, far below. "Caymus has got to be tired by now." He turned and looked at King Garrin. "And he's not fighting kittens."

Garrin nodded, then he stared down at the battlefield that had consumed his city for a few moments. His face, drained of color, was covered in lines of worry and stress as he tried to see a way to help from here, miles away from where the fighting was taking place. "I am not losing this city," he repeated, though not as loudly, this time.

Then, the king's eyes widened. His face showed obvious excitement, but also concern, as he turned to Be'Var. "You said earlier that Caymus is fireproof now, yes?"

Be'Var frowned. He didn't know where this was going, but he already didn't like it. "I said that, yes. He learned it from the Falaar."

Garrin nodded once. "How fireproof?"

Be'Var made a face. "*How* fireproof?"

Garrin nodded again, quickly, impatiently. "Yes," he said. "Is there a limit to how much he can handle?"

Be'Var eyed Garrin suspiciously. "I don't know this 'Unburning' Aspect, myself," he said, cautiously, "but immune to fire is immune to fire," he continued, "however much of it there is, or however hot it gets. As far as I know he could even stand walking through that slud—"

Be'Var froze in mid-sentence, his eyes widening. "You're not really going to try it, are you?"

"I am *not* losing this city," the king replied.

Before Be'Var could argue, or even think of an argument to make, Garrin was turning to Charles, who was now standing behind them, a signal flag in each hand. "Charles," he said, "I have another order for our catapult team."

~~~

"KNIGHT!"

Caymus turned in the direction of the sound, not knowing what to make of it, not quite knowing where it had come from, only that it had seemed to emanate from what remained of the gate. All around him, skirmishes between man and krealite paused as others did the same.

He'd never heard that voice before, and yet he knew it well. The impressions from his sword told him the voice was that of an emissary of the Sograve, an agent of the realm of kreal. It was the voice of the commander of the Black Moon Army, their Chieftain. It was that voice which had directed this same army up the wall of a gully, toward him, just a few days ago. That voice had ended the lives of the men who had been a prince's closest companions.

Now, it was calling out for him.

As though united in a single purpose, like the ripples of a stone in a pond, the warriors of Black Moon pulled away from their opponents and moved backward, toward the remnants of the gate. Even the krealite insect Caymus had just been engaged with took a few steps back, keeping a wary eye on him as it retreated. The broken wall that had been the Grass-Guard Gate seemed to fill with the black shapes, as though a wave of darkness had permeated it.

Caymus took a deep breath, steadied himself, prepared for what was coming. He and his fellows had done a great deal of damage to Black
~~~

Moon this day. Now, everything that remained of it was coming for him, and for him only.

"Get back!" he yelled over his shoulder at the soldiers. "Everybody get back!" The press of bodies that was about to come at him was going to be intense; he might be able to withstand the force, but it would certainly crush anybody that got in its way.

He turned around, making sure everyone had heard him, making sure that his friends were, at least for the moment, out of harm's way. Milo and Aiella were standing on the roof of a nearby building. Caymus took a moment to wonder how the building was still there. The last time he'd noticed the structure, it and several others had been on fire, all set to burn to the ground.

Aiella looked tired, though she seemed worried and angry too, her gaze centered on him. Caymus couldn't remember having ever seen such a raw display of emotion on the young woman's face. She must have been worried for his safety, so much so that only Milo's bracing arm was keeping her from charging off the roof to try and save him. He'd have to thank Milo, should he ever get the chance, for that. At least the two of them were safe up there.

He realized just how important that was to him, there, in that moment. He'd been so worried about saving the world yesterday, but in the last few hours, the world had become a trivial, abstract thing, something he couldn't protect nor even care much about. All Caymus really wanted to save, he was beginning to understand, were the people he cared about. Rill, Milo, Sannet, Gwenna, Be'Var, Garrin...Aiella.

Caymus wasn't afforded much time to think about his friends, though. The mass of darkness had spread out from the wall and had formed a circle about him. Now, it was moving in, closing on him from every direction at once. He took his last few moments of peace to try to form some manner of defense. As he concentrated on shaping the flames of his sword, he placed the tip of the blade on the ground next to him and spun himself in a circle. As the metal scraped across stone, he narrowed the conduit, increasing the intensity of the fire as much as he could, and lent as much heat as possible to the cobblestones around him. Those bits of rock that couldn't actually catch fire began to melt into slag in a wide circle at his feet.

He spun three more times, imparting more fire to the ground, causing the circle of burning, boiling earth to grow about a foot in width. Once he stopped spinning, he found he was pleased with the result. If they were all going to attack at once, he was, at the very least, going to cause them some difficulty in getting to him.

He didn't watch for movement. Rather, a slight twitch in the flesh of his neck heralded the first opponent to reach him: the insectoid krealite he'd been fighting before was approaching from behind. Without even turning to look, he turned and dragged his sword, with both hands, through the air. He shaped the flame so that it preceded the blade by about an inch, poured as much of the Conflagration into it as possible. The creature had made a point of stepping over the small moat of lava that surrounded him, and so its thorax was exposed.

"Fire burns," Be'Var had said. Caymus let the fire burn. The chitin sizzled as the leading edge of the flame passed through. The blade itself had little more than ash and char to cut by the time it reached the creature's center.

He realized what the sword was now. It was a remarkable weapon, yes, with properties of hardness and sharpness that he didn't yet understand. But it was also a conduit, an enduring one, much the same as the one on the roof of the Temple. The sword was a link between himself and the Conflagration, a way for him to call on the raw power of his benefactor without having to open a conduit of his own. Even the memories of the previous knight were somehow cataloged within the Conflagration, and the sword gave him windows into those, too.

The weapon was much more than just burning steel. When Caymus fought with the sword of the Conflagration's champion, he fought with the combined might and experience of the entire realm of fire at his side.

Caymus moved hardly at all as another of the monsters came, as did two of the soldiers. These soldiers were blacker of flesh, more taken by the Sograve, than most of the others, but he realized it hardly mattered anymore. The Conflagration itself was working through him now; before its might, everything burned. A sword, raised to parry his blade, melted under the searing heat and dripped down the arm of its wielder even as that wielder's head was cleaved in half. Armor burned away under his strokes. Blood and sweat vaporized.

Again, they pressed in: more and more of them. Caymus slashed out, remembering not only the things the sword had to tell him about battle, but also a short lesson just outside of Otvia. *Strike hard*, he thought. *Their shields will not save them.*

He had expected the bodies of his slain foes to begin piling up around him, yet the forces of Black Moon remained unimpeded, save for the circle of boiling street. A few of the bodies of the krealites he'd struck down still burned about him, of course, but many more had already turned to ash, their remnants drifting on a hot wind. A number of the krealite insects had done their disappearing trick, too; having been injured, they simply vanished into the earth. Caymus felt like the tide of battle was turning. One by one, he was cutting down his enemy's forces. He didn't have time to think about it though, couldn't spare a moment to celebrate his success. He had to focus on keeping himself alive. He was doing well so far, but there were a lot of soldiers left.

And there was the Chieftain, too. Caymus knew he was out there somewhere, that he was close by. The sensation of the kreal that emanated from him was stronger than it was in any of the others. The insects, the soldiers, were ashen, gray. Their commander was pure darkness, and he was getting closer.

Caymus supposed a good ten minutes must have passed before the first krealite blade touched him. Two swords and a battle-axe had come at him at once. He managed to cut through the first of the swords and the axe, killing their owners, but he had been unable to escape the reach of the second sword.

The weapon's edge was sharp. It punched through the leather at Caymus lower back and sunk into his flesh a good three inches. Caymus winced, but even as he turned to decapitate the soldier that had stabbed him, he was reaching inward to burn any kreal from his body—there was none; once again, he found that the weapon was coated with paint, rather than poison—and to sear the wound and stop any bleeding.

In that moment, there was pain and surprise but, more than that, there was relief. He'd been concerned, earlier in the day, when he'd realized that his mastery of the Unburning might interfere with his ability to cauterize his own flesh. In fact, the act had turned out to be easy, as though some manner of intuition had taken over, allowing just that tiny part of his body to be vulnerable to the flames for just that instant. He wondered how much of that was the sword teaching him what to do, and how much was true instinct.

He had a problem now, though. The wound hurt. He was fairly certain the blade had reached a kidney. The pain was something he could fight through, but he knew it was going to hinder his movements. The wound wasn't going to hobble him or anything, but he could already feel the slight hitch it was causing in his steps. Under normal circumstances, it wouldn't be an issue, but being attacked on all sides by hundreds or thousands of soldiers, not to mention huge, otherworldly insects, was a long way from "normal circumstances."

Grimacing, he spun, shaping a burst of fire all around him, trying to open up some space so to maneuver. The motion helped, gave him a moment's room to breathe, but only a moment's. Within the space of a second, he was being attacked again.

Three of the attacking blades caused him no trouble, but the fourth came dangerously close to his achilles tendon.

Caymus could feel himself beginning to worry. There were still so many of them to deal with, and the Chieftain was getting closer. The fact that he was so self-aware, so conscious of his worry, only frustrated him further, distracted him from the task at hand. Worry was not something he had time for right now.

A few more minutes passed, and as the battle continued, Caymus became so concerned with his own defense that he wasn't able to execute his attacks properly. His arcs were becoming shortened, his swings half-hearted. Even the molten rock around him was beginning to cool. He'd killed hundreds of krealites already, but there were still so many more, and they were pressing in, getting closer.

Just as he was becoming certain that he was going to lose his footing, that the forces of Black Moon were finally going to press him to the ground and smother him, he felt the help he needed falling down on him from the sky.

Caymus couldn't help but laugh out loud. He wondered which of his friends had taken upon himself the responsibility of firing Rill's fire-sludge at him. It didn't matter. The feeling of comradeship, the sensation that he wasn't in this fight alone, gave him new strength.

He knew he didn't have to worry about the sludge itself: he could handle even that immense heat. The container the sludge was in, however, a small barrel twice the size of his head, was coming at him too. He'd need to find a way of staying out of its path if he wanted to avoid a concussion. For a moment, he held back on his attacks and, instead, concentrated on the arc of the projectile.

He discovered that he needn't have worried. The barrel wasn't coming straight at him, but would instead fly over his head by a couple of yards. He smiled. The setup was nearly too perfect. He took a deep breath, waited until the thing was about to sail over him, then he jumped as high as he could and struck the container with his flaming blade.

The resulting explosion was incredible. Burning fire-sludge rained down all about him. Most of the stuff, in keeping with its inertia, sprayed over the Black Moon soldiers behind Caymus, but the sheer force of his strike had been enough to send a good deal of sludge the other way, too. All around him, his enemies either writhed about on the ground or died instantly as fire seared through their flesh.

As the krealites burned around him, Caymus planted his sword in the ground and took a knee, catching his breath. He hadn't realized until he'd stopped moving just how tired the constant fighting had made him, how hard his lungs were working just to keep him standing. He looked about himself, trying to judge how many of the enemy might be left. Several dozen, burning or no, still remained in this market square, but more kept pouring through the gate or funneling in through other side streets. They gathered at the edges of the flames, waiting, glaring, preparing for another assault.

The fight wasn't nearly over yet.

After a few minutes, the flames began to die out, having severely pockmarked the ground. The very moment they could cross the ground safely, the Black Moon soldiers approached. Caymus stood, pulled his sword from the ground, refreshed the circle of fire about him, and waited. As the dark figures stepped closer, he noted that, for the first time, only the men were visible. Not a single one of the huge insects was anywhere in sight.

The Black Moon soldiers gathered around him, stepping over pools of still-burning sludge. One of them was about to press his first attack when another barrel came out of the sky. This one had been aimed to hit before reaching Caymus, rather than after, so he didn't have to react to it at all. He felt the flaming barrel hit one of the soldiers, then explode against the ground, again showering everything with Rill's sludge.

Caymus felt the burning liquid on his skin as though it were the warm sun on his face. It gave him a feeling of peace to be so coated in the terrible concoction. He noticed, too, that the leather armor he wore seemed as immune to the flames as was he. It seemed the Unburning could be extended beyond his own skin.

The krealites, however, didn't fare as well. Again, ashen-skinned warriors writhed and died around the market. Those that had been outside of the projectile's radius watched in amazement as Caymus, their tormentor, also burned under the stuff, but to absolutely no effect. He smiled. He could actually see their resolve withering away as they began looking at each other with fear in their eyes. For the first time, they were facing an enemy that was able to hurt them. For the first time, they could lose.

Then, it happened. Caymus actually felt the exact moment that the soldiers of the Black Moon Army lost their will to fight. He wasn't sure what the sensation had been at first—it had felt like the snapping of a strap pulled with too much force—but an instant later they began their surrender. Weapons clattered to the ground. Men turned and ran. Heads bowed and bodies pressed themselves to the ground in supplication. He marveled at what he was seeing: he felt as though, rather than a collection of individuals, he was watching a single organism giving up the fight.

He could hear, too, sounds of celebration from the Kepren soldiers. The noise was modest at first—a cheer and a laugh from a single voice—but as more voices joined in, the intensity increased. Caymus frowned and took a deep breath as he turned to the hole in the wall between the Grass and Guard Districts. They shouldn't be celebrating; the fight wasn't done yet. He could feel the presence—just one more presence—coming their way.

Not all of Black Moon had given up. Not yet.

When he saw the Chieftain step through the broken masonry, past the fleeing forms of ash-skinned soldiers, Caymus felt a sensation of memory. The memory wasn't his own; it came from the sword. Sometime, in the depths of forgotten history, another knight had seen this same image, the leader of a defeated army crawling out from behind his forces to offer one last round of resistance.

The Chieftain was easily as tall as Caymus, and probably a few inches taller. The armor he wore, armor which covered the entirety of him, was fashioned from the plates of the insects Caymus had been fighting for so long now. The armor was deepest black, as though the figure wasn't made of anything, but rather constituted a hole in the world that light simply vanished into.

Black horns, like those of a bull, reached forward from the top of his helmet. The helmet seemed to be connected to his breastplate by a weave of articulating blackness, as though it wasn't designed to be removed. Caymus wondered if this thing even had a face.

As the Chieftain of Black Moon, the Sograve's agent, stepped slowly closer, it reached over its shoulder and retrieved a sword that was easily a match for Caymus's in size, if not in color. The sword was blackness itself. It seemed to disappear when it crossed before the armor. A dark, smoky substance emanated from the length of the blade, too, as though death itself was trying to escape from the weapon.

Caymus gritted his teeth as, without taunt or preamble, the figure took the sword in both hands and began jogging, and then running, toward him.

He knew he would not be able to burn this foe.

Kreal itself, in its purest form, was completely unable to react to the element of fire. Caymus had been able to burn his opponents thus far because those agents, even the insects, had existed in the Quatrain before becoming servants of the Sograve, and were thus partially made of the Quatrain's elements. The kreal could take the place of the elements in a person's body, but it could never completely replace them without killing the host. Even during Caymus's training in the Conflagration, the things he'd fought had been forms that lived in places between the elemental realms, and so had been impure.

This thing was not of the Quatrain, was not impure in any way. It had come here from the Sograve, had been constructed there, then had been sent here and given life. It would not burn, no matter how intense the flame, no matter if it were under the directed fury of a being of the Conflagration itself. Even the Knight of the Flame would not be able to set this being alight. Caymus would have to defeat his last foe by martial skill alone.

Thoughts and memories of battle flitted through Caymus's head as the krealite struck out with the kreal sword, swinging wide in a horizontal arc. Caymus stepped backward and avoided the blade completely. The thing was fast; that would make things a lot harder. He knew exactly where to strike the Chieftain in order to kill it; his memories told him that he would have to push his blade straight down at the base of the giant form's neck. The thing was so quick though, that any attempt he made to place his blade there would leave him wide open to attack.

Again, the kreal incarnate attacked, striking downward. Caymus raised his weapon and deflected the blade, then rotated his shoulders and turned the block into a counterattack. His opponent was ready for that, though, and was out of reach by the time his sword made its arc.

Again, it attacked. Again, Caymus defended, only just getting his sword placed in time to protect himself. He looked for a moment to counter, but the dark blade was already swinging again. This time, he stepped to the side, avoiding the attack. He brought his sword up again, intending to go for a leg, only to find himself needing to block again.

The cycle repeated, over and over. The Black Moon Chieftain moved so swiftly, was so light on its feet, that Caymus was forced to stay on the defensive, blocking and dodging. He kept trying to claim a moment to attack, but each time, before he could get his blade in a position to strike, his opponent was already attacking again, not giving him time to press his own offensive.

Caymus's memories didn't include the speed of this thing. What he remembered of the last krealite emissary he'd faced—that the last knight had faced—was that it had been heavy, lumbering, and slow. At first, he wondered if the sword's memories were deceiving him somehow, but he supposed that was unlikely, that it was more likely that the denizens of the Sograve had learned something since the last time they had sent one of their own against the Knight of the Flame.

In a heart-wrenching moment, he wondered if he was going to be able to win this fight.

Another barrel of fire-sludge fell out of the sky, and the two combatants were covered in the fiery substance. The krealite, however, paid the burning liquid no more mind than did Caymus, and instead just pressed its attack. Caymus felt just a little more hope drain away.

He found his thoughts running to his friends. Rill was likely the one lobbing the fire bombs at him. Be'Var would be stitching soldiers back together. Milo and Aiella, standing only a few yards away, had done so well today. If he failed in this fight, if he didn't find a way to beat this one, last opponent right now, they would die; the krealite Chieftain would rally the remaining Black Moon soldiers and his friends would die.

Somehow, he had to beat this thing. Somehow, he had to press his attack. With all the defending he'd done already, he'd gotten a good understanding of the way the Chieftain moved, how its joints were put together. He just needed to get that one attack in.

He just hoped he'd figure out what to do quickly. He'd been exhausted before this fight had even started. If he didn't have a very good idea in the next few minutes, simple fatigue would decide which of the two combatants walked away from this.

"You must not try to be as quick as me." The memory caught him off-guard. He hadn't given thought to his sparring session with Aiella since the day it had happened. Now the recollection of it jumped into his consciousness, unbidden. It surprised him so much that he nearly missed his next block and caught a blade in his shoulder. The sword's ability to keep memories, it seemed, did not flow in only a single direction. It was trying to tell him something.

Then, in that moment, he knew what he had to do.

When he squeezed the conduit that was his sword, making it burst into fiercer flame, he got the distinct impression, despite the lack of a face, that the krealite was laughing at him. He didn't care. He was about to really need that connection.

Caymus knew he would have to trick his opponent to get what he wanted, but that his subterfuge would rely on waiting for precisely the right moment before striking. He would need *exactly* the right circumstance to appear before he could get that one, decisive blow in. Thinking back over the course of this fight, he knew he'd felt such a circumstance a few times already; he just hoped another appeared soon.

"Protect your face, neck, and heart," she'd said.

He protected his face, neck and heart. Then, a few moments later, and he felt what he needed.

He'd just forcibly blocked a side-swing, his sword held vertically, ahead of his left shoulder, and the Chieftain was rearing back for a straight thrust. Instead of stepping sideways, moving his sword to his center, and getting ready to parry the thrust, however, Caymus reversed his grip and brought the blade in front of his right shoulder, as though he expected another side-swing. He wondered if the tension he felt was showing in his face. This had to work.

The Chieftain took the bait. The black-clad figure stood on its back foot, and then, with both hands and with all possible might, it leaned forward to bury the blade in Caymus's chest.

Caymus took a deep breath. He would need every possible ounce of his concentration and focus to survive the next moment.

He didn't move, other than to shift his body a couple of inches to the right. He saw a bright flash in the middle of his vision before he felt any actual pain, but by the time the dark blade had punctured all the way through his back, skewering his left lung, he was in indescribable agony. Before he could think about his wound though, he found the Chieftain's neck, exposed now that the krealite had leaned so far forward, choked up on his sword, and placed the tip of his down-turned blade there.

As he pushed, completely blinded by pain, he shaped the flames of the sword, pulling them into himself, into the wound that went all the way through him. As his sword sank down into his enemy, piercing heart and severing spinal cord, he forced a torrent of flame around the blade in his chest, sealing up the flesh around the intruding object.

The two of them collapsed together: the krealite chieftain dead, Caymus barely alive. He still couldn't see, but he felt his hands drop away from the hilt of his weapon, felt it settle in his vanquished enemy's flesh. Caymus let his body go, allowed himself to drop down on top of the broken body of his foe. As his weight fell, he felt the kreal blade, still buried to the hilt in his chest, rock slightly, its sharpness making additional cuts into the seared flesh. He tried to roll onto his side, so as to let neither blade nor hilt touch the ground. He didn't know if he succeeded.

Time stopped passing for Caymus, then. He knew his chest hurt, knew he was wheezing, but he couldn't quite remember why. He was comfortable enough where he was, though. He felt secure, despite the pain. The crackling of flames all around soothed him, reminded him of campfires back home.

When he heard the shouting voices, he turned his head to see where they were coming from, then he remembered he was still blind. He could still feel, though. On the other side of the flames, he felt a few figures moving about. One of them seemed light, as though not quite tethered to the ground. That had to be Milo; Caymus was glad Milo had survived.

One of the other figures was smaller than the others, and it seemed just a little cooler, too. That could only be Aiella. He really liked Aiella. She was intelligent, had a lot of interesting things to say, and was easily the most beautiful woman he'd ever seen.

They seemed to be yelling at him, but they were separated by a wall of crackling fire and he couldn't understand them. With some effort, he reached out to the flames and cut off the conduits that connected them to the Conflagration.

The last thing Caymus thought, as his friends ran toward him, was that they seemed really worried about something.

He hoped they were alright.

Epilogue

Be'Var, despite the fact that he still didn't quite believe his eyes, had to admit that he was impressed. "He's actually getting better at this, isn't he?"

Rill, too, watched with a look of amused astonishment on his face as Milo seemed to simply drift upward again. "Better?" he said. "You mean he's done this before today?"

Be'Var nodded and couldn't quite suppress a smile. "Started it last week." In fact, Milo had gotten the idea to actually try and learn how to fly a couple of months previously, after having watched Perra soaring about during a particularly lazy afternoon. "At first, he was just kind of floating around on those air columns of his, but it's looking more and more like actual flight these days."

"That's absolutely incredible," Rill said, then tilted his head and narrowed his eyes, "if a little strange."

Be'Var let out a blast of a laugh. He couldn't remember the last time he'd been this content. "If you think it's strange," he said, pointing up at Perra, flying just a handful of yards away from the air priest, "just imagine how the bird feels!"

Rill laughed too. "You think he can hear us from up there?"

Be'Var shrugged. "Only one way to find out." He cupped his hands to his mouth. "Milo!" he shouted, "get down here, you flaming, flying idiot!"

Milo did appear to be able to hear them. Be'Var could make out just the slightest shift in the man's arms—and the wings attached to them—that usually precluded a long, lazy turn. Then, the air priest made a slow descent to the battlements of the Keep's inner wall, where Be'Var and Rill stood waiting. Be'Var was curious about how much of Milo's new ability was due to the columns of air he was able to create, and how much had to do with those false wings of his. As he watched the man gliding down, he got the distinct impression that the wings were tied to his arms more securely than before. He wondered if Milo'd had the idea of flight in mind when he'd made them in the first place.

At the last instant, just prior to landing, Milo swooped up a couple of feet, got his legs under him, then dropped to the ground. "Hello, gentlemen!" Milo said, a ridiculously pleased look on his face. "Is it that time, already?"

Be'Var was trying to wear the expression he usually employed to suggest that he didn't suffer fools gladly, but he was failing to get it right. Instead, he just shook his head. "It is," he said. "Come on," he continued, turning to walk down the rampart, "let's get the flaming thing over with."

Milo and Rill followed closely behind. "Aw, come on, Be'Var," said Milo, fiddling with the feathers that hung from his arms, "don't be like that. This is supposed to be fun!"

"Fun..." Be'Var huffed. "Pointless is never fun."

"I disagree," said Rill, walking next to Milo. "Most of the really fun people I know are a bit pointless, too."

Be'Var turned to look over his shoulder at Rill. Rill just smiled back at him, so he pointed his eyes forward again. Burn him, but that boy had gotten cheeky since Draya made him a lieutenant.

The three of them walked along the top of the wall for a while, heading towards one of the towers that would take them inside the Keep itself. As they walked, Be'Var heard the sounds of swordplay and the shouting of young men. He looked over the side of the wall to see a number of them, all practicing the sticking of their swords through the armor of a couple of dead krealite insects.

Be'Var marveled at the sight. Just a few months ago, these boys, these defenders of Kepren, had thought these creatures to be invincible. They had collectively trembled at the very thought of the black chitin approaching the walls of their city. Now, they were learning how to cut down the bastards. The soldiers thought their newfound skills were terribly important, but Be'Var knew that wasn't the point; it was the change in their attitudes, the knowledge that, yes, they could actually fight this enemy, that was the important thing.

He was glad, too, that they had the bodies to practice with. When Caymus had beaten that black-hearted, no-faced leader of the Black Moon Army, the Chieftain's body, as well as the bodies of many of the insects, had simply vanished into the ground, the way so many of them had vanished before. Be'Var wasn't sure why that had happened. He'd not thought that a dead thing could have performed that particular trick. Had they not been dead? Or had some otherworldly force reached out from the Sograve and pulled them back? That thought, in particular, gave him the shivers.

About a dozen of the insects had remained above ground, however. Most of the corpses had been commandeered by the engineers, who had been busy studying them, trying to figure out ways to use the alien element in their designs. The Keep-Marshal himself had needed to intervene on the soldiers' behalf in the end, taking a couple of the bodies so that the fighting men could learn and practice the set and push attack.

"Looks like they're getting the hang of it," said Milo as they reached the large door of one of the Keep's five towers. Be'Var opened the door and they began their descent down a long flight of spiral stairs.

"They really are," said Rill. "I spent some time down there myself, today."

Be'Var looked up and over his shoulder. "I wasn't aware that you needed the practice."

Rill shrugged, his head down. "Never had the chance before now," he said. "Caymus was the one sticking swords in 'em, and until the day that Black Moon showed up, I'd never seen anybody but Merkan kill one without using fire. That first night at the Temple, even in Otvia, my strategy was always to keep as far away from them as possible."

The mention of the day when Black Moon had arrived reminded Be'Var of a question he'd been meaning to ask, though he had to admit he didn't much care for bringing the subject up. He waited until they'd reached the bottom of the tower and were passing through one of the Keep's wide, stone hallways before he slowed to let the other two catch him up. "Did you ever speak to Roland's parents?" he asked, once they were walking three abreast.

Rill seemed to deflate a little bit. "I did," he said. "I managed to steal away for a couple of hours, a few days after the battle."

Be'Var didn't say anything. He knew the subject was a sore one for Rill, and he didn't want to push. Sannet had always been one of Rill's better friends at the Temple, and that would have made giving that rather horrifying news to his mother and father particularly difficult. Be'Var didn't envy the boy the responsibility, especially since he'd been the one to catch Roland and put him into the arms of a royal inquisitor. It was a heavy burden: perhaps too heavy.

They walked on awhile, going through another wide doorway. The hard stone of the floor had given way to polished marble before Rill continued. "His father said Sannet's brother had always been angry. 'Exceptional jealousy' was the term he used." As they rounded a corner, he heaved a big sigh. "It sounded like he was sad about Roland, but not very surprised."

"I'd like to know how the krealites got to him," Milo said.

"So would I," said Rill. Then, after a moment, "So would they."

So would I, Be'Var thought. He'd caught sight of the lad around

Flamehearth a couple of times since that first encounter with him in Caymus's room, but he'd never paid him much mind. He'd been surprised to find out that Sannet had a brother in the first place, in fact, and he found the whole mess confusing. Why would a boy, even one so angry as Roland, decide to throw his lot in with the force that was invading his world, that would eventually destroy everything he knew? Be'Var had surmised that some krealite emissary must have offered him something: something his young, inexperienced mind couldn't say no to. Perhaps that Mrowvain character had turned him.

Of course, maybe he'd just hated his brother that much.

"Hey," Milo said, brightening a little, "I never thought: should we be fetching Miss Aiella?"

Be'Var chuckled, glad for the change of subject. "What?" he said, arching an eyebrow at his young friend. "Do you really think she's not already there?"

Milo gave him one of those mischievous smiles that he had such a ready supply of. "Hmmm, yes, I suppose she probably is, isn't she?"

Be'Var had long suspected that Brocke's daughter held feelings for Caymus that went further than comradeship. She'd spent a great deal of time at Flamehearth while the boy had taken his long nap, after all. He—and everyone else, for that matter—had been surprised, however, at the fierce devotion she'd displayed, both on and since the day Black Moon was defeated.

Be'Var knew he didn't have the full picture, but from what he'd pieced together from the stories the soldiers told, she was the reason Caymus had survived that day. It seemed that the very moment the boy had put out the fires that the engineers had been lobbing at him, she had ordered Milo, in no uncertain terms, to find Be'Var and bring him at once.

Milo, for his part, had wasted absolutely no time in completing his task—Be'Var never particularly wanted to ride down the side of the White Spire on a column of air again—but all the time that the air priest had been away, Aiella had been the one who had kept Caymus going. She was the one who had kept him still and safe. When others had moved to lay hands on him, she'd shouted at them until they'd backed away again. When the body of the Chieftain, over which Caymus had been slumped, had disappeared into the ground, she had held his mass of dead weight up all by herself, preventing the blade in his chest from being jostled, even by a hair's breadth.

Caymus had been conscious the entire time. He'd later told Be'Var that he'd been completely blind from the moment the sword had gone into him—that was something Be'Var had seen before; the shock of such a grievous injury could sometimes take a man's sight for a while—and that it had been Aiella's soothing voice in his ear that had convinced him he was still alive, and that he wanted to stay that way.

Milo had also reported that the girl had pulled more water from the ground that day than should have been possible, saving a great deal of the city from destruction by fire. That fact was one in which her father had shown great interest, once he'd found out.

Be'Var had spent the better part of a week removing the sickly, black blade from Caymus's chest. At first, he'd thought the task impossible, but he'd eventually discovered that he could make a slow kind of progress if he moved the blade only a little at a time, stopping after each movement to seal up the bleeds. He'd lost count of how many times he'd repeated that process, but he'd eventually managed to pull the blade free without killing the boy. He was particularly proud of that fact that Caymus still had use of the lung that had been skewered after he'd finished.

Aiella had been there for all of it, from the moving of the body back to Flamehearth, to the slow removal of the sword, to keeping the boy company until he'd finally regained his sight, nine days after the attack.

"That Caymus," Garrin had said when he'd learned that their savior was going to live, "I swear, since I've known him, he's spent more time in bed than on his feet!"

Be'Var shook his head, bemusedly, at the memory. Garrin, too, had spent a lot of time in bed, lately. He'd argued at first, but he'd eventually been convinced that his people, glad as they were for his service and leadership during the battle, could take care of things for a while. In the three months it had taken for Be'Var to fully knit Caymus's flesh back together, the northern and western gates had been mostly rebuilt; dead soldiers had been buried or burned, each according to his religion; and the civilian population of Kepren, only a handful of whom had actually been killed in the attack, had gotten to the general business of putting their city back together.

Be'Var found that he was smiling as the trio entered the open doors of a grand hall. He didn't usually care much for events like these, but he was going to make an exception in this case.

Inside the hall, dozens of people stood waiting for the ceremony to begin. Dukes Fel and Chenswig were there, of course—Korwinder had been struck with a sudden sense of duty just before the battle; he hadn't survived his wounds—as were King Garrin and Ambassadors Brocke and Cull, of Creveya. Keep-Marshal Tanner was talking to a pretty woman in a bright yellow dress, an impressively large goblet in his hand. Everyone from Flamehearth Mission was in attendance; Keeper Elia gave him a nod and a wink when she noticed the three of them approaching. Even Kavuu, the headman of the Falaar down south, who had taught Caymus how to walk through fire without getting singed, was standing in one corner with three of his people, including Tavrin and Gwenna. Be'Var hadn't understood why Gwenna had suddenly decided to live out in the desert the way she had, but he'd eventually accepted the idea. He was glad that she had been able to be here for this, though; it was right that she should be in attendance.

A few dozen other people whom Be'Var didn't know were also present. He'd been told that a number of other important individuals, be they noblemen, priests, or merchants, had been invited to attend. Be'Var didn't really like having all these strangers here, but he supposed that if he was going to go through with this ceremony, the more people that saw it, the better.

Standing in the middle of everything, a foot or two from the dais at the far end of the hall, was Caymus himself. Somebody had decided he needed a set of armor and had constructed one from leather, mail, and even a few plates; somebody had also decided that the whole thing would look better painted with hues of red and orange. Be'Var thought it was a bit much, really, but he had to admit it drew the eye—nearly, in fact, as much as the huge sword strapped to his back. He still wondered how that blade of his wasn't constantly scraping across the ground.

Standing next to Caymus, as was her custom of late, was Aiella, her blue robes of state arrayed about her, her hair spilling down in dark waves. Be'Var decided there must still exist some uncertainty between the two of them. They stood close enough to each other that anyone could tell there was something there, yet they were a bit too far apart for that something to be anything intimate. Based on the quick glances they both kept darting around the room, the conversation they were engaged in wasn't one they wanted others to overhear.

"I can't believe she talked me into this," Be'Var grunted.

Milo laughed and slapped a hand on his shoulder. "She told me you were the one who brought it up!"

"I only found some reference to it an old book." Be'Var protested. "I didn't expect to actually have to perform the flaming thing."

In truth, when Be'Var had first read about this particular event in one of the old tomes, buried deep in the bowels of the Royal Library—to which Garrin, since becoming king, had finally given him access—he'd thought a bit of ceremony might be a good idea, that it might bolster Caymus's reputation, especially among Kepren's upper classes. He had not, however, actually been planning on performing it himself, at least not so soon. Then, Aiella had caught wind of the idea, and she'd pestered him for days with that overly reasonably way of hers until he'd finally agreed to go through with it. Now, here he was, about to carry out this service, this ritual that nobody in living memory had ever seen.

At least if he got it wrong, nobody would know to correct him.

"Well," he said, looking around the room and taking a deep breath, "I suppose we'd better get it over with."

When Aiella saw him coming, she had the good grace to take a few steps away from Caymus, leaving him alone before the dais, though not before giving his hand a squeeze.

"You ready for this, boy?" Be'Var said as he stood to one side of his former student.

Caymus smiled a big, easy-going smile. One would never suspect that smile had been at death's door just a handful of weeks ago, or that those huge hands of his had struck down hundreds of men. "Shouldn't be too hard, right?" he said.

Be'Var just clicked his tongue, then managed the single step up to the dais and took his position. He waited a few moments for the low murmur of a dozen conversations to die down. After those few moments passed, however, and he didn't have silence, he reminded himself that he wasn't a patient man.

"Quiet, all of you!" he yelled out. When the voices stopped and everybody looked at him questioningly, he said, "We're starting."

He waited for a few more moments, drinking in the silence, then began.

"By now," he said, loud enough for all to hear, "everyone here knows about the krealites, about this element that has invaded our world, about how it has destroyed many of the cities to the North, and how it then sent the Black Moon Army south, through the Greatstones, to destroy the rest of us."

There was a general murmur of agreement.

"By now," he continued, "everyone here also knows," he smiled, "that the dark army was beaten, that our enemy's great force was stopped, here, in Kepren."

A few small cheers went up, but most of the room stayed quiet.

"The last time forces such as the kreal, elements from realms we've never even heard of, tried to lay a claim on our world, they were beaten by an alliance that, to this day, hasn't been broken. We don't know a lot about how that alliance came about, but we do know that each of the four elements of our world—earth, air, fire, and water—chose champions, representatives of the elemental realms, to fight on their behalves."

He turned to look at Caymus. "These champions were called 'knights', and the world hasn't seen one for a very long time." Caymus, his eyes locked on Be'Var, wasn't smiling. He seemed to be taking this very seriously. Be'Var turned to address the crowd again. "We recently discovered that there's a bit of a ceremony that goes along with the title. I have been convinced," he darted his eyes at Aiella, "that, now that the elements are choosing champions again, we also need to revive the ceremony. So. Here we are."

Be'Var looked at the faces around the room. Most were smiling, some nodding in agreement. Several women and even a couple of the men were dabbing their eyes with handkerchiefs. He had to admit he was surprised at the response. He'd never met most of the people gathered here today, but he'd been certain that they'd all be too busy thinking about their own problems to really care about kreal, about Caymus, or about anything to do with this war. He'd been expecting indifference, boredom, or, at best, confusion. The overwhelming impression Be'Var felt from the gathered faces, though, was hope.

He was reminded of something Caymus had told him about his trial in the Conduit, all those months ago. "Hope" was the word Caymus had given when the Lords had asked him what was in his heart, though he'd never known why. Be'Var understood now. Strength and valor might have been a knight's weapons, but hope was his stock-in-trade, what he had to offer the people around him.

He'd never been as proud of Caymus as he was in that very moment.

He looked down at his pupil-turned-champion. "The sword, please, Caymus."

Caymus nodded, then he reached over his back and pulled the huge, two-handed sword he kept there, the weapon of the Conflagration's champion. When he reversed it, then offered the hilt to Be'Var, a few gasps arose from the crowd. Be'Var, too, might have been a bit worried, but he had, in fact, handled the sword before, knew that he was strong enough to lift it, at least long enough to perform this part of the ceremony. He *was* an experienced blacksmith, after all.

When Be'Var had a firm hold on the grip, and Caymus released it fully into his care, he raised the blade up in front of him. It was so long that it nearly touched the ceiling. He nodded at the young man before him. "Kneel, Caymus Bolwerc."

Caymus did as instructed. He got down on one knee. He also hung his head.

Be'Var then lowered the blade, flat side down. "Now stand," he touched the blade to one shoulder, "as Knight Caymus Bolwerc," he touched the other shoulder, "Knight of the Flame, Champion of the Conflagration, and Sword of Kepren."

Be'Var and Garrin had spent a long evening deciding on the latter title. Garrin had wanted to call him the "Shield" of Kepren. Be'Var had spent several hours, and a few mugs of ale, explaining why that hadn't been appropriate.

As Caymus got back to his feet, a huge roar of celebration went up in the room. Before Be'Var could even return the knight's sword, a certain young woman in a blue dress had run into his arms and was fiercely embracing him.

As others walked up to shake the knight's hand, pat him on the back, or otherwise congratulate him, Be'Var decided he would just hold onto the sword for now. He'd return it when there was less chance that somebody might get injured.

After all, there was a knight in the world for the first time anybody could remember. It was only fitting that everyone should get a good look at him.

~~~

King Garrin rested his goblet on the stone parapet as he looked out to the North from one of the Keep's towers. The sun had set in the western sky mere moments earlier, and the horizon was awash with red clouds. "It was a good day," he said. "I think we all needed it."

"I think you're right," Be'Var said, from over Garrin's shoulder. "I hadn't realized just how much until we were in the middle of it."

Garrin turned to say something to him, but Be'Var was looking down into the marshaling yard where Caymus, Milo, Aiella, and Rill were talking and laughing.

"It did my daughter's heart good, I believe," Brocke said, from over the other shoulder, "though I do not know that I like that she is so close to it."

Garrin grinned. "I don't think you're going to get much choice in the matter," he turned to look at Brocke, who was sniffing that powder of his again, "Mister Ambassador." Brocke didn't answer. He just stared down in obvious discontentment and drank his wine.

"She could do worse, I think," said Be'Var. "They both could. Anyway," he continued, "we old men need to stay out of the affairs of the young people."

"Now, now," Garrin said, managing the beginnings of a smile, "I hope you're not lumping me in with the old men."

Brocke and Be'Var both laughed. "Have you not noticed?" Brocke said. "You are a king now. I do not care your actual age. When you take the crown of a city such as Kepren, you are immediately one of the old men."

Garrin tried to laugh at the thought, but he wasn't really in a laughing sort of mood. "They're out there still, gentlemen," he said, picking up his goblet and gesturing northward with it. "Black Moon's gone, completely annihilated, but we can be sure that wasn't all this Sograve had to throw at us, that there's a lot more of them out there."

"The Summit, too, has heard these things," said Brocke, his smile
~~~

vanishing with the words. "It seems they are making a base of power in Caranaar."

"Or what's left of Caranaar," Be'Var said.

"Yes," agreed Brocke.

Garrin sighed. "I was fool enough to hope we'd beaten them for good," he said, "that we'd beat their big army and the rest would just give up and slink away." He looked down into his goblet as he swirled the last of his drink around. "But it's not true, is it?"

"It isn't," Be'Var said.

"What do they want?" Garrin nearly shouted. He was surprised at just how frustrated he sounded, how much raw emotion was in his voice. Had he really been sitting on this for so long? He hoped not: keeping things bottled up was something his father had done, a mistake he didn't want to repeat.

"They want this world," Be'Var said.

"Yes, of course," Garrin said. He turned around and leaned back against the rampart, his elbow up on the stone. "But what does that actually mean? I understand that they're trying to become a part of the world somehow, that they're trying to force out the elements we know, but..." He wasn't quite sure how to express the thought.

"But, what does that have to do with attacking cities and killing people?" Be'Var asked.

Garrin pointed with his goblet. "Precisely!"

But Be'Var only shook his head. "I don't know." As the master of the Conflagration sighed and took a long drink of wine, he seemed to suddenly age a good twenty years. "There's so much I don't know yet," he said, "so many things we haven't figured out about our enemy's motivations."

Garrin pressed him. "Go on."

"Well, I mean," Be'Var said, "why are some of the soldiers more kreal than others? Have they just been exposed to some kind of krealite substance longer? If so, what are they being exposed to? We know that if you get cut with a kreal-covered blade, it just kills you. What about the insects? They aren't natural insects that have been exposed to kreal, so where do they come from? Why did they come from the North? Why did they come south? Was Kepren their end-goal, or were they just going through us to get somewhere else?" He raised his eyebrows and pointed a finger at Garrin. "And where are the other knights, the champions for the other elements? Shouldn't we have seen something of at least one of them by now?"

Garrin finally managed to smile; he supposed that had something to do with knowing somebody else was at least as frustrated as he was. Maybe Brocke was right; maybe he was one of the old men, after all.

Be'Var put the pointing finger away, then he brought his goblet to his lips and looked out at the orange sky. Brocke was putting away that snuff box of his. Garrin sighed and turned to gaze at the sunset, too. Be'Var was right: there was too much they didn't know. The difference was that now he was the king and so it was his responsibility to answer the questions that Be'Var had just voiced.

A sharp sensation of cold hit his hand, and he pulled it back. "What was—"

Another hit him, this time in the face. He turned. Be'Var and Brocke both seemed to be feeling it, too. What was happening? Were they under attack?

After he heard the staccato, pattering sound around him, and then reached up to feel the wet on his face, he found himself laughing out loud.

It was raining in Kepren, for the first time in more than two years.

When he heard the cheers coming from the city below him, Garrin, the King of Kepren, felt a joy he'd never before known. He lifted his head and grinned into the cold, cold rain. He didn't know how, but with the help of the men at his side, and of the young people in the yard down below him, the people—*his* people—were going to survive this war.

Greetings from Southampton!

Well, you're here at the end of Knight of the Flame, and I'm hoping that means you enjoyed reading it as much as I did writing it.

There's this weird subset of the population who feel a constant compulsion to tell stories about the characters, scenes, and ideas that are always constantly occupying space in their heads. There's another subset of that subset who actually go through the process of writing those stories down. Finally there's the subset of *that* subset who have the gall to think, "Hey, maybe I could make a living doing this!?"

That third group? Yeah, those are my people. I honestly think we're all pretty nuts, but we don't seem to be able to help ourselves.

You're probably used to hearing this from self-professed "indies" like myself, but if you enjoyed this book and you want to see the next one come out sooner, **please, please, please Leave a Review** on the storefront you bought it from. Reviews are the things that tell the poor, struggling shopkeepers (you know, like Amazon and Apple) which books are worth keeping in the window displays. The more visible the books are, the more of them that get sold. And the more of *my* books that get sold, the less attention I have to pay to working my day job to pay the rent, and the more I can focus on just getting the next book out.

More review equals faster releases. Simple as that.

Oh, and you should totally subscribe to my mailing list at www.hjohnspriggs.com! You'll get the latest information about my new stuff, and the occasional preview of upcoming work. And in case you're worried about spam: don't be. I don't send anything unless it's really worth sending, and I'd quite literally walk through fire before I'd give away or sell my readers' information.

Thanks.

(Really, thank you so, so much. What I do is fun, but in the end it's just words on paper. It takes someone like you to come along and actually read it…then, it's a story.)

-H John

Books by H John Spriggs

Children of the Old War

i. Knight of the Flame
ii. Winds of a Growing Storm
iii. Sect of the Rounded Stone

ACKNOWLEDGEMENTS

A number of people had a hand in the creation of this book. Thanks to Andrew Ripley and Mark Tabler, who, from the very first chapters, let me know I was on the right track. Thanks also to Linda Nichols, Michael Wambeek, Chris Brumfit, Alan Cook, and Sean Burdick, who helped to sand out the rough edges ad really make the story shine. I couldn't not mention Jeremy Ellis, whose imagination helped conceive of the idea of Caymus, many years ago.

And thanks, of course, to Joyce, my mom, who always knew this book would happen.

ABOUT THE AUTHOR

H John Spriggs was born in Scotland, grew up in Arizona, and spend a few years here and there ever since. He now lives with his wife on the southern coast of England.

Made in the USA
Columbia, SC
12 September 2021